THE COMPLETE STORIES

Bernard Malamud is the author of seven novels – *The Natural* (1952), *The Assistant* (1957), *A New Life* (1961), *The Fixer* (1967), *The Tenants* (1971), *Dubin's Lives* (1979), *God's Grace* (1982) – and the unfinished *The People*. His many awards include two National Book Awards (for *The Magic Barrel* and *The Fixer*), the Pulitzer Prize (for *The Fixer*), and the Gold Medal of the American Academy and Institute of Arts and Letters. He served as president of the PEN American Center from 1979 to 1981, and taught for many years at Bennington College. Bernard Malamud died in 1986.

D0989381

Bernard Malamud

THE COMPLETE STORIES

EDITED AND INTRODUCED BY
Robert Giroux

VINTAGE

Published by Vintage 1998

2 4 6 8 10 9 7 5 3 1

First published in the United States of America by
Farrar, Straus and Giroux 1997

First published in the United Kingdom by
Vintage 1998

Vintage
Random House, 20 Vauxhall Bridge Road,
London SW1V 2SA

Random House Australia (Pty) Limited
20 Alfred Street, Milsons Point, Sydney
New South Wales 2061, Australia

Random House New Zealand Limited
18 Poland Road, Glenfield,
Auckland 10, New Zealand

Random House South Africa (Pty) Limited
Endulini, 5A Jubilee Road, Parktown 2193,
South Africa

Random House UK Limited Reg. No. 954009

A CIP catalogue record for this book
is available from the British Library

ISBN 0 09 927734 4

Papers used by Random House UK Ltd are natural,
recyclable products made from wood grown in sustain-
able forests. The manufacturing processes conform to the
environmental regulations of the country of origin

Printed and bound in Great Britain by
Mackays of Chatham PLC, Chatham, Kent

CONTENTS

APPENDIX

INTRODUCTION

by Robert Giroux

"Working alone to create stories is not a bad way to live our loneliness," Bernard Malamud wrote not long before his death, in a characteristically modest statement which identifies a major theme of his writing. And as a result of his lonely work, readers have gained a body of short fiction unlike that of any other writer. Robert Alter called these stories "products of a unique imagination . . . Only Bernard Malamud could have written them." In his memoir "Long Work, Short Life," Malamud acknowledged: "My writing has drawn, out of a reluctant soul, a measure of astonishment at the nature of life." Between 1940 (when he began) and his death in 1986, he produced some of the most original and memorable stories of his era. This book brings them all together for the first time.

He started out in the early 1940s by publishing stories in noncommercial magazines—"meaning I didn't get paid for them but was happy to have them published"—until in 1949 *Harper's Bazaar* bought "The Cost of Living" and his professional career was launched. At Harcourt, Brace in 1952 I took on his first novel, *The Natural*, and we signed a two-book contract, intending that his second book would be a collection of stories. I did this because with the help of my friend Catharine Carver (then the first-reader at *Partisan Review*) I had read his unpublished story "The Magic Barrel," which revealed his mastery of the short-story form. I was happy to become the editor and publisher of an important new writer.

Before Bern's second book was ready, I moved from Harcourt,

Brace to become vice president and editor in chief at Farrar, Straus
and Company. I thought I had lost him, owing to the two-book contract, but things worked out surprisingly. When Bern told me Harcourt had turned down his new book, I blurted: "I can't believe they'd
reject your stories!" and he said, "No, it's a novel, *The Assistant.* Would
you like to read it?" It was excellent, and Farrar, Straus published the
novel in 1957. The next year, we brought out *The Magic Barrel* (as
his collection was called); it won the National Book Award, the first
such award for the firm. Thus began the splendid cavalcade of eight
novels and four volumes of stories that constitute his *oeuvre.* When
FSG republished *The Natural* in 1961, all his books were in print on
our list.

A fellow writer once called Malamud a "stern moralist." Moralist, of course, but stern was not his style. I came to admire the
character of this gentle man more and more. As Bern's talent bur-
geoned, our personal relationship deepened into a close and abiding
friendship. We shared many interests, especially a love of music and
(with his wife, Ann) of opera. Bern and I were born not only in the
same year but in the same month; in the Depression we had both
worked our way through college in New York; and nothing was more
important to each of us than the book. Once, as a birthday present,
he gave me a rare item, Thomas Merton's translation of Guigo the
Carthusian's "On the Solitary Life," in a limited edition from the
press of his Bennington colleague Claude Fredericks. During Bern's
presidency of the PEN American Center (1979–81), when FSG was
awarded the fifth annual Publisher Citation, he arranged for the ceremony to take place on my birthday. (The citation bears his personal
accent: "For distinctive and continuous service to international letters,
to the dignity and freedom of writers, and to the free transmission of
the printed word across the barriers of poverty, ignorance, censorship
and repression.")

There's a famous joke about a movie producer who was asked if
he'd read *The Wings of the Dove* and answered, "Not personally." One
memorable evening at Bennington College, when Governor Snelling
presented Bern with the Vermont Arts Council Award, it was clear
that *he* had read Malamud personally. The spirits of Bern's departed
colleagues Shirley Jackson and Stanley Edgar Hyman permeated the
proceedings, and the whole ceremony became a family affair. Also,
there was an unexpected Malamudian experience in Japan, where I
lectured under the USIA cultural exchange program in five cities, in
four of which only Ernest Hemingway seemed to be of interest. But

at the University of Hiroshima, when Professor Katsuhiro Jinsaki asked me to meet with his students in American literature, I was delighted when the class asked only about Bernard Malamud, whose books they knew thoroughly. I thought this would surprise Bern on my return, but he grinned and said, "Professor Jinsaki and I have had a voluminous correspondence. He's *the* Malamud expert."

•

Bernard Malamud was born in Brooklyn on April 26, 1914, the elder of the two sons of Bertha Fidelman and Max Malamud, immigrants from Russia. They had worked hard to establish a local late-night grocery store, a setting destined to become familiar in their son's writing. After changing locations over the years, they finally settled on McDonald Avenue, where the family lived in rooms over the store.

In 1929, when Bern was fifteen, his mother died and his father remarried. ("After the death of my mother, I had had a stepmother and a thin family life," he revealed.) Eugene, his younger brother, was twice hospitalized for schizophrenia and died at age fifty-five. Bern went to school at P.S. 181 in Brooklyn, graduated in 1932 from Erasmus Hall high school, and entered City College in New York, where he received his B.A. in 1936. "I had hoped to write short stories after graduation from City College during the Depression," he explained, "but they were long in coming. I had ideas and felt I was on the verge of sustained work. But at that time I had no means of earning a living, and as the son of a poor man, a poor grocer, I could not stand the thought of living off him, a generous and self-denying person . . . I registered for a teacher's examination and afterwards worked a year at $4.50 a day as a teacher-in-training in a high school [Lafayette] in Brooklyn." He recorded how he felt when he took civil service exams for postal clerk and letter carrier: "This is mad, I thought, or I am. Yet I told myself the kind of work I might get didn't matter so long as I was working for time to write."

In the spring of 1940 he accepted a civil service job at the census bureau in Washington, D.C. "All morning I conscientiously checked estimates of drainage ditch statistics, as they appeared in various counties in the United States. Although the work hardly thrilled me, I worked diligently and was promoted after three months . . . After lunch I kept my head bent low while I was writing stories at my desk." It was a lonely rooming-house existence in the capital. That summer he wrote a non-fiction piece for *The Washington Post*, about the fall of France after the German Army was "obscenely jubilant in conquered Paris." He recalled, "I felt unhappy, as though mourning the death of a civilization I loved, yet somehow I managed to celebrate ongoing life and related acts. Though I was often lonely, I stayed in the rooming house night after night trying to invent stories I needn't be ashamed of." One such story, "Armistice," the first in this book, is about the fall of France as it affects an American grocer and his son.

Bern earned his master's degree in English literature at Columbia University in 1942, with a thesis on Thomas Hardy's poetry, and by 1943 his first stories had begun to appear in little magazines like *Assembly*, *Threshold*, *American Prefaces*, and *New Threshold*. In 1945 he married Ann de Chiara; their son, Paul, was born in 1947 and their daughter, Janna, in 1952. He received an offer in 1949 to teach at Oregon State College. A severe critic of his own work, he destroyed the manuscript of his first completed novel, *The Light Sleeper*, "one night in Oregon because I thought I could do better." His first book, then, was *The Natural*, a novel about the reality and fantasy of baseball, published in 1952. He dedicated it to his father, who died shortly thereafter. ("What does a writer need most? When I ask this question, I think of my father.") He wrote "The Magic Barrel" in a carrel in the basement of the college library. *Partisan Review* published it in 1954. In 1956–57, on sabbatical leave, he traveled in Europe and lived in Rome on a Rockefeller grant sponsored by *Partisan Review*, a period from which his stories with Italian settings are drawn. *The Assistant*, published in 1957, won the Rosenthal Award of the American Academy and Institute of Arts and Letters. *The Magic Barrel* was published in 1958, followed by six novels: *A New Life* (1961), *The Fixer* (1966), *The Tenants* (1971), *Dubin's Lives* (1979), *God's Grace* (1982), and the unfinished *The People* (1989), which appeared posthumously. The other collections of stories were *Idiots First* (1963); *Pictures of Fidelman* (1969), a book of related stories set in Italy; and *Rembrandt's Hat* (1973). In September 1961 he joined the faculty of Bennington College, where he taught for the rest of his life.

He won both the Pulitzer Prize and the National Book Award for *The Fixer*. New York University honored him with the Elmer H. Bobst Award and the American Academy of Arts and Letters awarded him their prestigious Gold Medal for Fiction in 1983. (The latter is given only at five-year intervals, and it was presented by his friend Ralph Ellison.) In 1985 he received a major Italian award, the Mondello Prize, at an annual literary festival in Sicily. One night in March 1986, when the Malamuds were dinner guests of Roger and Dorothea Straus, Bern stated that he was four chapters from the end of his first draft of *The*

People and believed it would be finished by the fall. The next afternoon, March 18, he died of a heart attack after working at his desk.

.

The Complete Stories of Bernard Malamud includes fifty-five stories, starting in 1940 with "Armistice" and closing with the last two stories he wrote in the 1980s, while experimenting with new forms. (In his 1983 notes he calls them "fictive biographies" and "biographed stories." "In Kew Gardens," about Virginia Woolf, and "Alma Redeemed," about Alma Mahler, were both published in 1984; the odd biographical details of the lives of these famous women sound fantastic but are literally true—that is his point.) The fifty-five stories are arranged as accurately as possible in the order of composition rather than publication. They reveal an astonishing development over forty years, from the realism of the grocery-store and Brooklyn background stories to the fantasy and freedom of stories like "The Jewbird," "Talking Horse," "Angel Levine," and "The Magic Barrel."

Only one story, "Suppose a Wedding," about the family of an unmarried daughter, is in dramatic form. As far as anyone knows, Bern made no other attempt to write a play, though he was always interested in the theater. He told me his uncle Charles Fidelman had been a prompter at the Yiddish Theater on Second Avenue and had toured with a repertory company in Buenos Aires. "Suppose a Wedding" was first published in 1963 in London in the *New Statesman*. (In 1996 it was set to music as an opera by Dr. Leonard Lehrman.) Another early story, "A Confession of Murder," was in fact written as the first chapter of a novel, *The Man Nobody Could Lift*, which he abandoned. Since it is a self-contained narrative with a surprise ending which he preserved, his executors decided to include it as an uncollected story. "Steady Customer," written in 1943, was recently discovered in *New Threshold*. (That issue of the magazine also ran an early story by Madeleine L'Engle, written when she was a Smith undergraduate, and a piece against "Jim Crow" by Eleanor Roosevelt.)

.

Flannery O'Connor, a great story writer herself (whose work Bern admired), quietly revealed what she thought of his genius in a letter to her friend "A" on June 14, 1958: "I have discovered a short-story writer who is better than any of them, including myself. Go to the library and get a book called *The Magic Barrel* by Bernard Malamud." Richard Gilman in his excellent *New Republic* memorial piece, "Malamud's

Grace," called him "a story-teller in an era when most of our best writers have been suspicious of straightforward narrative. He was both [a realist and a fantasist]. I don't mean he alternated between reality and fantasy, but that at his best the line between the two was obliterated. Observation gave way to imagining." Gilman added that "a story like 'The Jewbird' (to my mind perhaps his finest), a piece that appears all whimsy and allegorical effort, is anchored in pebbly actuality." In her moving tribute to Malamud at the memorial service held for him at the 92nd Street Y, Cynthia Ozick remembered his reading of his story "The Silver Crown," which was "so electrifying that I wished with all my heart it was mine."

Both Gilman and Ozick rightly praised his highly individual stylistic gifts. Ozick mentioned the "heat of a Malamudian sentence." Gilman cited "the pleasures of the text, the little fates of language," giving these examples: "He drew on his cold embittered clothing" (*Idiots First*); "Life, despite their frantic yoohooings, had passed them by" ("The Magic Barrel"); "He pitied her, her daughter, the world. Who not?" ("The Girl of My Dreams"); "His heart, like a fragile pitcher, toppled from the shelf and bump bumped down the stairs, cracking at the bottom" ("The Death of Me"); "The window was open so the skinny bird flew in. Flappity-flap with its frazzled black wings. That's how it goes. It's open, you're in. Closed, you're out, and that's your fate" ("The Jewbird"); "Exaltation having gone where exaltation goes" ("The Last Mohican").

Ozick asked: "Is he an American Master? Of course. He not only wrote in the American language, he augmented it with fresh plasticity, he shaped our English into startling new configurations . . . He wrote about suffering Jews, about poor Jews, about grocers and fixers and birds and horses and angels in Harlem and matchmakers and salesmen and rabbis and landlords and tenants and egg candlers and writers and chimpanzees; he wrote about the plentitude and unity of the world."

At the memorial service Daniel Stern stated that Malamud "came as close to making a religion of art as is possible; a religion of suffering and comedy, taking the Jew as his starting point for what was most human in humankind. All men are Jews—perhaps his most famous and most mysterious line."

Over the years I considered myself fortunate to be Bernard Malamud's editor, and even more fortunate to be his friend. In 1983, when he put together *The Stories of Bernard Malamud,* the last book published during his lifetime, I was honored that he dedicated it to me. But even more I treasure his written inscription: "For Bob, my first and only editor." His preface says, "Art celebrates life and gives us our measure." His art has given us his measure and it is great.

•

In compiling this book I have had the generous help of Alice Birney, curator of the Bernard Malamud papers at the Library of Congress; Paul Elie, editor at FSG; Daniel Stern and Tim Seldes, with whom I serve as co-executors of the Malamud literary estate; and Ann Malamud, whose support, as usual, has been invaluable. I am grateful to them for their assistance.

B M

The Complete Stories

❧ B M ❧

Armistice

When he was a boy, Morris Lieberman saw a burly Russian peasant seize a wagon wheel that was lying against the side of a blacksmith's shop, swing it around, and hurl it at a fleeing Jewish sexton. The wheel caught the Jew in the back, crushing his spine. In speechless terror, he lay on the ground before his burning house, waiting to die.

Thirty years later Morris, a widower who owned a small grocery and delicatessen store in a Scandinavian neighborhood in Brooklyn, could recall the scene of the pogrom with the twisting fright that he had felt at fifteen. He often experienced the same fear since the Nazis had come to power.

The reports of their persecution of the Jews that he heard over the radio filled him with dread, but he never stopped listening to them. His fourteen-year-old son, Leonard, a thin, studious boy, saw how overwrought his father became and tried to shut off the radio, but the grocer would not allow him to. He listened, and at night did not sleep, because in listening he shared the woes inflicted upon his race.

When the war began, Morris placed his hope for the salvation of the Jews in his trust of the French army. He lived close to his radio, listening to the bulletins and praying for a French victory in the conflict which he called "this righteous war."

On the May day in 1940 when the Germans ripped open the French lines at Sedan, his long-growing anxiety became intolerable. Between waiting on customers, or when he was preparing salads in the kitchen at the rear of the store, he switched on the radio and heard, with increasing dismay, the flood of reports which never seemed to contain any good news. The Belgians surrendered. The British retreated at Dunkerque, and in mid-June, the Nazis, speeding toward Paris in their lorries, were passing large herds of conquered Frenchmen resting in the fields.

Day after day, as the battle progressed, Morris sat on the edge of the cot in the kitchen listening to the additions to his sorrow, nodding his head the way the Jews do in mourning, then rousing himself to hope for the miracle that would save the French as it had saved the Jews in the wilderness. At three o'clock, he shut off the radio, because Leonard came home from school about then. The boy, seeing the harmful effect of the war on his father's health, had begun to plead with him not to listen to so many news broadcasts, and Morris pacified him by pretending that he no longer thought of the war. Each afternoon Leonard remained behind the counter while his father slept on the cot. From the dream-filled, raw sleep of these afternoons, the grocer managed to derive enough strength to endure the long day and his own bitter thoughts.

The salesmen from the wholesale grocery houses and the drivers who served Morris were amazed at the way he suffered. They told him that the war had nothing to do with America and that he was taking it too seriously. Some of the others made him the object of their ridicule outside the store. One of them, Gus Wagner, who delivered the delicatessen meats and provisions, was not afraid to laugh at Morris to his face.

Gus was a heavy man, with a strong, full head and a fleshy face. Although born in America, and a member of the AEF in 1918, his imagination was fired by the Nazi conquests and he believed that they had the strength and power to conquer the world. He kept a scrapbook filled with clippings and pictures of the German army. He was deeply impressed by the Panzer divisions, and when he read accounts of battles in which they tore through the enemy's lines, his mind glowed with excitement. He did not reveal his feelings directly because he considered his business first. As it was, he poked fun at the grocer for wanting the French to win.

Each afternoon, with his basket of liverwursts and bolognas on his arm, Gus strode into the store and swung the basket onto the table in the kitchen. The grocer as usual was sitting on the cot, listening to the radio.

"Hello, Morris," Gus said, pretending surprise. "What does it say on the radio?" He sat down heavily and laughed.

When things were going especially well for the Germans, Gus dropped his attitude of pretense and said openly, "You better get used to it, Morris. The Germans will wipe out the Frenchmen."

Morris disliked these remarks, but he said nothing. He allowed Gus to talk as he did because he had known the meat man for nine years. Once they had nearly been friends. After the death of Morris's wife four years ago, Gus stayed longer than usual and joined Morris in a cup of coffee. Occasionally he repaired a hole in the screen door or fixed the plug for the electric slicing machine.

Leonard had driven them apart. The boy disliked the meat man and always tried to avoid him. He was nauseated by Gus's laughter, which he called a cackle, and he would not allow his father to do business with Gus in the kitchen when he was having his milk and crackers after school.

Gus knew how the boy felt about him and he was deeply annoyed. He was angered too when the boy added up the figures on the meat bills and found errors. Gus was careless in arithmetic, which often caused trouble. Once Morris mentioned a five-dollar prize that Leonard had won in mathematics and Gus said, "You better watch out, Morris. He's a skinny kid. If he studies too much, he'll get consumption."

Morris was frightened. He felt that Gus was wishing harm upon Leonard. Their relations became cooler, and after that Gus spoke more freely about politics and the war, often expressing his contempt for the French.

The Germans took Paris and pushed on toward the west and south. Morris, drained of his energy, prayed that the ordeal would soon be over. Then the Reynaud cabinet fell. Marshal Pétain addressed a request to the Germans for "peace with honor." In the dark Compiègne forest, Hitler sat in Marshal Foch's railroad car, listening to his terms being read to the French delegation.

That night, after closing his store, Morris disconnected the radio and carried it upstairs. In his bedroom, the door shut tightly so Leonard would not be awakened, he tuned in softly to the midnight broadcast and learned that the French had accepted Hitler's terms and would sign the armistice tomorrow. Morris shut off the radio. An age-old weariness filled him. He wanted to sleep but he knew that he could not.

Morris turned out the lights, removed his shirt and shoes in the dark, and sat smoking in the large bedroom that had once belonged to him and his wife.

The door opened softly, and Leonard looked into the room. By the light of the street lamp which shone through the window, the boy could see his father in the chair. It made him think of the time when his mother was in the hospital and his father sat in the chair all night.

Leonard entered the bedroom in his bare feet. "Pa," he said, putting his arm around his father's shoulders, "go to sleep."

"I can't sleep, Leonard."

"Pa, you got to. You work sixteen hours."

"Oh, my son," cried Morris, with sudden emotion, putting his arms around Leonard, "what will become of us?"

The boy became afraid.

"Pa," he said, "go to sleep. Please, you got to."

"All right, I'll go," said Morris. He crushed his cigarette in the ashtray and got into bed. The boy watched him until he turned over on his right side, which was the side he slept on; then he returned to his room.

Later Morris rose and sat by the window, looking into the street. The night was cool. The breeze swayed the street lamp, which creaked and moved the circle of light that fell upon the street.

"What will become of us?" he muttered to himself. His mind went back to the days when he was a boy studying Jewish history. The Jews lived in an interminable exodus. Long lines trudged forever with their bundles on their shoulders.

He dozed and dreamed that he had fled from Germany into France. The Nazis had found out where he lived in Paris. He sat in a chair in a dark room waiting for them to come. His hair had grown grayer. The moonlight fell on his sloping shoulders, then moved into the darkness. He rose and climbed out onto a ledge overlooking the lighted city of Paris. He fell. Something clumped to the sidewalk. Morris groaned and awoke. He heard the purring of a truck's motor and he knew that the driver was dropping the bundles of morning newspapers in front of the stationery store on the corner.

The dark was soft with gray. Morris crawled into bed and began to dream again. It was Sunday at suppertime. The store was crowded with customers. Suddenly Gus was there. He waved a copy of *Social Justice* and cried out, "The Protocols of Zion! The Protocols of Zion!" The customers began to leave. "Gus," Morris pleaded, "the customers, the customers—"

He awoke shivering and lay awake until the alarm rang.

After he had dragged in the bread and milk boxes and had waited on the deaf man who always came early, Morris went to the corner for a paper. The armistice was signed. Morris looked around to see if the street had changed, but everything was the same, though he could hardly understand why. Leonard came down for his coffee and roll. He took fifty cents from the till and left for school.

The day was warm and Morris was tired. He grew uneasy when he thought of Gus. He knew that today he would have difficulty controlling himself if Gus made some of his remarks.

At three o'clock, when Morris was slicing small potatoes for potato salad, Gus strode into the store and swung his basket onto the table.

"Well, Morris"—he laughed—"why don't you turn the radio on? Let's hear the news."

Morris tried to control himself, but his bitterness overcame him. "I see you're happy today, Gus. What great cause has died?"

The meat man laughed, but he did not like that remark.

"Come on, Morris," he said, "let's do business before your skinny kid comes home and wants the bill signed by a certified public accountant."

"He looks out for my interests," answered Morris. "He's a good mathematics student," he added.

"That's the sixth time I heard that," said Gus.

"You'll never hear it about your children."

Gus lost his temper. "What the hell's the matter with you Jews?" he asked. "Do you think you own all the brains in the world?"

"Gus," Morris cried, "you talk like a Nazi."

"I'm a hundred percent American. I fought in the war," answered Gus.

Leonard came into the store and heard the loud voices. He ran into the kitchen and saw the two men arguing. A feeling of shame and nausea overcame him.

"Pa," he begged, "don't fight."

Morris was still angry. "If you're not a Nazi," he said to Gus, "why are you so glad the French lost?"

"Who's glad?" asked Gus. Suddenly he felt proud and he said, "They deserved to lose, the way they starved the German people. Why the hell do you want them to win?"

"Pa," said Leonard again.

"I want them to win because they are fighting for democracy."

"Like hell," said Gus. "You want them to win because they're protecting the Jews—like that lousy Léon Blum."

"You Nazi, you," Morris shouted angrily, coming from behind the table. "You Nazi! You don't deserve to live in America!"

"Papa," cried Leonard, holding him, "don't fight, please, please."

"Mind your own business, you little bastard," said Gus, pushing Leonard away.

A sob broke from Leonard's throat. He began to cry.

Gus paused, seeing that he had gone too far.

Morris Lieberman's face was white. He put his arm around the boy and kissed him again and again.

"No, no. No more, Leonard. Don't cry. I'm sorry. I give you my word. No more."

Gus looked on without speaking. His face was still red with anger, but he was afraid that he would lose Morris's business. He pulled two liverwursts and a bologna from his basket.

"The meat's on the table," he said. "Pay me tomorrow."

Gus glanced contemptuously at the grocer comforting his son, who was quiet now, and he walked out of the store. He threw the basket into his truck, got in, and drove off.

As he rode amid the cars on the avenue, he thought of the boy crying and his father holding him. It was always like that with the Jews. Tears and people holding each other. Why feel sorry for them?

Gus sat up straight at the wheel, his face grim. He thought of the armistice and imagined that he was in Paris. His truck was a massive tank rumbling with the others through the wide boulevards. The French, on the sidewalks, were overpowered with fear.

He drove tensely, his eyes unsmiling. He knew that if he relaxed the picture would fade.

1940

Spring Rain

George Fisher was still lying awake, thinking of the accident which he had seen on 121st Street. A young man had been struck by an automobile, and they had carried him to the drugstore on Broadway. The druggist couldn't do anything for him, so they waited for an ambulance. The man lay on the druggist's table in the back of the store looking at the ceiling. He knew he was going to die.

George felt deeply sorry for the man, who seemed to be in his late twenties. The stoical way in which he took the accident convinced George that he was a person of fine character. He knew that the man was not afraid of death, and he wanted to speak to him and tell him that he too was not afraid to die; but the words never formed themselves on his thin lips. George went home, choked with unspoken words.

Lying in bed in his dark room, George heard his daughter, Florence, put the key in the lock. He heard her whisper to Paul, "Do you want to come in for a minute?"

"No," said Paul after a while, "I've got a nine o'clock class tomorrow."

"Then good night," said Florence and she closed the door hard.

George thought, This is the first decent boy Florence has gone out with, and she can't get anywhere with him. She's like her mother. She doesn't know how to handle decent people. He raised his head and looked at Beatie, half expecting her to wake up because his thoughts sounded so loud to him, but she didn't move.

This was one of George's sleepless nights. They came just after he had finished reading an interesting novel, and he lay awake imagining that all those things were happening to him. In his sleepless nights George thought of the things that had happened to him during the day, and he said those words that people saw on his lips, but which they never heard him speak. He said to the dying young man, "I'm not afraid to die either." He said to the heroine in the novel, "You understand my loneliness. I can tell you these things." He told his wife and daughter what he thought of them.

"Beatie," he said, "you made me talk once, but it wasn't you. It was the sea and the darkness and the sound of the water sucking the beams of the pier. Those poetical things I said about how lonely men are—I said them because you were pretty, with dark red hair, and I was afraid because I was a small man with thin lips, and I was afraid that I could not have you. You didn't love me, but you said yes for Riverside Drive and your apartment and your two fur coats and the people who come here to play bridge and mah-jongg."

He said to Florence, "What a disappointment you are. I loved you when you were a child, but now you're selfish and small. I lost my last bit of feeling for you when you didn't want to go to college. The best thing you ever did was to bring an educated boy like Paul into the house, but you'll never keep him."

George spoke these thoughts to himself until the first gray of the April dawn drifted into the bedroom and made the silhouette of Beatie in the other bed clearer. Then George turned over and slept for a while.

In the morning, at breakfast, he said to Florence, "Did you have a good time?"

"Oh, leave me alone," answered Florence.

"Leave her alone," said Beatie. "You know she's cranky in the morning."

"I'm not cranky," said Florence, almost crying. "It's Paul. He never takes me anyplace."

"What did you do last night?" asked Beatie.

"What we always do," answered Florence. "We went for a walk. I can't even get him into a movie."

"Does he have money?" asked Beatie. "Maybe he's working his way through college."

"No," said Florence, "he's got money. His father is a big buyer. Oh, what's the use? I'll never get him to take me out."

"Be patient," Beatie told her. "Next time, either I or your father will suggest it to him."

"I won't," said George.

"No, you won't," answered Beatie, "but I will."

George drank his coffee and left.

When he came home for dinner, there was a note for George saying that Beatie and Florence had eaten early because Beatie was going to Forest Hills to play bridge and Florence had a date to go to the movies with her girl friend. The maid served George, and later he went into the living room to read the papers and listen to the war news.

The bell rang. George rose, calling out to the maid, who was coming from her room, that he would answer the bell. It was Paul, wearing an old hat and a raincoat, wet on the shoulders.

George was glad that Florence and Beatie were not there.

"Come in, Paul. Is it raining?"

"It's drizzling."

Paul entered without taking off his raincoat. "Where's Florence?" he asked.

"She went to the pictures with a friend of hers. Her mother is playing bridge or mah-jongg somewhere. Did Florence know you were coming?"

"No, she didn't know."

Paul looked disappointed. He walked to the door.

"Well, I'm sorry," said George, hoping that the boy would stay.

Paul turned at the door. "Mr. Fisher."

"Yes?" said George.

"Are you busy now?"

"No, I'm not."

"How about going for a walk with me?"

"Didn't you say it was raining?"

"It's only spring rain," said Paul. "Put on your raincoat and an old hat."

"Yes," said George, "a walk will do me good." He went into his room for a pair of rubbers. As he was putting them on, he could feel a sensation of excitement, but he didn't think of it. He put on his black raincoat and last year's hat.

As soon as they came into the street and the cold mist fell on his face, George could feel the excitement flow through his body. They crossed the street, passed Grant's Tomb, and walked toward the George Washington Bridge.

The sky was filled with a floating white mist which clung to the street lamps. A wet wind blew across the dark Hudson from New Jersey and carried within it the smell of spring. Sometimes the wind blew the cold mist into George's eyes, and it shocked him as if it were electricity. He took long steps to keep up with Paul, and he secretly rejoiced in what they were doing. He felt a little like crying, but he did not let Paul guess.

Paul was talking. He told stories about his professors in Columbia at which George laughed. Then Paul surprised George by telling him that he was studying architecture. He pointed out the various details of the houses they were passing and told him what they were derived from. George was very much interested. He always liked to know where things came from.

They slowed down, waited for traffic to stop, crossed Riverside Drive again, and walked over to Broadway to a tavern. Paul ordered a sandwich and a bottle of beer, and George did the same. They talked about the war; then George ordered two more bottles of beer for Paul and him, and they began to talk about people. George told the boy the story of the young man who had died in the drugstore. He felt a strange happiness to see how the story affected Paul.

Somebody put a nickel into the electric phonograph, and it played a tango. The tango added to George's pleasure, and he sat there thinking how fluently he had talked.

Paul had grown quiet. He drank some beer, then he began to speak about Florence. George was uneasy and a little bit frightened. He was afraid that the boy was going to tell him something that he did not want to know and that his good time would be over.

"Florence is beautiful with that red hair," said Paul, as if he were talking to himself.

George said nothing.

"Mr. Fisher," said Paul, lowering his glass and looking up, "there's something I want you to know."

"Me?"

"Mr. Fisher," Paul told him earnestly, "Florence is in love with me. She told me that. I want to love her because I'm lonely, but I don't know—I can't love her. I can't reach her. She's not like you. We go for a walk along the Drive, and I can't reach her. Then she says I'm moody, and she wants to go to the movies."

George could feel his heart beating strongly. He felt that he was listening to secrets, yet they were not secrets because he had known them all his life. He wanted to talk—to tell Paul that he was like him. He wanted to tell him how lonely he had been all his life and how he lay awake at night, dreaming and thinking until the gray morning drifted into the room. But he didn't.

"I know what you mean, Paul," he said.

They walked home in the rain, which was coming down hard now.

•

When he got in, George saw that both Beatie and Florence had gone to bed. He removed his rubbers and hung his wet hat and raincoat in the bathroom. He stepped into his slippers, but he decided not to undress because he did not feel like sleeping. He was aware of a fullness of emotion within him.

George went over to the radio and turned on some jazz softly. He lit a cigar and put out the lamps. For a while he stood in the dark, listening to the soft music. Then he went to the window and drew aside the curtain.

The spring rain was falling everywhere. On the dark mass of the Jersey shore. On the flowing river. Across the street the rain was droning on the leaves of the tall maples, wet in the lamplight, and swaying in the wind. The wind blew the rain hard and sharp across the window, and George felt tears on his cheeks.

A great hunger for words rose in him. He wanted to talk. He wanted to say things that he had never said before. He wanted to tell them that he had discovered himself and that never again would he be lost and silent. Once more he possessed the world and loved it. He loved Paul, and he loved Florence, and he loved the young man who had died.

I must tell her, he thought. He opened the door of Florence's room. She was sleeping. He could hear her quiet breathing.

"Florence," he called softly, "Florence."

She was instantly awake. "What's the matter?" she whispered.

The words rushed to his lips. "Paul, Paul was here."

She rose on her elbow, her long hair falling over her shoulder. "Paul? What did he say?"

George tried to speak, but the words were suddenly immovable. He could never tell her what Paul had said. A feeling of sorrow for Florence stabbed him.

"He didn't say anything," he stammered. "We walked—went for a walk."

Florence sighed and lay down again. The wind blew the spring rain against the windows and they listened to the sound it made falling in the street.

The Grocery Store

They sat in the kitchen in the rear of the grocery store, and Rosen, the salesman from G. and S., chewing a cigar stump in the corner of his mouth, quickly and monotonously read off the items from a mimeographed list that was clipped to the inside cover of his large pink-sheeted order book. Ida Kaplan, her small, fleshy chin raised, was listening attentively as Rosen read this week's specials and their prices. She looked up, annoyed at her husband, whose eyes showed that he wasn't listening.

"Sam," she called sharply, "listen please to Rosen."

"I'm listening," said Sam absently. He was a heavy man with thick, sloping shoulders and graying hair which looked grayer still in the glare of the large, unshaded electric bulb. The sharp light bothered his eyes, and water constantly trickled over his reddened eyelids. He was tired and he yawned ceaselessly.

Rosen stopped for a minute and smiled cynically at the grocer. The salesman shifted his large body into a more comfortable position on the backless chair and automatically continued to drone forth the list of grocery items: "G. and S. grape jam, $1.80 a dozen; G. and S. grape jelly, $1.60 a dozen; Gulden's mustard, $2.76 a carton; G. and S. canned grapefruit juice Number 2, $1.00 a dozen; Heckers flour, 3½ lbs., $2.52 a half barrel—"

Rosen stopped abruptly, removed his cigar, and said, "Well, whaddayasay, Sam, you gonna order one item at least?"

"Read," said Sam, stirring a bit, "I'm listening."

"You listening, yes," said Ida, "but you not thinking."

Rosen gripped the wet cigar butt between his teeth and went on reading: "Kippered herrings, $2.40 a dozen; Jell-O, 65¢ a dozen; junket, $1.00 a dozen."

Sam forced himself to listen for a moment, then his mind wandered. What was the use? True, the shelves were threadbare and the store needed goods, but how could he afford to place an order? Ever since the A&P supermarket had moved into the neighborhood, he had done less than half his original business. The store was down to $160 a week, just barely enough to pay for rent, gas, electricity, and a few other expenses. A dull feeling of misery gnawed at his heart. Eighteen hours a day, from 6 a.m. to midnight, sitting in the back of a grocery store waiting for a customer to come in for a bottle of milk and a loaf of bread and maybe—*maybe* a can of sardines. Nineteen impoverished years in the grocery business to this end. Nineteen years of standing on his feet for endless hours until the blue veins bulged out of his legs and grew hard and stiff so that every step he took was a step of pain. For what? For what, dear God? The feeling of misery crept to his stomach. Sam shivered. He felt sick.

"Sam," cried Ida, "listen, for godsake."

"I'm listening," Sam said, in a loud, annoyed tone.

Rosen looked up in surprise. "I read the whole list," he declared.

"I heard," Sam said.

"So what did you decide to order?" asked Ida.

"Nothing."

"Nothing!" she cried shrilly.

In disgust, Rosen snapped his order book shut. He put on his woolen muffler and began to button his overcoat.

"Jack Rosen takes the trouble to come out on a windy, snowy February night and he don't even get an order for a lousy box of matches. That's a nice how-d'ye-do," he said sarcastically.

"Sam, we need goods," said Ida.

"So how'll we pay for the goods—with toothpicks?"

Ida grew angry. "Please," she said haughtily, "please, to me you will speak with respect. I wasn't brought up in my father's house a grocer should—you'll excuse me—a grocer should spit on me every time he talks."

"She's right," said Rosen.

"Who asked you?" Sam said, looking up at the salesman.

"I'm talking for your own good," said Rosen.

"Please," said Sam, "you'll be quiet. You are a salesman of groceries, not a counselor of human relations."

"It happens that I am also a human being."

"This is not the point," Sam declared. "I'm doing business with Rosen, the salesman, not the human being, if any."

Rosen quickly snatched his hat off the table. "What business?" he cried. "Who's doing business? On a freezing February night in winter I leave my wife and child and my warm house and drive twelve miles through the snow and the ice to give you a chance to fill up your fly-specked shelves with some goods, and you act like you're doing me a favor to say no. To hell with such business. It's not for Jack Rosen."

"Rosen," said Sam, looking at him calmly, "in my eyes you are common."

"Common?" spluttered the salesman. "I'm common?" he asked in astonishment. His manner changed. He slipped his book into the brief-case, snapped it shut, and gripped the handle with his gloved hand. "What's the use," he said philosophically. "Why should Jack Rosen waste his time talking to a two-bit grocer who don't think enough of his place of business to wash the windows or to sweep the snow off the side-walk so that a customer can come in? Such a person is a peasant in his heart. He belongs in czarist Russia. The advantages of the new world he don't understand or appreciate."

"A philosopher," sneered Sam, "a G. and S. wholesale groceries' philosopher."

The salesman snatched up his bag and strode out of the store. He slammed the front door hard. Several cans in the window toppled and fell.

Ida looked at her husband with loathing. Her small, stout body trembled with indignation.

"His every word was like it come from God," she said vehemently. "Who ever saw a man should sit in the back of the store all day long and never go inside, maybe to wipe off the shelves or clean out under the counter the boxes, or to think how to improve his store a customer should come in?"

Sam said nothing.

"Who ever heard there should be a grocer," continued Ida, shaking her head scornfully, "who don't think enough about his place of business and his wife, he should go outside and sweep off the snow from the sidewalk a customer should be able to come to the door. It's a shame and a disgrace that a man with a place of business is so lazy he won't get up from a chair. A shame and a disgrace."

"Enough," said Sam quietly.

"I deserve better," she said, raising her voice.

"Enough," he said again.

"Get up," she cried. "Get up and clean the sidewalk."

He turned to her angrily. "Please," he cried, "don't give me orders."

Ida rose and stood near his chair. "Sam, clean off the sidewalk," she shouted in her shrill voice.

"Shut up!" he shouted.

"Clean off the sidewalk!" Her voice was thick with rage.

"Shut up," he roared, rising angrily. "Shut up, you bastard, you."

Ida looked at him uncomprehendingly; then her lips twisted grotesquely, her cheeks bunched up like a gargoyle's, and her body shook with sobs as the hot tears flowed. She sank down into her chair, lowered her head on her arms, and cried with a bitter squealing sound.

Sam groaned inwardly. The words had leaped from his tongue, and now she was crying again. The miserable feeling ground itself into his bones. He cursed the store and his profitless life.

"Where's the shovel?" he asked, defeated.

She did not look up.

He searched for it in the store and found it in the hallway near the cellar door. Sam bounced the shovel against the floor to shake off the cobwebs and then went outside.

The icy February wind wrapped him in a tight, cold jacket, and the frozen snow on the ground gripped his feet like a steel vise. His apron flapped, and the wind blew his thin hair into his eyes. A wave of desperation rolled over him, but he fought against it. Sam bent over, scooped up a pile of snow, and heaved it into the gutter, where it fell and broke. His face was whipped into an icy ruddiness, and cold water ran from his eyes.

Mr. Fine, a retired policeman, one of Sam's customers, trudged by, heavily bundled up.

"For godsake, Sam," he boomed in his loud voice, "put on something warm."

The tenants on the top floor, a young Italian couple, came out of the house on their way to the movies. "You'll catch pneumonia, Mr. Kaplan," said Mrs. Costa.

"That's what I told him," Mr. Fine called back.

"At least put a coat on, Sam," advised Patsy Costa.

"I'm almost through," Sam grunted.

"It's your health," said Patsy. He and his wife pushed their way through the wind and the snow, going to the movies. Sam continued to shovel up the snow and heave it into the gutter.

When he finished cleaning the sidewalk, Sam was half frozen. His nose was running and his eyes were bleary. He went inside quickly. The warmth of the store struck him so hard that the back of his head began to ache, and he knew at once that he had made a mistake in not putting on an overcoat and gloves. He reeled and suddenly felt weak, as if his bones had dissolved and were no longer holding up his body. Sam leaned against the counter to keep himself from falling. When the dizziness went away, he dragged the wet shovel across the floor and put it back in the hall.

Ida was no longer crying. Her eyes were red and she looked away from him as he came into the kitchen. Sam still felt cold. He moved his chair close to the stove and picked up the Jewish paper, but his eyes were so tired that he could not make out the words. He closed them and let the paper slip to the floor. The overpowering warmth of the stove thawed out his chilled body, and he grew sleepy. As he was dozing off, he heard the front door open. With a start, Sam opened his eyes to see if Ida had gone inside. No, she sat at the table in frigid silence. His eyelids shut and opened again. Sam rose with an effort and shuffled into the store. The customer wanted a loaf of bread and ten cents' worth of store cheese. Sam waited on her and returned to his place by the stove. He closed his eyes again and sneezed violently. His nose was running. As he was searching for his handkerchief, the store door opened again.

"Go inside," he said to Ida, "I must take a aspirin."

She did not move.

"I have a cold," he said.

She gave no sign that she had heard.

With a look of disgust, he walked into the store and waited on the customer. In the kitchen, he began to sneeze again. Sam shook two aspirins out of the bottle and lifted them to his mouth with his palm, then he drank some water. As he sat down by the stove, he felt the cold grip him inside and he shivered.

"I'm sick," he said to his wife, but Ida paid no attention to him.

"I'm sick," he repeated miserably. "I'm going upstairs to sleep. Maybe tomorrow I'll feel a little better."

"If you go upstairs now," Ida said, with her back turned toward him, "I will not go in the store."

"So don't go," he said angrily.

"I will not come downstairs tomorrow," she threatened coldly.

"So don't come down," he said brokenly. "The way I feel, I hope the store drops dead. Nineteen years is enough. I can't stand any more. My heart feels dried up. I suffered too much in my life."

He went into the hall. She could hear his slow, heavy footsteps on the stairs and the door closing upstairs.

Ida looked at the clock. It was ten-thirty. For a moment she was tempted to close the store, but she decided not to. The A&P was closed. It was the only time they could hope to make a few cents. She thought about her life and grew despondent. After twenty-two years of married life, a cold flat and an impoverished grocery store. She looked out at the store, hating every inch of it, the dirty window, the empty shelves, showing old brown wallpaper where there were no cans, the old-fashioned wooden icebox, the soiled marble counters, the hard floor, the meagerness, the poverty, and the hard years of toil—for what?—to be insulted by a man without understanding or appreciation of her sacrifices, and to be left alone while he went upstairs to sleep. She could hear the wind blowing outside and she felt cold. The stove needed to be shaken and filled with coal, but she was too tired. Ida decided to close the store. It wasn't worth keeping open. Better for her to go to sleep and come down as late as she chose tomorrow. Let him have to prepare his own breakfast and dinner. Let him wash the kitchen floor and scrub out the icebox. Let him do all the things she did, then he would learn how to speak to her. She locked the front door, put out the window lights, and pulled the cord of each ceiling lamp, extinguishing the light, as she made her way toward the hall door.

Suddenly she heard a sharp tapping against the store window. Ida looked out and saw the dark form of a man who was rapping a coin against the glass.

A bottle of milk, thought Ida.

"Tomorrow," she called out. "The store is now closed."

The man stopped for a second, and she thought with relief that he was going away, but once again he began to rap the coin sharply and insistently. He waved his hands and shouted at her. A woman joined him.

"Mrs. Kaplan!" she called, "Mrs. Kaplan!"

Ida recognized Mrs. Costa. A great fright tore at her heart, and she rushed over to the door.

"What's the matter?" she cried when she opened it.

"Gas," said Patsy. "Gas in the hall. Where's Sam?"

"Oh, my God," cried Ida, pressing her hands against her bosom. "Oh, my God," she cried, "Sam is upstairs."

"Gimme the key, quick," said Patsy.

"Give him the key, Mrs. Kaplan," said Mrs. Costa excitedly.

Ida grew faint. "Oh, my God," she cried.

"Gimme the key," Patsy repeated urgently.

Ida found it in the pocket of her sweater and handed it to Patsy. He ran upstairs, two steps at a time, his wife running after him. Ida closed the store and followed them upstairs. The odor of gas was heavy.

"Oh, my God," she cried over and over again.

Patsy was opening all the windows, and his wife was shaking Sam in his bed. The sharp heavy stink of the gas tore at Ida's nostils as she came into the room.

"Sam!" she shrieked, "Sam!"

He woke from his sleep with a shock. "What's the matter?" he cried, his voice filled with fear.

"Oh, why did you do it?" cried Mrs. Costa in the dark. "Why did you do it?"

"I thank God he's alive," said Patsy.

Ida moaned and squeezed her hands against her bosom.

"What's the matter?" cried Sam. Then he smelled the gas, and for a moment he was paralyzed with fright.

Patsy put on the light. Sam's face was a dark red. He was perspiring from every pore. He pulled up the quilt to cover his shoulders.

"Why did you do it for, Sam?" asked Patsy.

"What? What?" Sam said excitedly, "what did I do?"

"The gas. You turned on the gas radiator without making the light."

"It wasn't lit?" cried Sam in astonishment.

"No," said Mrs. Costa.

Sam grew quieter. He lay back. "I made a mistake," he said. "This is the first time I made such a mistake."

"Didn't you do it on purpose?" asked Mrs. Costa.

"What on purpose? Why on purpose?" Sam asked.

"We thought——"

"No," said Sam, "no, I made a mistake. Maybe the match was no good."

"Then you shoulda smelled the gas," said Patsy.

"No, I got a cold."

"The only thing that saved you was you got a lot of air. You're lucky this flat ain't windproof."

"Yes, I'm lucky," Sam agreed.

"I told you to put on a coat," said Mrs. Costa. "He was standing out in the snow without a coat," she said to Ida.

Ida was pale and silent.

"Well, come on," said Patsy, taking his wife by the arm, "everybody wants to go to sleep."

"Good night," said Mrs. Costa.

"Leave the windows open for a coupla minutes more, and don't light no matches," advised Patsy.

"I'm much obliged to you for your trouble you took," said Sam.

"Don't mention it at all," said Patsy, "but next time take more care."

"It was a mistake," said Sam. "Nothing more, I assure you."

The Costas left. Ida saw them to the door and turned the lock. Sam covered himself more securely with the quilt. The house was freezing with the windows open. He was afraid he would begin to sneeze again. Ida said nothing. Sam fell asleep very soon.

Ida waited until the house was free of the smell of gas. Then she closed the windows. Before undressing, she looked at the radiator and saw that the stopcock was closed. She got into bed, utterly fatigued, and fell asleep immediately.

It seemed to Ida that she had slept only a short time when she awoke suddenly. Frightened, she looked at Sam, but he was bulked up beside her with the covers over his head. She listened to his deep, heavy breathing, and the momentary fear left her. Ida was fully awake now, and the events of the day tumbled quickly through her brain. She thought of the episode of the gas, and a sharp streak of pain ripped through every nerve in her body. Had Sam really tried to take his life? Had he? She wanted to wake him and ask him, but she was afraid. She turned over and tried to sleep again, but she couldn't.

Ida reached over to the night table and looked at the luminous face of the clock. It was four-twenty-five. The alarm would ring at six. Sam would get up and she would ask him, then maybe she could sleep. She closed her eyes, but still no sleep came. She opened them and kept them open.

A faint tinkling on the window caused her to look out. By the light of the street lamp she could see that it was snowing again. The flakes drifted down slowly and silently. They seemed to hang in the air, then the wind rose and blew them against the windows. The windows rattled softly; then everything became quiet again, except for the ticking of the clock.

Ida reached over for the clock and shut off the alarm. It was nearly five. At six o'clock she would get up, dress, and go downstairs. She would pull in the milk box and the bread. Then she would sweep the store, and then the snow from the sidewalk. Let Sam sleep. Later, if he felt better, he could come downstairs. Ida looked at the clock again. Five past five. The sleep would do him good.

Benefit Performance

Maurice Rosenfeld was conscious of himself as he took the key from his pocket and inserted it into the door of his small apartment. The Jewish actor saw his graying hair, the thick black eyebrows, the hunch of disappointment in his shoulders, and the sardonic grimness of his face accentuated by the twisted line of the lips. Rosenfeld turned the key in the lock, aware that he was playing his role well. Tragedy in the twisting of a key, he thought.

"Who's there?" said a voice from inside the apartment.

Surprised, Rosenfeld pushed open the door and saw that it was his daughter who had called out. Sophie was lying in her bed, which became the couch when it was folded together, and her bedroom became the living room. There was one other room, a small one, where Rosenfeld and his wife slept, and an alcove for the kitchen. When her father was working and came home late after the performance, Sophie would set up three screens around her bed so that she would not be awakened by the light which he put on while heating up some milk for himself before going to bed. The screens served another purpose. Whenever Sophie and her father quarreled, she set them up and let him rant outside. Deprived of her presence, he became silent and sulked. She sat on her sofa, reading a magazine by the light of her own lamp and blessing the screens for giving her privacy and preserving her dignity.

The screens were stacked up in the corner, and Rosenfeld was surprised to see his daughter in bed.

"What's the matter?" he said.

"I'm not well," she answered.

"Where's Momma?"

"She went to work."

"Today she's working?"

"She had half a day off. She's working from five to ten."

Rosenfeld looked around. The table in the alcove was not set and it was nearly suppertime.

"She left me to eat, something?"

"No, she thought you were going to eat with Markowitz. Is there anything doing?"

"No," he said bitterly, "nothing is doing. The Jewish theayter is deep in hell. Since the war, the Jews stay home. Everybody else goes out for a good time to forget their troubles, but Jews stay home and worry. Second Avenue is like a tomb."

"What did Markowitz want to see you for?" Sophie asked.

"A benefit, something. I should act in a benefit for Isaac Levin."

"Don't worry," she said, "you had a good season last year."

"I'm too young to live on memories," he said.

Sophie had no answer to that.

"If you want me to make you something, I'll get up," she said.

He walked into the kitchen and looked into the pots on the gas range.

"No, I'll make for myself. Here is some potatoes and carrots left over. I'll warm them up."

"Warm up the hamburger in the oven. Momma made one for me, but I couldn't eat it."

Rosenfeld pulled down the door of the broiler and glanced distastefully at the hamburger on the wire grill. "No, it burns me my stomach when I eat chopmeat," he said, closing the broiler door.

"How is your stomach?" she asked.

He placed his hand underneath his heart. "Today I got gas." He was moved by her solicitousness.

"How are you feeling?" he asked her.

"Like always. The first day is bad."

"It will go away."

"Yes, I know," she said.

•

He lit the flame under the vegetables and began to stir the mashed potatoes. They were lumpy. The remnants of his appetite disappeared.

Sophie saw the look on his face and said, "Put some butter in the potatoes." For a moment Rosenfeld did not move, but when Sophie repeated her suggestion, he opened the icebox.

"What butter?" he said, looking among the bottles and the fruit. "Here is no butter."

Sophie reached for her housecoat, drew it on over her head, and pulled up the zipper. Then she stepped into her slippers.

"I'll put some milk in," she said.

Without wanting to, he was beginning to grow angry.

"Who wants you to? Stay in bed. I'll take care myself of the—the supper," he ended sarcastically.

"Poppa," she said, "don't be stubborn. I've got to get up anyway."

"For me you don't have to get up."

"I said I have to get up anyway."

"What's the matter?"

"Someone is coming."

He turned toward her. "Who's coming?"

"Pa, let's not start that."

"Who's coming?"

"I don't want to fight. I'm sick today."

"Who's coming, answer me."

"Ephraim."

"The plum-ber?" He was sarcastic.

"Please, Pa, don't fight."

"*I* should fight with a plum-ber?"

"You always insult him."

"*I* insult a plum-ber? He insults *me* to come here."

"He's not coming to see you. He's coming to see me."

"He insults *you* to come here. What does a plum-ber, who didn't even finish high school, want with you? You don't need a plum-ber."

"I don't care what I need, Poppa, I'm twenty-eight years old," she said.

"But a plum-ber!"

"He's a good boy. I've known him for twelve years, since we were in high school. He's honest and he makes a nice steady living."

"All right," Rosenfeld said angrily. "So *I* don't make a steady living. So go on, spill some more salt on my bleeding wounds."

"Poppa, don't act, please. I only said *he* made a steady living. I didn't say anything about you."

"Who's acting?" he shouted, banging the icebox door shut and turning quickly. "Even if I didn't support you and your mother steady, at least I showed you the world and brought you in company with the greatest Jewish actors of our times. Adler, Schwartz, Ben-Ami, Goldenburg, all of them have been in my house. You heard the best conversation about life, about books and music and all kinds art. You toured with me everywhere. You were in South America. You were in England. You were in Chicago, Boston, Detroit. You got a father whose Shylock in Yiddish even the American critics came to see and raved about it. *This* is living. *This* is life. Not with a plum-ber. So who is he going to bring into your house, some more plum-bers, they should sit in the kitchen and talk about pipes and how to fix a leak in the toilet? This is living? This is conversation? When he comes here, does he open his mouth? The only thing he says is yes and no, yes and no—like a machine. This is not for you."

Sophie had listened to her father in silence.

"Poppa, that's not fair," she said quietly, "you make him afraid to talk to you."

The answer seemed to satisfy him.

"Don't be so much in the hurry," he said more calmly. "You can get better."

"Please drop the subject."

•

The bell rang. Sophie pressed the buzzer.

"Poppa, for godsake, please be nice to him."

He said nothing but turned to his cooking, and she went into the bathroom.

Ephraim knocked on the door.

"Come in!"

The door opened and he walked in. He was tall, very well built, and neatly dressed. His hair was carefully slicked back, but his hands were beefy and red from constant washing in hot water, which did not remove the calluses on his palms or the grease pockets underneath his nails. He was embarrassed to find only Sophie's father in.

"Is Sophie here?" he asked.

"Good evening," said Rosenfeld sarcastically.

Ephraim blushed.

"Good evening," he said. "Is Sophie here?"

"She will be here in a minute."

"Thank you very much." He remained standing.

Rosenfeld poured some milk into the potatoes and stirred them with a fork. "So you working now in the project houses?" he asked.

Ephraim was surprised to be addressed so politely. "No," he said. "We're working in the Brooklyn Navy Yard on the new ships."

"Hmm, must be a lot of toilets on the battleships?" Rosenfeld asked.

Ephraim did not answer him. Sophie came out of the bathroom with her hair neatly combed and a small blue ribbon in it to match the blue in her housecoat.

"Hello, Eph," she said.

He nodded.

"Sit down," she said, placing a chair near her bed. "I'll get back into bed." She lifted her feet out of the slippers, fixed the pillow so she could sit up, and covered herself with her blanket. Ephraim was facing her. Over his shoulder she could see her father scooping out the vegetables onto a plate. Then he sat down at the table and began to mash them.

"What's new, Eph?" she asked.

He sat with his elbows resting on his knees, the fingers of both hands interlocked.

"Nothing new," he said.

"Did you work today?"

"Only half a day. I got three weeks overtime."

"What else is new?"

He shrugged his shoulders.

"Did you hear about Edith and Mortie?" she asked.

"No," he said. Rosenfeld lowered his fork.

"They got married Sunday."

"That's good," he said.

"Oh, another thing, I bought tickets for the Russian War Relief at Madison Square Garden. Can you go Friday night?"

"Yes," he said. Rosenfeld banged his fork down on his plate. Ephraim did not turn and Sophie did not look up. They were silent for a moment, and then Sophie began again.

"Oh, I forgot," she said, "I wrote to Washington for those civil-service requirements for you. Did your mother tell you?"

"Yes," he said.

Rosenfeld banged his fist on the table. "Yes and no, yes and no," he shouted. "Don't you know no other words?"

Ephraim did not turn around.

"Poppa, *please*," begged Sophie.

"Yes and no," shouted her father, "yes and no. Is this the way to talk to an educated girl?"

Ephraim turned around and said with dignity, "I'm not talking to you. I'm talking to your daughter."

"You not *talking* to her. You *insulting* her with yes and no. This is not talk."

"I'm not an actor," said Ephraim. "I work with my hands."

"Don't open your mouth to insult me."

Ephraim's jaw was trembling. "You insulted me first."

"Please, please," cried Sophie. "Poppa, if you don't stop, I'm going to put up the screens."

"So put up the screens to hide the plum-ber," her father taunted.

"At least a plumber can support a wife and don't have to send her out to work for him," cried Ephraim, his voice full of emotion.

"Oh, Ephraim, don't," moaned Sophie.

For a moment Rosenfeld was stunned. Then his face reddened and he began to stutter, "You nothing, you. You nothing," he cried. His lips moved noiselessly as he tried to find words to say. Suddenly he caught himself and paused. He rose slowly. Rosenfeld crossed his arms over his breast, then raised them ceilingward and began to speak deliberately in fluent Yiddish.

"Hear me earnestly, great and good God. Hear the story of the afflictions of a second Job. Hear how the years have poured misery upon me, so that in my age, when most men are gathering their harvest of sweet flowers, I cull nothing but weeds.

"I have a daughter, O God, upon whom I have lavished my deepest affection, whom I have given every opportunity for growth and education, who has become so mad in her desire for carnal satisfaction that she is ready to bestow herself upon a man unworthy to touch the hem of her garment, to a common, ordinary, wordless, plum-ber, who has neither ideals nor—"

"Poppa," screamed Sophie, "Poppa, stop it!"

Rosenfeld stopped and a look of unutterable woe appeared on his face. He lowered his arms and turned his head toward Ephraim, his nostrils raised in scorn.

"Plum-ber," he said bitterly.

Ephraim looked at him with hatred. He tried to move, but couldn't.

"You cheap actor," he cried suddenly, with venomous fury. "You can go straight to hell!" He strode over to the door, tore it open, and banged it so furiously that the room seemed to shake.

By degrees Rosenfeld lowered his head. His shoulders hunched in disappointment, and he saw himself, with his graying hair, a tragic figure. Again he raised his head slowly and looked in Sophie's direction. She was already setting up the screens. Rosenfeld moved toward the table in the alcove and glanced down at the vegetables on the plate. They bored him. He went over to the gas range, carefully lit the flame under the broiler, and pulled down the door to see whether the hamburger was cooking. It was. He closed the door, lowered the flame a bit, and said quietly:

"Tonight I will eat chopmeat."

1943

The Place

Is Different Now

Late one warm night in July, a week after they had let Wally Mullane out of the hospital on Welfare Island, he was back in his old neighborhood, searching for a place to sleep. He tried the stores on the avenue first, but they were closed, even the candy store on the corner. The hall doors were all shut, and the cellars padlocked. He peered into the barbershop window and cursed his luck for getting there so late, because Mr. Davido would have let him sleep on one of the barber chairs.

He walked for a block along the avenue, past the stores, and turned in on Third Street, where the rows of frame houses began. In the middle of the block, he crossed the street and slipped into an alley between two old-fashioned frame houses. He tried the garage doors, but they were locked too. As he came out of the alley, he spotted a white-topped prowl car with shaded lights moving slowly down the street, close to the curb, under the trees. Ducking back into the alley, he hid behind a tree in the back yard and waited there nervously for the police car to go by. If the car stopped, he would run. He would climb the fences and come out in his mother's yard on Fourth Street, but he didn't like the idea. The lights moved by. In five minutes Wally sneaked out of the alley and walked quickly up the street. He wanted to try the cellars of the private houses but was afraid to because someone might wake and take him for a burglar. They would call the police, and it would be just his luck if his brother Jimmy was driving one of the radio cars.

All night long Wally hunted through the neighborhood, up Fourth, then Fifth Street, then along the parkway, all the way from the cemetery to the railroad cut, which was a block from the avenue and ran parallel to it. He thought of sleeping in the BMT elevated station but didn't have a nickel, so that was out. The coal yard near the railroad cut was out too, because they kept a watchman there. At five o'clock, tired from wandering, he turned into Fourth Street again and stood under a tree, across the street from his mother's house. He wanted to go into the cellar and sleep there, but he thought of Jimmy and his sister Agnes and said to hell with that.

Wally walked slowly down the avenue to the El station and stood on the corner watching it grow light. Gray light seeped into the morning sky, and the quiet streets were full of thinning, warm darkness. It made Wally feel sad. The neighborhood looked the same but wasn't. He thought of the fellows who were gone now and he thought of his friend Vincent Davido, the barber's son, who had been gone since before the war. He thought of himself not having set foot in his own house for years, and it made him feel like crying.

There was an empty milk box in front of the delicatessen. Wally dragged it across the sidewalk and placed it against the El pillar to have a backrest. He was tired but didn't want to fall asleep, because soon the people would be going up to the station and he wanted to see if there was anyone he knew. He thought if he saw two or three people he knew, maybe they would give him about fifty cents and he would have enough for a beer and some ham and eggs.

Just before the sun came up, Wally fell asleep. The people buying their papers at the newsstand looked at him before they went upstairs to the station. Not many of them knew him. A fat man in a gray suit who recognized him stood on the corner with a disgusted look on his face, watching Wally sleep. Wally sat heavy-bellied on the milk box, with his head leaning back against the pillar and his mouth open. His straw-colored hair was slicked back. His face, red and smudged, was unshaven and thick with loose flesh. He had on a brown suit, oily with filth, black shoes, and a soiled shirt, with a rag of a brown tie knotted at the collar.

"The bastard's always drunk," said the fat man to the man from the candy store who had come out to collect the pennies on the newsstand. The storekeeper nodded.

At eight o'clock, a water truck turned the corner of Second Street and rumbled along the avenue toward the El, shooting two fanlike sprays of water out of its iron belly. The water foamed white where it hit the sizzling asphalt and shot up a powdery mist into the air. As the truck turned under the El, the floating cool mist settled upon Wally's sweating face and he woke up. He looked around wildly, but it wasn't Jimmy and the feeling of fright went away.

The day was heavy with wet, blistering heat, and Wally had a headache. His stomach rumbled and his tongue was sour. He wanted to eat but he didn't have a cent.

Several people walked past him on their way to work, and Wally looked at their faces but saw no one he knew. He didn't like to ask strangers for money. It was different if you knew them. Looking into the candy-store window to see the time, he was annoyed that it was eight-twenty-five. From long experience Wally knew that he had missed his best chances. The factory workers and those who worked in the stores had passed by very early in the morning, and the white-collar employees who followed them about an hour or so later were also gone. Only the stragglers and the women shoppers were left. You couldn't get much out of them. Wally thought he would wait awhile, and if no one came along soon, he'd go over to the fruit store and ask them if they had any spoiled fruit.

At half past eight, Mr. Davido, who lived on the top floor above the delicatessen, came out of the house to open his barbershop across the street. He was shocked when he saw Wally standing on the corner. How strange it is, he thought, when you see something that looks as if it was always there and everything seems the same once more.

The barber was a small, dark-skinned man nearing sixty. His fuzzy hair was gray, and he wore old-fashioned pince-nez with a black ribbon attached to them. His arms were short and heavy, and his fingers were stubby, but he maneuvered them well when he was shaving someone or cutting his hair. The customers knew how quickly and surely those short fingers moved when a man was in a hurry to get out of the shop. When there was no hurry, Mr. Davido worked slowly. Sometimes, as he was cutting a man's hair, the man would happen to look into the mirror and see the barber staring absently out the window, his lips pursed and his eyes filled with quiet sadness. Then, in a minute, he would raise his brows and begin cutting again, his short, stubby fingers snipping quickly to make up for time he had lost.

"Hey, Wally," he said, "where you keep yourself? You don't come aroun for a long time."

"I was sick," Wally said. "I was in a hospital."

"Whatsamatter, Wally, you still drinkin poison whiskey?"

"Nah, I ain't allowed to drink anymore. I got diabetes. They took a blood test an it showed diabetes."

Mr. Davido frowned and shook his head. "Take care of yourself," he said.

"I had a bad time. I almost got gangrene. When you get that, they amputate your legs off."

"How you get that, Wally?"

"From my brother Jimmy when he beat me up. My whole legs was swollen. The doctor said it was a miracle I didn't get gangrene."

Wally looked up the avenue as he talked. The barber followed his glance.

"You better keep away from your brother."

"I'm watchin out."

"You better leave this neighborhood, Wally. Your brother told you he don't like you in this neighborhood. There's a lot of jobs nowadays, Wally. Why don't you get some kind of a job and get a furnish room to live?"

"Yeah, I'm thinkin of gettin a job."

"Look every day," said the barber.

"I'll look," said Wally.

"You better look now. Go to the employment agency."

"I'll go," said Wally. "First I'm lookin for somebody. There's a lot of strange faces here. The neighborhood is changed."

"That's right," said the barber, "a lot of the young single fellows is gone. I can tell in the shop. The married men don't come in for shaves like the single fellows, only haircuts. They buy electric razors. The single fellows was sports."

"I guess everyone is gone or they got married," said Wally.

"They went to the war but some never came back, and a lot of them moved away to other places."

"Did you ever hear from Vincent?" Wally asked.

"No."

"I just thought I'd ask you."

"No," said the barber. There was silence for a minute; then he said, "Come over later, Wally. I shave you."

"When?"

"Later."

Wally watched Mr. Davido cross the avenue and go past the drugstore and laundry to his barbershop. Before he went in, he took a key from his vest pocket and wound up the barber pole. The red spiral, followed by the white and blue spirals, went round and round.

A man and a woman walked by, and Wally thought he recognized the man, but whoever he was lowered his eyes and passed by. Wally looked after him contemptuously.

He became tired of watching the stragglers and drifted over to the newsstand to read the headlines. Mr. Margolies, the owner of the candy store, came out again and picked up the pennies on the stand.

Wally was sore. "What's the matter, you think I'm gonna steal your lousy pennies?"

"Please," said Mr. Margolies, "to you I don't have to explain my business."

"I'm sorry I ever spent a cent in your joint."

Mr. Margolies's face grew red. "Go way, you troublemaker, you. Go way from here," he cried, flipping his hand.

"Aw, screwball."

A strong hand grasped Wally's shoulder and swung him around. For an instant he went blind with fear and his body sagged, but when he saw it was his oldest sister, Agnes, standing there with his mother, he straightened, pretending he hadn't been afraid.

"What'd you do now, you drunken slob?" said Agnes in her thick voice.

"I didn't do anything."

Mr. Margolies had seen the look on Wally's face. "He didn't do anything," he said. "He was only blocking the stand so the customers couldn't get near the papers."

Then he retreated into the store.

"You were told to stay out of this neighborhood," rasped Agnes. She was a tall, redheaded woman, very strongly built. Her shoulders were broad, and her thick breasts hung heavily against her yellow dress.

"I was just standin here."

"Who is that, Agnes?" asked his mother, peering through thick glasses.

"It's Wallace," Agnes said disgustedly.

"Hello, Ma," Wally said in a soft voice.

"Wallace, where have you been?" Mrs. Mullane was a stout woman, big-bellied and stoop-shouldered. Her pink scalp shone through her thin white hair, which she kept up with two amber-colored combs. Her eyes blinked under her thick glasses and she clung tightly to her daughter's arm for fear she would walk into something she couldn't see.

"I was in the hospital, Ma. Jimmy beat me up."

"And rightly so, you drunken bum," said Agnes. "You had your chances. Jimmy used to give you money to go to the agencies for a job, and the minute he had his back turned, you hit the bottle."

"It was the Depression. I couldn't get a job."

"You mean nobody would take you after the BMT canned you for spendin the nickel collections on the racehorses."

"Aw, shut up."

"You're a disgrace to your mother and your family. The least you could do is to get out of here and stay out. We suffered enough on account of you."

Wally changed his tone. "I'm sick. The doctor said I got diabetes."

Agnes said nothing.

"Wallace," his mother asked, "did you take a shower?"

"No, Ma."

"You ought to take one."

"I have no place."

Agnes grasped her mother's arm. "I'm takin your mother to the eye hospital."

"Wait awhile, Agnes," said Mrs. Mullane pettishly. "Wallace, are you wearing a clean shirt?"

"No, I ain't, Ma."

"Well, you come home for one."

"Jimmy'd break his back."

"He needs a clean shirt," insisted Mrs. Mullane.

"I got one in the laundry," said Wally.

"Well, then take it out, Wallace."

"I ain't got the money."

"Ma, don't give any money to him. He'll only throw it away on drink."

"He ought to have a clean shirt."

She opened her pocketbook and fumbled in her change purse.

"A shirt is twenty cents," said Agnes.

Mrs. Mullane peered at the coin she held in her hand. "Is this a dime, Agnes?"

"No, it's a penny. Let me get it for you." Agnes took two dimes from the change purse and dropped them into Wally's outstretched palm.

"Here, bum."

He let it go by. "Do you think I could have a little something to eat with, Ma?"

"No," said Agnes. She gripped her mother's elbow and walked forward.

"Change your shirt, Wallace," Mrs. Mullane called to him from the El steps. Wally watched them go upstairs and disappear into the station.

He felt weak, his legs unsteady. Thinking it was because his stomach was empty, he decided to get some pretzels and beer with the dimes. Later, he could get some spoiled fruit from the fruit store and would ask Mr. Davido for some bread. Wally walked along under the El to Mc-Cafferty's tavern, near the railroad cut.

Opening the screen door, he glanced along the bar and was almost paralyzed with fright. His brother Jimmy, in uniform, was standing at the rear of the bar drinking a beer. Wally's heart banged hard as he stepped back and closed the screen door. It slipped from his hand and slammed shut. The men at the bar looked up, and Jimmy saw Wally through the door.

"Jesus Christ!"

Wally was already running. He heard the door slam and knew Jimmy was coming after him. Though he strained every muscle in his heavy, jouncing body, he could hear Jimmy's footsteps coming nearer. Wally sped down the block, across the tracks of the railroad siding, and into the coal yard. He ran past some men loading a coal truck and crossed the cobblestoned yard, with his brother coming after him. Wally's lungs hurt. He wanted to run inside the coal loft and hide, but he knew he would be cornered there. He looked around wildly, then made for the hill of coal near the fence. He scrambled up. Jimmy came up after him, but Wally kicked down the coal and it hit Jimmy on the face and chest. He slipped and cursed, but gripped his club and came up again. At the top of the coal pile, Wally boosted himself up on the fence and dropped heavily to the other side. As he hit the earth his legs shook, but fear would not let him stop. He ran across a back yard and thumped up the inclined wooden cellar door, jumping clumsily over a picket fence. Out of the corner of his eye he saw Jimmy hoisting himself over the coal-yard fence. Wally wanted to get into the delicatessen man's back yard so he could go down to the cellar and come out on the avenue. Mr. Davido would let him hide in the toilet of the barbershop.

Wally ran across the flower bed in the next back yard and lifted himself over the picket fence. His sweaty palms slipped and he pitched forward, his pants cuff caught on one of the pointed boards. His hands were in the soft earth of an iris bed, and he dangled from the picket fence by one leg. He wriggled his leg and pulled frantically. The cuff tore away and he fell into the flower bed. He pushed himself up, but before he could move, Jimmy had hurdled the fence and tackled him. Wally fell on the ground, the breath knocked out of him. He lay there whimpering.

"You dirty bastard," Jimmy said. "I'll break your goddamn back."

He swung his club down on Wally's legs. Wally shrieked and tried to pull in his legs, but Jimmy held him down and whacked him across the thighs and buttocks. Wally tried to shield his legs with his arms, but Jimmy beat him harder.

"Oh, please, please, please," cried Wally, wriggling under his brother's blows, "please, Jimmy, my legs, my legs. Don't hit my legs!"

"You scum."

"My legs," screamed Wally, "my legs, I'll get gangrene, my legs, my legs!"

The pain burned through his body. He felt nauseated. "My legs," he moaned.

Jimmy let up. He wiped his wet face and said, "I told you to stay the hell outta this neighborhood. If I see you here again, I'll murder you."

Looking up, Wally saw two frightened women gazing at them out of their windows. Jimmy brushed off his uniform and went over to the cellar door. He pulled it open and walked downstairs.

Wally lay still among the trampled flowers.

"Why didn't the policeman arrest him?" asked Mrs. Werner, the delicatessen man's wife.

"It's the policeman's brother," explained Mrs. Margolies.

He lay on his stomach, arms outstretched, and his cheek pressed against the ground. His nose was bleeding, but he was too exhausted to move. The sweat ran down his arms and the back of his coat was stained dark with it. For a long while he had no thoughts; then the nausea subsided a little, and bits of things floated through his mind. He recalled how he used to play in the coal yard with Jimmy when they were kids. He thought of the Fourth Street boys coasting down the snow-covered sides of the railroad cut in the winter. Then he thought of standing in front of the candy store on quiet summer evenings, with his shirtsleeves rolled up, smoking and fooling around with Vincent and the guys, talking about women, good times, and ballplayers, while they all waited for the late papers to come in. He thought about Vincent, and he remembered the day Vincent went away. It was during the Depression, and the unemployed guys stood on the corner, smoking and chewing gum and making remarks to the girls who passed by. Like Wally, Vincent had quit going to the agencies, and he stayed on the corner with the rest of them, smoking and spitting around. A girl passed by and Vincent said something to her which made the guys laugh. Mr. Davido was looking out the window of the barbershop across the street. He slammed down the scissors and left the customer sitting in the chair. His face was red as he crossed the street. He grabbed Vincent by the arm and struck him hard across the face, shouting, "You bum, why don't you go look for a job?" Vincent's face turned gray. He didn't say anything, but walked away, and they never saw him again. That's how it was.

Mrs. Margolies said, "He's laying there for a long time. Do you think he's dead?"

"No," said Mrs. Werner, "I just saw him move."

Wally pushed himself up and stumbled down the stone steps of the cellar. Groping his way along the wall, he came up the stairs in front of the delicatessen. He searched through his pockets for the twenty cents his mother had given him but couldn't find them. The nausea came back and he wanted a place to sit down and rest. He crossed the street, walking unsteadily toward the barbershop.

Mr. Davido was standing near the window, sharpening a straight razor on a piece of sandstone. The sight of Wally that morning had brought up old memories, and he was thinking about Vincent. As he rubbed the razor round and round on the lathered sandstone, he glanced up and saw Wally staggering across the street. His pants were torn and covered with dirt, and his face was bloody. Wally opened the screen door, but Mr. Davido said sharply, "Stay outta here now, you're drunk."

"Honest I ain't," said Wally. "I didn't have a drop."

"Why you look like that?"

"Jimmy caught me and almost killed me. My legs must be black and blue." Wally lowered himself into a chair.

"I'm sorry, Wally." Mr. Davido got him some water, and Wally swallowed a little.

"Come on, Wally, on the chair," the barber said heartily. "I shave you an you rest an feel cooler."

He helped Wally onto the barber's chair; then he lowered the back and raised the front so that Wally lay stretched out as if he were on a bed. The barber swung a towel around his neck and began to rub a blob of hot lather into his beard. It was a tough beard and hadn't been shaved for a week. Mr. Davido rubbed the lather in deeply with his gentle, stubby fingers.

As he was rubbing Wally's beard, the barber looked at him in the mirror and thought how he had changed. The barber's eyes grew sad as he recalled how things used to be, and he turned away to look out the window. He thought about his son Vincent. How wonderful it would be if Vincent came home someday, he would put his arms around his boy and kiss him on the cheek . . .

Wally was also thinking how it used to be. He remembered how it was when he looked in the mirror before going out on Saturday night. He had a yellow mustache and wore a green hat. He remembered his expensive suits and the white carnation in his buttonhole and a good cigar to smoke.

He opened his eyes.

"You know," he said, "the place is different now."

"Yes," said the barber, looking out the window.

Wally closed his eyes.

Mr. Davido looked down at him. Wally was breathing quietly. His lips were pulled together tightly, and the tears were rolling down his cheeks. The barber slowly raised the lather until it mixed with the tears.

1943

Steady Customer

The two lunch waitresses had heard the sad news from Mr. Mollendorf when they came in at ten-thirty, and for the rest of the day their eyes were red and swollen from crying. After lunch, when things grew slow, they sat on the bench in front of the wall mirror in the rear of the restaurant and they would look at Eileen's empty tables, and then they would begin to cry again. At four o'clock, after the two girls for the evening meal had hung up their raincoats and umbrellas and had changed into their uniforms, Gracie and Clara told them, and the four of them began to cry.

"She was only twenty-eight," wept Mary, and the sobs grew louder as the girls thought of Eileen lying dead in the hospital after her gallbladder operation.

At four-fifteen, Mr. Mollendorf, the chef and owner of the restaurant, came out of the kitchen in his apron and chef's cap and asked them please to control themselves and set the tables for the evening meal. It was a sad thing that had happened, but this was a business establishment from which they all drew their living, and it wasn't good for the customers to be served by a bunch of crying women. As he turned to go into the kitchen, something occurred to Mr. Mollendorf and he said, "Which one of you girls wants to serve Eileen's station tonight?"

No one spoke. They were almost horrified at the thought.

"The one who serves it tonight can serve it all the time from now on," said Mr. Mollendorf.

No one answered him. They knew Eileen's station was the best in the restaurant, good for at least a dollar more each night, but no one spoke.

"Well, what about you, Gracie? You were her best friend," said the boss.

"No, please, no, Mr. Mollendorf. Honest, I just couldn't."

"Clara? You could use a little extra money."

"No, thanks, Mr. Mollendorf."

"Mary?"

"No, sir."

"Elsie?"

"No, thank you."

Mr. Mollendorf shrugged his shoulders. "In that case, okay," he said. "Now I just got to call the agency for a new girl and give her the best station."

The girls, neatly attired in their trim black-and-white uniforms, were silent. They all looked so frightened Mr. Mollendorf felt sorry for them.

"Okay, girls," he said in a kind voice, "don't worry. I'm hurt too. She was a very fine person, very fine, and only twenty-eight years." He wiped his eye with the back of his hand and then went back into the kitchen.

"He ain't so bad," said Mary. They all agreed Mr. Mollendorf was all right. They set the tables for the evening meal. The afternoon dragged on and it began to rain harder outside.

"Even the heavens are crying," said Mary.

"I guess the supper will be spoiled," said Clara.

"Let it," Elsie said. "I don't feel like working anyway, when I think of her laying there dead in the hospital."

"You know what?" said Gracie quietly.

"What?"

"Her—her steady customer—"

The girls had forgotten him. In spite of themselves, the tears came once more.

"When he comes in, I'm not gonna let any new girl wait on him," Gracie told them, "I'm gonna wait on him myself."

"That's right, Gracie," Clara agreed. "You couldn't let a stranger tell him. It just—well, it wouldn't be right."

At five-thirty, the new girl came from the agency. She carried her uniform in a cardboard dress box from Klein's. Mr. Mollendorf told Gracie to take her downstairs to change, then give her the bill of fare and show her where things were. Gracie took the new waitress, whose name was Rose, downstairs to the lockers. Then she told Rose about Eileen and her operation.

"I'm very sorry to hear that," said Rose, "truly I am. I don't want to enrich myself on the dead."

"No, nobody does."

"Leastways not I."

Gracie told her about Eileen's steady customer. "When he comes in, will you mind if I serve him?" she asked. "You know, it's more personal."

"I understand perfectly," Rose said. "Anything I can do, I will gladly do it."

"Thanks."

"Were they goin together?"

"Well—not exactly, but they woulda soon. He's been coming here every night for the past two years and he always sits at Eileen's table. She knew exactly what he wanted. All he does is give the meat order, everything else is the same. First, he has fruit cup, then green-pea soup with croutons or vegetable soup—it's all according what we're serving—then he has his meat order—medium, with string beans and mashed potatoes, and then homemade apple pie or blueberry pie, if blueberries are in season, and coffee with two creams, because he likes it light. Eileen knew exactly what he wanted. He didn't have to say two words."

"He musta been used to her."

"Yeah, and he liked her. At first he was shy and didn't talk to her much, but after about five or six months she sorta won him around with her smile and her nice ways and he began to talk to her. Eileen always said he was very smart. He used to know everything about current events and the war and stuff like that."

"Do you think he'll take it bad?"

"Yeah," said Gracie, "I think so—that's why I want to tell him myself. You know how it is."

"Yes I know," Rose said sentimentally.

•

Rose had changed into her uniform, which was also black with a white collar and cuffs and a white apron. A customer could tell that she hadn't worked there before, because her shoes were black whereas the other girls wore white shoes.

Gracie introduced Rose to the girls and showed her Eileen's section. "He sits in this seat here," she said, pointing to the third table along the wall. "You can recognize him because he's thin and sorta blond and he always reads the *World-Telegram*."

"If I see him, I'll call you," said Rose.

"That's right."

They went back to the bench near the mirror and the girls sat there talking in quiet tones. They told Rose stories of Eileen's goodness—how she never got married because she was supporting her old mother, whom her two married brothers had neglected, and how pretty and good-natured she was, never getting angry at a girl who cut in ahead of her in the kitchen, and how she was always smiling so that everyone liked her.

The girls watched the rain streaming down the windows. The restaurant was empty and seemed emptier still when they looked at each of the tables so neatly set with silverware and white napkins and tablecloths. At the front of the store the cashier read a book, and the waitresses sat at the back in the half darkness, thinking about the things people think when somebody has just died.

•

"What time does this guy come in?" Rose asked Gracie while they were getting desserts in the kitchen.

"Usually half past seven."

Rose looked at her wristwatch. "It's ten to eight."

"Sometimes he don't come in. Maybe on account of the rain he won't come in tonight," Gracie said.

"I hope he does."

When Gracie went outside again, she saw him hanging up his coat near his regular table and her heart skipped a beat. She served her desserts and caught Rose's eye. Rose looked and saw him reading the *World-Telegram*. She smiled knowingly. The other waitresses saw the interchange of glances and the atmosphere grew tense.

Gracie straightened her apron and tried to calm herself. She decided to say nothing and let him ask. She went over to the table in Eileen's section and poured a glass of water for the man. He looked up from his newspaper. His eyes were a kind of dull blue and his hair was dry and thinning on top. He was mildly surprised at seeing Gracie.

"Shall—shall I give you the order?"

"Yes, sir." She would tell him when he asked her where Eileen was. Gracie girded herself for the moment. The girls were at their tasks, looking up to see what was going on.

"Well," he said, lightly rubbing his cheek with his long, bony fingers, "I usually take a fruit cup, and green-pea soup with croutons. Then tonight I'll have chopped steak—medium, please, and string beans and mashed potatoes."

Gracie wrote quickly.

"I usually take blueberry pie and coffee with two creams for dessert."

She closed her book and stood there for a minute, waiting for him to ask about Eileen, but he turned to his paper. She was disappointed. He looked up again.

"Did I—is something wrong?"

"No, sir." She walked hurriedly into the kitchen, her face set hard.

•

Two of the girls gathered around her in the kitchen.

"Did you tell him?" asked Mary.

"No, he didn't even ask where she was."

Mary's face fell. "Oh," she exclaimed, disappointed.

"That's the way they are," said Clara philosophically. "They don't know whether you're dead or alive and they don't care."

"Yeah," said Gracie.

"Maybe he thinks she's off tonight," Mary suggested.

Gracie brightened. "You got somethin," she said, "except he knew she was off Thursdays, and this is Tuesday."

"Yes, but maybe he forgot."

"Tell him outright," said Clara, "tell him outright and see what he says."

"Yes, maybe I'll do that."

Gracie got the bread and butter, some salad, and a fruit cup. She set the food down on his table, and he lowered his newspaper.

"Sir," she said.

He looked up, almost frightened.

"Being you're a steady customer," she said, "I thought you might be interested to know that Eileen, the girl who usually serves here—well, she's—she passed away this morning in the hospital from a gallbladder operation."

Gracie wasn't able to control herself. Her mouth was distorted and the tears began to roll down her cheeks. The girls knew that she had told him.

He didn't know what to say. He swallowed and was embarrassed, and he looked around nervously at the other tables.

"I—I see," he said, his voice curiously uncontrolled. "I'm sorry." His eyes dropped to the paper. Gracie blinked the tears out of her eyes and pressed her lips tightly together. She walked quickly away.

"The hell with him," she said to Clara in the kitchen. "The hell with him. I only hope he croaks."

"He deserves it," Clara said.

Gracie called Rose over. She tore out his check from her order book. "Here," she said, "serve him. I can't stand his guts."

"Did you tell him?" asked Rose.

"I told him all right, but nothing to what I'd like to tell him."

"They're all alike," said Clara.

The word went around to the other girls, and they looked at him scornfully as they walked past his table with their loaded trays. Rose served him mechanically. She removed his fruit dish and shoved down the soup. He seemed not to notice. His eyes were on his paper.

The girls were angry and talked about him in the kitchen.

"You'd think he'd show a little loyalty," said Mary.

"Didn't he ask more about it?"

"No, he just said, 'I see. I'm sorry'—cold like, and he didn't say another word."

"I'd like to ram this chopped steak down his throat," Rose said vehemently.

"Me too," said Clara.

They went out again, but they could not control their glances. Before long, the customers were staring in the direction of the man. From the scornful faces of the waitresses they knew that something was wrong.

Once, he glanced up and he saw the people looking at him. His eyes fell quickly, and his hand trembled as he cut his meat. Then suddenly he wiped his lips and laid his napkin on the table. He picked up his check and took his hat and coat from the hook on the wall. His face was very white. He quickly paid his check and left.

The girls were stunned. They stood frozen, their serving suspended. When the door closed behind him, they gathered together some soiled dishes and hurried into the kitchen.

"Did you see that?" asked Clara. "He left right in the middle of the meal."

"He must've felt sick about Eileen," said Mary.

"Maybe he saw how we felt about him," Gracie said.

"No, I don't think so. I think Mary's right," Clara said. "Some guys are like that. They don't talk much, but inside they eat their heart out."

"I don't know," said Gracie.

"For godsakes, girls," called Mr. Mollendorf, "I'm running a restaurant here, not a meeting hall. Go back to your tables."

The group broke up. They filed out into the restaurant through the swinging doors.

"I'm convinced," Clara said to Gracie, "I'm convinced he really and truly loved her."

1943

The Literary Life of

Laban Goldman

Coming upstairs, Laban Goldman was rehearsing arguments against taking his wife to the movies so that he could attend his regular classes in night school, when he met Mrs. Campbell, his neighbor, who lived in the apartment next door.

"Look, Mrs. Campbell," said Laban, holding up a newspaper. "Again! This time in *The Brooklyn Eagle*."

"Another letter?" Mrs. Campbell said. "How do you do it?"

"They like the way I express myself on the subject of divorce." He pointed to his letter in the newspaper.

"I'll read it over later," Mrs. Campbell said. "Joe brings home the *Eagle*. He cuts out your letters. You know, he showed everyone the one about tolerance. Everyone thought the sentiments were very excellent."

"You mean my *New York Times* letter?" Laban beamed.

"Yes, it had excellent sentiments," said Mrs. Campbell, continuing downstairs. "Maybe someday you ought to write a book."

A tremor of bittersweet joy shook Laban Goldman. "With all my heart, I concur with your hope," he called down after her.

"Nobody can tell," Mrs. Campbell said.

Laban opened the door of his apartment and stepped into the hallway. The meeting with Mrs. Campbell had given him confidence. He felt that his arguments would take on added eloquence. As he was hanging up his hat and coat on the clothes tree in the hall, he heard his wife talking on the telephone.

"Laban?" she called.

"Yes." He tried to make it sound cold.

Emma came into the hallway. She was a small woman, heavily built.

"Sylvia is calling," she said.

He held up the paper. "The editor printed a letter," he said quickly. "It means I will have to go to school tonight."

Emma clutched her hands and pressed them to her bosom. "Laban," she cried, "you promised me."

"Tomorrow night."

"No, tonight!"

"Tomorrow night."

"Laban!" she screamed.

He held his ground. "Don't make an issue," he said. "Tomorrow is the same picture."

Emma bounded over to the telephone. "Sylvia," she cried, "you see, now he doesn't go."

Laban tried to duck into his room, but she was too quick for him.

"Telephone," she announced coldly. Wearily he walked over to the phone.

"Poppa," said Sylvia, "why have you broken your promise that you gave to Momma?"

"Listen, Sylvia, for a minute, without talking. I didn't break my promise. All I want to do is to delay or postpone it till tomorrow, and she jumps to conclusions."

"You promised me today," cried Emma, who was standing there, listening.

"Please," he said, "have the common decency to refrain from talking when I'm talking to someone else."

"You are talking to my daughter," she declared with dignity.

"I am well aware and conscious that your daughter is your daughter."

"All the time big words," she taunted.

"Poppa, don't fight," said Sylvia over the telephone. "You promised you would take Momma to the movies tonight."

"It just so happens that my presence is required in school tonight. *The Brooklyn Eagle* printed a vital letter I wrote, and Mr. Taub, my English teacher, likes to discuss them in class."

"Can't it wait till tomorrow?"

"The issue is alive and pertinent today. Tomorrow, today's paper will be yesterday's."

"What is the letter about?"

"It's a sociological subject of import. You will read it."

"Poppa, this can't go on," said Sylvia sharply. "I have two young children to take care of. I can't keep tearing myself away from my family every other night to take Momma to the movies. It's your duty to take her out."

"I have no alternative."

"What do you mean, Poppa?"

"My education comes first."

"You can get just as much education four nights a week as you can five."

"That will not hold water mathematically," he said.

"Poppa, you're a pretty smart man. Couldn't you stay home just one night a week, say on Wednesdays, and take Momma out?"

"To me, the movies are not worth it."

"You mean your wife is not worth it," broke in Emma again.

"I wasn't talking to you," said Laban.

"Don't fight, *please*," said Sylvia. "Poppa, try to be considerate."

"I'm *too* considerate," Laban said. "That's why I didn't advance in my whole life up to now. It's about time I showed some consideration for myself."

"I'm not going to argue with you about that anymore, but I warn you, Poppa, you will have to take more responsibility about Momma. It isn't fair to let her stay home all alone at night."

"That's her problem."

"It's yours," broke in Emma.

Laban lost his temper. "It's yours," he shouted.

"Goodbye, Poppa," said Sylvia hastily. "Tell Momma I'll come over at eight o'clock."

Laban hung up the receiver. His wife's face was red. Her whole body was heaving with indignation.

"To who you married," she asked bitterly, "to the night school?"

"Twenty-seven years I have been married to you in a life which I got nothing from it," he said.

"You got to eat," she said, "you got to sleep, and you got a nice house. From your wife who brought up your child, I will say nothing."

"This is ancient history," sneered Laban. "Tell me, please, have I got understanding? Did I get encouragement to study to take civil-service examinations so I am now a government clerk who is making twenty-six hundred dollars a year and always well provided for his family? Did I get encouragement to study subjects in high school?

Did I get praise when I wrote letters to the editor which the best papers in New York saw fit to print them? Answer me this."

"Hear thou me, Laban—" began Emma in Yiddish.

"Talk English, please," Laban shouted. "When in Rome, do what the Romans do."

"I don't express myself so good in English."

"So go to school and learn."

Emma completely lost her temper. "Big words I need to clean the house? School I need to cook for you?" she shouted.

"You don't have to cook for me!"

"I don't have to cook?" she asked sarcastically. "So good!" Emma drew herself up. "So tonight, cook your own supper!" She stomped angrily into the hall and turned at the door of her room. "And when you'll get an ulcer from your cooking," she said, "so write a letter to the editor." She banged the door of her room shut.

•

Laban went into his room and stuffed his books and newspaper into his briefcase. "She makes my whole life disagreeable," he muttered. He put on his hat and coat and went downstairs. His first impulse had been to go to the restaurant, but his appetite was gone, so he went to the cafeteria on the corner of the avenue near the school. The quarrel had depressed him because he had counted on avoiding it. He ate half a sandwich, drank his coffee, and hurried off to school.

He went through his biology and geometry classes without paying much attention to the discussions, but his interest picked up in his Spanish class when Miss Moscowitz, who was also in his English class, came into the room. Laban nodded to her. She was a tall, thin young woman in her early thirties. Except for her glasses and a few pockmarks on her cheek, almost entirely hidden by the careful use of rouge, she wasn't bad-looking. She and Laban were the shining lights of their English class, and it thrilled him to think how he would impress her with his letter. He debated with himself on the procedure of introducing the letter into the discussion. Should he ask Mr. Taub for permission to read the letter to the class, or should he wait for a favorable moment and surprise the class by reading the letter then? He decided to wait. When he thought how dramatic the scene would be, Laban's excitement grew. The bell rang. He gathered up his books and, without waiting for Miss Moscowitz, walked toward his English room.

Mr. Taub began the lesson with a discussion on the element of fate in *Romeo and Juliet*, the play the class had just read. The class, adults and young people, both American and foreign-born, gave their opinions on the subject as Laban nervously sought for an opening. He was usually very active in this type of discussion, but he decided not to participate too much tonight in order to give his full attention to discovering a subject relevant to the letter. Miss Moscowitz was particularly effective in her answers. She analyzed the various elements of the plot with such impressive clarity that the class held its breath as she talked. Laban squirmed uncomfortably in his seat as the period grew shorter. He knew that he would feel miserable if he had not read his letter, especially since he had not even participated in the discussion. Mr. Taub brought up another question: "How did the lovers themselves contribute to their tragedy?"

Again Miss Moscowitz's hand shot up. The teacher looked around, but no hands were raised so he nodded to her.

"Their passion was the cause of the tragedy," said Miss Moscowitz, rising from her seat; but before she could go on, Laban Goldman's hand was waving in the air.

"Ah, Mr. Goldman," said the teacher, "we haven't heard from you tonight. Suppose we let him go on, Miss Moscowitz?"

"Gladly," she said, resuming her seat.

Laban rose and nodded to Miss Moscowitz. He tried to appear at ease, but his whole body was throbbing with excitement. He stepped into the aisle, thrust his right hand into his trouser pocket, and cleared his throat.

"A young woman like Miss Moscowitz should be complimented on her very clear and visionary answers. There was once a poet who quoted 'Passions spin the plot,' and Miss Moscowitz saw that this quotation is also true in this play. The youthful lovers, Romeo and Juliet, both of them were so overwhelmed and disturbed by their youthful ardor for each other that they could not discern or see clearly what their problems would be. This is not true only of these Shakespeare lovers, but also of all people in particular. When a man is young, he is carried away by his ardor and passion for a woman with the obvious and apparent result that he don't take into consideration his wife's real characteristics—whether she is suited to be his mate in mind as well as in the body. The result of this incongruence is very frequently tragedy or, nowadays, divorce. On this subject I would like to quote you some words of mine which were printed in a newspaper, *The Brooklyn Eagle*, today."

He paused and looked at the teacher.

"Please do," said Mr. Taub. The class buzzed with interest.

Laban's hands trembled as he took the paper from his briefcase. He cleared his throat again.

To the Editor of *The Brooklyn Eagle*:

I would like to point out to your attention that there are many important problems that we are forgetting on account of the war. It is not my purpose or intention to disavow the war, but it is my purpose to say a few words on the subject of divorce.

New York State is back in the dark ages where this problem is concerned. Many a man of unstained reputation has his life filled with the darkness of tragedy because he will not allow his reputation to be defiled or soiled. I refer to adultery, which, outside of desertion, which takes too long, is the only practicable means of securing a divorce in this state. When will we become enlightened enough to learn that incompatibility "breeds contempt," and that such a condition festers in the mind the way adultery festers in the body?

In view of this fact, there is only one conclusion—that we ought to have a law here to provide us with divorce on the grounds of incompatibility. I consider this to be *Quod Erat Demonstrandum*.

Laban Goldman
Brooklyn, January 28, 1942

Laban lowered his paper, and in the pause that ensued he said, "I don't have to explain to the people in this class who are taking Geometry 1 or 2 what this Latin quotation means."

The class was deeply impressed. They applauded as Laban sat down. His legs trembled, but he was filled with the great happiness of triumph.

"Thank you, Mr. Goldman," said Mr. Taub. "It pleases me to see that you are continuing your literary pursuits, and I should like the class to note that there was a definite Introduction, Body, and Conclusion in Mr. Goldman's composition—that is to say—his letter. Without having seen the paper, I feel sure that there are three paragraphs in the letter he read to us. Isn't that so, Mr. Goldman?"

"Absolutely!" said Laban. "I invite all to inspect the evidence."

Miss Moscowitz's hand shot up. The teacher nodded.

"I don't know how the class feels, but I for one am honored to be in a class with a man of Mr. Goldman's obvious experience and literary talent. I thought that the gist of the letter was definitely very excellent."

The class applauded as she sat down. The bell rang, and school was over for the night.

•

Laban caught up with Miss Moscowitz in the hall and walked downstairs with her. "The bell rang too soon before I could reciprocate the way you felt about me," he said.

"Oh, thank you," said Miss Moscowitz, her face lighting with happiness. "That makes it mutual."

"Without doubt," said Laban, as they were continuing downstairs. He felt very good.

The students poured out into the street and began to disperse in many directions, but Laban did not feel like going home. The glow of triumph was warm within him, and he felt that he wanted to talk. He tipped his hat and said, "Miss Moscowitz, I realize I am a middle-aged man and you are a young woman, but I am young in my mind so I would like to continue our conversation. Would you care to accompany me to the cafeteria, we should have some coffee?"

"Gladly," said Miss Moscowitz, "and I am not such a young woman. Besides, I get along better with a more mature man."

Very much pleased, he took her arm and led her up the block to the cafeteria on the corner. Miss Moscowitz arranged the silverware and the paper napkins on the table while he went for the coffee and cake.

As they sipped their coffee, Laban felt twenty years younger, and a sense of gladness filled his heart. It seemed to him that his past was like a soiled garment which he had cast off. Now his vision was sharp and he saw things clearly. When he looked at Miss Moscowitz, he was surprised and pleased to see how pretty she was. Within him, a great torrent of words was fighting for release.

"You know, Miss Moscowitz—" he began.

"Please call me Ruth," she said.

"Ah, Ruth, ever faithful in the Bible," Laban mused. "My name is Laban."

"Laban, that's a distinguished name."

"It's also a biblical name. What I started out to say," he went on, "was to tell you the background of my letter which they printed today."

"Oh, please do, I am definitely interested."

"Well, that letter is true and autobiographical," he said impressively.

"Without meaning to be personal, how?" she asked.

"Well, I'll tell you in a nutshell," Laban said. "You are a woman of intelligence and you will understand. What I meant," he went on, acknowledging her smile with a nod, "what I meant was that I was the main character in the letter." He sought carefully for his words. "Like Romeo and Juliet, I was influenced by passion when I was a young man, and the result was I married a woman who was incompatible with my mind."

"I'm very sorry," said Miss Moscowitz.

Laban grew moody. "She has no interest in the subjects I'm interested in. She don't read much and she don't know the elementary facts about psychology and the world."

Miss Moscowitz was silent.

"If I had married someone with my own interests when I was young," he mused, "—someone like you, why I can assure you that this day I would be a writer. I had great dreams for writing, and with my experience and understanding of life, I can assure you that I would write some very fine books."

"I believe you," she said. "I really do."

He sighed and looked out of the window.

Miss Moscowitz glanced over his shoulder and saw a short, stout woman with a red, angry face bearing down upon them. She held a cup of coffee in her hand and was trying to keep it from spilling as she pushed her way toward Laban's table. A young woman was trying to restrain her. Miss Moscowitz sized up the situation at once.

"Mr. Goldman," she said in a tight voice, "your wife is coming."

He was startled and half rose, but Emma was already upon them.

"So this is night school!" she cried angrily, banging the half-spilled cup of coffee on the table. "This is education every night?"

"Momma, please," begged Sylvia, "everyone is looking."

"He is a married man, you housebreaker!" Emma shouted at Miss Moscowitz.

Miss Moscowitz rose. Her face had grown pale, and the pockmarks were quite visible.

"I can assure you that the only relationship that I have had with Mr. Goldman is purely platonic. He is a member of my English class," she said with dignity.

"Big words," sneered Emma.

"Be still," Laban cried. He turned to Miss Moscowitz. "I apologize to you, Miss Moscowitz. This is my cross I bear," he said bitterly.

"Poppa, please," begged Sylvia.

Miss Moscowitz picked up her books.

"Wait," called Laban, "I will pay your check."

"Over my dead body," cried Emma.

"That will not be necessary," said Miss Moscowitz. "Good night." She paid her check and went out through the revolving door.

"You ignoramus, you," shouted Laban, "look what you did!"

"Oh, he's cursing me," Emma wailed, bursting into tears.

"Oh, Poppa, this is so mortifying," said Sylvia. "Everyone is staring at us."

"Let them look," he said. "Let them see what a man of sensitivity and understanding has to suffer because of incompatible ignorance." He snatched up his briefcase, thrust his hat on his head, and strode over to the door. He tossed a coin on the counter and pushed through the revolving door into the street. Emma was still sobbing at the table, and Sylvia was trying to comfort her.

Laban turned at the corner and walked down the avenue in the direction away from his home. The good feeling was gone and a mood of depression settled upon him as he thought about the scene in the cafeteria. To his surprise he saw things clearly, more clearly than he ever had before. He thought about his life with quiet objectivity and he enjoyed the calmness that came to him as he did so. The events of the day flowed into his thoughts, and Laban remembered his triumph in the classroom. The feeling of depression lifted.

"Ah," he sighed, as he walked along, "with my experience, what a book I could really write!"

1943

❧ B M ❧

The Cost of Living

Winter had fled the city streets but Sam Tomashevsky's face, when he stumbled into the back room of his grocery store, was a blizzard. Sura, sitting at the round table eating bread and a salted tomato, looked up in fright, and the tomato turned a deeper red. She gulped the bite she had bitten and with pudgy fist socked her chest to make it go down. The gesture already was one of mourning, for she knew from the wordless sight of him there was trouble.

"My God," Sam croaked.

She screamed, making him shudder, and he fell wearily into a chair. Sura was standing, enraged and frightened.

"Speak, for God's sake."

"Next door," Sam muttered.

"What happened next door?"—upping her voice.

"Comes a store!"

"What kind of a store?" The cry was piercing.

He waved his arms in rage. "A grocery comes next door."

"Oi." She bit her knuckle and sank down moaning. It could not have been worse.

They had, all winter, been haunted by the empty store. An Italian shoemaker had owned it for years, and then a streamlined shoe-repair shop had opened up next block where they had two men in red smocks hammering away in the window and everyone stopped to look. Pellegrino's business had slackened off as if someone was shutting a faucet, and one day he had looked at his workbench, and when everything stopped jumping, it loomed up ugly and empty. All morning he had sat motionless, but in the afternoon he put down the hammer he had been clutching and got his jacket and an old darkened Panama hat a customer had never called for when he used to do hat cleaning and blocking; then he went into the neighborhood, asking among his former customers for work they might want done. He collected two pairs of shoes, a man's brown-and-white ones for summertime and a pair of lady's dancing slippers. At the same time, Sam found his own soles and heels had been worn paper thin for being so many hours on his feet—he could feel the cold floorboards under him as he walked—and that made three pairs altogether, which was what Mr. Pellegrino had that week—and another pair the week after. When the time came for him to pay next month's rent he sold everything to a junkman and bought candy to peddle with in the streets, but after a while no one saw the shoemaker anymore, a stocky man with round eyeglasses and a bristling mustache, wearing a summer hat in wintertime.

When they tore up the counters and other fixtures and moved them out, when the store was empty except for the sink glowing in the rear, Sam would occasionally stand there at night, everyone on the block but him closed, peering into the window exuding darkness. Often while gazing through the dusty plate glass, which gave him back the image of a grocer gazing out, he felt as he had when he was a boy in Kamenets-Podolski and going—the three of them—to the river; they would, as they passed, swoop a frightened glance into a tall wooden house, eerily narrow, topped by a strange double-steepled roof, where there had once been a ghastly murder and now the place was haunted. Returning late, at times in early moonlight, they walked a distance away, speechless, listening to the ravenous silence of the house, room after room fallen into deeper stillness, and in the midmost a pit of churning quiet from which, if you thought about it, evil erupted. And so it seemed in the dark recesses of the empty store, where so many shoes had been leathered and hammered into life, and so many people had left something of themselves in the coming and going, that even in emptiness the store contained some memory of their presences, unspoken echoes in declining tiers, and that in a sense was what was so frightening. Afterwards when Sam went by the store, even in daylight he was afraid to look, and quickly walked past, as they had the haunted house when he was a boy.

But whenever he shut his eyes the empty store was stuck in his mind, a long black hole eternally revolving so that while he slept he was not asleep but within, revolving: what if it should happen to me? What if after twenty-seven years of toil (he should years ago have got out), what if after all of that, your own store, a place of business . . . after all the years, the years, the thousands of cans he had wiped off and packed away, the milk cases dragged in like rocks from the street before dawn in freeze or heat; insults, petty thievery, doling of credit to the impoverished by the poor; the peeling ceiling, fly-specked shelves, puffed cans, dirt, swollen veins, the back-breaking sixteen-hour day like a heavy hand slapping, upon awaking, the skull, pushing the head down to bend the body's bones; the hours; the work, the years, my God, and where is my life now? Who will save me now, and where will I go, where? Often he had thought these thoughts, subdued after months; and the garish FOR RENT sign had yellowed and fallen in the window so how could anyone know the place was to let? But they did. Today when he had all but laid the ghost of fear, a streamer in red cracked him across the eyes: National Grocery Will Open Another Of Its Bargain Price Stores On These Premises, and the woe went into him and his heart bled.

At last Sam raised his head and told her, "I will go to the landlord next door."

Sura looked at him through puffy eyelids. "So what will you say?"

"I will talk to him."

Ordinarily she would have said, "Sam, don't be a fool," but she let him go.

Averting his head from the glare of the new red sign in the window, he entered the hall next door. As he labored up the steps the bleak light of the skylight fell on him and grew heavier as he ascended. He went unwillingly, not knowing what he would say to the landlord. Reaching the top floor, he paused before the door at the jabbering in Italian of a woman bewailing her fate. Sam already had one foot on the top stair, ready to descend, when he heard the coffee advertisement and realized it had been a radio play. Now the radio was off, the hallway oppressively silent. He listened and at first heard no voices inside, so he knocked without allowing himself to think anymore. He was a little frightened and lived in suspense until the slow heavy steps of the landlord, who was also the barber across the street, reached the door, and it was—after some impatient fumbling with the lock—opened.

When the barber saw Sam in the hall he was disturbed, and Sam at once knew why he had not been in the grocery store even once in the past two weeks. However, the barber, becoming cordial, invited Sam to step into the kitchen, where his wife and a stranger were seated at the table eating from piled-high plates of spaghetti.

"Thanks," said Sam shyly. "I just ate."

The barber came out into the hall, shutting the door behind him. He glanced vaguely down the stairway and turned to Sam. His movements were unresolved. Since the death of his son in the war he had become absentminded; and sometimes when he walked one had the impression he was dragging something.

"Is it true?" Sam asked in embarrassment. "What it says downstairs on the sign?"

"Sam," the barber began heavily. He stopped to wipe his mouth with a paper napkin he held in his hand and said, "Sam, you know this store I had no rent for it for seven months?"

"I know."

"I can't afford. I was waiting for maybe a liquor store or a hardware, but I don't have no offers from them. Last month this chain store make me an offer and then I wait five weeks for something else. I had to take it, I couldn't help myself."

Shadows thickened in the darkness. In a sense Pellegrino was present, standing with them at the top of the stairs.

"When will they move in?" Sam sighed.

"Not till May."

The grocer was too faint to say anything. They stared at each other, not knowing what to suggest. But the barber forced a laugh and said the chain store wouldn't hurt Sam's business.

"Why not?"

"Because you carry different brands of goods and when the customers want those brands they go to you."

"Why should they go to me if my prices are higher?"

"A chain store brings more customers and they might like things that you got."

Sam felt ashamed. He did not doubt the barber's sincerity, but his stock was meager and he could not imagine chain store customers interested in what he had to sell.

Holding Sam by the arm, the barber told him in confidential tones of a friend who had a meat store next to an A&P supermarket and was making out very well.

Sam tried hard to believe he would make out well but couldn't.

"So did you sign with them the lease yet?" he asked.

"Friday," said the barber.

"Friday?" Sam had a wild hope. "Maybe," he said, trying to hold it down, "maybe I could find you, before Friday, a new tenant?"

"What kind of a tenant?"

"A tenant," Sam said.

"What kind of store is he interested?"

Sam tried to think. "A shoe store," he said.

"Shoemaker?"

"No, a shoe store where they sell shoes."

The barber pondered it. At last he said if Sam could get a tenant he wouldn't sign the lease with the chain store.

As Sam descended the stairs the light from the top-floor bulb diminished on his shoulders but not the heaviness, for he had no one in mind to take the store.

However, before Friday he thought of two people. One was the red-haired salesman for a wholesale grocery jobber, who had lately been recounting his investments in new stores; but when Sam spoke to him on the phone he said he was only interested in high-income grocery stores, which was no solution to the problem. The other man he hesitated to call, because he didn't like him. That was I. Kaufman, a former dry-goods merchant, with a wart under his left eyebrow. Kaufman had made some fortunate real estate deals and had become quite wealthy. Years ago he and Sam had stores next to one another on Marcy Avenue in Williamsburg. Sam took him for a lout and was not above saying so, for which Sura often ridiculed him, seeing how Kaufman had prospered, and where Sam was. Yet they stayed on comparatively good terms, perhaps because the grocer never asked for favors. When Kaufman happened to be around in the Buick, he usually dropped in, which Sam increasingly disliked, for Kaufman gave advice without stint and Sura sandpapered it in when he had left.

Despite qualms he telephoned him. Kaufman was pontifically surprised and said yes he would see what he could do. On Friday morning the barber took the red sign out of the window so as not to prejudice a possible deal. When Kaufman marched in with his cane that forenoon, Sam, who for once, at Sura's request, had dispensed with his apron, explained to him they had thought of the empty store next door as perfect for a shoe store because the neighborhood had none and the rent was reasonable. And since Kaufman was always investing in one project or another they thought he might be interested in this. The barber came over from across the street and unlocked the door. Kaufman clomped into the empty store, appraised the structure of the place, tested the floor, peered through the barred window into the back yard, and, squinting, totaled with moving lips how much shelving was necessary and at what cost. Then he asked the barber how much rent and the barber named a modest figure.

Kaufman nodded sagely and said nothing to either of them there, but in the grocery store he vehemently berated Sam for wasting his time.

"I didn't want to make you ashamed in front of the goy," he said in anger, even his wart red, "but who do you think, if he is in his right mind, will open a shoe store in this stinky neighborhood?"

Before departing, he gave good advice the way a tube bloops toothpaste, and ended by saying to Sam, "If a chain store grocery comes in you're finished. Get out of here before the birds pick the meat out of your bones."

Then he drove off in his Buick. Sura was about to begin a commentary, but Sam pounded his fist on the table and that ended it. That evening the barber pasted the red sign back on the window, for he had signed the lease.

Lying awake nights, Sam knew what was going on inside the store, though he never went near it. He could see carpenters sawing the sweet-smelling pine that willingly yielded to the sharp blade and became in tiers the shelves rising almost to the ceiling. The painters arrived, a long man and a short one he was positive he knew, their faces covered with paint drops. They thickly calcimined the ceiling and painted everything in bright colors, impractical for a grocery but pleasing to the eye. Electricians appeared with fluorescent lamps which obliterated the yellow darkness of globed bulbs; and then the fixture men hauled down from their vans the long marble-top counters and gleaming enameled three-windowed refrigerator, for cooking, medium, and best butter; and a case for frozen foods, creamy white, the latest thing. As he was admiring it all, he turned to see if anyone was watching him, and when he had reassured himself, and turned again to look through the window, it had been whitened so he could see nothing more. He had to get up then to smoke a cigarette and was tempted to put on his pants and go in slippers quietly down the stairs to see if the window was really soaped up. That it might be kept him there, so he returned to bed, and being still unable to sleep he worked until he had polished, with a bit of rag, a small hole in the center of the white window, and enlarged that till he could make out everything clearly. The store was assembled now, spic-and-span, roomy, ready to receive the goods; it was a pleasure to come in. He whispered to himself this would be good if it was mine, but then the alarm banged in his ear and he had to get up and drag in the milk cases. At 8 a.m. three enormous trucks rolled down the block and six young men in white duck jackets jumped off and packed the store in seven hours. All day Sam's heart beat so hard he sometimes fondled it with his hand as though trying to calm a bird that wanted to fly off.

When the chain store opened in the middle of May, with a horseshoe wreath of roses in the window, Sura counted up that night and proclaimed they were ten dollars short; which wasn't so bad, Sam said, till she reminded him ten times six was sixty. She openly wept, sobbing they must do *something*, driving Sam to a thorough wiping of the shelves with wet cloths she handed him, oiling the floor, and washing, inside and out, the front window, which she redecorated with white tissue paper from the five-and-ten. Then she told him to call the wholesaler, who read off this week's specials; and when they were delivered, Sam packed three cases of cans in a towering pyramid in the window. Only no one seemed to buy. They were fifty dollars short the next week and Sam thought, If it stays like this we can exist, and he cut the price of beer, lettering with black crayon on wrapping paper a sign for the window that beer was reduced in price, thus selling fully five cases more that day, though Sura nagged what was the good of it if they made no profit—lost on paper bags—and the customers who came in for beer went next door for bread and canned goods? Yet Sam still hoped, but the next week they were seventy-two behind, and in two weeks a clean hundred. The chain store, with a manager and two clerks, was busy all day, but with Sam there was never, anymore, anything resembling a rush. Then he discovered that they carried, next door, every brand he had and many he hadn't, and he felt for the barber a furious anger.

That summer, usually better for his business, was bad, and the fall was worse. The store was so silent it got to be a piercing pleasure when someone opened the door. They sat long hours under the unshaded bulb in the rear, reading and rereading the newspaper, and looking up hopefully when anyone passed by in the street, though trying not to look when they could tell he was going next door. Sam now kept open an hour longer, till midnight, although that wearied him greatly, but he was able, during the extra hour, to pick up a dollar or two among the housewives who had run out of milk, or needed a last-minute loaf of bread for school sandwiches. To cut expenses he put out one of the two lights in the window and a lamp in the store. He had the phone removed, bought his paper bags from peddlers, shaved every second day, and, although he would not admit it, ate less. Then in an unexpected burst of optimism he ordered eighteen cases of goods from the jobber and filled the empty sections of his shelves with low-priced items clearly marked, but, as Sura said, who saw them if nobody came in? People he had seen every day for ten, fifteen, even twenty years disappeared as if they had moved or died. Sometimes when he was delivering a small order somewhere he saw a former customer who either quickly crossed the street or ducked the other way and walked around the block. The barber, too, avoided him and he avoided the barber. Sam schemed to give short weight on loose items but couldn't bring himself to. He considered canvassing the neighborhood from house to house for orders he would personally deliver but then remembered Mr. Pellegrino and gave up the idea. Sura, who had all their married life nagged him, now sat silent in the back. When Sam counted the receipts for the first week in December he knew he could no longer hope. The wind blew outside and the store was cold. He offered it for sale but no one would take it.

One morning Sura got up and slowly ripped her cheeks with her fingernails. Sam went across the street for a haircut. He had formerly had his hair cut once a month, but now it had grown ten weeks and was thickly pelted at the back of the neck. The barber cut it with his eyes shut. Then Sam called an auctioneer, who moved in with two lively assistants and a red auction flag that flapped and furled in the icy breeze as though it were a holiday. The money they got was not a quarter of the sum needed to pay the creditors. Sam and Sura closed the store and moved away. So long as he lived he would not return to the old neighborhood, afraid his store was standing empty, and he dreaded to look through the window.

1949

❧ B M ❧

The Prison

Though he tried not to think of it, at twenty-nine Tommy Castelli's life was a screaming bore. It wasn't just Rosa or the store they tended for profits counted in pennies, or the unendurably slow hours and endless drivel that went with selling candy, cigarettes, and soda water; it was this sick-in-the-stomach feeling of being trapped in old mistakes, even some he had made before Rosa changed Tony into Tommy. He had been as Tony a kid of many dreams and schemes, especially getting out of this tenement-crowded, kid-squawking neighborhood, with its lousy poverty, but everything had fouled up against him before he could. When he was sixteen he quit the vocational school where they were making him into a shoemaker, and began to hang out with the gray-hatted, thick-soled-shoe boys, who had the spare time and the mazuma and showed it in fat wonderful rolls down in the cellar clubs to all who would look, and everybody did, popeyed. They were the ones who had bought the silver caffè espresso urn and later the television, and they arranged the pizza parties and had the girls down; but it was getting in with them and their cars, leading to the holdup of a liquor store, that had started all the present trouble. Lucky for him the coal-and-ice man who was their landlord knew the leader in the district, and they arranged something so nobody bothered him after that. Then before he knew what was going on—he had been frightened sick by the whole mess—there was his father cooking up a deal with Rosa Agnello's old man that Tony would marry her and the father-in-law would, out of his savings, open a candy store for him to make an honest living. He wouldn't spit on a candy store, and Rosa was too plain and lank a chick for his personal taste, so he beat it off to Texas and bummed around in too much space, and when he came back everybody said it was for Rosa and the candy store, and it was all arranged again and he, without saying no, was in it.

That was how he had landed on Prince Street in the Village, working from eight in the morning to almost midnight every day, except for an hour off each afternoon when he went upstairs to sleep, and on Tuesdays, when the store was closed and he slept some more and went at night alone to the movies. He was too tired always for schemes now, but once he tried to make a little cash on the side by secretly taking in punchboards some syndicate was distributing in the neighborhood, on which he collected a nice cut and in this way saved fifty-five bucks that Rosa didn't know about; but then the syndicate was written up by a newspaper, and the punchboards all disappeared. Another time, when Rosa was at her mother's house, he took a chance and let them put in a slot machine that could guarantee a nice piece of change if he kept it long enough. He knew of course he couldn't hide it from her, so when she came and screamed when she saw it, he was ready and patient, for once not yelling back when she yelled, and he explained it was not the same as gambling because anybody who played it got a roll of mints every time he put in a nickel. Also the machine would supply them a few extra dollars cash they could use to buy television so he could see the fights without going to a bar; but Rosa wouldn't let up screaming, and later her father came in shouting that he was a criminal and chopped the machine apart with a plumber's hammer. The next day the cops raided for slot machines and gave out summonses wherever they found them, and though Tommy's place was practically the only candy store in the neighborhood that didn't have one, he felt bad about the machine for a long time.

Mornings had been his best time of day because Rosa stayed upstairs cleaning, and since few people came into the store till noon, he could sit around alone, a toothpick in his teeth, looking over the *News* and *Mirror* on the fountain counter, or maybe gab with one of the old cellar-club guys who had happened to come by for a pack of butts, about a horse that was running that day or how the numbers were paying lately; or just sit there, drinking coffee and thinking how far away he could get on the fifty-five he had stashed away in the cellar. Generally the mornings were this way, but after the slot machine, usually the whole day stank and he along with it. Time rotted in him, and all he could think of, the whole morning, was going to sleep in the afternoon, and he would wake up with the sour remembrance of the long night in the store ahead of him, while everybody else was doing as he damn pleased. He cursed the candy store and Rosa, and cursed, from its beginning, his unhappy life.

It was on one of these bad mornings that a ten-year-old girl from around the block came in and asked for two rolls of colored tissue paper, one red and one yellow. He wanted to tell her to go to hell and stop bothering, but instead went with bad grace to the rear, where Rosa, whose bright idea it was to keep the stuff, had put it. He went from force of habit, for the girl had been coming in every Monday since the summer for the same thing, because her rock-faced mother, who looked as if she arranged her own widowhood, took care of some small kids after school and gave them the paper to cut out dolls and such things. The girl, whose name he didn't know, resembled her mother, except her features were not quite so sharp and she had very light skin with dark eyes; but she was a plain kid and would be more so at twenty. He had noticed, when he went to get the paper, that she always hung back as if afraid to go where it was dark, though he kept the comics there and most of the other kids had to be slapped away from them; and that when he brought her the tissue paper her skin seemed to grow whiter and her eyes shone. She always handed him two hot dimes and went out without glancing back.

It happened that Rosa, who trusted nobody, had just hung a mirror on the back wall, and as Tommy opened the drawer to get the girl her paper this Monday morning that he felt so bad, he looked up and saw in the glass something that made it seem as if he were dreaming. The girl had disappeared, but he saw a white hand reach into the candy case for a chocolate bar and for another, then she came forth from behind the counter and stood there, innocently waiting for him. He felt at first like grabbing her by the neck and socking till she threw up, but he had been caught, as he sometimes was, by this thought of how his Uncle Dom, years ago before he went away, used to take with him Tony alone of all the kids, when he went crabbing to Sheepshead Bay. Once they went at night and threw the baited wire traps into the water and after a while pulled them up and they had this green lobster in one, and just then this fat-faced cop came along and said they had to throw it back unless it was nine inches. Dom said it was nine inches, but the cop said not to be a wise guy so Dom measured it and it was ten, and they laughed about that lobster all night. Then he remembered how he had felt after Dom was gone, and tears filled his eyes. He found himself thinking about the way his life had turned out, and then about this girl, moved that she was so young and a thief. He felt he ought to do something for her, warn her to cut it out before she got trapped and fouled up her life before it got started. His urge to do this was strong, but when he went forward she looked up frightened because he had taken so long. The fear in her eyes bothered him and he didn't say anything. She thrust out the dimes, grabbed at the tissue rolls, and ran out of the store.

He had to sit down. He kept trying to make the desire to speak to her go away, but it came back stronger than ever. He asked himself what difference does it make if she swipes candy—so she swipes it; and the role of reformer was strange and distasteful to him, yet he could not convince himself that what he felt he must do was unimportant. But he worried he would not know what to say to her. Always he had trouble speaking right, stumbled over words, especially in new situations. He was afraid he would sound like a jerk and she would not take him seriously. He had to tell her in a sure way so that even if it scared her, she would understand he had done it to set her straight. He mentioned her to no one but often thought about her, always looking around whenever he went outside to raise the awning or wash the window, to see if any of the girls playing in the street was her, but they never were. The following Monday, an hour after opening the store he had smoked a full pack of butts. He thought he had found what he wanted to say but was afraid for some reason she wouldn't come in, or if she did, this time she would be afraid to take the candy. He wasn't sure he wanted that to happen until he had said what he had to say. But at about eleven, while he was reading the *News*, she appeared, asking for the tissue paper, her eyes shining so he had to look away. He knew she meant to steal. Going to the rear he slowly opened the drawer, keeping his head lowered as he sneaked a look into the glass and saw her slide behind the counter. His heart beat hard and his feet felt nailed to the floor. He tried to remember what he had intended to do, but his mind was like a dark, empty room so he let her, in the end, slip away and stood tongue-tied, the dimes burning his palm.

Afterwards, he told himself that he hadn't spoken to her because it was while she still had the candy on her, and she would have been scared worse than he wanted. When he went upstairs, instead of sleeping, he sat at the kitchen window, looking out into the back yard. He blamed himself for being too soft, too chicken, but then he thought, no, there was a better way to do it. He would do it indirectly, slip her a hint he knew, and he was pretty sure that would stop her. Sometime after, he would explain her why it was good she had stopped. So next time he cleaned out this candy platter she helped herself from, thinking she might get wise he was on to her, but she seemed not to, only hesitated with her hand before she took two candy bars from the next plate and dropped them into the black patent-leather purse she always had with her. The time after that he cleaned out the whole top shelf, and still she was not suspicious, and reached down to the next and took something different. One Monday he put some loose change, nickels and dimes, on the candy plate, but she left them there, only taking the candy, which bothered him a little. Rosa asked him what he was mooning about so much and why was he eating chocolate lately. He didn't answer her, and she began to look suspiciously at the women who came in, not excluding the little girls; and he would have been glad to rap her in the teeth, but it didn't matter as long as she didn't know what he had on his mind. At the same time he figured he would have to do something sure soon, or it would get harder for the girl to stop her stealing. He had to be strong about it. Then he thought of a plan that satisfied him. He would leave two bars on the plate and put in the wrapper of one a note she could read when she was alone. He tried out on paper many messages to her, and the one that seemed best he cleanly printed on a strip of cardboard and slipped it under the wrapper of one chocolate bar. It said, "Don't do this anymore or you will suffer your whole life." He puzzled whether to sign it A Friend or Your Friend and finally chose Your Friend.

This was Friday, and he could not hold his impatience for Monday. But on Monday she did not appear. He waited for a long time, until Rosa came down, then he had to go up and the girl still hadn't come. He was greatly disappointed because she had never failed to come before. He lay on the bed, his shoes on, staring at the ceiling. He felt hurt, the sucker she had played him for and was now finished with because she probably had another on her hook. The more he thought about it the worse he felt. He worked up a splitting headache that kept him from sleeping, then he suddenly slept and woke without it. But he had awaked depressed, saddened. He thought about Dom getting out of jail and going away God knows where. He wondered whether he would ever meet up with him somewhere, if he took the fifty-five bucks and left. Then he remembered Dom was a pretty old guy now, and he might not know him if they did meet. He thought about life. You never really got what you wanted. No matter how hard you tried you made mistakes and couldn't get past them. You could never see the sky outside or the ocean because you were in a prison, except nobody called it a prison, and if you did they didn't know what you were talking about, or they said they didn't. A pall settled on him. He lay motionless, without thought or sympathy for himself or anybody.

But when he finally went downstairs, ironically amused that Rosa had allowed him so long a time off without bitching, there were people in the store and he could hear her screeching. Shoving his way through the crowd he saw in one sickening look that she had caught the girl with the candy bars and was shaking her so hard the kid's head bounced back and forth like a balloon on a stick. With a curse he tore her away from the girl, whose sickly face showed the depth of her fright.

"Whatsamatter," he shouted at Rosa, "you want her blood?"

"She's a thief," cried Rosa.

"Shut your face."

To stop her yowling he slapped her across her mouth, but it was a harder crack than he had intended. Rosa fell back with a gasp. She did not cry but looked around dazedly at everybody, and tried to smile, and everybody there could see her teeth were flecked with blood.

"Go home," Tommy ordered the girl, but then there was a movement near the door and her mother came into the store.

"What happened?" she said.

"She stole my candy," Rosa cried.

"I let her take it," said Tommy.

1950

The First Seven Years

Feld, the shoemaker, was annoyed that his helper, Sobel, was so insensitive to his reverie that he wouldn't for a minute cease his fanatic pounding at the other bench. He gave him a look, but Sobel's bald head was bent over the last as he worked, and he didn't notice. The shoemaker shrugged and continued to peer through the partly frosted window at the nearsighted haze of falling February snow. Neither the shifting white blur outside nor the sudden deep remembrance of the snowy Polish village where he had wasted his youth could turn his thoughts from Max the college boy (a constant visitor in the mind since early that morning when Feld saw him trudging through the snowdrifts on his way to school), whom he so much respected because of the sacrifices he had made throughout the years—in winter or direst heat—to further his education. An old wish returned to haunt the shoemaker: that he had had a son instead of a daughter, but this blew away in the snow, for Feld, if anything, was a practical man. Yet he could not help but contrast the diligence of the boy, who was a peddler's son, with Miriam's unconcern for an education. True, she was always with a book in her hand, yet when the opportunity arose for a college education, she had said no, she would rather find a job. He had begged her to go, pointing out how many fathers could not afford to send their children to college, but she said she wanted to be independent. As for education, what was it, she asked, but books, which Sobel, who diligently read the classics, would as usual advise her on. Her answer greatly grieved her father.

A figure emerged from the snow and the door opened. At the counter the man withdrew from a wet paper bag a pair of battered shoes for repair. Who he was the shoemaker for a moment had no idea, then his heart trembled as he realized, before he had thoroughly discerned the face, that Max himself was standing there, embarrassedly explaining what he wanted done to his old shoes. Though Feld listened eagerly, he couldn't hear a word, for the opportunity that had burst upon him was deafening.

He couldn't exactly recall when the thought had occurred to him, because it was clear he had more than once considered suggesting to the boy that he go out with Miriam. But he had not dared speak, for if Max said no, how would he face him again? Or suppose Miriam, who harped so often on independence, blew up in anger and shouted at him for his meddling? Still, the chance was too good to let by: all it meant was an introduction. They might long ago have become friends had they happened to meet somewhere, therefore was it not his duty—an obligation—to bring them together, nothing more, a harmless connivance to replace an accidental encounter in the subway, let's say, or a mutual friend's introduction in the street? Just let him once see and talk to her and he would for sure be interested. As for Miriam, what possible harm for a working girl in an office, who met only loudmouthed salesmen and illiterate shipping clerks, to make the acquaintance of a fine scholarly boy? Maybe he would awaken in her a desire to go to college; if not—the shoemaker's mind at last came to grips with the truth—let her marry an educated man and live a better life.

When Max finished describing what he wanted done to his shoes, Feld marked them, both with enormous holes in the soles which he pretended not to notice, with large white-chalk X's and the rubber heels, thinned to the nails, he marked with O's, though it troubled him he might have mixed up the letters. Max inquired the price, and the shoemaker cleared his throat and asked the boy, above Sobel's insistent hammering, would he please step through the side door there into the hall. Though surprised, Max did as the shoemaker requested, and Feld went in after him. For a minute they were both silent, because Sobel had stopped banging, and it seemed they understood neither was to say anything until the noise began again. When it did, loudly, the shoemaker quickly told Max why he had asked to talk to him.

"Ever since you went to high school," he said, in the dimly lit hallway, "I watched you in the morning go to the subway to school,

and I said always to myself, this is a fine boy that he wants so much
an education."

"Thanks," Max said, nervously alert. He was tall and grotesquely
thin, with sharply cut features, particularly a beak-like nose. He was
wearing a loose, long, slushy overcoat that hung down to his ankles,
looking like a rug draped over his bony shoulders, and a soggy old
brown hat, as battered as the shoes he had brought in.

"I am a businessman," the shoemaker abruptly said to conceal
his embarrassment, "so I will explain you right away why I talk to
you. I have a girl, my daughter Miriam—she is nineteen—a very
nice girl and also so pretty that everybody looks on her when she
passes by in the street. She is smart, always with a book, and I thought
to myself that a boy like you, an educated boy—I thought maybe
you will be interested sometime to meet a girl like this." He laughed
a bit when he had finished and was tempted to say more but had the
good sense not to.

Max stared down like a hawk. For an uncomfortable second he
was silent, then he asked, "Did you say nineteen?"

"Yes."

"Would it be all right to inquire if you have a picture of her?"

"Just a minute." The shoemaker went into the store and hastily
returned with a snapshot that Max held up to the light.

"She's all right," he said.

Feld waited.

"And is she sensible—not the flighty kind?"

"She is very sensible."

After another short pause, Max said it was okay with him if he
met her.

"Here is my telephone," said the shoemaker, hurriedly handing
him a slip of paper. "Call her up. She comes home from work six
o'clock."

Max folded the paper and tucked it away into his worn leather
wallet.

"About the shoes," he said. "How much did you say they will
cost me?"

"Don't worry about the price."

"I just like to have an idea."

"A dollar—dollar fifty. A dollar fifty," the shoemaker said.

At once he felt bad, for he usually charged $2.25 for this kind
of job. Either he should have asked the regular price or done the work
for nothing.

Later, as he entered the store, he was startled by a violent clanging and looked up to see Sobel pounding upon the naked last. It broke, the iron striking the floor and jumping with a thump against the wall, but before the enraged shoemaker could cry out, the assistant had torn his hat and coat off the hook and rushed out into the snow.

.

So Feld, who had looked forward to anticipating how it would go with his daughter and Max, instead had a great worry on his mind. Without his temperamental helper he was a lost man, especially as it was years now since he had carried the store alone. The shoemaker had for an age suffered from a heart condition that threatened collapse if he dared exert himself. Five years ago, after an attack, it had appeared as though he would have either to sacrifice his business on the auction block and live on a pittance thereafter or put himself at the mercy of some unscrupulous employee who would in the end probably ruin him. But just at the moment of his darkest despair, this Polish refugee, Sobel, had appeared one night out of the street and begged for work. He was a stocky man, poorly dressed, with a bald head that had once been blond, a severely plain face, and soft blue eyes prone to tears over the sad books he read, a young man but old—no one would have guessed thirty. Though he confessed he knew nothing of shoemaking, he said he was apt and would work for very little if Feld taught him the trade. Thinking that with, after all, a landsman, he would have less to fear than from a complete stranger, Feld took him on and within six weeks the refugee rebuilt as good a shoe as he, and not long thereafter expertly ran the business for the thoroughly relieved shoemaker.

Feld could trust him with anything and did, frequently going home after an hour or two at the store, leaving all the money in the till, knowing Sobel would guard every cent of it. The amazing thing was that he demanded so little. His wants were few; in money he wasn't interested—in nothing but books, it seemed—which he one by one lent to Miriam, together with his profuse, queer written comments, manufactured during his lonely rooming house evenings, thick pads of commentary which the shoemaker peered at and twitched his shoulders over as his daughter, from her fourteenth year, read page by sanctified page, as if the word of God were inscribed on them. To protect Sobel, Feld himself had to see that he received more than he asked for. Yet his conscience bothered him for not insisting that the assistant accept a better wage than he was getting, though Feld had honestly told him he could earn a handsome salary if he worked elsewhere, or maybe opened a place of his own. But the assistant answered, somewhat ungraciously, that he was not interested in going elsewhere, and though Feld frequently asked himself, What keeps him here? why does he stay? he finally answered it that the man, no doubt because of his terrible experiences as a refugee, was afraid of the world.

After the incident with the broken last, angered by Sobel's behavior, the shoemaker decided to let him stew for a week in the rooming house, although his own strength was taxed dangerously and the business suffered. However, after several sharp nagging warnings from both his wife and daughter, he went finally in search of Sobel, as he had once before, quite recently, when over some fancied slight—Feld had merely asked him not to give Miriam so many books to read because her eyes were strained and red—the assistant had left the place in a huff, an incident which, as usual, came to nothing, for he had returned after the shoemaker had talked to him and taken his seat at the bench. But this time, after Feld had plodded through the snow to Sobel's house—he had thought of sending Miriam but the idea became repugnant to him—the burly landlady at the door informed him in a nasal voice that Sobel was not at home, and though Feld knew this was a nasty lie, for where had the refugee to go? still for some reason he was not completely sure of   it may have been the cold and his fatigue—he decided not to insist on seeing him. Instead he went home and hired a new helper.

Thus he settled the matter, though not entirely to his satisfaction, for he had much more to do than before, and so, for example, could no longer lie late in bed mornings because he had to get up to open the store for the new assistant, a speechless, dark man with an irritating rasp as he worked, whom he would not trust with the key as he had Sobel. Furthermore, this one, though able to do a fair repair job, knew nothing of grades of leather or prices, so Feld had to make his own purchases; and every night at closing time it was necessary to count the money in the till and lock up. However, he was not dissatisfied, for he lived much in his thoughts of Max and Miriam. The college boy had called her, and they had arranged a meeting for this coming Friday night. The shoemaker would personally have preferred Saturday, which he felt would make it a date of the first magnitude, but he learned Friday was Miriam's choice, so he said nothing. The day of the week did not matter. What mattered was the aftermath. Would they like each other and want to be friends? He sighed at all the time that would have to go by before he knew for sure. Often he was tempted to talk to Miriam about the boy, to ask whether she thought she would like his type—he had told her only that he considered Max a nice boy and had suggested he call her—but the one time he tried she snapped at him—justly—how should she know?

At last Friday came. Feld was not feeling particularly well so he stayed in bed, and Mrs. Feld thought it better to remain in the bedroom with him when Max called. Miriam received the boy, and her parents could hear their voices, his throaty one, as they talked. Just before leaving, Miriam brought Max to the bedroom door and he stood there a minute, a tall, slightly hunched figure wearing a thick, droopy suit, and apparently at ease as he greeted the shoemaker and his wife, which was surely a good sign. And Miriam, although she had worked all day, looked fresh and pretty. She was a large-framed girl with a well-shaped body, and she had a fine open face and soft hair. They made, Feld thought, a first-class couple.

Miriam returned after 11:30. Her mother was already asleep, but the shoemaker got out of bed and after locating his bathrobe went into the kitchen, where Miriam, to his surprise, sat at the table, reading.

"So where did you go?" Feld asked pleasantly.

"For a walk," she said, not looking up.

"I advised him," Feld said, clearing his throat, "he shouldn't spend so much money."

"I didn't care."

The shoemaker boiled up some water for tea and sat down at the table with a cupful and a thick slice of lemon.

"So how," he sighed after a sip, "did you enjoy?"

"It was all right."

He was silent. She must have sensed his disappointment, for she added, "You can't really tell much the first time."

"You will see him again?"

Turning a page, she said that Max had asked for another date.

"For when?"

"Saturday."

"So what did you say?"

"What did I say?" she asked, delaying for a moment—"I said yes."

Afterwards she inquired about Sobel, and Feld, without exactly knowing why, said the assistant had got another job. Miriam said nothing more and went on reading. The shoemaker's conscience did not trouble him; he was satisfied with the Saturday date.

During the week, by placing here and there a deft question, he managed to get from Miriam some information about Max. It surprised him to learn that the boy was not studying to be either a doctor or lawyer but was taking a business course leading to a degree in accountancy. Feld was a little disappointed because he thought of accountants as bookkeepers and would have preferred "a higher profession." However, it was not long before he had investigated the subject and discovered that Certified Public Accountants were highly respected people, so he was thoroughly content as Saturday approached. But because Saturday was a busy day, he was much in the store and therefore did not see Max when he came to call for Miriam. From his wife he learned there had been nothing especially revealing about their greeting. Max had rung the bell and Miriam had got her coat and left with him—nothing more. Feld did not probe, for his wife was not particularly observant. Instead, he waited up for Miriam with a newspaper on his lap, which he scarcely looked at, so lost was he in thinking of the future. He awoke to find her in the room with him, tiredly removing her hat. Greeting her, he was suddenly inexplicably afraid to ask anything about the evening. But since she volunteered nothing he was at last forced to inquire how she had enjoyed herself. Miriam began something noncommittal, but apparently changed her mind, for she said after a minute, "I was bored."

When Feld had sufficiently recovered from his anguished disappointment to ask why, she answered without hesitation, "Because he's nothing more than a materialist."

"What means this word?"

"He has no soul. He's only interested in things."

He considered her statement for a long time, then asked, "Will you see him again?"

"He didn't ask."

"Suppose he will ask you?"

"I won't see him."

He did not argue; however, as the days went by he hoped increasingly she would change her mind. He wished the boy would telephone, because he was sure there was more to him than Miriam, with her inexperienced eye, could discern. But Max didn't call. As a matter of fact he took a different route to school, no longer passing the shoemaker's store, and Feld was deeply hurt.

Then one afternoon Max came in and asked for his shoes. The shoemaker took them down from the shelf where he had placed them, apart from the other pairs. He had done the work himself and the soles and heels were well built and firm. The shoes had been highly polished and somehow looked better than new. Max's Adam's apple went up once when he saw them, and his eyes had little lights in them.

"How much?" he asked, without directly looking at the shoe-maker.

"Like I told you before," Feld answered sadly. "One dollar fifty cents."

Max handed him two crumpled bills and received in return a newly minted silver half dollar.

He left. Miriam had not been mentioned. That night the shoe-maker discovered that his new assistant had been all the while stealing from him, and he suffered a heart attack.

•

Though the attack was very mild, he lay in bed for three weeks. Miriam spoke of going for Sobel, but sick as he was Feld rose in wrath against the idea. Yet in his heart he knew there was no other way, and the first weary day back in the shop thoroughly convinced him, so that night after supper he dragged himself to Sobel's rooming house.

He toiled up the stairs, though he knew it was bad for him, and at the top knocked at the door. Sobel opened it and the shoemaker entered. The room was a small, poor one, with a single window facing the street. It contained a narrow cot, a low table, and several stacks of books piled haphazardly around on the floor along the wall, which made him think how queer Sobel was, to be uneducated and read so much. He had once asked him, Sobel, why you read so much? and the assistant could not answer him. Did you ever study in a college someplace? he had asked, but Sobel shook his head. He read, he said, to know. But to know what, the shoemaker demanded, and to know, why? Sobel never explained, which proved he read so much because he was queer.

Feld sat down to recover his breath. The assistant was resting on his bed with his heavy back to the wall. His shirt and trousers were clean, and his stubby fingers, away from the shoemaker's bench, were strangely pallid. His face was thin and pale, as if he had been shut in this room since the day he had bolted from the store.

"So when you will come back to work?" Feld asked him.

To his surprise, Sobel burst out, "Never."

Jumping up, he strode over to the window that looked out upon the miserable street. "Why should I come back?" he cried.

"I will raise your wages."

"Who cares for your wages!"

The shoemaker, knowing he didn't care, was at a loss what else to say.

"What do you want from me, Sobel?"

"Nothing."

"I always treated you like you was my son."

Sobel vehemently denied it. "So why you look for strange boys in the street they should go out with Miriam? Why you don't think of me?"

The shoemaker's hands and feet turned freezing cold. His voice became so hoarse he couldn't speak. At last he cleared his throat and croaked, "So what has my daughter got to do with a shoemaker thirty-five years old who works for me?"

"Why do you think I worked so long for you?" Sobel cried out. "For the stingy wages I sacrificed five years of my life so you could have to eat and drink and where to sleep?"

"Then for what?" shouted the shoemaker.

"For Miriam," he blurted—"for her."

The shoemaker, after a time, managed to say, "I pay wages in cash, Sobel," and lapsed into silence. Though he was seething with excitement, his mind was coldly clear, and he had to admit to himself he had sensed all along that Sobel felt this way. He had never so much as thought it consciously, but he had felt it and was afraid.

"Miriam knows?" he muttered hoarsely.

"She knows."

"You told her?"

"No."

"Then how does she know?"

"How does she know?" Sobel said. "Because she knows. She knows who I am and what is in my heart."

Feld had a sudden insight. In some devious way, with his books and commentary, Sobel had given Miriam to understand that he loved her. The shoemaker felt a terrible anger at him for his deceit.

"Sobel, you are crazy," he said bitterly. "She will never marry a man so old and ugly like you."

Sobel turned black with rage. He cursed the shoemaker, but then, though he trembled to hold it in, his eyes filled with tears and he broke into deep sobs. With his back to Feld, he stood at the window, fists clenched, and his shoulders shook with his choked sobbing.

Watching him, the shoemaker's anger diminished. His teeth were on edge with pity for the man, and his eyes grew moist. How strange and sad that a refugee, a grown man, bald and old with his miseries, who had by the skin of his teeth escaped Hitler's incinerators, should fall in love, when he had got to America, with a girl less than half his age. Day after day, for five years he had sat at his bench, cutting and hammering away, waiting for the girl to become a woman, unable to ease his heart with speech, knowing no protest but desperation.

"Ugly I didn't mean," he said half aloud.

Then he realized that what he had called ugly was not Sobel but Miriam's life if she married him. He felt for his daughter a strange and gripping sorrow, as if she were already Sobel's bride, the wife, after all, of a shoemaker, and had in her life no more than her mother had had. And all his dreams for her—why he had slaved and destroyed his heart with anxiety and labor—all these dreams of a better life were dead.

The room was quiet. Sobel was standing by the window reading, and it was curious that when he read he looked young.

"She is only nineteen," Feld said brokenly. "This is too young yet to get married. Don't ask her for two years more, till she is twenty-one, then you can talk to her."

Sobel didn't answer. Feld rose and left. He went slowly down the stairs but once outside, though it was an icy night and the crisp falling snow whitened the street, he walked with a stronger stride.

But the next morning, when the shoemaker arrived, heavy-hearted, to open the store, he saw he needn't have come, for his assistant was already seated at the last, pounding leather for his love.

1950

The Death of Me

Marcus was a tailor, long ago before the war, a buoyant man with a bushy head of graying hair, fine fragile brows, and benevolent hands, who comparatively late in life had become a clothier. Because he had prospered, so to say, into ill health, he had to employ an assistant tailor in the rear room, who made alterations on garments but could not, when the work piled high, handle the pressing, so that it became necessary to put on a presser; therefore though the store did well, it did not do too well.

It might have done better but the presser, Josip Bruzak, a heavy, beery, perspiring Pole, who worked in undershirt and felt slippers, his pants loose on his beefy hips, the legs crumpling around his ankles, conceived a violent dislike for Emilio Vizo, the tailor—or it worked the other way, Marcus wasn't sure—a thin, dry, pigeon-chested Sicilian, who bore or returned the Pole a steely malice. Because of their quarrels the business suffered.

Why they should fight as they did, fluttering and snarling like angry cocks, and using, in the bargain, terrible language, loud coarse words that affronted the customers and sometimes made the embarrassed Marcus feel dizzy to the point of fainting, mystified the clothier, who knew their troubles and felt they were, as people, much alike. Bruzak, who lived in a half-ruined rooming house near the East River, constantly guzzled beer at work and kept a dozen bottles in a rusty pan full of ice. When Marcus, in the beginning, objected, Josip, always respectful to the clothier, locked away the pan and disappeared through the back door into the tavern down the block where he had his glass, in the process wasting so much precious time it paid Marcus to tell him to go back to the pan. Every day at lunch Josip pulled out of the drawer a small sharp knife and cut chunks of the hard garlic salami he ate with puffy lumps of white bread, washing it all down with beer and then black coffee brewed on the one-burner gas stove for the tailor's iron. Sometimes he cooked up a soupy mess of cabbage which stank up the store, but on the whole neither the salami nor the cabbage interested him, and for days he seemed weary and uneasy until the mailman brought him, about every third week, a letter from the other side. When the letters came, he more than once tore them in half with his bumbling fingers; he forgot his work and, sitting on a backless chair, fished out of the same drawer where he kept his salami a pair of cracked eyeglasses which he attached to his ears by means of looped cords he had tied on in place of the broken sidepieces. Then he read the tissue sheets he held in his fist, a crabbed Polish writing in faded brown ink whose every word he uttered aloud so that Marcus, who understood the language but preferred not to hear, heard. Before the presser had dipped two sentences into the letter, his face dissolved and he cried, tears smearing his cheeks and chin so that it looked as though he had been sprayed with something to kill flies. At the end he fell into a roar of sobbing, a terrible thing to behold, which incapacitated him for hours and wasted the morning.

Marcus had often thought of telling him to read his letters at home, but the news in them wrung his heart and he could not bring himself to scold Josip, who was, by the way, a master presser. Once he began on a pile of suits, the steaming machine hissed without letup, and every garment came out neat, without puff or excessive crease, and the arms, legs, and pleats were as sharp as knives. As for the news in the letters, it was always the same, concerning the sad experiences of his tubercular wife and unfortunate fourteen-year-old son, whom Josip, except in pictures, had never seen, a boy who lived, literally, in the mud with the pigs, and was also sick, so that even if his father saved up money for his passage to America, and the boy could obtain a visa, he would never get past the immigration doctors. Marcus more than once gave the presser a suit of clothes to send to his son, and occasionally some cash, but he wondered if these things ever got to him. He had the uncomfortable thought that Josip, in the last fourteen years, might have brought the boy over had he wanted, his wife too, before she had contracted tuberculosis, but for some reason he preferred to weep over them where they were.

Emilio, the tailor, was another lone wolf. Every day he had a forty-cent lunch in the diner about three blocks away but returned early to read his *Corriere*. His strangeness was that he was always whispering to himself. No one could understand what he said, but it was sibilant and insistent, and wherever he stood, one could hear his hissing voice urging something, or moaning softly, though he never wept. He whispered when he sewed a button on, or shortened a sleeve, or when he used the iron. Whispering when he hung up his coat in the morning, he was still whispering when he put on his black hat, wriggled his sparse shoulders into his coat, and left, in loneliness, the store at night. Only once did he hint what the whispering was about; when the clothier, noticing his pallor one morning, brought him a cup of coffee, in gratitude the tailor confided that his wife, who had returned last week, had left him again this, and he held up the outstretched fingers of one bony hand to show she had five times run out on him. Marcus offered the man his sympathy, and thereafter, when he heard the tailor whispering in the rear of the store, could always picture the wife coming back to him from wherever she had been, saying she was this time—she swore—going to stay for good, but at night when they were in bed and he was whispering about her in the dark, she would think to herself she was sick of this and in the morning was gone. And so the man's ceaseless whisper irritated Marcus; he had to leave the store to hear silence, yet he kept Emilio on because he was a fine tailor, a demon with a needle, who could sew up a perfect cuff in less time than it takes an ordinary workman to take measurements, the kind of tailor who, when you were looking for one, was very rare.

For more than a year, despite the fact that they both made noises in the rear room, neither the presser nor the tailor seemed to notice one another; then one day, as though an invisible wall between them had fallen, they were at each other's throat. Marcus, it appeared, walked in at the very birth of their venom, when, leaving a customer in the store one afternoon, he went back to get a piece of marking chalk and came on a sight that froze him. There they were in the afternoon sunlight that flooded the rear of the shop, momentarily blinding the clothier so that he had time to think he couldn't possibly be seeing what he saw—the two at opposite corners staring stilly at one another—a live, almost hairy staring of intense hatred. The sneering Pole in one trembling hand squeezed a heavy wooden pressing block, while the livid tailor, his back like a cat's against the wall, held aloft in his rigid fingers a pair of cutter's shears.

"What is it?" Marcus shouted when he had recovered his voice, but neither of them would break the stone silence and remained as when he had discovered them, glaring across the shop at the other, the tailor's lips moving and the presser breathing like a dog in heat, an eeriness about them that Marcus had never suspected.

"My God," he cried, his body drenched in cold creeping wetness, "tell me what happened here." But neither uttered a sound, so he shrieked through the constriction in his throat, which made the words grate awfully, "Go back to work—" hardly believing they would obey; and when they did, Bruzak turning like a lump back to the machine and the tailor stiffly to his hot iron, Marcus was softened by their compliance and, speaking as if to children, said with tears in his eyes, "Boys, remember, don't fight."

Afterwards the clothier stood alone in the shade of the store, staring through the glass of the front door at nothing at all; lost, in thinking of them at his very back, in a horrid world of gray grass and mottled sunlight, of moaning and blood-smell. They had made him dizzy. He lowered himself into the leather chair, praying no customer would enter until he had sufficiently recovered from his nausea. So, sighing, he shut his eyes and felt his skull liven with new terror to see them both engaged in round pursuit in his mind. One ran hot after the other, lumbering but in flight, who had stolen his box of broken buttons. Skirting the lit and smoking sands, they scrambled high up a craggy cliff, locked in two-handed struggle, teetering on the ledge, till one slipped in slime and pulled the other with him. Reaching forth empty hands, they clutched nothing in stiffened fingers, as Marcus, the watcher, shrieked without sound at their evanescence.

He sat dizzily until these thoughts had left him.

When he was again himself, remembrance made it a kind of dream. He denied any untoward incident had happened; yet, knowing it had, called it a triviality—hadn't he, in the factory he had worked in on coming to America, often seen such fights among the men?—trivial things they all forgot, no matter how momentarily fierce.

However, on the very next day, and thereafter without skipping a day, the two in the back broke out of their hatred into thunderous quarreling that did damage to the business; in ugly voices they called each other dirty names, embarrassing the clothier so that he threw the measuring tape he wore like a garment on his shoulders once around his neck. Customer and clothier glanced nervously at each other, and Marcus quickly ran through the measurements; the customer, who as a rule liked to linger in talk of his new clothes, left hurriedly after paying cash, to escape the drone of disgusting names hurled about in the back yet clearly heard in front so that no one had privacy.

Not only would they curse and heap destruction on each other but they muttered in their respective tongues other dreadful things. The clothier understood Josip shouting he would tear off someone's genitals and rub the bloody mess in salt; so he guessed Emilio was shrieking the same things, and was saddened and maddened at once.

He went many times to the rear, pleading with them, and they listened to his every word with interest and tolerance, because the clothier, besides being a kind man—this showed in his eyes—was also eloquent, which they both enjoyed. Yet, whatever his words, they did no good, for the minute he had finished and turned his back on them they began again. Embittered, Marcus withdrew into the store and sat nursing his misery under the yellow-faced clock ticking away yellow minutes, till it was time to stop—it was amazing they got anything done—and go home.

His urge was to bounce them out on their behinds but he couldn't conceive where to find two others who were such skilled and, in essence, proficient workers, without having to pay a fortune in gold. Therefore, with reform uppermost in his mind, he caught Emilio one noon as he was leaving for lunch, whispered him into a corner, and said, "Listen, Emilio, you're the smart one, tell me why do you fight? Why do you hate him and why does he hate you, and why do you use such bad words?"

Though he enjoyed the whispering and was soft in the clothier's palms, the tailor, who liked these little attentions, lowered his eyes and blushed darkly, but either would not or could not reply.

So Marcus sat under the clock all afternoon with his fingers in his ears. And he caught the presser on his way out that evening and said to him, "Please, Josip, tell me what he did to you. Josip, why do you fight, you have a sick wife and boy?" But Josip, who also felt an affection for the clothier—he was, despite Polish, no anti-Semite—merely caught him in his hammy arms and, though he had to clutch at his trousers, which were falling and impeding his movements, hugged Marcus in a ponderous polka, then with a cackle pushed him aside and, in his beer jag, danced away.

When they began the same dirty hullabaloo the next morning and drove a customer out at once, the clothier stormed into the rear and they turned from their cursing—both fatigued and green-gray to the gills—and listened to Marcus begging, shaming, weeping, but especially paid heed when he, who found screeching unsuited to him, dropped it and gave advice and little preachments in a low, becoming tone. He was a tall man and, because of his illness, quite thin. What flesh remained had wasted further in these troublesome months, and his hair was white now so that, as he stood before them, expostulating, exhorting, he was in appearance like an old hermit, if not a saint, and the workers showed respect and keen interest as he spoke.

It was a homily about his long-dead dear father, when they were all children living in a rutted village of small huts, a gaunt family of ten—nine boys and an undersized girl. Oh, they were marvelously poor: on occasion he had chewed bark and even grass, bloating his belly, and often the boys bit one another, including the sister, upon the arms and neck in rage at their hunger.

"So my poor father, who had a long beard down to here"—he stooped, reaching his hand to his knee, and at once tears sprang up in Josip's eyes—"my father said, 'Children, we are poor people and strangers wherever we go, let us at least live in peace, or if not—' "

But the clothier was not able to finish because the presser, plumped down on the backless chair where he read his letters, swaying a little, had begun to whimper and then bawl, and the tailor, who was making odd clicking noises in his throat, had to turn away.

"Promise," Marcus begged, "that you won't fight anymore."

Josip wept his promise, and Emilio, with wet eyes, gravely nodded.

This, the clothier exulted, was fellowship and, with a blessing on both their heads, departed, but even before he was altogether gone the air behind him was greased with their fury.

Twenty-four hours later he fenced them in. A carpenter came and built a thick partition, halving the presser's and tailor's work space, and for once there was astonished quiet between them. They were, in fact, absolutely silent for a full week. Marcus, had he had the energy, would have jumped in joy, and kicked his heels together. He noticed, of course, that the presser occasionally stopped pressing and came befuddled to the new door to see if the tailor was still there, and though the tailor did the same, it went no further than that. Thereafter Emilio Vizo no longer whispered to himself and Josip Bruzak touched no beer; and when the emaciated letters arrived from the other side, he took them home to read by the dirty window of his dark room; when night came, though there was electricity, he preferred to read by candlelight.

One Monday morning he opened his table drawer to get at his garlic salami and found it had been roughly broken in two. With his pointed knife, he rushed at the tailor, who, at that very moment, because someone had battered his black hat, was coming at him with his burning iron. He caught the presser along the calf of the arm and opened a smelly purple wound, just as Josip stuck him in the groin, and the knife hung there for a minute.

Roaring, wailing, the clothier ran in and, despite their wounds, sent them packing. When he had left, they locked themselves together and choked necks.

Marcus rushed in again, shouting, "No, no, please, *please*," flailing his withered arms, nauseated, enervated (all he could hear in the uproar was the thundering clock), and his heart, like a fragile pitcher, toppled from the shelf and bump bumped down the stairs, cracking at the bottom, the shards flying everywhere.

Although the old Jew's eyes were glazed as he crumpled, the assassins could plainly read in them, What did I tell you? *You see?*

1957

🙥 B M 🙥

The Bill

Though the street was somewhere near a river, it was landlocked and narrow, a crooked row of aged brick tenement buildings. A child throwing a ball straight up saw a bit of pale sky. On the corner, opposite the blackened tenement where Schlegel worked as janitor, stood another like it except that this included the only store on the street—going down five stone steps into the basement, a small, dark delicatessen owned by Mr. and Mrs. F. Panessa, really a hole in the wall.

They had just bought it with the last of their money, Mrs. Panessa told the janitor's wife, so as not to have to depend on either of their daughters, both of whom, Mrs. Schlegel understood, were married to selfish men who had badly affected their characters. To be completely independent of them, Panessa, a retired factory worker, withdrew his three thousand of savings and bought this little delicatessen store. When Mrs. Schlegel, looking around—though she knew the delicatessen quite well for the many years she and Willy had been janitors across the way—when she asked, "Why did you buy this one?" Mrs. Panessa cheerfully replied because it was a small place and they would not have to overwork; Panessa was sixty-three. They were not here to coin money but to support themselves without working too hard. After talking it over many nights and days, they had decided that the store would at least give them a living. She gazed into Etta Schlegel's gaunt eyes and Etta said she hoped so.

She told Willy about the new people across the street who had bought out the Jew, and said to buy there if there was a chance; she meant by that they would continue to shop at the self-service, but when they had forgotten to buy something, they could go to Panessa's. Willy did as he was told. He was tall and broad-backed, with a heavy face seamed dark from the coal and ashes he shoveled around all winter, and his hair often looked gray from the dust the wind whirled up at him out of the ashcans, when he was lining them up for the sanitation truck. Always in overalls—he complained he never stopped working—he would drift across the street and down the steps when something was needed and, lighting his pipe, would stand around talking to Mrs. Panessa as her husband, a small bent man with a fitful smile, stood behind the counter waiting for the janitor after a long interval of talk to ask, upon reflection, for a dime's worth of this or that, the whole business never amounting to more than half a dollar. Then one day Willy got to talking about how the tenants goaded him all the time, and what the cruel and stingy landlord could think up for him to do in that smelly five-floor dungeon. He was absorbed by what he was saying and before he knew it had run up a three-dollar order, though all he had on him was fifty cents. Willy looked like a dog that had just had a licking, but Mr. Panessa, after clearing his throat, chirped up it didn't matter, he could pay the rest whenever he wanted. He said that everything was run on credit, business and everything else, because after all what was credit but the fact that people were human beings, and if you were really a human being you gave credit to somebody else and he gave credit to you. That surprised Willy because he had never heard a storekeeper say it before. After a couple of days he paid the two-fifty, but when Panessa said he could trust whenever he felt like it, Willy sucked a flame into his pipe, then began to order all sorts of things.

When he brought home two large bagfuls of stuff, Etta shouted he must be crazy. Willy answered he had charged everything and paid no cash.

"But we have to pay sometime, don't we?" Etta shouted. "And we have to pay higher prices than in the self-service." She said then what she always said, "We're poor people, Willy. We can't afford too much."

Though Willy saw the justice of her remarks, despite her scolding he still went across the street and trusted. Once he had a crumpled ten-dollar bill in his pants pocket and the amount came to less than four, but he didn't offer to pay, and let Panessa write it in the book.

Etta knew he had the money so she screamed when he admitted he had bought on credit.

"Why are you doing it for? Why don't you pay if you have the money?"

He didn't answer, but after a time he said there were other things he had to buy once in a while. He went into the furnace room and came out with a wrapped package which he opened, and it contained a beaded black dress.

Etta cried over the dress and said she would never wear it because the only time he ever brought her anything was when he had done something wrong. Thereafter she let him do all the grocery shopping and she did not speak when he bought on trust.

•

Willy continued to buy at Panessa's. It seemed they were always waiting for him to come in. They lived in three tiny rooms on the floor above the store, and when Mrs. Panessa saw him out of her window, she ran down to the store. Willy came up from his basement, crossed the street, and went down the steps into the delicatessen, looming large as he opened the door. Every time he bought, it was never less than two dollars' worth, and sometimes it would go as high as five. Mrs. Panessa would pack everything into a deep double bag, after Panessa had called off each item and written the price with a smeary black pencil into his looseleaf notebook. Whenever Willy walked in, Panessa would open the book, wet his fingertip, and flip through a number of blank pages till he found Willy's account in the center of the book. After the order was packed and tied up, Panessa added the amount, touching each figure with his pencil, hissing to himself as he added, and Mrs. Panessa's bird eyes would follow the figuring until Panessa wrote down a sum, and the new total sum (after Panessa had glanced up at Willy and saw that Willy was looking) was twice underscored and then Panessa shut the book. Willy, with his loose unlit pipe in his mouth, did not move until the book was put away under the counter; then he roused himself and embracing the bundles—with which they offered to help him across the street though he always refused—plunged out of the store.

One day when the sum total came to eighty-three dollars and some cents, Panessa, lifting his head and smiling, asked Willy when he could pay something on the account. The very next day Willy stopped buying at Panessa's and after that Etta, with her cord market bag, began to shop again at the self-service, and neither of them went across the street for as much as a pound of prunes or a box of salt they had meant to buy but had forgotten.

Etta, when she returned from shopping at the self-service, scraped the wall on her side of the street to get as far away as possible from Panessa's.

Later she asked Willy if he had paid them anything.

He said no.

"When will you?"

He said he didn't know.

A month went by, then Etta met Mrs. Panessa around the corner, and though Mrs. Panessa, looking unhappy, said nothing about the bill, Etta came home and reminded Willy.

"Leave me alone," he said, "I got enough trouble of my own."

"What kind of trouble have you got, Willy?"

"The goddamn tenants and the goddamn landlord," he shouted and slammed the door.

When he returned he said, "What have I got that I can pay? Ain't I a poor man every day of my life?"

She was sitting at the table and lowered her arms and put her head down on them and wept.

"With what?" he shouted, his face lit dark and webbed. "With the meat off of my bones? With the ashes in my eyes. With the piss I mop up on the floors. With the cold in my lungs when I sleep."

He felt for Panessa and his wife a grating hatred and vowed never to pay because he hated them so much, especially the humpback behind the counter. If he ever smiled at him again with those goddamn eyes he would lift him off the floor and crack his bent bones.

That night he went out and got drunk and lay till morning in the gutter. When he returned, with filthy clothes and bloodied eyes, Etta held up to him the picture of their four-year-old son who had died of diphtheria, and Willy, weeping splashy tears, swore he would never touch another drop.

Each morning he went out to line up the ashcans he never looked the full way across the street.

"Give credit," he mimicked, "give credit."

Hard times set in. The landlord ordered cut down on heat, cut down on hot water. He cut down on Willy's expense money and wages. The tenants were angered. All day they pestered Willy like clusters of flies and he told them what the landlord had ordered. Then they cursed Willy and Willy cursed them. They telephoned the Board of Health, but when the inspectors arrived they said the temperature was within the legal minimum though the house was drafty. However, the tenants still complained they were cold and goaded Willy about it all day, but he said he was cold too. He said he was freezing but no one believed him.

One day he looked up from lining up four ashcans for the sanitation truck to remove and saw Mr. and Mrs. Panessa staring at him from the store. They were staring up through the glass front door and when he looked at them at first his eyes blurred, and they appeared to be two scrawny, loose-feathered birds.

He went down the block to get a wrench from another janitor, and when he got back they then reminded him of two skinny leafless bushes sprouting up through the wooden floor. He could see through the bushes to the empty shelves.

In the spring, when the grass shoots were sticking up in the cracks in the sidewalk, he told Etta, "I'm only waiting till I can pay it all."

"How, Willy?"

"We can save up."

"How?"

"How much do we save a month?"

"Nothing."

"How much have you got hid away?"

"Nothing anymore."

"I'll pay them bit by bit. I will, by Jesus."

The trouble was there was no place they could get the money. Sometimes when he was trying to think of the different ways there were to get money his thoughts ran ahead and he saw what it would be like when he paid. He would wrap the wad of bills with a thick rubber band and then go up the stairs and cross the street and go down the five steps into the store. He would say to Panessa, "Here it is, little old man, and I bet you didn't think I would do it, and I don't suppose nobody else did and sometimes me myself, but here it is in bucks all held together by a fat rubber band." After hefting the wad a little, he placed it, like making a move on a checkerboard, squarely in the center of the counter, and the diminutive man and his wife both unpeeled it, squeaking and squealing over each blackened buck, and marveling that so many ones had been put together into such a small pack.

Such was the dream Willy dreamed, but he could never make it come true.

He worked hard to. He got up early and scrubbed the stairs from cellar to roof with soap and a hard brush, then went over that with a wet mop. He cleaned the woodwork too and oiled the banister till it shone the whole zigzag way down, and rubbed the mailboxes in the vestibule with metal polish and a soft rag until you could see your face in them. He saw his own heavy face with a surprising yellow mustache he had recently grown and the tan felt cap he wore that a tenant had left behind in a closetful of junk when he had moved. Etta helped him and they cleaned the whole cellar and the dark courtyard under the crisscrossed clotheslines, and they were quick to respond to any kind of request, even from tenants they didn't like, for sink or toilet repairs. Both worked themselves to exhaustion every day, but as they knew from the beginning, no extra money came in.

One morning when Willy was shining up the mailboxes, he found in his own a letter for him. Removing his cap, he opened the envelope and held the paper to the light as he read the trembling writing. It was from Mrs. Panessa, who wrote her husband was sick across the street, and she had no money in the house so could he pay her just ten dollars and the rest could wait for later.

He tore the letter to bits and hid all day in the cellar. That night, Etta, who had been searching for him in the streets, found him behind the furnace amid the pipes, and she asked him what he was doing there.

He explained about the letter.

"Hiding won't do you any good at all," she said hopelessly.

"What should I do then?"

"Go to sleep, I guess."

He went to sleep but the next morning burst out of his covers, pulled on his overalls, and ran out of the house with an overcoat flung over his shoulders. Around the corner he found a pawnshop, where he got ten dollars for the coat and was gleeful.

But when he ran back, there was a hearse or something across the street and two men in black were carrying this small and narrow pine box out of the house.

"Who's dead, a child?" he asked one of the tenants.

"No, a man named Mr. Panessa."

Willy couldn't speak. His throat had turned to bone.

After the pine box was squeezed through the vestibule doors, Mrs. Panessa, grieved all over, tottered out alone. Willy turned his head away although he thought she wouldn't recognize him because of his new mustache and tan cap.

"What'd he die of?" he whispered to the tenant.

"I really couldn't say."

But Mrs. Panessa, walking behind the box, had heard.

"Old age," she shrilly called back.

He tried to say some sweet thing but his tongue hung in his mouth like dead fruit on a tree, and his heart was a black-painted window.

Mrs. Panessa moved away to live first with one stone-faced daughter, then with the other. And the bill was never paid.

1957

❧ B M ❧

The Loan

The sweet, the heady smell of Lieb's white bread drew customers in droves long before the loaves were baked. Alert behind the counter, Bessie, Lieb's second wife, discerned a stranger among them, a frail, gnarled man with a hard hat who hung, disjoined, at the edge of the crowd. Though the stranger looked harmless enough among the aggressive purchasers of baked goods, she was at once concerned. Her glance questioned him but he signaled with a deprecatory nod of his hatted head that he would wait—glad to (forever)—though his face glittered with misery. If suffering had marked him, he no longer sought to conceal the sign; the shining was his own—him—now. So he frightened Bessie.

She made quick hash of the customers, and when they, after her annihilating service, were gone, she returned him her stare.

He tipped his hat. "Pardon me—Kobotsky. Is Lieb the baker here?"

"Who Kobotsky?"

"An old friend"—frightening her further.

"From where?"

"From long ago."

"What do you want to see him?"

The question insulted, so Kobotsky was reluctant to say.

As if drawn into the shop by the magic of a voice the baker, shirtless, appeared from the rear. His pink fleshy arms had been deep in dough. For a hat he wore jauntily a flour-covered brown paper sack. His peering glasses were dusty with flour, and the inquisitive face white with it, so that he resembled a paunchy ghost; but the ghost, through the glasses, was Kobotsky, not he.

"Kobotsky," the baker cried almost with a sob, for it was so many years gone Kobotsky reminded him of, when they were both at least young, and circumstances were—ah, different. Unable, for sentimental reasons, to refrain from smarting tears, he jabbed them away with a thrust of the hand.

Kobotsky removed his hat—he had grown all but bald where Lieb was gray—and patted his flushed forehead with an immaculate handkerchief.

Lieb sprang forward with a stool. "Sit, Kobotsky."

"Not here," Bessie murmured.

"Customers," she explained to Kobotsky. "Soon comes the supper rush."

"Better in the back," nodded Kobotsky.

So that was where they went, happier for the privacy. But it happened that no customers came so Bessie went in to hear.

Kobotsky sat enthroned on a tall stool in a corner of the room, stoop-shouldered, his black coat and hat on, the stiff, gray-veined hands drooping over thin thighs. Lieb, peering through full moons, eased his bones on a flour sack. Bessie lent an attentive ear, but the visitor was dumb. Embarrassed, Lieb did the talking: ah, of old times. The world was new. We were, Kobotsky, young. Do you remember how both together, immigrants out of steerage, we registered in night school?

"Haben, hatte, gehabt." He cackled at the sound of it.

No word from the gaunt one on the stool. Bessie fluttered around an impatient duster. She shot a glance into the shop: empty.

Lieb, acting the life of the party, recited, to cheer his friend: " 'Come,' said the wind to the trees one day, 'Come over the meadow with me and play.' Remember, Kobotsky?"

Bessie sniffed aloud. "Lieb, the bread!"

The baker bounced up, strode over to the gas oven, and pulled one of the tiered doors down. Just in time he yanked out the trays of brown breads in hot pans, and set them on the tin-top worktable.

Bessie clucked at the narrow escape.

Lieb peered into the shop. "Customers," he said triumphantly. Flushed, she went in. Kobotsky, with wetted lips, watched her go. Lieb set to work molding the risen dough in a huge bowl into two trays of pans. Soon the bread was baking, but Bessie was back.

The honey odor of the new loaves distracted Kobotsky. He breathed the fragrance as if this were the first air he was tasting, and even beat his fist against his chest at the delicious smell.

"Oh, my God," he all but wept. "Wonderful."

"With tears," Lieb said humbly, pointing to the large bowl of dough.

Kobotsky nodded.

For thirty years, the baker explained, he was never with a penny to his name. One day, out of misery, he had wept into the dough. Thereafter his bread was such it brought customers in from everywhere.

"My cakes they don't like so much, but my bread and rolls they run miles to buy."

•

Kobotsky blew his nose, then peeked into the shop: three customers.

"Lieb"—a whisper.

Despite himself the baker stiffened.

The visitor's eyes swept back to Bessie out front, then, under raised brows, questioned the baker.

Lieb, however, remained mute.

Kobotsky coughed to clear his throat. "Lieb, I need two hundred dollars." His voice broke.

Lieb slowly sank onto the sack. He knew—had known. From the minute of Kobotsky's appearance he had weighed in his thoughts the possibility of this against the remembrance of the lost and bitter hundred, fifteen years ago. Kobotsky swore he had repaid it, Lieb said no. Afterwards a broken friendship. It took years to blot out of the system the memoried outrage.

Kobotsky bowed his head.

At least admit you were wrong, Lieb thought, waiting a cruelly long time.

Kobotsky stared at his crippled hands. Once a cutter of furs, driven by arthritis out of the business.

Lieb gazed too. The bottom of a truss bit into his belly. Both eyes were cloudy with cataracts. Though the doctor swore he would see after the operation, he feared otherwise.

He sighed. The wrong was in the past. Forgiven: forgiven at the dim sight of him.

"For myself, positively, but she"—Lieb nodded toward the shop

—"is a second wife. Everything is in her name." He held up empty hands.

Kobotsky's eyes were shut.

"But I will ask her—" Lieb looked doubtful.

"My wife needs—"

The baker raised a palm. "Don't speak."

"Tell her—"

"Leave it to me."

He seized the broom and circled the room, raising clouds of white dust.

When Bessie, breathless, got back she threw one look at them, and with tightened lips waited adamant.

Lieb hastily scoured the pots in the iron sink, stored the bread pans under the table, and stacked the fragrant loaves. He put one eye to the slot of the oven: baking, all baking.

Facing Bessie, he broke into a sweat so hot it momentarily stunned him.

Kobotsky squirmed atop the stool.

"Bessie," said the baker at last, "this is my old friend."

She nodded gravely.

Kobotsky lifted his hat.

"His mother—God bless her—gave me many times a plate hot soup. Also when I came to this country, for years I ate at his table. His wife is a very fine person—Dora—you will someday meet her—"

Kobotsky softly groaned.

"So why I didn't meet her yet?" Bessie said, after a dozen years still jealous of the first wife's prerogatives.

"You will."

"Why didn't I?"

"Lieb—" pleaded Kobotsky.

"Because I didn't see her myself fifteen years," Lieb admitted.

"Why not?" she pounced.

Lieb paused. "A mistake."

Kobotsky turned away.

"My fault," said Lieb.

"Because you never go anyplace," Bessie spat out. "Because you live always in the shop. Because it means nothing to you to have friends."

Lieb solemnly agreed.

"Now she is sick," he announced. "The doctor must operate. This will cost two hundred dollars. I promised Kobotsky—"

Bessie screamed.

Hat in hand, Kobotsky got off the stool.

Pressing a palm to her bosom, Bessie lifted her arm to her eyes. She tottered. They both ran forward to steady her but she did not fall. Kobotsky retreated quickly to the stool and Lieb returned to the sink.

Bessie, her face like the inside of a loaf, quietly addressed the visitor. "I have pity for your wife but we can't help you. I am sorry, Mr. Kobotsky, we are poor people, we don't have the money."

"A mistake," Lieb cried, enraged.

Bessie strode over to the shelf and tore out a bill box. She dumped its contents on the table, the papers flying everywhere.

"Bills," she shouted.

Kobotsky hunched his shoulders.

"Bessie, we have in the bank——"

"No——"

"I saw the bankbook."

"So what if you saved a few dollars, so have you got life insurance?"

He made no answer.

"Can you get?" she taunted.

The front door banged. It banged often. The shop was crowded with customers clamoring for bread. Bessie stomped out to wait on them.

•

In the rear the wounded stirred. Kobotsky, with bony fingers, buttoned his overcoat.

"Sit," sighed the baker.

"Lieb, I am sorry——"

Kobotsky sat, his face lit with sadness.

When Bessie finally was rid of the rush, Lieb went into the shop. He spoke to her quietly, almost in a whisper, and she answered as quietly, but it took only a minute to start them quarreling.

Kobotsky slipped off the stool. He went to the sink, wet half his handkerchief, and held it to his dry eyes. Folding the damp handkerchief, he thrust it into his overcoat pocket, then took out a small penknife and quickly pared his fingernails.

As he entered the shop, Lieb was pleading with Bessie, reciting the embittered hours of his toil, the enduring drudgery. And now that he had a penny to his name, what was there to live for if he could not share it with a dear friend? But Bessie had her back to him.

"Please," Kobotsky said, "don't fight. I will go away now."

Lieb gazed at him in exasperation. Bessie stayed with head averted.

"Yes," Kobotsky sighed, "the money I wanted for Dora, but she is not sick, Lieb, she is dead."

"Ai," Lieb cried, wringing his hands.

Bessie faced the visitor, pallid.

"Not now," he spoke kindly, "five years ago."

Lieb groaned.

"The money I need for a stone on her grave. She never had a stone. Next Sunday is five years that she is dead and every year I promise her, 'Dora, this year I will give you your stone,' and every year I gave her nothing."

The grave, to his everlasting shame, lay uncovered before all eyes. He had long ago paid a fifty-dollar deposit for a headstone with her name on it in clearly chiseled letters, but had never got the rest of the money. If there wasn't one thing to do with it there was always another: first an operation; the second year he couldn't work, imprisoned again by arthritis; the third a widowed sister lost her only son and the little Kobotsky earned had to help support her; the fourth incapacitated by boils that made him ashamed to walk out into the street. This year he was at least working, but only for just enough to eat and sleep, so Dora still lay without a stone, and for aught he knew he would someday return to the cemetery and find her grave gone.

Tears sprang into the baker's eyes. One gaze at Bessie's face—and the odd looseness of her neck and shoulders—told him that she too was moved. Ah, he had won out. She would now say yes, give the money, and they would then all sit down at the table and eat together.

•

But Bessie, though weeping, shook her head, and before they could guess what, had blurted out the story of her afflictions: how the Bolsheviki came when she was a little girl and dragged her beloved father into the snowy fields without his shoes; the shots scattered the blackbirds in the trees and the snow oozed blood; how, when she was married a year, her husband, a sweet and gentle man, an educated accountant—rare in those days and that place—died of typhus in Warsaw; and how she, abandoned in her grief, years later found sanctuary in the home of an older brother in Germany, who sacrificed his own chances to send her, before the war, to America, and himself ended, with wife and daughter, in one of Hitler's incinerators.

"So I came to America and met here a poor baker, a poor man—who was always in his life poor—without a cent and without enjoyment, and I married him, God knows why, and with my both hands, working day and night, I fixed up for him his piece of business and we make now, after twelve years, a little living. But Lieb is not a healthy man, also with eyes that he needs an operation, and this is not yet everything. Suppose, God forbid, that he died, what will I do alone by myself? Where will I go, where, and who will take care of me if I have nothing?"

The baker, who had often heard this tale, munched, as he listened, chunks of bread.

When she had finished he tossed the shell of a loaf away. Kobotsky, at the end of the story, held his hands over his ears.

Tears streaming from her eyes, Bessie raised her head and suspiciously sniffed the air. Screeching suddenly, she ran into the rear and with a cry wrenched open the oven door. A cloud of smoke billowed out at her. The loaves in the trays were blackened bricks—charred corpses.

Kobotsky and the baker embraced and sighed over their lost youth. They pressed mouths together and parted forever.

1952

B M

A Confession of Murder

With the doing of the deed embedded in his mind like a child's grave in the earth, Farr shut the door and walked heavy-hearted down the stairs. At the third-floor landing he stopped to look out the small dirty window, across the harbor. The late-winter day was sullen, but Farr could see the ocean in the distance. Although he was carrying the weapon, a stone sash weight in a brown paper bag, heedless of the danger he set it down on the window ledge and stared at the water. It seemed to Farr that he had never loved the sea as he did now. Although he had not crossed it—he thought he would during the war but didn't—and had never gone any of the different ways it led, he felt he someday ought to. As he gazed, the water seemed to come alive in sunlight, flowing with slanted white sails. Moved to grief at the lovely sight he remained at the window with unseeing eyes until he remembered to go.

He went down the creaking stairs to the black, airless cellar. Farr pulled the rasping chain above the electric bulb and, when the dim light fell on him, searched around for a hiding place. As his hand uncoiled he realized with horror that he had forgotten the sash weight. He bounded up three flights of stairs, coming to a halt as he saw through the banister that an old woman was standing at the window, resting her bundle on the ledge—on the sash weight itself! Agitated, Farr watched to see whether she would discover the bloody thing, but she too was looking at the water and made no move to go. When she finally left, Farr, who had been lurking on the landing below, ran up, seized the package, and fled down to the cellar.

There he was tempted to draw the weapon out of the paper to inspect it but did not dare. He hunted for a place to bury it but felt secure nowhere. At last he tore open the asbestos covering of an insulated water pipe overhead and shoved the sash weight into the wool. As he was smoothing the asbestos he heard footsteps above and broke into a chilling sweat at the fear he was being followed. Stealthily he put out the light, sneaked close to the wall, and crouched in the pitch dark behind a dusty dresser abandoned there. He waited with indrawn breath for whoever he was to come limping down. Farr planned to yell into his face, escape up the stairs.

No one came down. Farr was afraid to abandon the hiding place, stricken at the thought that it was not a stranger but his father, miraculously recovered from his wound, who sought him there, as he had in the past, shouting in drunken rage against his son, stalking him in the dark, threatening to beat his head off with his belt buckle if he did not reveal himself. The memory of this so deeply affected Farr that he groaned aloud. It did not console him that his father had at last paid a terrible price for all the misery he had inflicted on him.

Farr trudged up the steps out of the cellar. In the street he felt unspeakable relief to be out of the grimy tenement house. He brushed the cobwebs off his brown hat and spanked a whitewash smear off the back of his long overcoat. Then he went down the block to where the houses ended and stood at the water's edge. The wind, whipping whitecaps along the surface of the harbor water, struck him with force. He held tightly to his hat. A flight of sparrows sprang across the sky, flying over the ships at anchor and disappearing in the distance. The aroma of roasting coffee filled Farr's hungry nostrils, but just then he saw some eggshells bobbing in the water and a dead rat floating. Surfeited, he turned away.

A skinny man in a green suit was standing at his elbow. "Sure looks like snow." The man wore no overcoat and his soiled shirt was open at the collar. His face and hands were tinged blue. Farr cupped a match to his cigarette, puffing quickly. He would have walked away but was afraid of being followed, so he stayed.

"Just a whiff of a butt makes me hungry to the bottom of my belly," said the man.

Farr listened, looking away.

After a minute the man, staring absently at the water, said, "The chill bites deep when there's no food between it and the marrow."

Suspecting him of planning to trick him, Farr warned himself to confess nothing. They'd have to ram a crowbar through his teeth to pry his jaws open.

"You wouldn't know it from the look of me," said the man, "but I'm a gentleman at heart." He wore a strained smile and held forth a trembling hand. Farr reached into his pants pocket, where he had five crumpled dollars plus a large assortment of coins. He pulled out a fistful of change, selected a nickel and five pennies, and dropped them into the man's outstretched hand.

Without thanking Farr, he drew back his arm and pitched the money into the water. Farr's suspicions awoke. He hurried up the block, glancing back from time to time to see if he was being followed, but the man had dropped out of sight.

He turned on the half run up the treeless avenue, angered with the bum for spoiling his view of the harbor. Yet though Farr was now passing the pawnshops, which reminded him of things he did not like to remember, his spirits rose. He accounted for this strange and unexpected change in him by his having done the deed. For an age he had been tormented by the desire to do it, had grown silent, lonely, sullen, until the decision came that the doing was the only way out. Much too long the plan had festered in his mind, waiting for an action, but now that it was done he at last felt free of the rank desire, the suppressed rage and fear that had embittered and thwarted his existence. It was done; he was content. As he walked, the vista of the narrow avenue, a street he had lived his life along, broadened, and he could see miles ahead, down to the suspension bridge in the distance, and was aware of people walking along as separate beings, not part of the mass he remembered avoiding so often as he'd trudged along here at various times of day and night.

·

One of the pawnshop windows caught his eye. Farr reluctantly stopped, yet he scanned it eagerly. There among the wedding bands, watches, knives, crucifixes, and the rest, among the stringed musical instruments and brasses hanging on pegs on the wall, he found what his eye sought—his mandolin—and felt a throb of pity for it. But Farr had not been working for more than a year—had left the place one rainy day in the fall—and the only way, thereafter, that he could keep himself in cigarette, newspaper, and movie money was to part, one by one, with the things he had bought for himself in a better time: a portable typewriter, used perhaps now and then to peck out a letter ordering a magazine; a pair of ice skates worn twice; a fine wristwatch he had bought on his birthday; and lately, with everything else gone, he had sold this little mandolin he'd liked so well, which he had taught himself to strum as he sang, and it was this bit of self-made music that he missed most. He considered redeeming it with the same five one-dollar bills he had got for it a month ago, but didn't relish the thought of strumming alone in his room; so sighing, Farr tore himself away from the window.

•

At the next corner stood Gus's Tavern. Farr, who had not gone in in an age, after a struggle entered, gazing around as if in a cathedral. Gus, older, with a folded apron around his paunch and an open vest over his white shirt, was standing behind the bar polishing beer glasses. When he saw Farr he put down the glass he was shining and observed him in astonishment.

"Well, throw me for a jackass if 'tisn't the old Punch-Ball King of South Second!"

Farr grunted awkwardly at the old appellation. "Surprised, Gus?"

"That's the least of it. Where in the name of mud have you been these many months—or is it years?"

"In the house mostly," Farr answered huskily.

Gus continued to regard him closely, to Farr's discomfort. "You've changed a lot, Eddie, haven't you now? I ask everybody whatever has become of the old Punch-Ball King and nobody says they ever see you. You used to haunt the streets when you were a kid."

Farr blinked but didn't reply.

"Married?" Gus winked.

"No," Farr said, embarrassed. He stole a glance at the door. It was still there.

Gus clucked. "How well I remember standing on the curbstone watching you play. *Flippo* with his left hand and the ball spins up. *Biffo* with his right, a tremendous sock lifting it far over the heads of all the fielders. How old were you then, Eddie?"

Farr made no attempt to think. "Fifteen, I guess."

An expression of sorrow lit Gus's eyes. "It comes back to me now. You were the same age as my Marty."

Farr's tongue tightened. It was beyond him to speak of the dead.

Himself again after a while, Gus sighed, "Ah yes, Eddie, you missed your true calling."

"One beer," Farr said, digging into his pocket for the change.

Gus drew a beer, shaved it, and set it before him.

"Put your pennies away. Any old friend of my Marty's needn't be thirsty here."

Farr gulped through the froth. A cold beer went with how good he now felt. He thought he might even break into a jig step or two.

Gus was still watching him. Farr, finding he couldn't drink, set the glass down.

After a pause Gus asked, "Do you still ever sing, Eddie?"

"Not so much anymore."

"Do me a favor and sing some old-time tune."

Farr looked around, but they were alone. Pretending to be strumming his mandolin, he sang, "In the good old summertime, in the good old summertime."

"Your voice has changed, Eddie," said Gus, "but it's still pleasing to the ear."

Farr then sang, "Ah, sweet mystery of life, at last I've found you."

Gus's eyes went wet and he blew his nose. "A fine little singer was lost to the world somewhere along the line."

Farr hung his head.

"What are your plans now, Eddie?"

The question scared him. Luckily, two customers came in and stood at the bar. Gus went to them, and Farr did not have to answer.

He picked up the beer and pointed with one finger to a booth in the rear.

Gus nodded. "Only don't leave without saying goodbye."

Farr promised.

•

He sat in the booth, thinking of Marty. Farr often thought and dreamed about him, but though he knew him best as a boy he dreamed of him as a man, mostly as he was during the days and nights they stood on street corners, waiting to be called into the army. There didn't seem anything to do then but wait till they were called in, so they spent most of their time smoking, throwing the bull, and making wisecracks at the girls who passed by. Marty, strangely inactive for the wild kid he had been—never knowing what wild thing to do next—was a blond fellow whose good looks the girls liked, but he never stopped wisecracking at them, whether he knew them or not. One day he said something dirty to this Jewish girl who passed by and she burst into tears. Gus, who had happened to be watching out of the upstairs window, heard what Marty said, ran down in his slippers, and smacked him hard across the teeth. Marty spat blood. Farr went sick to the pit of his stomach at the sound of the sock. He later threw up. And that was the last any of them had ever seen of Marty, because he enlisted in the army and never came out again. Gus got a telegram one day saying that he was killed in action, and he never really got over it.

⋅

Farr was whispering to himself about Marty when he gazed up and saw this dark-haired woman standing by his table, looking as if she had slyly watched his startled eyes find her. Half rising, he remembered to remove his hat.

"Remember me, Ed? Helen Melisatos—Gus told me to say hello."

He knew she was this Greek girl—only she'd been very pretty then—who had once lived in the same tenement house with him. One summer night they had gone together up to the roof.

"Sure," said Farr. "Sure I remember you."

Her body had broadened but her face and hair were not bad, and her dark brown eyes seemed still to be expecting something that she would never get.

She sat down, telling him to sit.

He did, placing his hat next to him on the seat.

She lit a cigarette and smoked for a long time. A man called her from the bar but she shook her head. He left without her.

Her lips moved hungrily. Although he could at first hear no voice, she seemed, against his will, to be telling him a story he didn't want to hear. It was about this boy and a girl, a slim dark girl with soft eyes, seventeen then, wearing this nice white dress on a hot summer night. They'd been kissing. Then she had slipped off her undergarment and lain back, uncovered, on the tar-papered roof. With heart thudding he watched her, and when she said to kneel he kneeled, and then she said it was hot and why didn't he take off his pants. He wanted to love her with their clothes on. When he got his pants off he stopped and couldn't go on. What do you think of a guy who would do a thing like that to a girl? He wasn't much of a lover, was he? She was smiling broadly now, and she spoke in an older, disillusioned voice, "You're different, Ed." And she said, "You used to talk a lot."

He listened intently but said nothing.

"But you still ain't a bad-looking guy. How old are you, anyway?"

"Twenty-eight, going on twenty-nine."

"Married?"

"Not yet," he said quickly. "How about you?"

"I had enough," Helen said.

He cagily asked her another question to keep her talking about herself. "How's your brother George?"

"He lives in Athens now. He went back with my mother after the war. My father died here."

Farr put on his hat.

"Going someplace, Ed?"

"No." He whispered to himself that he must say nothing about his own father.

She shrugged.

"Drink?" he asked.

She lifted her half-full whiskey glass. "Order yourself."

"I got my beer." But when he took up the glass it was empty.

"Still absentminded?" She smiled.

"My mind's okay," Farr said.

"I bet you're still a virgin?"

"I bet you're not." Farr grinned and drained a drop from the glass.

"Remember that night on the roof?"

He harshly said he didn't want to hear about it.

"I couldn't believe in myself for a long time after that," Helen said.

"I don't want to hear about it."

She sat silent, not looking at him. She sat silent so long his confidence finally ebbed back.

"Remember," he said, "when you had that sweet-sixteen party in your house, your mother gave us that Greek coffee that had jelly in the bottom of the little cup?"

She said she remembered.

"Let me buy you a drink." Farr reached into his pocket. He was smoking and squinted as he counted the coins.

He caught Gus's eye and ordered whiskey for her, but Gus wouldn't take anything for it. Farr then slid a coin into the jukebox.

"Dance?" he said, fighting a panicky feeling.

"No."

Vastly relieved, he went to the bar and ordered another beer. This time Gus let him pay. Farr cashed one of his dollar bills.

"Nothing like old friends, eh, Eddie?"

"Yeah," said Farr happily. He lit a cigarette and steered the beer over to the table. Helen had another whiskey and Farr another beer. He got used to the way her eyes looked at him over her glass.

After a time Helen asked him if he had had supper.

A violent hunger seized him as he remembered his last meal had been breakfast.

He said no.

"Come on up to my place. I'll fix you something good."

Farr whispered to himself that he ought to go. He ought to, and later talk her into going up to the roof with him. If he did it to her now, maybe he would feel better and then things that had gone wrong would go right. You could never tell.

Her face was flushed, and all the time she was grinning at him in a dirty way.

Farr whispered something and she strained to catch it but couldn't. "What the hell are you saying?"

"Nothing."

"Come on up with me, kid," she urged. "After, I'll show you how to make a man out of yourself."

His head fell with a bang against the tabletop. His eyes were shut, and he wouldn't move.

"Imagine a guy your age who never made love," Helen taunted.

He answered nothing and she began cursing him, her face lit in livid anger. Finally she got up, a little unsteady on her feet. "Why don't you go and drop dead?"

He said he would.

•

Farr walked again in the darkened streets. He stopped at the heavy wooden doors of the Catholic church. Pulling one open, he glanced hastily inside and saw the holy-water basin. He wondered what would happen if he went in and gargled a mouthful. A girl in a brown coat and purple bandanna came out of the church and Farr asked her when was confession.

She looked up at him in fright and quickly said, "Saturday."

He thanked her and walked away. It was Monday.

She ran after him and said she could arrange for him to see the priest if he wanted to.

He said no, that he was not a Catholic.

Though his coat reached to his ankles, his legs were cold. So were the soles of his feet. He walked as if he were dragging a burden. The burden was the way he felt. The good feeling had gone and this old one was heavier now than anything he remembered. He would not mind the cold so much if he could only get rid of this dismal heaviness. His brain felt like a rock. Still it grew heavier. That was the unaccountable thing. He wondered how heavy it could get. If it got any heavier, he would keel over in the street and nobody'd be able to lift him. They would all give up and leave him lying with his head sunk in asphalt.

On the next street shone two green lamps on both sides of some stone steps leading into a dark and dirty building. It was a police station. Farr stood across the street from it, but nobody went in or came out. Finally it grew freezing cold. He blew into his fists, looked around to see if he was being followed, and then went in.

He was grateful for the warmth. The sergeant sat at the desk writing. He was a bald-headed man with a bulbous nose, which he frequently scratched with his little finger. His second and third fingers had ink stains on them from a leaky fountain pen. The sergeant glanced up in surprise, and Farr did not care for his face.

"What's yours?" he said.

Farr's tongue was like a sash weight. Unable to speak, he hung his head.

"Remove your hat."

Farr took it off.

"Come to the point," said the sergeant, scratching his nose.

Farr at last confessed to a crime.

"Such as what?" said the sergeant.

Farr's lips twitched and assumed odd shapes. "I killed somebody."

"Who, for instance?"

"My father."

The sergeant's incredulous look vanished. "Ah, that's too bad."

He wrote Farr's name down in a large ledger, blotted it, and told him to wait on a bench by the wall.

"I got to locate a detective to talk to you, but as it happens nobody's around just now. You picked suppertime to come in."

Farr sat on the bench with his hat on. After a while a heavyset man came through the door, carrying a paper bag and a pint container of coffee.

"Say, Wolff," called the sergeant.

Wolff slowly turned around. He had broad, bent shoulders and a thick mustache. His large black hat was broad-brimmed.

The sergeant pointed his pen at Farr. "A confession of murder."

Wolff's eyebrows went up slightly. "Where's Burns or Newman?"

"Supper. You're the only one that's around right now."

The detective glanced uneasily at Farr. "Come on," he said.

Farr got up and followed him. The detective walked heavily up the wooden stairs. Halfway up he stopped, sighed inaudibly, and went up more slowly.

"Hold this," he said at the top of the stairs.

Farr held the bag of food and the coffee. The hot container

warmed his cold hand. Wolff unlocked a door with a key, then took his
supper from Farr, and they went inside. The church bell in the neighborhood bonged seven times.

Wolff routinely frisked Farr. He sat down heavily at his desk, tore
open the paper bag, and unwrapped his food. He had three meat-and-
cheese sandwiches and a paper dish of cabbage salad which he ate with
a small plastic fork that annoyed him. As he was eating he remembered
the coffee and twisted the top off the container. His hand shook a little
as he poured the steaming coffee into a white cup without a handle.

He ate with his hat on. Farr held his in his lap. He enjoyed the
warmth of the room and the peaceful sight of someone eating.

"My first square today," said Wolff. "Busy from morning."

Farr nodded.

"One thing after another."

"I know."

Wolff, as he ate, kept his eyes fastened on Farr. "Take your coat
off. It's hot here."

"No, thanks." He was now sorry he had come.

The detective finished up quickly. He rolled the papers on his desk
and what remained of the food into a ball and dumped it into the wastebasket. Then he got up and washed his hands in a closet sink. At his
desk he lit a cigar, puffed with pleasure two or three times, put it to the
side in an ashtray, and said, "What's this confession?"

Although Farr struggled with himself to speak, he couldn't.

Wolff grew restless. "Murder, did somebody say?"

Farr sighed deeply.

"Your mother?" Wolff asked sympathetically.

"No, my father."

"Oh ho," said Wolff.

Farr gazed at the floor.

The detective opened a black pocket notebook and found a pencil
stub.

"Name?" he said.

"You mean mine?" asked Farr.

"Yours—who else?"

"My father's."

"First yours."

"Farr, Edward."

"His?"

"Herman J. Farr."

"Age of victim?"

Farr tried to think. "I don't know."

"You don't know your own father's age?"

"No."

"How old are you?"

"Twenty-nine, going on thirty."

"That you know?"

Farr didn't answer.

Wolff wrote down something in the book.

"What was his occupation?"

"Upholsterer."

"And yours?"

"None," Farr said, in embarrassment.

"Unemployed?"

"Yes."

"What's your regular work?"

"I have none in particular."

"A jack of all trades." Wolff broke the ash off in the tray and took another puff of the cigar. "Address?"

"80 South Second."

"Your father too?"

"Yes."

"That where the body is?"

Farr nodded absently.

The detective then slipped the notebook into his pocket.

"What did you use to kill him with?"

Farr paused, wet his dry lips, and said, "A blunt instrument."

"You don't say? What kind of a blunt instrument?"

"A window sash weight."

"What'd you do with it?"

"I hid it."

"Whereabouts?"

"In the cellar where we live."

Wolff carefully tapped his cigar out in the ashtray and leaned forward. "So tell me," he said, "why does a man kill his father?"

Alarmed, Farr half rose from his chair.

"Sit down," said the detective.

Farr sat down.

"I asked you why did you kill him?"

Farr gnawed on his lip till it bled.

"Come on, come on," said Wolff, "we have to have the motive."

"I don't know."

"Who then should know—I?"

Farr tried frantically to think why. Because he had had nothing in his life and what he had done was a way of having something?

"What did you do it for, I said," Wolff asked sternly.

"I had to—" Farr had risen.

"What do you mean 'had to'?"

"I had no love for him. He ruined my life."

"Is that a reason to kill your father?"

"Yes," Farr shouted. "For that and everything else."

"What else?"

"Leave me alone. Can't you see I'm an unhappy man?"

Wolff sat back in his chair. "You don't say."

"Sarcasm won't get you anyplace," Farr cried angrily. "Be humble with suffering people."

"I don't need any advice on how to run my profession."

"Try to remember a man is not a beast." Trembling, Farr resumed his seat.

"Are you a man?" Wolff asked slyly.

"No, I have failed."

"Then you are a beast?"

"Insofar as I am not a man."

They stared at each other. Wolff flattened his mustache with his fingertips. Suddenly he opened his drawer and took out a picture.

"Do you recognize this woman?"

Farr stared at the wrinkled face of an old crone. "No."

"She was raped and murdered on the top floor of an apartment house in your neighborhood."

Farr covered his ears with his hands.

The detective laid the picture back in the drawer. He fished out another.

"Here's a boy aged about six or seven. He was brutally stabbed to death in an empty lot on South Eighth. Did you ever see him before?"

He thrust the picture close to Farr's face.

When Farr looked into the boy's innocent eyes he burst into tears.

Wolff put the picture away. He pulled on the dead cigar, then examined it and threw it away.

"Come on," he said, tiredly rising.

•

The cellar was full of violent presences. Farr went fearfully down the steps.

Wolff flashed his light on the crisscrossed pipes overhead. "Which one?"

Farr pointed.

The detective brushed aside some cobwebs and felt along the pipe with his fingers. He found the loose asbestos and from the wool inside plucked forth the sash weight.

Farr audibly sucked in his breath.

In the yellow glow of the hall lamp upstairs the detective took the sash weight out of the bag and examined it. Farr shut his eyes.

"What floor do you live on?"

"Fourth."

Wolff looked up uneasily. They trudged up the stairs, Farr leading.

"Not so fast," said Wolff.

Farr slowed down. As they passed the third-floor window he looked out to sea, but all was dark. On the next floor he stopped before a warped door with a top panel of frosted glass.

"In here," Farr said at last.

"Have you got the key?"

Farr turned the knob and the door fell open, bumping loudly against the wall. The corridor to the kitchen was black. The detective's light pierced it, lighting up a wooden table and two wooden chairs.

"Go on in."

"I'm afraid," whispered Farr.

"Go on, I said."

He stepped reluctantly forward.

"Where is he?" said the detective.

"In the bedroom." He spoke hoarsely.

"Show me."

Farr led him through a small windowless room containing a cot and some books and magazines on the floor. Wolff's light shone on him.

"In there." Farr pointed to the door.

"Open it."

"No."

"Open, I said."

"For godsake, don't make me."

"Open."

Farr thought quickly: in the dark there he would upset the detective and make a hasty escape into the street.

"For the last time, I said open."

Farr pushed the door and it squeaked open on its hinges. The long, narrow bedroom was heavy with darkness. Wolff's light hit the metal headboard of an old double bed, sunken in the middle.

A groan rose from the bed. Farr groaned too, his hair on end.

"Murder," said the groan, "terrible, terrible."

A white bloodless face rose into the light, old and staring.

"Who's there?" cried Wolff.

"Oh, my dreams, my dreams," wept the old man, "I dreamed I was bein murdered."

Flinging aside the worn quilt, he slid out of bed and hopped in bare feet on the cold floor, skinny in his long underwear. He groped toward them.

Farr whispered wild things to himself.

The detective found the light chain and pulled it.

The old man saw the stranger in the room. "And who are you, might I ask?"

"Theodore Wolff, detective from the Sixty-second Precinct." He flashed his shield.

Herman Farr blinked in surprise and shame. He hastily got into the pants that had been draped across a chair and, stepping into misshapen slippers, raised suspenders over his shoulders.

"I must've overslept my nap. I usually have supper cookin at six and we eat half past six, him and I." He suddenly asked, "What are you doin here if you're a detective?"

"I came here with your son."

"He didn't do anything wrong?" asked the old man, frightened.

"I don't know. That's what I came to find out."

"Come into the kitchen," said Herman Farr. "The light's better."

They went into the kitchen. Herman Farr got a third chair from the bedroom and they sat around the wooden table, Farr waxen and fatigued, his father gaunt and bony-faced, with loose skin sprouting gray stubble, and on the long side of the table, the heavyset Wolff, wearing his black hat.

"Where are my glasses?" complained Herman Farr. He got up and found them on a shelf above the gas stove. The lenses were thick and magnified his watery eyes.

"Until now I couldn't tell the nature of your face," he said to the detective.

Wolff grunted.

"Now what's the trouble here?" said Herman Farr, staring at his son.

Farr sneered at him.

The detective removed the sash weight from the paper bag and laid it on the table. Farr gazed at it as if it were a snake uncoiling.

"Ever see this before?"

Herman Farr stared stupidly at the sash weight, one hand clawing the back of the other.

"Where'd you get it?" he cried in a quavering voice.

"Answer my question first."

"Yes. It belongs to me, though I wish to Christ I had never seen it."

"It's yours?" said Wolff.

"That's right. I had it hid in my trunk."

"What's this stain on it here?"

Farr gazed in fascination where the detective pointed.

Herman Farr said he didn't know.

"It's a bloodstain," Wolff said.

"Ah, so it is," sighed Herman Farr, his mouth trembling. "I'll tell you the truth. My wife—may God rest her soul—once tried to hit me with it."

Farr laughed out loud.

"Is this your blood?" asked Wolff.

"No, by the livin mercy. It's hers."

They were all astonished.

"Are you telling the truth?" said Wolff sternly.

"I'd give my soul if I only wasn't."

"Did you hit her with it?"

Herman Farr lifted his glasses and with a clotted yellow handkerchief wiped the tears from his flowing eyes.

"A sin is never lost. Once, in a drunken fit, enraged as I was by my long-lastin poverty, I swung it at her and opened a wound on her head. The blood is hers. I could never blame her for wantin to kill me with it. She tried it one night when I was at my supper, but the thing fell out of her hand and smashed the plate. I nearly jumped out of my shoes. Seein it fall I realized the extent of my wickedness and kept the sash weight hid away at the bottom of my trunk as a memory of my sins."

Wolff scratched a match under the table, paused, and shook it out. Farr smoked the last cigarette in his crushed pack. The old man wept into his dirty handkerchief.

"I have deserved a violent endin of my life if anybody ever did. In my younger days I was a beast—cruel, and a weaklin. I treated them both very badly." He nodded to Farr. "As he more than once said it, I killed her a little every day. Many times—may the livin God keep tor-turin me for it—I beat her black and blue, once bloodyin her nose on a frosty morning when she complained of the cold, and another time pushin her down a flight of stairs. As for him, I more than once skinned his back with my belt buckle."

Farr crushed his cigarette and snapped it into the sink.

Wolff then lit a cigar and puffed slowly.

The old man wept openly. "This young man is the livin witness of my terrible deeds, but he don't know half the depths of my sufferin since that poor soul left this world, or the terrible nature of my nightly dreams."

"When did she die?" the detective asked.

"Sixteen years ago, and he has never forgiven me, carryin his ha-tred like a fire in his heart, although she, good soul, forgave me in his presence at the time of her last illness. 'Herman,' she said, 'I'm goin to a place where I would be ill at ease if I didn't forgive you,' and with that she went to her peace. But my son has hated me throughout the years, and I can't look at him without seein it in his eyes. 'Tis true, he has sometimes been kind to a helpless old man, and when my arthritis was so bad that I couldn't move, he more than once brought a plate of soup to my bed and fed me with a spoon, but in the depths of his soul my change has made no difference to him and he hates me now as he did then, though I've repented on sore knees a thousand times. I have often said to him, 'What's done is done, and judge me for what I have since become'—for he is an intelligent man and reads books you and I never heard of—but on this thing he won't yield or be reasoned with."

"Did he ever try to hurt you?"

"No more than to nag or snarl at me. No, for all he does nowadays is to sit alone in his room and read and reflect, although his learnin doesn't in the least unbend his mind to me. Of course I don't approve him givin up his job, because with these puffed and crippled hands I am lucky when I can work half time, but there are all sorts in the world and some have greater need for reflection than others. He has been in-clined in that direction since he was a lad, although I did not notice his quiet and solitary ways until after he had returned from the army."

"What did he do then?" said Wolff.

"He worked for a year at his old job, then gave it up and became a hospital orderly. But he couldn't stand it long and he quit and stayed home."

Farr looked out the dark fire-escape window and saw himself walking along the dreary edge of a desolate beach, the wind wailing at his feet, driftwood taking on frightening shapes, and his footsteps fading behind, to appear on the ground before him as he walked along the vast, silent shore . . .

Wolff rubbed the cigar out against the sole of his shoe. "You want to know why I'm here?" he said to Herman Farr.

"Yes."

"He came to the station house around suppertime and made a statement that he had murdered you with this sash weight."

The old man groaned. "Not that I don't deserve the fate."

"He thought he actually did it," Wolff said.

"It's his overactive imagination on account of not gettin any exercise to speak of. I've told him that many times but he don't listen to what I say. I can't describe to you the things he talks about in his sleep. Many a night they keep me awake."

"Do you see this sash weight?" Wolff asked Farr.

"I do," he said, with eyes shut.

"Do you still maintain that you hit or attempted to hit your father with it?"

Farr stared rigidly at the wall. He thought, If I answer I'll go crazy. *I mustn't. I mustn't.*

"He thinks he did," Wolff said. "You can see he's insane."

Herman Farr cried out as though he had been stabbed in the throat.

Farr shouted, "What about that boy I killed? You showed me his picture."

"That boy was my son," Wolff said. "He died ten years ago of terrible sickness."

Farr rose and thrust forth his wrists.

The detective shook his head. "No cuffs. We'll just call the ambulance."

Farr wildly swung his fist, catching the detective on the jaw. Wolff's chair toppled and he fell heavily to the floor. Amid the confusion and shouting by Herman Farr that he was the one who deserved hanging, Farr fled down the ill-lighted stairs with murder in his heart. In the street he flung his coins into the sky.

❧ B M ❦

Riding Pants

After a supper of fried kidneys and brains—he was thoroughly sick of every kind of meat—Herm quickly cleared the table and piled the dirty dishes in with the oily pans in the metal sink. He planned to leave like the wind, but in the thinking of it hesitated just long enough for his father to get his tongue free.

"Herm," said the butcher in a tired but angry voice as he stroked the fat-to-bursting beef-livered cat that looked like him, "you better think of getting them fancy pants off and giving me a hand. I never heard of a boy of sixteen years wearing riding pants for all day when he should be thinking to start some steady work."

He was sitting, with the cat on his knees, in a rocker in the harshly lit kitchen behind the butcher shop where they always ate since the death of the butcher's wife. He had on—it never seemed otherwise—his white store jacket with the bloody sleeves, and apron, also blood-smeared and tight around his bulging belly, and the stupid yellow pancake of a straw hat that he wore in storm, sleet, or dead of winter. His mustache was gray, his lips thin, and his eyes, once blue as ice, were dark with fatigue.

"Not in a butcher store, Pa," Herm answered.

"What's the matter with one?" said the butcher, sitting up and looking around with exaggerated movements of the head.

Herm turned away. "Blood," he said sideways, "and chicken feathers."

The butcher slumped back in the chair.

"The Lord made certain creatures designed for man to satisfy his craving for food. Meat and fowl are full of proteins and vitamins. Somebody has to carve the animal and trim the meat clear of bone and gristle. There's no shame attached to such work. I did it my whole life long and never stole a cent from no one."

Herm considered whether there was a concealed stab in his words but he could find none. He had not stolen anything since he was thirteen and the butcher was never one to carry a long grudge.

"Meat might be good, but I don't have to like it."

"What *do* you like, Herm?"

Herm thought of his riding pants and the leather boots he was saving for. He knew, though, what his father meant—that he never stuck to a job. After he quit school he had a paper route, but the pay was chicken feed, so he left that and did lawn-mowing and cellar-cleaning, but that was not steady enough, so he quit that too, but not before he had enough to buy a pair of riding pants.

Since he could think of nothing to say, he tried to walk out, but his father called him back.

"Herm, I'm a mighty tired man since your momma died. I don't get near enough rest and I need it. I can't afford to pay a butcher's clerk because my take is not good. As a matter of fact it's bad. I'm every day losing customers for the reason that I can't give them the service they're entitled to. I know you're favorable to delivering orders but I need more of your help. You didn't like high school and asked me to sign you out. I did that, but you haven't been doing anything worthwhile for the past two months, so I decided I could use you in here. What do you say?"

"What am I supposed to say?"

"Yes or no, damn it."

"Then no, damn it," Herm said, his face flaring. "I hate butcher stores. I hate guts and chicken feathers, and I want to live my own kind of life and not yours."

And though the butcher called and called, he ran out of the store.

That night, while Herm was asleep, the butcher took his riding pants and locked them in the closet of his bedroom, but Herm guessed where they were and the next day went to the hardware store down the block, bought a skeleton key for a dime, and sneaked his riding pants out of his father's closet.

•

When Herm had just learned to ride he liked to go often, though he didn't always enjoy it. In the beginning he was too conscious of the horse's body, the massive frame he had to straddle, each independent rippling muscle, and the danger that he might have his head kicked in if he fell under the thundering hooves. And the worst of it was that sometimes while riding he was conscious of the interior layout of the horse, where the different cuts of round, rump, and flank were, as if the horse were stripped and labeled on a chart, posted, as a steer was, on the wall in the back of the store. He kept thinking of this the night he was out on Girlie, the roan they told him he wasn't ready for, and she had got the reins from him and turned and ran the way she wanted, shaking him away when he tried to hold her back, till she came to the stable with him on her like a sack of beans and everybody laughing. After that he had made up his mind to quit horses, and did, but one spring night he went back and took out Girlie, who, though lively, was docile to his touch and went with him everywhere and did everything he wanted; and the next morning he took his last twenty-five dollars out of the savings account and bought the riding pants, and that same night dreamed he was on a horse that dissolved under him as he rode but there he was with his riding pants on galloping away on thin air.

.

Herm woke to hear the sound of a cleaver on the wooden block down in the store. As it was still night he jumped out of bed frightened and searched for his riding pants. They were not in the bottom drawer where he had hidden them under a pile of his mother's clothes, so he ran to his father's closet and saw it was open and the butcher not in bed. In his pajamas Herm raced downstairs and tried to get into the butcher shop, but he was locked out and stood by the door crying as his father chopped the tightly rolled pants as if they were a bologna, with the slices falling off at each sock of the cleaver onto the floor, where the cat sniffed the uncurled remains.

.

He woke with the moon on his bed, rose and went on bare toes into his father's room, which looked so different now that it was no longer his mother's, and tried to find the butcher's trousers. They were hanging on a chair but without the store keys in the pockets, or the bill-fold, he realized blushing. Some loose change clinked and the butcher stirred in the creaking bed. Herm stood desperately still but, when his father had quieted, hung the pants and tiptoed back to his room. He pushed up the window softly, deciding he would slide down the telephone wires to the back yard and get in that way. Once within the store he would find a knife, catch the cat, and dismember it, leaving the pieces for his father to find in the morning; but not his son.

Testing the waterspout, he found it too shaky, but the wires held his weight, so he slid slowly down to the ground. Then he climbed up the sill and tried to push on the window. The butcher had latched it, not knowing Herm had loosened the screws of the latch; it gave and he was able to climb in. As his foot touched the floor, he thought he heard something scamper away but wasn't sure. Afraid to pull the light on because the Holmes police usually passed along the block this time of night, he said softly in the dark, "Here, kitty, here, kitty kitty," and felt around on the pile of burlap bags, but the cat was not where she usually slept.

He felt his way into the store and looked in the windows and they too were empty except for the pulpy blood droppings from the chickens that had hung on the hooks. He tried the paper-bag slots behind the counter and the cat was not there either, so he called again, "Here, kitty kitty kitty," but could not find it. Then he noticed the icebox door had been left ajar, which surprised him, because the butcher always yelled whenever anyone kept it open too long. He went in thinking of course the damn cat was there, poking its greedy head into the bowl of slightly sour chicken livers the butcher conveniently kept on the bottom shelf.

"Here, kitty," he whispered as he stepped into the box, and was completely unprepared when the door slammed shut behind him. He thought at first, so what, it could be opened from the inside, but then it flashed on him that the butcher had vaguely mentioned he was having trouble with the door handle and the locksmith was taking it away till tomorrow. He thought then, Oh, my God, I'm trapped here and will freeze to death, and his skull all but cracked with terror. Fumbling his way to the door, he worked frantically on the lock with his numbed fingers, wishing he had at least switched on the light from outside where the switch was, and he could feel the hole where the handle had been but was unable to get his comb or house key in to turn it. He thought if he had a screwdriver that might do it, or he could unscrew the metal plate and pick the lock apart, and for a second his heart leaped in expectation that he had taken a knife with him, but he hadn't.

Holding his head back to escape the impaling hooks, he reached his hand along the shelves on the side of the icebox and then the top shelf, cautiously feeling if the butcher had maybe left some tool around. His hand moved forward and stopped; it took him a minute to comprehend it was not going farther, because his fingers had entered a moist bony cavern; he felt suddenly shocked, as if he were touching the inside of an electric socket, but the hole was in a pig's head where an eye had been. Stepping back, he tripped over something he thought was the cat, but when he touched it, it was a bag of damp squirmy guts. As he flung it away he lost his balance and his face brushed against the clammy open side of a bleeding lamb. He sat down in the sawdust on the floor and bit his knuckles.

After a time, his fright prevented any further disgust. He tried to reason out what to do, but there was nothing he could think of, so he tried to think what time it was and could he live till his father came down to open the store. He had heard of people staying alive by beating their arms together and walking back and forth till help came, but when he tried that it tired him more, so that he began to feel very sleepy, and though he knew he oughtn't, he sat down again. He might have cried, but the tears were frozen in, and he began to wonder from afar if there was some quicker way to die. By now the icebox had filled with white mist, and from the distance, through the haze, a winged black horse moved toward him. This is it, he thought, and got up to mount it, but his foot slipped from the stirrup and he fell forward, his head bonging against the door, which opened, and he fell out on the floor.

•

He woke in the morning with a cutting headache and would have stayed in bed but was too hungry, so he dressed and went downstairs. He had six dollars in his pocket, all he owned in the world; he intended to have breakfast and after that pretend to go for a newspaper and never come back again.

The butcher was sitting in the rocker, sleepily stroking the cat. Neither he nor Herm spoke. There were some slices of uncooked bacon on a plate on the table and two eggs in a cardboard carton, but he could not look at them. He poured himself a cup of black coffee and drank it with an unbuttered roll.

A customer came into the store and the butcher rose with a sigh to serve her. The cat jumped off his lap and followed him. They looked like brothers. Herm turned away. This was the last he would see of either of them.

He heard a woman's resounding voice ordering some porterhouse steak and a chunk of calf's liver, nice and juicy for the dogs, and recognized her as Mrs. Gibbs, the doctor's wife, whom all the storekeepers treated like the Empress of Japan, all but kissing her rear end, especially his father, and this was what he wanted his own son to do. Then he heard the butcher go into the icebox and he shivered. The butcher came out and hacked at something with the cleaver and Herm shivered again. Finally the lady, who had talked loud and steadily, the butcher always assenting, was served. The door closed behind her corpulent bulk and the store was quiet. The butcher returned and sat in his chair, fanning his red face with his straw hat, his bald head glistening with sweat. It took him a half hour to recover every time he waited on her.

When the door opened again a few minutes later, it almost seemed as if he would not be able to get up, but Mrs. Gibbs's bellow brought him immediately to his feet. "Coming," he called with a sudden frog in his throat and hurried inside. Then Herm heard her yelling about something, but her voice was so powerful the sound blurred. He got up and stood at the door.

It was her, all right, a tub of a woman with a large hat, a meaty face, and a thick rump covered in mink.

"You stupid dope," she shouted at the butcher, "you don't even know how to wrap a package. You let the liver blood run all over my fur. My coat is ruined."

The anguished butcher attempted to apologize, but her voice beat him down. He tried to apologize with his hands and his rolling eyes and with his yellow straw hat, but she would have none of it. When he went forth with a clean rag and tried to wipe the mink, she drove him back with an angry yelp. The door shut with a bang. On the counter stood her dripping bag. Herm could see his father had tried to save paper.

He went back to the table. About a half hour later the butcher came in. His face was deathly white and he looked like a white scarecrow with a yellow straw hat. He sat in the rocker without rocking. The cat tried to jump into his lap but he wouldn't let it and sat there looking into the back yard and far away.

Herm too was looking into the back yard. He was thinking of all the places he could go where there were horses. He wanted to be where there were many and he could ride them all.

But then he got up and reached for the blood-smeared apron hanging on a hook. He looped the loop over his head and tied the strings around him. They covered where the riding pants had been, but he felt as though he still had them on.

The Girl of My Dreams

After Mitka had burned the manuscript of his heartbroken novel in the blackened bottom of Mrs. Lutz's rusty trash can in her back yard, although the emotional landlady tried all sorts of bait and schemes to lure him forth, and he could tell as he lay abed, from the new sounds on the floor and her penetrating perfume, that there was an unattached female loose on the premises (wondrous possibility of yore), he resisted all and with a twist of the key had locked himself a prisoner in his room, only venturing out after midnight for crackers and tea and an occasional can of fruit; and this went on for too many weeks to count.

In the late fall, after a long year and a half of voyaging among more than twenty publishers, the novel had returned to stay and he had hurled it into a barrel burning autumn leaves, stirring the mess with a long length of pipe, to get the inner sheets afire. Overhead a few dead apples hung like forgotten Christmas ornaments upon the leafless tree. The sparks, as he stirred, flew to the apples, the withered fruit representing not only creation gone for nothing (three long years), but all his hopes, and the proud ideas he had given his book; and Mitka, although not a sentimentalist, felt as if he had burned (it took a thick two hours) an everlasting hollow in himself.

Into the fire also went a sheaf of odd-size papers (why he had saved them he would never know): copies of letters to literary agents and their replies; mostly, however, printed rejection forms, with perhaps three typed notes from lady editors, saying they were returning the MS of his novel, among other reasons—but this prevailed—because of the symbolism, the fact that it was obscure. Only one of the ladies had written let's hear from you again. Though he cursed them to damnation it did not cause the acceptance of his book. Yet for a year Mitka labored over a new one, up to the time of the return of the old manuscript, when, upon rereading that, then the new work, he discovered the same symbolism, more obscure than ever; so he shoved the second book aside. True, at odd moments he sneaked out of bed to try a new thought with his pen, but the words refused to budge; besides he had lost the belief that anything he said could make significant meaning, and if it perhaps did, that it could be conveyed in all its truth and drama to some publisher's reader in his aseptic office high above Madison Avenue; so he wrote nothing for months —although Mrs. Lutz actively mourned—and vowed never to write again though he felt the vow was worthless, because he couldn't write anyway whether he had vowed or no.

·

So Mitka sat alone and still in his faded yellow-papered room, the badly colored Orozco reproduction he had picked up, showing Mexican peasants bent and suffering, thumbtacked above the peeling mantelpiece, and stared through sore eyes at the antics of pigeons on the roof across the street; or aimlessly followed traffic—not people—in the street; he slept for good or ill a great deal, had bad dreams, some horrific, and awaking, looked long at the ceiling, which never represented the sky although he imagined it snowing; listened to music if it came from the distance, and occasionally attempted to read some historical or philosophical work but shut it with a bang if it lit the imagination and made him think of writing. At times he cautioned himself, Mitka, this will have to end or you will, but the warning did not change his ways. He grew wan and thin, and once when he beheld his meager thighs as he dressed, if he were a weeper he would have wept.

Now Mrs. Lutz, herself a writer—a bad one but always interested in writers and had them in her house whenever she could fish one up (her introductory inquisition masterfully sniffed this fact among the first) even when she could ill afford it—Mrs. Lutz knew all this about Mitka and she daily attempted some unsuccessful ministration. She tried tempting him down to her kitchen with spry descriptions of lunch: steaming soup, Mitka, with soft white rolls, calf's foot jelly, rice with tomato sauce, celery hearts, delicious breast of chicken—beef if he preferred—and his choice of satisfying sweets; also with fat notes slipped under his door in sealed envelopes, describing when she was a little girl, and the intimate details of her sad life since with Mr. Lutz, imploring a better fate on Mitka; or she left at the door all sorts of books fished out of her ancient library that he never looked at, magazines with stories marked, "You can do better," and when it arrived, her own copy, for him to read first, of the *Writer's Journal.* All these attempts having this day failed—his door shut (Mitka voiceless) though she had hid in the hall an hour to await its opening—Mrs. Lutz dropped to one horsy knee and with her keyhole eye peeked in: he lay outstretched in bed.

"Mitka," she wailed, "how thin you have grown—a skeleton—it frightens me. Come downstairs and eat."

He remained motionless, so she enticed him otherwise: "Here are clean sheets on my arm, let me refresh your bed and air the room."

He groaned for her to go away.

Mrs. Lutz groped a minute. "We have with us a new guest on your floor, girl by the name of Beatrice—a real beauty, Mitka, and a writer too."

He was silent but, she knew, listening.

"I'd say a tender twenty-one or -two, pinched waist, firm breasts, pretty face, and you should see her little panties hanging on the line—like flowers all."

"What does she write?" he solemnly inquired.

Mrs. Lutz found herself coughing.

"Advertising copy, as I understand, but she would like to write verse."

He turned away, wordless.

She left a tray in the hall—a bowl of hot soup whose odor nearly drove him mad, two folded sheets, pillowcase, fresh towels, and a copy of that morning's *Globe.*

•

After he had ravished the soup and all but chewed the linen, he tore open the *Globe* to confirm that he was missing nothing. The headlines told him: correct. He was about to crumple the paper and pitch it out the window when he recalled "The Open Globe" on the editorial page, a column he hadn't looked at in years. In the past he had reached for the paper with five cents and trembling fingers, for "The Open Globe," come-one, come-all to the public, to every writer under a rock, inviting contributions in the form of stories at five bucks the thousand-word throw. Though he now hated the memory of it, it was his repeated acceptance here—a dozen stories in less than half a year (he had bought a blue suit and a two-pound jar of jam)—that had started him writing the novel (requiescat); from that to the second abortion, to the impotence and murderous self-hatred that had descended upon him afterwards. Open Globe, indeed. He gnashed his teeth but the holes in them hurt. Yet the not unsweet remembrance of past triumphs—the quarter of a million potential readers every time he appeared in print, all within a single city so that *everybody* knew when he was in (people reading him in buses, at cafeteria tables, park benches, as Mitka the Magician lurked around, watching for smiles and tears); also flattering letters from publishers' editors, fan letters too, from the most unlikely people —fame is the purr, the yip the yay. Remembering, he cast a momentarily dewy eye upon the column and, having done so, devoured the print.

The story socked in the belly. This girl, Madeleine Thorn, who wrote the piece as "I"—though she only traced herself here and there she came at once alive to him—he pictured her as maybe twenty-three, slim yet soft-bodied, the face whiplashed with understanding—that Thorn was not for nothing; anyway, there she was that day, running up and down the stairs in joy and terror. She too lived in a rooming house, at work on her novel, bit by bit, nights, after a depleting secretarial grind each day; page by page, each neatly typed and slipped into the carton under her bed. At the very end of the book a last chapter to go of the first draft, she had one night got out the carton and lay on the bed, rereading, to see if the book was any good. Page after page she dropped on the floor, at last falling asleep, worried she hadn't got it right, wearied at how much rewriting (this sank in by degrees) she would have to do, when the light of the risen sun struck her eyes and she pounced up, realizing she had forgotten to set the alarm. With a sweep of the hand she shot the typewritten sheets under the bed, washed, slipped on a fresh dress, and ran a comb through her hair. Down the stairs she ran and out of the house.

At work, strangely a good day. The novel again came together in the mind and she memo'd what she'd have to do—not very much really—to make it the decent book she had hoped to write. Home, happy, holding flowers, to be met on the first floor by the landlady, flouncing and all smiles: guess what I've gone and done for you today; describing new curtains, matching bedspread, a rug no less, to keep your tootsies warm, and surprise! the room spring-cleaned from top to bottom. Oh my God. The girl tore up the stairs. Falling on her hands and knees in her room she searched under the bed: an empty carton. Downstairs like dark light. Where, landlady, are the typewritten papers that were under my bed? She spoke with her hand to her throat. "Oh, those that I found on the floor, honey? I thought you meant for me to sweep the mess out and so I did." Madeleine, controlling her voice: "Are they perhaps in the garbage? I—don't believe they collect it till Thursday." "No, love, I burned them in the barrel this morning. The smoke made my eyes smart for a whole hour." Curtain. Groaning, Mitka collapsed on the bed.

·

He was convinced it was every bit of it true. He saw the crazy dame dumping the manuscript into the barrel and stirring it until every blessed page was aflame. He groaned at the burning—years of precious work. The tale haunted him. He wanted to escape it—leave the room and abandon the dismal memory of misery, but where would he go and what do without a penny in his pocket? So he lay on the bed and whether awake or asleep dreamed the recurrent dream of the burning barrel (in it their books commingled), suffering her agony as well as his own. The barrel, a symbol he had not conceived before, belched flame, shot word-sparks, poured smoke as thick as oil. It turned red hot, a sickly yellow, black—loaded high with the ashes of human bones— guess whose. When his imagination calmed, a sorrow for her afflicted him. The last chapter—irony of it. He yearned all day to assuage her grief, express sympathy in some loving word or gesture, assure her she would write it again, only better. Around midnight he could bear his thoughts no longer. He thrust a sheet of paper into the portable, twirled the roller, and in the strange stillness of the house clacked out to her a note c/o *Globe*, expressing his sorrow—a writer himself—but don't give up, write it again. Sincerely, Mitka. He found an envelope and sticky stamp in his desk drawer. Against his better judgment he sneaked out and mailed it.

Immediately he regretted it. Was he in his right mind? *All right*, so he had written to her, but what if she wrote back? Who wanted, who needed a correspondence? He simply hadn't the strength for it. There-fore he was glad there continued to be no mail—not since he had burned his book in November, and this was February. Yet on the way out to forage some food for himself when the house was sleeping, ridi-culing himself, holding a lit match he peered into the mailbox. The next night he felt inside the slot with his fingers: empty, served him right. Silly business. He had all but forgotten her story; that is, thought of it less each day. Yet if the girl by some mischance should write, Mrs. Lutz usually opened the box and brought up whatever mail herself—

any excuse to waste his time. The next morning he heard the courier carrying her bulk lightly up the stairs and knew the girl had answered. Steady, Mitka. Despite a warning to himself of the dream world he was in, his heart pounded as the old tease coyly knocked. He didn't answer. Gurgling, "For you, Mitka darling," she at last slipped it under the door—her favorite pastime. Waiting till she had moved on so as not to give her the satisfaction of hearing him go for it, he sprang off the bed and tore the envelope open. "Dear Mr. Mitka (a most feminine handwriting): Thank you for the expression of your kind sympathy, sincerely, M.T." That was all, no return address, no nothing. Giving himself a horse bray he dropped the business into the basket. He brayed louder the next day: there was another epistle, the story wasn't true— she had invented every word; but the truth was she was lonely and would he care to write again?

•

Nothing comes easy for Mitka but eventually he wrote to her. He had plenty of time and nothing else to do. He told himself he had answered her letter because she was lonely—all right, because they both were. Ultimately he admitted that he wrote because he couldn't do the other kind of writing, and this, though he was no escapist, solaced him a bit. Mitka sensed that although he had vowed never to go back to it, he hoped the correspondence would return him to his abandoned book. (Sterile writer seeking end of sterility through satisfying epistolary intercourse with lady writer.) Clearly then, he was trying with these letters to put an end to the hatred of self for not working, for having no ideas, for cutting himself off from them. Ah, Mitka. He sighed at this weakness, to depend on others. Yet though his letters were often harsh, provocative, even unkind, they drew from her warm responses, receptive, soft, willing; and so it was not long (who can resist it? he bitterly assailed himself) before he had brought up the subject of their meeting. He broached it first and she (with reluctance) gave in, for wasn't it better, she had asked, not to intrude the person?

The meeting was arranged for a Monday evening at the branch public library near where she worked—her bookish preference; himself, he would have chosen the freedom of a street corner. She would, she said, be wearing a sort of reddish babushka. Now Mitka found himself actively wondering what she looked like. Her letters showed her sensible, modest, honest, but what of the human body? Though he liked his women, among other things, to be lookers, he guessed she wasn't. Partly from hints dropped by her, partly his intuition. He pictured her as comely yet hefty. But what of it as long as she was womanly, intelligent, brave? A man like him nowadays had need of something special.

The March evening was zippy outside but cupped in it the breath of spring. Mitka opened both windows and allowed the free air to blow on him. About to go—there came a quick knock on the door. "Telephone," a girl's voice sang out. Probably the advertising Beatrice. He waited till she was gone, then unlocked the door and stepped into the hall for his first phone call of the year. As he picked up the receiver a crack of light showed in the corner. He stared and the door shut tight. The landlady's fault, she built him up among the roomers as a sort of freak. "My writer upstairs."

"Mitka?" It was Madeleine.

"Speaking."

"Mitka, do you know why I'm calling?"

"How should I know?"

"I'm half drunk on wine."

"Save it till later."

"Because I am afraid."

"Afraid of what?"

"I do so love your letters and would hate to lose them. Do we have to meet?"

"Yes," he hissed.

"Suppose I am not what you expect?"

"Leave that to me."

She sighed. "All right then—"

"You'll be there?"

No sound from her.

"For godsake, don't frustrate me now."

"Yes, Mitka." She hung up.

·

Sensitive kid. He plucked his very last buck out of the drawer and quickly left the room, to hurry to the library before she could change her mind and leave. But Mrs. Lutz, in flannel bathrobe, caught him at the bottom of the stairs. Her gray hair wild, her voice broken. "Mitka, why have you shunned me so long? I have waited months for a single word. How can you be so cruel?"

"Please." He shoved her aside and ran out of the house. Nutty dame. The balmy current in the air swept away the unpleasantness, carried a sob to his throat. He walked briskly, more alive than for many a season.

The library was an old stone structure. He searched in circulation amid rows of books on sagging floors but found only the yawning librarian. The children's room was dark. In reference, a lone middle-aged female sat at a long table, reading; on the table stood her bulky market bag. Mitka searched the room and was turning to look elsewhere when a monstrous insight tore at his scalp: *this was she.* He stared unbelievingly, his heart a dishrag. Rage possessed him. Hefty she was but yes, eyeglassed, and marvelously plain; Christ, didn't know color even—the babushka a sickly running orange. Ah, colossal trickery—was ever man so cruelly defrauded? His impulse was to escape into breathable air but she held him there by serenely reading the printed page—(sly one, she knew the tiger in the room). Had she for a split second gazed up with wavering lids he'd have bolted sure; instead she buttoned her eyes to the book and let him duck if he so willed. This infuriated him further. Who wanted charity from the old girl? Mitka strode (in misery) toward her table.

"Madeleine?" He mocked the name. (Writer maims bird in flight. Enough not enough.)

She looked up with a shy and stricken smile. "Mitka?"

"The same—" He cynically bowed.

"Madeleine is my daughter's name, which I borrowed for my story. Mine is Olga really."

A pox on her lies—yet he hopefully asked, "Did she send you?"

She smiled sadly. "No, I am the one. Sit, Mitka."

He sat sullenly, harboring murderous thoughts: to hack her to pieces and incinerate the remains in Mrs. Lutz's barrel.

"They'll be closing soon," she said. "Where shall we go?"

He was motionless, stunned.

"I know a beer place around the corner where we can refresh ourselves," Olga suggested.

She buttoned a drab coat over a gray sweater. At length he rose. She got up too and followed him, hauling her market bag down the stone steps.

In the street he took the bag—it felt full of rocks—and trailed her around the corner into the beer joint.

Along the wall opposite the beat-up bar ran a row of dark booths. Olga sought one in the rear.

"For peace and privacy."

He laid the bag on the table. "The place smells."

They sat facing each other. He grew increasingly depressed at the thought of spending the evening with her. The irony of it—immured for months in a rat hole, to come forth for this. He'd go back now and entomb himself forever.

•

She removed her coat. "You'd have liked me when I was young, Mitka. I had a sylphlike figure and glorious hair. I was much sought after by men. I was not what you would call sexy but they knew I had it."

Mitka looked away.

"I had verve and a quality of wholeness. I loved life. In many ways I was too rich for my husband. He couldn't understand my nature and this caused him to leave me—mind you, with two small children."

She saw he wasn't listening. Olga sighed and burst into tears.

The waiter came.

"One beer. Bring the lady whiskey."

She used two handkerchiefs, one to blow her nose in, the other to dry her eyes.

"You see, Mitka, I told you so."

Her humility touched him. "I see." Why hadn't he, fool, not listened?

She gazed at him with sadly smiling eyes. Without glasses she looked better.

"You're exactly the way I pictured you, except for your thinness, which surprises me."

Olga reached into her market bag and brought out several packages. She unwrapped bread, sausage, herring, Italian cheese, soft salami, pickles, and a large turkey drumstick.

"Sometimes I favor myself with these little treats. Eat, Mitka."

Another landlady. Set Mitka adrift and he enticed somebody's mama. But he ate, grateful she had provided an occupation.

The waiter brought the drinks. "What's going on here, a picnic?"

"We're writers," Olga explained.

"The boss will be pleased."

"Never mind him, eat, Mitka."

He ate listlessly. A man had to live. Or did he? When had he felt this low? Probably never.

Olga sipped her whiskey. "Eat, it's self-expression."

He expressed himself by finishing off the salami, also half the loaf of bread, cheese, and herring. His appetite grew. Searching within the bag Olga brought out a package of sliced corned beef and a ripe pear. He made a sandwich of the meat. On top of that the cold beer was tasty.

"How is the writing going now, Mitka?"

He lowered the glass but changed his mind and gulped the rest.

"Don't speak of it."

"Be uphearted, not down. Work every day."

He gnawed the turkey drumstick.

"That's what I do. I've been writing for over twenty years and sometimes—for one reason or another—it gets so bad that I don't feel like going on. But what I do then is relax for a short while and then change to another story. After my juices are flowing again I go back to the other and usually that starts off once more. Or sometimes I discover that it isn't worth bothering over. After you've been writing so long as I you'll learn a system to keep yourself going. It depends on your view of life. If you're mature you'll find out how to work."

"My writing is a mess," he sighed, "a fog, a blot."

"You'll invent your way out," said Olga, "if you only keep trying."

•

They sat awhile longer. Olga told him of her childhood and when she was a girl. She would have talked longer but Mitka was restless. He was wondering, what after this? Where would he drag that dead cat, his soul?

Olga put what was left of the food into the market bag.

In the street he asked where to.

"The bus, I guess. I live on the other side of the river with my son, his vinegary wife, and their little daughter."

He took her bag—a lightened load—and walked with it in one hand, a cigarette in the other, toward the bus terminal.

"I wish you'd known my daughter, Mitka."

"So why not?" he asked hopefully, surprised he hadn't brought up this before, because she was all the time in the back of his mind.

"She had flowing hair and a sweet hourglass figure. Her nature was beyond compare. You'd have loved her."

"What's the matter, is she married?"

"She died at twenty—at the fount of life. All my stories are actually about her. Someday I'll collect the best and see if I can get them published."

He all but crumpled, then walked unsteadily on. For Madeleine he had this night come out of his burrow, to hold her against his lonely heart, but she had burst into fragments, a meteor in reverse, scattered in the far-flung sky, as he stood below, a man mourning.

They came at last to the terminal and Mitka put Olga on the bus.

"Will we meet again, Mitka?"

"Better no," he said.

"Why not?"

"It makes me sad."

"Won't you write either? You'll never know what your letters meant to me. I was like a young girl waiting for the mailman."

"Who knows?" He got off the bus.

She called him to the window. "Don't worry about your work, and get more fresh air. Build up your body. Good health will help your writing."

His face showed nothing but he pitied her, her daughter, the world. Who not?

"Character is what counts in the pinches, of course properly mixed with talent. When you saw me in the library and stayed I thought, There is a man of character."

"Good night," Mitka said.

"Good night, my dear. Write soon."

She sat back in her seat and the bus roared out of the depot. As it turned the corner she waved from the window.

Mitka walked the other way. He was momentarily uneasy, until he realized he felt no pangs of hunger. On what he had eaten tonight he could live for a week. Mitka, the camel.

•

Spring. It gripped and held him. Though he fought the intimacy he was the night's prisoner as he moved toward Mrs. Lutz's.

He thought of the old girl. He'd go home now and drape her from head to foot in flowing white. They would jounce together up the stairs, then (strictly a one-marriage man) he would swing her across the threshold, holding her where the fat overflowed her corset as they waltzed around his writing chamber.

1953

The Magic Barrel

Not long ago there lived in uptown New York, in a small, almost meager room, though crowded with books, Leo Finkle, a rabbinical student at the Yeshiva University. Finkle, after six years of study, was to be ordained in June and had been advised by an acquaintance that he might find it easier to win himself a congregation if he were married. Since he had no present prospects of marriage, after two tormented days of turning it over in his mind, he called in Pinye Salzman, a marriage broker whose two-line advertisement he had read in the *Forward*.

The matchmaker appeared one night out of the dark fourth-floor hallway of the graystone rooming house where Finkle lived, grasping a black, strapped portfolio that had been worn thin with use. Salzman, who had been long in the business, was of slight but dignified build, wearing an old hat, and an overcoat too short and tight for him. He smelled frankly of fish, which he loved to eat, and although he was missing a few teeth, his presence was not displeasing, because of an amiable manner curiously contrasted with mournful eyes. His voice, his lips, his wisp of beard, his bony fingers were animated, but give him a moment of repose and his mild blue eyes revealed a depth of sadness, a characteristic that put Leo a little at ease although the situation, for him, was inherently tense.

He at once informed Salzman why he had asked him to come, explaining that but for his parents, who had married comparatively late in life, he was alone in the world. He had for six years devoted himself almost entirely to his studies, as a result of which, understandably, he had found himself without time for social life and the company of young women. Therefore he thought it the better part of trial and error—of embarrassing fumbling—to call in an experienced person to advise him on these matters. He remarked in passing that the function of the marriage broker was ancient and honorable, highly approved in the Jewish community, because it made practical the necessary without hindering joy. Moreover, his own parents had been brought together by a matchmaker. They had made, if not a financially profitable marriage—since neither had possessed any worldly goods to speak of—at least a successful one in the sense of their everlasting devotion to each other. Salzman listened in embarrassed surprise, sensing a sort of apology. Later, however, he experienced a glow of pride in his work, an emotion that had left him years ago, and he heartily approved of Finkle.

The two went to their business. Leo had led Salzman to the only clear place in the room, a table near a window that overlooked the lamp-lit city. He seated himself at the matchmaker's side but facing him, attempting by an act of will to suppress the unpleasant tickle in his throat. Salzman eagerly unstrapped his portfolio and removed a loose rubber band from a thin packet of much-handled cards. As he flipped through them, a gesture and sound that physically hurt Leo, the student pretended not to see and gazed steadfastly out the window. Although it was still February, winter was on its last legs, signs of which he had for the first time in years begun to notice. He now observed the round white moon, moving high in the sky through a cloud menagerie, and watched with half-open mouth as it penetrated a huge hen, and dropped out of her like an egg laying itself. Salzman, though pretending through eyeglasses he had just slipped on to be engaged in scanning the writing on the cards, stole occasional glances at the young man's distinguished face, noting with pleasure the long, severe scholar's nose, brown eyes heavy with learning, sensitive yet ascetic lips, and a certain almost hollow quality of the dark cheeks. He gazed around at shelves upon shelves of books and let out a soft, contented sigh.

When Leo's eyes fell upon the cards, he counted six spread out in Salzman's hand.

"So few?" he asked in disappointment.

"You wouldn't believe me how much cards I got in my office," Salzman replied. "The drawers are already filled to the top, so I keep them now in a barrel, but is every girl good for a new rabbi?"

Leo blushed at this, regretting all he had revealed of himself in a curriculum vitae he had sent to Salzman. He had thought it best to acquaint him with his strict standards and specifications but, in having done so, felt he had told the marriage broker more than was absolutely necessary.

He hesitantly inquired, "Do you keep photographs of your clients on file?"

"First comes family, amount of dowry, also what kind promises," Salzman replied, unbuttoning his tight coat and settling himself in the chair. "After comes pictures, rabbi."

"Call me Mr. Finkle. I'm not yet a rabbi."

Salzman said he would, but instead called him doctor, which he changed to rabbi when Leo was not listening too attentively.

Salzman adjusted his horn-rimmed spectacles, gently cleared his throat, and read in an eager voice the contents of the top card:

"Sophie P. Twenty-four years. Widow one year. No children. Educated high school and two years college. Father promises eight thousand dollars. Has wonderful wholesale business. Also real estate. On the mother's side comes teachers, also one actor. Well known on Second Avenue."

Leo gazed up in surprise. "Did you say a widow?"

"A widow don't mean spoiled, rabbi. She lived with her husband maybe four months. He was a sick boy she made a mistake to marry him."

"Marrying a widow has never entered my mind."

"This is because you have no experience. A widow, especially if she is young and healthy like this girl, is a wonderful person to marry. She will be thankful to you the rest of her life. Believe me, if I was looking now for a bride, I would marry a widow."

Leo reflected, then shook his head.

Salzman hunched his shoulders in an almost imperceptible gesture of disappointment. He placed the card down on the wooden table and began to read another:

"Lily H. High school teacher. Regular. Not a substitute. Has savings and new Dodge car. Lived in Paris one year. Father is successful dentist thirty-five years. Interested in professional man. Well-Americanized family. Wonderful opportunity.

"I know her personally," said Salzman. "I wish you could see this girl. She is a doll. Also very intelligent. All day you could talk to her about books and theayter and whatnot. She also knows current events."

"I don't believe you mentioned her age?"

"Her age?" Salzman said, raising his brows. "Her age is thirty-two years."

Leo said after a while, "I'm afraid that seems a little too old."

Salzman let out a laugh. "So how old are you, rabbi?"

"Twenty-seven."

"So what is the difference, tell me, between twenty-seven and thirty-two? My own wife is seven years older than me. So what did I suffer?— Nothing. If Rothschild's a daughter wants to marry you, would you say on account her age, no?"

"Yes," Leo said dryly.

Salzman shook off the no in the yes. "Five years don't mean a thing. I give you my word that when you will live with her for one week you will forget her age. What does it mean five years—that she lived more and knows more than somebody who is younger? On this girl, God bless her, years are not wasted. Each one that it comes makes better the bargain."

"What subject does she teach in high school?"

"Languages. If you heard the way she speaks French, you will think it is music. I am in the business twenty-five years, and I recommend her with my whole heart. Believe me, I know what I'm talking, rabbi."

"What's on the next card?" Leo said abruptly.

Salzman reluctantly turned up the third card:

"Ruth K. Nineteen years. Honor student. Father offers thirteen thousand cash to the right bridegroom. He is a medical doctor. Stomach specialist with marvelous practice. Brother-in-law owns own garment business. Particular people."

Salzman looked as if he had read his trump card.

"Did you say nineteen?" Leo asked with interest.

"On the dot."

"Is she attractive?" He blushed. "Pretty?"

Salzman kissed his fingertips. "A little doll. On this I give you my word. Let me call the father tonight and you will see what means pretty."

But Leo was troubled. "You're sure she's that young?"

"This I am positive. The father will show you the birth certificate."

"Are you positive there isn't something wrong with her?" Leo insisted.

"Who says there is wrong?"

"I don't understand why an American girl her age should go to a marriage broker."

A smile spread over Salzman's face.

"So for the same reason you went, she comes."

Leo flushed. "I am pressed for time."

Salzman, realizing he had been tactless, quickly explained. "The father came, not her. He wants she should have the best, so he looks around himself. When we will locate the right boy he will introduce him and encourage. This makes a better marriage than if a young girl without experience takes for herself. I don't have to tell you this."

"But don't you think this young girl believes in love?" Leo spoke uneasily.

Salzman was about to guffaw but caught himself and said soberly, "Love comes with the right person, not before."

Leo parted dry lips but did not speak. Noticing that Salzman had snatched a glance at the next card, he cleverly asked, "How is her health?"

"Perfect," Salzman said, breathing with difficulty. "Of course, she is a little lame on her right foot from an auto accident that it happened to her when she was twelve years, but nobody notices on account she is so brilliant and also beautiful."

Leo got up heavily and went to the window. He felt curiously bitter and upbraided himself for having called in the marriage broker. Finally, he shook his head.

"Why not?" Salzman persisted, the pitch of his voice rising.

"Because I detest stomach specialists."

"So what do you care what is his business? After you marry her do you need him? Who says he must come every Friday night in your house?"

Ashamed of the way the talk was going, Leo dismissed Salzman, who went home with heavy, melancholy eyes.

Though he had felt only relief at the marriage broker's departure, Leo was in low spirits the next day. He explained it as arising from Salzman's failure to produce a suitable bride for him. He did not care for his type of clientele. But when Leo found himself hesitating whether to seek out another matchmaker, one more polished than Pinye, he wondered if it could be—his protestations to the contrary, and although he honored his father and mother—that he did not, in essence, care for the matchmaking institution? This thought he quickly put out of mind yet found himself still upset. All day he ran around in the woods—missed an important appointment, forgot to give out his laundry, walked out of a Broadway cafeteria without paying and had to run back with the ticket in his hand; had even not recognized his landlady in the street when she passed with a friend and courteously called out, "A good evening to you, Dr. Finkle." By nightfall, however, he had regained sufficient calm to sink his nose into a book and there found peace from his thoughts.

Almost at once there came a knock on the door. Before Leo could say enter, Salzman, commercial Cupid, was standing in the room. His face was gray and meager, his expression hungry, and he looked as if he would expire on his feet. Yet the marriage broker managed, by some trick of the muscles, to display a broad smile.

"So good evening. I am invited?"

Leo nodded, disturbed to see him again, yet unwilling to ask the man to leave.

Beaming still, Salzman laid his portfolio on the table. "Rabbi, I got for you tonight good news."

"I've asked you not to call me rabbi. I'm still a student."

"Your worries are finished. I have for you a first-class bride."

"Leave me in peace concerning this subject." Leo pretended lack of interest.

"The world will dance at your wedding."

"Please, Mr. Salzman, no more."

"But first must come back my strength," Salzman said weakly. He fumbled with the portfolio straps and took out of the leather case an oily paper bag, from which he extracted a hard, seeded roll and a small smoked whitefish. With a quick motion of his hand he stripped the fish out of its skin and began ravenously to chew. "All day in a rush," he muttered.

Leo watched him eat.

"A sliced tomato you have maybe?" Salzman hesitantly inquired.

"No."

The marriage broker shut his eyes and ate. When he had finished he carefully cleaned up the crumbs and rolled up the remains of the fish, in the paper bag. His spectacled eyes roamed the room until he discovered, amid some piles of books, a one-burner gas stove. Lifting his hat he humbly asked, "A glass tea you got, rabbi?"

Conscience-stricken, Leo rose and brewed the tea. He served it with a chunk of lemon and two cubes of lump sugar, delighting Salzman.

After he had drunk his tea, Salzman's strength and good spirits were restored.

"So tell me, rabbi," he said amiably, "you considered some more the three clients I mentioned yesterday?"

"There was no need to consider."

"Why not?"

"None of them suits me."

"What then suits you?"

Leo let it pass because he could give only a confused answer.

Without waiting for a reply, Salzman asked, "You remember this girl I talked to you—the high school teacher?"

"Age thirty-two?"

But, surprisingly, Salzman's face lit in a smile. "Age twenty-nine."

Leo shot him a look. "Reduced from thirty-two?"

"A mistake," Salzman avowed. "I talked today with the dentist. He took me to his safety deposit box and showed me the birth certificate. She was twenty-nine years last August. They made her a party in the mountains where she went for her vacation. When her father spoke to me the first time I forgot to write the age and I told you thirty-two, but now I remember this was a different client, a widow."

"The same one you told me about, I thought she was twenty-four?"

"A different. Am I responsible that the world is filled with widows?"

"No, but I'm not interested in them, nor, for that matter, in schoolteachers."

Salzman pulled his clasped hands to his breast. Looking at the ceiling he devoutly exclaimed, "Yiddishe kinder, what can I say to somebody that he is not interested in high school teachers? So what then you are interested?"

Leo flushed but controlled himself.

"In what else will you be interested," Salzman went on, "if you not interested in this fine girl that she speaks four languages and has personally in the bank ten thousand dollars? Also her father guarantees further twelve thousand. Also she has a new car, wonderful clothes, talks on all subjects, and she will give you a first-class home and children. How near do we come in our life to paradise?"

"If she's so wonderful, why wasn't she married ten years ago?"

"Why?" said Salzman with a heavy laugh. "—Why? Because she is *partikiler*. This is why. She wants the *best*."

Leo was silent, amused at how he had entangled himself. But Salzman had aroused his interest in Lily H., and he began seriously to consider calling on her. When the marriage broker observed how intently Leo's mind was at work on the facts he had supplied, he felt certain they would soon come to an agreement.

•

Late Saturday afternoon, conscious of Salzman, Leo Finkle walked with Lily Hirschorn along Riverside Drive. He walked briskly and erectly, wearing with distinction the black fedora he had that morning taken with trepidation out of the dusty hat box on his closet shelf, and the heavy black Saturday coat he had thoroughly whisked clean. Leo also owned a walking stick, a present from a distant relative, but quickly put temptation aside and did not use it. Lily, petite and not unpretty, had on something signifying the approach of spring. She was au courant, animatedly, with all sorts of subjects, and he weighed her words and found her surprisingly sound—score another for Salzman, whom he uneasily sensed to be somewhere around, hiding perhaps high in a tree along the street, flashing the lady signals with a pocket mirror; or perhaps a cloven-hoofed Pan, piping nuptial ditties as he danced his invisible way before them, strewing wild buds on the walk and purple grapes in their path, symbolizing fruit of a union, though there was of course still none.

Lily startled Leo by remarking, "I was thinking of Mr. Salzman, a curious figure, wouldn't you say?"

Not certain what to answer, he nodded.

She bravely went on, blushing, "I for one am grateful for his introducing us. Aren't you?"

He courteously replied, "I am."

"I mean," she said with a little laugh—and it was all in good taste, or at least gave the effect of being not in bad—"do you mind that we came together so?"

He was not displeased with her honesty, recognizing that she meant to set the relationship aright, and understanding that it took a certain amount of experience in life, and courage, to want to do it quite that way. One had to have some sort of past to make that kind of beginning.

He said that he did not mind. Salzman's function was traditional and honorable—valuable for what it might achieve, which, he pointed out, was frequently nothing.

Lily agreed with a sigh. They walked on for a while and she said after a long silence, again with a nervous laugh, "Would you mind if I asked you something a little bit personal? Frankly, I find the subject fascinating." Although Leo shrugged, she went on half-embarrassedly, "How was it that you came to your calling? I mean, was it a sudden passionate inspiration?"

Leo, after a time, slowly replied, "I was always interested in the Law."

"You saw revealed in it the presence of the Highest?"

He nodded and changed the subject. "I understand that you spent a little time in Paris, Miss Hirschorn?"

"Oh, did Mr. Salzman tell you, Rabbi Finkle?" Leo winced but she went on, "It was ages ago and almost forgotten. I remember I had to return for my sister's wedding."

And Lily would not be put off. "When," she asked in a slightly trembly voice, "did you become enamored of God?"

He stared at her. Then it came to him that she was talking about not Leo Finkle but a total stranger, some mystical figure, perhaps even passionate prophet that Salzman had dreamed up for her—no relation to the living or dead. Leo trembled with rage and weakness. The trickster had obviously sold her a bill of goods, just as he had him, who'd expected to become acquainted with a young lady of twenty-nine, only to behold, the moment he had laid eyes upon her strained and anxious face, a woman past thirty-five and aging rapidly. Only his self-control had kept him this long in her presence.

"I am not," he said gravely, "a talented religious person," and, in seeking words to go on, found himself possessed by shame and fear. "I think," he said in a strained manner, "that I came to God not because I loved Him but because I did not."

This confession he spoke harshly because its unexpectedness shook him.

Lily wilted. Leo saw a profusion of loaves of bread go flying like ducks high over his head, not unlike the winged loaves by which he had counted himself to sleep last night. Mercifully, then, it snowed, which he would not put past Salzman's machinations.

•

He was infuriated with the marriage broker and swore he would throw him out of the room the moment he reappeared. But Salzman did not come that night, and when Leo's anger had subsided, an unaccountable despair grew in its place. At first he thought this was caused by his disappointment in Lily, but before long it became evident that he had involved himself with Salzman without a true knowledge of his own intent. He gradually realized—with an emptiness that seized him with six hands—that he had called in the broker to find him a bride because he was incapable of doing it himself. This terrifying insight he had derived as a result of his meeting and conversation with Lily Hirschorn. Her probing questions had somehow irritated him into revealing—to himself more than her—the true nature of his relationship to God, and from that it had come upon him, with shocking force, that apart from his parents, he had never loved anyone. Or perhaps it went the other way, that he did not love God so well as he might, because he had not loved man. It seemed to Leo that his whole life stood starkly revealed and he saw himself for the first time as he truly was—unloved and loveless. This bitter but somehow not fully unexpected revelation brought him to a point of panic, controlled only by extraordinary effort. He covered his face with his hands and cried.

The week that followed was the worst of his life. He did not eat and lost weight. His beard darkened and grew ragged. He stopped attending seminars and almost never opened a book. He seriously considered leaving the Yeshiva, although he was deeply troubled at the thought of the loss of all his years of study—saw them like pages torn from a book, strewn over the city—and at the devastating effect of this decision upon his parents. But he had lived without knowledge of himself, and never in the Five Books and all the Commentaries—mea culpa—had the truth been revealed to him. He did not know where to turn, and in all this desolating loneliness there was no *to whom*, although he often thought of Lily but not once could bring himself to go downstairs and make the call. He became touchy and irritable, especially with his landlady, who asked him all manner of personal questions; on the other hand, sensing his own disagreeableness, he waylaid her on the stairs and apologized abjectly, until, mortified, she ran from him. Out of this, however, he drew the consolation that he was a Jew and that a Jew suffered. But gradually, as the long and terrible week drew to a close, he regained his composure and some idea of purpose in life: to go on as planned. Although he was imperfect, the ideal was not. As for his quest of a bride, the thought of continuing afflicted him with anxiety and heartburn, yet perhaps with this new knowledge of himself he would be more successful than in the past. Perhaps love would now come to him and a bride to that love. And for this sanctified seeking who needed a Salzman?

The marriage broker, a skeleton with haunted eyes, returned that very night. He looked, withal, the picture of frustrated expectancy—as if he had steadfastly waited the week at Miss Lily Hirschorn's side for a telephone call that never came.

Casually coughing, Salzman came immediately to the point: "So how did you like her?"

Leo's anger rose and he could not refrain from chiding the matchmaker: "Why did you lie to me, Salzman?"

Salzman's pale face went dead white, the world had snowed on him.

"Did you not state that she was twenty-nine?" Leo insisted.

"I give you my word——"

"She was thirty-five, if a day. *At least* thirty-five."

"Of this don't be too sure. Her father told me——"

"Never mind. The worst of it is that you lied to her."

"How did I lie to her, tell me?"

"You told her things about me that weren't true. You made me out to be more, consequently less than I am. She had in mind a totally different person, a sort of semi-mystical Wonder Rabbi."

"All I said, you was a religious man."

"I can imagine."

Salzman sighed. "This is my weakness that I have," he confessed. "My wife says to me I shouldn't be a salesman, but when I have two fine people that they would be wonderful to be married, I am so happy that I talk too much." He smiled wanly. "This is why Salzman is a poor man."

Leo's anger left him. "Well, Salzman, I'm afraid that's all."

The marriage broker fastened hungry eyes on him.

"You don't want anymore a bride?"

"I do," said Leo, "but I have decided to seek her in another way. I am no longer interested in an arranged marriage. To be frank, I now admit the necessity of premarital love. That is, I want to be in love with the one I marry."

"Love?" said Salzman, astounded. After a moment he remarked, "For us, our love is our life, not for the ladies. In the ghetto they——"

"I know, I know," said Leo. "I've thought of it often. Love, I have said to myself, should be a product of living and worship rather than its own end. Yet for myself I find it necessary to establish the level of my need and fulfill it."

Salzman shrugged but answered, "Listen, rabbi, if you want love, this I can find for you also. I have such beautiful clients that you will love them the minute your eyes will see them."

Leo smiled unhappily. "I'm afraid you don't understand."

But Salzman hastily unstrapped his portfolio and withdrew a manila packet from it.

"Pictures," he said, quickly laying the envelope on the table.

Leo called after him to take the pictures away, but as if on the wings of the wind, Salzman had disappeared.

March came. Leo had returned to his regular routine. Although he felt not quite himself yet—lacked energy—he was making plans for a more active social life. Of course it would cost something, but he was an expert in cutting corners; and when there were no corners left he would make circles rounder. All the while Salzman's pictures had lain on the table, gathering dust. Occasionally as Leo sat studying, or enjoying a cup of tea, his eyes fell on the manila envelope, but he never opened it.

The days went by and no social life to speak of developed with a member of the opposite sex—it was difficult, given the circumstances of his situation. One morning Leo toiled up the stairs to his room and stared out the window at the city. Although the day was bright his view of it was dark. For some time he watched the people in the street below hurrying along and then turned with a heavy heart to his little room. On the table was the packet. With a sudden relentless gesture he tore it open. For a half hour he stood by the table in a state of excitement, examining the photographs of the ladies Salzman had included. Finally, with a deep sigh he put them down. There were six, of varying degrees of attractiveness, but look at them long enough and they all became Lily Hirschorn: all past their prime, all starved behind bright smiles, not a true personality in the lot. Life, despite their frantic yoohooings, had passed them by; they were pictures in a briefcase that stank of fish. After a while, however, as Leo attempted to return the photographs into the envelope, he found in it another, a snapshot of the type taken by a machine for a quarter. He gazed at it a moment and let out a low cry.

Her face deeply moved him. Why, he could at first not say. It gave him the impression of youth—spring flowers, yet age—a sense of having been used to the bone, wasted; this came from the eyes, which were hauntingly familiar, yet absolutely strange. He had a vivid impression that he had met her before, but try as he might he could not place her although he could almost recall her name, as if he had read it in her own handwriting. No, this couldn't be; he would have remembered her. It was not, he affirmed, that she had an extraordinary beauty—no, though her face was attractive enough; it was that *something* about her moved him. Feature for feature, even some of the ladies of the photographs could do better; but she leaped forth to his heart—had *lived*, or wanted to—more than just wanted, perhaps regretted how she had lived—had somehow deeply suffered: it could be seen in the depths of those reluctant eyes, and from the way the light enclosed and shone from her, and within her, opening realms of possibility: this was her own. Her he desired. His head ached and eyes narrowed with the intensity of his gazing, then as if an obscure fog had blown up in the mind, he experienced fear of her and was aware that he had received an impression, somehow, of evil. He shuddered, saying softly, It is thus with us all. Leo brewed some tea in a small pot and sat sipping it without sugar, to calm himself. But before he had finished drinking, again with excitement he examined the face and found it good: good for Leo Finkle. Only such a one could understand him and help him seek whatever he was seeking. She might, perhaps, love him. How she had happened to be among the discards in Salzman's barrel he could never guess, but he knew he must urgently go find her.

Leo rushed downstairs, grabbed up the Bronx telephone book, and searched for Salzman's home address. He was not listed, nor was his office. Neither was he in the Manhattan book. But Leo remembered having written down the address on a slip of paper after he had read Salzman's advertisement in the "personals" column of the *Forward*. He ran up to his room and tore through his papers, without luck. It was exasperating. Just when he needed the matchmaker he was nowhere to be found. Fortunately Leo remembered to look in his wallet. There on a card he found his name written and a Bronx address. No phone number was listed, the reason—Leo now recalled—he had originally communicated with Salzman by letter. He got on his coat, put a hat on over his skullcap, and hurried to the subway station. All the way to the far end of the Bronx he sat on the edge of his seat. He was more than once tempted to take out the picture and see if the girl's face was as he remembered, but he refrained, allowing the snapshot to remain in his inside coat pocket, content to have her so close. When the train pulled into the station he was waiting at the door and bolted out. He quickly located the street Salzman had advertised.

The building he sought was less than a block from the subway, but it was not an office building, nor even a loft, nor a store in which one could rent office space. It was a very old tenement house. Leo found Salzman's name in pencil on a soiled tag under the bell and climbed three dark flights to his apartment. When he knocked, the door was opened by a thin, asthmatic, gray-haired woman, in felt slippers.

"Yes?" she said, expecting nothing. She listened without listening. He could have sworn he had seen her, too, before but knew it was an illusion.

"Salzman—does he live here? Pinye Salzman," he said, "the matchmaker?"

She stared at him a long minute. "Of course."

He felt embarrassed. "Is he in?"

"No." Her mouth, though left open, offered nothing more.

"The matter is urgent. Can you tell me where his office is?"

"In the air." She pointed upward.

"You mean he has no office?" Leo asked.

"In his socks."

He peered into the apartment. It was sunless and dingy, one large room divided by a half-open curtain, beyond which he could see a sagging metal bed. The near side of the room was crowded with rickety chairs, old bureaus, a three-legged table, racks of cooking utensils, and all the apparatus of a kitchen. But there was no sign of Salzman or his magic barrel, probably also a figment of the imagination. An odor of frying fish made Leo weak to the knees.

"Where is he?" he insisted. "I've got to see your husband."

At length she answered, "So who knows where he is? Every time he thinks a new thought he runs to a different place. Go home, he will find you."

"Tell him Leo Finkle."

She gave no sign she had heard.

He walked downstairs, depressed.

But Salzman, breathless, stood waiting at his door.

Leo was astounded and overjoyed. "How did you get here before me?"

"I rushed."

"Come inside."

They entered. Leo fixed tea, and a sardine sandwich for Salzman. As they were drinking he reached behind him for the packet of pictures and handed them to the marriage broker.

Salzman put down his glass and said expectantly, "You found somebody you like?"

"Not among these."

The marriage broker turned away.

"Here is the one I want." Leo held forth the snapshot.

Salzman slipped on his glasses and took the picture into his trembling hand. He turned ghastly and let out a groan.

"What's the matter?" cried Leo.

"Excuse me. Was an accident this picture. She isn't for you."

Salzman frantically shoved the manila packet into his portfolio. He thrust the snapshot into his pocket and fled down the stairs.

Leo, after momentary paralysis, gave chase and cornered the marriage broker in the vestibule. The landlady made hysterical outcries but neither of them listened.

"Give me back the picture, Salzman."

"No." The pain in his eyes was terrible.

"Tell me who she is then."

"This I can't tell you. Excuse me."

He made to depart, but Leo, forgetting himself, seized the matchmaker by his tight coat and shook him frenziedly.

"Please," sighed Salzman. *"Please."*

Leo ashamedly let him go. "Tell me who she is," he begged. "It's very important for me to know."

"She is not for you. She is a wild one—wild, without shame. This is not a bride for a rabbi."

"What do you mean wild?"

"Like an animal. Like a dog. For her to be poor was a sin. This is why to me she is dead now."

"In God's name, what do you mean?"

"Her I can't introduce to you," Salzman cried.

"Why are you so excited?"

"Why, he asks," Salzman said, bursting into tears. "This is my baby, my Stella, she should burn in hell."

•

Leo hurried up to bed and hid under the covers. Under the covers he thought his life through. Although he soon fell asleep he could not sleep her out of his mind. He woke, beating his breast. Though he prayed to be rid of her, his prayers went unanswered. Through days of torment he endlessly struggled not to love her; fearing success, he escaped it. He then concluded to convert her to goodness, himself to God. The idea alternately nauseated and exalted him.

He perhaps did not know that he had come to a final decision until he encountered Salzman in a Broadway cafeteria. He was sitting alone at a rear table, sucking the bony remains of a fish. The marriage broker appeared haggard, and transparent to the point of vanishing.

Salzman looked up at first without recognizing him. Leo had grown a pointed beard and his eyes were weighted with wisdom.

"Salzman," he said, "love has at last come to my heart."

"Who can love from a picture?" mocked the marriage broker.

"It is not impossible."

"If you can love her, then you can love anybody. Let me show you some new clients that they just sent me their photographs. One is a little doll."

"Just her I want," Leo murmured.

"Don't be a fool, doctor. Don't bother with her."

"Put me in touch with her, Salzman," Leo said humbly. "Perhaps I can be of service."

Salzman had stopped eating and Leo understood with emotion that it was now arranged.

Leaving the cafeteria, he was, however, afflicted by a tormenting suspicion that Salzman had planned it all to happen this way.

•

Leo was informed by letter that she would meet him on a certain corner, and she was there one spring night, waiting under a street lamp. He appeared, carrying a small bouquet of violets and rosebuds. Stella stood by the lamppost, smoking. She wore white with red shoes, which fitted his expectations, although in a troubled moment he had imagined the dress red, and only the shoes white. She waited uneasily and shyly. From afar he saw that her eyes—clearly her father's—were filled with desperate innocence. He pictured, in her, his own redemption. Violins and lit candles revolved in the sky. Leo ran forward with flowers outthrust.

Around the corner, Salzman, leaning against a wall, chanted prayers for the dead.

1953

The Mourners

Kessler, formerly an egg candler, lived alone on social security. Though past sixty-five, he might have found well-paying work with more than one butter and egg wholesaler, for he sorted and graded with speed and accuracy, but he was a quarrelsome type and considered a troublemaker, so the wholesalers did without him. Therefore, after a time he retired, living with few wants on his old-age pension. Kessler inhabited a small cheap flat on the top floor of a decrepit tenement on the East Side. Perhaps because he lived above so many stairs, no one bothered to visit him. He was much alone, as he had been most of his life. At one time he'd had a family, but unable to stand his wife or children, always in his way, he had after some years walked out on them. He never saw them thereafter because he never sought them, and they did not seek him. Thirty years had passed. He had no idea where they were, nor did he think much about it.

In the tenement, although he had lived there ten years, he was more or less unknown. The tenants on both sides of his flat on the fifth floor, an Italian family of three middle-aged sons and their wizened mother, and a sullen, childless German couple named Hoffman, never said hello to him, nor did he greet any of them on the way up or down the narrow wooden stairs. Others of the house recognized Kessler when they passed him in the street, but they thought he lived elsewhere on the block. Ignace, the small, bent-back janitor, knew him best, for they had several times played two-handed pinochle; but Ignace, usually the loser because he lacked skill at cards, had stopped going up after a time. He complained to his wife that he couldn't stand the stink there, that the filthy flat with its junky furniture made him sick. The janitor had spread the word about Kessler to the others on the floor, and they shunned him as a dirty old man. Kessler understood this but had contempt for them all.

One day Ignace and Kessler began a quarrel over the way the egg candler piled oily bags overflowing with garbage into the dumbwaiter, instead of using a pail. One word shot off another, and they were soon calling each other savage names, when Kessler slammed the door in the janitor's face. Ignace ran down five flights of stairs and loudly cursed out the old man to his impassive wife. It happened that Gruber, the landlord, a fat man with a consistently worried face, who wore yards of baggy clothes, was in the building, making a check of plumbing repairs, and to him the enraged Ignace related the trouble he was having with Kessler. He described, holding his nose, the smell in Kessler's flat, and called him the dirtiest person he ever saw. Gruber knew his janitor was exaggerating, but he felt burdened by financial worries which shot his blood pressure up to astonishing heights, so he settled it quickly by saying, "Give him notice." None of the tenants in the house had held a written lease since the war, and Gruber felt confident, in case somebody asked questions, that he could easily justify his dismissal of Kessler as an undesirable tenant. It had occurred to him that Ignace could then slap a cheap coat of paint on the walls, and the flat would be let to someone for five dollars more than the old man was paying.

That night after supper, Ignace victoriously ascended the stairs and knocked on Kessler's door. The egg candler opened it and, seeing who stood there, immediately slammed it shut. Ignace shouted through the door, "Mr. Gruber says to give notice. We don't want you around here. Your dirt stinks the whole house." There was silence, but Ignace waited, relishing what he had said. Although after five minutes he still heard no sound, the janitor stayed there, picturing the old Jew trembling behind the locked door. He spoke again, "You got two weeks' notice till the first, then you better move out or Mr. Gruber and myself will throw you out." Ignace watched as the door slowly opened. To his surprise he found himself frightened at the old man's appearance. He looked, in the act of opening the door, like a corpse adjusting his coffin lid. But if he appeared dead, his voice was alive. It rose terrifyingly harsh from his throat, and he sprayed curses over all the years of Ignace's life. His eyes were reddened, his cheeks sunken, and his wisp of beard moved agitatedly. He seemed to be losing weight as he shouted. The janitor no longer had any heart for the matter, but he could not bear so many insults all at once, so he cried out, "You dirty old bum, you better get out and don't make so much trouble." To this the enraged Kessler swore they would first have to kill him and drag him out dead.

On the morning of the first of December, Ignace found in his letter box a soiled folded paper containing Kessler's twenty-five dollars. He showed it to Gruber that evening when the landlord came to collect the rent money. Gruber, after a minute of absently contemplating the money, frowned disgustedly.

"I thought I told you to give notice."

"Yes, Mr. Gruber," Ignace agreed. "I gave him."

"That's a helluva chutzpah," said Gruber. "Gimme the keys."

Ignace brought the ring of passkeys, and Gruber, breathing heavily, began the lumbering climb up the long avenue of stairs. Although he rested on each landing, the fatigue of climbing, and his profuse flowing perspiration, heightened his irritation.

Arriving at the top floor he banged his fist on Kessler's door. "Gruber, the landlord. Open up here."

There was no answer, no movement within, so Gruber inserted his key into the lock and twisted. Kessler had barricaded the door with a chest and some chairs. Gruber had to put his shoulder to the door and shove before he could step into the hallway of the badly lit two-and-a-half-room flat. The old man, his face drained of blood, was standing in the kitchen doorway.

"I warned you to scram outta here," Gruber said loudly. "Move out or I'll telephone the city marshal."

"Mr. Gruber—" began Kessler.

"Don't bother me with your lousy excuses, just beat it." He gazed around. "It looks like a junk shop and it smells like a toilet. It'll take me a month to clean up here."

"This smell is only cabbage that I am cooking for my supper. Wait, I'll open a window and it will go away."

"When you go away, it'll go away." Gruber took out his bulky wallet, counted out twelve dollars, added fifty cents, and plunked the money on top of the chest. "You got two more weeks till the fifteenth, then you gotta be out or I will get a dispossess. Don't talk back talk. Get outta here and go somewhere that they don't know you and maybe you'll get a place."

"No, Mr. Gruber," Kessler cried passionately. "I didn't do nothing, and I will stay here."

"Don't monkey with my blood pressure," said Gruber. "If you're not out by the fifteenth, I will personally throw you on your bony ass."

Then he left and walked heavily down the stairs.

The fifteenth came and Ignace found the twelve-fifty in his letter box. He telephoned Gruber and told him.

"I'll get a dispossess," Gruber shouted. He instructed the janitor to write out a note saying to Kessler that his money was refused, and to stick it under his door. This Ignace did. Kessler returned the money to the letter box, but again Ignace wrote a note and slipped it, with the money, under the old man's door.

After another day Kessler received a copy of his eviction notice. It said to appear in court on Friday at 10 a.m. to show cause why he should not be evicted for continued neglect and destruction of rental property. The official notice filled Kessler with great fright because he had never in his life been to court. He did not appear on the day he had been ordered to.

That same afternoon the marshal came with two brawny assistants. Ignace opened Kessler's lock for them, and as they pushed their way into the flat, the janitor hastily ran down the stairs to hide in the cellar. Despite Kessler's wailing and carrying on, the two assistants methodically removed his meager furniture and set it out on the sidewalk. After that they got Kessler out, though they had to break open the bathroom door because the old man had locked himself in there. He shouted, struggled, pleaded with his neighbors to help him, but they looked on in a silent group outside the door. The two assistants, holding the old man tightly by the arms and skinny legs, carried him, kicking and moaning, down the stairs. They sat him in the street on a chair amid his junk. Upstairs, the marshal bolted the door with a lock Ignace had supplied, signed a paper which he handed to the janitor's wife, and then drove off in an automobile with his assistants.

Kessler sat on a split chair on the sidewalk. It was raining and the rain soon turned to sleet, but he still sat there. People passing by skirted the pile of his belongings. They stared at Kessler and he stared at nothing. He wore no hat or coat, and the snow fell on him, making him look like a piece of his dispossessed goods. Soon the wizened Italian woman from the top floor returned to the house with two of her sons, each carrying a loaded shopping bag. When she recognized Kessler sitting amid his furniture, she began to shriek. She shrieked in Italian at Kessler although he paid no attention to her. She stood on the stoop, shrunken, gesticulating with thin arms, her loose mouth working angrily. Her sons tried to calm her, but still she shrieked. Several of the neighbors came down to see who was making the racket. Finally, the two sons, unable to think what else to do, set down their shopping bags, lifted Kessler out of the chair, and carried him up the stairs. Hoffman, Kessler's other neighbor, working with a small triangular file, cut open the padlock, and Kessler was carried into the flat from which he had been evicted. Ignace screeched at everybody, calling them filthy names, but the three men went downstairs and hauled up Kessler's chairs, his broken table, chest, and ancient metal bed. They piled all the furniture into the bedroom. Kessler sat on the edge of the bed and wept. After a while, after the old Italian woman had sent in a soup plate full of hot macaroni seasoned with tomato sauce and grated cheese, they left.

Ignace phoned Gruber. The landlord was eating and the food turned to lumps in his throat. "I'll throw them all out, the bastards," he yelled. He put on his hat, got into his car, and drove through the slush to the tenement. All the time he was thinking of his worries: high repair costs; it was hard to keep the place together; maybe the building would someday collapse. He had read of such things. All of a sudden the front of the building parted from the rest and fell like a breaking wave into the street. Gruber cursed the old man for taking him from his supper. When he got to the house, he snatched Ignace's keys and ascended the sagging stairs. Ignace tried to follow, but Gruber told him to stay the hell in his hole. When the landlord was not looking, Ignace crept up after him.

Gruber turned the key and let himself into Kessler's dark flat. He pulled the light chain and found the old man sitting limply on the side of the bed. On the floor at his feet lay a plate of stiffened macaroni.

"What do you think you're doing here?" Gruber thundered.

The old man sat motionless.

"Don't you know it's against the law? This is trespassing and you're breaking the law. Answer me."

Kessler remained mute.

Gruber mopped his brow with a large yellowed handkerchief.

"Listen, my friend, you're gonna make lots of trouble for yourself. If they catch you in here you might go to the workhouse. I'm only try-ing to advise you."

To his surprise Kessler looked at him with wet, brimming eyes.

"What did I did to you?" he bitterly wept. "Who throws out of his house a man that he lived there ten years and pays every month on time his rent? What did I do, tell me? Who hurts a man without a reason? Are you Hitler or a Jew?" He was hitting his chest with his fist.

Gruber removed his hat. He listened carefully, at first at a loss what to say, but then answered: "Listen, Kessler, it's not personal. I own this house and it's falling apart. My bills are sky-high. If the tenants don't take care they have to go. You don't take care and you fight with my janitor, so you have to go. Leave in the morning, and I won't say another word. But if you don't leave the flat, you'll get the heave-ho again. I'll call the marshal."

"Mr. Gruber," said Kessler, "I won't go. Kill me if you want it, but I won't go."

Ignace hurried away from the door as Gruber left in anger. The next morning, after a restless night of worries, the landlord set out to drive to the city marshal's office. On the way he stopped at a candy store for a pack of cigarettes and there decided once more to speak to Kessler. A thought had occurred to him: he would offer to get the old man into a public home.

He drove to the tenement and knocked on Ignace's door.

"Is the old gink still up there?"

"I don't know if so, Mr. Gruber." The janitor was ill at ease.

"What do you mean you don't know?"

"I didn't see him go out. Before, I looked in his keyhole but nothing moves."

"So why didn't you open the door with your key?"

"I was afraid," Ignace answered nervously.

"What are you afraid?"

Ignace wouldn't say.

A fright went through Gruber but he didn't show it. He grabbed the keys and walked ponderously up the stairs, hurrying every so often.

No one answered his knock. As he unlocked the door he broke into heavy sweat.

But the old man was there, alive, sitting without shoes on the bedroom floor.

"Listen, Kessler," said the landlord, relieved although his head pounded. "I got an idea that, if you do it the way I say, your troubles are over."

He explained his proposal to Kessler, but the egg candler was not listening. His eyes were downcast, and his body swayed slowly sideways. As the landlord talked on, the old man was thinking of what had whirled through his mind as he had sat out on the sidewalk in the falling snow. He had thought through his miserable life, remembering how, as a young man, he had abandoned his family, walking out on his wife and three innocent children, without even in some way attempting to provide for them; without, in all the intervening years—so God help him—once trying to discover if they were alive or dead. How, in so short a life, could a man do so much wrong? This thought smote him to the heart and he recalled the past without end and moaned and tore at his flesh with his nails.

Gruber was frightened at the extent of Kessler's suffering. Maybe I should let him stay, he thought. Then as he watched the old man, he realized he was bunched up there on the floor engaged in an act of mourning. There he sat, white from fasting, rocking back and forth, his beard dwindled to a shade of itself.

Something's wrong here—Gruber tried to imagine what and found it all oppressive. He felt he ought to run out, get away, but then saw himself fall and go tumbling down the five flights of stairs; he groaned at the broken picture of himself lying at the bottom. Only he was still there in Kessler's bedroom, listening to the old man praying. Somebody's dead, Gruber muttered. He figured Kessler had got bad news, yet instinctively he knew he hadn't. Then it struck him with a terrible force that the mourner was mourning him: it was *he* who was dead.

The landlord was agonized. Sweating brutally, he felt an enormous constricted weight in him that forced itself up until his head was at the point of bursting. For a full minute he awaited a stroke; but the feeling painfully passed, leaving him miserable.

When after a while, he gazed around the room, it was clean, drenched in daylight, and fragrant. Gruber then suffered unbearable remorse for the way he had treated the old man. With a cry of shame he pulled the sheet off Kessler's bed and, wrapping it around himself, sank to the floor and became a mourner.

1955

Angel Levine

Manischevitz, a tailor, in his fifty-first year suffered many reverses and indignities. Previously a man of comfortable means, he overnight lost all he had when his establishment caught fire, after a metal container of cleaning fluid exploded, and burned to the ground. Although Manischevitz was insured against fire, damage suits by two customers who had been hurt in the flames deprived him of every penny he had saved. At almost the same time, his son, of much promise, was killed in the war, and his daughter, without so much as a word of warning, married a lout and disappeared with him as off the face of the earth. Thereafter Manischevitz was victimized by excruciating backaches and found himself unable to work even as a presser—the only kind of work available to him—for more than an hour or two daily, because beyond that the pain from standing was maddening. His Fanny, a good wife and mother, who had taken in washing and sewing, began before his eyes to waste away. Suffering shortness of breath, she at last became seriously ill and took to her bed. The doctor, a former customer of Manischevitz, who out of pity treated them, at first had difficulty diagnosing her ailment, but later put it down as hardening of the arteries at an advanced stage. He took Manischevitz aside, prescribed complete rest for her, and in whispers gave him to know there was little hope.

Throughout his trials Manischevitz had remained somewhat stoic, almost unbelieving that all this had descended on his head, as if it were happening, let us say, to an acquaintance or some distant relative; it was, in sheer quantity of woe, incomprehensible. It was also ridiculous, unjust, and because he had always been a religious man, an affront to God. Manischevitz believed this in all his suffering. When his burden had grown too crushingly heavy to be borne he prayed in his chair with shut hollow eyes: "My dear God, sweetheart, did I deserve that this should happen to me?" Then recognizing the worthlessness of it, he set aside the complaint and prayed humbly for assistance: "Give Fanny back her health, and to me for myself that I shouldn't feel pain in every step. Help now or tomorrow is too late." And Manischevitz wept.

•

Manischevitz's flat, which he had moved into after the disastrous fire, was a meager one, furnished with a few sticks of chairs, a table, and bed, in one of the poorer sections of the city. There were three rooms: a small, poorly papered living room; an apology for a kitchen with a wooden icebox; and the comparatively large bedroom where Fanny lay in a sagging secondhand bed, gasping for breath. The bedroom was the warmest room in the house and it was here, after his outburst to God, that Manischevitz, by the light of two small bulbs overhead, sat reading his Jewish newspaper. He was not truly reading because his thoughts were everywhere; however the print offered a convenient resting place for his eyes, and a word or two, when he permitted himself to comprehend them, had the momentary effect of helping him forget his troubles. After a short while he discovered, to his surprise, that he was actively scanning the news, searching for an item of great interest to him. Exactly what he thought he would read he couldn't say—until he realized, with some astonishment, that he was expecting to discover something about himself. Manischevitz put his paper down and looked up with the distinct impression that someone had come into the apartment, though he could not remember having heard the sound of the door opening. He looked around: the room was very still, Fanny sleeping, for once, quietly. Half frightened, he watched her until he was satisfied she wasn't dead; then, still disturbed by the thought of an unannounced visitor, he stumbled into the living room and there had the shock of his life, for at the table sat a black man reading a newspaper he had folded up to fit into one hand.

"What do you want here?" Manischevitz asked in fright.

The Negro put down the paper and glanced up with a gentle expression. "Good evening." He seemed not to be sure of himself, as if he had got into the wrong house. He was a large man, bonily built, with a heavy head covered by a hard derby, which he made no attempt to remove. His eyes seemed sad, but his lips, above which he wore a slight mustache, sought to smile; he was not otherwise prepossessing. The cuffs of his sleeves, Manischevitz noted, were frayed to the lining, and the dark suit was badly fitted. He had very large feet. Recovering from his fright, Manischevitz guessed he had left the door open and was being visited by a case worker from the Welfare Department—some came at night—for he had recently applied for welfare. Therefore he lowered himself into a chair opposite the Negro, trying, before the man's uncertain smile, to feel comfortable. The former tailor sat stiffly but patiently at the table, waiting for the investigator to take out his pad and pencil and begin asking questions; but before long he became convinced the man intended to do nothing of the sort.

"Who are you?" Manischevitz at last asked uneasily.

"If I may, insofar as one is able to, identify myself, I bear the name of Alexander Levine."

In spite of his troubles Manischevitz felt a smile growing on his lips. "You said Levine?" he politely inquired.

The Negro nodded. "That is exactly right."

Carrying the jest further, Manischevitz asked, "You are maybe Jewish?"

"All my life I was, willingly."

The tailor hesitated. He had heard of black Jews but had never met one. It gave an unusual sensation.

Recognizing in afterthought something odd about the tense of Levine's remark, he said doubtfully, "You ain't Jewish anymore?"

Levine at this point removed his hat, revealing a very white part in his black hair, but quickly replaced it. He replied, "I have recently been disincarnated into an angel. As such, I offer you my humble assistance, if to offer is within my province and power—in the best sense." He lowered his eyes in apology. "Which calls for added explanation: I am what I am granted to be, and at present the completion is in the future."

"What kind of angel is this?" Manischevitz gravely asked.

"A bona fide angel of God, within prescribed limitations," answered Levine, "not to be confused with the members of any particular sect, order, or organization here on earth operating under a similar name."

Manischevitz was thoroughly disturbed. He had been expecting something, but not this. What sort of mockery was it—provided that Levine was an angel—of a faithful servant who had from childhood lived in the synagogues, concerned with the word of God?

To test Levine he asked, "Then where are your wings?"

The Negro blushed as well as he could. Manischevitz understood this from his altered expression. "Under certain circumstances we lose privileges and prerogatives upon returning to earth, no matter for what purpose or endeavoring to assist whomsoever."

"So tell me," Manischevitz said triumphantly, "how did you get here?"

"I was translated."

Still troubled, the tailor said, "If you are a Jew, say the blessing for bread."

Levine recited it in sonorous Hebrew.

Although moved by the familiar words Manischevitz still felt doubt he was dealing with an angel.

"If you are an angel," he demanded somewhat angrily, "give me the proof."

Levine wet his lips. "Frankly, I cannot perform either miracles or near-miracles, due to the fact that I am in a condition of probation. How long that will persist or even consist depends on the outcome."

Manischevitz racked his brains for some means of causing Levine positively to reveal his true identity, when the Negro spoke again:

"It was given me to understand that both your wife and you require assistance of a salubrious nature?"

The tailor could not rid himself of the feeling that he was the butt of a jokester. Is this what a Jewish angel looks like? he asked himself. This I am not convinced.

He asked a last question. "So if God sends to me an angel, why a black? Why not a white that there are so many of them?"

"It was my turn to go next," Levine explained.

Manischevitz could not be persuaded. "I think you are a faker."

Levine slowly rose. His eyes indicated disappointment and worry. "Mr. Manischevitz," he said tonelessly, "if you should desire me to be of assistance to you any time in the near future, or possibly before, I can be found"—he glanced at his fingernails—"in Harlem."

He was by then gone.

．

The next day Manischevitz felt some relief from his backache and was able to work four hours at pressing. The day after, he put in six hours; and the third day four again. Fanny sat up a little and asked for some halvah to suck. But after the fourth day the stabbing, breaking ache afflicted his back, and Fanny again lay supine, breathing with blue-lipped difficulty.

Manischevitz was profoundly disappointed at the return of his active pain and suffering. He had hoped for a longer interval of easement, long enough to have a thought other than of himself and his troubles. Day by day, minute after minute, he lived in pain, pain his only memory, questioning the necessity of it, inveighing, though with affection, against God. Why *so much*, Gottenyu? If He wanted to teach His servant a lesson for some reason, some cause—the nature of His nature— to teach him, say, for reasons of his weakness, his pride, perhaps, during his years of prosperity, his frequent neglect of God—to give him a little lesson, why then any of the tragedies that had happened to him, any *one* would have sufficed to chasten him. But *all together*—the loss of both his children, his means of livelihood, Fanny's health and his—that was too much to ask one frail-boned man to endure. Who, after all, was Manischevitz that he had been given so much to suffer? A tailor. Certainly not a man of talent. Upon him suffering was largely wasted. It went nowhere, into nothing: into more suffering. His pain did not earn him bread, nor fill the cracks in the wall, nor lift, in the middle of the night, the kitchen table; only lay upon him, sleepless, so sharply oppressive that he could many times have cried out yet not heard himself this misery.

In this mood he gave no thought to Mr. Alexander Levine, but at moments when the pain wavered, slightly diminishing, he sometimes wondered if he had been mistaken to dismiss him. A black Jew and angel to boot—very hard to believe, but suppose he *had* been sent to succor him, and he, Manischevitz, was in his blindness too blind to understand? It was this thought that put him on the knife-point of agony.

Therefore the tailor, after much self-questioning and continuing doubt, decided he would seek the self-styled angel in Harlem. Of course he had great difficulty because he had not asked for specific directions, and movement was tedious to him. The subway took him to 116th Street, and from there he wandered in the open dark world. It was vast and its lights lit nothing. Everywhere were shadows, often moving. Manischevitz hobbled along with the aid of a cane and, not knowing where to seek in the blackened tenement buildings, would look fruitlessly through store windows. In the stores he saw people and everybody was black. It was an amazing thing to observe. When he was too tired, too unhappy to go farther, Manischevitz stopped in front of a tailor's shop. Out of familiarity with the appearance of it, with some sadness he entered. The tailor, an old skinny man with a mop of woolly gray hair, was sitting cross-legged on his workbench, sewing a pair of tuxedo pants that had a razor slit all the way down the seat.

"You'll excuse me, please, gentleman," said Manischevitz, admir-

ing the tailor's deft thimbled fingerwork, "but you know maybe somebody by the name Alexander Levine?"

The tailor, who, Manischevitz thought, seemed a little antagonis-
tic to him, scratched his scalp.

"Cain't say I ever heared dat name."

"Alex-ander Lev-ine," Manischevitz repeated it.

The man shook his head. "Cain't say I heared."

Manischevitz remembered to say: "He is an angel, maybe."

"Oh, *him*," said the tailor, clucking. "He hang out in dat honky-
tonk down here a ways." He pointed with his skinny finger and returned to sewing the pants.

Manischevitz crossed the street against a red light and was almost
run down by a taxi. On the block after the next, the sixth store from the
corner was a cabaret, and the name in sparkling lights was Bella's.
Ashamed to go in, Manischevitz gazed through the neon-lit window,
and when the dancing couples had parted and drifted away, he discovered at a table on the side, toward the rear, Alexander Levine.

He was sitting alone, a cigarette butt hanging from the corner of
his mouth, playing solitaire with a dirty pack of cards, and Manischevitz
felt a touch of pity for him, because Levine had deteriorated in appearance. His derby hat was dented and had a gray smudge. His ill-fitting
suit was shabbier, as if he had been sleeping in it. His shoes and trouser
cuffs were muddy, and his face covered with an impenetrable stubble
the color of licorice. Manischevitz, though deeply disappointed, was
about to enter, when a big-breasted Negress in a purple evening gown
appeared before Levine's table and, with much laughter through many
white teeth, broke into a vigorous shimmy. Levine looked at Manischevitz with a haunted expression, but the tailor was too paralyzed to
move or acknowledge it. As Bella's gyrations continued Levine rose, his
eyes lit in excitement. She embraced him with vigor, both his hands
clasped around her restless buttocks, and they tangoed together across
the floor, loudly applauded by the customers. She seemed to have lifted
Levine off his feet and his large shoes hung limp as they danced. They
slid past the windows where Manischevitz, white-faced, stood staring
in. Levine winked slyly and the tailor left for home.

·

Fanny lay at death's door. Through shrunken lips she muttered
concerning her childhood, the sorrows of the marriage bed, the loss of
her children; yet wept to live. Manischevitz tried not to listen, but even
without ears he would have heard. It was not a gift. The doctor panted

up the stairs, a broad but bland, unshaven man (it was Sunday), and soon shook his head. A day at most, or two. He left at once to spare himself Manischevitz's multiplied sorrow; the man who never stopped hurting. He would someday get him into a public home.

Manischevitz visited a synagogue and there spoke to God, but God had absented Himself. The tailor searched his heart and found no hope. When she died, he would live dead. He considered taking his life although he knew he wouldn't. Yet it was something to consider. Considering, you existed. He railed against God— Can you love a rock, a broom, an emptiness? Baring his chest, he smote the naked bones, cursing himself for having, beyond belief, believed.

Asleep in a chair that afternoon, he dreamed of Levine. He was standing before a faded mirror, preening small decaying opalescent wings. "This means," mumbled Manischevitz, as he broke out of sleep, "that it is possible he could be an angel." Begging a neighbor lady to look in on Fanny and occasionally wet her lips with water, he drew on his thin coat, gripped his walking stick, exchanged some pennies for a subway token, and rode to Harlem. He knew this act was the last desperate one of his woe: to go seeking a black magician to restore his wife to invalidism. Yet if there was no choice, he did at least what was chosen.

He hobbled to Bella's, but the place seemed to have changed hands. It was now, as he breathed, a synagogue in a store. In the front, toward him, were several rows of empty wooden benches. In the rear stood the Ark, its portals of rough wood covered with rainbows of sequins; under it a long table on which lay the sacred scroll unrolled, illuminated by the dim light from a bulb on a chain overhead. Around the table, as if frozen to it and the scroll, which they all touched with their fingers, sat four Negroes wearing skullcaps. Now as they read the Holy Word, Manischevitz could, through the plate-glass window, hear the singsong chant of their voices. One of them was old, with a gray beard. One was bubble-eyed. One was humpbacked. The fourth was a boy, no older than thirteen. Their heads moved in rhythmic swaying. Touched by this sight from his childhood and youth, Manischevitz entered and stood silent in the rear.

"Neshoma," said bubble eyes, pointing to the word with a stubby finger. "Now what dat mean?"

"That's the word that means soul," said the boy. He wore eyeglasses.

"Let's git on wid de commentary," said the old man.

"Ain't necessary," said the humpback. "Souls is immaterial substance. That's all. The soul is derived in that manner. The immateriality is derived from the substance, and they both, causally an otherwise, derived from the soul. There can be no higher."

"That's the highest."

"Over de top."

"Wait a minute," said bubble eyes. "I don't see what is dat immaterial substance. How come de one gits hitched up to de odder?" He addressed the humpback.

"Ask me somethin hard. Because it is substanceless immateriality. It couldn't be closer together, like all the parts of the body under one skin—closer."

"Hear now," said the old man.

"All you done is switched de words."

"It's the primum mobile, the substanceless substance from which comes all things that were incepted in the idea—you, me, and everything and -body else."

"Now how did all dat happen? Make it sound simple."

"It de speerit," said the old man. "On de face of de water moved de speerit. An dat was good. It say so in de Book. From de speerit ariz de man."

"But now listen here. How come it become substance if it all de time a spirit?"

"God alone done dat."

"Holy! Holy! Praise His Name."

"But has dis spirit got some kind of a shade or color?" asked bubble eyes, deadpan.

"Man, of course not. A spirit is a spirit."

"Then how come we is colored?" he said with a triumphant glare.

"Ain't got nothing to do wid dat."

"I still like to know."

"God put the spirit in all things," answered the boy. "He put it in the green leaves and the yellow flowers. He put it with the gold in the fishes and the blue in the sky. That's how come it came to us."

"Amen."

"Praise Lawd and utter loud His speechless Name."

"Blow de bugle till it bust the sky."

They fell silent, intent upon the next word. Manischevitz, with doubt, approached them.

"You'll excuse me," he said. "I am looking for Alexander Levine. You know him maybe?"

"That's the angel," said the boy.

"Oh, *him*," snuffed bubble eyes.

"You'll find him at Bella's. It's the establishment right down the street," the humpback said.

Manischevitz said he was sorry that he could not stay, thanked them, and limped across the street. It was already night. The city was dark and he could barely find his way.

But Bella's was bursting with jazz and the blues. Through the window Manischevitz recognized the dancing crowd and among them sought Levine. He was sitting loose-lipped at Bella's side table. They were tippling from an almost empty whiskey fifth. Levine had shed his old clothes, wore a shiny new checkered suit, pearl-gray derby hat, cigar, and big, two-tone, button shoes. To the tailor's dismay, a drunken look had settled upon his formerly dignified face. He leaned toward Bella, tickled her earlobe with his pinky while whispering words that sent her into gales of raucous laughter. She fondled his knee.

Manischevitz, girding himself, pushed open the door and was not welcomed.

"This place reserved."

"Beat it, pale puss."

"Exit, Yankel, Semitic trash."

But he moved toward the table where Levine sat, the crowd breaking before him as he hobbled forward.

"Mr. Levine," he spoke in a trembly voice. "Is here Manischevitz."

Levine glared blearily. "Speak yo piece, son."

Manischevitz shivered. His back plagued him. Tremors tormented his legs. He looked around, everybody was all ears.

"You'll excuse me. I would like to talk to you in a private place."

"Speak, Ah is a private pusson."

Bella laughed piercingly. "Stop it, boy, you killin me."

Manischevitz, no end disturbed, considered fleeing, but Levine addressed him:

"Kindly state the pu'pose of yo communication with yo's truly."

The tailor wet cracked lips. "You are Jewish. This I am sure."

Levine rose, nostrils flaring. "Anythin else yo got to say?"

Manischevitz's tongue lay like a slab of stone.

"Speak now or fo'ever hold off."

Tears blinded the tailor's eyes. Was ever man so tried? Should he say he believed a half-drunk Negro was an angel?

The silence slowly petrified.

Manischevitz was recalling scenes of his youth as a wheel in his mind whirred: believe, do not, yes, no, yes, no. The pointer pointed to yes, to between yes and no, to no, no it was yes. He sighed. It moved but one still had to make a choice.

"I think you are an angel from God." He said it in a broken voice, thinking, If you said it, it was said. If you believed it, you must say it. If you believed, you believed.

The hush broke. Everybody talked but the music began and they went on dancing. Bella, grown bored, picked up the cards and dealt herself a hand.

Levine burst into tears. "How you have humiliated me."

Manischevitz apologized.

"Wait'll I freshen up." Levine went to the men's room and returned in his old suit.

No one said goodbye as they left.

They rode to the flat via subway. As they walked up the stairs Manischevitz pointed with his cane at his door.

"That's all been taken care of," Levine said. "You go in while I take off."

Disappointed that it was so soon over, but torn by curiosity, Manischevitz followed the angel up three flights to the roof. When he got there the door was already padlocked.

Luckily he could see through a small broken window. He heard an odd noise, as though of a whirring of wings, and, when he strained for a wider view, could have sworn he saw a dark figure borne aloft on a pair of strong black wings.

A feather drifted down. Manischevitz gasped as it turned white, but it was only snowing.

He rushed downstairs. In the flat Fanny wielded a dust mop under the bed, and then upon the cobwebs on the wall.

"A wonderful thing, Fanny," Manischevitz said. "Believe me, there are Jews everywhere."

1955

A Summer's Reading

George Stoyonovich was a neighborhood boy who had quit high school on an impulse when he was sixteen, run out of patience, and though he was ashamed every time he went looking for a job, when people asked him if he had finished and he had to say no, he never went back to school. This summer was a hard time for jobs and he had none. Having so much time on his hands, George thought of going to summer school, but the kids in his classes would be too young. He also considered registering in a night high school, only he didn't like the idea of the teachers always telling him what to do. He felt they had not respected him. The result was he stayed off the streets and in his room most of the day. He was close to twenty and had needs with the neighborhood girls, but no money to spend, and he couldn't get more than an occasional few cents because his father was poor, and his sister, Sophie, who resembled George, a tall bony girl of twenty-three, earned very little and what she had she kept for herself. Their mother was dead, and Sophie had to take care of the house.

Very early in the morning George's father got up to go to work in a fish market. Sophie left at about eight for her long ride in the subway to a cafeteria in the Bronx. George had his coffee by himself, then hung around in the house. When the house, a five-room railroad flat above a butcher store, got on his nerves he cleaned it up—mopped the floors with a wet mop and put things away. But most of the time he sat in his room. In the afternoons he listened to the ball game.

Otherwise he had a couple of old copies of the *World Almanac* he had bought long ago, and he liked to read in them and also the magazines and newspapers that Sophie brought home, that had been left on the tables in the cafeteria. They were mostly picture magazines about movie stars and sports figures, also usually the *News* and *Mirror*. Sophie herself read whatever fell into her hands, although she sometimes read good books.

She once asked George what he did in his room all day and he said he read a lot too.

"Of what besides what I bring home? Do you ever read any worthwhile books?"

"Some," George answered, although he really didn't. He had tried to read a book or two that Sophie had in the house but found he was in no mood for them. Lately he couldn't stand made-up stories, they got on his nerves. He wished he had some hobby to work at— as a kid he was good in carpentry, but where could he work at it? Sometimes during the day he went for walks, but mostly he did his walking after the hot sun had gone down and it was cooler in the streets.

In the evening after supper George left the house and wandered in the neighborhood. During the sultry days some of the storekeepers and their wives sat in chairs on the thick, broken sidewalks in front of their shops, fanning themselves, and George walked past them and the guys hanging out on the candy store corner. A couple of them he had known his whole life, but nobody recognized each other. He had no place special to go, but generally, saving it till the last, he left the neighborhood and walked for blocks till he came to a darkly lit little park with benches and trees and an iron railing, giving it a feeling of privacy. He sat on a bench here, watching the leafy trees and the flowers blooming on the inside of the railing, thinking of a better life for himself. He thought of the jobs he had had since he had quit school—delivery boy, stock clerk, runner, lately working in a factory—and he was dissatisfied with all of them. He felt he would someday like to have a good job and live in a private house with a porch, on a street with trees. He wanted to have some dough in his pocket to buy things with, and a girl to go with, so as not to be so lonely, especially on Saturday nights. He wanted people to like and respect him. He thought about these things often but mostly when he was alone at night. Around midnight he got up and drifted back to his hot and stony neighborhood.

One time while on his walk George met Mr. Cattanzara coming

home very late from work. He wondered if he was drunk but then could tell he wasn't. Mr. Cattanzara, a stocky, bald-headed man who worked in a change booth in an IRT station, lived on the next block after George's, above a shoe repair store. Nights, during the hot weather, he sat on his stoop in an undershirt, reading *The New York Times* in the light of the shoemaker's window. He read it from the first page to the last, then went up to sleep. And all the time he was reading the paper, his wife, a fat woman with a white face, leaned out of the window, gazing into the street, her thick white arms folded under her loose breast, on the window ledge.

Once in a while Mr. Cattanzara came home drunk, but it was a quiet drunk. He never made any trouble, only walked stiffly up the street and slowly climbed the stairs into the hall. Though drunk, he looked the same as always, except for his tight walk, the quietness, and that his eyes were wet. George liked Mr. Cattanzara because he remembered him giving him nickels to buy lemon ice with when he was a squirt. Mr. Cattanzara was a different type than those in the neighborhood. He asked different questions than the others when he met you, and he seemed to know what went on in all the newspapers. He read them, as his fat sick wife watched from the window.

"What are you doing with yourself this summer, George?" Mr. Cattanzara asked. "I see you walkin around at nights."

George felt embarrassed. "I like to walk."

"What are you doin in the day now?"

"Nothing much just right now. I'm waiting for a job." Since it shamed him to admit he wasn't working, George said, "I'm staying home—but I'm reading a lot to pick up my education."

Mr. Cattanzara looked interested. He mopped his hot face with a red handkerchief.

"What are you readin?"

George hesitated, then said, "I got a list of books in the library once, and now I'm gonna read them this summer." He felt strange and a little unhappy saying this, but he wanted Mr. Cattanzara to respect him.

"How many books are there on it?"

"I never counted them. Maybe around a hundred."

Mr. Cattanzara whistled through his teeth.

"I figure if I did that," George went on earnestly, "it would help me in my education. I don't mean the kind they give you in high school. I want to know different things than they learn there, if you know what I mean."

The change maker nodded. "Still and all, one hundred books is a pretty big load for one summer."

"It might take longer."

"After you're finished with some, maybe you and I can shoot the breeze about them?" said Mr. Cattanzara.

"When I'm finished," George answered.

Mr. Cattanzara went home and George continued on his walk. After that, though he had the urge to, George did nothing different from usual. He still took his walks at night, ending up in the little park. But one evening the shoemaker on the next block stopped George to say he was a good boy, and George figured that Mr. Cattanzara had told him all about the books he was reading. From the shoemaker it must have gone down the street, because George saw a couple of people smiling kindly at him, though nobody spoke to him personally. He felt a little better around the neighborhood and liked it more, though not so much he would want to live in it forever. He had never exactly disliked the people in it, yet he had never liked them very much either. It was the fault of the neighborhood. To his surprise, George found out that his father and Sophie knew about his reading too. His father was too shy to say anything about it—he was never much of a talker in his whole life—but Sophie was softer to George, and she showed him in other ways she was proud of him.

As the summer went on George felt in a good mood about things. He cleaned the house every day, as a favor to Sophie, and he enjoyed the ball games more. Sophie gave him a buck a week allowance, and though it still wasn't enough and he had to use it carefully, it was a helluva lot better than just having two bits now and then. What he bought with the money—cigarettes mostly, an occasional beer or movie ticket—he got a big kick out of. Life wasn't so bad if you knew how to appreciate it. Occasionally he bought a paperback book from the newsstand, but he never got around to reading it, though he was glad to have a couple of books in his room. But he read thoroughly Sophie's magazines and newspapers. And at night was the most enjoyable time, because when he passed the storekeepers sitting outside their stores, he could tell they regarded him highly. He walked erect, and though he did not say much to them, or they to him, he could feel approval on all sides. A couple of nights he felt so good that he skipped the park at the end of the evening. He just wandered in the neighborhood, where people had known him from the time he was a kid playing punchball whenever there was a game of it going; he wandered there, then came home and got undressed for bed, feeling fine.

For a few weeks he had talked only once with Mr. Cattanzara, and though the change maker had said nothing more about the books, asked no questions, his silence made George a little uneasy. For a while George didn't pass in front of Mr. Cattanzara's house anymore, until one night, forgetting himself, he approached it from a different direction than he usually did when he did. It was already past midnight. The street, except for one or two people, was deserted, and George was surprised when he saw Mr. Cattanzara still reading his newspaper by the light of the street lamp overhead. His impulse was to stop at the stoop and talk to him. He wasn't sure what he wanted to say, though he felt the words would come when he began to talk; but the more he thought about it, the more the idea scared him, and he decided he'd better not. He even considered beating it home by another street, but he was too near Mr. Cattanzara, and the change maker might see him as he ran, and get annoyed. So George unobtrusively crossed the street, trying to make it seem as if he had to look in a store window on the other side, which he did, and then went on, uncomfortable at what he was doing. He feared Mr. Cattanzara would glance up from his paper and call him a dirty rat for walking on the other side of the street, but all he did was sit there, sweating through his undershirt, his bald head shining in the dim light as he read his *Times*, and upstairs his fat wife leaned out of the window, seeming to read the paper along with him. George thought she would spy him and yell out to Mr. Cattanzara, but she never moved her eyes off her husband.

George made up his mind to stay away from the change maker until he had got some of his softback books read, but when he started them and saw they were mostly story books, he lost his interest and didn't bother to finish them. He lost his interest in reading other things too. Sophie's magazines and newspapers went unread. She saw them piling up on a chair in his room and asked why he was no longer looking at them, and George told her it was because of all the other reading he had to do. Sophie said she had guessed that was it. So for most of the day, George had the radio on, turning to music when he was sick of the human voice. He kept the house fairly neat, and Sophie said nothing on the days when he neglected it. She was still kind and gave him his extra buck, though things weren't so good for him as they had been before.

But they were good enough, considering. Also his night walks invariably picked him up, no matter how bad the day was. Then one night George saw Mr. Cattanzara coming down the street toward him. George was about to turn and run but he recognized from Mr. Cattanzara's walk that he was drunk, and if so, probably he would not even bother to notice him. So George kept on walking straight ahead until he came abreast of Mr. Cattanzara, and though he felt wound up enough to pop into the sky, he was not surprised when Mr. Cattanzara passed him without a word, walking slowly, his face and body stiff. George drew a breath in relief at his narrow escape, when he heard his name called, and there stood Mr. Cattanzara at his elbow, smelling like the inside of a beer barrel. His eyes were sad as he gazed at George, and George felt so intensely uncomfortable he was tempted to shove the drunk aside and continue on his walk.

But he couldn't act that way to him, and besides, Mr. Cattanzara took a nickel out of his pants pocket and handed it to him.

"Go buy yourself a lemon ice, Georgie."

"It's not that time anymore, Mr. Cattanzara," George said, "I am a big guy now."

"No, you ain't," said Mr. Cattanzara, to which George made no reply he could think of.

"How are all your books comin along now?" Mr. Cattanzara asked. Though he tried to stand steady, he swayed a little.

"Fine, I guess," said George, feeling the red crawling up his face.

"You ain't sure?" The change maker smiled slyly, a way George had never seen him smile.

"Sure I'm sure. They're fine."

Though his head swayed in little arcs, Mr. Cattanzara's eyes were steady. He had small blue eyes which could hurt if you looked at them too long.

"George," he said, "name me one book on that list that you read this summer, and I will drink to your health."

"I don't want anybody drinking to me."

"Name me one so I can ask you a question on it. Who can tell, if it's a good book maybe I might wanna read it myself."

George knew he looked passable on the outside, but inside he was crumbling apart.

Unable to reply, he shut his eyes, but when—years later—he opened them, he saw that Mr. Cattanzara had, out of pity, gone away, but in his ears he still heard the words he had said when he left: "George, don't do what I did."

The next night he was afraid to leave his room, and though Sophie argued with him he wouldn't open the door.

"What are you doing in there?" she asked.

"Nothing."

"Aren't you reading?"

"No."

She was silent a minute, then asked, "Where do you keep the books you read? I never see any in your room outside of a few cheap trashy ones."

He wouldn't tell her.

"In that case you're not worth a buck of my hard-earned money. Why should I break my back for you? Go on out, you bum, and get a job."

He stayed in his room for almost a week, except to sneak into the kitchen when nobody was home. Sophie railed at him, then begged him to come out, and his old father wept, but George wouldn't budge, though the weather was terrible and his small room stifling. He found it very hard to breathe, each breath was like drawing a flame into his lungs.

One night, unable to stand the heat anymore, he burst into the street at 1 a.m., a shadow of himself. He hoped to sneak to the park without being seen, but there were people all over the block, wilted and listless, waiting for a breeze. George lowered his eyes and walked, in disgrace, away from them, but before long he discovered they were still friendly to him. He figured Mr. Cattanzara hadn't told on him. Maybe when he woke up out of his drunk the next morning, he had forgotten all about meeting George. George felt his confidence slowly come back to him.

That same night a man on a street corner asked him if it was true that he had finished reading so many books, and George admitted he had. The man said it was a wonderful thing for a boy his age to read so much.

"Yeah," George said, but he felt relieved. He hoped nobody would mention the books anymore, and when, after a couple of days, he accidentally met Mr. Cattanzara again, *he* didn't, though George had the idea he was the one who had started the rumor that he had finished all the books.

One evening in the fall, George ran out of his house to the library, where he hadn't been in years. There were books all over the place, wherever he looked, and though he was struggling to control an inward trembling, he easily counted off a hundred, then sat down at a table to read.

1956

❧ B M ❧

Take Pity

Davidov, the census-taker, opened the door without knocking, limped into the room, and sat wearily down. Out came his notebook and he was on the job. Rosen, the ex–coffee salesman, wasted, eyes despairing, sat motionless, cross-legged, on his cot. The square, clean, but cold room, lit by a dim globe, was sparsely furnished: the cot, a folding chair, small table, old unpainted chests—no closets but who needed them?—and a small sink with a rough piece of green, institutional soap on its holder—you could smell it across the room. The worn black shade over the single narrow window was drawn to the ledge, surprising Davidov.

"What's the matter you don't pull the shade up?" he remarked.

Rosen ultimately sighed. "Let it stay."

"Why? Outside is light."

"Who needs light?"

"What then you need?"

"Light I don't need," replied Rosen.

Davidov, sour-faced, flipped through the closely scrawled pages of his notebook until he found a clean one. He attempted to scratch in a word with his fountain pen but it had run dry, so he fished a pencil stub out of his vest pocket and sharpened it with a cracked razor blade. Rosen paid no attention to the feathery shavings falling to the floor. He looked restless, seemed to be listening to or for something, although Davidov was convinced there was absolutely nothing to listen to. It was only when the census-taker somewhat irritably and

with increasing loudness repeated a question that Rosen stirred and
identified himself. He was about to furnish an address but caught
himself and shrugged.

Davidov did not comment on the salesman's gesture. "So begin,"
he nodded.

"Who knows where to begin?" Rosen stared at the drawn shade.
"Do they know here where to begin?"

"Philosophy we are not interested," said Davidov. "Start in how
you met her."

"Who?" pretended Rosen.

"Her," he snapped.

"So if I got to begin, how you know about her already?" Rosen
asked triumphantly.

Davidov spoke wearily, "You mentioned before."

Rosen remembered. They had questioned him upon his arrival
and he now recalled blurting out her name. It was perhaps something
in the air. It did not permit you to retain what you remembered. That
was part of the cure, if—you wanted a cure.

"Where I met her—?" Rosen murmured. "I met her where she
always was in the back room there in that hole in the wall that it
was a waste of time for me I went there. Maybe I sold them a half
a bag of coffee a month. This is not business."

"In business we are not interested."

"What then you are interested?" Rosen mimicked Davidov's tone.
Davidov clammed up coldly.

Rosen knew they had him where it hurt, so he went on: "The
husband was maybe forty, Axel Kalish, a Polish refugee. He worked
like a blind horse when he got to America, and saved maybe two,
three thousand dollars that he bought with the money this pisher
grocery in a dead neighborhood where he didn't have a chance. He
called my company up for credit and they sent me I should see. I
recommended okay because I felt sorry. He had a wife, Eva, you know
already about her, and two darling girls, one five and one three, little
dolls, Fega and Surale, that I didn't want them to suffer. So right
away I told him, without tricks, 'Kiddo, this is a mistake. This place
is a grave. Here they will bury you if you don't get out quick!' "

Rosen sighed deeply.

"So?" Davidov had thus far written nothing, irking the ex-
salesman.

"So?— Nothing. He didn't get out. After a couple months he
tried to sell but nobody bought, so he stayed and starved. They never

made expenses. Every day they got poorer you couldn't look in their faces. 'Don't be a damn fool,' I told him, 'go in bankruptcy.' But he couldn't stand to lose all his capital, and he was also afraid it would be hard to find a job. 'My God,' I said, 'do anything. Be a painter, a janitor, a junk man, but get out of here before everybody is a skeleton.'

"This he finally agreed with me, but before he could go in auction he dropped dead."

Davidov made a note. "How did he die?"

"On this I am not an expert," Rosen replied. "You know better than me."

"How did he die?" Davidov spoke impatiently. "Say in one word."

"From what he died?—he died, that's all."

"Answer, please, this question."

"Broke in him something. That's how."

"Broke what?"

"Broke what breaks. He was talking to me how bitter was his life, and he touched me on my sleeve to say something else, but the next minute his face got small and he fell down dead, the wife screaming, the little girls crying that it made in my heart pain. I am myself a sick man and when I saw him laying on the floor, I said to myself, 'Rosen, say goodbye, this guy is finished.' So I said it."

Rosen got up from the cot and strayed despondently around the room, avoiding the window. Davidov was occupying the only chair, so the ex-salesman was finally forced to sit on the edge of the bed again. This irritated him. He badly wanted a cigarette but disliked asking for one.

Davidov permitted him a short interval of silence, then leafed impatiently through his notebook. Rosen, to needle the census-taker, said nothing.

"So what happened?" Davidov finally demanded.

Rosen spoke with ashes in his mouth. "After the funeral—" He paused, tried to wet his lips, then went on: "He belonged to a society that they buried him, and he also left a thousand dollars insurance, but after the funeral I said to her, 'Eva, listen to me. Take the money and your children and run away from here. Let the creditors take the store. What will they get?— Nothing.'

"But she answered me, 'Where will I go, where, with my two orphans that their father left them to starve?'

" 'Go anywhere,' I said. 'Go to your relatives.'

"She laughed like laughs somebody who hasn't got no joy. 'My relatives Hitler took away from me.'

" 'What about Axel—surely an uncle somewheres?'

" 'Nobody,' she said. 'I will stay here like my Axel wanted. With the insurance I will buy new stock and fix up the store. Every week I will decorate the window, and in this way gradually will come in new customers—'

" 'Eva, my darling girl—'

" 'A millionaire I don't expect to be. All I want is I should make a little living and take care on my girls. We will live in the back here like before, and in this way I can work and watch them, too.'

" 'Eva,' I said, 'you are a nice-looking young woman, only thirty-eight years. Don't throw away your life here. Don't flush in the toilet—you should excuse me—the thousand poor dollars from your dead husband. Believe me, I know from such stores. After thirty-five years' experience I know a graveyard when I smell it. Go better someplace and find a job. You're young yet. Sometime you will meet somebody and get married.'

" 'No, Rosen, not me,' she said. 'With marriage I am finished. Nobody wants a poor widow with two children.'

" 'This I don't believe it.'

" 'I know,' she said.

"Never in my life I saw so bitter a woman's face.

" 'No,' I said. 'No.'

" 'Yes, Rosen, yes. In my whole life I never had anything. In my whole life I always suffered. I don't expect better. This is my life.'

"I said no and she said yes. What could I do? I am a man with only one kidney, and worse than that, that I won't mention it. When I talked she didn't listen, so I stopped to talk. Who can argue with a widow?"

The ex-salesman glanced up at Davidov but the census-taker did not reply. "What happened then?" he asked.

"What happened?" mocked Rosen. "Happened what happens."

Davidov's face grew red.

"What happened, happened," Rosen said hastily. "She ordered from the wholesalers all kinds goods that she paid for them cash. All week she opened boxes and packed on the shelves cans, jars, packages. Also she cleaned, and she washed, and she mopped with oil the floor. With tissue paper she made new decorations in the window, everything should look nice—but who came in? Nobody except a few poor customers from the tenement around the corner. And when they came? When was closed the supermarkets and they needed some little item that they forgot to buy, like a quart milk, fifteen cents' cheese, a small can sardines for lunch. In a few months was again dusty the cans on the shelves, and her money was gone. Credit she couldn't get except from me, and from me she got because I paid out of my pocket the company. This she didn't know. She worked, she dressed clean, she waited that the store should get better. Little by little the shelves got empty, but where was the profit? They ate it up. When I looked on the little girls I knew what she didn't tell me. Their faces were white, they were thin, they were hungry. She kept the little food that was left, on the shelves. One night I brought in a nice piece of sirloin, but I could see from her eyes that she didn't like that I did it. So what else could I do? I have a heart and I am human."

Here the ex-salesman wept.

Davidov pretended not to see though once he peeked.

Rosen blew his nose, then went on more calmly, "When the children were sleeping we sat in the dark there, in the back, and not once in four hours opened the door should come in a customer. 'Eva, for Godsakes, *run away*,' I said.

" 'I have no place to go,' she said.

" 'I will give you where you can go, and please don't say to me no. I am a bachelor, this you know. I got whatever I need and more besides. Let me help you and the children. Money don't interest me. Interests me good health, but I can't buy it. I'll tell you what I will do. Let this place go to the creditors and move into a two-family house that I own, which the top floor is now empty. Rent will cost you nothing. In the meantime you can go and find a job. I will also pay the downstairs lady to take care of the girls—God bless them—until you will come home. With your wages you will buy the food, if you need clothes, and also save a little. This you can use when you get married someday. What do you say?'

"She didn't answer me. She only looked on me in such a way, with such burning eyes, like I was small and ugly. For the first time I thought to myself, Rosen, this woman don't like you.

" 'Thank you very kindly, my friend Mr. Rosen,' she answered me, 'but charity we are not needing. I got yet a paying business, and it will get better when times are better. Now is bad times. When comes again good times will get better the business.'

" 'Who charity?' I cried to her. 'What charity? Speaks to you your husband's a friend.'

" 'Mr. Rosen, my husband didn't have no friends.'

" 'Can't you see that I want to help the children?'

" 'The children have their mother.'

" 'Eva, what's the matter with you?' I said. 'Why do you make sound bad something that I mean it should be good?'

"This she didn't answer. I felt sick in my stomach, and was coming also a headache, so I left.

"All night I didn't sleep, and then all of a sudden I figured out a reason why she was worried. She was worried I would ask for some kind of payment except cash. She got the wrong man. Anyway, this made me think of something that I didn't think about before. I thought now to ask her to marry me. What did she have to lose? I could take care of myself without any trouble to them. Fega and Surale would have a father he could give them for the movies, or sometime to buy a little doll to play with, and when I died, would go to them my investments and insurance policies.

"The next day I spoke to her.

" 'For myself, Eva, I don't want a thing. Absolutely not a thing. For you and your girls—everything. I am not a strong man, Eva. In fact, I am sick. I tell you this you should understand I don't expect to live long. But even for a few years would be nice to have a little family.'

"She was with her back to me and didn't speak.

"When she turned around again her face was white but the mouth was like iron.

" 'No, Mr. Rosen.'

" 'Why not, tell me?'

" 'I had enough with sick men.' She began to cry. 'Please, Mr. Rosen. Go home.'

"I didn't have strength I should argue with her, so I went home. I went home but hurt me in my mind. All day long and all night I felt bad. My back pained me where was missing my kidney. Also too much smoking. I tried to understand this woman but I couldn't. Why should somebody that her two children were starving always say no to a man that he wanted to help her? What did I do to her bad? Am I maybe a murderer she should hate me so much? All that I felt in my heart was pity for her and the children, but I couldn't convince her. Then I went back and begged her she should let me help them, and once more she told me no.

" 'Eva,' I said, 'I don't blame you that you don't want a sick man. So come with me to a marriage broker and we will find you a strong, healthy husband that he will support you and your girls. I will give the dowry.'

"She screamed, 'On this I don't need your help, Rosen!'

"I didn't say no more. What more could I say? All day long, from early in the morning till late in the night she worked like an animal. All day she mopped, she washed with soap and a brush the shelves, the few cans she polished, but the store was still rotten. The little girls I was afraid to look at. I could see in their faces their bones. They were tired, they were weak. Little Surale held with her hand all the time the dress of Fega. Once when I saw them in the street I gave them some cakes, but when I tried the next day to give them something else, the mother shouldn't know, Fega answered me, 'We can't take, Momma says today is a fast day.'

"I went inside. I made my voice soft. 'Eva, on my bended knees, I am a man with nothing in this world. Allow me that I should have a little pleasure before I die. Allow me that I should help you to stock up once more the store.'

"So what did she do? She cried, it was terrible to see. And after she cried, what did she say? She told me to go away and I shouldn't come back. I felt like to pick up a chair and break her head.

"In my house I was too weak to eat. For two days I took in my mouth nothing except maybe a spoon of chicken noodle soup, or maybe a glass tea without sugar. This wasn't good for me. My health felt bad.

"Then I made up a scheme that I was a friend of Axel's who lived in Jersey. I said I owed Axel seven hundred dollars that he lent me this money fifteen years ago, before he got married. I said I did not have the whole money now, but I would send her every week twenty dollars till it was paid up the debt. I put inside the letter two tens and gave it to a friend of mine, also a salesman, he should mail it in Newark so she wouldn't be suspicious who wrote the letters."

To Rosen's surprise Davidov had stopped writing. The book was full, so he tossed it onto the table, yawned, yet listened amiably. His curiosity had died.

Rosen got up and fingered the notebook. He tried to read the small distorted handwriting but could not make out a single word.

"It's not English and it's not Yiddish," he said. "Could it be in Hebrew?"

"No," answered Davidov. "It's an old-fashioned language they don't use it nowadays."

"Oh?" Rosen returned to the cot. He saw no purpose in going on now that it was not required, but he felt he had to.

"Came back all the letters," he said dully. "The first she opened it, then pasted back again the envelope, but the rest she didn't even open."

" 'Here,' I said to myself, 'is a very strange thing—a person that you can never give her anything. —But I will give.'

"I went then to my lawyer and we made out a will that everything

I had—all my investments, my two houses that I owned, also furniture, my car, the checking account—every cent would go to her, and when she died, the rest would be left for the two girls. The same with my insurance. They would be my beneficiaries. Then I signed and went home. In the kitchen I turned on the gas and put my head in the stove.

"Let her say now no."

Davidov, scratching his stubbled cheek, nodded. This was the part he already knew. He got up and, before Rosen could cry no, idly raised the window shade.

It was twilight in space but a woman stood before the window.

Rosen with a bound was off his cot to see.

It was Eva, staring at him with haunted, beseeching eyes. She raised her arms to him.

Infuriated, the ex-salesman shook his fist.

"Whore, bastard, bitch," he shouted at her. "Go 'way from here. Go home to your children."

Davidov made no move to hinder him as Rosen rammed down the window shade.

1956

❧ B M ❧

The Elevator

Eleonora was an Umbrian girl whom the portiere's wife had brought up to the Agostinis' first-floor apartment after their two unhappy experiences with Italian maids, not long after they had arrived in Rome from Chicago. She was about twenty-three, thin, and with bent bony shoulders which she embarrassedly characterized as gobbo—hunchbacked. But she was not unattractive and had an interesting profile, George Agostini thought. Her full face was not so interesting; like the portinaia's, also an Umbrian, it was too broad and round, and her left brown eye was slightly wider than her right. It also looked sadder than her right eye.

She was an active girl, always moving in her noisy slippers at a half trot across the marble floors of the furnished two-bedroom apartment, getting things done without having to be told, and handling the two children very well. After the second girl was let go, George had wished they didn't have to be bothered with a full-time live-in maid. He had suggested that maybe Grace ought to go back to sharing the signora's maid—their landlady across the hall—for three hours a day, paying her on an hourly basis, as they had when they first moved in after a rough month of apartment hunting. But when George mentioned this, Grace made a gesture of tearing her red hair, so he said nothing more. It wasn't that he didn't want her to have the girl—she certainly needed one with all the time it took to shop in six or seven stores instead of one supermarket, and she was even without a washing machine, with all the kids' things to do; but George felt he wasn't comfortable with a maid always around. He didn't like people waiting on him, or watching him eat. George was heavy, and sensitive about it. He also didn't like her standing back to let him enter a room first. He didn't want her saying "Comanda" the minute he spoke her name. Furthermore he wasn't happy about the tiny maid's room the girl lived in, or her sinkless bathroom, with its cramped sitzbath and no water heater. Grace, whose people had always been much better off than his, said everybody in Italy had maids and he would get used to it. George hadn't got used to the first two girls, but he did find that Eleonora bothered him less. He liked her more as a person and felt sorry for her. She looked as though she had more on her back than her bent shoulders.

One afternoon about a week and a half after Eleonora had come to them, when George arrived home from the FAO office where he worked, during the long lunch break, Grace said the maid was in her room crying.

"What for?" George said, worried.

"I don't know."

"Didn't you ask her?"

"Sure I did, but all I could gather was that she's had a sad life. You're the linguist around here, why don't you ask her?"

"What are you so annoyed about?"

"Because I feel like a fool, frankly, not knowing what it's all about."

"Tell me what happened."

"She came out of the hall crying, about an hour ago," Grace said. "I had sent her up to the roof with a bundle of wash to do in one of the tubs up there instead of our bathtub, so she doesn't have to lug the heavy wet stuff up to the lines on the roof but can hang it out right away. Anyway, she wasn't gone five minutes before she was back crying, and that was when she answered me about her sad life. I wanted to tell her I have a sad life too. We've been in Rome close to two months and I haven't even been able to see St. Peter's. When will I ever see anything?"

"Let's talk about her," George said. "Do you know what happened in the hall?"

"I told you I didn't. After she came back, I went down to the ground floor to talk to the portinaia—she has some smattering of English—and she told me that Eleonora had been married but had lost her husband. He died or something when she was eighteen. Then she had a baby by another guy who didn't stay around long enough to see if he recognized it, and that, I suppose, is why she finds life so sad."

"Did the portinaia say whether the kid is still alive?" George asked.

"Yes. She keeps it in a convent school."

"Maybe that's what got her down," he suggested. "She thinks of her kid being away from her and then feels bad."

"So she starts to cry in the hall?"

"Why not in the hall? Why not anywhere so long as you feel like crying? Maybe I ought to talk to her."

Grace nodded. Her face was flushed, and George knew she was troubled.

He went into the corridor and knocked on the door of the maid's room. "Permesso," George said.

"Prego." Eleonora had been lying on the bed but was respectfully on her feet when George entered. He could see she had been crying. Her eyes were red and her face pale. She looked scared, and George's throat went dry.

"Eleonora, I am sorry to see you like this," he said in Italian. "Is there something either my wife or I can do to help you?"

"No, Signore," she said quietly.

"What happened to you out in the hall?"

Her eyes glistened but she held back the tears. "Nothing. One feels like crying, so she cries. Do these things have a reason?"

"Are you satisfied with conditions here?" George asked her.

"Yes."

"If there is something we can do for you, I want you to tell us."

"Please don't trouble yourself about me." She lifted the bottom of her skirt, at the same time bending her head to dry her eyes on it. Her bare legs were hairy but shapely.

"No trouble at all," George said. He closed the door softly.

"Let her rest," he said to Grace.

"Damn! Just when I have to go out."

But in a few minutes Eleonora came out and went on with her work in the kitchen. They said nothing more and neither did she. Then at three George left for the office, and Grace put on her hat and went off to her Italian class and then to St. Peter's.

That night when George got home from work, Grace called him into their bedroom and said she now knew what had created all the commotion that afternoon. First the signora, after returning from an appointment with her doctor, had bounded in from across the hall, and Grace had gathered from the hot stew the old woman was in that she was complaining about their maid. The portinaia then happened to come up with the six o'clock mail, and the signora laced into her for bringing an inferior type of maid into the house. Finally, when the signora had left, the portinaia told Grace that the old lady had been the one who had made Eleonora cry. She had apparently forbidden the girl to use the elevator. She would listen behind the door, and as soon as she heard someone putting the key into the elevator lock, she would fling open her door, and if it was Eleonora, as she had suspected, she would cry out, "The key is not for you. The key is not for you." She would stand in front of the elevator, waving her arms to prevent her from entering. "Use the stairs," she cried, "the stairs are for walking. There is no need to fly, or God would have given you wings."

"Anyway," Grace went on, "Eleonora must have been outwitting her or something, because what she would do, according to the portinaia, was go upstairs to the next floor and call the elevator from there. But today the signora got suspicious and followed Eleonora up the stairs. She gave her a bad time up there. When she blew in here before, Eleonora got so scared that she ran to her room and locked the door. The signora said she would have to ask us not to give our girl the key anymore. She shook her keys at me."

"What did you say after that?" George asked.

"Nothing. I wasn't going to pick a fight with her even if I could speak the language. A month of hunting apartments was enough for me."

"We have a lease," said George.

"Leases have been broken."

"She wouldn't do it—she needs the money."

"I wouldn't bet on it," said Grace.

"It burns me up," George said. "Why shouldn't the girl use the elevator to lug the clothes up to the roof? Five floors is a long haul."

"Apparently none of the other girls does," Grace said. "I saw one of them carrying a basket of wash up the stairs on her head."

"They ought to join the acrobats' union."

"We have to stick to their customs."

"I'd still like to tell the old dame off."

"This is Rome, George, not Chicago. You came here of your own free will."

"Where's Eleonora?" George asked.

"In the kitchen."

George went into the kitchen. Eleonora was washing the children's supper dishes in a pan of hot water. When George came in she looked up with fear, the fear in her left eye shining more brightly than in her right.

"I'm sorry about the business in the hall," George said with sympathy, "but why didn't you tell me about it this afternoon?"

"I don't want to make trouble."

"Would you like me to talk to the signora?"

"No, no."

"I want you to ride in the elevator if you want to."

"Thank you, but it doesn't matter."

"Then why are you crying?"

"I'm always crying, Signore. Don't bother to notice it."

"Have it your own way," George said.

He thought that ended it, but a week later as he came into the building at lunchtime he saw Eleonora getting into the elevator with a laundry bundle. The portinaia had just opened the door for her with her key, but when she saw George she quickly ducked down the stairs to the basement. George got on the elevator with Eleonora. Her face was crimson.

"I see you don't mind using the elevator," he said.

"Ah, Signore"—she shrugged—"we must all try to improve ourselves."

"Are you no longer afraid of the signora?"

"Her girl told me the signora is sick," Eleonora said happily.

Eleonora's luck held, George learned, because the signora stayed too sick to be watching the elevator, and one day after the maid rode up in it to the roof, she met a plumber's helper working on the washtubs, Fabrizio Occhiogrosso, who asked her to go out with him on her next afternoon off. Eleonora, who had been doing little on her Thursday and Sunday afternoons off, mostly spending her time with the portinaia, readily accepted. Fabrizio, a short man with pointed shoes, a thick trunk, hairy arms, and the swarthy face of a Spaniard, came for her on his motorbike and away they would go together, she sitting on the seat behind him, holding both arms around his belly. She sat astride the seat, and when Fabrizio, after impatiently revving the Vespa, roared up the narrow street, the wind fluttered her skirt and her bare legs were exposed above the knees.

"Where do they go?" George once asked Grace.

"She says he has a room on the Via della Purificazione."

"Do they always go to his room?"

"She says they sometimes ride to the Borghese Gardens or go to the movies."

One night in early December, after the maid had mentioned that Fabrizio was her fiancé now, George and Grace stood at their living-room window looking down into the street as Eleonora got on the motorbike and it raced off out of sight.

"I hope she knows what she's doing," he muttered in a worried tone. "I don't much take to Fabrizio."

"So long as she doesn't get pregnant too soon. I'd hate to lose her."

George was silent for a time, then remarked, "How responsible do you suppose we are for her morals?"

"Her morals?" laughed Grace. "Are you batty?"

"I never had a maid before," George said.

"This is our third."

"I mean in principle."

"Stop mothering the world," said Grace.

Then one Sunday after midnight Eleonora came home on the verge of fainting. What George had thought might happen had. Fabrizio had taken off into the night on his motorbike. When they had arrived at his room early that evening, a girl from Perugia was sitting on his bed. The portiere had let her in after she had showed him an engagement ring and a snapshot of her and Fabrizio in a rowboat. When Eleonora demanded to know who this one was, the plumber's helper did not bother to explain but ran down the stairs, mounted his Vespa, and drove away. The girl disappeared. Eleonora wandered the streets for hours, then returned to Fabrizio's room. The portiere told her that he had been back, packed his valise, and left for Perugia, the young lady riding on the back seat.

Eleonora dragged herself home. When she got up the next morning to make breakfast she was a skeleton of herself and the gobbo looked like a hill. She said nothing and they asked nothing. What Grace wanted to know she later got from the portinaia. Eleonora no longer ran through her chores but did everything wearily, each movement like flowing stone. Afraid she would collapse, George advised her to take a week off and go home. He would pay her salary and give her something extra for the bus.

"No, Signore," she said dully, "it is better for me to work." She said, "I have been through so much, more is not noticeable."

But then she had to notice it. One afternoon she absentmindedly picked up Grace's keys and got on the elevator with a bag of clothes to be washed. The signora, having recovered her health, was waiting for her. She flung open the door, grabbed Eleonora by the arm as she was about to close the elevator door, and dragged her out.

"Whore," she cried, "don't steal the privileges of your betters. Use the stairs."

Grace opened the apartment door to see what the shouting was about, and Eleonora, with a yowl, rushed past her. She locked herself in her room and sat there all afternoon without moving. She wept copiously. Grace, on the verge of exhaustion, could do nothing with her. When George came home from work that evening he tried to coax her out, but she shouted at him to leave her alone.

George was thoroughly fed up. "I've had enough," he said. He thought out how he would handle the signora, then told Grace he was going across the hall.

"Don't do it," she shouted, but he was already on his way.

George knocked on the signora's door. She was a woman of past sixty-five, a widow, always dressed in black. Her face was long and gray, but her eyes were bright black. Her husband had left her these two apartments across the hall from each other that he had owned outright. She lived in the smaller and rented the other, furnished, at a good rent. George knew that this was her only source of income. She had once been a schoolteacher.

"Scusi, Signora," said George, "I have come with a request."

"Prego." She asked him to sit.

George took a chair near the terrace window. "I would really appreciate it, Signora, if you will let our girl go into the elevator with the laundry when my wife sends her up to the tubs. She is not a fortunate person and we would like to make her life a little easier for her."

"I am sorry," answered the signora with dignity, "but I can't permit her to enter the elevator."

"She's a good girl and you have upset her very much."

"Good," said the signora, "I am glad. She must remember her place, even if you don't. This is Italy, not America. You must understand that we have to live with these people long after you, who come to stay for a year or two, return to your own country."

"Signora, she does no harm in the elevator. We are not asking you to ride with her. After all, the elevators are a convenience for all who live in this house and therefore ought to be open for those who work for us here."

"No," said the signora.

"Why not think it over and let me know your answer tomorrow? I assure you I wouldn't ask this if I didn't think it was important."

"I have thought it over," she said stiffly, "and I have given you the same answer I will give tomorrow."

George got up. "In that case," he said, "if you won't listen to reason, I consider my lease with you ended. You have had your last month's rent. We will move on the first of February."

The signora looked as if she had just swallowed a fork.

"The lease is a sacred contract," she said, trembling. "It is against the law to break it."

"I consider that you have already broken it," George said quietly, "by creating conditions that make it very hard for my family to function in this apartment. I am simply acknowledging a situation that already exists."

"If you move out, I will take a lawyer and make you pay for the whole year."

"A lawyer will cost you half the rent he might collect," George answered. "And if my lawyer is better than yours, you will get nothing and owe your lawyer besides."

"Oh, you Americans," said the signora bitterly. "How well I understand you. Your money is your dirty foot with which you kick the world. Who wants you here," she cried, "with your soaps and toothpastes and your dirty gangster movies!"

"I would like to remind you that my origin is Italian," George said.

"You have long ago forgotten your origin," she shouted.

George left the apartment and went back to his own.

"I'll bet you did it," Grace greeted him. Her face was ashen.

"I did," said George.

"I'll bet you fixed us good. Oh, you ought to be proud. How will we ever find another apartment in the dead of winter with two kids?"

She left George and locked herself in the children's bedroom. They were both awake and got out of bed to be with her.

George sat in the living room in the dark. I did it, he was thinking.

After a while the doorbell rang. He got up and put on the light. It was the signora and she looked unwell. She entered the living room at George's invitation and sat there with great dignity.

"I am sorry I raised my voice to a guest in my house," she said. Her mouth was loose and her eyes glistened.

"I am sorry I offended you," George said.

She did not speak for a while, then said, "Let the girl use the elevator." The signora broke into tears.

When she had dried her eyes, she said, "You have no idea how bad things have become since the war. The girls are disrespectful. Their demands are endless, it is impossible to keep up with them. They talk back, they take every advantage. They crown themselves with privileges. It is a struggle to keep them in their place. After all, what have we left when we lose our self-respect?" The signora wept heartbrokenly.

After she had gone, George stood at the window. Across the street a beggar played a flute.

I didn't do it well, George thought. He felt depressed.

On her afternoon off Eleonora rode up and down on the elevator.

1957

✿ B M ✿

An Apology

Early one morning, during a wearying hot spell in the city, a police car that happened to be cruising along Canal Street drew over to the curb and one of the two policemen in the car leaned out of the window and fingered a come-here to an old man wearing a black derby hat, who carried a large carton on his back, held by clothesline rope to his shoulder, and dragged a smaller carton with his other hand.

"Hey, Mac."

But the peddler, either not hearing or paying no attention, went on. At that, the policeman, the younger of the two, pushed open the door and sprang out. He strode over to the peddler and, shoving the large carton on his back, swung him around as if he were straw. The peddler stared at him in frightened astonishment. He was a gaunt, shriveled man with very large eyes which at the moment gave the effect of turning lights, so that the policeman was a little surprised, though not for long.

"Are you deaf?" he said.

The peddler's lips moved in a way that suggested he might be, but at last he cried out, "Why do you push me?" and again surprised the policeman with the amount of wail that rang in his voice.

"Why didn't you stop when I called you?"

"So who knows you called me? Did you say my name?"

"What is your name?"

The peddler clamped his sparse yellow teeth rigidly together.

"And where's your license?"

"What license?—who license?"

"None of your wisecracks—your license to peddle. We saw you peddle."

The peddler did not deny it.

"What's in the big box?"

"Hundred watt."

"Hundred what?"

"Lights."

"What's in the other?"

"Sixty watt."

"Don't you know it's against the law to peddle without a license?"

Without answering, the peddler looked around, but there was no one in sight except the other policeman in the car and his eyes were shut as if he was catching a little lost sleep.

The policeman on the sidewalk opened his black summons book.

"Spill it, Pop, where do you live?"

The peddler stared down at the cracked sidewalk.

"Hurry up, Lou," called the policeman from the car. He was an older man, though not so old as the peddler.

"Just a second, Walter, this old guy here is balky."

With his pencil he prodded the peddler, who was still staring at the sidewalk but who then spoke, saying he had no money to buy a license.

"But you have the money to buy bulbs. Don't you know you're cheating the city when you don't pay the legitimate fees?"

" . . . "

"Talk, will you?"

"Come on, Lou."

"Come on yourself, this nanny goat won't talk."

The other policeman slowly got out of the car, a heavy man with gray hair and a red face shiny with perspiration.

"You better give him the information he wants, mister."

The peddler, holding himself stiff, stared between them. By this time some people had gathered and were looking on, but Lou scattered them with a wave of his arm.

"All right, Walter, give me a hand. This bird goes to the station house."

Walter looked at him with some doubt, but Lou said, "Resisting an officer in the performance of his duty."

He took the peddler's arm and urged him forward. The carton of bulbs slipped off his shoulder, pulling him to his knees.

"Veh is mir."

Walter helped him up and they lifted him into the car. The young cop hauled the large carton to the rear of the car, opened the trunk, and shoved it in sideways. As they drove off, a man in front of one of the stores held up a box and shouted, "Hey, you forgot this one," but neither of them turned to look back, and the peddler didn't seem to be listening.

•

On their way to the station house they passed the Brooklyn Bridge.

"Just a second, Lou," said Walter. "Could you drive across the bridge now and stop at my house? My feet are perspiring and I'd like to change my shirt."

"After we get this character booked."

But Walter querulously insisted it would take too long, and though Lou didn't want to drive him home he finally gave in. Neither of them spoke on the way to Walter's house, which was not far from the bridge, on a nice quiet street of three-story brownstone houses with young trees in front of them, newly planted not far from the curb.

When Walter got out, he said to the peddler, "If you were in Germany they would have killed you. All we were trying to do was give you a summons that would maybe cost you a buck fine." Then he went up the stone steps.

After a while Lou became impatient waiting for him and honked the horn. A window shade on the second floor slid up and Walter in his underwear called down, "Just five minutes, Lou—I'm just drying my feet."

He came down all spry and they drove back several blocks and onto the bridge. Midway across, they had to slow down in a long traffic line, and to their astonishment the peddler pushed open the door and reeled out upon the bridge, miraculously ducking out of the way of the trailers and trucks coming from the other direction. He scooted across the pedestrians' walk and clambered with ferocious strength up on the railing of the bridge.

But Lou, who was very quick, immediately pursued him and managed to get his hand on the peddler's coattails as he stood poised on the railing for the jump.

With a yank Lou pulled him to the ground. The back of his head struck against the sidewalk and his derby hat bounced up, twirled, and landed at his feet. However, he did not lose consciousness. He lay on the ground moaning and tearing with clawlike fingers at his chest and arms.

Both the policemen stood there looking down at him, not sure what to do since there was absolutely no bleeding. As they were talking it over, a fat woman with moist eyes who, despite the heat, was wearing a white shawl over her head and carrying, with the handle over her pudgy arm, a large basket of salted five-cent pretzels passed by and stopped out of curiosity to see what had happened.

Seeing the man on the ground she called out, "Bloostein!" but he did not look at her and continued tearing at his arms.

"Do you know him?" Lou asked her.

"It's Bloostein. I know him from the neighborhood."

"Where does he live?"

She thought for a minute but didn't know. "My father said he used to own a store on Second Avenue but he lost it. Then his missus died and also his daughter was killed in a fire. Now he's got the seven years' itch and they can't cure it in the clinic. They say he peddles with light bulbs."

"Don't you know his address?"

"Not me. What did he do?"

"It doesn't matter what he tried to do," said Walter.

"Goodbye, Bloostein, I have to go to the schoolyard," the fat lady apologized. She picked up the basket and went with her pretzels down the bridge.

By now Bloostein had stopped his frantic scratching and lay quietly on the sidewalk. The sun shone straight into his eyes but he did nothing to shield them.

Lou, who was quite pale, looked at Walter and Walter said, "Let him go."

They got him up on his feet, dusted his coat, and placed his dented hat on his head. Lou said he would get the bulbs out of the car, but Walter said, "Not here, down at the foot of the bridge."

They helped Bloostein back to the car and in a few minutes let him go with his carton of bulbs at the foot of the bridge, not far from the place where they had first chanced to see him.

•

But that night, after their tour of duty, when Lou drove him home, Walter got out of the car and saw, after a moment of disbelief, that Bloostein himself was waiting for him in front of his house.

"Hey, Lou," he called, but Lou had already driven off so he had to face the peddler alone. Bloostein looked, with his carton of bulbs, much as he had that morning, except for the smudge where the dent on his derby hat had been, and his eyes were fleshy with fatigue.

"What do you want here?" Walter said to him.

The peddler parted his lips, then pointed to his carton. "My little box lights."

"What about it?"

"What did you do with them?"

Walter thought a few seconds and remembered the other box of bulbs.

"You sure you haven't gone back and hid them somewhere?" he asked sternly.

Bloostein wouldn't look at him.

The policeman felt very hot. "All right, we'll try and locate them, but first I have to have my supper. I'm hungry."

He went up the steps and turned to say something more, but a woman came out of the house and he raised his hat to her and went in.

After supper he would have liked very much to relax in front of the radio, but instead he changed out of his uniform, said he was going to the corner, and walked, conscious of his heavy disappointment, down the stairs.

Bloostein was planted where he had left him.

"My car's in the garage." Walter went slowly up the street, Bloostein following with his carton of bulbs on his back.

At the garage Walter motioned him into the car. Bloostein lifted the carton into the back seat and got in with it. Walter drove out and over the bridge to Canal Street, to the place where they had taken the peddler into the car.

He parked and went into three of the stores there, flashing his badge and asking if anyone knew who had got the bulbs they had forgotten. No one knew for sure, but the clerk in the third store thought it might be someone next door whose name and address he gave to Walter.

Before returning to the car Walter went into a tavern and had a few beers. Over the fourth he had a hunch and called the police property clerk, who said he had taken in no electric bulbs that day. Walter walked out and asked Bloostein how many bulbs he had had in the carton.

"Five dozen."

"At how much—wholesale?"

"Eight cents."

"That's four-eighty," he figured. Taking a five-dollar bill from his wallet, he handed it to Bloostein, who wouldn't accept it.

"What do you want, the purple heart?"

"My little box lights."

Walter then kidded, "Now you're gonna take a little ride."

They then rode to the address he had been given but no one knew where the one who had the bulbs was. Finally a bald-headed, stocky man in an undershirt came down from the top floor and said he was the man's uncle and what did Walter want.

Walter convinced him it wasn't serious. "It's just that he happens to know where these bulbs are that we left behind by mistake after an arrest."

The uncle said if it wasn't really serious he would give him the address of the social club where he could find his nephew. The address was a lot farther uptown and on the East Side.

"This is foolish," Walter said to himself as he came out of the house. He thought maybe he could take his time and Bloostein might go away, so he stopped at another beer parlor and had several more as he watched a ten-round fight on television.

He came out sweaty from the beers.

But Bloostein was there.

Walter scratched under his arm. "What's good for an itch?" he said. When he got into the car he thought he was a little bit drunk but it didn't bother him and he drove to the social club on the East Side where a dance was going on. He asked the ticket taker in a tuxedo if this nephew was around.

The ticket taker, whose right eye was very crossed, assured him that nobody by the name mentioned was there.

"It's really not very important," Walter said. "Just about a small carton of bulbs he happens to be holding for this old geezer outside."

"I wouldn't know anything about it."

"It's nothing to worry about."

Walter stood by the door a few minutes and watched the dancers, but there was no one whose face he could recognize.

"He's really not there."

"I don't doubt your word."

Afterward he said it was a nice dance but he had to leave.

"Stay awhile," said the ticket taker.

"I have to go," said Walter. "I have a date with a back-seat driver."

The ticket taker winked with his good eye, which had a comical effect, but Walter didn't smile and soon he left.

"Still here, kid?" he asked Bloostein.

•

He started the car and drove back to Sixth Avenue, where he stopped at a liquor store and bought himself a fifth of whiskey. In the car he tore the wrapper off the bottle and took a long pull.

"Drink?" He offered the bottle to Bloostein.

Bloostein was perched like a skinny owl on the back seat gazing at him.

Walter capped the bottle but did not start the car. He sat for a long time at the wheel, moodily meditating. At the point where he was beginning to feel down in the dumps, he got a sudden idea. The idea was so simple and good he quickly started the motor and drove downtown straight to Canal, where there was a hardware store that stayed open to midnight. He almost ran into the place and in ten minutes came out with a wrapped carton containing five dozen 60-watt bulbs.

"The joyride's finished, my friend."

The peddler got out and Walter unloaded the large carton and left it standing on the sidewalk near the smaller one.

He drove off quickly.

•

Going over the bridge he felt relieved, yet at the same time a little anxious to get to sleep because he had to be up at six. He garaged the car and then walked home and upstairs, taking care to move about softly in the bathroom so as not to waken his son, a light sleeper, or his wife, who slept heavily but couldn't get back to sleep once she had been waked up. Undressing, he got into bed with her, but though the night was hot he felt like a cake of ice covered with a sheet. After a while he got up, raised the shade, and stood by the window.

The quiet street was drenched in moonlight, and warm dark shadows fell from the tender trees. But in the tree shadow in front of the house were two strange oblongs and a gnarled, grotesque-hatted silhouette that stretched a tormented distance down the block. Walter's heart pounded heavily, for he knew it was Bloostein.

He put on his robe and straw slippers and ran down the stairs.

"What's wrong?"

Bloostein stared at the moonlit sidewalk.

"What do you want?"

" . . . "

"You better go, Bloostein. This is too late for monkey business. You got your bulbs. Now you better just go home and leave me alone. I hate to have to call the police. Just go home."

Then he lumbered up the stone steps and the flight of carpeted stairs. Inside the bedroom he could hear his son moan in his sleep. Walter lay down and slept, but was awakened by the sound of soft rain. Getting up, he stared out. There was the peddler in the rain, with his white upraised face looking at the window, so near he might be standing on stilts.

Hastening into the hall, Walter rummaged in a closet for an umbrella but couldn't find one. Then his wife woke and called in a loud whisper, "Who's there?" He stood motionless and she listened a minute and evidently went back to sleep. Then because he couldn't find the umbrella he got out a light summer blanket, brought it into the little storage room next to the bedroom, and, taking the screen out of the window, threw the blanket out to Bloostein so he wouldn't get too wet. The white blanket seemed to float down.

•

He returned to bed, by an effort of the will keeping himself there for hours. Then he noticed that the rain had stopped and he got up to make sure. The blanket lay heaped where it had fallen on the sidewalk. Bloostein was standing away from it, under the tree.

Walter's straw slippers squeaked as he walked down the stairs. The heat had broken and now a breeze came through the street, shivering the leaves in summer cold.

In the doorway he thought, What's my hurry? I can wait him out till six, then just let the mummy try to follow me into the station house.

"Bloostein," he said, going down the steps, but as the old man looked up, he felt a sickening emptiness.

Staring down at the sidewalk he thought about everything. At last he raised his head and slowly said, "Bloostein, I owe you an apology. I'm really sorry the whole thing happened. I haven't been able to sleep. From my heart I'm truly sorry."

Bloostein gazed at him with enormous eyes reflecting the moon. He answered nothing, but it seemed he had shrunk and so had his shadow.

Walter said good night. He went up and lay down under the sheet.

"What's the matter?" said his wife.

"Nothing."

She turned over on her side. "Don't wake Sonny."

"No."

He rose and went to the window. Raising the shade, he stared out. Yes, gone. He, his boxes of lights and soft summer blanket. He looked again, but the long, moon-whitened street had never been so empty.

1957

The Last Mohican

Fidelman, a self-confessed failure as a painter, came to Italy to prepare a critical study of Giotto, the opening chapter of which he had
carried across the ocean in a new pigskin-leather briefcase, now
gripped in his perspiring hand. Also new were his gum-soled oxblood
shoes, a tweed suit he had on despite the late-September sun slanting
hot in the Roman sky, although there was a lighter one in his bag;
and a Dacron shirt and set of cotton-Dacron underwear, good for quick
and easy washing for the traveler. His suitcase, a bulky, two-strapped
affair which embarrassed him slightly, he had borrowed from his
sister, Bessie. He planned, if he had any money left at the end of the
year, to buy a new one in Florence. Although he had been in not
much of a mood when he had left the U.S.A., Fidelman revived in
Naples, and at the moment, as he stood in front of the Rome railroad
station, after twenty minutes still absorbed in his first sight of the
Eternal City, he was conscious of a certain exaltation that devolved
on him after he had discovered that directly across the many-vehicled
piazza stood the remains of the Baths of Diocletian. Fidelman remembered having read that Michelangelo had had a hand in converting
the baths into a church and convent, the latter ultimately changed
into the museum that presently was there. "Imagine," he muttered.
"Imagine all that history."

In the midst of his imagining, Fidelman experienced the sensation of suddenly seeing himself as he was, to the pinpoint, outside
and in, not without bittersweet pleasure; and as the well-known image

of his face rose before him he was taken by the depth of pure feeling
in his eyes, slightly magnified by glasses, and the sensitivity of his
elongated nostrils and often tremulous lips, nose divided from lips by
a mustache of recent vintage that looked, Fidelman thought, as if it
had been sculptured there, adding to his dignified appearance although he was a little on the short side. But almost at the same
moment, this unexpectedly intense sense of his being—it was more
than appearance—faded, exaltation having gone where exaltation
goes, and Fidelman became aware that there was an exterior source
to the strange, almost tri-dimensional reflection of himself he had felt
as well as seen. Behind him, a short distance to the right, he had
noticed a stranger—give a skeleton a couple of pounds—loitering
near a bronze statue on a stone pedestal of the heavy-dugged Etruscan
wolf suckling the infants Romulus and Remus, the man contemplating Fidelman already acquisitively so as to suggest to the traveler that
he had been mirrored (lock, stock, barrel) in the other's gaze for some
time, perhaps since he had stepped off the train. Casually studying
him, though pretending no, Fidelman beheld a person of about his
own height, oddly dressed in brown knickers and black, knee-length
woolen socks drawn up over slightly bowed, broomstick legs, these
grounded in small, porous, pointed shoes. His yellowed shirt was open
at the gaunt throat, both sleeves rolled up over skinny, hairy arms.
The stranger's high forehead was bronzed, his black hair thick behind
small ears, the dark, close-shaven beard tight on the face; his experienced nose was weighted at the tip, and the soft brown eyes, above
all, *wanted*. Though his expression suggested humility, he all but
licked his lips as he approached the ex-painter.

"Shalom," he greeted Fidelman.

"Shalom," the other hesitantly replied, uttering the word—so
far as he recalled—for the first time in his life. My God, he
thought, a handout for sure. My first hello in Rome and it has to be
a schnorrer.

The stranger extended a smiling hand. "Susskind," he said, "Shimon Susskind."

"Arthur Fidelman." Transferring his briefcase to under his left
arm while standing astride the big suitcase, he shook hands with
Susskind. A blue-smocked porter came by, glanced at Fidelman's bag,
looked at him, then walked away.

Whether he knew it or not Susskind was rubbing his palms
contemplatively together.

"Parla italiano?"

"Not with ease, although I read it fluently. You might say I need practice."

"Yiddish?"

"I express myself best in English."

"Let it be English then." Susskind spoke with a slight British intonation. "I knew you were Jewish," he said, "the minute my eyes saw you."

Fidelman chose to ignore the remark. "Where did you pick up your knowledge of English?"

"In Israel."

Israel interested Fidelman. "You live there?"

"Once, not now," Susskind answered vaguely. He seemed suddenly bored.

"How so?"

Susskind twitched a shoulder. "Too much heavy labor for a man of my modest health. Also I couldn't stand the suspense."

Fidelman nodded.

"Furthermore, the desert air makes me constipated. In Rome I am lighthearted."

"A Jewish refugee from Israel, no less," Fidelman said good-humoredly.

"I'm always running," Susskind answered mirthlessly. If he was lighthearted, he had yet to show it.

"Where else from, if I may ask?"

"Where else but Germany, Hungary, Poland? Where not?"

"Ah, that's so long ago." Fidelman then noticed the gray in the man's hair. "Well, I'd better be going," he said. He picked up his bag as two porters hovered uncertainly nearby.

But Susskind offered certain services. "You got a hotel?"

"All picked and reserved."

"How long are you staying?"

What business is it of his? However, Fidelman courteously replied, "Two weeks in Rome, the rest of the year in Florence, with a few side trips to Siena, Assisi, Padua, and maybe also Venice."

"You wish a guide in Rome?"

"Are you a guide?"

"Why not?"

"No," said Fidelman. "I'll look as I go along to museums, libraries, et cetera."

This caught Susskind's attention. "What are you, a professor?"

Fidelman couldn't help blushing. "Not exactly, really just a student."

"From which institution?"

He coughed a little. "By that I mean a professional student, you might say. Call me Trofimov, from Chekhov. If there's something to learn I want to learn it."

"You have some kind of a project?" the other persisted. "A grant?"

"No grant. My money is hard-earned. I worked and saved a long time to take a year in Italy. I made certain sacrifices. As for a project, I'm writing on the painter Giotto. He was one of the most important—"

"You don't have to tell me about Giotto," Susskind interrupted with a little smile.

"You've studied his work?"

"Who doesn't know Giotto?"

"That's interesting to me," said Fidelman, secretly irritated. "How do you happen to know him?"

"How do you mean?"

"I've given a good deal of time and study to his work."

"So I know him, too."

I'd better get this over with before it begins to amount to something, Fidelman thought. He set down his bag and fished with a finger in his leather coin purse. The two porters watched with interest, one taking a sandwich out of his pocket, unwrapping the newspaper, and beginning to eat.

"This is for yourself," Fidelman said.

Susskind hardly glanced at the coin as he let it drop into his pants pocket. The porters then left.

The refugee had an odd way of standing motionless, like a cigar-store Indian about to burst into flight. "In your luggage," he said vaguely, "would you maybe have a suit you can't use? I could use a suit."

At last he comes to the point. Fidelman, though annoyed, controlled himself. "All I have is a change from the one you now see me wearing. Don't get the wrong idea about me, Mr. Susskind. I'm not rich. In fact, I'm poor. Don't let a few new clothes deceive you. I owe my sister money for them."

Susskind glanced down at his shabby, baggy knickers. "I haven't had a suit for years. The one I was wearing when I ran away from Germany fell apart. One day I was walking around naked."

"Isn't there a welfare organization that could help you out—some group in the Jewish community interested in refugees?"

"The Jewish organizations wish to give me what they wish, not what I wish," Susskind replied bitterly. "The only thing they offer me is a ticket back to Israel."

"Why don't you take it?"

"I told you already, here I feel free."

"Freedom is a relative term."

"Don't tell me about freedom."

He knows all about that, too, Fidelman thought. "So you feel free," he said, "but how do you live?"

Susskind coughed, a brutal cough.

Fidelman was about to say something more on the subject of freedom but left it unsaid. Jesus, I'll be saddled with him all day if I don't watch out.

"I'd better be getting off to the hotel." He bent again for his bag.

Susskind touched him on the shoulder, and when Fidelman exasperatedly straightened up, the half dollar he had given the man was staring him in the eye.

"On this we both lose money."

"How do you mean?"

"Today the lira sells six twenty-three on the dollar, but for specie they only give you five hundred."

"In that case, give it here and I'll let you have a dollar." From his wallet Fidelman quickly extracted a crisp bill and handed it to the refugee.

"Not more?" Susskind sighed.

"Not more," the student answered emphatically.

"Maybe you would like to see Diocletian's bath? There are some enjoyable Roman coffins inside. I will guide you for another dollar."

"No thanks." Fidelman said goodbye and, lifting the suitcase, lugged it to the curb. A porter appeared and the student, after some hesitation, let him carry it toward the line of small dark-green taxis in the piazza. The porter offered to carry the briefcase too, but Fidelman wouldn't part with it. He gave the cabdriver the address of the hotel, and the taxi took off with a lurch. Fidelman at last relaxed. Susskind, he noticed, had disappeared. Gone with his breeze, he thought. But on the way to the hotel he had an uneasy feeling that the refugee, crouched low, might be clinging to the little tire on the back of the cab; he didn't look out to see.

•

Fidelman had reserved a room in an inexpensive hotel not far from the station, with its very convenient bus terminal. Then, as was his habit, he got himself quickly and tightly organized. He was always concerned with not wasting time, as if it were his only wealth—not true, of course, though Fidelman admitted he was ambitious—and he soon arranged a schedule that made the most of his working hours. Mornings he usually visited the Italian libraries, searching their catalogues and archives, read in poor light, and made profuse notes. He napped for an hour after lunch, then at four, when the churches and museums were reopening, hurried off to them with lists of frescoes and paintings he must see. He was anxious to get to Florence, at the same time a little unhappy at all he would not have time to take in in Rome. Fidelman promised himself to return again if he could afford it, perhaps in the spring, and look at anything he pleased.

After dark he managed to unwind and relax. He ate as the Romans did, late, enjoyed a half liter of white wine, and smoked a cigarette. Afterwards he liked to wander—especially in the old sections near the Tiber. He had read that here, under his feet, were the ruins of ancient Rome. It was an inspiring business, he, Arthur Fidelman, after all born a Bronx boy, walking around in all this history. History was mysterious, the remembrance of things unknown, in a way burdensome, in a way a sensuous experience. It uplifted and depressed, why he did not know, except that it excited his thoughts more than he thought good for him. This kind of excitement was all right up to a point, perfect maybe for a creative artist, but less so for a critic. A critic, he thought, should live on beans. He walked for miles along the winding river, gazing at the starstrewn skies. Once, after a couple of days in the Vatican Museum, he saw flights of angels—gold, blue, white—intermingled in the sky. "My God, I got to stop using my eyes so much," Fidelman said to himself. But back in his room he sometimes wrote till morning.

Late one night, about a week after his arrival in Rome, as Fidelman was writing notes on the Byzantine-style mosaics he had seen during the day, there was a knock on the door, and though the student, immersed in his work, was not conscious he had said "Avanti," he must have, for the door opened and, instead of an angel, in came Susskind in his shirt and baggy knickers.

Fidelman, who had all but forgotten the refugee, certainly never thought of him, half rose in astonishment. "Susskind," he exclaimed, "how did you get in here?"

Susskind for a moment stood motionless, then answered with a weary smile, "I'll tell you the truth, I know the desk clerk."

"But how did you know where I live?"

"I saw you walking in the street so I followed you."

"You mean you saw me accidentally?"

"How else? Did you leave me your address?"

Fidelman resumed his seat. "What can I do for you, Susskind?" He spoke grimly.

The refugee cleared his throat. "Professor, the days are warm but the nights are cold. You see how I go around naked." He held forth bluish arms, goosefleshed. "I came to ask you to reconsider about giving away your old suit."

"And who says it's an old suit?" Despite himself, Fidelman's voice thickened.

"One suit is new, so the other is old."

"Not precisely. I am afraid I have no suit for you, Susskind. The one I presently have hanging in the closet is a little more than a year old and I can't afford to give it away. Besides, it's gabardine, more like a summer suit."

"On me it will be for all seasons."

After a moment's reflection, Fidelman drew out his billfold and counted four single dollars. These he handed to Susskind.

"Buy yourself a warm sweater."

Susskind also counted the money. "If four," he said, "why not five?"

Fidelman flushed. The man's warped nerve. "Because I happen to have four available," he answered. "That's twenty-five hundred lire. You should be able to buy a warm sweater and have something left over besides."

"I need a suit," Susskind said. "The days are warm but the nights are cold." He rubbed his arms. "What else I need I won't tell you."

"At least roll down your sleeves if you're so cold."

"That won't help me."

"Listen, Susskind," Fidelman said gently, "I would gladly give you the suit if I could afford to, but I can't. I have barely enough money to squeeze out a year for myself here. I've already told you I am indebted to my sister. Why don't you try to get yourself a job somewhere, no matter how menial? I'm sure that in a short while you'll work yourself up into a decent position."

"A job, he says," Susskind muttered gloomily. "Do you know what it means to get a job in Italy? Who will give me a job?"

"Who gives anybody a job? They have to go out and look for it."

"You don't understand, professor. I am an Israeli citizen and this means I can only work for an Israeli company. How many Israeli companies are there here?—maybe two, El Al and Zim, and even if they had a job, they wouldn't give it to me because I have lost my passport.

I would be better off now if I were stateless. A stateless person shows his laissez-passer and sometimes he can find a small job."

"But if you lost your passport why didn't you put in for a duplicate?"

"I did, but did they give it to me?"

"Why not?"

"Why not? They say I sold it."

"Had they reason to think that?"

"I swear to you somebody stole it from me."

"Under such circumstances," Fidelman asked, "how do you live?"

"How do I live?" He chomped with his teeth. "I eat air."

"Seriously?"

"Seriously, on air. I also peddle," he confessed, "but to peddle you need a license, and that the Italians won't give me. When they caught me peddling I was interned for six months in a work camp."

"Didn't they attempt to deport you?"

"They did, but I sold my mother's old wedding ring that I kept in my pocket so many years. The Italians are a humane people. They took the money and let me go, but they told me not to peddle anymore."

"So what do you do now?"

"I peddle. What should I do, beg?—I peddle. But last spring I got sick and gave my little money away to the doctors. I still have a bad cough." He coughed fruitily. "Now I have no capital to buy stock with. Listen, professor, maybe we can go in partnership together? Lend me twenty thousand lire and I will buy ladies' nylon stockings. After I sell them I will return you your money."

"I have no funds to invest, Susskind."

"You will get it back, with interest."

"I honestly am sorry for you," Fidelman said, "but why don't you at least do something practical? Why don't you go to the Joint Distribution Committee, for instance, and ask them to assist you? That's their business."

"I already told you why. They wish me to go back, but I wish to stay here."

"I still think going back would be the best thing for you."

"No," cried Susskind angrily.

"If that's your decision, freely made, then why pick on me? Am I responsible for you then, Susskind?"

"Who else?" Susskind loudly replied.

"Lower your voice, please, people are sleeping around here," said Fidelman, beginning to perspire. "Why should I be?"

"You know what responsibility means?"

"I think so."

"Then you are responsible. Because you are a man. Because you are a Jew, aren't you?"

"Yes, goddamn it, but I'm not the only one in the whole wide world. Without prejudice, I refuse the obligation. I am a single individual and can't take on everybody's personal burden. I have the weight of my own to contend with."

He reached for his billfold and plucked out another dollar.

"This makes five. It's more than I can afford, but take it and after this please leave me alone. I have made my contribution."

Susskind stood there, oddly motionless, an impassioned statue, and for a moment Fidelman wondered if he would stay all night, but at last the refugee thrust forth a stiff arm, took the fifth dollar, and departed.

Early the next morning Fidelman moved out of the hotel into another, less convenient for him, but far away from Shimon Susskind and his endless demands.

•

This was Tuesday. On Wednesday, after a busy morning in the library, Fidelman entered a nearby trattoria and ordered a plate of spaghetti with tomato sauce. He was reading his *Messagero*, anticipating the coming of the food, for he was unusually hungry, when he sensed a presence at the table. He looked up, expecting the waiter, but beheld instead Susskind standing there, alas, unchanged.

Is there no escape from him? thought Fidelman, severely vexed. Is this why I came to Rome?

"Shalom, professor," Susskind said, keeping his eyes off the table. "I was passing and saw you sitting here alone, so I came in to say shalom."

"Susskind," Fidelman said in anger, "have you been following me again?"

"How could I follow you?" asked the astonished Susskind. "Do I know where you live now?"

Though Fidelman blushed a little, he told himself he owed nobody an explanation. So he had found out he had moved—good.

"My feet are tired. Can I sit five minutes?"

"Sit."

Susskind drew out a chair. The spaghetti arrived, steaming hot. Fidelman sprinkled it with cheese and wound his fork into several tender strands. One of the strings of spaghetti seemed to stretch for miles, so he stopped at a certain point and swallowed the forkful. Having foolishly neglected to cut the long spaghetti string he was left sucking it, seemingly endlessly. This embarrassed him.

Susskind watched with rapt attention.

Fidelman at last reached the end of the long spaghetti, patted his mouth with a napkin, and paused in his eating.

"Would you care for a plateful?"

Susskind, eyes hungry, hesitated. "Thanks," he said.

"Thanks yes or thanks no?"

"Thanks no." The eyes looked away.

Fidelman resumed eating, carefully winding his fork; he had had not too much practice with this sort of thing and was soon involved in the same dilemma with the spaghetti. Seeing Susskind still watching him, he became tense.

"We are not Italians, professor," the refugee said. "Cut it in small pieces with your knife. Then you will swallow it easier."

"I'll handle it as I please," Fidelman responded testily. "This is my business. You attend to yours."

"My business," Susskind sighed, "don't exist. This morning I had to let a wonderful chance get away from me. I had a chance to buy ladies' stockings at three hundred lire if I had money to buy half a gross. I could easily sell them for five hundred a pair. We would have made a nice profit."

"The news doesn't interest me."

"So if not ladies' stockings, I can also get sweaters, scarves, men's socks, also cheap leather goods, ceramics—whatever would interest you."

"What interests me is what you did with the money I gave you for a sweater."

"It's getting cold, professor," Susskind said worriedly. "Soon comes the November rains, and in winter the tramontana. I thought I ought to save your money to buy a couple of kilos of chestnuts and a bag of charcoal for my burner. If you sit all day on a busy street corner you can sometimes make a thousand lire. Italians like hot chestnuts. But if I do this I will need some warm clothes, maybe a suit."

"A suit," Fidelman remarked sarcastically, "why not an overcoat?"

"I have a coat, poor that it is, but now I need a suit. How can anybody come in company without a suit?"

Fidelman's hand trembled as he laid down his fork. "To my mind you are utterly irresponsible and I won't be saddled with you. I have the right to choose my own problems and the right to my privacy."

"Don't get excited, professor, it's bad for your digestion. Eat in peace." Susskind got up and left the trattoria.

Fidelman hadn't the appetite to finish his spaghetti. He paid the bill, waited ten minutes, then departed, glancing around from time to time to see if he was being followed. He headed down the sloping street to a small piazza where he saw a couple of cabs. Not that he could afford one, but he wanted to make sure Susskind didn't tail him back to his new hotel. He would warn the clerk at the desk never to allow anybody of the refugee's name or description even to make inquiries about him.

Susskind, however, stepped out from behind a plashing fountain at the center of the little piazza. Modestly addressing the speechless Fidelman, he said, "I don't wish to take only, professor. If I had something to give you, I would gladly give it to you."

"Thanks," snapped Fidelman, "just give me some peace of mind."

"That you have to find yourself," Susskind answered.

In the taxi Fidelman decided to leave for Florence the next day, rather than at the end of the week, and once and for all be done with the pest.

That night, after returning to his room from an unpleasurable walk in the Trastevere—he had a headache from too much wine at supper—Fidelman found his door ajar and at once recalled that he had forgotten to lock it, although he had as usual left the key with the desk clerk. He was at first frightened, but when he tried the armadio in which he kept his clothes and suitcase, it was shut tight. Hastily unlocking it, he was relieved to see his blue gabardine suit—a one-button-jacket affair, the trousers a little frayed at the cuffs, but all in good shape and usable for years to come—hanging amid some shirts the maid had pressed for him; and when he examined the contents of the suitcase he found nothing missing, including, thank God, his passport and traveler's checks. Gazing around the room, Fidelman saw all in place. Satisfied, he picked up a book and read ten pages before he thought of his briefcase. He jumped to his feet and began to search everywhere, remembering distinctly that it had been on the night table as he had lain on the bed that afternoon, rereading his chapter. He searched under the bed and behind the night table, then again throughout the room, even on top of and behind the armadio. Fidelman hopelessly opened every drawer, no matter how small, but found neither the briefcase nor, what was worse, the chapter in it.

With a groan he sank down on the bed, insulting himself for not having made a copy of the manuscript, because he had more than once warned himself that something like this might happen to it. But he hadn't because there were some revisions he had contemplated making, and he had planned to retype the entire chapter before beginning the next. He thought now of complaining to the owner of the hotel, who lived on the floor below, but it was already past midnight and he realized nothing could be done until morning. Who could have taken it? The maid or the hall porter? It seemed unlikely they would risk their jobs to steal a piece of leather goods that would bring them only a few thousand lire in a pawnshop. Possibly a sneak thief? He would ask tomorrow if other persons on the floor were missing something. He somehow doubted it. If a thief, he would then and there have ditched the chapter and stuffed the briefcase with Fidelman's oxblood shoes, left by the bed, and the fifteen-dollar R. H. Macy sweater that lay in full view on the desk. But if not the maid or porter or a sneak thief, then who? Though Fidelman had not the slightest shred of evidence to support his suspicions, he could think of only one person—Susskind. This thought stung him. But if Susskind, why? Out of pique, perhaps, that he had not been given the suit he had coveted, nor was able to pry it out of the armadio? Try as he would, Fidelman could think of no one else and no other reason. Somehow the peddler had followed him home (he suspected their meeting at the fountain) and had got into his room while he was out to supper.

Fidelman's sleep that night was wretched. He dreamed of pursuing the refugee in the Jewish catacombs under the ancient Appian Way, threatening him with a blow on the presumptuous head with a seven-flamed candelabrum he clutched in his hand; while Susskind, clever ghost, who knew the ins and outs of all the crypts and alleys, eluded him at every turn. Then Fidelman's candles all blew out, leaving him sightless and alone in the cemeterial dark; but when the student arose in the morning and wearily drew up the blinds, the yellow Italian sun winked him cheerfully in both bleary eyes.

•

Fidelman postponed going to Florence. He reported his loss to the Questura, and though the police were polite and eager to help, they could do nothing for him. On the form on which the inspector noted the complaint, he listed the briefcase as worth ten thousand lire, and for "valore del manuscritto" he drew a line. Fidelman, after giving the matter a good deal of thought, did not report Susskind, first, because he had absolutely no proof, for the desk clerk swore he had seen no stranger around in knickers; second, because he was afraid of the consequences for the refugee if he was written down "suspected thief" as

well as "unlicensed peddler" and inveterate refugee. He tried instead to
rewrite the chapter, which he felt sure he knew by heart, but when he
sat down at the desk, there were important thoughts, whole paragraphs,
even pages, that went blank in the mind. He considered sending to
America for his notes for the chapter, but they were in a barrel in his
sister's attic in Levittown, among many notes for other projects. The
thought of Bessie, a mother of five, poking around in his things, and the
work entailed in sorting the cards, then getting them packaged and
mailed to him across the ocean, wearied Fidelman unspeakably; he was
certain she would send the wrong ones. He laid down his pen and went
into the street, seeking Susskind. He searched for him in neighborhoods
where he had seen him before, and though Fidelman spent hours looking, literally days, Susskind never appeared; or if he perhaps did, the
sight of Fidelman caused him to vanish. And when the student inquired
about him at the Israeli consulate, the clerk, a new man on the job, said
he had no record of such a person or his lost passport; on the other hand,
he was known at the Joint Distribution Committee, but by name and
address only, an impossibility, Fidelman thought. They gave him a
number to go to but the place had long since been torn down to make
way for an apartment house.

Time went without work, without accomplishment. To put an end
to this appalling waste Fidelman tried to force himself back into his
routine of research and picture viewing. He moved out of the hotel,
which he now could not stand for the harm it had done him (leaving a
telephone number and urging he be called if the slightest clue turned
up), and he took a room in a small pensione near the stazione and here
had breakfast and supper rather than go out. He was much concerned
with expenditures and carefully recorded them in a notebook he had
acquired for the purpose. Nights, instead of wandering in the city, feast-
ing himself upon its beauty and mystery, he kept his eyes glued to paper, sitting steadfastly at his desk in an attempt to re-create his initial
chapter, because he was lost without a beginning. He had tried writing
the second chapter from notes in his possession, but it had come to nothing. Always Fidelman needed something solid behind him before he
could advance, some worthwhile accomplishment upon which to build
another. He worked late, but his mood, or inspiration, or whatever it
was, had deserted him, leaving him with growing anxiety, almost dis-
orientation; of not knowing—it seemed to him for the first time in
months—what he must do next, a feeling that was torture. Therefore
he again took up his search for the refugee. He thought now that once
he had settled it, knew that the man had or hadn't stolen his chapter—

whether he recovered it or not seemed at the moment immaterial—just the knowing of it would ease his mind and again he would *feel* like working, the crucial element.

Daily he combed the crowded streets, searching for Susskind wherever people peddled. On successive Sunday mornings he took the long ride to the Porta Portese market and hunted for hours among the piles of secondhand goods and junk lining the back streets, hoping his briefcase would magically appear, though it never did. He visited the open market at Piazza Fontanella Borghese, and observed the ambulant vendors at Piazza Dante. He looked among fruit and vegetable stalls set up in the streets, whenever he chanced upon them, and dawdled on busy street corners after dark, among beggars and fly-by-night peddlers. After the first cold snap at the end of October, when the chestnut sellers appeared throughout the city, huddled over pails of glowing coals, he sought in their faces the missing Susskind. Where in all of modern and ancient Rome was he? The man lived in the open air—he had to appear somewhere. Sometimes when riding in a bus or tram, Fidelman thought he had glimpsed somebody in a crowd, dressed in the refugee's clothes, and he invariably got off to run after whoever it was—once a man standing in front of the Banco di Santo Spirito, gone when Fidelman breathlessly arrived; and another time he overtook a person in knickers, but this one wore a monocle. Sir Ian Susskind?

In November it rained. Fidelman wore a blue beret with his trench coat and a pair of black Italian shoes, smaller, despite their pointed toes, than his burly oxbloods, which overheated his feet and whose color he detested. But instead of visiting museums he frequented movie houses, sitting in the cheapest seats and regretting the cost. He was, at odd hours in certain streets, several times accosted by prostitutes, some heartbreakingly pretty, one a slender, unhappy-looking girl with bags under her eyes whom he desired mightily, but Fidelman feared for his health. He had got to know the face of Rome and spoke Italian fairly fluently, but his heart was burdened, and in his blood raged a murderous hatred of the bandy-legged refugee—although there were times when he bethought himself he might be wrong—so Fidelman more than once cursed him to perdition.

•

One Friday night, as the first star glowed over the Tiber, Fidelman, walking aimlessly along the left riverbank, came upon a synagogue and wandered in among a crowd of Sephardim with Italianate faces. One by one they paused before a sink in an antechamber to dip their hands under a flowing faucet, then in the house of worship touched with loose fingers their brows, mouths, and breasts as they bowed to the Ark, Fidelman doing likewise. Where in the world am I? Three rabbis rose from a bench and the service began, a long prayer, sometimes chanted, sometimes accompanied by invisible organ music, but no Susskind anywhere. Fidelman sat at a desk-like pew in the last row, where he could inspect the congregants yet keep an eye on the door. The synagogue was unheated and the cold rose like an exudation from the marble floor. The student's freezing nose burned like a lit candle. He got up to go, but the beadle, a stout man in a high hat and short caftan, wearing a long thick silver chain around his neck, fixed the student with his powerful left eye.

"From New York?" he inquired, slowly approaching.

Half the congregation turned to see who.

"State, not city," answered Fidelman, nursing an active guilt for the attention he was attracting. Then, taking advantage of a pause, he whispered, "Do you happen to know a man named Susskind? He wears knickers."

"A relative?" The beadle gazed at him sadly.

"Not exactly."

"My own son—killed in the Ardeatine Caves." Tears stood forth in his eyes.

"Ah, for that I'm sorry."

But the beadle had exhausted the subject. He wiped his wet lids with pudgy fingers and the curious Sephardim turned back to their prayer books.

"Which Susskind?" the beadle wanted to know.

"Shimon."

He scratched his ear. "Look in the ghetto."

"I looked."

"Look again."

The beadle walked slowly away and Fidelman sneaked out.

The ghetto lay behind the synagogue for several crooked, well-packed blocks, encompassing aristocratic palazzi ruined by age and unbearable numbers, their discolored façades strung with lines of withered wet wash, the fountains in the piazzas dirt-laden, dry. And dark stone tenements, built partly on centuries-old ghetto walls, inclined toward one another across narrow, cobblestoned streets. In and among the impoverished houses were the wholesale establishments of wealthy Jews, dark holes ending in jeweled interiors, silks and silver of all colors. In the mazed streets wandered the present-day poor, Fidelman among them, oppressed by history, although, he joked to himself, it added years to his life.

A white moon shone upon the ghetto, lighting it like dark day. Once he thought he saw a ghost he knew by sight, and hastily followed him through a thick stone passage to a blank wall where shone in white letters under a tiny electric bulb: VIETATO URINARE. Here was a smell but no Susskind.

For thirty lire the student bought a dwarfed, blackened banana from a street vendor (not S) on a bicycle, and stopped to eat. A crowd of ragazzi gathered to watch.

"Anybody here know Susskind, a refugee wearing knickers?" Fidelman announced, stooping to point the banana where the pants went beneath the knees. He also made his legs a trifle bowed but nobody noticed.

There was no response until he had finished his fruit, then a thin-faced boy with brown liquescent eyes out of Murillo piped: "He sometimes works in the Cimitero Verano, the Jewish section."

There too? thought Fidelman. "Works in the cemetery?" he inquired. "With a shovel?"

"He prays for the dead," the boy answered, "for a small fee."

Fidelman bought him a quick banana and the others dispersed.

In the cemetery, deserted on the Sabbath—he should have come Sunday—Fidelman went among the graves, reading legends carved on tombstones, many topped with small brass candelabra, whilst withered yellow chrysanthemums lay on the stone tablets of other graves, dropped stealthily, Fidelman imagined, on All Souls' Day—a festival in another part of the cemetery—by renegade sons and daughters unable to bear the sight of their dead bereft of flowers, while the crypts of the goyim were lit and in bloom. Many were burial places, he read on the stained stones, of those who, for one reason or another, had died in the late large war, including an empty place, it said under a six-pointed star engraved upon a marble slab that lay on the ground, for "My beloved father / Betrayed by the damned Fascists / Murdered at Auschwitz by the barbarous Nazis / *O Crime Orribile*." But no Susskind.

•

Three months had gone by since Fidelman's arrival in Rome. Should he, he many times asked himself, leave the city and this foolish search? Why not off to Florence, and there amid the art splendors of the world, be inspired to resume his work? But the loss of his first chapter was like a spell cast over him. There were times he scorned it as a man-made thing, like all such, replaceable; other times he feared it was not the chapter per se, but that his volatile curiosity had become somehow entangled with Susskind's strange personality— Had he repaid generosity by stealing a man's life work? Was he so distorted? To satisfy himself, to know man, Fidelman had to know, though at what a cost in precious time and effort. Sometimes he smiled wryly at all this; ridiculous, the chapter grieved him for itself only—the precious thing he had created, then lost—especially when he got to thinking of the long diligent labor, how painstakingly he had built each idea, how cleverly mastered problems of order, form, how impressive the finished product, Giotto reborn! It broke the heart. What else, if after months he was here, still seeking?

And Fidelman was unchangingly convinced that Susskind had taken it, or why would he still be hiding? He sighed much and gained weight. Mulling over his frustrated career, on the backs of envelopes containing unanswered letters from his sister, Bessie, he aimlessly sketched little angels flying. Once, studying his minuscule drawings, it occurred to him that he might someday return to painting, but the thought was more painful than Fidelman could bear.

One bright morning in mid-December, after a good night's sleep, his first in weeks, he vowed he would have another look at the Navicella and then be off to Florence. Shortly before noon he visited the porch of St. Peter's, trying, from his remembrance of Giotto's sketch, to see the mosaic as it had been before its many restorations. He hazarded a note or two in shaky handwriting, then left the church and was walking down the sweeping flight of stairs, when he beheld at the bottom—his heart misgave him, was he still seeing pictures, a sneaky apostle added to the overloaded boatful?—ecco Susskind! The refugee, in beret and long green G.I. raincoat, from under whose skirts showed his black-stockinged, rooster's ankles—indicating knickers going on above though hidden—was selling black-and-white rosaries to all who would buy. He had several strands of beads in one hand, while in the palm of the other a few gilded medallions glinted in the winter sun. Despite his outer clothing, Susskind looked, it must be said, unchanged, not a pound more of meat or muscle, the face, though aged, ageless. Gazing at him, the student ground his teeth in remembrance. He was tempted quickly to hide, and unobserved observe the thief; but his impatience, after the long, unhappy search, was too much for him. With controlled trepidation he approached Susskind on his left as the refugee was busily engaged on the right, urging a sale of beads upon a woman drenched in black.

"Beads, rosaries, say your prayers with holy beads."

"Greetings, Susskind," Fidelman said, coming shakily down the stairs, dissembling the Unified Man, all peace and contentment. "One looks for you everywhere and finds you here. Wie gehts?"

Susskind, though his eyes flickered, showed no surprise to speak of. For a moment his expression seemed to say he had no idea who this was, had forgotten Fidelman's existence, but then at last remembered —somebody long ago from another country, whom you smiled on, then forgot.

"Still here?" he perhaps ironically joked.

"Still." Fidelman was embarrassed at his voice slipping.

"Rome holds you?"

"Rome," faltered Fidelman, "—the air." He breathed deep and exhaled with emotion.

Noticing the refugee was not truly attentive, his eyes roving upon potential customers, Fidelman, girding himself, remarked, "By the way, Susskind, you didn't happen to notice—did you?—the briefcase I was carrying with me around the time we met in September?"

"Briefcase—what kind?" This he said absently, his eyes on the church doors.

"Pigskin. I had in it"—here Fidelman's voice could be heard cracking—"a chapter of a critical work on Giotto I was writing. You know, I'm sure, the Trecento painter?"

"Who doesn't know Giotto?"

"Do you happen to recall whether you saw, if, that is—" He stopped, at a loss for words other than accusatory.

"Excuse me—business." Susskind broke away and bounced up the steps two at a time. A man he approached shied away. He had beads, didn't need others.

Fidelman had followed the refugee. "Reward," he muttered up close to his ear. "Fifteen thousand for the chapter, and who has it can keep the brand-new briefcase. That's his business, no questions asked. Fair enough?"

Susskind spied a lady tourist, including camera and guidebook. "Beads—holy beads." He held up both hands but she was just a Lutheran, passing through.

"Slow today," Susskind complained as they walked down the stairs, "but maybe it's the items. Everybody has the same. If I had some big ceramics of the Holy Mother, they go like hot cakes—a good investment for somebody with a little cash."

"Use the reward for that," Fidelman cagily whispered, "buy Holy Mothers."

If he heard, Susskind gave no sign. At the sight of a family of nine emerging from the main portal above, the refugee, calling addio over his shoulder, fairly flew up the steps. But Fidelman uttered no response. I'll get the rat yet. He went off to hide behind a high fountain in the square. But the flying spume raised by the wind wet him, so he retreated behind a massive column and peeked out at short intervals to keep the peddler in sight.

At two o'clock, when St. Peter's closed to visitors, Susskind dumped his goods into his raincoat pockets and locked up shop. Fidelman followed him all the way home, indeed the ghetto, although along a street he had not consciously been on before, which led into an alley where the refugee pulled open a left-handed door and, without transition, was "home." Fidelman, sneaking up close, caught a dim glimpse of an overgrown closet containing bed and table. He found no address on wall or door, nor, to his surprise, any door lock. This for a moment depressed him. It meant Susskind had nothing worth stealing. Of his own, that is. The student promised himself to return tomorrow, when the occupant was elsewhere.

Return he did, in the morning, while the entrepreneur was out selling religious articles, glanced around once, and was quickly inside. He shivered—a pitch-black freezing cave. Fidelman scratched up a thick match and confirmed bed and table, also a rickety chair, but no heat or light except a drippy candle stub in a saucer on the table. He lit the yellow candle and searched all over the place. In the table drawer a few eating implements plus safety razor, though where he shaved was a mystery, probably a public toilet. On a shelf above the thin-blanketed bed stood half a flask of red wine, part of a package of spaghetti, and a hard panino. Also an unexpected little fish bowl with a bony goldfish swimming around in arctic seas. The fish, reflecting the candle flame, gulped repeatedly, threshing its frigid tail as Fidelman watched. He loves pets, thought the student. Under the bed he found a chamber pot, but nowhere a briefcase with a fine critical chapter in it. The place was not more than an icebox someone probably had lent the refugee to come in out of the rain. Alas, Fidelman sighed. Back in the pensione, it took a hot-water bottle two hours to thaw him out; but from the visit he never fully recovered.

•

In this latest dream of Fidelman's he was spending the day in a cemetery all crowded with tombstones, when up out of an empty grave rose this long-nosed brown shade, Virgilio Susskind, beckoning.

Fidelman hurried over.

"Have you read Tolstoy?"

"Sparingly."

"Why is art?" asked the shade, drifting off.

Fidelman, willy-nilly, followed, and the ghost, as it vanished, led him up steps going through the ghetto and into a marble synagogue.

The student, left alone, for no reason he could think of lay down upon the stone floor, his shoulders keeping strangely warm as he stared at the sunlit vault above. The fresco therein revealed this saint in fading blue, the sky flowing from his head, handing an old knight in a thin red robe his gold cloak. Nearby stood a humble horse and two stone hills.

Giotto. San Francesco dona le vesti al cavaliere povero.

Fidelman awoke running. He stuffed his blue gabardine into a paper bag, caught a bus, and knocked early on Susskind's heavy portal.

"Avanti." The refugee, already garbed in beret and raincoat (probably his pajamas), was standing at the table, lighting the candle with a flaming sheet of paper. To Fidelman the paper looked like the underside of a typewritten page. Despite himself, the student recalled in letters of fire his entire chapter.

"Here, Susskind," he said in a trembling voice, offering the bundle, "I bring you my suit. Wear it in good health."

The refugee glanced at it without expression. "What do you wish for it?"

"Nothing at all." Fidelman laid the bag on the table, called goodbye, and left.

He soon heard footsteps clattering after him across the cobblestones.

"Excuse me, I kept this under my mattress for you." Susskind thrust at him the pigskin briefcase.

Fidelman savagely opened it, searching frenziedly in each compartment, but the bag was empty. The refugee was already in flight. With a bellow the student started after him. "You bastard, you burned my chapter!"

"Have mercy," cried Susskind, "I did you a favor."

"I'll do you one and cut your throat."

"The words were there but the spirit was missing."

In a towering rage, Fidelman forced a burst of speed, but the refugee, light as the wind in his marvelous knickers, his green coattails flying, rapidly gained ground.

The ghetto Jews, framed in amazement in their medieval windows, stared at the wild pursuit. But in the middle of it, Fidelman, stout and short of breath, moved by all he had lately learned, had a triumphant insight.

"Susskind, come back," he shouted, half sobbing. "The suit is yours. All is forgiven."

He came to a dead halt but the refugee ran on. When last seen he was still running.

1958

❧ B M ❧

The Lady of the Lake

Henry Levin, an ambitious, handsome thirty, who walked the floors in Macy's book department wearing a white flower in his lapel, having recently come into a small inheritance, quit, and went abroad seeking romance. In Paris, for no reason he was sure of, except that he was tired of the past—tired of the limitations it had imposed upon him; although he had signed the hotel register with his right name, Levin took to calling himself Henry R. Freeman. Freeman lived for a short while in a little hotel on a narrow gas lamp–lit street near the Luxembourg Gardens. In the beginning he liked the sense of foreignness of the city—of things different, anything likely to happen. He liked, he said to himself, the possible combinations. But not much did happen; he met no one he particularly cared for (he had sometimes in the past deceived himself about women, they had come to less than he had expected); and since the heat was hot and tourists underfoot, he felt he must flee. He boarded the Milan express and, after Dijon, developed a painful, palpitating anxiety. This grew so troublesome that he had serious visions of leaping off the train, but reason prevailed and he rode on. However, he did not get to Milan. Nearing Stresa, after a quick, astonished look at Lake Maggiore, Freeman, a nature lover from early childhood, pulled his suitcase off the rack and hurriedly left the train. He at once felt better.

An hour later he was established in a pensione in a villa not far from the line of assorted hotels fronting the Stresa shore. The padrona, a talkative woman, much interested in her guests, complained that

June and July had been lost in unseasonable cold and wet. Many had cancelled; there were few Americans around. This didn't exactly disturb Freeman, who had had his full share of Coney Island. He lived in an airy, French-windowed room, including soft bed and spacious bath, and though personally the shower type, was glad of the change. He was very fond of the balcony at his window, where he loved to read, or study Italian, glancing up often to gaze at the water. The long blue lake, sometimes green, sometimes gold, went out of sight among distant mountains. He liked the red-roofed town of Pallanza on the opposite shore, and especially the four beautiful islands in the water, tiny but teeming with palazzi, tall trees, gardens, visible statuary. The sight of these islands aroused in Freeman a deep emotion; each a universe—how often do we come across one in a lifetime?— filled him with expectancy. Of what, he wasn't sure. Freeman still hoped for what he hadn't, what few got in the world and many dared not think of; to wit, love, adventure, freedom. Alas, the words by now sounded slightly comical. Yet there were times, when he was staring at the islands, if you pushed him a little he could almost cry. Ah, what names of beauty: Isola Bella, dei Pescatori, Madre, and del Dongo. Travel is truly broadening, he thought; who ever got emotional over Welfare Island?

But the islands, the two he visited, let him down. Freeman walked off the vaporetto at Isola Bella amid a crowd of late-season tourists in all languages, especially German, who were at once beset by many vendors of cheap trinkets. And he discovered there were guided tours only—strictly no unsupervised wandering—the pink palazzo full of old junk, surrounded by artificial formal gardens, including grottoes made of seashells, the stone statuary a tasteless laugh. And although Isola dei Pescatori had some honest atmosphere, old houses hugging crooked streets, thick nets drying in piles near fishermen's dories drawn up among trees; again there were tourists snapping all in pictures, and the whole town catering to them. Everybody had something to sell you could buy better in Macy's basement. Freeman returned to his pensione, disappointed. The islands, beautiful from afar, up close were so much stage scenery. He complained thus to the padrona and she urged him to visit Isola del Dongo. "More natural," she persuaded him. "You never saw such unusual gardens. And the palazzo is historical, full of the tombs of famous men of the region, including a cardinal who became a saint. Napoleon, the emperor, slept there. The French have always loved this island. Their writers have wept at its beauty."

However, Freeman showed little interest. "Gardens I've seen in my time." So, when restive, he wandered in the back streets of Stresa, watching the men playing at boccia, avoiding the laden store windows. Drifting by devious routes back to the lake, he sat at a bench in the small park, watching the lingering sunset over the dark mountains and thinking of a life of adventure. He watched alone, talked now and then to stray Italians—almost everybody spoke a good broken English—and lived too much on himself. On weekends, there was, however, a buzz of merriment in the streets. Excursionists from around Milan arrived in busloads. All day they hurried to their picnics; at night one of them pulled an accordion out of the bus and played sad Venetian or happy Neapolitan songs. Then the young Italians and their girls got up and danced in tight embrace in the public square; but not Freeman.

One evening at sunset, the calm waters so marvelously painted they drew him from inactivity, he hired a rowboat, and for want of any-place more exciting to go, rowed toward the Isola del Dongo. He had no intention other than reaching it, then turning back, a round trip completed. Two-thirds of the way there, he began to row with growing un-easiness which soon became dread, because a stiff breeze had risen, driving the sucking waves against the side of the boat. It was a warm wind, but a wind was a wind and the water was wet. Freeman didn't row well—had learned late in his twenties, despite the nearness of Central Park—and he swam poorly, always swallowing water, never enough breath to get anywhere; clearly a landlubber from the word go. He strongly considered returning to Stresa—it was at least a half mile to the island, then a mile and a half in return—but chided himself for his timidity. He had, after all, hired the boat for an hour; so he kept rowing though he feared the risk. However, the waves were not too bad and he had discovered the trick of letting them hit the prow head-on. Although he handled his oars awkwardly, Freeman, to his surprise, made good time. The wind now helped rather than hindered; and daylight—reassuring—still lingered in the sky among streaks of red.

At last Freeman neared the island. Like Isola Bella, it rose in ter-races through hedged gardens crowded with statuary, to a palazzo on top. But the padrona had told the truth—this island looked more inter-esting than the others, the vegetation lush, wilder, exotic birds flying around. By now the place was bathed in mist, and despite the thicken-ing dark, Freeman recaptured the sense of awe and beauty he had felt upon first beholding the islands. At the same time he recalled a sad memory of unlived life, his own, of all that had slipped through his fingers. Amid these thoughts he was startled by a movement in the garden by the water's edge. It had momentarily seemed as though a statue had come to life, but Freeman quickly realized a woman was standing this side of a low marble wall, watching the water. He could not, of course, make out her face, though he sensed she was young; only the skirt of her white dress moved in the breeze. He imagined someone waiting for her lover, and was tempted to speak to her, but then the wind blew up strongly and the waves rocked his rowboat. Freeman hastily turned the boat with one oar and, pulling hard, took off. The wind drenched him with spray, the rowboat bobbed among nasty waves, the going grew frighteningly rough. He had visions of drowning, the rowboat swamped, poor Freeman slowly sinking to the bottom, striving fruitlessly to reach the top. But as he rowed, his heart like a metal disk in his mouth, and still rowed on, gradually he overcame his fears; also the waves and wind. Although the lake was by now black, though the sky still dimly reflected white, turning from time to time to peer ahead, he guided himself by the flickering lights of the Stresa shore. It rained hard as he landed, but Freeman, as he beached the boat, considered his adventure an accomplishment and ate a hearty supper at an expensive restaurant.

The curtains billowing in his sunny room the next morning woke him. Freeman rose, shaved, bathed, and after breakfast got a haircut. Wearing his bathing trunks under slacks, he sneaked onto the Hotel Excelsior beach for a dip, short but refreshing. In the early afternoon he read his Italian lesson on the balcony, then snatched a snooze. At four-thirty—he felt he really hadn't made up his mind until then—Freeman boarded the vaporetto making its hourly tour of the islands. After touching at Isola Madre, the boat headed for the Isola del Dongo. As they were approaching the island, coming from the direction opposite that which Freeman had taken last night, he observed a lanky boy in bathing trunks sunning himself on a raft in the lake—nobody he recognized. When the vaporetto landed at the dock on the southern side of the island, to Freeman's surprise and deep regret, the area was crowded with the usual stalls piled high with tourist gewgaws. And though he had hoped otherwise, inspection of the island was strictly in the guide's footsteps, and vietato trying to go anywhere alone. You paid a hundred lire for a ticket, then trailed behind this unshaven, sad-looking clown, who stabbed a jaunty cane at the sky as he announced in three languages to the tourists who followed him: "Please not stray nor wander. The family del Dongo, one of the most illustrious of Italy, so requests. Only thus ees eet able to remain open thees magnificent eestorical palatz and supreme jardens for the inspection by the members of all nations."

They tailed the guide at a fast clip through the palace, through long halls hung with tapestries and elaborate mirrors, enormous rooms filled with antique furniture, old books, paintings, statuary—a lot of it in better taste than the stuff he had seen on the other island; and he visited where Napoleon had slept—a bed. Yet Freeman secretly touched the counterpane, though not quickly enough to escape the all-seeing eye of the Italian guide, who wrathfully raised his cane to the level of Freeman's heart and explosively shouted, "Basta!" This embarrassed Freeman and two British ladies carrying parasols. He felt bad until the group—about twenty—were led into the garden. Gazing from here, the highest point of the island, at the panorama of the golden-blue lake, Freeman gasped. And the luxuriant vegetation of the island was daring, voluptuous. They went among orange and lemon trees (he had never known that lemon was a perfume), magnolia, oleander—the guide called out the names. Everywhere were flowers in great profusion, huge camellias, rhododendron, jasmine, roses in innumerable colors and varieties, all bathed in intoxicating floral fragrance. Freeman's head swam; he felt dizzy, slightly off his rocker at this extraordinary assailment of his senses. At the same time, though it was an "underground" reaction, he experienced a painful, contracting remembrance—more like a warning—of personal poverty. This he had difficulty accounting for, because he usually held a decent opinion of himself. When the comical guide bounced forward, with his cane indicating cedars, eucalyptus, camphor, and pepper trees, the former floorwalker, overcome by all he was for the first time seeing, at the same moment choked by almost breathless excitement, fell behind the group of tourists, and pretended to inspect the berries of a pepper tree. As the guide hurried forward, Freeman, although not positive he had planned it so, ducked behind the pepper tree, ran along a path beside a tall laurel shrub and down two flights of stairs; he hopped over a marble wall and went hastily through a small wood, expectant, seeking, he thought only God knew what.

He figured he was headed in the direction of the garden by the water where he had seen the girl in the white dress last night, but after several minutes of involved wandering, Freeman came upon a little beach, a pebbly strand, leading down stone steps into the lake. About a hundred feet away a raft was anchored, nobody on it. Exhausted by the excitement, a little moody, Freeman sat down under a tree to rest. When he glanced up, a girl in a white bathing suit was coming up the steps out of the water. Freeman stared as she sloshed up the shore, her wet skin glistening in bright sunlight. She had seen him and quickly bent for a towel she had left on a blanket, draped it over her shoulders, and modestly held the ends together over her high-arched breast. Her wet black hair fell upon her shoulders. She stared at Freeman. He rose, forming words of apology in his mind. A haze that had been before his eyes evaporated. Freeman grew pale and the girl blushed.

Freeman was, of course, a New York City boy from way back. As the girl stood there unselfconsciously regarding him—it could not have been longer than thirty seconds—he was aware of his background and certain other disadvantages; but he also knew he wasn't a bad-looking guy, even, it could be said, quite on the handsome side. Though a pin-prick bald at the back of his noggin—not more than a dime could adequately cover—his head of hair was alive, expressive; Freeman's gray eyes were clear, unenvious, nose well molded, the mouth generous. He had well-proportioned arms and legs and his stomach lay respectfully flat. He was a bit short, but on him, he knew, it barely showed. One of his former girlfriends had told him she sometimes thought of him as tall. This counterbalanced the occasions when he had thought of himself as short. Yet though he knew he made a good appearance, Freeman feared this moment, partly because of all he hungered for from life, and partly because of the uncountable obstacles existing between strangers, may the word forever perish.

She, apparently, had no fear of their meeting; as a matter of surprising fact, seemed to welcome it, immediately curious about him. She had, of course, the advantage of position—which included receiving, so to speak, the guest-intruder. And she had grace to lean on; herself also favored physically—mama, what a queenly high-assed form—itself the cause of grace. Her dark, sharp Italian face had that quality of beauty which holds the mark of history, the beauty of a people and civilization. The large brown eyes, under straight slender brows, were filled with sweet light; her lips were purely cut as if from red flowers; her nose was perhaps the one touch of imperfection that perfected the rest—a trifle long and thin. Despite the effect, a little of sculpture, her ovoid face, tapering to a small chin, was soft, suffused with the loveliness of youth. She was about twenty-three or -four. And when Freeman had, to a small degree, calmed down, he discovered in her eyes a hidden hunger, or memory thereof; perhaps it was sadness; and he felt he was, for this reason, if not unknown others, sincerely welcomed. Had he, oh, God, at last met his fate?

"Si è perduto?" the girl asked, smiling, still tightly holding her white towel. Freeman understood and answered in English. "No, I came on my own. On purpose you might say." He had in mind to ask her if she remembered having seen him before, namely in last night's row-boat, but didn't.

"Are you an American?" she inquired, her Italian accent pleas-antly touched with an English one.

"That's right."

The girl studied him for a full minute, and then hesitantly asked, "Are you, perhaps, Jewish?"

Freeman suppressed a groan. Though secretly shocked by the question, it was not, in a way, unexpected. Yet he did not look Jewish, could pass as not—had. So without batting an eyelash, he said, no, he wasn't. And a moment later added, though he personally had nothing against them.

"It was just a thought. You Americans are so varied," she ex-plained vaguely.

"I understand," he said, "but have no worry." Lifting his hat, he introduced himself: "Henry R. Freeman, traveling abroad."

"My name," she said, after an absentminded pause, "is Isabella del Dongo."

Safe on first, thought Freeman. "I'm proud to know you." He bowed. She gave him her hand with a gentle smile. He was about to surprise it with a kiss when the comical guide appeared at a wall a few terraces above. He gazed at them in astonishment, then let out a yell and ran down the stairs, waving his cane like a rapier.

"Transgressor," he shouted at Freeman.

The girl said something to calm him, but the guide was too fur-ious to listen. He grabbed Freeman's arm, yanking him toward the stairs. And though Freeman, in the interest of good manners, barely re-sisted, the guide whacked him across the seat of the pants; but the ex-floorwalker did not complain.

Though his departure from the island had been, to put it mildly, an embarrassment (the girl had vanished after her unsuccessful mo-mentary intercession), Freeman dreamed of a triumphant return. The big thing so far was that she, a knockout, had taken to him; he had been favored by her. Just why, he couldn't exactly tell, but he could tell yes, had seen in her eyes. Yet wondering if yes why yes—an old habit—Freeman, among other reasons he had already thought of, namely the thus and therefore of man-woman attraction—laid it to the fact that he was different, had dared. He had, specifically, dared to duck the guide and be waiting for her at the edge of the lake when she came out of it.

And she was different too (which of course quickened her response to him). Not only in her looks and background, but of course different as regards past. (He had been reading with fascination about the del Dongos in all the local guidebooks.) Her past he could see boiling in her all the way back to the knights of old, and then some; his own history was something else again, but men were malleable, and he wasn't afraid of attempting to create certain daring combinations: Isabella and Henry Freeman. Hoping to meet someone like her was his main reason for having come abroad. And he had also felt he would be appreciated more by a European woman; his personality, that is. Yet, since their lives were *so* different, Freeman had moments of grave doubt, wondered what trials he was in for if he went after her, as he had every intention of doing: with her unknown family—other things of that sort. And he was in afterthought worried because she had asked him if he was Jewish. Why had the question popped out of her pretty mouth before they had even met? He had never before been asked anything like this by a girl, under let's call it similar circumstances. Just when they were looking each other over. He was puzzled because he absolutely did not look Jewish. But then he figured her question might have been a "test" of some kind, she making it a point, when a man attracted her, quickly to determine his "eligibility." Maybe she had once had some sort of unhappy experience with a Jew? Unlikely, but possible, they were now everywhere. Freeman finally explained it to himself as "one of those things," perhaps a queer thought that had for no good reason impulsively entered her mind. And because it was queer, his answer, without elaboration, was sufficient. With ancient history why bother? All these things—the odds against him, whetted his adventurous appetite.

He was in the grip of an almost unbearable excitement and must see her again soon, often, become her friend—not more than a beginning but where begin? He considered calling her on the telephone, if there was one in a palazzo where Napoleon had slept. But if the maid or somebody answered the phone first, he would have a ridiculous time identifying himself; so he settled for sending her a note. Freeman wrote a few lines on good stationery he had bought for the purpose, asking if he might have the pleasure of seeing her again under circumstances favorable to leisurely conversation. He suggested a carriage ride to one of the other lakes in the neighborhood, and signed his name not Levin, of course, but Freeman. Later he told the padrona that anything addressed to that name was meant for him. She was always to refer to him as Mr. Freeman. He gave no explanation, although the padrona raised interested brows; but after he had slipped her—for reasons of friendship—

a thousand lire, her expression became serene. Having mailed the letter, he felt time descend on him like an intricate trap. How would he ever endure until she answered? That evening he impatiently hired a row-boat and headed for Isola del Dongo. The water was glassy smooth but when he arrived the palazzo was dark, almost gloomy, not a single window lit; the whole island looked dead. He saw no one, though he imagined her presence. Freeman thought of tying up at a dock and searching around a bit, but it seemed like folly. Rowing back to Stresa, he was stopped by the lake patrol and compelled to show his passport. An officer advised him not to row on the lake after dark; he might have an accident. The next morning, wearing sunglasses, a light straw, recently purchased, and a seersucker suit, he boarded the vaporetto and soon landed on the island of his dreams, together with the usual group of tourists. But the fanatic guide at once spied Freeman and, waving his cane like a schoolmaster's rod, called on him to depart peacefully. Fearing a scene that the girl would surely hear of, Freeman left at once, greatly annoyed. The padrona, that night, in a confidential mood, warned him not to have anything to do with anybody on the Isola del Dongo. The family had a perfidious history and was known for its deceit and trickery.

On Sunday, at the low point of a depression after an afternoon nap, Freeman heard a knock on his door. A long-legged boy in short pants and a torn shirt handed him an envelope, the corner embossed with somebody's coat of arms. Breathlessly, Freeman tore it open and extracted a sheet of thin bluish paper with a few lines of spidery writing on it: "You may come this afternoon at six. Ernesto will accompany you. I. del D." It was already after five. Freeman was overwhelmed, giddy with pleasure.

"Tu sei Ernesto?" he asked the boy.

The boy, perhaps eleven or twelve, who had been watching Freeman with large curious eyes, shook his head. "No, signore. Sono Giacobbe."

"Dov'è Ernesto?"

The boy pointed vaguely at the window, which Freeman took to mean that whoever he was was waiting at the lakefront.

Freeman changed in the bathroom, emerging in a jiffy with his new straw hat on and the seersucker suit. "Let's go." He ran down the stairs, the boy running after him.

At the dock, to Freeman's startled surprise, "Ernesto" turned out to be the temperamental guide with the pestiferous cane, probably a majordomo in the palazzo, long with the family. Now a guide in another context, he was obviously an unwilling one, to judge from his expression. Perhaps a few wise words had subdued him, and though haughty still, he settled for a show of politeness. Freeman greeted him courteously. The guide sat not in the ritzy launch Freeman had expected to see, but at the stern of an oversize, weatherbeaten rowboat, a cross between a fishing dory and small lifeboat. Preceded by the boy, Freeman climbed in over the unoccupied part of the rear seat, then, as Giacobbe took his place at the oars, hesitantly sat down next to Ernesto. One of the boatmen on the shore gave them a shove off and the boy began to row. The big boat seemed hard to maneuver, but Giacobbe, working deftly with a pair of long, heavy oars, managed with ease. He rowed quickly from the shore and toward the island where Isabella was waiting.

Freeman, though heartened to be off, contented, loving the wide airy world, wasn't comfortable sitting so snug with Ernesto, who smelled freshly of garlic. The talkative guide was a silent traveler. A dead cheroot hung from the corner of his mouth, and from time to time he absently poked his cane in the slats at the bottom of the boat; if there was no leak, Freeman thought, he would create one. He seemed tired, as if he had been carousing all night and had found no time to rest. Once he removed his black felt hat to mop his head with a handkerchief, and Freeman realized he was bald and looked surprisingly old.

Though tempted to say something pleasant to the old man—no hard feelings on this marvelous journey, Freeman had no idea where to begin. What would he reply to a grunt? After a time of prolonged silence, now a bit on edge, Freeman remarked, "Maybe I'd better row and give the boy a rest?"

"As you weesh." Ernesto shrugged.

Freeman traded places with the boy, then wished he hadn't. The oars were impossibly heavy; he rowed badly, allowing the left oar to sink deeper into the water than the right, thus twisting the boat off course. It was like pulling a hearse, and as he awkwardly splashed the oars around, he was embarrassedly aware of the boy and Ernesto, alike in their dark eyes and greedy beaks, a pair of odd birds, openly staring at him. He wished them far far away from the beautiful island and in exasperation pulled harder. By dint of determined effort, though his palms were painfully blistered, he began to row rhythmically, and the boat went along more smoothly. Freeman gazed up in triumph but they were no longer watching him, the boy trailing a straw in the water, the guide staring dreamily into the distance.

After a while, as if having studied Freeman and decided, when all was said and done, that he wasn't exactly a villain, Ernesto spoke in a not unfriendly tone.

"Everybody says how reech ees America?" he remarked.

"Rich enough," Freeman grunted.

"Also thees ees the same with you?" The guide spoke with a half-embarrassed smile around his drooping cheroot butt.

"I'm comfortable," Freeman replied, and in honesty added, "but I have to work for a living."

"For the young people ees a nice life, no? I mean there ees always what to eat, and for the woman een the house many remarkable machines?"

"Many," Freeman said. Nothing comes from nothing, he thought. He's been asked to ask questions. Freeman then gave the guide an earful on the American standard of living, and he meant living. This for whatever it was worth to such as the Italian aristocracy. He hoped for the best. You could never tell the needs and desires of others.

Ernesto, as if memorizing what he had just heard, watched Freeman row for a while.

"Are you in biziness?" he ultimately asked.

Freeman searched around and came up with "Sort of in public relations."

Ernesto now threw away his butt. "Excuse me that I ask. How much does one earn in thees biziness in America?"

Calculating quickly, Freeman replied, "I personally average about a hundred dollars a week. That comes to about a quarter million lire every month."

Ernesto repeated the sum, holding on to his hat in the breeze. The boy's eyes had widened. Freeman hid a satisfied smile.

"And your father?" Here the guide paused, searching Freeman's face.

"What about him?" asked Freeman, tensing.

"What ees hees trade?"

"Was. He's dead—insurance."

Ernesto removed his respectful hat, letting the sunlight bathe his bald head. They said nothing more until they had reached the island, then Freeman, consolidating possible gain, asked him in a complimentary tone where he had learned his English.

"Everywhere," Ernesto replied, with a weary smile, and Freeman, alert for each shift in the prevailing wind, felt that if he hadn't made a bosom friend, he had at least softened an enemy; and that, on home grounds, was going good.

They landed and watched the boy tie up the boat; Freeman asked Ernesto where the signorina was. The guide, now looking bored by it all, pointed his cane at the top terraces, a sweeping gesture that seemed to take in the whole upper half of the luscious island. Freeman hoped the man would not insist on accompanying him and interfering with his meeting with the girl; but when he looked down from looking up without sighting Isabella, both Ernesto and Giacobbe had made themselves scarce. Leave it to the Italians at this sort of thing, Freeman thought.

Warning himself to be careful, tactful, he went quickly up the stairs. At each terrace he glanced around, then ran up to the next, his hat already in his hand. He found her, after wandering through profusions of flowers, where he had guessed she would be, alone in the garden behind the palazzo. She was sitting on an old stone bench near a little marble fountain, whose jets from the mouths of mocking elves sparkled in mellow sunlight.

Beholding her, the lovely face, sharply incised, yet soft in its femininity, the dark eyes pensive, her hair loosely knotted at the nape of her graceful neck, Freeman ached to his oar-blistered fingers. She was wearing a linen blouse of some soft shade of red that fell gently upon her breasts, and a long, slender black skirt; her tanned legs were without stockings; and on her narrow feet she wore sandals. As Freeman approached her, walking slowly to keep from loping, she brushed back a strand of hair, a gesture so beautiful it saddened him, because it was gone in the doing; and though Freeman, on this miraculous Sunday evening, was aware of his indefatigable reality, he could not help thinking as he dwelt upon her lost gesture that she might be as elusive as it, as evanescent; and so might this island be, and so, despite all the days he had lived through, good, bad, and boring, that too often sneaked into his thoughts—so, indeed, might he today, tomorrow. He went toward her with a deep sense of the transitoriness of things, but this feeling was overwhelmed by one of pure joy when she rose to give him her hand.

"Welcome," Isabella said, blushing; she seemed happy, yet, in her manner, a little agitated to see him—perhaps one and the same thing —and he wanted then and there to embrace her but could not work up the nerve. Although he felt in her presence a fulfillment, as if they had already confessed love for one another, at the same time Freeman sensed an uneasiness in her which made him think, though he fought the idea, that they were far away from love; or at least were approaching it through opaque mystery. But that's what happened, Freeman, who had often been in love, told himself. Until you were lovers you were strangers.

In conversation he was at first formal. "I thank you for your kind note. I have been looking forward to seeing you."

She turned toward the palazzo. "My people are out. They have gone to a wedding on another island. May I show you something of the palace?"

He was at this news both pleased and disappointed. He did not at the moment feel like meeting her family. Yet if she had presented him, it would have been a good sign.

They walked for a while in the garden, then Isabella took Freeman's hand and led him through a heavy door into the large rococo palazzo.

"What would you care to see?"

Though he had superficially been through two floors of the building, wanting to be led by her, this close to him, Freeman replied, "Whatever you want me to."

She took him first to the chamber where Napoleon had slept. "It wasn't Napoleon himself who slept here," Isabella explained. "He slept on Isola Bella. His brother Joseph may have been here, or perhaps Pauline, with one of her lovers. No one is sure."

"Oh ho, a trick," said Freeman.

"We often pretend," she remarked. "This is a poor country."

They entered the main picture gallery. Isabella pointed out the Titians, Tintorettos, Bellinis, making Freeman breathless; then at the door of the room she turned with an embarrassed smile and said that most of the paintings in the gallery were copies.

"Copies?" Freeman was shocked.

"Yes, although there are some fair originals from the Lombard school."

"All the Titians are copies?"

"All."

This slightly depressed him. "What about the statuary—also copies?"

"For the most part."

His face fell.

"Is something the matter?"

"Only that I couldn't tell the fake from the real."

"Oh, but many of the copies are exceedingly beautiful," Isabella said. "It would take an expert to tell they weren't originals."

"I guess I've got a lot to learn," Freeman said.

At this she squeezed his hand and he felt better.

But the tapestries, she remarked as they traversed the long hall hung with them, which darkened as the sun set, were genuine and valuable. They meant little to Freeman: long floor-to-ceiling, bluish-green fabrics of woodland scenes: stags, unicorns, and tigers disporting themselves, though in one picture, the tiger killed the unicorn. Isabella hurried past this and led Freeman into a room he had not been in before, hung with tapestries of somber scenes from the *Inferno*. One before which they stopped was of a writhing leper, spotted from head to foot with pustulating sores which he tore at with his nails, but the itch went on forever.

"What did he do to deserve his fate?" Freeman inquired.

"He falsely said he could fly."

"For that you go to hell?"

She did not reply. The hall had become gloomily dark, so they left.

From the garden close by the beach where the raft was anchored, they watched the water turn all colors. Isabella had little to say about herself—she seemed to be quite often pensive—and Freeman, concerned with the complexities of the future, though his heart contained multitudes, found himself comparatively silent. When the night was complete, as the moon was rising, Isabella said she would be gone for a moment, and stepped behind a shrub. When she came forth, Freeman had this utterly amazing vision of her, naked, but before he could even focus his eyes on her flowerlike behind, she was already in the water, swimming for the raft. After an anguished consideration of could he swim that far or would he drown, Freeman, eager to see her from up close (she was sitting on the raft, showing her breasts to the moon), shed his clothes behind the shrub where her delicate things lay, and walked down the stone steps into the warm water. He swam awkwardly, hating the picture he must make in her eyes, Apollo Belvedere slightly maimed; and still suffered visions of drowning in twelve feet of water. Or suppose she had to jump in to rescue him? However, nothing risked, nothing gained, so he splashed on and made the raft with breath to spare, his worries always greater than their cause.

But when he had pulled himself up on the raft, to his dismay, Isabella was no longer there. He caught a glimpse of her on the shore, darting behind the shrub. Nursing gloomy thoughts, Freeman rested awhile, then, when he had sneezed twice and presupposed a nasty cold, jumped into the water and splashed his way back to the island. Isabella, already clothed, was waiting with a towel. She threw it to Freeman as he came up the steps, and withdrew while he dried himself and dressed. When he came forth in his seersucker, she offered salami, prosciutto, cheese, bread, and red wine, from a large platter delivered from the kitchen. Freeman, for a while angered at the runaround on the raft, re-

laxed with the wine and feeling of freshness after a bath. The mosquitoes behaved long enough for him to say he loved her. Isabella kissed
him tenderly, then Ernesto and Giacobbe appeared and rowed him back
to Stresa.

Monday morning Freeman didn't know what to do with himself.
He awoke with restless memories, enormously potent, many satisfying,
some burdensome; they ate him, he ate them. He felt he should somehow have made every minute with her better, hadn't begun to say half
of what he had wanted—the kind of man he was, what they could get
out of life together. And he regretted that he hadn't gotten quickly to
the raft, still excited by what might have happened if he had reached it
before she had left. But a memory was only a memory—you could forget, not change it. On the other hand, he was pleased, surprised by what
he had accomplished: the evening alone with her, the trusting, intimate
sight of her beautiful body, her kiss, the unspoken promise of love. His
desire for her was so splendid it hurt. He wandered through the afternoon, dreaming of her, staring often at the glittering islands in the
opaque lake. By nightfall he was exhausted and went to sleep oppressed
by all he had lived through.

It was strange, he thought, as he lay in bed waiting to sleep, that
of all his buzzing worries he was worried most about one. If Isabella
loved him, as he now felt she did or would before very long; with the
strength of this love they could conquer their problems as they arose.
He anticipated a good handful, stirred up, in all probability, by her family; but life in the U.S.A. was considered by many Italians, including
aristocrats (else why had Ernesto been sent to sniff out conditions
there?), a fine thing for their marriageable daughters. Given this additional advantage, things would somehow get worked out, especially if
Isabella, an independent girl, gazed a little eagerly at the star-spangled
shore. Her family would give before flight in her eyes. No, the worry
that troubled him most was the lie he had told her, that he wasn't a Jew.
He could, of course, confess, say she knew Levin, not Freeman, man of
adventure, but that might ruin all, since it was quite clear she wanted
nothing to do with a Jew, or why, at first sight, had she asked so searching a question? Or he might admit nothing and let her, more or less,
find out after she had lived awhile in the States and seen it was no crime
to be Jewish; that a man's past was, it could safely be said, expendable.
Yet this treatment, if the surprise was upsetting, might cause recrimi-
nations later on. Another solution might be one he had thought of often:
to change his name (he had considered Le Vin but preferred Freeman)
and forget he had ever been born Jewish. There was no question of

hurting family, or being embarrassed by them, he the only son of both parents dead. Cousins lived in Toledo, Ohio, where they would always live and never bother. And when he brought Isabella to America they could skip N.Y.C. and go to live in a place like San Francisco, where nobody knew him and nobody "would know." To arrange such details and prepare other minor changes was why he figured on a trip or two home before they were married; he was prepared for that. As for the wedding itself, since he would have to marry her here to get her out of Italy, it would probably have to be in a church, but he would go along with that to hasten things. It was done every day. Thus he decided, although it did not entirely satisfy him; not so much the denial of being Jewish—what had it brought him but headaches, inferiorities, unhappy memories?—as the lie to the beloved. At first sight love and a lie; it lay on his heart like a sore. Yet, if that was the way it had to be, it was the way.

He awoke the next morning, beset by a swarm of doubts concerning his plans and possibilities. When would he see Isabella again, let alone marry her? ("When?" he had whispered before getting into the boat, and she had vaguely promised, "Soon.") Soon was brutally endless. The mail brought nothing and Freeman grew dismayed. Had he, he asked himself, been constructing a hopeless fantasy, wish seducing probability? Was he inventing a situation that didn't exist, namely, her feeling for him, the possibility of a future with her? He was desperately casting about for something to keep his mood from turning dark blue, when a knock sounded on his door. The padrona, he thought, because she often came up for one unimportant thing or another, but to his unspeakable joy it was Cupid in short pants—Giacobbe holding forth the familiar envelope. She would meet him, Isabella wrote, at two o'clock in the piazza where the electric tram took off for Mt. Mottarone, from whose summit one saw the beautiful panorama of lakes and mountains in the region. Would he share this with her?

Although he had quashed the morning's anxiety, Freeman was there at 1 p.m., smoking impatiently. His sun rose as she appeared, but as she came toward him he noticed she was not quite looking at him (in the distance he could see Giacobbe rowing away), her face neutral, inexpressive. He was at first concerned, but she had, after all, written the letter to him, so he wondered what hot nails she had had to walk on to get off the island. He must sometime during the day drop the word "elope" to see if she savored it. But whatever was bothering her, Isabella immediately shook off. She smiled as she greeted him; he hoped for her lips but got instead her polite fingers. These he kissed in broad daylight (let the spies tell Papa) and she shyly withdrew her hand. She was wearing—it surprised him, though he gave her credit for resisting foolish pressures—exactly the same blouse and skirt she had worn on Sunday. They boarded the tram with a dozen tourists and sat alone on the open seat in front; as a reward for managing this she permitted Freeman to hold her hand. He sighed. The tram, drawn by an old electric locomotive, moved slowly through the town and more slowly up the slope of the mountain. They rode for close to two hours, watching the lake fall as the mountains rose. Isabella, apart from pointing to something now and then, was again silent, withdrawn, but Freeman, allowing her her own rate at flowering, for the moment without plans, was practically contented. A long vote for an endless journey; but the tram at last came to a stop and they walked through a field thick with wildflowers, up the slope to the summit of the mountain. Though the tourists followed in a crowd, the mountaintop was broad and they stood near its edge, to all intents and purposes alone. Below them, on the green undulating plains of Piedmont and Lombardy, seven lakes were scattered, each a mirror reflecting whose fate? And high in the distance rose a ring of astonishing snow-clad Alps. Ah, he murmured, and fell silent.

"We say here," Isabella said, " 'un pezzo di paradiso caduto dal cielo.' "

"You can say it again." Freeman was deeply moved by the sublimity of the distant Alps. She named the white peaks from Mt. Rosa to the Jungfrau. Gazing at them, he felt he had grown a head taller and was inspired to accomplish a feat men would wonder at.

"Isabella—" Freeman turned to ask her to marry him; but she was standing apart from him, her face pale.

Pointing to the snowy mountains, her hand moving in a gentle arc, she asked, "Don't those peaks—those seven—look like a menorah?"

"Like a what?" Freeman politely inquired. He had a sudden frightening remembrance of her seeing him naked as he came out of the lake and felt constrained to tell her that circumcision was de rigueur in stateside hospitals; but he didn't dare. She may not have noticed.

"Like a seven-branched candelabrum holding white candles in the sky?" Isabella asked.

"Something like that."

"Or do you see the Virgin's crown adorned with jewels?"

"Maybe the crown," he faltered. "It all depends how you look at it."

They left the mountain and went down to the water. The tram

ride was faster going down. At the lakefront, as they were waiting for Giacobbe to come with the rowboat, Isabella, her eyes troubled, told Freeman she had a confession to make. He, still eager to propose, hoped she would finally say she loved him. Instead, she said, "My name is not del Dongo. It is Isabella della Seta. The del Dongos have not been on the island in years. We are the caretakers of the palace, my father, brother, and I. We are poor people."

"Caretakers?" Freeman was astonished.

"Yes."

"Ernesto is your father?" His voice rose.

She nodded.

"Was it his idea for you to say you were somebody else?"

"No, mine. He did what I asked him to. He has wanted me to go to America, but under the right circumstances."

"So you had to pretend," he said bitterly. He was more greatly disturbed than he could account for, as if he had been expecting just this to happen.

She blushed and turned away. "I was not sure of the circumstances. I wanted you to stay until I knew you better."

"Why didn't you say so?"

"Perhaps I wasn't serious in the beginning. I said what I thought you wanted to hear. At the same time I wished you to stay. I thought you would be clearer to me after a while."

"Clearer how?"

"I don't really know." Her eyes searched his, then she dropped her glance.

"I'm not hiding anything," he said. He wanted to say more but warned himself not to.

"That's what I was afraid of."

Giacobbe had come with the boat and steadied it for his sister. They were alike as the proverbial peas—two dark Italian faces, the Middle Ages looking out of their eyes. Isabella got into the boat and Giacobbe pushed off with one oar. She waved from afar.

Freeman went back to his pensione in a turmoil, hurt where it hurts—in his dreams, thinking he should have noticed before how worn her blouse and skirt were, should have seen more than he had. It was this that irked. He called himself a damn fool for making up fairy tales—Freeman in love with the Italian aristocracy. He thought of taking off for Venice or Florence, but his heart ached for love of her, and he could not forget that he had originally come in the simple hope of finding a girl worth marrying. If the desire had developed complications, the fault was mostly his own. After an hour in his room, burdened by an overpowering loneliness, Freeman felt he must have her. She mustn't get away from him. So what if the countess had become a care-taker? She was a natural-born queen, whether by del Dongo or any other name. So she had lied to him, but so had he to her; they were quits on that score and his conscience was calm. He felt things would be eas-ier all around now that the air had been cleared.

Freeman ran down to the dock; the sun had set and the boatmen were home, swallowing spaghetti. He was considering untying one of the rowboats and paying tomorrow, when he caught sight of someone sitting on a bench—Ernesto, in his hot winter hat, smoking a cheroot. He was resting his wrists on the handle of his cane, his chin on them.

"You weesh a boat?" the guide asked in a not unkindly tone.

"With all my heart. Did Isabella send you?"

"No."

He came because she was unhappy, Freeman guessed—maybe crying. There's a father for you, a real magician despite his appearance. He waves his stick and up pops Freeman for his little girl.

"Get een," said Ernesto.

"I'll row," said Freeman. He had almost added "Father," but had caught himself. As if guessing the jest, Ernesto smiled, a little sadly. But he sat at the stern of the boat, enjoying the ride.

In the middle of the lake, seeing the mountains surrounding it lit in the last glow of daylight, Freeman thought of the "menorah" in the Alps. Where had she got the word, he wondered, and decided anywhere, a book or picture. But wherever she had, he must settle this subject once and for all tonight.

When the boat touched the dock, the pale moon rose. Ernesto tied up, and handed Freeman a flashlight.

"Een the jarden," he said tiredly, pointing with his cane.

"Don't wait up." Freeman hastened to the garden at the lake's edge, where the roots of trees hung like hoary beards above the water; the flashlight didn't work, but the moon and his memory were enough. Isabella, God bless her, was standing at the low wall among the moonlit statuary: stags, tigers, and unicorns, poets and painters, shepherds with pipes, and playful shepherdesses, gazing at the light shimmering on the water.

She was wearing white, the figure of a future bride; perhaps it was an altered wedding dress—he would not be surprised if a hand-me-down, the way they saved clothes in this poor country. He had pleasant thoughts of buying her some nifty outfits.

She was motionless, her back toward him—though he could picture her bosom breathing. When he said good evening, lifting his light straw, she turned to him with a sweet smile. He tenderly kissed her lips; this she let him do, softly returning the same.

"Goodbye," Isabella whispered.

"To whom goodbye?" Freeman affectionately mocked. "I have come to marry you."

She gazed at him with eyes moistly bright, then came the soft, inevitable thunder: "Are you a Jew?"

Why should I lie? he thought; she's mine for the asking. But then he trembled with the fear of at the last moment losing her, so Freeman answered, though his scalp prickled, "How many no's make never? Why do you persist with such foolish questions?"

"Because I hoped you were." Slowly she unbuttoned her bodice, arousing Freeman, though he was thoroughly confused as to her intent. When she revealed her breasts—he could have wept at their beauty (now recalling a former invitation to gaze at them, but he had arrived too late on the raft)—to his horror he discerned tattooed on the soft and tender flesh a bluish line of distorted numbers.

"Buchenwald," Isabella said, "when I was a little girl. The Fascists sent us there. The Nazis did it."

Freeman groaned, incensed at the cruelty, stunned by the desecration.

"I can't marry you. We are Jews. My past is meaningful to me. I treasure what I suffered for."

"Jews," he muttered, "—you? Oh, God, why did you keep this from me too?"

"I did not wish to tell you something you would not welcome. I thought at one time it was possible you were—I hoped but was wrong."

"Isabella—" he cried brokenly. "Listen, I—I am—"

He groped for her breasts, to clutch, kiss, or suckle them; but she had stepped among the statues, and when he vainly sought her in the veiled mist that had risen from the lake, still calling her name, Freeman embraced only moonlit stone.

Behold the Key

One beautiful late-autumn day in Rome, Carl Schneider, a graduate student in Italian studies at Columbia University, left a real estate agent's office after a depressing morning of apartment hunting and walked up Via Veneto, disappointed in finding himself so dissatisfied in this city of his dreams. Rome, a city of perpetual surprise, had surprised unhappily. He felt unpleasantly lonely for the first time since he had been married, and found himself desiring the lovely Italian women he passed in the street, especially the few who looked as if they had money. He had been a damn fool, he thought, to come here with so little of it in his pocket.

He had, last spring, been turned down for a Fulbright fellowship and had had no peace with himself until he decided to go to Rome anyway to do his Ph.D. on the Risorgimento from firsthand sources, at the same time enjoying Italy. This plan had for years aroused his happiest expectations. Norma thought he was crazy to want to take off with two kids under six and all their savings—$3,600, most of it earned by her, but Carl argued that people had to do something different with their lives occasionally or they went to pot. He was twenty-eight—his years weighed on him—and she was thirty, and when else could they go if not now? He was confident, since he knew the language, that they could get settled satisfactorily in a short time. Norma had her doubts. It all came to nothing until her mother, a widow, offered to pay their passage across; then Norma said yes, though still with misgiving.

"We've read prices are terrible in Rome. How do we know we'll get along on what we have?"

"You got to take a chance once in a while," Carl said.

"Up to a point, with two kids," Norma replied; but she took the chance and they sailed out of season—the sixteenth of October, arriving in Naples on the twenty-sixth and going on at once to Rome, in the hope they would save money if they found an apartment quickly, though Norma wanted to see Capri and Carl would have liked to spend a little time in Pompeii.

In Rome, though Carl had no trouble getting around or making himself understood, they had immediate rough going trying to locate an inexpensive furnished flat. They had figured on a two-bedroom apartment, Carl to work in theirs; or one bedroom and a large maid's room where the kids would sleep. Although they searched across the city they could locate nothing decent within their means, fifty to fifty-five thousand lire a month, a top of about ninety dollars. Carl turned up some inexpensive places but in hopeless Trastevere sections; elsewhere there was always some other fatal flaw: no heat, missing furniture, sometimes no running water or sanitation.

To make bad worse, during their second week at the dark little pensione where they were staying, the children developed nasty intestinal disorders, little Mike having to be carried to the bathroom ten times one memorable night, and Christine running a temperature of 105; so Norma, who didn't trust the milk or cleanliness of the pensione, suggested they would be better off in a hotel. When Christine's fever abated they moved into the Sora Cecilia, a second-class albergo recommended by a Fulbright fellow they had met. It was a four-story building full of high-ceilinged, boxlike rooms. The toilets were in the hall, but the rent was comparatively low. About the only other virtue of the place was that it was near the Piazza Navone, a lovely seventeenth-century square, walled by many magnificently picturesque, wine-colored houses. Within the piazza three fountains played, whose water and sculpture Carl and Norma enjoyed, but which they soon became insensible to during their sad little walks with the kids, as the days passed and they still found themselves homeless.

Carl had in the beginning avoided the real estate agents to save the commission—5 percent of the full year's rent; but when he gave in and visited their offices they said it was too late to get anything at the price he wanted to pay.

"You should have come in July," one agent said.

"I'm here now."

He threw up his hands. "I believe in miracles but who can make them?" Better to pay seventy-five-thousand and so live comfortable like other Americans.

"I can't afford it, not with heat extra."

"Then you will sit out the winter in the hotel."

"I appreciate your concern." Carl left, embittered.

However, they sometimes called him to witness an occasional "miracle." One man showed him a pleasant apartment overlooking some prince or other's formal garden. The rent was sixty thousand, and Carl would have taken it had he not later learned from the tenant next door—he had returned because he distrusted the agent—that the flat was heated electrically, which would cost twenty thousand a month over the sixty thousand rent. Another "miracle" was the offer by this agent's cousin of a single studio room on the Via Margutta, for forty thousand. And from time to time a lady agent called Norma to tell her about this miraculous place in the Parioli: eight stunning rooms, three bedrooms, double service, American-style kitchen with refrigerator, garage—marvelous for an American family: price, two hundred thousand.

"Please, no more," Norma said.

"I'll go mad," said Carl. He was nervous over the way time was flying, almost a month gone, he having given none of it to his work. And Norma, washing the kids' things in the hotel sink, in an unheated, cluttered room, was obviously unhappy. Furthermore, the hotel bill last week had come to twenty thousand lire, and it was costing them two thousand more a day to eat badly, even though Norma was cooking the children's food in their room on a hotplate they had bought.

"Carl, maybe I'd better go to work?"

"I'm tired of your working," he answered. "You'll have no fun."

"What fun am I having? All I've seen is the Colosseum." She then suggested they could rent an unfurnished flat and build their own furniture.

"Where would I get the tools?" he said. "And what about the cost of wood in a country where it's cheaper to lay down marble floors? And who'll do my reading for me while I'm building and finishing the stuff?"

"All right," Norma said. "Forget I said anything."

"What about taking a seventy-five-thousand place but staying only for five or six months?" Carl said.

"Can you get your research done in five or six months?"

"No."

"I thought your research was the main reason we came here."
Norma then wished she had never heard of Italy.

"That's enough of that," said Carl.

He felt helpless, blamed himself for coming—bringing all this
on Norma and the kids. He could not understand why things were
going so badly. When he was not blaming himself he was blaming
the Italians. They were aloof, evasive, indifferent to his plight. He
couldn't communicate with them in their own language, whatever it
was. He couldn't get them to say what was what, to awaken their
hearts to his needs. He felt his plans, his hopes caving in, and feared
disenchantment with Italy unless they soon found an apartment.

•

At the Porta Pinciana, near the tram, Carl felt himself tapped on
the shoulder. A bushy-haired Italian, clutching a worn briefcase, was
standing in the sun on the sidewalk. His hair rose in all directions. His
eyes were gentle; not sad, but they had been. He wore a clean white
shirt, rag of a tie, and a black jacket that had crawled a little up his back.
His trousers were of denim, and his porous, sharp-pointed shoes, neatly
shined, were summer shoes.

"Excuse me," he said with an uneasy smile. "I am Vasco Bevilacqua. Weesh you an apotament?"

"How did you guess?" Carl said.

"I follow you," the Italian answered, making a gesture in the air,
"when you leave the agencia. I am myself agencia. I like to help Americans. They are wonderful people."

"You're a real estate agent?"

"Eet is just."

"Parliamo italiano?"

"You spik?" He seemed disappointed. "Ma non è italiano?"

Carl told him he was an American student of Italian history and
culture, had studied the language for years.

Bevilacqua then explained that, although he had no regular office,
nor, for that matter, a car, he had managed to collect several exclusive
listings. He had got these, he said, from friends who knew he was starting a business, and they made it a habit to inform him of apartments
recently vacated in their buildings or those of friends, for which service
he of course tipped them out of his commissions. The regular agents,
he went on, demanded a heartless 5 percent. He requested only 3. He
charged less because his expenses, frankly, were low, and also because

of his great affection for Americans. He asked Carl how many rooms he was looking for and what he was willing to pay.

Carl hesitated. The man, though pleasant, was no bona fide agent, probably had no license. He had heard about these two-bit operators and was about to say he wasn't interested but Bevilacqua's eyes pleaded with him not to say it.

Carl figured he had nothing to lose. Maybe he does have a place I might be interested in. He told the Italian what he was looking for and how much he expected to pay.

Bevilacqua's face lit up. "In weech zone do you seek?" he asked with emotion.

"Anyplace fairly decent," Carl said in Italian. "It doesn't have to be perfect."

"Not the Parioli?"

"Not the Parioli only. It would depend on the rent."

Bevilacqua held his briefcase between his knees and fished in his shirt pocket. He drew out a sheet of very thin paper, unfolded it, and read the penciled writing, with wrinkled brows. After a while he thrust the paper back into his pocket and retrieved his briefcase.

"Let me have your telephone number," he said in Italian. "I will examine my other listings and give you a ring."

"Listen," Carl said, "if you've got a good place to show me, all right. If not, please don't waste my time."

Bevilacqua looked hurt. "I give you my word," he said, placing his big hand on his chest, "tomorrow you will have your apartment. May my mother give birth to a goat if I fail you."

He put down in a little book where Carl was staying. "I'll be over at thirteen sharp to show you some miraculous places," he said.

"Can't you make it in the morning?"

Bevilacqua was apologetic. "My hours are now from thirteen to sixteen." He said he hoped to expand his time later, and Carl guessed he was working his real estate venture during his lunch and siesta time, probably from some underpaid clerk's job.

He said he would expect him at thirteen sharp.

Bevilacqua, his expression now so serious he seemed to be listening to it, bowed, and walked away in his funny shoes.

•

He showed up at the hotel at ten to two, wearing a small black fedora, his hair beaten down with pomade whose odor sprang into the lobby. Carl was waiting restlessly near the desk, doubting he would show up, when Bevilacqua came running through the door, clutching his briefcase.

"Ready?" he said breathlessly.

"Since one o'clock," Carl answered.

"Ah, that's what comes of not owning your own car," Bevilacqua explained. "My bus had a flat tire."

Carl looked at him but his face was deadpan. "Well, let's get on," the student said.

"I have three places to show you." Bevilacqua told him the first address, a two-bedroom apartment at just fifty thousand.

On the bus they clung to straps in a tight crowd, the Italian raising himself on his toes and looking around at every stop to see where they were. Twice he asked Carl the time, and when Carl told him, his lips moved soundlessly. After a time Bevilacqua roused himself, smiled, and remarked, "What do you think of Marilyn Monroe?"

"I haven't much thought of her," Carl said.

Bevilacqua looked puzzled. "Don't you go to the movies?"

"Once in a while."

The Italian made a short speech on the wonder of American films. "In Italy they always make us look at what we have just lived through." He fell into silence again. Carl noticed that he was holding in his hand a wooden figurine of a hunchback with a high hat, whose poor gobbo he was rubbing with his thumb, for luck.

"For us both," Carl hoped. He was still restless, still worried.

But their luck was nil at the first place, an ocher-colored house behind an iron gate.

"Third floor?" Carl asked, after the unhappy realization that he had been here before.

"Exactly. How did you guess?"

"I've seen the apartment," he answered gloomily. He remembered having seen an ad. If that was how Bevilacqua got his listings, they might as well quit now.

"But what's wrong with it?" the Italian asked, visibly disappointed.

"Bad heating."

"How is that possible?"

"They have a single gas heater in the living room but nothing in the bedrooms. They were supposed to have steam heat installed in the building in September, but the contract fell through when the price of steam pipe went up. With two kids, I wouldn't want to spend the winter in a cold flat."

"Cretins," muttered Bevilacqua. "The portiere said the heat was perfect."

He consulted his paper. "I have a place in the Prati district, two fine bedrooms and combined living and dining room. Also an American-type refrigerator in the kitchen."

"Has the apartment been advertised in the papers?"

"Absolutely no. My cousin called me about this one last night— but the rent is fifty-five thousand."

"Let's see it anyway," Carl said.

It was an old house, formerly a villa, which had been cut up into apartments. Across the street stood a little park with tall, tufted pine trees, just the thing for the kids. Bevilacqua located the portiere, who led them up the stairs, all the while saying how good the flat was. Although Carl discovered at once that there was no hot water in the kitchen sink and it would have to be carried in from the bathroom, the flat made a good impression on him. But then in the master bedroom he noticed that one wall was wet and there was a disagreeable odor in the room.

The portiere quickly explained that a water pipe had burst in the wall, but they would have it fixed in a week.

"It smells like a sewer pipe," said Carl.

"But they will have it fixed this week," Bevilacqua said.

"I couldn't live a week with that smell in the room."

"You mean you are not interested in the apartment?" the Italian said fretfully.

Carl nodded. Bevilacqua's face fell. He blew his nose and they left the house. Outside he regained his calm. "You can't trust your own mother nowadays. I called the portiere this morning and he guaranteed me the house was without a fault."

"He must have been kidding you."

"It makes no difference. I have an exceptional place in mind for you now, but we've got to hurry."

Carl halfheartedly asked where it was.

The Italian looked embarrassed. "In the Parioli, a wonderful section, as you know. Your wife won't have to look far for friends—there are Americans all over. Also Japanese and Indians, if you have international tastes."

"The Parioli," Carl muttered. "How much?"

"Only sixty-five thousand," Bevilacqua said, staring at the ground.

"Only? Still, it must be a dump at that price."

"It's really very nice—new, and with a good-size nuptial bedroom and one small, besides the usual things, including a fine kitchen. You will personally love the magnificent terrace."

"Have you seen the place?"

"I spoke to the maid and she says the owner is very anxious to rent. They are moving, for business reasons, to Turin next week. The maid is an old friend of mine. She swears the place is perfect."

Carl considered it. Sixty-five thousand meant close to a hundred and five dollars. "Well," he said after a while, "let's have a look at it."

•

They caught a tram and found seats together, Bevilacqua impatiently glancing out of the window whenever they stopped. On the way he told Carl about his hard life. He was the eighth of twelve children, only five now alive. Nobody was really ever not hungry, though they ate spaghetti by the bucketful. He had to leave school at ten and go to work. In the war he was wounded twice, once by the Americans advancing, and once by the Germans retreating. His father was killed in an Allied bombardment of Rome, the same that had cracked open his mother's grave in the Cimitero Verano.

"The British pinpointed their targets," he said, "but the Americans dropped bombs everywhere. This was the advantage of your great wealth."

Carl said he was sorry about the bombardments.

"Nevertheless, I like the Americans better," Bevilacqua went on. "They are more like Italians—open. That's why I like to help them when they come here. The British are more closed. They talk with tight lips." He made sounds with tight lips.

As they were walking toward Piazza Euclide, he asked Carl if he had an American cigarette on him.

"I don't smoke," Carl said apologetically.

Bevilacqua shrugged and walked faster.

The house he took Carl to was a new one on Via Archimede, an attractive street that wound up and around a hill. It was crowded with long-balconied apartment buildings in bright colors. Carl thought he would be happy to live in one of them. It was a short thought, he wouldn't let it get too long.

They rode up to the fifth floor, and the maid, a dark girl with fuzzy cheeks, showed them through the neat apartment.

"Is sixty-five thousand correct?" Carl asked her.

She said yes.

The flat was so good that Carl, moved by elation and fear, began to pray.

"I told you you'd like it," Bevilacqua said, rubbing his palms. "I'll draw up the contract tonight."

"Let's see the bedroom now," Carl said.

But first the maid led them onto a broad terrace to show them the view of the city. The sight excited Carl—the variety of architecture from ancient to modern times, where history had been and still, in its own aftermath, sensuously flowed, a sea of roofs, towers, domes; and in the background, golden-domed St. Peter's. This marvelous city, Carl thought.

"Now the bedroom," he said.

"Yes, the bedroom." The maid led them through double doors into the "camera matrimoniale," spacious, and tastefully furnished, containing handsome mahogany twin beds.

"They'll do," Carl said, to hide his joy, "though I personally prefer a double bed."

"I also," said the maid, "but you can move one in."

"These will do."

"But they won't be here," she said.

"What do you mean they won't be here?" Bevilacqua demanded.

"Nothing will be left. Everything goes to Turin."

Carl's beautiful hopes took another long dive into a dirty cellar.

Bevilacqua flung his hat on the floor, landed on it with both feet, and punched himself on the head with his fists.

The maid swore she had told him on the phone that the apartment was for rent unfurnished.

He began to yell at her and she shouted at him. Carl left, broken-backed. Bevilacqua caught up with him in the street. It was a quarter to four and he had to rush off to work. He held his hat and ran down the hill.

"I weel show you a terreefic place tomorrow," he called over his shoulder.

"Over my dead body," said Carl.

On the way to the hotel he was drenched in a heavy rainfall, the first of many in the late autumn.

•

The next morning the hotel phone rang at seven-thirty. The children awoke, Mike crying. Carl, dreading the day, groped for the ringing phone. Outside it was still raining.

"Pronto."

It was a cheery Bevilacqua. "I call you from my job. I 'ave found for you an apotament een weech you can move tomorrow if you like."

"Go to hell."

"Cosa?"

"Why do you call so early? You woke the children."

"Excuse me," Bevilacqua said in Italian. "I wanted to give you the good news."

"What goddamn good news?"

"I have found a first-class apartment for you near the Monte Sacro. It has only one bedroom but also a combined living and dining room with a double daybed, and a glass-enclosed terrace studio for your studies, and a small maid's room. There is no garage but you have no car. Price forty-five thousand—less than you expected. The apartment is on the ground floor and there is also a garden for your children to play in. Your wife will go crazy when she sees it."

"So will I," Carl said. "Is it furnished?"

Bevilacqua coughed. "Of course."

"Of course. Have you been there?"

He cleared his throat. "Not yet. I just discovered it this minute. The secretary of my office, Mrs. Gaspari, told me about it. The apartment is directly under hers. She will make a wonderful neighbor for you. I will come to your hotel precisely at thirteen and a quarter."

"Give yourself time. Make it fourteen."

"You will be ready?"

"Yes."

But when he had hung up, his feeling of dread had grown. He felt afraid to leave the hotel and confessed this to Norma.

"Would you like me to go this time?" she asked.

He considered it but said no.

"Poor Carl."

" 'The great adventure.' "

"Don't be bitter. It makes me miserable."

They had breakfast in the room—tea, bread and jam, fruit. They were cold, but there was to be no heat, it said on a card tacked on the door, until December. Norma put sweaters on the kids. Both had colds. Carl opened a book but could not concentrate and settled for *Il Messaggero*. Norma telephoned the lady agent; she said she would ring back when there was something new to show.

Bevilacqua called up from the lobby at one-forty.

"Coming," Carl said, his heart heavy.

The Italian was standing in wet shoes near the door. He held his briefcase and a dripping large umbrella but had left his hat home. Even in the damp his bushy hair stood upright. He looked slightly miserable.

They left the hotel, Bevilacqua walking quickly by Carl's side, maneuvering to keep the umbrella over both of them. On the Piazza Navona a woman was feeding a dozen stray cats in the rain. She had spread a newspaper on the ground and the cats were grabbing hard strings of last night's macaroni. Carl felt the recurrence of his loneliness.

A packet of garbage thrown out of a window hit their umbrella and bounced off. The garbage spilled on the ground. A white-faced man, staring out of a third-floor window, pointed to the cats. Carl shook his fist at him.

Bevilacqua was moodily talking about himself. "In eight years of hard work I advanced myself only from thirty thousand lire to fifty-five thousand a month. The cretin who sits on my left in the office has his desk at the door and makes forty thousand extra in tips just to give callers an appointment with the big boss. If I had that desk I would double what he takes in."

"Have you thought of changing jobs?"

"Certainly, but I could never start at the salary I am now earning. And there are twenty people who will jump into my job at half the pay."

"Tough," Carl said.

"For every piece of bread, we have twenty open mouths. You Americans are the lucky ones."

"Yes, in that way."

"In what way no?"

"We have no piazzas."

Bevilacqua shrugged one shoulder. "Can you blame me for wanting to advance myself?"

"Of course not. I wish you the best."

"I wish the best to all Americans," Bevilacqua declared. "I like to help them."

"And I to all Italians and pray them to let me live among them for a while."

"Today it will be arranged. Tomorrow you will move in. I feel luck in my bones. My wife kissed St. Peter's toe yesterday."

Traffic was heavy, a stream of gnats—Vespas, Fiats, Renaults—roared at them from both directions, nobody slowing down to let them pass. They plowed across dangerously. At the bus stop the crowd rushed for the doors when the bus swerved to the curb. It moved away with its rear door open, four people hanging on the step.

I can do as well in Times Square, Carl thought.

•

In a half hour, after a short walk from the bus stop, they arrived at a broad, tree-lined street. Bevilacqua pointed to a yellow apartment house on the corner they were approaching. All over it were terraces, the ledges loaded with flower pots and stone boxes dropping ivy over the walls. Carl would not allow himself to think the place had impressed him.

Bevilacqua nervously rang the portiere's bell. He was again rubbing the hunchback's gobbo. A thickset man in a blue smock came up from the basement. His face was heavy and he wore a full black mustache. Bevilacqua gave him the number of the apartment they wanted to see.

"Ah, there I can't help you," said the portiere. "I haven't got the key."

"Here we go again," Carl muttered.

"Patience," Bevilacqua counseled. He spoke to the portiere in a dialect Carl couldn't follow. The portiere made a long speech in the same dialect.

"Come upstairs," said Bevilacqua.

"Upstairs where?"

"To the lady I told you about, the secretary of my office. She lives on the first floor. We will wait there comfortably until we can get the key to the apartment."

"Where is it?"

"The portiere isn't sure. He says a certain Contessa owns the apartment but she let her lover live in it. Now the Contessa decided to get married so she asked the lover to move, but he took the key with him."

"It's that simple," said Carl.

"The portiere will telephone the Contessa's lawyer, who takes care of her affairs. He must have another key. While he makes the call we will wait in Mrs. Gaspari's apartment. She will make you an American coffee. You'll like her husband too, he works for an American company."

"Never mind the coffee," Carl said. "Isn't there some way we can get a look into the flat? For all I know it may not be worth waiting for. Since it's on the ground floor maybe we can have a look through the windows?"

"The windows are covered by shutters which can be raised from the inside only."

They walked up to the secretary's apartment. She was a dark woman of thirty, with extraordinary legs, and bad teeth when she smiled.

"Is the apartment worth seeing?" Carl asked her.

"It's just like mine, with the exception of having a garden. Would you care to see mine?"

"If I may."

"Please."

She led him through her rooms. Bevilacqua remained on the sofa in the living room, his damp briefcase on his knees. He opened the straps, took out a chunk of bread, and chewed thoughtfully.

Carl admitted to himself that he liked the flat. The building was comparatively new, had gone up after the war. The one bedroom was a disadvantage, but the kids could have it and he and Norma would sleep on the daybed in the living room. The terrace studio was perfect for a workroom. He had looked out of the bedroom window and seen the garden, a wonderful place for children to play.

"Is the rent really forty-five thousand?" he asked.

"Exactly."

"And it is furnished?"

"In quite good taste."

"Why doesn't the Contessa ask more for it?"

"She has other things on her mind," Mrs. Gaspari laughed. "Oh, see," she said, "the rain has stopped and the sun is coming out. It is a good sign." She was standing close to him.

What's in it for her? Carl thought and then remembered she would share Bevilacqua's poor 3 percent.

He felt his lips moving. He tried to stop the prayer but it went on. When he had finished, it began again. The apartment was fine, the garden just the thing for the kids. The price was better than he had hoped.

In the living room Bevilacqua was talking to the portiere. "He couldn't reach the lawyer," he said glumly.

"Let me try," Mrs. Gaspari said. The portiere gave her the number and left. She dialed the lawyer but found he had gone for the day. She got his house number and telephoned there. The busy signal came. She waited a minute, then dialed again.

Bevilacqua took two small hard apples from his briefcase and offered one to Carl. Carl shook his head. The Italian peeled the apples with his penknife and ate both. He dropped the skins and cores into his briefcase, then locked the straps.

"Maybe we could take the door down," Carl suggested. "It shouldn't be hard to pull the hinges."

"The hinges are on the inside," Bevilacqua said.

"I doubt if the Contessa would rent to you," said Mrs. Gaspari from the telephone, "if you got in by force."

"If I had the lover here," Bevilacqua said, "I would break his neck for stealing the key."

"Still busy," said Mrs. Gaspari.

"Where does the Contessa live?" Carl asked. "Maybe I could take a taxi over."

"I believe she moved recently," Mrs. Gaspari said. "I once had her address but I have no longer."

"Would the portiere know it?"

"Possibly." She called the portiere on the house phone but all he would give her was the Contessa's telephone number. The Contessa wasn't home, her maid said, so they telephoned the lawyer and again got a busy signal. Carl was by now irritated.

Mrs. Gaspari called the telephone operator, giving the Contessa's number and requesting her home address. The telephone operator found the old one but could not locate the new.

"Stupid," said Mrs. Gaspari. Once more she dialed the lawyer.

"I have him," she announced over the mouthpiece. "Buon giorno, Avvocato." Her voice was candy.

Carl heard her ask the lawyer if he had a duplicate key and the lawyer replied for three minutes.

She banged down the phone. "He has no key. Apparently there is only one."

"To hell with all this." Carl got up. "I'm going back to the United States."

It was raining again. A sharp crack of thunder split the sky, and Bevilacqua, abandoning his briefcase, rose in fright.

•

"I'm licked," Carl said to Norma, the next morning. "Call the agents and tell them we're ready to pay seventy-five. We've got to get out of this joint."

"Not before we speak to the Contessa. I'll tell her my troubles and break her heart."

"You'll get involved and you'll get nowhere," Carl warned her.

"Please call her anyway."

"I haven't got her number. I didn't think of asking for it."

"Find it. You're good at research."

He considered phoning Mrs. Gaspari for the number but remembered she was at work, and he didn't have that number. Recalling the address of the apartment house, he looked it up in the phone book. Then he telephoned the portiere and asked for the Contessa's address and her phone number.

"I'll call you back," said the portiere, eating as he spoke. "Give me your telephone."

"Why bother? Give me her number and save yourself the trouble."

"I have strict orders from the Contessa never to give her number to strangers. They call up on the phone and annoy her."

"I'm not a stranger. I want to rent her flat."

The portiere cleared his throat. "Where are you staying?"

"Albergo Sora Cecilia."

"I'll call you back in a quarter of an hour."

"Have it your way." He gave the portiere his name.

In forty minutes the phone rang and Carl reached for it. "Pronto."

"Signore Schneider?" It was a man's voice—a trifle high.

"Speaking."

"Permit me," the man said, in fluent though accented English. "I am Aldo De Vecchis. It would please me to speak to you in person."

"Are you a real estate agent?"

"Not precisely, but it refers to the apartment of the Contessa. I am the former occupant."

"The man with the key?" Carl asked quickly.

"It is I."

"Where are you now?"

"In the foyer downstairs."

"Come up, please."

"Excuse me, but if you will permit, I would prefer to speak to you here."

"I'll be right down."

"The lover," he said to Norma.

"Oh, God."

He rushed down in the elevator. A thin man in a green suit with cuffless trousers was waiting in the lobby. He was about forty, his face small, his hair wet black, and he wore at a tilt the brownest hat Carl had ever seen. Though his shirt collar was frayed, he looked impeccable. Into the air around him leaked the odor of cologne.

"De Vecchis," he bowed. His eyes, in a slightly pockmarked face, were restless.

"I'm Carl Schneider. How'd you get my number?"

De Vecchis seemed not to have heard. "I hope you are enjoying your visit here."

"I'd enjoy it more if I had a house to live in."

"Precisely. But what is your impression of Italy?"

"I like the people."

"There are too many of them." De Vecchis looked restlessly around. "Where may we speak? My time is short."

"Ah," said Carl. He pointed to a little room where people wrote letters. "In there."

•

They entered and sat at a table, alone in the room.

De Vecchis felt in his pocket for something, perhaps a cigarette, but came up with nothing. "I won't waste your time," he said. "You wish the apartment you saw yesterday? I wish you to have it, it is most desirable. There is also with it a garden of roses. You will love it on a summer night when Rome is hot. However, the practical matter is this. Are you willing to invest a few lire to obtain the privilege of entry?"

"The key?" Carl knew but asked.

"Precisely. To be frank I am not in good straits. To that is added the psychological disadvantage of the aftermath of a love affair with a most difficult woman. I leave you to imagine my present condition. Notwithstanding, the apartment I offer is attractive and the rent, as I understand, is for Americans not too high. Surely this has its value for you?" He attempted a smile but it died in birth.

"I am a graduate student of Italian studies," Carl said, giving him the facts. "I've invested all of my savings in this trip abroad to get my Ph.D. dissertation done. I have a wife to support and two children."

"I hear that your government is most generous to the Fulbright fellows?"

"You don't understand. I am not a Fulbright fellow."

"Whatever it is," De Vecchis said, drumming his fingertips on the table, "the price of the key is eighty thousand lire."

Carl laughed mirthlessly.

"I beg your pardon?"

Carl rose.

"Is the price too high?"

"It's impossible."

De Vecchis rubbed his brow nervously. "Very well, since not all Americans are rich Americans—you see, I am objective—I will reduce the sum by one half. For less than a month's rent the key is yours."

"Thanks. No dice."

"Please? I don't understand your expression."

"I can't afford it. I'd still have a commission to pay the agent."

"Oh? Then why don't you forget him? I will issue orders to the portiere to allow you to move in immediately. This evening, if you prefer. The Contessa's lawyer will draw up the lease free of charge. And although she is difficult to her lovers, she is an angel to her tenants."

"I'd like to forget the agent," Carl said, "but I can't."

De Vecchis gnawed his lip. "I will make it twenty-five thousand," he said, "but this is my last and absolute word."

"No, thanks. I won't be a party to a bribe."

De Vecchis rose, his small face tight, pale. "It is people like you who drive us to the hands of Communists. You try to buy us—our votes, our culture, and then you dare speak of bribes."

He strode out of the room and through the lobby.

Five minutes later the phone rang. "Fifteen thousand is my final offer." His voice was thick.

"Not a cent," said Carl.

Norma stared at him.

De Vecchis slammed the phone.

•

The portiere telephoned. He had looked everywhere, he said, but had lost the Contessa's address.

"What about her phone number?" Carl asked.

"It was changed when she moved. The numbers are confused in my mind, the old with the new."

"Look here," Carl said, "I'll tell the Contessa you sent De Vecchis to see me about her apartment."

"How can you tell her if you don't know her number?" the portiere asked with curiosity. "It isn't listed in the book."

"I'll ask Mrs. Gaspari for it when she gets home from work, then I'll call the Contessa and tell her what you did."

"What did I do? Tell me exactly."

"You sent her former lover, a man she wants to get rid of, to try to squeeze money out of me for something that is none of his business—namely her apartment."

"Is there no other way than this?" asked the portiere.

"If you tell me her address I will give you one thousand lire." Carl felt his tongue thicken.

"How shameful," Norma said from the sink, where she was washing clothes.

"Not more than one thousand?" asked the portiere.

"Not till I move in."

The portiere then told him the Contessa's last name and her new address. "Don't repeat where you got it."

Carl swore he wouldn't.

He left the hotel on the run, got into a cab, and drove across the Tiber to the Via Cassia, in the country.

The Contessa's maid admitted him into a fabulous place with mosaic floors, gilded furniture, and a marble bust of the Contessa's great-grandfather in the foyer where Carl waited. In twenty minutes the Contessa appeared, a plain-looking woman, past fifty, with dyed blond hair, black eyebrows, and a short, tight dress. The skin on her arms was wrinkled, but her bosom was enormous and she smelled like a rose garden.

"Please, you must be quick," she said impatiently. "There is so much to do. I am preparing for my wedding."

"Contessa," said Carl, "excuse me for rushing in like this, but my wife and I have a desperate need for an apartment and we know that yours on the Via Tirreno is vacant. I'm an American student of Italian life and manners. We've been in Italy almost a month and are still living in a third-rate hotel. My wife is unhappy. The children have miserable colds. I'll be glad to pay you fifty thousand lire, instead of the forty-five you ask, if you will kindly let us move in today."

"Listen," said the Contessa, "I come from an honorable family. Don't try to bribe me."

Carl blushed. "I mean nothing more than to give you proof of my good will."

"In any case, my lawyer attends to my real estate matters."

"He hasn't the key."

"Why hasn't he?"

"The former occupant took it with him."

"The fool," she said.

"Do you happen to have a duplicate?"

"I never keep duplicate keys. They all get mixed up and I never know which is which."

"Could we have one made?"

"Ask my lawyer."

"I called this morning but he's out of town. May I make a suggestion, Contessa? Could we have a window or a door forced? I will pay the cost of repair."

The Contessa's eyes glinted. "Of course not," she said huffily. "I will have no destruction of my property. We've had enough of that sort of thing here. You Americans have no idea what we've lived through."

"But doesn't it mean something to you to have a reliable tenant in your apartment? What good is it standing empty? Say the word and I'll bring you the rent in an hour."

"Come back in two weeks, young man, after I finish my honeymoon."

"In two weeks I may be dead," Carl said.

The Contessa laughed.

Outside, he met Bevilacqua. He had a black eye and a stricken expression.

"So you've betrayed me?" the Italian said hoarsely.

"What do you mean 'betrayed'? Who are you, Jesus Christ?"

"I hear you went to De Vecchis and begged for the key, with plans to move in without telling me."

"How could I keep that a secret with your pal Mrs. Gaspari living right over my head? The minute I moved in she'd tell you, then you'd be over on horseback to collect."

"That's right," said Bevilacqua. "I didn't think of it."

"Who gave you the black eye?" Carl asked.

"De Vecchis. He's as strong as a wild pig. I met him at the apartment and asked for the key. He called me dirty names. We had a fight and he hit me in the eye with his elbow. How did you make out with the Contessa?"

"Not well. Did you come to see her?"

"Vaguely."

"Go in and beg her to let me move in, for God's sake. Maybe she'll listen to a countryman."

"Don't ask me to eat a horse," said Bevilacqua.

•

That night Carl dreamed they had moved out of the hotel into the Contessa's apartment. The children were in the garden, playing among the roses. In the morning he decided to go to the portiere and offer him ten thousand lire if he would have a new key made, however they did it—door up or door down.

When he arrived at the apartment house the portiere and Bevilacqua were there with a toothless man, on his knees, poking a hooked wire into the door lock. In two minutes it clicked open.

With a gasp they all entered. From room to room they wandered like dead men. The place was a ruin. The furniture had been smashed with a dull axe. The slashed sofa revealed its inner springs. Rugs were cut up, crockery broken, books wildly torn and scattered. The white walls had been splashed with red wine, except one in the living room which was decorated with dirty words in six languages, printed in orange lipstick.

"Mamma mia," muttered the toothless locksmith, crossing himself. The portiere slowly turned yellow. Bevilacqua wept.

De Vecchis, in his pea-green suit, appeared in the doorway. "Ecco la chiave!" He held it triumphantly aloft.

"Assassin!" shouted Bevilacqua. "Turd! May your bones grow hair and rot."

"He lives for my death," he cried to Carl, "I for his. This is our condition."

"You lie," said Carl. "I love this country."

De Vecchis flung the key at them and ran. Bevilacqua, the light of hatred in his eyes, ducked, and the key hit Carl on the forehead, leaving a mark he could not rub out.

1958

❧ B M ❧

The Maid's Shoes

The maid had left her name with the porter's wife. She said she was looking for steady work and would take anything but preferred not to work for an old woman. Still, if she had to she would. She was forty-five and looked older. Her face was worn but her hair was black, and her eyes and lips were pretty. She had few good teeth. When she laughed she was embarrassed around the mouth. Although it was cold in early October, that year in Rome, and the chestnut vendors were already bent over their pans of glowing charcoals, the maid wore only a threadbare black cotton dress which had a split down the left side, where about two inches of seam had opened on the hip, exposing her underwear. She had sewn the seam several times but this was one of the times it was open again. Her heavy but well-formed legs were bare and she wore house slippers as she talked to the portinaia; she had done a single day's washing for a signora down the street and carried her shoes in a paper bag. There were three comparatively new apartment houses on the hilly street and she left her name in each.

The portinaia, a dumpy woman wearing a brown tweed skirt she had got from an English family that had once lived in the building, said she would remember the maid but then she forgot; she forgot until an American professor moved into a furnished apartment on the fifth floor and asked her to help him find a maid. The portinaia brought him a girl from the neighborhood, a girl of sixteen, recently from Umbria, who came with her aunt. But the professor, Orlando Krantz, did not like the way the aunt played up certain qualities of the girl, so he sent her away. He told the portinaia he was looking for an older woman, someone he wouldn't have to worry about. Then the portinaia thought of the maid who had left her name and address, and she went to her house on the Via Appia Antica near the catacombs and told her an American was looking for a maid, mezzo servizio; she would give him her name if the maid agreed to make it worth her while. The maid, whose name was Rosa, shrugged her shoulders and looked stiffly down the street. She said she had nothing to offer the portinaia.

"Look at what I'm wearing," she said. "Look at this junk pile, can you call it a house? I live here with my son and his bitch of a wife who counts every spoonful of soup in my mouth. They treat me like dirt and dirt is all I have to my name."

"In that case I can do nothing for you," the portinaia said. "I have myself and my husband to think of." But she returned from the bus stop and said she would recommend the maid to the American professor if she gave her five thousand lire the first time she was paid.

"How much will he pay?" the maid asked the portinaia.

"I would ask for eighteen thousand a month. Tell him you have to spend two hundred lire a day for carfare."

"That's almost right," Rosa said. "It will cost me forty one way and forty back. But if he pays me eighteen thousand I'll give you five if you sign that's all I owe you."

"I will sign," said the portinaia, and she recommended the maid to the American professor.

Orlando Krantz was a nervous man of sixty. He had mild gray eyes, a broad mouth, and a pointed clefted chin. His round head was bald and he had a bit of a belly, although the rest of him was quite thin. He was a somewhat odd-looking man but an authority in law, the portinaia told Rosa. The professor sat at a table in his study, writing all day, yet was up every half hour on some pretext or other to look nervously around. He worried how things were going and often came out of his study to see. He would watch Rosa working, then went in and wrote. In a half hour he would come out, ostensibly to wash his hands in the bathroom or drink a glass of cold water, but he was really passing by to see what she was doing. She was doing what she had to. Rosa worked quickly, especially when he was watching. She seemed, he thought, to be unhappy, but that was none of his business. Their lives, he knew, were full of troubles, often sordid; it was best to be detached.

This was the professor's second year in Italy; he had spent the

first in Milan, and the second was in Rome. He had rented a large
three-bedroom apartment, one of which he used as a study. His wife
and daughter, who had returned for a visit to the States in August,
would have the other bedrooms; they were due back before not too
long. When the ladies returned, he had told Rosa, he would put her
on full-time. There was a maid's room where she could sleep; indeed,
which she already used as her own though she was in the apartment
only from nine till four. Rosa agreed to a full-time arrangement because it would mean all her meals in and no rent to pay her son and
his dog-faced wife.

While they were waiting for Mrs. Krantz and the daughter to
arrive, Rosa did the marketing and cooking. She made the professor's
breakfast when she came in, and his lunch at one. She offered to stay
later than four, to prepare his supper, which he ate at six, but he
preferred to take that meal out. After shopping she cleaned the house,
thoroughly mopping the marble floors with a wet rag she pushed
around with a stick, though the floors did not look particularly dusty
to him. She also washed and ironed his laundry. She was a good
worker, her slippers clip-clopping as she hurried from one room to
the next, and she frequently finished up about an hour or so before
she was due to go home; so she retired to the maid's room and there
read *Tempo* or *Epoca*, or sometimes a love story in photographs, with
the words printed in italics under each picture. Often she pulled her
bed down and lay in it under blankets, to keep warm. The weather
had turned rainy, and now the apartment was uncomfortably cold.
The custom of the condominium in this apartment house was not to
heat until the fifteenth of November, and if it was cold before then,
as it was now, the people of the house had to do the best they could.
The cold disturbed the professor, who wrote with his gloves and hat
on, and increased his nervousness so that he was out to look at her
more often. He wore a heavy blue bathrobe over his clothes; sometimes the bathrobe belt was wrapped around a hot-water bottle he
had placed against the lower part of his back, under the suit coat.
Sometimes he sat on the hot-water bag as he wrote, a sight that caused
Rosa, when she once saw this, to smile behind her hand. If he left
the hot-water bag in the dining room after lunch, Rosa asked if she
might use it. As a rule he allowed her to, and then she did her work
with the rubber bag pressed against her stomach with her elbow. She
said she had trouble with her liver. That was why the professor did
not mind her going to the maid's room to lie down before leaving,
after she had finished her work.

Once after Rosa had gone home, smelling tobacco smoke in the corridor near her room, the professor entered it to investigate. The room was not more than an elongated cubicle with a narrow bed that lifted sideways against the wall; there was also a small green cabinet, and an adjoining tiny bathroom containing a toilet and a sitz bath fed by a cold-water tap. She often did the laundry on a washboard in the sitz bath, but never, so far as he knew, had bathed in it. The day before her daughter-in-law's name day she had asked permission to take a hot bath in his tub in the big bathroom, and though he had hesitated a moment, the professor finally said yes. In her room, he opened a drawer at the bottom of the cabinet and found a hoard of cigarette butts in it, the butts he had left in ashtrays. He noticed, too, that she had collected his old newspapers and magazines from the wastebaskets. She also saved cord, paper bags, and rubber bands; also pencil stubs he had thrown away. After he found that out, he occasionally gave her some meat left over from lunch, and cheese that had gone dry, to take with her. For this she brought him flowers. She also brought a dirty egg or two her daughter-in-law's hen had laid, but he thanked her and said the yolks were too strong for his taste. He noticed that she needed a pair of shoes, for those she put on to go home in were split in two places, and she wore the same black dress with the tear in it every day, which embarrassed him when he had to speak to her; however, he thought he would refer these matters to his wife when she arrived.

As jobs went, Rosa knew she had a good one. The professor paid well and promptly, and he never ordered her around in the haughty manner of some of her Italian employers. This one was nervous and fussy but not a bad sort. His main fault was his silence. Though he could speak a better than passable Italian, he preferred, when not at work, to sit in an armchair in the living room, reading. Only two souls in the whole apartment, you would think they would want to say something to each other once in a while. Sometimes when she served him a cup of coffee as he read, she tried to get in a word about her troubles. She wanted to tell him about her long, impoverished widowhood, how badly her son had turned out, and what her miserable daughter-in-law was like to live with. But though he listened courteously, although they shared the same roof, and even the same hot-water bottle and bathtub, they almost never shared speech. He said no more to her than a crow would, and clearly showed he preferred to be left alone. So she left him alone and was lonely in the apartment. Working for foreigners had its advantages, she thought, but it also had disadvantages.

After a while the professor noticed that the telephone was ringing regularly for Rosa each afternoon during the time she usually was
resting in her room. In the following week, instead of staying in the
house until four, after her telephone call she asked permission to leave.
At first she said her liver was bothering her, but later she stopped
giving excuses. Although he did not much approve of this sort of
thing, suspecting she would take advantage of him if he was too
liberal in granting favors, he informed her that, until his wife arrived,
she might leave at three on two afternoons of the week, provided that
all her duties were fully discharged. He knew that everything was
done before she left but thought he ought to say it. She listened
meekly—her eyes aglow, lips twitching—and meekly agreed. He pre-
sumed, when he happened to think about it afterwards, that Rosa had
a good spot here, by any standard, and she ought soon to show it in
her face, change her unhappy expression for one less so. However,
this did not happen, for when he chanced to observe her, even on
days when she was leaving early, she seemed sadly preoccupied, sighed
much, as if something on her heart was weighing her down.

He never asked what, preferring not to become involved in whatever it was. These people had endless troubles, and if you let yourself
get involved in them you got endlessly involved. He knew of one
woman, the wife of a colleague, who had said to her maid: "Lucrezia,
I am sympathetic to your condition but I don't want to hear about
it." This, the professor reflected, was basically good policy. It kept
employer-employee relationships where they belonged—on an objective level. He was, after all, leaving Italy in April and would never
in his life see Rosa again. It would do her a lot more good if, say, he
sent her a small check at Christmas, than if he needlessly immersed
himself in her miseries now. The professor knew he was nervous and
often impatient, and he was sometimes sorry for his nature; but he
was what he was and preferred to stay aloof from what did not closely
and personally concern him.

But Rosa would not have it so. One morning she knocked on his
study door, and when he said avanti, she went in embarrassedly, so
that even before she began to speak he was himself embarrassed.

"Professore," Rosa said, unhappily, "please excuse me for bothering your work, but I have to talk to somebody."

"I happen to be very busy," he said, growing a little angry. "Can
it wait awhile?"

"It'll take only a minute. Your troubles hang on all your life but
it doesn't take long to tell them."

"Is it your liver complaint?" he asked.

"No. I need your advice. You're an educated man and I'm no more than an ignorant peasant."

"What kind of advice?" he asked impatiently.

"Call it anything you like. The fact is I have to speak to somebody. I can't talk to my son, even if it were possible in this case. When I open my mouth he roars like a bull. And my daughter-in-law isn't worth wasting my breath on. Sometimes, on the roof, when we're hanging the wash, I say a few words to the portinaia, but she isn't a sympathetic person so I have to come to you, I'll tell you why."

Before he could say how he felt about hearing her confidences, Rosa had launched into a story about this middle-aged government worker in the tax bureau, whom she had happened to meet in the neighborhood. He was married, had four children, and sometimes worked as a carpenter after leaving his office at two o'clock each day. His name was Armando; it was he who telephoned her every afternoon. They had met recently on a bus, and he had, after two or three meetings, seeing that her shoes weren't fit to wear, urged her to let him buy her a new pair. She had told him not to be foolish. One could see he had very little, and it was enough that he took her to the movies twice a week. She had said that, yet every time they met he talked about the shoes he wanted to buy her.

"I'm only human," Rosa frankly told the professor, "and I need the shoes badly, but you know how these things go. If I put on his shoes they may carry me to his bed. That's why I thought I would ask you if I ought to take them."

The professor's face and bald head were flushed. "I don't see how I can possibly advise you—"

"You're the educated one," she said.

"However," he went on, "since the situation is still essentially hypothetical, I will go so far as to say you ought to tell this generous gentleman that his responsibilities should be to his family. He would do well not to offer you gifts, as you will do, not to accept them. If you don't, he can't possibly make any claims upon you or your person. This is all I care to say. Since you have requested advice, I've given it, but I won't say any more."

Rosa sighed. "The truth of it is I could use a pair of shoes. Mine look as though they've been chewed by goats. I haven't had a new pair in six years."

But the professor had nothing more to add.

After Rosa had gone for the day, in thinking about her problem, he decided to buy her a pair of shoes. He was concerned that she might be expecting something of the sort, had planned, so to speak, to have it work out this way. But since this was conjecture only, evidence entirely lacking, he would assume, until proof to the contrary became available, that she had no ulterior motive in asking his advice. He considered giving her five thousand lire to make the purchase of the shoes herself and relieve him of the trouble, but he was doubtful, for there was no guarantee she would use the money for the agreed purpose. Suppose she came in the next day, saying she had had a liver attack that had necessitated calling the doctor, who had charged three thousand lire for his visit; therefore would the professor, in view of these unhappy circumstances, supply an additional three thousand for the shoes? That would never do, so the next morning, when the maid was at the grocer's, the professor slipped into her room and quickly traced on paper the outline of her miserable shoe—a task but he accomplished it quickly. That evening, in a store on the same piazza as the restaurant where he liked to eat, he bought Rosa a pair of brown shoes for fifty-five hundred lire, slightly more than he had planned to spend; but they were a solid pair of ties, walking shoes with a medium heel, a practical gift.

He gave them to Rosa the next day, a Wednesday. He felt embarrassed to be doing that, because he realized that despite his warnings to her, he had permitted himself to meddle in her affairs; but he considered giving her the shoes a psychologically proper move in more ways than one. In presenting her with them he said, "Rosa, I have perhaps a solution to suggest in the matter you discussed with me. Here is a pair of new shoes for you. Tell your friend you must refuse his. And when you do, perhaps it would be advisable also to inform him that you intend to see him a little less frequently from now on."

Rosa was overjoyed at the professor's kindness. She attempted to kiss his hand but he thrust it behind him and retired to his study. On Thursday, when he opened the apartment door to her ring, she was wearing his shoes. She carried a large paper bag from which she offered the professor three small oranges still on a branch with green leaves. He said she needn't have brought them, but Rosa, smiling half-hiddenly in order not to show her teeth, said that she wanted him to see how grateful she was. Later she requested permission to leave at three so she could show Armando her new shoes.

He said dryly, "You may go at that hour if your work is done."

She thanked him profusely. Hastening through her tasks, she left shortly after three, but not before the professor, in his hat, gloves, and bathrobe, standing at his open study door as he was inspecting the corridor floor she had just mopped, saw her hurrying out of the apartment, wearing a pair of dressy black needle-point pumps. This angered him; and when Rosa appeared the next morning, though she begged him not to when he said she had made a fool of him and he was firing her to teach her a lesson, the professor did. She wept, pleading for another chance, but he would not change his mind. So she desolately wrapped up the odds and ends in her room in a news-paper and left, still crying. Afterwards he was upset and very nervous. He could not stand the cold that day and he could not work.

A week later, the morning the heat was turned on, Rosa appeared at the apartment door and begged to have her job back. She was distraught, said her son had hit her, and gently touched her puffed black-and-blue lip. With tears in her eyes, although she didn't cry, Rosa explained it was no fault of hers that she had accepted both pairs of shoes. Armando had given her his pair first; had, out of jealousy of a possible rival, forced her to take them. Then when the professor had kindly offered his pair of shoes, she had wanted to refuse them but was afraid of angering him and losing her job. This was God's truth, so help her St. Peter. She would, she promised, find Armando, whom she had not seen in a week, and return his shoes if the professor would take her back. If he didn't, she would throw herself into the Tiber. He, though he didn't care for talk of this kind, felt a certain sympathy for her. He was disappointed in himself at the way he had handled her. It would have been better to have said a few appropriate words on the subject of honesty and then philo-sophically dropped the matter. In firing her he had only made things difficult for them both, because, in the meantime, he had tried two other maids and found them unsuitable. One stole, the other was lazy. As a result the house was a mess, impossible for him to work in, although the portinaia came up for an hour each morning to clean. It was his good fortune that Rosa had appeared at the door just then. When she removed her coat, he noticed with satisfaction that the tear in her dress had finally been mended.

She went grimly to work, dusting, polishing, cleaning everything in sight. She unmade beds, then made them, swept under them, mopped, polished head- and footboards, adorned the beds with newly pressed spreads. Though she had just got her job back and worked with her usual efficiency, she worked, he observed, in sadness, fre-quently sighing, attempting a smile only when his eye was on her. This is their nature, he thought; they have hard lives. To spare her further blows by her son he gave her permission to live in. He offered extra money to buy meat for her supper but she refused it, saying pasta would do. Pasta and green salad was all she ate at night. Occasionally she boiled an artichoke left over from lunch and ate it with oil and vinegar. He invited her to drink the white wine in the cupboard and take fruit. Once in a while she did, always telling what and how much, though he repeatedly asked her not to. The apartment was nicely in order. Though the phone rang, as usual, daily at three, only seldom did she leave the house after she had talked to Armando.

Then one dismal morning Rosa came to the professor and in her distraught way confessed she was pregnant. Her face was lit in despair; her white underwear shone through her black dress.

He felt annoyance, disgust, blaming himself for having re-employed her.

"You must leave at once," he said, trying to keep his voice from trembling.

"I can't," she said. "My son will kill me. In God's name, help me, professore."

He was infuriated by her stupidity. "Your sexual adventures are none of my responsibility.

"Was it this Armando?" he asked almost savagely.

She nodded.

"Have you informed him?"

"He says he can't believe it." She tried to smile but couldn't.

"I'll convince him," he said. "Do you have his telephone number?"

She told it to him. He called Armando at his office, identified himself, and asked the government clerk to come at once to the apartment. "You have a grave responsibility to Rosa."

"I have a grave responsibility to my family," Armando answered.

"You might have considered them before this."

"All right, I'll come over tomorrow after work. It's impossible today. I have a carpentering contract to finish up."

"She'll expect you," the professor said.

When he hung up he felt less angry, although still more emotional than he cared to feel. "Are you quite sure of your condition?" he asked her, "that you are pregnant?"

"Yes." She was crying now. "Tomorrow is my son's birthday. What a beautiful present it will be for him to find out his mother's a whore. He'll break my bones, if not with his hands, then with his teeth."

"It hardly seems likely you can conceive, considering your age."

"My mother gave birth at fifty."

"Isn't there a possibility you are mistaken?"

"I don't know. It's never been this way before. After all, I've been a widow—"

"Well, you'd better find out."

"Yes, I want to," Rosa said. "I want to see the midwife in my neighborhood but I haven't got a single lira. I spent all I had left when I wasn't working, and I had to borrow carfare to get here. Armando can't help me just now. He has to pay for his wife's teeth this week. She has very bad teeth, poor thing. That's why I came to you. Could you advance me two thousand of my pay so I can be examined by the midwife?"

After a minute he counted two one-thousand-lire notes out of his wallet. "Go to her now," he said. He was about to add that if she was pregnant, not to come back, but he was afraid she might do something desperate, or lie to him so she could go on working. He didn't want her around anymore. When he thought of his wife and daughter arriving amid this mess, he felt sick with nervousness. He wanted to get rid of the maid as soon as possible.

The next day Rosa came in at twelve instead of nine. Her dark face was pale. "Excuse me for being late," she murmured. "I was praying at my husband's grave."

"That's all right," the professor said. "But did you go to the midwife?"

"Not yet."

"Why not?" Though angry he spoke calmly.

She stared at the floor.

"Please answer my question."

"I was going to say I lost the two thousand lire on the bus, but after being at my husband's grave I'll tell you the truth. After all, it's bound to come out."

This is terrible, he thought, it's unending. "What did you do with the money?"

"That's what I mean," Rosa sighed. "I bought my son a present. Not that he deserves it, but it was his birthday." She burst into tears.

He stared at her a minute, then said, "Please come with me."

The professor left the apartment in his bathrobe, and Rosa followed. Opening the elevator door he stepped inside, holding the door for her. She entered the elevator.

They stopped two floors below. He got out and nearsightedly scanned the names on the brass plates above the bells. Finding the one he wanted, he pressed the button. A maid opened the door and let them in. She seemed frightened by Rosa's expression.

"Is the doctor in?" the professor asked the doctor's maid.

"I will see."

"Please ask him if he'll see me for a minute. I live in the building, two flights up."

"Sì, signore." She glanced again at Rosa, then went inside.

The Italian doctor came out, a short middle-aged man with a beard. The professor had once or twice passed him in the cortile of the apartment house. The doctor was buttoning his shirt cuff.

"I am sorry to trouble you, sir," said the professor. "This is my maid, who has been having some difficulty. She would like to determine whether she is pregnant. Can you assist her?"

The doctor looked at him, then at the maid, who had a handkerchief to her eyes.

"Let her come into my office."

"Thank you," said the professor. The doctor nodded.

The professor went up to his apartment. In a half hour the phone rang.

"Pronto."

It was the doctor. "She is not pregnant," he said. "She is frightened. She also has trouble with her liver."

"Can you be certain, doctor?"

"Yes."

"Thank you," said the professor. "If you write her a prescription, please have it charged to me, and also send me your bill."

"I will," said the doctor, and hung up.

Rosa came into the apartment. "The doctor told you?" the professor said. "You aren't pregnant."

"It's the Virgin's blessing," said Rosa.

Speaking quietly, he then told her she would have to go. "I'm sorry, Rosa, but I simply cannot be constantly caught up in this sort of thing. It upsets me and I can't work."

She turned her head away.

The doorbell rang. It was Armando, a small thin man in a long gray overcoat. He was wearing a rakish black Borsalino and a slight mustache. He had dark, worried eyes. He tipped his hat to them.

Rosa told him she was leaving the apartment.

"Then let me help you get your things," Armando said. He followed her to the maid's room and they wrapped Rosa's things in newspaper.

When they came out of the room, Armando carrying a shopping bag, Rosa holding a shoe box wrapped in a newspaper, the professor handed Rosa the remainder of her month's wages.

"I'm sorry," he said, "but I have my wife and daughter to think of. They'll be here in a few days."

She answered nothing. Armando, smoking a cigarette butt, gently opened the door for her and they left together.

Later the professor inspected the maid's room and saw that Rosa had taken all her belongings but the shoes he had given her. When his wife arrived in the apartment, shortly before Thanksgiving, she gave the shoes to the portinaia, who wore them a week, then gave them to her daughter-in-law.

1959

Idiots First

The thick ticking of the tin clock stopped. Mendel, dozing in the dark, awoke in fright. The pain returned as he listened. He drew on his cold embittered clothing, and wasted minutes sitting at the edge of the bed.

"Isaac," he ultimately sighed.

In the kitchen, Isaac, his astonished mouth open, held six peanuts in his palm. He placed each on the table. "One . . . two . . . nine."

He gathered each peanut and appeared in the doorway. Mendel, in loose hat and long overcoat, still sat on the bed. Isaac watched with small eyes and ears, thick hair graying the sides of his head.

"Schlaf," he nasally said.

"No," muttered Mendel. As if stifling he rose. "Come, Isaac."

He wound his old watch though the sight of the stopped clock nauseated him.

Isaac wanted to hold it to his ear.

"No, it's late." Mendel put the watch carefully away. In the drawer he found the little paper bag of crumpled ones and fives and slipped it into his overcoat pocket. He helped Isaac on with his coat.

Isaac looked at one dark window, then at the other. Mendel stared at both blank windows.

They went slowly down the darkly lit stairs, Mendel first, Isaac watching the moving shadows on the wall. To one long shadow he offered a peanut.

"Hungrig."

In the vestibule the old man gazed through the thin glass. The November night was cold and bleak. Opening the door he cautiously thrust his head out. Though he saw nothing he quickly shut the door.

"Ginzburg, that he came to see me yesterday," he whispered in Isaac's ear.

Isaac sucked air.

"You know who I mean?"

Isaac combed his chin with his fingers.

"That's the one, with the black whiskers. Don't talk to him or go with him if he asks you."

Isaac moaned.

"Young people he don't bother so much," Mendel said in afterthought.

It was suppertime and the street was empty but the store windows dimly lit their way to the corner. They crossed the deserted street and went on. Isaac, with a happy cry, pointed to the three golden balls. Mendel smiled but was exhausted when they got to the pawnshop.

The pawnbroker, a red-bearded man with black horn-rimmed glasses, was eating a whitefish at the rear of the store. He craned his head, saw them, and settled back to sip his tea.

In five minutes he came forward, patting his shapeless lips with a large white handkerchief.

Mendel, breathing heavily, handed him the worn gold watch. The pawnbroker, raising his glasses, screwed in his eyepiece. He turned the watch over once. "Eight dollars."

The dying man wet his cracked lips. "I must have thirty-five."

"So go to Rothschild."

"Cost me myself sixty."

"In 1905." The pawnbroker handed back the watch. It had stopped ticking. Mendel wound it slowly. It ticked hollowly.

"Isaac must go to my uncle that he lives in California."

"It's a free country," said the pawnbroker.

Isaac, watching a banjo, snickered.

"What's the matter with him?" the pawnbroker asked.

"So let be eight dollars," muttered Mendel, "but where will I get the rest till tonight?

"How much for my hat and coat?" he asked.

"No sale." The pawnbroker went behind the cage and wrote out a ticket. He locked the watch in a small drawer but Mendel still heard it ticking.

In the street he slipped the eight dollars into the paper bag, then searched in his pockets for a scrap of writing. Finding it, he strained to read the address by the light of the street lamp.

As they trudged to the subway, Mendel pointed to the sprinkled sky.

"Isaac, look how many stars are tonight."

"Eggs," said Isaac.

"First we will go to Mr. Fishbein, after we will eat."

They got off the train in upper Manhattan and had to walk several blocks before they located Fishbein's house.

"A regular palace," Mendel murmured, looking forward to a moment's warmth.

Isaac stared uneasily at the heavy door of the house.

Mendel rang. The servant, a man with long sideburns, came to the door and said Mr. and Mrs. Fishbein were dining and could see no one.

"He should eat in peace but we will wait till he finishes."

"Come back tomorrow morning. Tomorrow morning Mr. Fishbein will talk to you. He don't do business or charity at this time of the night."

"Charity I am not interested—"

"Come back tomorrow."

"Tell him it's life or death—"

"Whose life or death?"

"So if not his, then mine."

"Don't be such a big smart aleck."

"Look me in my face," said Mendel, "and tell me if I got time till tomorrow morning?"

The servant stared at him, then at Isaac, and reluctantly let them in.

The foyer was a vast high-ceilinged room with many oil paintings on the walls, voluminous silken draperies, a thick flowered rug at foot, and a marble staircase.

Mr. Fishbein, a paunchy bald-headed man with hairy nostrils and small patent-leather feet, ran lightly down the stairs, a large napkin tucked under a tuxedo coat button. He stopped on the fifth step from the bottom and examined his visitors.

"Who comes on Friday night to a man that he has guests, to spoil him his supper?"

"Excuse me that I bother you, Mr. Fishbein," Mendel said. "If I didn't come now I couldn't come tomorrow."

"Without more preliminaries, please state your business. I'm a hungry man."

"Hungrig," wailed Isaac.

Fishbein adjusted his pince-nez. "What's the matter with him?"

"This is my son Isaac. He is like this all his life."

Isaac mewled.

"I am sending him to California."

"Mr. Fishbein don't contribute to personal pleasure trips."

"I am a sick man and he must go tonight on the train to my Uncle Leo."

"I never give to unorganized charity," Fishbein said, "but if you are hungry I will invite you downstairs in my kitchen. We having tonight chicken with stuffed derma."

"All I ask is thirty-five dollars for the train ticket to my uncle in California. I have already the rest."

"Who is your uncle? How old a man?"

"Eighty-one years, a long life to him."

Fishbein burst into laughter. "Eighty-one years and you are sending him this halfwit."

Mendel, flailing both arms, cried, "Please, without names."

Fishbein politely conceded.

"Where is open the door there we go in the house," the sick man said. "If you will kindly give me thirty-five dollars, God will bless you. What is thirty-five dollars to Mr. Fishbein? Nothing. To me, for my boy, is everything."

Fishbein drew himself up to his tallest height.

"Private contributions I don't make—only to institutions. This is my fixed policy."

Mendel sank to his creaking knees on the rug.

"Please, Mr. Fishbein, if not thirty-five, give maybe twenty."

"Levinson!" Fishbein angrily called.

The servant with the long sideburns appeared at the top of the stairs.

"Show this party where is the door—unless he wishes to partake food before leaving the premises."

"For what I got chicken won't cure it," Mendel said.

"This way if you please," said Levinson, descending.

Isaac assisted his father up.

"Take him to an institution," Fishbein advised over the marble balustrade. He ran quickly up the stairs and they were at once outside, buffeted by winds.

The walk to the subway was tedious. The wind blew mournfully. Mendel, breathless, glanced furtively at shadows. Isaac, clutching his peanuts in his frozen fist, clung to his father's side. They entered a small park to rest for a minute on a stone bench under a leafless two-branched tree. The thick right branch was raised, the thin left one hung down. A very pale moon rose slowly. So did a stranger as they approached the bench.

"Gut yuntif," he said hoarsely.

Mendel, drained of blood, waved his wasted arms. Isaac yowled sickly. Then a bell chimed and it was only ten. Mendel let out a piercing anguished cry as the bearded stranger disappeared into the bushes. A policeman came running and, though he beat the bushes with his nightstick, could turn up nothing. Mendel and Isaac hurried out of the little park. When Mendel glanced back the dead tree had its thin arm raised, the thick one down. He moaned.

They boarded a trolley, stopping at the home of a former friend, but he had died years ago. On the same block they went into a cafeteria and ordered two fried eggs for Isaac. The tables were crowded except where a heavyset man sat eating soup with kasha. After one look at him they left in haste, although Isaac wept.

Mendel had another address on a slip of paper but the house was too far away, in Queens, so they stood in a doorway shivering.

What can I do, he frantically thought, in one short hour?

He remembered the furniture in the house. It was junk but might bring a few dollars. "Come, Isaac." They went once more to the pawnbroker's to talk to him, but the shop was dark and an iron gate—rings and gold watches glinting through it—was drawn tight across his place of business.

They huddled behind a telephone pole, both freezing. Isaac whimpered.

"See the big moon, Isaac. The whole sky is white."

He pointed but Isaac wouldn't look.

Mendel dreamed for a minute of the sky lit up, long sheets of light in all directions. Under the sky, in California, sat Uncle Leo drinking tea with lemon. Mendel felt warm but woke up cold.

Across the street stood an ancient brick synagogue.

He pounded on the huge door but no one appeared. He waited till he had breath and desperately knocked again. At last there were footsteps within, and the synagogue door creaked open on its massive brass hinges.

A darkly dressed sexton, holding a dripping candle, glared at them.

"Who knocks this time of night with so much noise on the synagogue door?"

Mendel told the sexton his troubles. "Please, I would like to speak to the rabbi."

"The rabbi is an old man. He sleeps now. His wife won't let you see him. Go home and come back tomorrow."

"To tomorrow I said goodbye already. I am a dying man."

Though the sexton seemed doubtful he pointed to an old wooden house next door. "In there he lives." He disappeared into the synagogue with his lit candle casting shadows around him.

Mendel, with Isaac clutching his sleeve, went up the wooden steps and rang the bell. After five minutes a big-faced, gray-haired bulky woman came out on the porch with a torn robe thrown over her nightdress. She emphatically said the rabbi was sleeping and could not be waked.

But as she was insisting, the rabbi himself tottered to the door. He listened a minute and said, "Who wants to see me let them come in."

They entered a cluttered room. The rabbi was an old skinny man with bent shoulders and a wisp of white beard. He wore a flannel nightgown and black skullcap; his feet were bare.

"Vey is mir," his wife muttered. "Put on shoes or tomorrow comes sure pneumonia." She was a woman with a big belly, years younger than her husband. Staring at Isaac, she turned away.

Mendel apologetically related his errand. "All I need more is thirty-five dollars."

"Thirty-five?" said the rabbi's wife. "Why not thirty-five thousand? Who has so much money? My husband is a poor rabbi. The doctors take away every penny."

"Dear friend," said the rabbi, "if I had I would give you."

"I got already seventy," Mendel said, heavy-hearted. "All I need more is thirty-five."

"God will give you," said the rabbi.

"In the grave," said Mendel. "I need tonight. Come, Isaac."

"Wait," called the rabbi.

He hurried inside, came out with a fur-lined caftan, and handed it to Mendel.

"Yascha," shrieked his wife, "not your new coat!"

"I got my old one. Who needs two coats for one body?"

"Yascha, I am screaming—"

"Who can go among poor people, tell me, in a new coat?"

"Yascha," she cried, "what can this man do with your coat? He needs tonight the money. The pawnbrokers are asleep."

"So let him wake them up."

"No." She grabbed the coat from Mendel.

He held on to a sleeve, wrestling her for the coat. Her I know, Mendel thought. "Shylock," he muttered. Her eyes glittered.

The rabbi groaned and tottered dizzily. His wife cried out as Mendel yanked the coat from her hands.

"Run," cried the rabbi.

"Run, Isaac."

They ran out of the house and down the steps.

"Stop, you thief," called the rabbi's wife.

The rabbi pressed both hands to his temples and fell to the floor.

"Help!" his wife wept. "Heart attack! Help!"

But Mendel and Isaac ran through the streets with the rabbi's new fur-lined caftan. After them noiselessly ran Ginzburg.

It was very late when Mendel bought the train ticket in the only booth open.

There was no time to stop for a sandwich so Isaac ate his peanuts and they hurried to the train in the vast deserted station.

"So in the morning," Mendel gasped as they ran, "there comes a man that he sells sandwiches and coffee. Eat but get change. When reaches California the train, will be waiting for you on the station Uncle Leo. If you don't recognize him he will recognize you. Tell him I send best regards."

But when they arrived at the gate to the platform it was shut, the light out.

Mendel, groaning, beat on the gate with his fists.

"Too late," said the uniformed ticket collector, a bulky, bearded man with hairy nostrils and a fishy smell.

He pointed to the station clock. "Already past twelve."

"But I see standing there still the train," Mendel said, hopping in his grief.

"It just left—in one more minute."

"A minute is enough. Just open the gate."

"Too late I told you."

Mendel socked his bony chest with both hands. "With my whole heart I beg you this little favor."

"Favors you had enough already. For you the train is gone. You shoulda been dead already at midnight. I told you that yesterday. This is the best I can do."

"Ginzburg!" Mendel shrank from him.

"Who else?" The voice was metallic, eyes glittered, the expression amused.

"For myself," the old man begged, "I don't ask a thing. But what will happen to my boy?"

Ginzburg shrugged slightly. "What will happen happens. This isn't my responsibility. I got enough to think about without worrying about somebody on one cylinder."

"What then is your responsibility?"

"To create conditions. To make happen what happens. I ain't in the anthropomorphic business."

"Whatever business you in, where is your pity?"

"This ain't my commodity. The law is the law."

"Which law is this?"

"The cosmic universal law, goddamnit, the one I got to follow myself."

"What kind of a law is it?" cried Mendel. "For godsake, don't you understand what I went through in my life with this poor boy? Look at him. For thirty-nine years, since the day he was born, I wait for him to grow up, but he don't. Do you understand what this means in a father's heart? Why don't you let him go to his uncle?" His voice had risen and he was shouting.

Isaac mewled loudly.

"Better calm down or you'll hurt somebody's feelings," Ginzburg said with a wink toward Isaac.

"All my life," Mendel cried, his body trembling, "what did I have? I was poor. I suffered from my health. When I worked I worked too hard. When I didn't work was worse. My wife died a young woman. But I didn't ask from anybody nothing. Now I ask a small favor. Be so kind, Mr. Ginzburg."

The ticket collector was picking his teeth with a matchstick.

"You ain't the only one, my friend, some got it worse than you. That's how it goes in this country."

"You dog you." Mendel lunged at Ginzburg's throat and began to choke. "You bastard, don't you understand what it means human?"

They struggled nose to nose. Ginzburg, though his astonished eyes bulged, began to laugh. "You pipsqueak nothing. I'll freeze you to pieces."

His eyes lit in rage and Mendel felt an unbearable cold like an icy dagger invading his body, all of his parts shriveling.

Now I die without helping Isaac.

A crowd gathered. Isaac yelped in fright.

Clinging to Ginzburg in his last agony, Mendel saw reflected in the ticket collector's eyes the depth of his terror. But he saw that Ginzburg, staring at himself in Mendel's eyes, saw mirrored in them the extent of his own awful wrath. He beheld a shimmering, starry, blinding light that produced darkness.

Ginzburg looked astounded. "Who me?"

His grip on the squirming old man slowly loosened, and Mendel, his heart barely beating, slumped to the ground.

"Go," Ginzburg muttered, "take him to the train."

"Let pass," he commanded a guard.

The crowd parted. Isaac helped his father up and they tottered down the steps to the platform where the train waited, lit and ready to go.

Mendel found Isaac a coach seat and hastily embraced him. "Help Uncle Leo, Isaakil. Also remember your father and mother."

"Be nice to him," he said to the conductor. "Show him where everything is."

He waited on the platform until the train began slowly to move. Isaac sat at the edge of his seat, his face strained in the direction of his journey. When the train was gone, Mendel ascended the stairs to see what had become of Ginzburg.

1961

Still Life

1

Months after vainly seeking a studio on the Via Margutta, del Babuino, della Croce, and elsewhere in that neighborhood, Arthur Fidelman settled for part of a crowded, windowy, attic-like atelier on a cobblestone street in the Trastevere, strung high with sheets and underwear. He had, a week before, in "personal notices" in the American-language newspaper in Rome, read: "Studio to share, cheap, many advantages, etc., A. Oliovino," and after much serious anguish (the curt advertisement having recalled dreams he had dreamed were dead), many indecisions, enunciations, and renunciations, Fidelman had, one very cold late-December morning, hurried to the address given, a worn four-story building with a yellowish façade stained brown along the edges. On the top floor, in a thickly cluttered artist's studio smelling aromatically of turpentine and oil paints, the inspiring sight of an easel lit in unwavering light from the three large windows setting the former art student on fire once more to paint, he had dealt not with a pittore, as expected, but with a pittrice, Annamaria Oliovino.

The pittrice, a thin, almost gaunt, high-voiced, restless type, with short black uncombed hair, violet mouth, distracted eyes and tense neck, a woman with narrow buttocks and piercing breasts, was in her way attractive if not in truth beautiful. She had on a thick black woolen sweater, eroded black velveteen culottes, black socks, and leather sandals spotted with drops of paint. Fidelman and she eyed each other stealthily and he realized at once she was, as a woman, indifferent to him or his type, who or which made no difference. But after ten minutes, despite the turmoil she exuded even as she dispassionately answered his hesitant questions, the art student, ever a sucker for strange beauty and all sorts of experiences, felt himself involved with and falling for her. Not my deep dish, he warned himself, aware of all the dangers to him and his renewed desire to create art; yet he was already half in love with her. It can't be, he thought in desperation; but it could. It had happened to him before. In her presence he tightly shut both eyes and wholeheartedly wished against what might be. Really he trembled, and though he labored to extricate his fate from hers, he was already a plucked bird, greased, and ready for frying. Fidelman protested within—cried out severely against the weak self, called himself ferocious names but could do not much, a victim of his familiar response, a too passionate fondness for strangers. So Annamaria, who had advertised a twenty-thousand-lire monthly rental, in the end doubled the sum, and Fidelman paid through both nostrils, cash for first and last months (should he attempt to fly by night) plus a deposit of ten thousand for possible damages. An hour later he moved in with his imitation-leather suitcase. This happened in the dead of winter. Below the cold sunlit windows stood two frozen umbrella pines and beyond, in the near distance, sparkled the icy Tiber.

The studio was well heated, Annamaria had insisted, but the cold leaked in through the wide windows. It was more a blast; the art student shivered but was kept warm by his hidden love for the pittrice. It took him most of a day to clear himself a space to work, about a third of the studio was as much as he could manage. He stacked her canvases five deep against her portion of the walls, curious to examine them, but Annamaria watched his every move (he noticed several self-portraits) although she was at the same time painting a monumental natura morta of a loaf of bread with two garlic bulbs ("Pane ed Aglii"). He moved stacks of *Oggi*, piles of postcards and yellowed letters, and a bundle of calendars going back to many years ago; also a Perugina candy box full of broken pieces of Etruscan pottery, one of small sea shells, and a third of medallions of various saints and of the Virgin, which she warned him to handle with care. He had uncovered a sagging cot by a dripping stone sink in his corner of the studio and there he slept. She furnished an old chafing dish and a broken table, and he bought a few household things he needed. Annamaria rented the art student an easel for a thousand lire a month. Her quarters were private, a room at the other end of the studio whose door she kept locked, handing him the key when he had to use the toilet. The wall was thin and the instrument noisy. He could hear the whistle and rush of her water, and though he tried to be quiet, because of the plumbing the bowl was always brimful and the pour of his stream embarrassed him. At night, if there was need, although he was tempted to use the sink, he fished out the yellowed, sedimented pot under his bed; once or twice, as he was using it in the thick of night, he had the impression she was awake and listening.

They painted in their overcoats, Annamaria wearing a black babushka, Fidelman a green wool hat pulled down over his frozen ears. She kept a pan of hot coals at her feet and every so often lifted a sandaled foot to toast it. The marble floor of the studio was sheer thick ice; Fidelman wore two pairs of tennis socks his sister, Bessie, had recently sent him from the States. Annamaria, a lefty, painted with a smeared leather glove on her hand, and theoretically his easel had been arranged so that he couldn't see what she was doing but he often sneaked looks at her work. The pittrice, to his surprise, painted with flicks of her fingers and wrists, peering at her performance with almost shut eyes. He noticed she alternated still lifes with huge lyric abstractions—massive whorls of red and gold exploding in all directions, these built on, entwined with, and ultimately concealing a small black religious cross, her first two brushstrokes on every abstract canvas. Once when Fidelman gathered the nerve to ask her why the cross, she answered it was the symbol that gave the painting its meaning.

He was eager to know more but she was impatient. "Eh," she shrugged, "who can explain art."

Though her response to his various attempts to become better acquainted were as a rule curt, and her voluntary attention to him, shorter still—she was able, apparently, to pretend he wasn't there—Fidelman's feeling for Annamaria grew, and he was as unhappy in love as he had ever been.

But he was patient, a persistent virtue, served her often in various capacities, for instance carrying down four flights of stairs her two bags of garbage shortly after supper—the portinaia was crippled and the portiere never around—sweeping the studio clean each morning, even running to retrieve a brush or paint tube when she happened to drop one—offering any service any time, you name it. She accepted these small favors without giving them notice.

One morning after reading a many-paged letter she had just got in the mail, Annamaria was sad, sullen, unable to work; she paced

around restlessly, it troubled him. But after feverishly painting a wid-
ening purple spiral that continued off the canvas, she regained a measure of repose. This heightened her beauty, lent it somehow a youthful
quality it didn't ordinarily have—he guessed her to be no older than
twenty-seven or -eight; so Fidelman, inspired by the change in her,
hoping it might foretoken better luck for him, approached Annamaria,
removed his hat, and suggested since she went out infrequently why
not lunch for a change at the trattoria at the corner, Guido's, where
workmen assembled and the veal and white wine were delicious? She,
to his surprise, after darting an uneasy glance out of the window at
the tops of the motionless umbrella pines, abruptly assented. They ate
well and conversed like human beings, although she mostly limited
herself to answering his modest questions. She informed Fidelman she
had come from Naples to Rome two years ago, although it seemed
much longer, and he told her he was from the United States. Being
so physically close to her, able to inhale the odor of her body—like
salted flowers—and intimately eating together, excited Fidelman, and
he sat very still, not to rock the boat and spill a drop of what was so
precious to him. Annamaria ate hungrily, her eyes usually lowered.
Once she looked at him with a shade of a smile and he felt beatitude;
the art student contemplated many such meals though he could ill
afford them, every cent he spent saved and sent by Bessie.

After zuppa inglese and a peeled apple she patted her lips with
a napkin and, still in good humor, suggested they take the bus to the
Piazza del Popolo and visit some painter friends of hers.

"I'll introduce you to Alberto Moravia."

"With pleasure," Fidelman said, bowing.

But when they stepped into the street and were walking to the
bus stop near the river a cold wind blew up and Annamaria turned
pale.

"Something wrong?" Fidelman inquired.

"The East Wind," she answered testily.

"What wind?"

"The Evil Eye," she said with irritation. "Malocchio."

He had heard something of the sort. They returned quickly to the
studio, their heads lowered against the noisy wind, the pittrice from
time to time furtively crossing herself. A black-habited old nun passed
them at the trattoria corner, from whom Annamaria turned in torment,
muttering, "Jettatura! Porca miseria!" When they were upstairs in the
studio she insisted Fidelman touch his testicles three times to undo or
dispel who knows what witchcraft, and he modestly obliged. Her re-

quest had inflamed him although he cautioned himself to remember it was, in purpose and essence, theological.

Later she received a visitor, a man who came to see her on Monday and Friday afternoons after his work in a government bureau. Her visitors, always men, whispered with her a minute, then left restlessly; most of them, excepting also Giancarlo Balducci, a cross-eyed illustrator—Fidelman never saw again. But the one who came oftenest stayed longest, a solemn gray-haired gent, Augusto Ottogalli, with watery blue eyes and missing side teeth, old enough to be her father for sure. He wore a slanted black fedora, and a shabby gray overcoat too large for him, greeted Fidelman vacantly, and made him inordinately jealous. When Augusto arrived in the afternoon the pittrice usually dropped anything she was doing and they retired to her room, at once locked and bolted. The art student wandered alone in the studio for dreadful hours. When Augusto ultimately emerged, looking disheveled, and if successful, defeated, Fidelman turned his back on him and the old man hastily let himself out of the door. After his visits, and only his, Annamaria did not appear in the studio for the rest of the day. Once when Fidelman knocked on her door to invite her out to supper, she told him to use the pot because she had a headache and was sound asleep. On another occasion when Augusto was locked long in her room with her, after a tormenting two hours Fidelman tiptoed over and put his jealous ear to the door. All he could hear was the buzz and sigh of their whispering. Peeking through the keyhole he saw them both in their overcoats, sitting on her bed, Augusto tightly clasping her hands, whispering passionately, his nose empurpled with emotion, Annamaria's white face averted. When the art student checked an hour afterwards, they were still at it, the old man imploring, the pittrice weeping. The next time, Augusto came with a priest, a portly, heavy-breathing man with a doubtful face. But as soon as they appeared in the studio Annamaria, enraged to fury, despite the impassioned entreatments of Augusto, began to throw at them anything of hers or Fidelman's she could lay hands on.

"Bloodsuckers!" she shouted, "scorpions! parasites!" until they had hastily retreated. Yet when Augusto, worn and harried, returned alone, without complaint she retired to her room with him.

2

Fidelman's work, despite the effort and despair he gave it, was going poorly. Every time he looked at unpainted canvas he saw harlequins, whores, tragic kings, fragmented musicians, the sick and the dread. Still, tradition was tradition and what if he should want to make more? Since he had always loved art history he considered embarking on a "Mother and Child," but was afraid her image would come out too much Bessie—after all, fifteen years between them. Or maybe a moving "Pietà," the dead son's body held like a broken wave in mama's frail arms? A curse on art history—he fought the fully prefigured picture though some of his former best paintings had jumped in every detail to the mind. Yet if so, where's true engagement? Sometimes I'd like to forget every picture I've seen, Fidelman thought. Almost in panic he sketched in charcoal a coattailed "Figure of a Jew Fleeing" and quickly hid it away. After that, ideas, prefigured or not, were scarce. "Astonish me," he muttered to himself, wondering whether to return to surrealism. He also considered a series of "Relations to Place and Space," constructions in squares and circles, the pleasures of tri-dimensional geometry of linear abstraction, only he had little heart for it. The furthest abstraction, Fidelman thought, is the blank canvas. A moment later he asked himself, if painting shows who you are, why should not painting?

After the incident with the priest Annamaria was despondent for a week, stayed in her room sometimes bitterly crying, Fidelman often standing helplessly by her door. However this was a prelude to a burst of creativity by the pittrice. Works by the dozens leaped from her brush and stylus. She continued her lyric abstractions based on the theme of a hidden cross and spent hours with a long black candle, burning holes in heavy white paper ("Buchi Spontanei"). Having mixed coffee grounds, sparkling bits of crushed mirror, and ground-up sea shells, she blew the dust on mucilaged paper ("Velo nella Nebbia"). She composed collages of rags and toilet tissue. After a dozen linear studies ("Linee Discendenti"), she experimented with gold leaf sprayed with umber, the whole while wet combed in long undulations with a fine comb. She framed this in a black frame and hung it on end like a diamond ("Luce di Candela"). Annamaria worked intently, her brow furrowed, violet mouth tightly pursed, eyes lit, nostrils palpitating in creative excitement. And when she had temporarily run out of new ideas she did a mythological bull in red clay ("La Donna Toro"), afterwards returning to nature morte with bunches of bananas; then self-portraits.

The pittrice occasionally took time out to see what Fidelman was up to, although not much, and then editing his efforts. She changed lines and altered figures, or swabbed paint over whole compositions that didn't appeal to her. There was not much that did, but Fidelman was grateful for any attention she gave his work, and even kept at it to incite her criticism. He could feel his heart beat in his teeth whenever she stood close to him modifying his work, he deeply breathing her intimate smell of sweating flowers. She used perfume only when Augusto came and it disappointed Fidelman that the old man should evoke the use of bottled fragrance; yet he was cheered that her natural odor, which he, so to say, got for free, was so much more exciting than the stuff she doused herself with for her decrepit Romeo. He had noticed she had a bit of soft belly but he loved the pliant roundness and often daydreamed of it. Thinking it might please her, for he pleased her rarely (he reveried how it would be once she understood the true depth of his love for her), the art student experimented with some of the things Annamaria had done—the spontaneous holes, for instance, several studies of "Lines Ascending," and two lyrical abstract expressionistic pieces based on, interwoven with, and ultimately concealing a Star of David, although for these attempts he soon discovered he had earned, instead of her good will, an increased measure of scorn.

However, Annamaria continued to eat lunch with him at Guido's, and more often than not, supper, although she said practically nothing during meals and afterwards let her eye roam over the faces of the men at the other tables. But there were times after they had eaten when she would agree to go for a short walk with Fidelman, if there was no serious wind; and once in a while they entered a movie in the Trastevere, for she hated to cross any of the bridges of the Tiber, and then only in a bus, sitting stiffly, staring ahead. As they were once riding, Fidelman seized the opportunity to hold her tense fist in his, but as soon as they were across the river she tore it out of his grasp. He was by now giving her presents—tubes of paints, the best brushes, a few yards of Belgian linen, which she accepted without comment; she also borrowed small sums from him, nothing startling—a hundred lire today, five hundred tomorrow. And she announced one morning that he would thereafter, since he used so much of both, have to pay additional for water and electricity—he already paid extra for the heatless heat. Fidelman, though continually worried about money, assented. He would have given his last lira to lie on her soft belly, but she offered niente, not so much as a caress; until one day, he was permitted to look on as she sketched herself nude in his presence. Since it was bitter cold the pittrice did this in two stages. First she removed her sweater and brassiere and, viewing herself in a long, faded mirror, quickly sketched the upper half of her body before it turned blue. He was dizzily enamored of her form and flesh. Hastily fastening the brassiere and pulling on her sweater, Annamaria stepped out of her sandals and peeled off her culottes, and white panties torn at the crotch, then drew the rest of herself down to her toes. The art student begged permission to sketch along with her but the pittrice denied it, so he had, as best one can, to commit to memory her lovely treasures—the hard, piercing breasts, narrow shapely buttocks, vine-hidden labia, the font and sweet beginning of time. After she had drawn herself and dressed, and when Augusto appeared and they had retired behind her bolted door, Fidelman sat motionless on his high stool before the glittering blue-skied windows, slowly turning to ice to faint strains of Bach.

3

The art student increased his services to Annamaria, her increase was scorn, or so it seemed. This severely bruised his spirit. What have I done to deserve such treatment? That I pay my plenty of rent on time? That I buy her all sorts of presents, not to mention two full meals a day? That I live in flaming hot and freezing cold? That I passionately adore each sweet-and-sour bit of her? He figured it bored her to see so much of him. For a week Fidelman disappeared during the day, sat in cold libraries or stood around in frosty museums. He tried painting after midnight and into the early-morning hours but the pittrice found out and unscrewed the bulbs before she went to bed. "Don't waste my electricity, this isn't America." He screwed in a dim blue bulb and worked silently from 1 a.m. to 5. At dawn he discovered he had painted a blue picture. Fidelman wandered in the streets of the city. At night he slept in the studio and could hear her sleeping in her room. She slept restlessly, dreamed badly, and often moaned. He dreamed he had three eyes.

For two weeks he spoke to no one but a dumpy four-and-a-half-foot female on the third floor, and to her usually to say no. Fidelman, having often heard the music of Bach drifting up from below, had tried to picture the lady piano player, imagining a quiet blonde with a slender body, a woman of grace and beauty. It had turned out to be Clelia Montemaggio, a middle-aged old-maid music teacher, who sat at an old upright piano, her apartment door open to let out the cooking smells, particularly fried fish on Friday. Once when coming up from bringing down the garbage, Fidelman had paused to listen to part of a partita at her door and she had lassoed him in for an espresso and pastry. He ate and listened to Bach, her plump bottom moving spryly on the bench as she played not badly. "Lo spirito," she called to him raptly over her shoulder, "l'architettura!" Fidelman nodded. Thereafter whenever she spied him in the hall she attempted to entice him with cream-filled pastries and J.S.B., whom she played apparently exclusively.

"Come een," she called in English, "I weel play for you. We weel talk. There is no use for too much solitude." But the art student, burdened by his, spurned hers.

Unable to work, he wandered in the streets in a desolate mood, his spirit dusty in a city of fountains and leaky water taps. Water, water everywhere, spouting, flowing, dripping, whispering secrets, love love love, but not for him. If Rome's so sexy, where's mine? Fidelman's Romeless Rome. It belonged least to those who yearned most for it. With slow steps he climbed the Pincio, if possible to raise his spirits gazing down at the rooftops of the city, spires, cupolas, towers, monuments, compounded history, and past time. It was in sight, possessable, all but its elusive spirit; after so long he was still straniero. He was then struck by a thought: if you could paint this sight, give it its quality in yours, the spirit belonged to you. History become aesthetic! Fidelman's scalp thickened. A wild rush of things he might paint swept sweetly through him: saints in good and bad health, whole or maimed, in gold and red; nude gray rabbis at Auschwitz, black or white Negroes—what not when *any* color dripped from your brush? And if these, so also ANNA-MARIA ES PULCHRA. He all but cheered. What more intimate possession of a woman! He would paint her, whether she permitted or not, posed or not—she was his to paint, he could with eyes shut. Maybe something will come after all of my love for her. His spirits elevated, Fidelman ran most of the way home.

It took him eight days, a labor of love. He tried her as nude and, although able to imagine every inch of her, could not commit it to canvas. Then he suffered until it occurred to him to paint her as "Virgin with Child." The idea astonished and elated him. Fidelman went feverishly to work and caught an immediate likeness in paint. Annamaria, saintly beautiful, held in her arms the infant resembling his little nephew Georgie. The pittrice, aware, of course, of his continuous activity, cast curious glances his way, but Fidelman, painting in the corner by the stone sink, kept the easel turned away from her. She pretended unconcern. Done for the day he covered the painting and carefully guarded it. The art student was painting Annamaria in a passion of tenderness for the infant at her breast, her face responsive to its innocence. When, on the ninth day, in trepidation Fidelman revealed his work, the pittrice's eyes clouded and her underlip curled. He was about to grab the canvas and smash it up all over the place when her expression fell apart. The art student postponed all movement but visible trembling. She seemed at first appalled, a darkness descended on her, she was undone. She wailed wordlessly, then sobbed, "You have seen my soul." They embraced tempestuously, her breasts stabbing him, Annamaria bawling on his shoulder. Fidelman kissed her wet face and salted lips, she murmuring as he fooled with the hook of her brassiere under her sweater, "Aspetta, aspetta, caro, Augusto viene." He was mad with expectation and suspense.

Augusto, who usually arrived punctually at four, did not appear that Friday afternoon. Uneasy as the hour approached, Annamaria seemed relieved as the streets grew dark. She had worked badly after viewing Fidelman's painting, sighed frequently, gazed at him with sweet-sad smiles. At six she gave in to his urging and they retired to her room, his unframed "Virgin with Child" already hanging above her bed, replacing a gaunt self-portrait. He was curiously disappointed in the picture—surfacy thin—and made a mental note to borrow it back in the morning to work on it more. But the conception, at least, deserved the reward. Annamaria cooked supper. She cut his meat for him and fed him forkfuls. She peeled Fidelman's orange and stirred sugar in his coffee. Afterwards, at his nod, she locked and bolted the studio and bedroom doors and they undressed and slipped under her blankets. How good to be for a change on this side of the locked door, Fidelman thought, relaxing marvelously. Annamaria, however, seemed tensely alert to the noises of the old building, including a parrot screeching, some shouting kids running up the stairs, a soprano singing "Ritorna, vincitor!" But she calmed down and then hotly embraced Fidelman. In the middle of a passionate kiss the doorbell rang.

Annamaria stiffened in his arms. "Diavolo! Augusto!"

"He'll go away," Fidelman advised. "Both doors locked."

But she was at once out of bed, drawing on her culottes. "Get dressed," she said.

He hopped up and hastily got into his pants.

Annamaria unlocked and unbolted the inner door and then the outer one. It was the postman waiting to collect ten lire for an overweight letter from Naples.

After she had read the long letter and wiped away a tear they undressed and got back into bed.

"Who is he to you?" Fidelman asked.

"Who?"

"Augusto."

"An old friend. Like a father. We went through much together."

"Were you lovers?"

"Look, if you want me, take me. If you want to ask questions, go back to school."

He determined to mind his business.

"Warm me," she said, "I'm freezing."

Fidelman stroked her slowly. After ten minutes she said, " 'Gioco di mano, gioco di villano.' Use your imagination."

He used his imagination and she responded with excitement. "Dolce tesoro," she whispered, flicking the tip of her tongue into his ear, then with little bites biting his earlobe.

The doorbell rang loudly.

"For Christ's sake, don't answer," Fidelman groaned. He tried to hold her down but she was already up, hunting her robe.

"Put on your pants," she hissed.

He had thoughts of waiting for her in bed but it ended with his dressing fully. She sent him to the door. It was the crippled portinaia, the art student having neglected to take down the garbage.

Annamaria furiously got the two bags and handed them to her.

In bed she was so cold her teeth chattered.

Tense with desire Fidelman warmed her.

"Angelo mio," she murmured. "Amore, possess me."

He was about to when she rose in a hurry. "The cursed door again!"

Fidelman gnashed his teeth. "I heard nothing."

In her torn yellow silk robe she hurried to the front door, opened and shut it, quickly locked and bolted it, did the same in her room, and slid into bed.

"You were right, it was nobody."

She embraced him, her hairy armpits perfumed. He responded with postponed passion.

"Enough of antipasto," Annamaria said. She reached for his member.

Overwrought, Fidelman, though fighting himself not to, spent himself in her hand. Although he mightily willed resurrection, his wilted flower bit the dust.

She furiously shoved him out of bed, into the studio, flinging his clothes after him.

"Pig, beast, onanist!"

4

At least she lets me love her. Daily Fidelman shopped, cooked, and
cleaned for her. Every morning he took her shopping sack off the hook,
went to the street market, and returned with the bag stuffed full of
greens, pasta, eggs, meat, cheese, wine, bread. Annamaria insisted on
three hearty meals a day although she had once told him she no longer
enjoyed eating. Twice he had seen her throw up her supper. What she
enjoyed he didn't know except it wasn't Fidelman. After he had served
her at her table he was allowed to eat alone in the studio. At two every
afternoon she took her siesta, and though it was forbidden to make
noise, he was allowed to wash the dishes, dust and clean her room, swab
the toilet bowl. She called, Fatso, and in he trotted to get her anything
she had run out of—drawing pencils, sanitary belt, safety pins. After
she waked from her nap, rain or shine, snow or hail, he was now compelled to leave the studio so she could work in peace and quiet. He wandered, in the tramontana, from one cold two-bit movie to another. At
seven he was back to prepare her supper, and twice a week Augusto's,
who sported a new black hat and spiffy overcoat, and pitied the art student with both wet blue eyes but wouldn't look at him. After supper,
another load of dishes, the garbage downstairs, and when Fidelman returned, with or without Augusto Annamaria was already closeted behind her bolted door. He checked through the keyhole on Mondays and
Fridays but she and the old gent were always fully clothed. Fidelman
had more than once complained to her that his punishment exceeded
his crime, but the pittrice said he was a type she would never have any
use for. In fact he did not exist for her. Not existing how could he paint,
although he told himself he must? He couldn't. He aimlessly froze
wherever he went, a mean cold that seared his lungs, although under
his overcoat he wore a new thick sweater Bessie had knitted for him,
and two woolen scarves around his neck. Since the night Annamaria
had kicked him out of bed he had not been warm; yet he often dreamed
of ultimate victory. Once when he was on his lonely way out of the
house—a night she was giving a party for some painter friends, Fidelman, a drooping butt in the corner of his mouth, carrying the garbage
bags, met Clelia Montemaggio coming up the stairs.

"You look like a frozen board," she said. "Come in and enjoy the
warmth and a little Bach."

Unable to unfreeze enough to say no, he continued down with the
garbage.

"Every man gets the woman he deserves," she called after him.

"Who got," Fidelman muttered. "Who gets."

He considered jumping into the Tiber but it was full of ice that winter.

One night at the end of February, Annamaria, to Fidelman's astonishment—it deeply affected him—said he might go with her to a party at Giancarlo Balducci's studio on the Via dell'Oca; she needed somebody to accompany her in the bus across the bridge and Augusto was flat on his back with the Asian flu. The party was lively—painters, sculptors, some writers, two diplomats, a prince and a visiting Hindu sociologist, their ladies, and three hotsy-totsy, scantily dressed, unattached girls. One of them, a shapely beauty with orange hair, bright eyes, and warm ways became interested in Fidelman, except that he was dazed by Annamaria, seeing her in a dress for the first time, a ravishing, rich, ruby-colored affair. The cross-eyed host had provided simply a huge cut-glass bowl of spiced mulled wine, and the guests dipped ceramic glasses into it, and guzzled away. Everyone but the art student seemed to be enjoying himself. One or two of the men disappeared into other rooms with female friends or acquaintances and Annamaria, in a gay mood, did a fast shimmy to rhythmic hand-clapping. She was drinking steadily and, when she wanted her glass filled, politely called him "Arturo." He began to have mild thoughts of possibly possessing her.

The party bloomed, at least forty, and turned wildish. Practical jokes were played. Fidelman realized his left shoe had been smeared with mustard. Balducci's black cat mewed at a fat lady's behind, a slice of sausage pinned to her dress. Before midnight there were two fistfights, Fidelman enjoying both but not getting involved, though once he was socked on the neck by a sculptor who had aimed at a painter. The girl with the orange hair, still interested in the art student, invited him to join her in Balducci's bedroom, but he continued to be devoted to Annamaria, his eyes tied to her every move. He was jealous of the illustrator who, whenever near her, nipped her bottom.

One of the sculptors, Orazio Pinello, a slender man with a darkish face, heavy black brows, and bleached blond hair, approached Fidelman. "Haven't we met before, caro?"

"Maybe," the art student said, perspiring lightly. "I'm Arthur Fidelman, an American painter."

"You don't say? Action painter?"

"Always active."

"I refer of course to Abstract Expressionism."

"Of course. Well, sort of. On and off."

"Haven't I seen some of your work around? Galleria Schneider?

Some symmetric, hard-edge, biomorphic forms? Not bad as I remember."

Fidelman thanked him, in full blush.

"Who are you here with?" Orazio Pinello asked.

"Annamaria Oliovino."

"Her?" said the sculptor. "But she's a fake."

"Is she?" Fidelman said with a sigh.

"Have you looked at her work?"

"With one eye. Her art is bad but I find her irresistible."

"Peccato." The sculptor shrugged and drifted away.

A minute later there was another fistfight, during which the bright-eyed orange head conked Fidelman with a Chinese vase. He went out cold, and when he came to, Annamaria and Balducci were undressing him in the illustrator's bedroom. Fidelman experienced an almost overwhelming pleasure, then Balducci explained that the art student had been chosen to pose in the nude for drawings both he and the pittrice would do of him. He explained there had been a discussion as to which of them did male nudes best and they had decided to settle it in a short contest. Two easels had been wheeled to the center of the studio; a half hour was allotted to the contestants, and the guests would judge who had done the better job. Though he at first objected because it was a cold night, Fidelman nevertheless felt warmish from wine so he agreed to pose; besides he was proud of his muscles and maybe if she sketched him nude it might arouse her interest for a tussle later. And if he wasn't painting he was at least being painted.

So the pittrice and Giancarlo Balducci, in paint-smeared smocks, worked for thirty minutes by the clock, the whole party silently looking on, with the exception of the orange-haired tart, who sat in the corner eating a prosciutto sandwich. Annamaria, her brow furrowed, lips pursed, drew intensely with crayon; Balducci worked calmly in colored chalk. The guests were absorbed, although after ten minutes the Hindu went home. A journalist locked himself in the painter's bedroom with orange head and would not admit his wife, who pounded on the door. Fidelman, standing barefoot on a bathmat, was eager to see what Annamaria was accomplishing but had to be patient. When the half hour was up he was permitted to look. Balducci had drawn a flock of green and black abstract testiculate circles. Fidelman shuddered. But Annamaria's drawing was representational, not Fidelman although of course inspired by him: a gigantic funereal phallus that resembled a broken-backed snake. The blond sculptor inspected it with half-closed eyes, then yawned and left. By now the party was over, the guests departed, lights out except for a few dripping white candles. Balducci was collecting his ceramic glasses and emptying ashtrays, and Annamaria had thrown up. The art student afterwards heard her begging the illustrator to sleep with her but Balducci complained of fatigue.

"I will if he won't," Fidelman offered.

Annamaria, enraged, spat on her picture of his unhappy phallus.

"Don't dare come near me," she cried. "Malocchio! Jettatura!"

5

The next morning he awoke sneezing, a nasty cold. How can I go on? Annamaria, showing no signs of pity or remorse, continued shrilly to berate him. "You've brought me nothing but bad luck since you came here. I'm letting you stay because you pay well but I warn you to keep out of my sight."

"But how——" he asked hoarsely.

"That doesn't concern me."

"——how will I paint?"

"Who cares? Paint at night."

"Without light——"

"Paint in the dark. I'll buy you a can of black paint."

"How can you be so cruel to a man who loves——"

"I'll scream," she said.

He left in anguish. Later while she was at her siesta he came back, got some of his things, and tried to paint in the hall. No dice. Fidelman wandered in the rain. He sat for hours on the Spanish Steps. Then he returned to the house and went slowly up the stairs. The door was locked. "Annamaria," he hoarsely called. Nobody answered. In the street he stood at the river wall, watching the dome of St. Peter's in the distance. Maybe a potion, Fidelman thought, or an amulet? He doubted either would work. How do you go about hanging yourself? In the late afternoon he went back to the house—would say he was sick, needed rest, possibly a doctor. He felt feverish. She could hardly refuse.

But she did, although explaining she felt bad herself. He held on to the banister as he went down the stairs. Clelia Montemaggio's door was open. Fidelman paused, then continued down, but she had seen him. "Come een, come een."

He went reluctantly in. She fed him camomile tea and panettone. He ate in a wolfish hurry as she seated herself at the piano.

"No Bach, please, my head aches from various troubles."

"Where's your dignity?" she asked.

"Try Chopin, that's lighter."

"Respect yourself, please."

Fidelman removed his hat as she began to play a Bach prelude, her bottom rhythmic on the bench. Though his cold oppressed him and he could hardly breathe, tonight the spirit, the architecture, moved him. He felt his face to see if he was crying but only his nose was wet. On the top of the piano Clelia had placed a bowl of white carnations in full bloom. Each white petal seemed a white flower. If I could paint those gorgeous flowers, Fidelman thought. If I could paint something. By Jesus, if I could paint myself, that'd show them! Astonished by the thought he ran out of the house.

The art student hastened to a costume shop and settled on a cassock and fuzzy black soup-bowl biretta, envisaging another Rembrandt: "Portrait of the Artist as Priest." He hurried with his bulky package back to the house. Annamaria was handing the garbage to the portinaia as Fidelman thrust his way into the studio. He quickly changed into the priest's vestments. The pittrice came in wildly to tell him where he got off, but when she saw Fidelman already painting himself as priest, with a moan she rushed into her room. He worked with smoking intensity and in no time created an amazing likeness. Annamaria, after stealthily re-entering the studio, with heaving bosom and agitated eyes closely followed his progress. At last, with a cry she threw herself at his feet.

"Forgive me, Father, for I have sinned——"

Dripping brush in hand, he stared down at her. "Please, I——"

"Oh, Father, if you knew how I have sinned. I've been a whore——"

After a moment's thought, Fidelman said, "If so, I absolve you."

"Not without penance. First listen to the rest. I've had no luck with men. They're all bastards. Or else I jinx them. If you want the truth I am an Evil Eye myself. Anybody who loves me is cursed."

He listened, fascinated.

"Augusto is really my uncle. After many others he became my lover. At least he's gentle. My father found out and swore he'd kill us both. When I got pregnant I was scared to death. A sin can go too far. Augusto told me to have the baby and leave it at an orphanage, but the night it was born I was confused and threw it into the Tiber. I was afraid it was an idiot."

She was sobbing. He drew back.

"Wait," she wept. "The next time in bed Augusto was impotent. Since then he's been imploring me to confess so he can get back his powers. But every time I step into the confessional my tongue turns to bone. The priest can't tear a word out of me. That's how it's been all my life, don't ask me why because I don't know."

She grabbed his knees. "Help me, Father, for Christ's sake."

Fidelman, after a short tormented time, said in a quavering voice, "I forgive you, my child."

"The penance," she wailed, "first the penance."

After reflecting, he replied, "Say one hundred times each, Our Father and Hail Mary."

"More," Annamaria wept. "More, more. Much more."

Gripping his knees so hard they shook she burrowed her head into his black-buttoned lap. He felt the surprised beginnings of an erection.

"In that case," Fidelman said, shuddering a little, "better undress."

"Only," Annamaria said, "if you keep your vestments on."

"Not the cassock, too clumsy."

"At least the biretta."

He agreed to that.

Annamaria undressed in a swoop. Her body was extraordinarily lovely, the flesh glowing. In her bed they tightly embraced. She clasped his buttocks, he cupped hers. Pumping slowly he nailed her to her cross.

1962

❧ B M ❧

Suppose a Wedding

(A SCENE OF A PLAY)

MAURICE FEUER *is a retired sick Jewish actor trying to influence his daughter,* ADELE, *in her choice of a husband. She is engaged to* LEON SINGER, *a young sporting-goods store owner from Newark.* FEUER *approves of* BEN GLICKMAN, *a poor beginning writer in the building—a tenement house off Second Avenue in Manhattan—who seems to share his values in life. At any rate* FEUER *likes him.* FLORENCE FEUER, *the actor's wife, once an actress now a beautician, who has also been around and garnered her kind of wisdom, is all for* LEON. *On a hot mid-August day* LEON *has driven in from New Jersey to surprise* ADELE, *when she arrives home from work, and take her to dinner. As the curtain rises,* LEON, *while waiting for her, is playing cards with* FEUER. *Because of the heat the apartment door is open and people occasionally pass by in the hall.*

LEON [*quietly*]: Rummy. This one is mine. [*He puts down his cards and begins to add up the score.*]

FEUER [*rising and pushing back his chair, he removes his glasses and, without warning, declaims emotionally in Yiddish*]: My God, you're killing your poor father, this is what you're doing. For your whole life I worked bitter hard to take care of you the way a father should. To feed and clothe you. To give you the best kind of education. To teach you what's right. And so how do you pay me back? You pay me back by becoming a tramp. By living with a married man, a cheap, dirty person who has absolutely no respect for you. A bum who used you like dirt. Worse than dirt. And now when he doesn't want you anymore and kicks you out of his bed, you come to me crying, begging I should take you back. My daughter, for what I went through with you, there's no more forgiveness. My heart is milked of tears. It's like a piece of rock. I don't want to see you again in my whole life. Go, but remember, you killed your father. [*He hangs his head.*]

LEON [*perplexed*]: What's that about?

FEUER [*assuming his identity as he puts on his glasses*]: Don't you understand Yiddish?

LEON: Only some of the words.

FEUER: Tst-tst. [*Sitting*] It's from a play I once played in the Second Avenue Theater, *Sein Tochter's Geliebter.* I was brilliant in this part—magnificent. All the critics raved about me even though the play was schmaltz. Even *The New York Times* sent somebody and he wrote in his review that Maurice Feuer is not only a wonderful actor, he is also a magician. What I could do with such a lousy play was unbelievable. I made it come to life. I made it believable.

[LEON *begins to deal out a new hand as* FEUER *goes on.*]

FEUER: I also played in *Greener Felder, Ghosts, The Dybbuk, The Cherry Orchard, Naches fon Kinder, Gott fon Nachoma,* and *Yoshe Kalb.* Schwartz played Reb Melech and I played Yoshe. I was brilliant—marvelous. The play ran three years in New York, and after we played in London, Paris, Prague, and Warsaw. We also brought it for a season in South America and played it in Rio, then for sixteen weeks in Buenos Aires . . . [*Struck by a memory* FEUER *falls silent.*]

LEON: It's your move.

[FEUER *absently takes a card and without looking gets rid of another.* LEON *picks up a card, examines it carefully, then drops it among the discards.*]

LEON: Your move.

[FEUER, *coming back to life, looks at a card and places it on the discard pile.*]

FEUER: This piece I recited to you is a father talking to his daughter. She took the wrong man and it ruined her life.

[LEON, *examining his cards, has nothing to say.*]

FEUER [*needling a little*]: You couldn't understand it?

LEON: Only partly. Still in all, when I had to I was able to give directions in Yiddish to an old baba with a wig who I met in downtown Newark, on how to get to Brooklyn, New York.

[*As they talk they continue the rummy game.*]

FEUER: Adele knows Yiddish perfect. She learned when she was a little girl. She used to write me letters in Yiddish—they were brilliant. She also had a wonderful handwriting.

LEON: Maybe she'll teach our kids.

[*He is unaware of* FEUER *regarding him ironically.*]

FEUER [*trying a new tack*]: Do you know something about Jewish history?

LEON [*amiably*]: Not very much. [*Afterthought*] If you're worried about religion, don't worry. I was bar mitzvahed.

FEUER: I'm not worried about anything. Tell me, do you know any of the big Yiddish writers—Peretz, Sholem Aleichem, Asch?

LEON: I've heard about them.

FEUER: Do you read serious books?

LEON: Sure, I belong to the Book Find Club.

FEUER: Why don't you pick your own books? Why did you go to college for?

LEON: I mostly do. It's no harm to belong to a good book club, it saves you time. [*Looking at his wristwatch*] What time is Adele due? It's getting late.

FEUER: Why didn't you telephone her so she would know you were coming? It's not expensive to telephone.

LEON: I thought I'd give her a surprise. My brother Mortie came into Newark this morning, and he did me the favor to take over the shop so I could get away early. We keep open Wednesday nights.

FEUER [*consulting an old pocket watch*]: She's late.

LEON: Rummy. I win again. [*He shows his cards.*]

FEUER [*hiding his annoyance*]: But my best roles were in Shakespeare—*Shylock, der Yid, Hamlet, der Yeshiva Bucher*—I was wonderful in the kaddish scene for his father, the dead king. And I also played *Kaynig Lear und sein Tochter.*

[*Rising and again removing his glasses, he recites in English*]:

"*Down from the waist they are Centaurs,*
 Though women all above;
 But to the girdle do the gods inherit,
 Beneath is all the fiends': there's hell, there's darkness,
 there is the sulphurous pit,
 Burning, scalding, stench, consumption; fie, fie,
 fie, pah, pah! Give me an ounce of civet, good
 apothecary, to sweeten my imagination."

[LEON, *as though this were not news to him, finishes adding up the score. He shuffles the cards thoroughly as* FEUER *puts on his glasses and, sitting, regards him objectively.*]

LEON: Another game? We're running even now, two and two. Almost the same points.

FEUER: The last one.

[LEON *deals again and the game goes on.*]

FEUER [*after playing a card, continuing to needle*]: Tell me, Leon, do you iike tragedy?

LEON: Do I like it?

FEUER: Do you like to see a tragedy on the stage or read tragic books?

LEON: I can take it or leave it. Generally my nature is cheerful.

FEUER [*building*]: But you went to college. You're a good businessman. Adele says you read *The New York Times* every day. In other words you're an intelligent person. So answer me this question: Why do all the best writers and poets write tragedy? And why does every theater play such plays and all kinds of people pay their good money to see tragedies? Why is that?

LEON: To tell the truth, I never had occasion to give it much thought.

FEUER [*a touch of malice*]: Do me a favor, think about it now.

LEON [*wary*]: I'm not so sure I can tell you exactly, but I suppose it's because a lot of life is like that. You realize what's what.

FEUER: What do you mean, "suppose"? Don't you know for sure? Think what we live through every day—accidents, murders, sickness, disappointments. The thought of death alone is enough.

LEON [*subdued*]: I know what you mean.

FEUER [*sarcasm evident*]: You think you know. Do you really know the condition of human existence? Do you know what the universe means? I'm not talking about who's dead but also about millions of people—in the millions—who live for nothing. They have nothing but poverty, disease, suffering. Or they live in a prison like the Russians. Is this your idea of a good life for everybody?

[BEN GLICKMAN *appears at the doorway, looks in hungrily, sees* LEON, *and goes on his way upstairs. Neither of the cardplayers has noticed him.*]

LEON: I wouldn't say that.

FEUER: If you know, you know conditions and you got to do something about them. A man has to be interested to ask for change where it is necessary, to help which way he can.

LEON: I try to help. I give regularly to charity, including the United Jewish Appeal.

FEUER: This isn't enough.

LEON: What do you do?

FEUER [*laying down his cards; emotionally*]: What do I do? I suffer for those who suffer. My heart bleeds for all the injustice in this world.

[LEON *is silently studying his cards.*]

FEUER [*picking up his hand, speaking quietly though still with a purpose*]: Do you ever think what happens to you—inside your soul, when you see a tragic play, for instance Shakespeare?

LEON [*suddenly recalling*]: I feel a catharsis through pity and terror.

FEUER [*after a pause*]: Don't quote me your college books. A writer writes tragedy so people don't forget that they are human. He shows us the conditions that exist. He organizes for us the meaning of our lives so it is clear to our eyes. That's why he writes it, that's why we play it. My best roles were tragic roles. I enjoyed them the most though I was also marvelous in comedy. "Leid macht auch lachen." [*He laughs dramatically, then quietly draws a card and lays down his hand triumphantly.*] Rummy!

LEON: You win. [*He begins to tot up the score.*] I guess I owe you exactly fifty-one cents. [*Taking out his change purse, he puts down two quarters and a penny and gently pushes the money toward* FEUER*'s side of the table.*]

FEUER [*casually; ignoring the money*]: So how is the baseball situation now, Leon?

LEON [*bites*]: I think the Yanks and Dodgers are leading as usual. [*Catching on*] I'm afraid I'm not following the situation very closely, Mr. Feuer.

FEUER: If you don't follow it, what do you talk about to your sporting-goods customers?

LEON [*patiently*]: Different things, though not necessarily sports. People are people—they talk about a lot of things. [*He slides the three coins a bit farther forward.*] You better put this away, Mr. Feuer.

FEUER: I'm not worried about the money. I play because I like to play. [*A thought strikes him.*] You know the story about the famous rabbi and the rich man? He was rich and a miser. The rabbi took him to the window and said, "What do you see, tell me?" The rich man looked and he said, "I see the street, what else should I see?" "What's in the street?" "What's in the street?" said the rich Jew, "people—they're walking in the street." Then the rabbi took him to a mirror in the room and he said, "What do you see now?" "What do I see now?" said the rich man. "Naturally I see myself, of course." "Aha," said the rabbi. "You'll notice in the window is glass, and there is also glass in the mirror. But the glass in the mirror has silver painted on the back, and once there's the silver you stop seeing everybody else and you see only yourself."

LEON [*still patient*]: The way I look at it is this: Rummy is a game of chance. If you play for cash the loser pays with cash and the winner accepts with good grace. [*Again he slides the coins toward* FEUER.]

FEUER [*pushing them back*]: Please don't tell me about manners. About manners I knew before you were born.

LEON: Mr. Feuer, if you want to insult me, there are better ways.

FEUER: Why should I insult you?

LEON: Please don't think I am a dope. It's as plain as anyone's nose that you don't like me, though I wish I knew why.

FEUER: I'll tell you why if you'll kindly tell me what you are living for. What is your philosophy of life?

LEON: I live because I'm alive.

FEUER: Good, but what do you *want* from your life? That's also important.

LEON [*beginning to show irritation*]: That's my business. Listen, Mr. Feuer, don't think I am so dense that I don't understand the reasons for this inquisition you gave me. You pretend you are cordial but it's for the purpose of needling me. I'm not so dense that I don't know what you're insinuating—that I'm not interested in the right things and also that I'm money-conscious. But that's all a camouflage. You have some pretty strong prejudices and that's why you're annoyed that Adele is going to marry me.

FEUER: That's a father's privilege.

LEON: I guess you have no respect for your daughter's judgment.

FEUER: I have plenty of respect, but she isn't your type. I don't say you're a bad person, but you aren't the right man for her.

LEON: Who's the right man?

FEUER: More an artistic type. Like her own nature.

LEON: That's just what I figured you would say, and if you'll excuse me, it's a batty point of view. A man is a man, not a profession. I've worked darn hard all my life for everything I have. I got myself a decent education which I paid for myself, even if it isn't a B.A. education. No matter what you think, if you look around, the world doesn't run on art. What it runs on I'm not going to argue with you but I'll say this: At the least you ought to respect me if for no other reason than because your daughter does. Just because I'm no long-hair writer doesn't make me unworthy of her, or for that matter, it doesn't make Adele unworthy of me. [*Rising*] Someday I hope you'll wake up to the facts of life.

[FLORENCE FEUER *appears on the stairs and momentarily pauses when she hears voices.*] People aren't the same as their businesses. I am not what I sell. And even if I happened to sell irradiated toilet seats, I still wouldn't worship them. I would use them for the purpose that they are intended.

[FLORENCE *enters the apartment.*]

FEUER: Whatever you sell or don't sell, if Adele marries somebody she don't love, she'll regret it.

FLORENCE [*gasping*]: Feuer—for God's sake! Leon, don't believe him—

LEON [*to* FLORENCE]: Hello, Mrs. Feuer. When Adele comes home, tell her I'll be back to take her out to dinner.

[*He leaves with dignity.* FLORENCE *sits down in the chair* LEON *has just occupied and slowly removes her shoes. For a minute she sits there not saying a word.* FEUER *is silent, too, then goes to the sink and pours himself a long glass of water. He stands there drinking thirstily.*]

FLORENCE [*with weary bitterness*]: What's the matter, Feuer, aren't you satisfied with all your miseries? What do you want from this poor girl's life? Do you hate her?

FEUER [*coolly*]: I'm doing her a favor.

FLORENCE: To ruin her life?

FEUER: To save it. This boy means well but he's a first-class mediocrity. I'm convinced for sure now.

FLORENCE [*wearily patient*]: Are you blind? Take your eyes in your hand and look again. How can you stay in the same room with Leon and not see what a fine person he is? The trouble is you're jealous.

FEUER: If I wasn't jealous of Maurice Schwartz why should I be jealous of Leon Singer?

FLORENCE: Why did you insult him for nothing?

FEUER: Who insulted him?

FLORENCE: You did. Why did he leave with his face so red?

FEUER: What am I, a diagnostician? All I asked him was a few honest questions. It's a father's privilege.

FLORENCE: I can imagine what you asked him.

FEUER: I asked him what he lived for. I asked him what's his philosophy, if any. I have a right to know.

FLORENCE: Why don't you ask yourself and leave him alone?

FEUER: I didn't ask him anything I don't ask myself.

FLORENCE: Please leave him alone. Adele picked him, not you. She's marrying him, not you. Leave them alone before you start a calamity.

FEUER: My opinion is she don't love him.

FLORENCE: Are you crazy? Who told you such a thing?

FEUER: She's not in love, she thinks she is.

FLORENCE: What are you now, a fortune-teller?—Miss Lonely-hearts? Have you loved so well that you know all about it?

FEUER: How well I loved *I* know. I also know her and I know she doesn't really love him.

FLORENCE: And I know you encouraged this boy upstairs to come here on his night off. Don't think I don't know you asked her to go out with him.

FEUER: She didn't go because he didn't ask. But yesterday he called her to go for a walk tonight, and she said yes.

FLORENCE [*rising*]: Oh, my God. [*She cracks her knuckles on her breasts.*] Does Leon know?

FEUER: Who cares if he knows?

FLORENCE [*angrily*]: Feuer, if you break up this engagement I will leave you. Cook your own vegetables.

[FEUER *glares at her.*]

FLORENCE: You ought to be ashamed to do this to her. What can she get from a poor writer without a steady job—even without a college education that you talk so much about—who writes all day without success?

FEUER: First you learn your art, then you have success. Someday he'll be a first-class writer.

FLORENCE: How do you know?

FEUER: He read me a story—it was brilliant.

FLORENCE: One story don't mean a thing.

FEUER: One is all I need.

FLORENCE [*intensely*]: What can a starving writer give her? A de-cent home? Can he afford to have children? Will he consider her first when she needs him, or his egotism? I want her to have a future, not a cold-water flat with a poor man.

FEUER: Maybe he won't be rich but he'll have a rich life. With him she could have a real excitement in her life—not a middle-class existence where the real pleasure is to go shopping for something you don't need. Don't underestimate Ben Glickman. I talked to him many times and I know his nature. This is a passionate man—how many are left in the world? He doesn't tell me what he has suffered but I can see in his eyes. He knows what life means and he knows what's real. He'll be good for Adele. He will understand her and love her like she needs to be loved.

FLORENCE: To me he looks sick, like a starved animal. And what are you talking about love when she doesn't even know him? What kind of foolishness is this? It's because you see yourself in him, that's who you see. You see another egoist.

FEUER: Who can talk to you? You're full of foolish anxieties you want to give me.

FLORENCE: Who else can I give them to?

FEUER: This isn't talk, it's confusion.

FLORENCE: You confuse her. Soon she won't know what she's doing. You confused me too.

FEUER: You confused yourself.

FLORENCE [*angrily*]: Egoist! Egoist! You don't deserve to have such a son-in-law.

FEUER [*sarcastic*]: Did I deserve to have such a wife?

FLORENCE [*rising*]: Never, you never deserved me.

[*She picks up her shoes, drops them into the living-room closet, and steps into slippers. Returning to the kitchen she opens the refrigerator door, takes out a few things, and begins wordlessly to prepare supper.* FEUER *is thumbing through a magazine she had brought home. After a minute* FLORENCE *goes to the hall door and quietly shuts it.*]

FEUER [*without turning his head*]: Don't close the door, it's too hot.

FLORENCE [*quietly*]: I want to talk to you one minute—private.

FEUER: Talk. But keep the door open. I'm suffocating.

FLORENCE: Please, Feuer, stop exaggerating. Stop performing. You won't die. All I want to do is talk to you without the neighbors' ears in our door.

FEUER [*shouting*]: Leave the door open, I told you.

FLORENCE [*opening it*]: You make me sick!

FEUER [*rising to the occasion*]: You made me sick!

FLORENCE [*though not wanting to, losing her temper*]: Blame yourself. You were sick to begin with from the day I met you. You spoiled my life.

FEUER: You spoiled it yourself.

FLORENCE [*vehemently*]: No, you spoiled it. You don't know where to stop. Every time you stab yourself you stab me twice. I used to be a nice person but you spoiled my nature. You're impossible to live with and impossible to talk to. You don't even converse anymore. When you open your mouth, right away you're yelling—it's always an argument.

FEUER: Who else is yelling if I may ask you?

FLORENCE: You spoiled my character.

FEUER: I didn't interfere with existing conditions.

FLORENCE [*on the verge of tears*]: You did, you did!

FEUER: If you believe this, you're lying to yourself.

FLORENCE: You're the one who lied. You lied about the choristers you couldn't stay away from them, even with a wife and child. I gave you my love but you couldn't say no to the chorus girls. If one of them looked at you you turned into a rooster. You had no will.

FEUER: I have a *magnificent* will.

FLORENCE: If her garter was loose you took off her stocking. If she took it off herself you helped her to take off the other.

FEUER [*bitterly*]: And which two-bit actors took off your stockings? And how many times in your married life?

FLORENCE: You started the whole dirty business. *You* started it. I never wanted that kind of a life, it wasn't my nature.

FEUER: It went on for years.

FLORENCE: You left me three times, once two whole years. Also many times you were on the road for months when I couldn't go. I was human. I made mistakes.

FEUER: You could've thought of your child instead of sending her from one place to another, in the hands of strangers who made her sick.

FLORENCE: Feuer, for God's sake, I can't stand any more. Why didn't you take care of her? Because you weren't there. Because you were busy in bed with somebody else.

FEUER [*blazing*]: You son of a bitch!

[FLORENCE *stares at him, then seems to crumple and slowly lowers herself into a chair. She puts her hands on the table, palms up, and, lowering her head, sobs into them. She sobs with her whole body, a wailing weeping.*

FEUER *goes to the door and quietly shuts it. He attempts to approach her but can't. He goes to the sink for another glass of water but pours it out without drinking, staring vaguely out the window. Wandering to the mirror, he stands there looking at himself, not enjoying what he sees. Gradually* FLORENCE *stops crying, raises her head, and sits quietly at the table, one hand shading her eyes. After a while she blows her nose, and wipes her eyes with a handkerchief.* FEUER, *after glaring at his image, in weariness lies down on the daybed.*]

FLORENCE [*very quietly*]: What's that smell?

FEUER [*wearily*]: Gas.

FLORENCE: What kind of gas?

FEUER: Human gas. Whatever you smell you want immediate identification.

FLORENCE [*after a while*]: Don't you feel well?

FEUER: Perfect.

FLORENCE [*still quietly*]: Did you take your pills today?

FEUER: I took. [*He jumps up from the bed and speaks suddenly, vehemently.*] Florence, I'm sorry. In my heart I love you. My tongue is filthy but not my heart.

FLORENCE [*after a pause*]: How can you love a son of a bitch?

FEUER: Don't poison me with my words. I have enough poison in me already. I say what I don't mean.

FLORENCE: What do you mean?

FEUER: I say that too.

FLORENCE [*still half stunned*]: How can anyone love a son of a bitch?

FEUER [*savagely striking his chest*]: I am the son of a bitch.

FLORENCE [*musing*]: It's my fault. I shouldn't fight with you. I don't know why I do it. Maybe it's change of life. What am I changing? Where is my life? It's true, I neglected her, she's the one who suffered. I still feel terrible about those days. But you left me. I had to work. I was out all day. At night I was afraid to be alone. I began to look for company. I was ashamed to let her see me so I sent her away. There was nobody to send her to so I sent her to strangers.

FEUER [*unable to restrain it*]: To friends of your lovers. To their relatives too.

FLORENCE: Have mercy on me, Feuer. My lovers I buried long ago. They're all dead. Don't dig them out of their graves. For what I did to my child I still suffer. You don't have to hurt me more. I know how to hurt myself. [*She cries quietly.*]

[FEUER *approaches her chair and stands behind her.*]

FEUER: I was a fool. I didn't know what I was doing. I didn't understand my own nature. I talked big but accomplished nothing. Even as an actor I wasn't one of the best. Thomashefsky, Jacob Adler, Schwartz—all were better than me. Their names are famous. Two years off the stage and my name is dead. This is what I deserve—I don't fool myself.

FLORENCE: You were a good actor.

FEUER: I wasn't a good actor and I am not a good man.

[*She rises and they embrace.*]

FLORENCE: I forgave you but you don't forgive me.

FEUER: I don't forgive myself.

FLORENCE [*again remembering*]: Three times you left me.

FEUER: I always came back.

FLORENCE: It took so long. I hurt her so much. [*She wipes her eyes with her fingers.*]

FEUER: Enough now. It was my fault too. I hurt her and I hurt you. Why did I hurt you?—because you were there to hurt. You were the only one [*He pauses—there was another but he doesn't say so*]—the only one who could stand me.

FLORENCE: You try to be good.

FEUER: No.

FLORENCE: Yes. [*After a minute*] Please do me a favor, Feuer, and I won't ask for anything else—let Leon alone. Let Adele alone. Let them find their life together. It's all I ask you. For her sake—or there will be terrible trouble.

[*The door opens and* ADELE *enters, discovering them in each other's arms.*]

ADELE [*sadly*]: Ah, you've been fighting again. [*She shuts the door.*]

[FLORENCE *goes to the sink, washes her eyes with cold water, and dries them with a kitchen towel.* FEUER, *after kissing* ADELE, *goes to the bathroom.*]

ADELE [*putting her purse and a paper down on the table*]: What were you fighting about?

FLORENCE: We weren't fighting. It was a disagreement. Leon was here.

ADELE: Leon? When?

FLORENCE: He came to surprise you. He wants you to eat dinner with him. Please, darling, go. He'll be right back in a few minutes.

ADELE: Where is he now?

FLORENCE: I don't know. I wasn't here. Papa told me. I think they were playing rummy and he said something to Leon.

ADELE: Nasty?

FLORENCE: Papa got sarcastic and Leon didn't like it. But he said he would come back soon.

ADELE: I wasn't expecting him tonight.

FLORENCE: It was a surprise.

ADELE: I wish he had at least called me. I already promised Ben I would go for a walk with him tonight.

FLORENCE: A walk is nothing.

ADELE: I promised.

FLORENCE: Adele, you're an engaged girl. Leon came all the way from Newark to take you to dinner. You ought to go.

ADELE: Being engaged doesn't mean I'm not entitled to a free minute to myself.

FLORENCE: Who said that? All I said was Leon was here. You can tell this boy upstairs you'll see him some other time.

ADELE: He called me up and I said yes.

FLORENCE: It isn't such a big promise.

ADELE: I can't understand why Leon didn't call.

FLORENCE: Call or not call, it's not nice to say no when he's already here. Adele, mamale, please see him tonight. I don't want you to walk with that boy. It's dangerous. [*She hadn't meant to say quite that.*]

ADELE: A walk isn't a wedding, Mama.

FLORENCE: It could be worse than a wedding.

ADELE: For God's sake, what do you mean?

FLORENCE [*cracking her knuckles on her bosom*]: You can walk to your grave with a little walk.

[FEUER *comes out of the bathroom, looks at himself earnestly in the mirror, mutters something derogatory, and enters the kitchen.*]

ADELE: Doesn't anyone trust me?

FEUER: I trust you.

FLORENCE [*to* ADELE]: Is this what you want all your life? [*Indicating the apartment.*]

ADELE: I don't see the relationship.

FLORENCE [*deeply troubled*]: For my sake don't go out with this writer. Don't make any more complications in your life. Life is complicated enough.

[*There is a knock on the door.*]

FLORENCE: Come in.

[LEON *enters, carrying a large bouquet of flowers.*]

FLORENCE: Leon!

LEON: Hello, everybody. [*To* ADELE] This is for you, honey.

ADELE: Hello, darling.

[*He hands her the flowers and they kiss.*]

LEON: Hello, Mrs. Feuer. Good evening, Mr. Feuer. [*He bears no grudges.*]

FEUER: Good evening.

[ADELE *hands the bouquet to her mother, who hunts for something to put it into. While she is doing that,* FEUER *takes up his newspaper, excuses himself, and, after drawing the curtain separating the rooms, sits on the daybed, reading.* FLORENCE, *disapproving the drawn curtain but glad to have* FEUER *out of the way, attends first to the flowers, then fixes her cold supper.* LEON *has seated himself at the table, and* ADELE, *after setting the vase of new flowers on the windowsill, is sitting near him.*]

FLORENCE: Leon, would you like to eat with us? It's not much—just a salad with smoked whitefish. Also a few potato pancakes, though not for Feuer—he can't eat them.

LEON: Thanks very much but I was thinking of asking Adele to go out and eat Chinese tonight. [*He looks at her.*]

ADELE: I'm sorry, Leon, if I had known you were coming I would have said yes. That is if you had called before Ben asked me. He's that friend of Papa's who writes. You met him.

LEON [*disappointed*]: Couldn't you break it with him, honey?

ADELE [*hesitantly*]: I'd rather not.

LEON: What's so special about this guy? I mean that you gave him the date? Is it because he's a writer?

ADELE [*defensively*]: You said I could go out once in a while if I felt like it.

LEON: I said it and I stick by it. All I want to know is why you're going out with him?

ADELE: I guess I have the feeling he's gone through a lot.

FLORENCE: Everybody goes through a lot—

ADELE: I like him, he's interesting. I like to talk to him.

LEON: I appreciate his problems, but the fact of it is I've come all the way from Newark, New Jersey, to be with the girl I'm engaged to—

FLORENCE: Mamale—

ADELE: Please, Mama—

[FLORENCE *removes her apron and retires behind the curtain.* FEUER, *who has been listening, raises his paper as she enters and pretends he's reading.* FLORENCE, *not sure she has made the right move, lights a cigarette and sits in the armchair, flipping through the pages of a magazine.*]

LEON [*lowering his voice*]: Honey, I don't dig it. I thought you'd surely be happy to have this kind of a surprise from me.

ADELE [*gently*]: I am. It's a nice surprise. But all I'm saying is I feel committed tonight. [*Aware of his concern*] Don't worry, it's not serious. Don't make anything serious out of it. It's just that he's a lonely person, I guess. You feel that when you're with him.

LEON: I'm lonely too. Couldn't you postpone it till tomorrow night?

ADELE: He's off tonight. Tomorrow he works.

LEON: Then till the next time he's off? I'll exchange him tonight for then. [*Again lowering his voice*] You haven't forgotten our plan to spend a week in the country together in September?

ADELE [*a little cold*]: I don't see what the relationship of this is with that.

LEON: Well, maybe there isn't, but why don't you think it over? I mean about tonight.

ADELE: I feel I ought to keep my word with him.

LEON [*edgy*]: What's the matter, Adele—you don't seem cordial at all. What is it, the atmosphere here?

ADELE: If you don't like the atmosphere, why do you come here?

LEON: I don't want to fight with you.

ADELE: I don't want to fight with you.

LEON [*after a minute*]: Maybe you're right. Give me a kiss and I'll call it quits.

ADELE: I'll kiss you because I like you.

[*They kiss.*]

ADELE [*gently*]: I'll postpone it with him if you really want me to.

FEUER [*from behind the curtain*]: Do what *you* want.

FLORENCE [*hushed whisper*]: Please, for God's sake, Feuer.

LEON [*as though he had heard nothing*]: Let's make a compromise. What time is he showing up here?

ADELE: I don't know, around eight, I suppose. He didn't say exactly.

LEON: All right, whatever time. [*He looks at his wristwatch.*] It's ten to six. We can still go out, have our Chinese meal, and I'll have you back in the car at fifteen after eight. Then you can go for a short walk and when you come back I'll be waiting and we can drive down to Coney Island.

ADELE: For the first suggestion, okay. I'll go to the Chinese restaurant with you. But I don't want to rush him, while we're walking, to get back for the drive. It's not that kind of date.

LEON [*annoyed*]: What kind of date is it?

ADELE: A very innocent one.

[*There's a knock on the door.* ADELE *gets up and opens it. Both* FLORENCE *and* FEUER *are attentive.* BEN *enters with a small bouquet of daffodils.*]

BEN: Am I too early?

[*No one answers as the curtain goes down.*]

Life Is Better Than Death

She seemed to remember the man from the same day last year. He was standing at a nearby grave, occasionally turning to look around, while Etta, a rosary in her hand, prayed for the repose of the soul of her husband, Armando. Sometimes she prayed he would move over and let her lie down with him so her heart might be eased. It was the second of November, All Souls' Day in the cimitero Campo Verano, in Rome, and it had begun to drizzle after she had laid down the bouquet of yellow chrysanthemums on the grave Armando wouldn't have had if it wasn't for a generous uncle, a doctor in Perugia. Without this uncle Etta had no idea where Armando would be buried, certainly in a much less attractive grave, though she would have resisted his often expressed desire to be cremated.

Etta worked for meager wages in a draper's shop and Armando had left no insurance. The bright large yellow flowers, glowing in November gloom on the faded grass, moved her and tears gushed forth. Although she felt uncomfortably feverish when she cried like that, Etta was glad she had, because crying seemed to be the only thing that relieved her. She was thirty, dressed in full mourning. Her figure was slim, her moist brown eyes red-rimmed and darkly ringed, the skin pale, and her features grown thin. Since the accidental death of Armando, a few months more than a year ago, she came almost daily during the long Roman afternoon to pray at his grave. She was devoted to his memory, ravaged within. Etta went to confession twice a week and took communion every Sunday. She lit candles for Armando at La Madonna Addolorata, and had a Mass offered once a month, more often when she had a little extra money. Whenever she returned to the cold flat she still lived in and could not give up because it had once also been his, Etta thought of Armando, recalling him as he had looked ten years ago, not as when he had died. Invariably she felt an oppressive pang and ate very little.

It was raining quietly when she finished her rosary. Etta dropped the beads into her purse and opened a black umbrella. The man from the other grave, wearing a darkish green hat and a tight black over- coat, had stopped a few feet behind her, cupping his small hands over a cigarette as he lit it. Seeing her turn from the grave he touched his hat. He was a short man with dark eyes and a barely visible mustache. He had meaty ears but was handsome.

"Your husband?" he asked respectfully, letting the smoke flow as he spoke, holding his cigarette cupped in his palm to keep it from getting wet.

She said it was.

He nodded in the direction of the grave where he had stood. "My wife. One day while I was on my job she was hurrying to meet a lover and was killed at once by a taxi in the Piazza Bologna." He spoke without bitterness, without apparent emotion, but his eyes were restless.

She noticed that he had put up his coat collar and was getting wet. Hesitantly she offered to share her umbrella with him on the way to the bus stop.

"Cesare Montaldo," he murmured, gravely accepting the um- brella and holding it high enough for both of them.

"Etta Oliva." She was, in her high heels, almost half a head taller than he.

They walked slowly along an avenue of damp cypresses to the gates of the cemetery, Etta keeping from him that she had been so deeply stricken by his story she could not get out even a sympathetic comment.

"Mourning is a hard business," Cesare said. "If people knew there'd be less death."

She sighed a slight smile.

Across the street from the bus stop was a bar with tables under a drawn awning. Cesare suggested coffee or perhaps an ice.

She thanked him and was about to refuse but his sad serious expression changed her mind and she went with him across the street. He guided her gently by the elbow, the other hand firmly holding the umbrella over them. She said she felt cold and they went inside.

He ordered an espresso but Etta settled for a piece of pastry, which she politely picked at with her fork. Between puffs of a cigarette he talked about himself. His voice was low and he spoke well. He was a freelance journalist, he said. Formerly he had worked in a government office but the work was boring so he had quit in disgust although he was in line for the directorship. "I would have directed the boredom." Now he was toying with the idea of going to America. He had a brother in Boston who wanted him to visit for several months and then decide whether he would emigrate permanently. The brother thought they could arrange that Cesare might come in through Canada. He had considered the idea but could not bring himself to break his ties with this kind of life for that. He seemed also to think that he would find it hard not to be able to go to his dead wife's grave when he was moved to do so. "You know how it is," he said, "with somebody you have once loved."

Etta felt for her handkerchief in her purse and touched her eyes.

"And you?" he asked sympathetically.

To her surprise she began to tell him her story. Though she had often related it to priests, she never had to anyone else, not even a friend. But she was telling it to a stranger because he seemed to be a man who would understand. And if later she regretted telling him, what difference would it make once he was gone?

She confessed she had prayed for her husband's death, and Cesare put down his coffee cup and sat with his cigarette between his lips, not puffing as she talked.

Armando, Etta said, had fallen in love with a cousin who had come during the summer from Perugia for a job in Rome. Her father had suggested that she live with them, and Armando and Etta, after talking it over, decided to let her stay for a while. They would save her rent to buy a secondhand television set so they could watch *Lascia o Raddoppia*, the quiz program that everyone in Rome watched on Thursday nights, and that way save themselves the embarrassment of waiting for invitations and having to accept them from neighbors they didn't like. The cousin came, Laura Ansaldo, a big-boned pretty girl of eighteen with thick brown hair and large eyes. She slept on the sofa in the living room, was easy to get along with, and made herself helpful in the kitchen before and after supper. Etta had liked her until she noticed that Armando had gone mad over the girl. She then tried to get rid of Laura but Armando threatened he would leave if she bothered her. One day Etta had come home from work and found them naked in the marriage bed, engaged in the act. She had screamed and wept. She called Laura a stinking whore and swore she would kill her if she didn't leave the house that minute. Armando was contrite. He promised he would send the girl back to Perugia, and the next day in the Stazione Termini had put her on the train. But the separation from her was more than he could bear. He grew nervous and miserable. Armando confessed himself one Saturday night and, for the first time in ten years, took communion, but instead of calming down he desired the girl more strongly. After a week he told Etta that he was going to get his cousin and bring her back to Rome.

"If you bring that whore here," Etta shouted, "I'll pray to Christ that you drop dead before you get back."

"In that case," Armando said, "start praying."

When he left the house she fell on her knees and prayed for his death.

That night Armando went with a friend to get Laura. The friend had a truck and was going to Assisi. On the way back he would pick them up in Perugia and drive to Rome. They started out when it was still twilight but it soon grew dark. Armando drove for a while, then felt sleepy and crawled into the back of the truck. The Perugian hills were foggy after a hot September day and the truck hit a rock in the road with a hard bump. Armando, in deep sleep, rolled out of the open tailgate of the truck, hitting the road with head and shoulders, then rolling down the hill. He was dead before he stopped rolling. When she heard of this Etta fainted away and it was two days before she could speak. After that she had prayed for her own death, and often did.

Etta turned her back to the other tables, though they were empty, and wept openly and quietly.

After a while Cesare squashed his butt. "Calma, signora. If God had wanted your husband to live he would still be living. Prayers have little relevance to the situation. To my way of thinking the whole thing was no more than a coincidence. It's best not to go too far with religion or it becomes troublesome."

"A prayer is a prayer," she said. "I suffer for mine."

Cesare pursed his lips. "But who can judge these things? They're much more complicated than most of us know. In the case of my wife I didn't pray for her death but I confess I might have wished it. Am I in a better position than you?"

"My prayer was a sin. You don't have that on your mind. It's worse than what you just might have thought."

"That's only a technical thing, signora."

"If Armando had lived," she said after a minute, "he would have been twenty-nine next month. I am a year older. But my life is useless now. I wait to join him."

He shook his head, seemed moved, and ordered an espresso for her.

Though Etta had stopped crying, for the first time in months she felt substantially disburdened.

Cesare would put her on the bus; as they were crossing the street he suggested they might meet now and then since they had so much in common.

"I live like a nun," she said.

He lifted his hat. "Coraggio," and she smiled at him for his kindness.

When she returned home that night the anguish of life without Armando recommenced. She remembered him as he had been when he was courting her and felt uneasy for having talked about him to Cesare. And she vowed for herself continued prayers, Rosaries, her own penitence to win him further indulgences in Purgatory.

Etta saw Cesare on a Sunday afternoon a week later. He had written her name in his little book and was able to locate her apartment in a house on the Via Nomentana through the help of a friend in the electric company.

When he knocked on her door she was surprised to see him, turned rather pale, though he hung back doubtfully. He said he had found out by accident where she lived and she asked for no details. Cesare had brought a small bunch of violets, which she embarrassedly accepted and put in water.

"You're looking better, signora," he said.

"My mourning for Armando goes on," she answered with a sad smile.

"Moderazione," he counseled, flicking his meaty ear with his finger. "You're still a young woman, and at that not bad-looking. You ought to acknowledge it to yourself. There are certain advantages to self-belief."

Etta made coffee and Cesare insisted on going out for a half dozen pastries.

He said as they were eating that he was considering emigrating if nothing better turned up soon. After a pause he said he had decided he had given more than his share to the dead. "I've been faithful to her memory but I have to think of myself once in a while. There comes a time when one has to return to life. It's only natural. Where there's life there's life."

She lowered her eyes and sipped her coffee.

Cesare set down his cup and got up. He put on his coat and thanked her. As he was buttoning his overcoat he said he would drop by again when he was in the neighborhood. He had a journalist friend who lived close by.

"Don't forget I'm still in mourning," Etta said.

He looked up at her respectfully. "Who can forget that, signora? Who would want to so long as you mourn?"

She then felt uneasy.

"You know my story." She spoke as though she was explaining again.

"I know," he said, "that we were both betrayed. They died and we suffer. My wife ate flowers and I belch."

"They suffer too. If Armando must suffer, I don't want it to be about me. I want him to feel that I'm still married to him." Her eyes were moist again.

"He's dead, signora. The marriage is over," Cesare said. "There's no marriage without his presence unless you expect the Holy Ghost." He spoke dryly, adding quietly, "Your needs are different from a dead man's, you're a healthy woman. Let's face the facts."

"Not spiritually," she said quickly.

"Spiritually and physically, there's no love in death."

She blushed and spoke in excitement. "There's love for the dead. Let him feel that I'm paying for my sin at the same time he is for his. To help him into heaven I keep myself pure. Let him feel that."

Cesare nodded and left, but Etta, after he had gone, continued to be troubled. She felt uneasy, could not define her mood, and stayed longer than usual at Armando's grave when she went the next day. She promised herself not to see Cesare again. In the next weeks she became a little miserly.

The journalist returned one evening almost a month later and Etta stood at the door in a way that indicated he would not be asked in. She had seen herself doing this if he appeared. But Cesare, with his hat in his hand, suggested a short stroll. The suggestion seemed so modest that she agreed. They walked down the Via Nomentana, Etta wearing her highest heels, Cesare unselfconsciously talking. He wore small patent-leather shoes and smoked as they strolled.

It was already early December, still late autumn rather than winter. A few leaves clung to a few trees and a warmish mist hung in the air. For a while Cesare talked of the political situation, but after an espresso in a bar on the Via Venti Settembre, as they were walking back he brought up the subject she had hoped to avoid. Cesare seemed suddenly to have lost his calm, unable to restrain what he had been planning to say. His voice was intense, his gestures impatient, his dark eyes restless. Although his outburst frightened her she could do nothing to prevent it.

"Signora," he said, "wherever your husband is you're not helping him by putting this penance on yourself. To help him, the best thing you can do is take up your normal life. Otherwise he will continue to suffer doubly, once for something he was guilty of, and the second time for the unfair burden your denial of life imposes on him."

"I am repenting my sins, not punishing him." She was too disturbed to say more, considered walking home wordless, then slamming the front door in his face; but she heard herself hastily saying, "If we became intimate it would be like adultery. We would be betraying the dead."

"Why is it you see everything in reverse?"

Cesare had stopped under a tree and almost jumped as he spoke. "They—*they* betrayed us. If you'll pardon me, signora, the truth is my wife was a pig. Your husband was a pig. We mourn because we hate them. Let's have the dignity to face the facts."

"No more," she moaned, hastily walking on. "Don't say anything else, I don't want to hear it."

"Etta," said Cesare passionately, walking after her, "this is my last word and then I'll nail my tongue to my jaw. Just remember this. If Our Lord Himself, this minute, let Armando rise from the dead to take up his life on earth, tonight—he would be lying in his cousin's bed."

She began to cry. Etta walked on, crying, realizing the truth of his remark. Cesare seemed to have said all he had wanted to, gently held her arm, breathing heavily as he escorted her back to her apartment. At the outer door, as she was trying to think how to get rid of him, how to end this, without waiting a minute he tipped his hat and walked off.

For more than a week Etta went through many torments. She felt a passionate desire to sleep with Cesare. Overnight her body became a torch. Her dreams were erotic. She saw Armando naked in bed with Laura, and in the same bed she saw herself with Cesare, clasping his body to hers. But she resisted—prayed, confessed her most lustful thoughts, and stayed for hours at Armando's grave to calm her mind.

Cesare knocked at her door one night, and because she was repelled when he suggested the marriage bed, she went with him to his rooms. Though she felt guilty afterwards she continued to visit Armando's grave, though less frequently, and she didn't tell Cesare that she had been to the cemetery when she went to his flat afterwards. Nor did he ask her, nor talk about his wife or Armando.

At first her uneasiness was intense. Etta felt as though she had committed adultery against the memory of her husband, but when she told herself over and over—there was no husband, he was dead; there was no husband, she was alone—she began to believe it. There was no husband, there was only his memory. She was not committing adultery. She was a lonely woman and had a lover, a widower, a gentle and affectionate man.

One night as they were lying in bed she asked Cesare about the possibility of marriage and he said that love was more important. They both knew how marriage destroyed love.

And when, two months later, she found she was pregnant and hurried that morning to Cesare's rooms to tell him, the journalist, in his pajamas, calmed her. "Let's not regret human life."

"It's your child," said Etta.

"I'll acknowledge it as mine," Cesare said, and Etta went home disturbed but happy.

The next day, when she returned at her usual hour, after having told Armando at his grave that she was at last going to have a baby, Cesare was gone.

"Moved," the landlady said, with a poof of her hand, and she didn't know where.

Though Etta's heart hurt and she mourned the loss of Cesare, try as she would she could not, even with the life in her womb, escape thinking of herself as a confirmed sinner; and she never returned to the cemetery to stand again at Armando's grave.

1963

❧ B M ❧

The Jewbird

The window was open so the skinny bird flew in. Flappity-flap with its frazzled black wings. That's how it goes. It's open, you're in. Closed, you're out, and that's your fate. The bird wearily flapped through the open kitchen window of Harry Cohen's top-floor apartment on First Avenue near the lower East River. On a rod on the wall hung an escaped-canary cage, its door wide open, but this black-type long-beaked bird—its ruffled head and small dull eyes, crossed a little, making it look like a dissipated crow—landed if not smack on Cohen's thick lamb chop, at least on the table, close by. The frozen-foods salesman was sitting at supper with his wife and young son on a hot August evening a year ago. Cohen, a heavy man with hairy chest and beefy shorts; Edie, in skinny yellow shorts and red halter; and their ten-year-old Morris (after her father)—Maurie, they called him, a nice kid though not overly bright—were all in the city after two weeks out, because Cohen's mother was dying. They had been enjoying Kingston, New York, but drove back when Mama got sick in her flat in the Bronx.

"Right on the table," said Cohen, putting down his beer glass and swatting at the bird. "Son of a bitch."

"Harry, take care with your language," Edie said, looking at Maurie, who watched every move.

The bird cawed hoarsely and with a flap of its bedraggled wings—feathers tufted this way and that—rose heavily to the top of the open kitchen door, where it perched staring down.

"Gevalt, a pogrom!"

"It's a talking bird," said Edie in astonishment.

"In Jewish," said Maurie.

"Wise guy," muttered Cohen. He gnawed on his chop, then put down the bone. "So if you can talk, say what's your business. What do you want here?"

"If you can't spare a lamb chop," said the bird, "I'll settle for a piece of herring with a crust of bread. You can't live on your nerve forever."

"This ain't a restaurant," Cohen replied. "All I'm asking is what brings you to this address?"

"The window was open," the bird sighed; adding after a moment, "I'm running. I'm flying but I'm also running."

"From whom?" asked Edie with interest.

"Anti-Semeets."

"Anti-Semites?" they all said.

"That's from who."

"What kind of anti-Semites bother a bird?" Edie asked.

"Any kind," said the bird, "also including eagles, vultures, and hawks. And once in a while some crows will take your eyes out."

"But aren't you a crow?"

"Me? I'm a Jewbird."

Cohen laughed heartily. "What do you mean by that?"

The bird began dovening. He prayed without Book or tallith, but with passion. Edie bowed her head, though not Cohen. And Maurie rocked back and forth with the prayers, looking up with one wide-open eye.

When the prayer was done Cohen remarked, "No hat, no phylacteries?"

"I'm an old radical."

"You're sure you're not some kind of a ghost or dybbuk?"

"Not a dybbuk," answered the bird, "though one of my relatives had such an experience once. It's all over now, thanks God. They freed her from a former lover, a crazy jealous man. She's now the mother of two wonderful children."

"Birds?" Cohen asked slyly.

"Why not?"

"What kind of birds?"

"Like me. Jewbirds."

Cohen tipped back in his chair and guffawed. "That's a big laugh. I heard of a Jewfish but not a Jewbird."

"We're once removed." The bird rested on one skinny leg, then on the other. "Please, could you spare maybe a piece of herring with a small crust of bread?"

Edie got up from the table.

"What are you doing?" Cohen asked her.

"I'll clear the dishes."

Cohen turned to the bird. "So what's your name, if you don't mind saying?"

"Call me Schwartz."

"He might be an old Jew changed into a bird by somebody," said Edie, removing a plate.

"Are you?" asked Harry, lighting a cigar.

"Who knows?" answered Schwartz. "Does God tell us everything?"

Maurie got up on his chair. "What kind of herring?" he asked the bird in excitement.

"Get down, Maurie, or you'll fall," ordered Cohen.

"If you haven't got matjes, I'll take schmaltz," said Schwartz.

"All we have is marinated, with slices of onion—in a jar," said Edie.

"If you'll open for me the jar I'll eat marinated. Do you have also, if you don't mind, a piece of rye bread—the spitz?"

Edie thought she had.

"Feed him out on the balcony," Cohen said. He spoke to the bird. "After that take off."

Schwartz closed both bird eyes. "I'm tired and it's a long way."

"Which direction are you headed, north or south?"

Schwartz, barely lifting his wings, shrugged.

"You don't know where you're going?"

"Where there's charity I'll go."

"Let him stay, Papa," said Maurie. "He's only a bird."

"So stay the night," Cohen said, "but not longer."

In the morning Cohen ordered the bird out of the house but Maurie cried, so Schwartz stayed for a while. Maurie was still on vacation from school and his friends were away. He was lonely and Edie enjoyed the fun he had playing with the bird.

"He's no trouble at all," she told Cohen, "and besides his appetite is very small."

"What'll you do when he makes dirty?"

"He flies across the street in a tree when he makes dirty, and if nobody passes below, who notices?"

"So all right," said Cohen, "but I'm dead set against it. I warn you he ain't gonna stay here long."

"What have you got against the poor bird?"

"Poor bird, my ass. He's a foxy bastard. He thinks he's a Jew."

"What difference does it make what he thinks?"

"A Jewbird, what a chutzpah. One false move and he's out on his drumsticks."

At Cohen's insistence Schwartz lived out on the balcony in a new wooden birdhouse Edie had bought him.

"With many thanks," said Schwartz, "though I would rather have a human roof over my head. You know how it is at my age. I like the warm, the windows, the smell of cooking. I would also be glad to see once in a while the *Jewish Morning Journal* and have now and then a schnapps because it helps my breathing, thanks God. But whatever you give me, you won't hear complaints."

However, when Cohen brought home a bird feeder full of dried corn, Schwartz said, "Impossible."

Cohen was annoyed. "What's the matter, crosseyes, is your life getting too good for you? Are you forgetting what it means to be migratory? I'll bet a helluva lot of crows you happen to be acquainted with, Jews or otherwise, would give their eyeteeth to eat this corn."

Schwartz did not answer. What can you say to a grubber yung?

"Not for my digestion," he later explained to Edie. "Cramps. Herring is better even if it makes you thirsty. At least rainwater don't cost anything." He laughed sadly in breathy caws.

And herring, thanks to Edie, who knew where to shop, was what Schwartz got, with an occasional piece of potato pancake, and even a bit of soupmeat when Cohen wasn't looking.

When school began in September, before Cohen would once again suggest giving the bird the boot, Edie prevailed on him to wait a little while until Maurie adjusted.

"To deprive him right now might hurt his schoolwork, and you know what trouble we had last year."

"So okay, but sooner or later the bird goes. That I promise you."

Schwartz, though nobody had asked him, took on full responsibility for Maurie's performance in school. In return for favors granted, when he was let in for an hour or two at night, he spent most of his time overseeing the boy's lessons. He sat on top of the dresser near Maurie's desk as he laboriously wrote out his homework. Maurie was a restless type and Schwartz gently kept him to his studies. He also listened to him practice his screechy violin, taking a few minutes off now and then to rest his ears in the bathroom. And they afterwards played dominoes. The boy was an indifferent checkers player and it was impossible to teach him chess. When he was sick, Schwartz read him comic books though he personally disliked them. But Maurie's work improved in school and even his violin teacher admitted his playing was better. Edie gave Schwartz credit for these improvements though the bird pooh-poohed them.

Yet he was proud there was nothing lower than C minuses on Maurie's report card, and on Edie's insistence celebrated with a little schnapps.

"If he keeps up like this," Cohen said, "I'll get him in an Ivy League college for sure."

"Oh, I hope so," sighed Edie.

But Schwartz shook his head. "He's a good boy—you don't have to worry. He won't be a shicker or a wife beater, God forbid, but a scholar he'll never be, if you know what I mean, although maybe a good mechanic. It's no disgrace in these times."

"If I was you," Cohen said, angered, "I'd keep my big snoot out of other people's private business."

"Harry, please," said Edie.

"My goddamn patience is wearing out. That crosseyes butts into everything."

Though he wasn't exactly a welcome guest in the house, Schwartz gained a few ounces, although he did not improve in appearance. He looked bedraggled as ever, his feathers unkempt, as though he had just flown out of a snowstorm. He spent, he admitted, little time taking care of himself. Too much to think about. "Also outside plumbing," he told Edie. Still there was more glow to his eyes so that though Cohen went on calling him crosseyes he said it less emphatically.

Liking his situation, Schwartz tried tactfully to stay out of Cohen's way, but one night when Edie was at the movies and Maurie was taking a hot shower, the frozen-foods salesman began a quarrel with the bird.

"For Christ sake, why don't you wash yourself sometimes? Why must you always stink like a dead fish?"

"Mr. Cohen, if you'll pardon me, if somebody eats garlic he will smell from garlic. I eat herring three times a day. Feed me flowers and I will smell like flowers."

"Who's obligated to feed you anything at all? You're lucky to get herring."

"Excuse me, I'm not complaining," said the bird. "You're complaining."

"What's more," said Cohen, "even from out on the balcony I can hear you snoring away like a pig. It keeps me awake nights."

"Snoring," said Schwartz, "isn't a crime, thanks God."

"All in all you are a goddamn pest and freeloader. Next thing you'll want to sleep in bed next to my wife."

"Mr. Cohen," said Schwartz, "on this rest assured. A bird is a bird."

"So you say, but how do I know you're a bird and not some kind of a goddamn devil?"

"If I was a devil you would know already. And I don't mean because your son's good marks."

"Shut up, you bastard bird," shouted Cohen.

"Grubber yung," cawed Schwartz, rising to the tips of his talons, his long wings outstretched.

Cohen was about to lunge for the bird's scrawny neck but Maurie came out of the bathroom, and for the rest of the evening until Schwartz's bedtime on the balcony, there was pretend peace.

But the quarrel had deeply disturbed Schwartz and he slept badly. His snoring woke him, and awake, he was fearful of what would become of him. Wanting to stay out of Cohen's way, he kept to the bird-house as much as possible. Cramped by it, he paced back and forth on the balcony ledge, or sat on the birdhouse roof, staring into space. In the evenings, while overseeing Maurie's lessons, he often fell asleep. Awakening, he nervously hopped around exploring the four corners of the room. He spent much time in Maurie's closet, and carefully examined his bureau drawers when they were left open. And once when he found a large paper bag on the floor, Schwartz poked his way into it to investigate what the possibilities were. The boy was amused to see the bird in the paper bag.

"He wants to build a nest," he said to his mother.

Edie, sensing Schwartz's unhappiness, spoke to him quietly.

"Maybe if you did some of the things my husband wants you, you would get along better with him."

"Give me a for instance," Schwartz said.

"Like take a bath, for instance."

"I'm too old for baths," said the bird. "My feathers fall out without baths."

"He says you have a bad smell."

"Everybody smells. Some people smell because of their thoughts or because who they are. My bad smell comes from the food I eat. What does his come from?"

"I better not ask him or it might make him mad," said Edie.

In late November Schwartz froze on the balcony in the fog and cold, and especially on rainy days he woke with stiff joints and could barely move his wings. Already he felt twinges of rheumatism. He would have liked to spend more time in the warm house, particularly when Maurie was in school and Cohen at work. But though Edie was goodhearted and might have sneaked him in in the morning, just to thaw out, he was afraid to ask her. In the meantime Cohen, who had been reading articles about the migration of birds, came out on the balcony one night after work when Edie was in the kitchen preparing pot roast and, peeking into the birdhouse, warned Schwartz to be on his way soon if he knew what was good for him. "Time to hit the flyways."

"Mr. Cohen, why do you hate me so much?" asked the bird. "What did I do to you?"

"Because you're an A-number-one troublemaker, that's why. What's more, whoever heard of a Jewbird? Now scat or it's open war."

But Schwartz stubbornly refused to depart so Cohen embarked on a campaign of harassing him, meanwhile hiding it from Edie and Maurie. Maurie hated violence and Cohen didn't want to leave a bad impression. He thought maybe if he played dirty tricks on the bird he would fly off without being physically kicked out. The vacation was over, let him make his easy living off the fat of somebody else's land. Cohen worried about the effect of the bird's departure on Maurie's schooling but decided to take the chance, first, because the boy now seemed to have the knack of studying—give the black bird-bastard credit—and second, because Schwartz was driving him bats by being there always, even in his dreams.

The frozen-foods salesman began his campaign against the bird by mixing watery cat food with the herring slices in Schwartz's dish. He also blew up and popped numerous paper bags outside the birdhouse as the bird slept, and when he had got Schwartz good and nervous, though not enough to leave, he brought a full-grown cat into the house, supposedly a gift for little Maurie, who had always wanted a pussy. The cat never stopped springing up at Schwartz whenever he saw him, one day managing to claw out several of his tail feathers. And even at lesson time, when the cat was usually excluded from Maurie's room, though somehow or other he quickly found his way in at the end of the lesson, Schwartz was desperately fearful of his life and flew from pinnacle to pinnacle—light fixture to clothestree to door top—in order to elude the beast's wet jaws.

Once when the bird complained to Edie how hazardous his existence was, she said, "Be patient, Mr. Schwartz. When the cat gets to know you better he won't try to catch you anymore."

"When he stops trying we will both be in Paradise," Schwartz answered. "Do me a favor and get rid of him. He makes my whole life worry. I'm losing feathers like a tree loses leaves."

"I'm awfully sorry but Maurie likes the pussy and sleeps with it."

What could Schwartz do? He worried but came to no decision, being afraid to leave. So he ate the herring garnished with cat food, tried hard not to hear the paper bags bursting like firecrackers outside the birdhouse at night, and lived terror-stricken, closer to the ceiling than the floor, as the cat, his tail flicking, endlessly watched him.

Weeks went by. Then on the day after Cohen's mother had died in her flat in the Bronx, when Maurie came home with a zero on an arithmetic test, Cohen, enraged, waited until Edie had taken the boy to his violin lesson, then openly attacked the bird. He chased him with a broom on the balcony and Schwartz frantically flew back and forth, finally escaping into his birdhouse. Cohen triumphantly reached in and, grabbing both skinny legs, dragged the bird out, cawing loudly, his wings wildly beating. He whirled the bird around and around his head. But Schwartz, as he moved in circles, managed to swoop down and catch Cohen's nose in his beak, and hung on for dear life. Cohen cried out in great pain, punched at the bird with his fist, and, tugging at its legs with all his might, pulled his nose free. Again he swung the yawking Schwartz around until the bird grew dizzy, then, with a furious heave, flung him into the night. Schwartz sank like a stone into the street. Cohen then tossed the birdhouse and feeder after him, listening at the ledge until they crashed on the sidewalk below. For a full hour, broom in hand, his heart palpitating and nose throbbing with pain, Cohen waited for Schwartz to return, but the brokenhearted bird didn't.

That's the end of that dirty bastard, the salesman thought and went in. Edie and Maurie had come home.

"Look," said Cohen, pointing to his bloody nose swollen three times its size, "what that sonofabitchy bird did. It's a permanent scar."

"Where is he now?" Edie asked, frightened.

"I threw him out and he flew away. Good riddance."

Nobody said no, though Edie touched a handkerchief to her eyes and Maurie rapidly tried the nine-times table and found he knew approximately half.

In the spring when the winter's snow had melted, the boy, moved by a memory, wandered in the neighborhood, looking for Schwartz. He found a dead black bird in a small lot by the river, his two wings broken, neck twisted, and both bird-eyes plucked clean.

"Who did it to you, Mr. Schwartz?" Maurie wept.

"Anti-Semeets," Edie said later.

1963

Black Is My Favorite Color

Charity Quietness sits in the toilet eating her two hard-boiled eggs while I'm having my ham sandwich and coffee in the kitchen. That's how it goes, only don't get the idea of ghettos. If there's a ghetto I'm the one that's in it. She's my cleaning woman from Father Divine and comes in once a week to my small three-room apartment on my day off from the liquor store. "Peace," she says to me. "Father reached on down and took me right up in Heaven." She's a small person with a flat body, frizzy hair, and a quiet face that the light shines out of, and Mama had such eyes before she died. The first time Charity Quietness came in to clean, a little more than a year and a half, I made the mistake to ask her to sit down at the kitchen table with me and eat her lunch. I was still feeling not so hot after Ornita left, but I'm the kind of a man—Nat Lime, forty-four, a bachelor with a daily growing bald spot on the back of my head, and I could lose frankly fifteen pounds—who enjoys company so long as he has it. So she cooked up her two hard-boiled eggs and sat down and took a small bite out of one of them. But after a minute she stopped chewing and she got up and carried the eggs in a cup to the bathroom, and since then she eats there. I said to her more than once, "Okay, Charity Quietness, so have it your way, eat the eggs in the kitchen by yourself and I'll eat when you're done," but she smiles absentminded, and eats in the toilet. It's my fate with colored people.

Although black is still my favorite color you wouldn't know it from my luck except in short quantities, even though I do all right in the liquor store business in Harlem, on Eighth Avenue between 110th and 111th. I speak with respect. A large part of my life I've had dealings with Negro people, most on a business basis but sometimes for friendly reasons with genuine feeling on both sides. I'm drawn to them. At this time of my life I should have one or two good colored friends, but the fault isn't necessarily mine. If they knew what was in my heart toward them, but how can you tell that to anybody nowadays? I've tried more than once but the language of the heart either is a dead language or else nobody understands it the way you speak it. Very few. What I'm saying is, personally for me there's only one human color and that's the color of blood. I like a black person if not because he's black, then because I'm white. It comes to the same thing. If I wasn't white my first choice would be black. I'm satisfied to be white because I have no other choice. Anyway, I got an eye for color. I appreciate. Who wants everybody to be the same? Maybe it's like some kind of a talent. Nat Lime might be a liquor dealer in Harlem, but once in the jungle in New Guinea in the Second World War, I got the idea, when I shot at a running Jap and missed him, that I had some kind of a talent, though maybe it's the kind where you have a good idea now and then, but in the end what do they come to? After all, it's a strange world.

Where Charity Quietness eats her eggs makes me think about Buster Wilson when we were both boys in the Williamsburg section of Brooklyn. There was this long block of run-down dirty frame houses in the middle of a not-so-hot white neighborhood full of pushcarts. The Negro houses looked to me like they had been born and died there, dead not long after the beginning of the world. I lived on the next street. My father was a cutter with arthritis in both hands, big red knuckles and fingers so swollen he didn't cut, and my mother was the one who went to work. She sold paper bags from a secondhand pushcart on Ellery Street. We didn't starve but nobody ate chicken unless we were sick, or the chicken was. This was my first acquaintance with a lot of black people and I used to poke around on their poor block. I think I thought, Brother, if there can be like this, what can't there be? I mean I caught an early idea what life was about. Anyway, I met Buster Wilson there. He used to play marbles by himself. I sat on the curb across the street, watching him shoot one marble lefty and the other one righty. The hand that won picked up the marbles. It wasn't so much of a game but he didn't ask me to come over. My idea was to be friendly, only he never encouraged, he discouraged. Why did I pick him out for a friend? Maybe because I had no others then, we were new in the neighborhood, from Manhattan. Also I liked his type. Buster did everything alone. He was a skinny kid and his brothers' clothes hung on him like worn-out potato sacks. He was a beanpole boy, about twelve, and I was then ten. His arms and legs were burnt-out matchsticks. He always wore a brown wool sweater, one arm half unraveled, the other went down to the wrist. His long and narrow head had a white part cut straight in the short woolly hair, maybe with a ruler there, by his father, a barber but too drunk to stay a barber. In those days though I had little myself I was old enough to know who was better off, and the whole block of colored houses made me feel bad in the daylight. But I went there as much as I could because the street was full of life. In the night it looked different, it's hard to tell a cripple in the dark. Sometimes I was afraid to walk by the houses when they were dark and quiet. I was afraid there were people looking at me that I couldn't see. I liked it better when they had parties at night and everybody had a good time. The musicians played their banjos and saxophones and the houses shook with the music and laughing. The young girls, with their pretty dresses and ribbons in their hair, caught me in my throat when I saw them through the windows.

But with the parties came drinking and fights. Sundays were bad days after the Saturday-night parties. I remember once that Buster's father, also long and loose, always wearing a dirty gray Homburg hat, chased another black man in the street with a half-inch chisel. The other one, maybe five feet high, lost his shoe and when they wrestled on the ground he was already bleeding through his suit, a thick red blood smearing the sidewalk. I was frightened by the blood and wanted to pour it back in the man who was bleeding from the chisel. On another time Buster's father was playing in a crap game with two big bouncy red dice, in the back of an alley between two middle houses. Then about six men started fistfighting there, and they ran out of the alley and hit each other in the street. The neighbors, including children, came out and watched, everybody afraid but nobody moving to do anything. I saw the same thing near my store in Harlem, years later, a big crowd watching two men in the street, their breaths hanging in the air on a winter night, murdering each other with switchblade knives, but nobody moved to call a cop. I didn't either. Anyway, I was just a young kid but I still remember how the cops drove up in a police paddy wagon and broke up the fight by hitting everybody they could hit with big nightsticks. This was in the days before La Guardia. Most of the fighters were knocked out cold, only one or two got away. Buster's father started to run back in his house but a cop ran after him and cracked him on his Homburg hat with a club, right on the front porch. Then the Negro men were lifted up by the cops, one at the arms and the other at the feet, and they heaved them in the paddy wagon. Buster's father hit the back of the wagon and fell, with his nose spouting very red blood, on top of three other men. I personally couldn't stand it, I was scared of the human race so I ran home, but I remember Buster watching without any expression in his eyes. I stole an extra fifteen cents from my mother's pocketbook and I ran back and asked Buster if he wanted to go to the movies, I would pay. He said yes. This was the first time he talked to me.

So we went more than once to the movies. But we never got to be friends. Maybe because it was a one-way proposition—from me to him. Which includes my invitations to go with me, my (poor mother's) movie money, Hershey chocolate bars, watermelon slices, even my best Nick Carter and Merriwell books that I spent hours picking up in the junk shops, and that he never gave me back. Once, he let me go in his house to get a match so we could smoke some butts we found, but it smelled so heavy, so impossible, I died till I got out of there. What I saw in the way of furniture I won't mention—the best was falling apart in pieces. Maybe we went to the movies altogether five or six matinees that spring and in the summertime, but when the shows were over he usually walked home by himself.

"Why don't you wait for me, Buster?" I said. "We're both going in the same direction."

But he was walking ahead and didn't hear me. Anyway he didn't answer.

One day when I wasn't expecting it he hit me in the teeth. I felt like crying but not because of the pain. I spit blood and said, "What did you hit me for? What did I do to you?"

"Because you a Jew bastard. Take your Jew movies and your Jew candy and shove them up your Jew ass."

And he ran away.

I thought to myself how was I to know he didn't like the movies. When I was a man I thought, You can't force it.

Years later, in the prime of my life, I met Mrs. Ornita Harris. She was standing by herself under an open umbrella at the bus stop, crosstown 110th, and I picked up her green glove that she had dropped on the wet sidewalk. It was in the end of November. Before I could ask her was it hers, she grabbed the glove out of my hand, closed her umbrella,

and stepped in the bus. I got on right after her. I was annoyed so I said,
"If you'll pardon me, miss, there's no law that you have to say thanks,
but at least don't make a criminal out of me."

"Well, I'm sorry," she said, "but I don't like white men trying to
do me favors."

I tipped my hat and that was that. In ten minutes I got off the bus
but she was already gone.

Who expected to see her again, but I did. She came into my store
about a week later for a bottle of Scotch.

"I would offer you a discount," I told her, "but I know you don't
like a certain kind of a favor and I'm not looking for a slap in the face."

Then she recognized me and got a little embarrassed.

"I'm sorry I misunderstood you that day."

"So mistakes happen."

The result was she took the discount. I gave her a dollar off.

She used to come in every two weeks for a fifth of Haig & Haig.
Sometimes I waited on her, sometimes my helpers, Jimmy or Mason,
also colored, but I said to give the discount. They both looked at me but
I had nothing to be ashamed. In the spring when she came in we used
to talk once in a while. She was a slim woman, dark, but not the most
dark, about thirty years I would say, also well built, with a combination
nice legs and a good-size bosom that I like. Her face was pretty, with
big eyes and high cheekbones, but lips a little thick and nose a little
broad. Sometimes she didn't feel like talking, she paid for the bottle,
less discount, and walked out. Her eyes were tired and she didn't look
to me like a happy woman.

I found out her husband was once a window cleaner on the big
buildings, but one day his safety belt broke and he fell fifteen stories.
After the funeral she got a job as a manicurist in a Times Square barbershop. I told her I was a bachelor and lived with my mother in a small
three-room apartment on West Eighty-third near Broadway. My
mother had cancer, and Ornita said she was very sorry.

One night in July we went out together. How that happened I'm
still not so sure. I guess I asked her and she didn't say no. Where do you
go out with a Negro woman? We went to the Village. We had a good
dinner and walked in Washington Square Park. It was a hot night. Nobody was surprised when they saw us, nobody looked at us like we were
against the law. If they looked maybe they saw my new lightweight suit
that I bought yesterday and my shiny bald spot when we walked under
a lamp, also how pretty she was for a man my type. We went in a movie
on West Eighth Street. I didn't want to go in but she said she had heard

about the picture. We went in like strangers and we came out like strangers. I wondered what was in her mind and I thought to myself, Whatever is in there it's not a certain white man that I know. All night long we went together like we were chained. After the movie she wouldn't let me take her back to Harlem. When I put her in a taxi she asked me, "Why did we bother?"

For the steak, I thought of saying. Instead I said, "You're worth the bother."

"Thanks anyway."

Kiddo, I thought to myself after the taxi left, you just found out what's what, now the best thing is forget her.

It's easy to say. In August we went out the second time. That was the night she wore a purple dress and I thought to myself, My God, what colors. Who paints that picture paints a masterpiece. Everybody looked at us but I had pleasure. That night when she took off her dress it was in a furnished room I had the sense to rent a few days before. With my sick mother, I couldn't ask her to come to my apartment, and she didn't want me to go home with her where she lived with her brother's family on West 115th near Lenox Avenue. Under her purple dress she wore a black slip, and when she took that off she had white underwear. When she took off the white underwear she was black again. But I know where the next white was, if you want to call it white. And that was the night I think I fell in love with her, the first time in my life, though I have liked one or two nice girls I used to go with when I was a boy. It was a serious proposition. I'm the kind of a man when I think of love I'm thinking of marriage. I guess that's why I am a bachelor.

That same week I had a holdup in my place, two big men—both black—with revolvers. One got excited when I rang open the cash register so he could take the money, and he hit me over the ear with his gun. I stayed in the hospital a couple of weeks. Otherwise I was insured. Ornita came to see me. She sat on a chair without talking much. Finally I saw she was uncomfortable so I suggested she ought to go home.

"I'm sorry it happened," she said.

"Don't talk like it's your fault."

When I got out of the hospital my mother was dead. She was a wonderful person. My father died when I was thirteen and all by herself she kept the family alive and together. I sat shiva for a week and remembered how she sold paper bags on her pushcart. I remembered her life and what she tried to teach me. Nathan, she said, if you ever forget you are a Jew a goy will remind you. Mama, I said, rest in peace on this subject. But if I do something you don't like, remember, on earth it's harder than where you are. Then when my week of mourning was finished, one night I said, "Ornita, let's get married. We're both honest people and if you love me like I love you it won't be such a bad time. If you don't like New York I'll sell out here and we'll move someplace else. Maybe to San Francisco, where nobody knows us. I was there for a week in the Second War and I saw white and colored living together."

"Nat," she answered me, "I like you but I'd be afraid. My husband woulda killed me."

"Your husband is dead."

"Not in my memory."

"In that case I'll wait."

"Do you know what it'd be like—I mean the life we could expect?"

"Ornita," I said, "I'm the kind of a man, if he picks his own way of life he's satisfied."

"What about children? Were you looking forward to half-Jewish polka dots?"

"I was looking forward to children."

"I can't," she said.

Can't is can't. I saw she was afraid and the best thing was not to push. Sometimes when we met she was so nervous that whatever we did she couldn't enjoy it. At the same time I still thought I had a chance. We were together more and more. I got rid of my furnished room and she came to my apartment—I gave away Mama's bed and bought a new one. She stayed with me all day on Sundays. When she wasn't so nervous she was affectionate, and if I know what love is, I had it. We went out a couple of times a week, the same way—usually I met her in Times Square and sent her home in a taxi, but I talked more about marriage and she talked less against it. One night she told me she was still trying to convince herself but she was almost convinced. I took an inventory of my liquor stock so I could put the store up for sale.

Ornita knew what I was doing. One day she quit her job, the next she took it back. She also went away a week to visit her sister in Philadelphia for a little rest. She came back tired but said maybe. Maybe is maybe so I'll wait. The way she said it, it was closer to yes. That was the winter two years ago. When she was in Philadelphia I called up a friend of mine from the army, now a CPA, and told him I would appreciate an invitation for an evening. He knew why. His wife said yes right away. When Ornita came back we went there. The wife made a fine dinner. It wasn't a bad time and they told us to come again. Ornita had a few drinks. She looked relaxed, wonderful. Later, because of a twenty-four-hour taxi strike I had to take her home on the subway. When we got to the 116th Street station she told me to go back on the train, and she would walk the couple of blocks to her house. I didn't like a woman walking alone on the streets at that time of the night. She said she never had any trouble but I insisted nothing doing. I said I would walk to her stoop with her and when she went upstairs I would go to the subway.

On the way there, on 115th in the middle of the block before Lenox, we were stopped by three men—maybe they were boys. One had a black hat with a half-inch brim, one a green cloth hat, and the third wore a black leather cap. The green hat was wearing a short coat and the other two had long ones. It was under a streetlight but the leather cap snapped a six-inch switchblade open in the light.

"What you doin with this white son of a bitch?" he said to Ornita.

"I'm minding my own business," she answered him, "and I wish you would too."

"Boys," I said, "we're all brothers. I'm a reliable merchant in the neighborhood. This young lady is my dear friend. We don't want any trouble. Please let us pass."

"You talk like a Jew landlord," said the green hat. "Fifty a week for a single room."

"No charge fo the rats," said the half-inch brim.

"Believe me, I'm no landlord. My store is Nathan's Liquors between Hundred Tenth and Eleventh. I also have two colored clerks, Mason and Jimmy, and they will tell you I pay good wages as well as I give discounts to certain customers."

"Shut your mouth, Jewboy," said the leather cap, and he moved the knife back and forth in front of my coat button. "No more black pussy for you."

"Speak with respect about this lady, please."

I got slapped on my mouth.

"That ain't no lady," said the long face in the half-inch brim, "that's black pussy. She deserve to have evvy bit of her hair shave off. How you like to have evvy bit of your hair shave off, black pussy?"

"Please leave me and this gentleman alone or I'm gonna scream long and loud. That's my house three doors down."

They slapped her. I never heard such a scream. Like her husband was falling fifteen stories.

I hit the one that slapped her and the next I knew I was laying in the gutter with a pain in my head. I thought, Goodbye, Nat, they'll stab me for sure, but all they did was take my wallet and run in three directions.

Ornita walked back with me to the subway and she wouldn't let me go home with her again.

"Just get home safely."

She looked terrible. Her face was gray and I still remembered her scream. It was a terrible winter night, very cold February, and it took me an hour and ten minutes to get home. I felt bad for leaving her but what could I do?

We had a date downtown the next night but she didn't show up, the first time.

In the morning I called her in her place of business.

"For God's sake, Ornita, if we got married and moved away we wouldn't have the kind of trouble that we had. We wouldn't come in that neighborhood anymore."

"Yes, we would. I have family there and don't want to move anyplace else. The truth of it is I can't marry you, Nat. I got troubles enough of my own."

"I coulda sworn you love me."

"Maybe I do but I can't marry you."

"For God's sake, why?"

"I got enough trouble of my own."

I went that night in a cab to her brother's house to see her. He was a quiet man with a thin mustache. "She gone," he said, "left for a long visit to some close relatives in the South. She said to tell you she appreciate your intentions but didn't think it will work out."

"Thank you kindly," I said.

Don't ask me how I got home.

Once, on Eighth Avenue, a couple of blocks from my store, I saw a blind man with a white cane tapping on the sidewalk. I figured we were going in the same direction so I took his arm.

"I can tell you're white," he said.

A heavy colored woman with a full shopping bag rushed after us.

"Never mind," she said, "I know where he live."

She pushed me with her shoulder and I hurt my leg on the fire hydrant.

That's how it is. I give my heart and they kick me in my teeth.

"Charity Quietness—you hear me?—come out of that goddamn toilet!"

❦ B M ❦

Naked Nude

1

Fidelman listlessly doodled all over a sheet of yellow paper. Odd indecipherable designs, ink-spotted blotched words, esoteric ideographs, tormented figures in a steaming sulfurous lake, including a stylish nude rising newborn from the water. Not bad at all, though more mannequin than Knidean Aphrodite. Scarpio, sharp-nosed on the former art student's gaunt left, looking up from his cards inspected her with his good eye.

"Not bad, who is she?"

"Nobody I really know."

"You must be hard up."

"It happens in art."

"Quiet," rumbled Angelo, the padrone, on Fidelman's fat right, his two-chinned face molded in lard. He flipped the top card.

Scarpio then turned up a deuce, making eight and a half and out. He cursed his Sainted Mother, Angelo wheezing. Fidelman showed four and his last hundred lire. He picked a cautious ace and sighed. Angelo, with seven showing, chose that passionate moment to get up and relieve himself.

"Wait for me," he ordered. "Watch the money, Scarpio."

"Who's that hanging?" Scarpio pointed to a long-coated figure loosely dangling from a gallows rope amid Fidelman's other drawings.

Who but Susskind, surely, a figure out of the far-off past.

"Just a friend."

"Which one?"

"Nobody you know."

"It better not be."

Scarpio picked up the yellow paper for a closer squint.

"But whose head?" he asked with interest. A long-nosed severed head bounced down the steps of the guillotine platform.

A man's head or his sex? Fidelman wondered. In either case a terrible wound.

"Looks a little like mine," he confessed. "At least the long jaw."

Scarpio pointed to a street scene. In front of American Express here's this starving white Negro pursued by a hooting mob of cowboys on horses.

Embarrassed by the recent past Fidelman blushed.

It was long after midnight. They sat motionless in Angelo's stuffy office, a small lit bulb hanging down over a square wooden table on which lay a pack of puffy cards, Fidelman's naked hundred-lire note, and a green bottle of Munich beer that the padrone of the Hotel du Ville, Milano, swilled from, between hands or games. Scarpio, his majordomo and secretary-lover, sipped an espresso, and Fidelman only watched, being without privileges. Each night they played sette e mezzo, jeenrummy, or baccarat and Fidelman lost the day's earnings, the few meager tips he had garnered from the whores for little services rendered. Angelo said nothing and took all.

Scarpio, snickering, understood the street scene. Fidelman, adrift penniless in the stony gray Milanese streets, had picked his first pocket, of an American tourist staring into a store window. The Texan, feeling the tug, and missing his wallet, had bellowed murder. A carabiniere looked wildly at Fidelman, who broke into a run, another well-dressed carabiniere on a horse clattering after him down the street, waving his sword. Angelo, cleaning his fingernails with his penknife in front of his hotel, saw Fidelman coming and ducked him around a corner, through a cellar door, into the Hotel du Ville, a joint for prostitutes who split their fees with the padrone for the use of a room. Angelo registered the former art student, gave him a tiny dark room, and, pointing a gun, relieved him of his passport, recently renewed, and the contents of the Texan's wallet. He warned him that if he so much as peeped to anybody, he would at once report him to the questura, where his brother presided, as a dangerous alien thief. The former art student, desperate to escape, needed money to travel, so he sneaked into Angelo's room one morning and, from the strapped suitcase under the bed, extracted fistfuls of lire, stuffing all his pockets. Scarpio, happening in, caught him at it and held a pointed dagger to

Fidelman's ribs—who fruitlessly pleaded they could both make a living from the suitcase—until the padrone appeared.

"A hunchback is straight only in the grave." Angelo slapped Fidelman's face first with one fat hand, then with the other, till it turned red and the tears freely flowed. He chained him to the bed in his room for a week. When Fidelman promised to behave he was released and appointed "mastro delle latrine," having to clean thirty toilets every day with a stiff brush, for room and board. He also assisted Teresa, the asthmatic, hairy-legged chambermaid, and ran errands for the whores. The former art student hoped to escape but the portiere or his assistant was at the door twenty-four hours a day. And thanks to the card games and his impassioned gambling Fidelman was without sufficient funds to go anywhere, if there was anywhere to go. And without a passport, so he stayed put.

Scarpio secretly felt Fidelman's thigh.

"Let go or I'll tell the padrone."

Angelo returned and flipped up a card. Queen. Seven and a half on the button. He pocketed Fidelman's last hundred lire.

"Go to bed," Angelo commanded. "It's a long day tomorrow."

Fidelman climbed up to his room on the fifth floor and stared out the window into the dark street to see how far down was death. Too far, so he undressed for bed. He looked every night and sometimes during the day. Teresa, screaming, had once held on to both his legs as Fidelman dangled half out of the window until one of the girls' naked customers, a barrel-chested man, rushed into the room and dragged him back in. Sometimes Fidelman wept in his sleep.

•

He awoke, cringing. Angelo and Scarpio had entered his room but nobody hit him.

"Search anywhere," he offered, "you won't find anything except maybe half a stale pastry."

"Shut up," said Angelo. "We came to make a proposition."

Fidelman slowly sat up. Scarpio produced the yellow sheet he had doodled on. "We notice you draw." He pointed a dirty fingernail at the nude figure.

"After a fashion," Fidelman said modestly. "I doodle and see what happens."

"Could you copy a painting?"

"What sort of painting?"

"A nude. Tiziano's 'Venus of Urbino.' The one after Giorgione."

"That one," said Fidelman, thinking. "I doubt that I could."

"Any fool can."

"Shut up, Scarpio," Angelo said. He sat his bulk at the foot of Fidelman's narrow bed. Scarpio, with his good eye, moodily inspected the cheerless view from the window.

"On Isola Bella in Lago Maggiore, about an hour from here," said Angelo, "there's a small castello full of lousy paintings, except for one which is a genuine Tiziano, authenticated by three art experts, including a brother-in-law of mine. It's worth half a million dollars but the owner is richer than Olivetti and won't sell though an American museum is breaking its head to get it."

"Very interesting," Fidelman said.

"Exactly," said Angelo. "Anyway, it's insured for at least $400,000. Of course if anyone stole it it would be impossible to sell."

"Then why bother?"

"Bother what?"

"Whatever it is," Fidelman said lamely.

"You'll learn more by listening," Angelo said. "Suppose it was stolen and held for ransom. What do you think of that?"

"Ransom?" said Fidelman.

"Ransom," Scarpio said from the window.

"At least $300,000," said Angelo. "It would be a bargain for the insurance company. They'd save a hundred thousand on the deal."

He outlined a plan. They had photographed the Titian on both sides, from all angles and several distances, and had collected from art books the best color plates. They also had the exact measurements of the canvas and every figure on it. If Fidelman could make a decent copy they would duplicate the frame and on a dark night sneak the reproduction into the castello gallery and exit with the original. The guards were stupid, and the advantage of the plan—instead of just slitting the canvas out of its frame—was that nobody would recognize the substitution for days, possibly longer. In the meantime they would row the picture across the lake and truck it out of the country down to the French Riviera. The Italian police had fantastic luck in recovering stolen paintings; one had a better chance in France. Once the picture was securely hidden, Angelo back at the hotel, Scarpio would get in touch with the insurance company. Imagine the sensation! Recognizing the brilliance of the execution, the company would have to kick in with the ransom money.

"If you make a good copy, you'll get yours," said Angelo.

"Mine? What would that be?" Fidelman asked.

"Your passport," Angelo said cagily. "Plus two hundred dollars in cash and a quick goodbye."

"Five hundred dollars," said Fidelman.

"Scarpio," said the padrone patiently, "show him what you have in your pants."

Scarpio unbuttoned his jacket and drew a long mean-looking dagger from a sheath under his belt. Fidelman, without trying, could feel the cold blade sinking into his ribs.

"Three fifty," he said. "I'll need plane fare."

"Three fifty," said Angelo. "Payable when you deliver the finished reproduction."

"And you pay for all supplies?"

"I pay all expenses within reason. But if you try any monkey tricks—snitch or double cross—you'll wake up with your head gone, or something worse."

"Tell me," Fidelman asked after a minute of contemplation, "what if I turn down the proposition? I mean in a friendly way?"

Angelo rose sternly from the creaking bed. "Then you'll stay here for the rest of your life. When you leave you leave in a coffin, very cheap wood."

"I see," said Fidelman.

"What do you say?"

"What more can I say?"

"Then it's settled," said Angelo.

"Take the morning off," said Scarpio.

"Thanks," Fidelman said.

Angelo glared. "First finish the toilet bowls."

•

Am I worthy? Fidelman thought. Can I do it? Do I dare? He had these and other doubts, felt melancholy, and wasted time.

Angelo one morning called him into his office. "Have a Munich beer."

"No, thanks."

"Cordial?"

"Nothing now."

"What's the matter with you? You look like you buried your mother."

Fidelman set down his mop and pail with a sigh and said nothing.

"Why don't you put those things away and get started?" the padrone asked. "I've had the portiere move six trunks and some broken furniture out of the storeroom where you have two big windows. Scarpio wheeled in an easel and he's bought you brushes, colors, and whatever else you need."

"It's west light, not very even."

Angelo shrugged. "It's the best I can do. This is our season and I can't spare any rooms. If you'd rather work at night we can set up some lamps. It's a waste of electricity but I'll make that concession to your temperament if you work fast and produce the goods."

"What's more I don't know the first thing about forging paintings," Fidelman said. "All I might do is just about copy the picture."

"That's all we ask. Leave the technical business to us. First do a decent drawing. When you're ready to paint I'll get you a piece of sixteenth-century Belgian linen that's been scraped clean of a former picture. You prime it with white lead and when it's dry you sketch. Once you finish the nude, Scarpio and I will bake it, put in the cracks, and age them with soot. We'll even stipple in fly spots before we varnish and glue. We'll do what's necessary. There are books on this subject and Scarpio reads like a demon. It isn't as complicated as you think."

"What about the truth of the colors?"

"I'll mix them for you. I've made a life study of Tiziano's work."

"Really?"

"Of course."

But Fidelman's eyes still looked unhappy.

"What's eating you now?" the padrone asked.

"It's stealing another painter's ideas and work."

The padrone wheezed. "Tiziano will forgive you. Didn't he steal the figure of the Urbino from Giorgione? Didn't Rubens steal the Andrian nude from Tiziano? Art steals and so does everybody. You stole a wallet and tried to steal my lire. It's the way of the world. We're only human."

"Isn't it sort of a desecration?"

"Everybody desecrates. We live off the dead and they live off us. Take for instance religion."

"I don't think I can do it without seeing the original," Fidelman said. "The color plates you gave me aren't true."

"Neither is the original anymore. You don't think Rembrandt painted in those sfumato browns? As for painting the Venus, you'll have to do the job here. If you copied it in the castello gallery one of those cretin guards might remember your face and the next thing you know you'd have trouble. So would we, probably, and we naturally wouldn't want that."

"I still ought to see it," Fidelman said obstinately.

The padrone then reluctantly consented to a one-day excursion to Isola Bella, assigning Scarpio to closely accompany the copyist.

•

On the vaporetto to the island, Scarpio, wearing dark glasses and a light straw hat, turned to Fidelman.

"In all confidence, what do you think of Angelo?"

"He's all right, I guess."

"Do you think he's handsome?"

"I haven't given it a thought. Possibly he was, once."

"You have many fine insights," said Scarpio. He pointed in the distance where the long blue lake disappeared amid towering Alps. "Locarno, sixty kilometers."

"You don't say." At the thought of Switzerland so close by, freedom swelled in Fidelman's heart, but he did nothing about it. Scarpio clung to him like a long-lost brother and sixty kilometers was a long swim with a knife in your back.

"That's the castello over there," the majordomo said. "It looks like a joint."

The castello was pink on a high terraced hill amid tall trees in formal gardens. It was full of tourists and bad paintings. But in the last gallery, "infinite riches in a little room," hung the "Venus of Urbino" alone.

What a miracle, thought Fidelman.

The golden brown-haired Venus, a woman of the real world, lay on her couch in serene beauty, her hand lightly touching her intimate mystery, the other holding red flowers, her nude body her truest accomplishment.

"I would have painted somebody in bed with her," Scarpio said.

"Shut up," said Fidelman.

Scarpio, hurt, left the gallery.

Fidelman, alone with Venus, worshipped the painting. What magnificent tones, what extraordinary flesh that can turn the body into spirit.

While Scarpio was out talking to the guard, the copyist hastily sketched the Venus and, with a Leica Angelo had borrowed from a friend for the purpose, took several new color shots.

Afterwards he approached the picture and kissed the lady's hands, thighs, and breasts, but as he was murmuring, "I love you," a guard struck him hard on the head with both fists.

That night as they returned on the rapido to Milano, Scarpio fell asleep, snoring. He awoke in a hurry, tugging at his dagger, but Fidelman hadn't moved.

2

The copyist threw himself into his work with passion. He had swallowed lightning and hoped it would strike whatever he touched. Yet he had nagging doubts he could do the job right and feared he would never escape alive from the Hotel du Ville. He tried at once to paint the Titian directly on canvas but hurriedly scraped it clean when he saw what a garish mess he had made. The Venus was insanely disproportionate and the maids in the background foreshortened into dwarfs. He then took Angelo's advice and made several drawings on paper to master the composition before committing it again to canvas.

Angelo and Scarpio came up every night and shook their heads over the drawings.

"Not even close," said the padrone.

"Far from it," said Scarpio.

"I'm trying," Fidelman said, anguished.

"Try harder," Angelo said grimly.

Fidelman had a sudden insight. "What happened to the last guy who tried?"

"He's still floating," Scarpio said.

"I'll need some practice," the copyist coughed. "My vision seems tight and the arm tires easily. I'd better go back to some exercises to loosen up."

"What kind of exercises?" Scarpio inquired.

"Nothing physical, just some warm-up nudes to get me going."

"Don't overdo it," Angelo said. "You've got about a month, not much more. There's a certain advantage in making the exchange of pictures during the tourist season."

"Only a month?"

The padrone nodded.

"Maybe you'd better trace it," Scarpio said.

"No."

"I'll tell you what," said Angelo. "I could get you an old reclining nude you could paint over. You might get the form of this one by altering the form of another."

"No."

"Why not?"

"It's not honest. I mean to myself."

Everyone tittered.

"Well, it's your headache," Angelo said.

Fidelman, unwilling to ask what happened if he failed, after they had left feverishly drew faster.

•

Things went badly for the copyist. Working all day and often into the very early morning hours, he tried everything he could think of. Since he always distorted the figure of Venus, though he carried it perfect in his mind, he went back to a study of Greek statuary with ruler and compass to compute the mathematical proportions of the ideal nude. Scarpio accompanied him to one or two museums. Fidelman also worked with the Vetruvian square in the circle, experimented with Dürer's intersecting circles and triangles, and studied Leonardo's schematic heads and bodies. Nothing doing. He drew paper dolls, not women, certainly not Venus. He drew girls who would not grow up. He then tried sketching every nude he could lay eyes on in the art books Scarpio brought him from the library, from the Esquiline goddess to "Les Demoiselles d'Avignon." Fidelman copied not badly many figures from classical statuary and modern painting, but when he returned to his Venus, with something of a laugh she eluded him. What am I, bewitched, the copyist asked himself, and if so by what? It's only a copy job so what's taking so long? He couldn't even guess until he happened to see a naked whore cross the hall and enter a friend's room. Maybe the ideal is cold and I like it hot? Nature over art? Inspiration—the live model? Fidelman knocked on the door and tried to persuade the girl to pose for him but she wouldn't for economic reasons. Neither would any of the others—there were four girls in the room.

A redhead among them called out to Fidelman, "Shame on you, Arturo, are you too good to bring up pizzas and coffee anymore?"

"I'm busy on a job for Angelo."

The girls laughed.

"Painting a picture, that is. A business proposition."

They laughed louder.

Their laughter further depressed his spirits. No inspiration from whores. Maybe too many naked women around made it impossible to draw a nude. Still he'd better try a live model, having tried everything else and failed.

In desperation, practically on the verge of panic because time was going so fast, he thought of Teresa, the chambermaid. She was a poor specimen of feminine beauty but the imagination could enhance anything. Fidelman asked her to pose for him, and Teresa, after a shy laugh, consented.

"I will if you promise not to tell anybody."

Fidelman promised.

She got undressed, a meager, bony girl, breathing heavily, and he drew her with flat chest, distended belly, thin hips, and hairy legs, unable to alter a single detail. Van Eyck would have loved her. When Teresa saw the drawing she wept profusely.

"I thought you would make me beautiful."

"I had that in mind."

"Then why didn't you?"

"It's hard to say," said Fidelman.

"I'm not in the least bit sexy," she wept.

Considering her body with half-open eyes, Fidelman told her to go borrow a long slip.

"Get one from one of the girls and I'll draw you sexy."

She returned in a frilly white slip and looked so attractive that, instead of painting her, Fidelman, with a lump in his throat, got her to lie down with him on a dusty mattress in the room. Clasping her slip-encased form, the copyist shut both eyes and concentrated on his elusive Venus. He felt about to recapture a rapturous experience and was looking forward to it, but at the last minute it turned into a limerick he didn't know he knew:

> *Whilst Titian was mixing rose madder,*
> *His model was crouched on a ladder;*
> *Her position to Titian suggested coition,*
> *So he stopped mixing madder and had 'er.*

Angelo entering the storeroom just then, let out a furious bellow. He fired Teresa on her naked knees pleading with him not to, and Fidelman had to go back to latrine duty the rest of the day.

"You might just as well keep me doing this permanently," Fidelman, disheartened, told the padrone in his office afterwards. "I'll never finish that cursed picture."

"Why not? What's eating you? I've treated you like a son."

"I'm blocked, that's what."

"Get to work, you'll feel better."

"I just can't paint."

"For what reason?"

"I don't know."

"Because you've had it too good here." Angelo angrily struck Fidelman across the face. When the copyist wept, he booted him hard in the rear.

That night Fidelman went on a hunger strike but the padrone, hearing of it, threatened force-feeding.

After midnight Fidelman stole some clothes from a sleeping whore, dressed quickly, tied on a kerchief, made up his eyes and lips, and walked out the door past Scarpio sitting on a bar stool, enjoying the night breeze. Having gone a block, fearing he would be chased, Fidelman broke into a high-heeled run but it was too late. Scarpio had recognized him in aftermath and called the portiere. Fidelman kicked off his slippers and ran furiously but the skirt impeded him. The major domo and portiere caught up with him and dragged him, kicking and struggling, back to the hotel. A carabiniere, hearing the commotion, appeared on the scene but, seeing how Fidelman was dressed, would do nothing for him. In the cellar Angelo hit him with a short rubber hose until he collapsed.

•

Fidelman lay in bed three days, refusing to eat or get up.

"What'll we do now?" Angelo, worried, whispered. "How about a fortune-teller? Either that or let's bury him."

"Astrology is better," Scarpio advised. "I'll check his planets. If that doesn't work we'll try psychology."

"Well, make it fast," said Angelo.

The next morning Scarpio entered Fidelman's room with an American breakfast on a tray and two thick books under his arm. Fidelman was still in bed, smoking a butt. He wouldn't eat.

Scarpio set down his books and took a chair close to the bed.

"What's your birthday, Arturo?" he asked gently, feeling Fidelman's pulse.

Fidelman told him, also the hour of birth and the place: Bronx, New York.

Scarpio, consulting the zodiacal tables, drew up Fidelman's horoscope on a sheet of paper and studied it thoroughly with his good eye. After a few minutes he shook his head. "It's no wonder."

"What's wrong?" Fidelman sat up weakly.

"Your Uranus and Venus are both in bad shape."

"My Venus?"

"She rules your fate." He studied the chart. "Taurus ascending, Venus afflicted. That's why you're blocked."

"Afflicted by what?"

"Sh," said Scarpio, "I'm checking your Mercury."

"Concentrate on Venus, when will she be better?"

Scarpio consulted the tables, jotted down some numbers and signs, and slowly turned pale. He searched through a few more pages of tables, then got up and stared out the dirty window.

"It's hard to tell. Do you believe in psychoanalysis?"

"Sort of."

"Maybe we'd better try that. Don't get up."

Fidelman's head fell back on the pillow.

Scarpio opened a thick book to its first chapter. "The thing to do is associate freely."

"If I don't get out of this whorehouse soon I'll surely die," said Fidelman.

"Do you have any memories of your mother?" Scarpio asked. "For instance, did you ever see her naked?"

"She died at my birth," Fidelman answered, on the verge of tears. "I was raised by my sister, Bessie."

"Go on, I'm listening," said Scarpio.

"I can't. My mind goes blank."

Scarpio turned to the next chapter, flipped through several pages, then rose with a sigh.

"It might be a medical matter. Take a physic tonight."

"I already have."

The major domo shrugged. "Life is complicated. Anyway, keep track of your dreams. Write them down as soon as you have them."

Fidelman puffed his butt.

That night he dreamed of Bessie about to bathe. He was peeking at her through the bathroom keyhole as she was preparing her bath. Openmouthed he watched her remove her robe and step into the tub. Her hefty well-proportioned body then was young and full in the right places; and in the dream Fidelman, then fourteen, looked at her with longing that amounted to anguish. The older Fidelman, the dreamer, considered doing a "La Baigneuse" right then and there, but when Bessie began to soap herself with Ivory soap, the boy slipped away into her room, opened her poor purse, filched fifty cents for the movies, and went on tiptoe down the stairs.

He was shutting the vestibule door with great relief when Arthur Fidelman woke with a headache. As he was scribbling down this dream he suddenly remembered what Angelo had said: "Everybody steals. We're all human."

A stupendous thought occurred to him: Suppose he personally were to steal the picture?

A marvelous idea all around. Fidelman heartily ate that morning's breakfast.

•

To steal the picture he had to paint one. Within another day the copyist successfully sketched Titian's painting and then began to work in oils on an old piece of Flemish linen that Angelo had hastily supplied him with after seeing the successful drawing. Fidelman underpainted the canvas and after it was dry began the figure of Venus as the conspirators looked on, sucking their breaths.

"Stay relaxed," begged Angelo, sweating. "Don't spoil it now. Remember you're painting the appearance of a picture. The original has already been painted. Give us a decent copy and we'll do the rest with chemistry."

"I'm worried about the brushstrokes."

"Nobody will notice them. Just keep in your mind that Tiziano painted resolutely with few strokes, his brush loaded with color. In the end he would paint with his fingers. Don't worry about that. We don't ask for perfection, just a good copy."

He rubbed his fat hands nervously.

But Fidelman painted as though he were painting the original. He worked alone late at night, when the conspirators were snoring, and he painted with what was left of his heart. He had caught the figure of the Venus, but when it came to her flesh, her thighs and breasts, he never thought he would make it. As he painted he seemed to remember every nude that had ever been done, Fidelman satyr, with Silenus beard and goatlegs dancing among them, piping and peeking at backside, frontside, or both, at the "Rokeby Venus," "Bathsheba," "Susanna," "Venus Anadyomene," "Olympia," at picnickers in dress or undress, bathers ditto, Vanitas or Truth, Niobe or Leda, in chase or embrace, hausfrau or whore, amorous ladies modest or brazen, single or in the crowds at the Turkish bath, in every conceivable shape or position, while he sported or disported until a trio of maenads pulled his curly beard and he galloped after them through the dusky woods. He was at the same time choked by remembered lust for all the women he had ever desired, from Bessie to Annamaria Oliovino, and for their garters, underpants, slips or half slips, brassieres, and stockings. Although thus tormented, Fidelman felt himself falling in love with the one he painted, every inch of her, including the ring on her pinky, bracelet on arm, the flowers she touched with her fingers, and the bright green earring that dangled from her eatable ear. He would have prayed her alive if he weren't certain she would fall in love, not with her famished creator, but surely the first Apollo Belvedere she laid eyes on. Is there, Fidelman asked himself, a world where love endures and is always satisfying? He answered in the negative. Still she was his as he painted, so he went on painting, planning never to finish, to be happy as he was in loving her, thus forever happy.

But he finished the picture on Saturday night, Angelo's gun pressed to his head. Then the Venus was taken from him and Scarpio and Angelo baked, smoked, stippled, and varnished, stretched and framed Fidelman's masterwork as the artist lay on his bed in his room in a state of collapse.

"The Venus of Urbino, c'est moi."

3

"What about my three hundred and fifty?" Fidelman asked Angelo during a card game in the padrone's stuffy office several days later. After completing the painting the copyist was again back on janitorial duty.

"You'll collect when we've got the Tiziano."

"I did my part."

"Don't question decisions."

"What about my passport?"

"Give it to him, Scarpio."

Scarpio handed him the passport. Fidelman flipped through the booklet and saw all the pages were intact.

"If you skiddoo now," Angelo warned him, "you'll get spit."

"Who's skiddooing?"

"So the plan is this: You and Scarpio will row out to the castello after midnight. The caretaker is an old man and half deaf. You hang our picture and breeze off with the other."

"If you wish," Fidelman suggested, "I'll gladly do the job myself. Alone, that is."

"Why alone?" said Scarpio suspiciously.

"Don't be foolish," Angelo said. "With the frame it weighs half a ton. Now listen to directions and don't give any. One reason I detest Americans is they never know their place."

Fidelman apologized.

"I'll follow in the putt-putt and wait for you halfway between

Isola Bella and Stresa in case we need a little extra speed at the last minute."

"Do you expect trouble?"

"Not a bit. If there's any trouble it'll be your fault. In that case watch out."

"Off with his head," said Scarpio. He played a deuce and took the pot.

Fidelman laughed politely.

The next night, Scarpio rowed a huge weatherbeaten rowboat, both oars muffled. It was a moonless night with touches of Alpine lightning in the distant sky. Fidelman sat on the stern, holding with both hands and balancing against his knees the large framed painting, heavily wrapped in monk's cloth and cellophane, and tied around with rope.

At the island the majordomo docked the boat and secured it. Fidelman, peering around in the dark, tried to memorize where they were. They carried the picture up two hundred steps, both puffing when they got to the formal gardens on top.

The castello was black except for a square of yellow light from the caretaker's turret window high above. As Scarpio snapped the lock of an embossed heavy wooden door with a strip of celluloid, the yellow window slowly opened and an old man peered down. They froze against the wall until the window was drawn shut.

"Fast," Scarpio hissed. "If anyone sees us they'll wake the whole island."

Pushing open the creaking door, they quickly carried the painting, growing heavier as they hurried, through an enormous room cluttered with cheap statuary and, by the light of the majordomo's flashlight, ascended a narrow flight of spiral stairs. They hastened in sneakers down a deep-shadowed, tapestried hall into the picture gallery, Fidelman stopping in his tracks when he beheld the Venus, the true and magnificent image of his counterfeit creation.

"Let's get to work." Scarpio quickly unknotted the rope and they unwrapped Fidelman's painting and leaned it against the wall. They were taking down the Titian when footsteps sounded unmistakably in the hall. Scarpio's flashlight went out.

"Sh, it's the caretaker. If he comes in I'll have to conk him."

"That'll destroy Angelo's plan—deceit, not force."

"I'll think of that when we're out of here."

They pressed their backs to the wall, Fidelman's clammy, as the old man's steps drew nearer. The copyist had anguished visions of losing the picture and made helter-skelter plans somehow to reclaim it. Then the footsteps faltered, came to a stop, and, after a moment of intense hesitation, moved in another direction. A door slammed and the sound was gone.

It took Fidelman several seconds to breathe. They waited in the dark without moving until Scarpio shone his light. Both Venuses were resting against the same wall. The major domo closely inspected each canvas with one eye shut, then signaled the painting on the left. "That's the one, let's wrap it up."

Fidelman broke into profuse sweat.

"Are you crazy? That's mine. Don't you know a work of art when you see it?" He pointed to the other picture.

"Art?" said Scarpio, removing his hat and turning pale. "Are you sure?" He peered at the painting.

"Without a doubt."

"Don't try to confuse me." He tapped the dagger under his coat.

"The lighter one is the Titian," Fidelman said through a dry throat. "You smoked mine a shade darker."

"I could have sworn yours was the lighter."

"No, Titian's. He used light varnishes. It's a historical fact."

"Of course." Scarpio mopped his brow with a soiled handkerchief. "The trouble is with my eyes. One is in bad shape and I overuse the other."

"Tst-tst," clucked Fidelman.

"Anyway, hurry up. Angelo's waiting on the lake. Remember, if there's any mistake he'll cut your throat first."

They hung the darker painting on the wall, quickly wrapped the lighter, and hastily carried it through the long hall and down the stairs, Fidelman leading the way with Scarpio's light.

At the dock the majordomo nervously turned to Fidelman. "Are you absolutely sure we have the right one?"

"I give you my word."

"I accept it but under the circumstances I'd better have another look. Shine the flashlight through your fingers."

Scarpio knelt to undo the wrapping once more, and Fidelman, trembling, brought the flashlight down hard on Scarpio's straw hat, the light shattering in his hand. The majordomo, pulling at his dagger, collapsed.

Fidelman had trouble loading the painting into the rowboat but finally got it in and settled, and quickly took off. In ten minutes he had rowed out of sight of the dark castled island. Not long afterwards he thought he heard Angelo's putt-putt behind him, and his heart beat erratically, but the padrone did not appear. He rowed as the waves deepened.

Locarno, sixty kilometers.

A wavering flash of lightning pierced the broken sky, lighting the agitated lake all the way to the Alps, as a dreadful thought assailed Fidelman: had he the right painting, after all? After a minute he pulled in his oars, listened once more for Angelo, and, hearing nothing, stepped to the stern of the rowboat, letting it drift as he frantically unwrapped the Venus.

In the pitch black, on the lake's choppy waters, he saw she was indeed his, and by the light of numerous matches adored his handiwork.

1963

✥ B M ✥

The German Refugee

Oskar Gassner sits in his cotton-mesh undershirt and summer bathrobe at the window of his stuffy, hot, dark hotel room on West Tenth Street as I cautiously knock. Outside, across the sky, a late-June green twilight fades in darkness. The refugee fumbles for the light and stares at me, hiding despair but not pain.

I was in those days a poor student and would brashly attempt to teach anybody anything for a buck an hour, although I have since learned better. Mostly I gave English lessons to recently arrived refugees. The college sent me, I had acquired a little experience. Already a few of my students were trying their broken English, theirs and mine, in the American marketplace. I was then just twenty, on my way into my senior year in college, a skinny, life-hungry kid, eating himself waiting for the next world war to start. It was a miserable cheat. Here I was panting to get going, and across the ocean Adolf Hitler, in black boots and a square mustache, was tearing up and spitting at all the flowers. Will I ever forget what went on with Danzig that summer?

Times were still hard from the Depression but I made a little living from the poor refugees. They were all over uptown Broadway in 1939. I had four I tutored—Karl Otto Alp, the former film star; Wolfgang Novak, once a brilliant economist; Friedrich Wilhelm Wolff, who had taught medieval history at Heidelberg; and after the night I met him in his disordered cheap hotel room, Oskar Gassner, the Berlin critic and journalist, at one time on the *Acht Uhr Abend-*

blatt. They were accomplished men. I had my nerve associating with them, but that's what a world crisis does for people, they get educated.

Oskar was maybe fifty, his thick hair turning gray. He had a big face and heavy hands. His shoulders sagged. His eyes, too, were heavy, a clouded blue; and as he stared at me after I had identified myself, doubt spread in them like underwater currents. It was as if, on seeing me, he had again been defeated. I had to wait until he came to. I stayed at the door in silence. In such cases I would rather be elsewhere, but I had to make a living. Finally he opened the door and I entered. Rather, he released it and I was in. "Bitte"—he offered me a seat and didn't know where to sit himself. He would attempt to say something and then stop, as though it could not possibly be said. The room was cluttered with clothing, boxes of books he had managed to get out of Germany, and some paintings. Oskar sat on a box and attempted to fan himself with his meaty hand. "Zis heat," he muttered, forcing his mind to the deed. "Impozzible. I do not know such heat." It was bad enough for me but terrible for him. He had difficulty breathing. He tried to speak, lifted a hand, and let it drop. He breathed as though he was fighting a war; and maybe he won because after ten minutes we sat and slowly talked.

Like most educated Germans Oskar had at one time studied English. Although he was certain he couldn't say a word he managed to put together a fairly decent, if sometimes comical English sentence. He misplaced consonants, mixed up nouns and verbs, and mangled idioms, yet we were able at once to communicate. We conversed in English, with an occasional assist by me in pidgin-German or Yiddish, what he called "Jiddish." He had been to America before, last year for a short visit. He had come a month before Kristallnacht, when the Nazis shattered the Jewish store windows and burnt all the synagogues, to see if he could find a job for himself; he had no relatives in America and getting a job would permit him quickly to enter the country. He had been promised something, not in journalism but, with the help of a foundation, as a lecturer. Then he returned to Berlin, and after a frightening delay of six months was permitted to emigrate. He had sold whatever he could, managed to get some paintings, gifts of Bauhaus friends, and some boxes of books out by bribing two Dutch border guards; he had said goodbye to his wife and left the accursed country. He gazed at me with cloudy eyes. "We parted amicably," he said in German, "my wife was gentile. Her mother was an appalling anti-Semite. They returned to live in Stettin." I asked no questions. Gentile is gentile, Germany is Germany.

His new job was in the Institute for Public Studies, in New York. He was to give a lecture a week in the fall term and, during next spring, a course, in English translation, in "The Literature of the Weimar Republic." He had never taught before and was afraid to. He was in that way to be introduced to the public, but the thought of giving the lecture in English just about paralyzed him. He didn't see how he could do it. "How is it pozzible? I cannot say two words. I cannot pronounziate. I will make a fool of myself." His melancholy deepened. Already in the two months since his arrival, and a round of diminishingly expensive hotel rooms, he had had two English tutors, and I was the third. The others had given him up, he said, because his progress was so poor, and he thought he also depressed them. He asked me whether I felt I could do something for him, or should he go to a speech specialist, someone, say, who charged five dollars an hour, and beg his assistance? "You could try him," I said, "and then come back to me." In those days I figured what I knew, I knew. At that he managed a smile. Still, I wanted him to make up his mind or it would be no confidence down the line. He said, after a while, he would stay with me. If he went to the five-dollar professor it might help his tongue but not his appetite. He would have no money left to eat with. The Institute had paid him in advance for the summer, but it was only three hundred dollars and all he had.

He looked at me dully. "Ich weiss nicht, wie ich weiter machen soll."

I figured it was time to move past the first step. Either we did that quickly or it would be like drilling rock for a long time.

"Let's stand at the mirror," I said.

He rose with a sigh and stood there beside me, I thin, elongated, red-headed, praying for success, his and mine; Oskar uneasy, fearful, finding it hard to face either of us in the faded round glass above his dresser.

"Please," I said to him, "could you say 'right'?"

"Ghight," he gargled.

"No—right. You put your tongue here." I showed him where as he tensely watched the mirror. I tensely watched him. "The tip of it curls behind the ridge on top, like this."

He placed his tongue where I showed him.

"Please," I said, "now say right."

Oskar's tongue fluttered. "Rright."

"That's good. Now say 'treasure'—that's harder."

"Tgheasure."

"The tongue goes up in front, not in the back of the mouth. Look."

He tried, his brow wet, eyes straining, "Trreasure."

"That's it."

"A miracle," Oskar murmured.

I said if he had done that he could do the rest.

We went for a bus ride up Fifth Avenue and then walked for a while around Central Park Lake. He had put on his German hat, with its hatband bow at the back, a broad-lapeled wool suit, a necktie twice as wide as the one I was wearing, and walked with a small-footed waddle. The night wasn't bad, it had got a bit cooler. There were a few large stars in the sky and they made me sad.

"Do you sink I will succezz?"

"Why not?" I asked.

Later he bought me a bottle of beer.

•

To many of these people, articulate as they were, the great loss was the loss of language—that they could not say what was in them to say. You have some subtle thought and it comes out like a piece of broken bottle. They could, of course, manage to communicate, but just to communicate was frustrating. As Karl Otto Alp, the ex–film star who became a buyer for Macy's, put it years later, "I felt like a child, or worse, often like a moron. I am left with myself unexpressed. What I know, indeed, what I am, becomes to me a burden. My tongue hangs useless." The same with Oskar it figures. There was a terrible sense of useless tongue, and I think the reason for his trouble with his other tutors was that to keep from drowning in things unsaid he wanted to swallow the ocean in a gulp: today he would learn English and tomorrow wow them with an impeccable Fourth of July speech, followed by a successful lecture at the Institute for Public Studies.

We performed our lessons slowly, step by step, everything in its place. After Oskar moved to a two-room apartment in a house on West Eighty-fifth Street, near the Drive, we met three times a week at four-thirty, worked an hour and a half, then, since it was too hot to cook, had supper at the Seventy-second Street Automat and conversed on my time. The lessons we divided into three parts: diction exercises and reading aloud; then grammar, because Oskar felt the necessity of it, and composition correction; with conversation, as I said, thrown in at supper. So far as I could see he was coming along. None of these exercises was giving him as much trouble as they apparently had in the past. He seemed to be learning and his mood lightened. There were moments of elation as he heard his accent flying off. For instance when sink became think. He stopped calling himself "hopelezz," and I became his "bezt teacher," a little joke I liked.

Neither of us said much about the lecture he had to give early in October, and I kept my fingers crossed. It was somehow to come out of what we were doing daily, I think I felt, but exactly how, I had no idea; and to tell the truth, though I didn't say so to Oskar, the lecture frightened me. That and the ten more to follow during the fall term. Later, when I learned that he had been attempting, with the help of the dictionary, to write in English and had produced "a complete disahster," I suggested maybe he ought to stick to German and we could afterwards both try to put it into passable English. I was cheating when I said that because my German is meager, enough to read simple stuff but certainly not good enough for serious translation; anyway, the idea was to get Oskar into production and worry about translating later. He sweated with it, from enervating morning to exhausted night, but no matter what language he tried, though he had been a professional writer for a generation and knew his subject cold, the lecture refused to move past page one.

It was a sticky, hot July, and the heat didn't help at all.

•

I had met Oskar at the end of June, and by the seventeenth of July we were no longer doing lessons. They had foundered on the "impozzible" lecture. He had worked on it each day in frenzy and growing despair. After writing more than a hundred opening pages he furiously flung his pen against the wall, shouting he could not longer write in that filthy tongue. He cursed the German language. He hated the damned country and the damned people. After that, what was bad became worse. When he gave up attempting to write the lecture, he stopped making progress in English. He seemed to forget what he already knew. His tongue thickened and the accent returned in all its fruitiness. The little he had to say was in handcuffed and tortured English. The only German I heard him speak was in a whisper to himself. I doubt he knew he was talking it. That ended our formal work together, though I did drop in every other day or so to sit with him. For hours he sat motionless in a large green velour armchair, hot enough to broil in, and through tall windows stared at the colorless sky above Eighty-fifth Street with a wet depressed eye.

Then once he said to me, "If I do not this legture prepare, I will take my life."

"Let's begin, Oskar," I said. "You dictate and I'll write. The ideas count, not the spelling."

He didn't answer so I stopped talking.

He had plunged into an involved melancholy. We sat for hours, often in profound silence. This was alarming to me, though I had already had some experience with such depression. Wolfgang Novak, the economist, though English came more easily to him, was another. His problems arose mainly, I think, from physical illness. And he felt a greater sense of the lost country than Oskar. Sometimes in the early evening I persuaded Oskar to come with me for a short walk on the Drive. The tail end of sunsets over the Palisades seemed to appeal to him. At least he looked. He would put on full regalia—hat, suit coat, tie, no matter how hot or what I suggested—and we went slowly down the stairs, I wondering whether he would make it to the bottom.

We walked slowly uptown, stopping to sit on a bench and watch night rise above the Hudson. When we returned to his room, if I sensed he had loosened up a bit, we listened to music on the radio; but if I tried to sneak in a news broadcast, he said to me, "Please, I cannot more stand of world misery." I shut off the radio. He was right, it was a time of no good news. I squeezed my brain. What could I tell him? Was it good news to be alive? Who could argue the point? Sometimes I read aloud to him—I remember he liked the first part of *Life on the Mississippi*. We still went to the Automat once or twice a week, he perhaps out of habit, because he didn't feel like going anywhere—I to get him out of his room. Oskar ate little, he toyed with a spoon. His eyes looked as though they had been squirted with a dark dye.

Once after a momentary cooling rainstorm we sat on newspapers on a wet bench overlooking the river and Oskar at last began to talk. In tormented English he conveyed his intense and everlasting hatred of the Nazis for destroying his career, uprooting his life, and flinging him like a piece of bleeding meat to the hawks. He cursed them thickly, the German nation, an inhuman, conscienceless, merciless people. "They are pigs mazquerading as peacogs," he said. "I feel certain that my wife, in her heart, was a Jew hater." It was a terrible bitterness, and eloquence beyond the words he spoke. He became silent again. I wanted to hear more about his wife but decided not to ask.

Afterwards in the dark, Oskar confessed that he had attempted suicide during his first week in America. He was living, at the end of May, in a small hotel, and had one night filled himself with barbiturates; but his phone had fallen off the table and the hotel operator had sent up the elevator boy, who found him unconscious and called the police. He was revived in the hospital.

"I did not mean to do it," he said, "it was a mistage."

"Don't ever think of it," I said, "it's total defeat."

"I don't," he said wearily, "because it is so arduouz to come bag to life."

"Please, for any reason whatever."

Afterwards when we were walking, he surprised me by saying, "Maybe we ought to try now the legture onze more."

We trudged back to the house and he sat at his hot desk, I trying to read as he slowly began to reconstruct the first page of his lecture. He wrote, of course, in German.

•

He got nowhere. We were back to sitting in silence in the heat. Sometimes, after a few minutes, I had to take off before his mood overcame mine. One afternoon I came unwillingly up the stairs—there were times I felt momentary surges of irritation with him—and was frightened to find Oskar's door ajar. When I knocked no one answered. As I stood there, chilled down the spine, I realized I was thinking about the possibility of his attempting suicide again. "Oskar?" I went into the apartment, looked into both rooms and the bathroom, but he wasn't there. I thought he might have drifted out to get something from a store and took the opportunity to look quickly around. There was nothing startling in the medicine chest, no pills but aspirin, no iodine. Thinking, for some reason, of a gun, I searched his desk drawer. In it I found a thin-paper airmail letter from Germany. Even if I had wanted to, I couldn't read the handwriting, but as I held it in my hand I did make out a sentence: "Ich bin dir siebenundzwanzig Jahre treu gewesen." There was no gun in the drawer. I shut it and stopped looking. It had occurred to me if you want to kill yourself all you need is a straight pin. When Oskar returned he said he had been sitting in the public library, unable to read.

Now we are once more enacting the changeless scene, curtain rising on two speechless characters in a furnished apartment, I in a straight-back chair, Oskar in the velour armchair that smothered rather than supported him, his flesh gray, the big gray face unfocused, sagging. I reached over to switch on the radio but he barely looked at me in a way that begged no. I then got up to leave but Oskar, clearing his throat, thickly asked me to stay. I stayed, thinking, was there more to this than I could see into? His problems, God knows, were real enough, but could there be something more than a refugee's displacement, alienation, financial insecurity, being in a strange land without friends or a speakable tongue? My speculation was the old one: not all drown in this ccean, why does he? After a while I shaped the thought and asked him was there something below the surface, invisible? I was full of this thing from college, and wondered if there mightn't be some unknown quantity in his depression that a psychiatrist maybe might help him with, enough to get him started on his lecture.

He meditated on this and after a few minutes haltingly said he had been psychoanalyzed in Vienna as a young man. "Just the jusual dreck," he said, "fears and fantazies that afterwaards no longer bothered me."

"They don't now?"

"Not."

"You've written many articles and lectures before," I said. "What I can't understand, though I know how hard the situation is, is why you can never get past page one."

He half lifted his hand. "It is a paralyzis of my will. The whole legture is clear in my mind, but the minute I write down a single word—or in English or in German—I have a terrible fear I will not be able to write the negst. As though someone has thrown a stone at a window and the whole house—the whole idea zmashes. This repeats, until I am dezperate."

He said the fear grew as he worked that he would die before he completed the lecture, or if not that, he would write it so disgracefully he would wish for death. The fear immobilized him.

"I have lozt faith. I do not—not longer possezz my former value of myself. In my life there has been too much illusion."

I tried to believe what I was saying: "Have confidence, the feeling will pass."

"Confidenze I have not. For this and alzo whatever elze I have lozt I thank the Nazis."

●

It was by then mid-August and things were growing steadily worse wherever one looked. The Poles were mobilizing for war. Oskar hardly moved. I was full of worries though I pretended calm weather.

He sat in his massive armchair, breathing like a wounded animal. "Who can write aboud Walt Whitman in such terrible times?"

"Why don't you change the subject?"

"It mages no differenze what is the subject. It is all uzelezz."

I came every day, as a friend, neglecting my other students and therefore my livelihood. I had a panicky feeling that if things went on as they were going they would end in Oskar's suicide; and I felt a frenzied desire to prevent that. What's more, I was sometimes afraid I was myself becoming melancholy, a new talent, call it, of taking less pleasure in my little pleasures. And the heat continued, oppressive, relentless. We thought of escape into the country, but neither of us had the money. One day I bought Oskar a secondhand electric fan—wondering why we hadn't thought of that before—and he sat in the breeze for hours each day, until after a week, shortly after the Soviet-Nazi non-aggression pact was signed, the motor gave out. He could not sleep at night and sat at his desk with a wet towel on his head, still attempting to write the lecture. He wrote reams on a treadmill, it came out nothing. When he slept in exhaustion he had fantastic frightening dreams of the Nazis inflicting torture, sometimes forcing him to look upon the corpses of those they had slain. In one dream he told me about he had gone back to Germany to visit his wife. She wasn't home and he had been directed to a cemetery. There, though the tombstone read another name, her blood seeped out of the earth above her shallow grave. He groaned aloud at the memory.

Afterwards he told me something about her. They had met as students, lived together, and were married at twenty-three. It wasn't a very happy marriage. She had turned into a sickly woman, unable to have children. "Something was wrong with her interior strugture."

Though I asked no questions, Oskar said, "I offered her to come with me here, but she refused this."

"For what reason?"

"She did not think I wished her to come."

"Did you?" I asked.

"Not," he said.

He explained he had lived with her for almost twenty-seven years under difficult circumstances. She had been ambivalent about their Jewish friends and his relatives, though outwardly she seemed not a prejudiced person. But her mother was always a dreadful anti-Semite.

"I have nothing to blame myzelf," Oskar said.

He took to his bed. I took to the New York Public Library. I read some of the German poets he was trying to write about, in English translation. Then I read *Leaves of Grass* and wrote down what I thought one or two of them had got from Whitman. One day, toward the end of August, I brought Oskar what I had written. It was in good part guessing, but my idea wasn't to do the lecture for him. He lay on his back, motionless, and listened sadly to what I had written. Then he said, no, it wasn't the love of death they had got from Whitman—that ran through German poetry—but it was most of all his feeling for Brudermen.sch, his humanity.

"But this does not grow long on German earth," he said, "and is soon deztroyed."

I said I was sorry I had got it wrong, but he thanked me anyway.

I left, defeated, and as I was going down the stairs heard the sound of sobbing. I will quit this, I thought, it has got to be too much for me. I can't drown with him.

I stayed home the next day, tasting a new kind of private misery too old for somebody my age, but that same night Oskar called me on the phone, blessing me wildly for having read those notes to him. He had got up to write me a letter to say what I had missed, and it ended in his having written half the lecture. He had slept all day and tonight intended to finish it up.

"I thank you," he said, "for much, alzo including your faith in me."

"Thank God," I said, not telling him I had just about lost it.

•

Oskar completed his lecture—wrote and rewrote it—during the first week in September. The Nazis had invaded Poland, and though we were greatly troubled, there was some sense of release; maybe the brave Poles would beat them. It took another week to translate the lecture, but here we had the assistance of Friedrich Wilhelm Wolff, the historian, a gentle, erudite man who liked translating and promised his help with future lectures. We then had about two weeks to work on Oskar's delivery. The weather had changed, and so, slowly, had he. He had awakened from defeat, battered, after a wearying battle. He had lost close to twenty pounds. His complexion was still gray; when I looked at his face I expected to see scars, but it had lost its flabby unfocused quality. His blue eyes had returned to life and he walked with quick steps, as though to pick up a few for all the steps he hadn't taken during those long hot days he had lain in his room.

We went back to our former routine, meeting three late afternoons a week for diction, grammar, and the other exercises. I taught him the phonetic alphabet and transcribed lists of words he was mispronouncing. He worked many hours trying to fit each sound in place, holding a matchstick between his teeth to keep his jaws apart as he exercised his tongue. All this can be a dreadfully boring business unless you think you have a future. Looking at him, I realized what's meant when somebody is called "another man."

The lecture, which I now knew by heart, went off well. The director of the Institute had invited a number of prominent people. Oskar was the first refugee they had employed, and there was a move to make the public cognizant of what was then a new ingredient in American life. Two reporters had come with a lady photographer. The auditorium of the Institute was crowded. I sat in the last row, promising to put up my hand if he couldn't be heard, but it wasn't necessary. Oskar, in a blue suit, his hair cut, was of course nervous, but you couldn't see it unless you studied him. When he stepped up to the lectern, spread out his manuscript, and spoke his first English sentence in public, my heart hesitated; only he and I, of everybody there, had any idea of the anguish he had been through. His enunciation wasn't at all bad—a few *s*'s for *th*'s, and he once said bag for back, but otherwise he did all right. He read poetry well—in both languages—and though Walt Whitman, in his mouth, sounded a little as though he had come to the shores of Long Island as a German immigrant, still the poetry read as poetry:

> *And I know the Spirit of God is the brother of my own,*
> *And that all the men ever born are also my brothers,*
> * and the women my sisters and lovers,*
> *And that the kelson of creation is love . . .*

Oskar read it as though he believed it. Warsaw had fallen, but the verses were somehow protective. I sat back conscious of two things: how easy it is to hide the deepest wounds; and the pride I felt in the job I had done.

•

Two days later I came up the stairs into Oskar's apartment to find a crowd there. The refugee, his face beet-red, lips bluish, a trace of froth in the corners of his mouth, lay on the floor in his limp pajamas, two firemen on their knees working over him with an inhalator. The windows were open and the air stank.

A policeman asked me who I was and I couldn't answer.

"No, oh no."

I said no but it was unchangeably yes. He had taken his life—gas—I hadn't even thought of the stove in the kitchen.

"Why?" I asked myself. "Why did he do it?" Maybe it was the fate of Poland on top of everything else, but the only answer anyone could come up with was Oskar's scribbled note that he wasn't well, and had left Martin Goldberg all his possessions. I am Martin Goldberg.

I was sick for a week, had no desire either to inherit or investigate, but I thought I ought to look through his things before the court impounded them, so I spent a morning sitting in the depths of Oskar's armchair, trying to read his correspondence. I had found in the top drawer a thin packet of letters from his wife and an airmail letter of recent date from his mother-in-law.

She writes in a tight script it takes me hours to decipher that her daughter, after Oskar abandons her, against her own mother's fervent pleas and anguish, is converted to Judaism by a vengeful rabbi. One night the Brown Shirts appear, and though the mother wildly waves her bronze crucifix in their faces, they drag Frau Gassner, together with the other Jews, out of the apartment house and transport them in lorries to a small border town in conquered Poland. There, it is rumored, she is shot in the head and topples into an open ditch with the naked Jewish men, their wives and children, some Polish soldiers, and a handful of Gypsies.

1963

❧ B M ❧

A Choice of Profession

Cronin, after discovering that his wife, Marge, had been two-timing
him with a friend, suffered months of crisis. He had loved Marge and
jealousy lingered unbearably. He lived through an anguish of degrad-
ing emotions and, a few months after his divorce, left a well-paying
job in Chicago to take up teaching. He had always wanted to teach.
Cronin taught composition and survey of literature in a small college
town in Northern California, and, after an initially exhilarating period, began to find it a bore. This caused him worry because he hoped
to be at peace in the profession. He wasn't sure whether it was true
boredom or simply not knowing whether he wanted to teach the rest
of his life. He was bored mostly outside the classroom—the endless
grading of papers and bookkeeping chores; and for a man of his type,
Cronin felt, he had too much to read. He also felt he had been asking
from teaching more than he was entitled to. He had always thought
of teaching as something religious and perhaps still did. It had to do
with giving oneself to others, a way of being he hadn't achieved in
his marriage. Cronin, a tall, bulky-shouldered man with sensitive eyes
and a full brown mustache, smoked too much. His trousers were usually smeared with cigarette ashes he brushed off his thighs; and lately,
after a period of forbearance, he had begun to drink. Apart from
students there were few women around who weren't married, and he
was alone too often. Though at the beginning he was invited to faculty
parties, he wanted nothing to do with the wives of his colleagues.

The fall wore away. Cronin remained aimlessly in town during the winter vacation. In the spring term a new student, an older girl, appeared in his literature class. Unlike most of the other girls, she wore bright attractive dresses and high heels. She wore her light hair in a bun from which strands slipped but she was otherwise feminine and neat, a mature woman, he realized. Although she wasn't really pretty, her face was open and attractive. Cronin wondered at her experienced eyes and deep-breasted figure. She had slender shoulders and fairly heavy but shapely legs. He thought at first she might be a faculty wife but she was without their combination of articulateness and timidity; he didn't think she was married. He also liked the way she listened to him in class. Many of the students, when he lectured or read poetry, looked sleepy, stupefied, or exalted, but she listened down to bedrock, as if she were expecting a message or had got it. Cronin noticed that the others in the class might listen to the poetry but she also listened to Cronin. Her name, not very charming, was Mary Lou Miller. He could tell she regarded him as a man, and after so long a dry, almost perilous season, he responded to her as a woman. Though Cronin wasn't planning to become involved with a student, he had at times considered taking up with one but resisted it on principle. He wanted to be protected in love by certain rules, but loving a student meant no rules to begin with.

He continued to be interested in her and she occasionally would wait at his desk after class and walk with him in the direction of his office. He often thought she had something personal to say to him, but when she spoke it was usually to say that one or another poem had moved her; her taste, he thought, was a little too inclusive. Mary Lou rarely recited in class. He found her a bit boring when they talked for more than five minutes, but that secretly pleased him because the attraction to her was quite strong and this was a form of insurance. One morning, during a free hour, he went to the registrar's office on some pretext or other and looked up her records. Cronin was surprised to discover she was twenty-four and only a first-year student. He, though he sometimes felt forty, was twenty-nine. Because they were so close in age, as well as for other reasons, he decided to ask her out. That same afternoon Mary Lou knocked on his office door and came in to see him about a quiz he had just returned. She had got a low C and it worried her. Cronin lit her cigarette and noticed that she watched him intently, his eyes, mustache, hands, as he explained what she might have written on her paper. They were sitting within a foot of one another, and when she raised both arms to fix her bun, the imprint of her large nipples on her dress caught his attention. It was during this talk in the office that he suggested they go for a drive one evening at the end of the week. Mary Lou agreed, saying maybe they could stop off somewhere for a drink, and Cronin, momentarily hesitating, said he thought they might. All the while they had been talking she was looking at him from some inner place in herself, and he had the feeling he had been appraising her superficially.

On the ride that night Mary Lou sat close to Cronin. She had at first sat at the door but soon her warm side was pressed to his though he had not seen her move. They had started at sunset and for an hour the sky was light. The Northern California winter, though colder than he had anticipated, was mild compared to a winter in Chicago, but Cronin was glad to be in touch with spring. He liked the lengthening days, and tonight it was a relief to be with a woman once more. The car passed through a number of neon-lit mountain towns neither of them had been in before, and Cronin noticed that every motel flashed vacancy signs. Part of his good mood was an awareness of the approach of a new season, and part that he had thought it over and decided there was nothing to worry about. She was a woman, no eighteen-year-old kid he would be taking advantage of. Nor was he married and about to commit adultery. He felt a sincere interest in her.

It was a pleasant evening drive in early March, and on their way back they stopped off at a bar in Red Bluff, about forty miles from the college, where it was unlikely anyone they knew would see them. The waiter brought drinks and when Mary Lou had finished hers she excused herself, went to the ladies room, and, upon returning, asked for another on the rocks. She had on a bright blue dress, rather short, and wore no stockings. During the week she used no lip rouge or nail polish; tonight she had both on and Cronin thought he liked her better without them. She smiled at him, her face, after she had had two, flushed. In repose her smile settled into the tail end of bitterness, an expression touched with cynicism, and he wondered about her. They had talked about themselves on the ride, she less than he, Cronin reticently. She had been brought up on a farm in Idaho. He had spent most of his life in Evanston, Illinois, where his grandfather, an evangelical minister, had lived and preached. Cronin's father had died when Cronin was fourteen. Mary Lou told him she had once been married and was now divorced. He had guessed something of the sort and at that point admitted he had been divorced himself. He could feel his leg touching hers under the table and realized it was her doing. Cronin, pretty much contented, had had one drink to her two, and he was nursing his first when she asked for a third. She had become quiet but when their eyes met she smiled again.

"Do you mind if I call you Mary Louise?" Cronin asked her.

"You can if you want to," she said, "but my real name is Mary Lou. That's on my birth certificate."

He asked her how long she had been married before her divorce.

"Oh, just about three years. One that I didn't live with him. How about yourself?"

"Two," said Cronin.

She drank from her glass. He liked the fact that she was satisfied with a few biographical details. A fuller exchange of information could come later.

He lit a cigarette, only his second since they had come in, whereas she squashed one butt to light another. He wondered why she was nervous.

"Happy?" Cronin asked.

"I'm okay, thanks." She crushed a newly lit cigarette, thought about it, and lit another.

She seemed about to say something, paused, and said, "How long have you been teaching, if you don't mind me asking you?"

Cronin wondered what was on her mind. "Not so long," he answered. "This is only my first year."

"You sure put a lot in it."

He could feel the calf of her leg pressed warmly against his; yet she was momentarily inattentive, vaguely looking around at the people in the bar.

"How about you?" he asked.

"In what ways?"

"How is it you started college so comparatively late?"

She finished her drink. "I never wanted to go when I graduated high school. Instead I worked a couple of years, then I joined the Wacs." She fell silent.

He asked if she wanted him to order another drink.

"Not right away." Mary Lou's eyes focused on his face. "First I want to tell you something about myself. Do you want to hear it?"

"Yes, if you want to tell me."

"It's about my life," Mary Lou said. "When I was in the Wacs I met this guy, Ray A. Miller, a T-5 from Providence, Rhode Island, and we got hitched in secret in Las Vegas. He was a first-class prick."

Cronin gazed at her, wondering if she had had one too many.

He considered suggesting they leave now but Mary Lou, sitting there solidly, smoking the last cigarette in her pack, told Cronin what she had started out to.

"I call him that word because that's what he was. He married me just to live easy off me. He talked me into doing what he wanted, and I was too goddamn stupid to say no, because at that time I loved him. After we left the service he set me up in this flea-bitten three-room apartment in San Francisco, where I was a call girl. He took the dough and I got the shit."

"Call girl?" Cronin almost groaned.

"A whore, if you want me to say it."

Cronin was overwhelmed. He felt a momentary constricting fright and a strange uneasy jealousy, followed by a sense of disappointment and unexpected loss.

"I'm sorry," he said. Her leg was tense against his but he let his stay though it seemed to him it trembled. His cigarette ash broke, and while brushing it off his thigh, Cronin managed to withdraw his leg from hers. Her face was impassive.

Mary Lou slowly fixed her bun, removing a large number of hairpins and placing them thickly back again.

"I suppose you have a bad opinion of me now?" she said to Cronin, after she had fixed her hair.

He said he had no opinion at all, though he knew he had. "I'm just sorry it happened."

She looked at him intently. "One thing I want you to know is I don't have that kind of a life anymore. I'm not interested in it. I'm interested in taking it as it comes or goes but not for money anymore. That won't happen to me again."

Cronin said he was surprised it ever had.

"It was just a job I had to do," Mary Lou explained. "That's how I thought about it. I kept on it because I was afraid Ray would walk out on me. He always knew what he wanted but I didn't. He was a strong type and I wasn't."

"Did he walk out?"

She nodded. "We were having fights about what to do with the dough. He said he was going to start some kind of a business but he never did."

"That's when you quit?"

She lowered her eyes. "Not all at once. I stayed for a while to get some money to go to college with. I didn't stay long and I haven't got enough, so I have to work in the cafeteria."

"When did you finally quit?"

"In three months, when I got arrested."

He asked about that.

"My apartment was raided by two San Francisco bulls. But it was my first offense so the judge paroled me. I'm paroled now and for one more year."

"I guess you've been through the mill," Cronin said, toying with his glass.

"I sure have," said Mary Lou, "but I'm not the same person I once was. I learned a lot."

"Would you care for a last drink before we leave?" he asked. "It's getting late. We've got an hour's drive."

"No, but thanks anyway."

"I'll just have a last drink."

The waiter brought Cronin a Scotch.

"Tell me why you told me this," he asked Mary Lou after he had drunk from his glass.

"I don't know for sure," she said. "Some of it is because I like you. I like the way you teach in your class. That's why I got the idea of telling you."

"But why, specifically?"

"Because everything's different now."

"The past doesn't bother you?"

"Not much. I wanted to tell you before this but I couldn't do it in your office without a drink to start me off."

"Do you want me to do anything for you?" Cronin asked her.

"For instance, what?" said Mary Lou.

"If you want to talk to anybody about yourself I could get you the name of a psychiatrist."

"Thanks," she said. "I don't need one. The guy I talk to about myself will have to do it for nothing, for kicks."

She asked Cronin for one of his cigarettes and smoked while he finished his drink.

As they were getting ready to leave, Mary Lou said, "The way I figure, it wasn't all my fault, but it's dead and gone now. I got the right to think of the future."

"You have," said Cronin.

On the ride home he felt more objective and not unsympathetic to the girl, yet he was still disappointed and, from time to time, irritated with himself.

"Anyway," Cronin told her, "you can work for a better way of life now."

"That's why I want an education for," Mary Lou said.

2

It took Cronin a surprisingly long time to get over having been let down by Mary Lou. He had built her up in his mind as a woman he might want to spend some time with, and the surprise of her revelation, and his disillusionment, lingered so long he felt unsettled. "What's this, Marge all over again?" He didn't want any more of that, and not from this girl. He saw her in class, as usual, three times a week. She seemed to listen with the same interest, maybe less interested, but she didn't approach him and no longer waited at his desk to walk with him to his office. Cronin understood that to mean he was to make the next move now that he knew, but he didn't make it. What could he say to her— that he wished he didn't know? Or now that he knew, sometimes when he glanced at her in class he pictured her being paid off by the last guy she had slept with. She was in his thoughts much of the time. He wondered what would have happened that night they were out if she hadn't made that confession. Could he have guessed from the way she performed in bed that she had been a professional? He continued to think of having her and sometimes the thought was so wearing he avoided looking at her in class. He found his desire hard to bear but after a month it wore down. She seemed not very interesting to him then, and he was often aware how hard her expression was. He felt sorry for her and occasionally smiled, and once in a while she seemed cynically to smile back.

Cronin had made friends with a painter, George Getz, an assistant professor in the art department, an active, prematurely bald man, with whom he went on sketching trips, usually on Saturday or Sunday afternoon. George sketched or did watercolors as Cronin looked on or sat against a tree, smoking. Sometimes he wandered along streams and in the woods. When the painter, married from youth and the father of three girls, was tied down during the weekend, Cronin drove off by himself or tried walking alone, though generally he cared little for walking in town, and wasn't sure which direction to go next. One fine Sunday in April, when George was busy with his family, Cronin started on a walk but it soon began to seem like work so he returned to his apartment and sat on the bed. Wanting company he searched in his mind for who, and after some doubts looked up Mary Lou Miller's number and dialed it. He wasn't sure why he had, though he knew it bothered him a little. "Hello there," she said. She had hesitated on hearing his voice but seemed cordial enough. Cronin wondered about a drive and she said she wouldn't mind. He called for her in his car. She looked a little distant when she came out and he was surprised at how attractive. He noticed she seemed to be prettier on warm days.

"How are things with you?" Cronin asked as he held the door open for her.

"All right, I guess. How are they with you?"

"Fine," Cronin said.

"How's the teaching?"

"Fine. I'm enjoying it more than I was."

Not much more but it was too much trouble to explain why.

She seemed at ease. They drove toward the mountains along some of the side roads he had explored with George, until they came to a long blue lake shaped like a bird in flight. Cronin parked the car and they went through a scattering of pine trees, down to the water. At his suggestion they walked part of the way around the lake, and back. It took more than an hour and Mary Lou said she hadn't walked that much in years.

"Life's pleasures are cheap," Cronin said.

"No, they're not," said Mary Lou.

He let it pass. They had said nothing about last time, there was nothing to say really. The beauty of the day had lightened Cronin's mood—he remembered having dreamed of Marge last night and had awakened uneasy. But Mary Lou's company, he admitted to himself, had made the walk around the lake enjoyable. She was wearing a yellow cotton dress that showed her figure off, and her hair, to the large thick knot on her neck, was for once neatly arranged. She was rather quiet, as though a word too much might defeat her, but once she loosened up they talked amiably. She seemed to Cronin, as he sat by her side gazing at the lake, no more nor less than any woman he had known. The way he presently saw it was that she was entitled to her mistakes. He was to his. Yet though he tried to forget what she had told him, the fact that she had been a whore kept nagging him. She had known many men, how large a crowd they would make following her now, he was afraid to guess. He had never known anyone like her, and that he was with her now struck him as somewhat strange. But Cronin thought what an unusual thing present time was. In the present a person is what she is becoming and not what she was. She was this heavy-but-shapely-legged girl in a yellow dress, sitting by his side as though she belonged there. Cronin thought this was an interesting lesson for him. The past interfered if you let it. People feared it because they thought it predicted the future. It didn't if you realized how much life changed, and concentrated on what it had changed to, and lived that. He began again to think of the possibility of friendship with Mary Lou.

She got up, brushing pine needles off her dress. "It's hot," she said. "Would you mind if I peeled and went in for a dip?"

"Go ahead," said Cronin.

"Why don't you come in yourself?" she asked. "You could keep your shorts on and later get dry in the sun."

"No, I don't think so," he said, "I'm not much of a swimmer."

"Neither am I," Mary Lou said, "but I like the water."

She unzipped her dress and pulled it over her head. Then she kicked off her shoes, stepped out of a half slip, and removed her white underwear. He enjoyed the fullness of her form, the beauty of her breasts. Mary Lou walked into the water, shivered, and began to swim. Cronin sat watching her, one arm around his knees as he smoked. After swimming a while, Mary Lou, her flesh lit in the sunlight, came out of the water, drew on her underpants, then let the sun dry her as she redid her damp hair. He was moved by her wet body after bathing.

When she had dressed, Cronin suggested they have dinner together and Mary Lou agreed. "But first you come up to my joint for a drink. I want to show you how I fixed it up."

He said he would like to.

On their ride back she was talkative. She told Cronin about her life as a child. Her father had been a small wheat farmer in Idaho. She had one married sister and two married brothers. She said the oldest brother was a big bastard.

"He's pretty rich by now," she said, "and he talks a lot about God's grace but in his heart he is a bastard. When I was thirteen one day he grabbed me in the barn and laid me though I didn't want to."

"Oh, Christ," said Cronin. "You committed incest?"

"It all happened when I was a kid."

"Why don't you keep these things to yourself?" Cronin said. "What makes you think I want to hear them?"

"I guess I felt I trusted you."

"Well, don't trust me," he shouted.

He drove to her house and let her off at the curb. Then he drove away.

The next morning Mary Lou did not appear in Cronin's class, and a few days later her drop-slip came through.

3

A week had gone by when Cronin one day saw her walking with George Getz, and his heart was flooded with jealous misery. He thought he was rid of his desire for the girl; but seeing her walking at the painter's side, talking animatedly, George interested, Mary Lou good to look at in a white summer dress and doing very well, thanks, without Cronin, awoke in him a sense of loss and jealousy. He thought he might be in love with her. Cronin watched them go up the stairs of the art building and, though he had no good reason to, pictured them in each other's arms, naked on George's studio couch. The effect was frightening.

My God, thought Cronin, here I am thinking of her with the same miserable feelings I had about Marge. I can't go through that again.

He fought to put her out of his mind—the insistent suspicion of an affair between her and the painter—but his memory of her body at the lake, and imagining the experience she had had with men, what she would do with George, for instance, and might have done with Cronin if they had become lovers, made things worse. Thinking of her experiences was like trying to stop the pain of a particular wound by stabbing yourself elsewhere. His only relief was to get drunk, but when that wore off the anguish was worse.

One morning he was so desperately jealous—the most useless of emotions, and especially useless in a situation where the girl really meant little to him, almost nothing, and the past, despite all his theorizing and good intentions, much too much—that he waited for them for hours, in the foyer of the school of architecture across the street from the art building. Cronin did not at first know why he was waiting but that he had to, perhaps to satisfy himself they were or weren't having an affair. He saw neither of them then, but on the next afternoon he followed the painter at a distance to Mary Lou's apartment. Cronin saw him go in shortly before 5 p.m., and was still unhappily waiting under a tree across the street, several houses down, when George came out at half past ten. Cronin was wakeful all night.

Terrified that this should mean so much to him, he tried to work out some means of relief. Should he telephone the girl and ask her back into his class so that they could once more be on good terms? Or if that meant trouble with the registrar's office, couldn't he just call and apologize for acting as he had, then offer to resume their friendship? Or could he scare George away by telling him about her past?

The painter was a family man, a careful sort, and Cronin felt sure he would end it with Mary Lou if he thought anyone suspected he was involved with her; he wanted to go on feeding his three girls. But telling him about her seemed such a stinking thing to do that Cronin couldn't face it. Still, things were so bad he finally decided to speak to George. He felt that if he could be sure the painter wasn't being intimate with her, his jealousy would die out and the girl fade in his thoughts.

He waited till George invited him on another sketching afternoon, and was glad to have the chance to bring it up then, rather than to have to seek the painter out in his office or studio. They were at the edge of the woods, George at work on a watercolor, when Cronin spoke of the girl and asked whether George knew that Mary Lou had once been a prostitute in San Francisco for a couple of years.

George wiped his brush with a rag, then asked Cronin where he had got his information.

Cronin said he had got it from her. "She was married to someone who set her up professionally and cut in on the take. After he left her she quit."

"What a son of a bitch," said George. He worked for a while, then turned to Cronin and asked, "Why do you tell me about it?"

"I thought you ought to know."

"Why ought I?"

"Isn't she a student of yours?"

"No, she isn't. She came to my office and offered to model for me. It's hard to get girls to pose in the nude around here so I said yes. That's all there is between us."

He seemed embarrassed.

Cronin looked away. "I didn't think there was anything between you. I just thought you would want to know, if she was your student. I didn't know she wasn't."

"Well," said George, "I know now, but I still intend to use her as a model."

"I don't see why not."

"Thanks for telling me, though," George said. "I've sometimes felt there's a bit of the slut in her. It wouldn't pay to get involved."

Cronin, feeling some repulsion for himself, then said, "To tell the truth, George, I'm not entirely innocent in this. I've wanted to take the girl to bed."

"Have you?"

"No."

"I almost did," George said.

Though Cronin wasn't sure the painter had or hadn't, he was certain he wouldn't dare be intimate with her now. When he got home he felt relief, mingled with shame that had him talking to himself, but he slept better that night.

4

A few nights later Mary Lou rang Cronin's doorbell, walked up the stairs, and, when she was admitted into his apartment, said she wanted to talk to him. Cronin, reading in pajamas and robe, offered her a Scotch but she refused. Her face was pale, her expression embittered. She was wearing Levi's and a baggy sweater; the hair spilled out of her bun.

"Look," Mary Lou said to Cronin, "I didn't come here for any favors, but did you say anything to Professor Getz about me? I mean what I told you about San Francisco?"

"Did he say I had?" Cronin asked.

"No, but we were being friendly and then he changed to me. I figure somebody must have told him something, and I thought nobody knew anything but you, so you must've told him."

Cronin admitted it. "I thought he ought to know, considering the circumstances."

"Such as what?" she asked sullenly.

He hesitated. "He's a married man with three kids. There could be serious trouble."

"That's his goddamn business."

He admitted that too. "I'm sorry, Mary Lou. All I can say is that my life has been confused and complicated lately."

"What about mine?" She was sitting in a chair, then turned her head and wept.

Cronin poured her a drink but Mary Lou wouldn't take it.

"The reason I told you those things is because I thought you were a guy I could trust and be friends with. Instead it was the opposite. I'm sorry what I told you got you so bothered, but there's a lot worse than that, and one thing I want you to know is it doesn't bother me anymore. I made my peace with my life."

"I haven't," said Cronin.

"I don't want to hear about it," said Mary Lou, and though he asked her to stay she left.

Afterwards he thought, She has learned something from her experience that I haven't learned from mine. And he felt sorry for Mary Lou, for the way he had treated her. It's not easy to be moral, Cronin thought. He decided, before he went to bed, not to come back to this college in the fall, to quit teaching.

•

On Commencement Day, Cronin met Mary Lou in the street, in her yellow dress, and they stopped to talk. She had put on weight but wasn't looking well, and as they talked her stomach rumbled. In embarrassment she covered her abdomen.

"It's from studying," she said. "I got awfully worried about my finals. The doctor in the infirmary said to watch out or I might wind up with an ulcer."

Cronin also advised her to take care. "Your health comes first."

They said goodbye. He never saw her again, but a year later, in Chicago, he had a card from her. She wrote she was still at college, majoring in education, and hoped someday to teach.

1963

❧ B M ❧

A Pimp's Revenge

F, ravaged Florentine, grieving, kicked apart a trial canvas, copy of one he had been working on for years, his foot through the poor mother's mouth, destroyed the son's insipid puss, age about ten. It deserved death for not coming to life. He stomped on them both, but not of course on the photograph still tacked to the easel ledge, sent years ago by sister, Bessie, together with her last meager check. "I found this old photo of you and Momma when you were a little boy. Thought you might like to have it, she's been dead these many years." Inch by enraged inch he rent the canvas, though cheap linen he could ill afford, and would gladly have cremated the remains if there were a place to. He swooped up the mess with both hands, grabbed some smeared drawings, ran down four rickety flights, and dumped all in the bowels of a huge burlap rubbish bag in front of the scabby mustard-walled house on Via S. Agostino. Fabio, the embittered dropsical landlord, asleep on his feet, awoke and begged for a few lire back rent but F ignored him. Across the broad piazza, Santo Spirito, nobly proportioned, stared him in the bushy-mustached face, but he would not look back. His impulse was to take the nearest bridge and jump off into the Arno, flowing again in green full flood after a dry summer; instead, he slowly ascended the stairs, pelted by the landlord's fruity curses. Upstairs in his desolate studio, he sat on his bed and wept. Then he lay with his head at the foot of the bed and wept.

The painter blew his nose at the open window and gazed for a reflective hour at the Tuscan hills in September haze. Otherwise, sunlight on the terraced silver-trunked olive trees, and San Miniato, sparkling, framed in the distance by black cypresses. Make an interesting impressionist oil, green and gold mosaics and those black trees of death, but that's been done. Not to mention Van Gogh's tormented cypresses. That's my trouble, everything's been done or is otherwise out of style—cubism, surrealism, action painting. If I could only guess what's next. Below, a stunted umbrella pine with a headful of black-and-white chirping swallows grew in the landlord's narrow yard, over a dilapidated henhouse that smelled to heaven, except that up here the smell was sweetened by the odor of red roof tiles. A small dirty white rooster crowed shrilly, the shrimpy brown hens clucking as they ran in dusty circles around three lemon trees in tubs. F's studio was a small room with a curtained kitchen alcove—several shelves, a stove and sink—the old-fashioned walls painted with faded rustic dancers, nymphs and shepherds, and on the ceiling a large scalloped cornucopia full of cracked and faded fruit.

He looked until the last of morning was gone, then briskly combed his thick mustache, sat at the table, and ate a hard anise biscuit as his eyes roamed over some quotations he had stenciled on the wall.

Constable: "Painting is for me another word for feeling."

Whistler: "A masterpiece is finished from the beginning."

Pollock: "What is it that escapes me? The human? That humanity is greater than art?"

Nietzsche: "Art is not an imitation of nature but its metaphysical supplement, raised up beside it in order to overcome it."

Picasso: "People seize on painting in order to cover up their nakedness."

Ah, if I had his genius.

Still, he felt better, picked up a fourteen-inch Madonna he had carved and sanded it busily. Then he painted green eyes, black hair, pink lips, and a sky-blue cloak, and waited around smoking until the statuette had dried. He wrapped it in a sheet of newspaper, dropped the package into a string bag, and went again downstairs, wearing sockless sandals, tight pants, and black beret. Sometimes he wore sunglasses.

At the corner he stepped into midstreet, repelled by the old crone's door, the fortune-teller, the eighth of seven sisters to hear her talk, six thick hairs sprouting from the wart on her chin; in order not to sneak in and ask, for one hundred lire, "Tell me, Signora, will I ever make it? Will I finish my five years' painting of Mother and Son? my sure masterpiece—I know it in my bones—if I ever get it done."

Her shrill sibylic reply made sense. "A good cook doesn't throw out yesterday's soup."

"But will it be as good, I mean. Very good, signora, maybe a masterwork?"

"Masters make masterworks."

"And what about my luck, when will it change from the usual?"

"When you do. Art is long, inspiration, short. Luck is fine, but don't stop breathing."

"Will I avoid an unhappy fate?"

"It all depends."

That or something like it for one hundred lire. No bargain.

F sighed. Still, it somehow encouraged.

A window shutter was drawn up with a clatter and a paper cone of garbage came flying out at him. He ducked as the oily bag split on the cobblestones behind him.

BEWARE OF FALLING MASONRY.

He turned the corner, barely avoiding three roaring Vespas.

Vita pericolosa. It had been a suffocating summer slowly deflated to cool autumn. He hurried, not to worry his hunger, past the fruit and vegetable stalls in the piazza, zigzagging through the Oltrarno streets as he approached Ponte Vecchio. Ah, the painter's eye! He enjoyed the narrow crowded noisy streets, the washing hung from windows. Tourists were all but gone, but the workshops were preparing for next year's migration, mechanics assembling picture frames, cutting leather, plastering tile mosaics; women plaiting straw. He sneezed passing through a tannery reek followed by hot stink of stable. Above the din of traffic an old forge rumbling. F hastened by a minuscule gallery where one of his action paintings had been hanging downside up for more than a year. He had made no protest, art lives on accidents.

At a small square, thick with stone benches where before the war there had been houses, the old and lame of the quarter sat amid beggars and berouged elderly whores, one nearby combing her reddish-gray locks. Another fed pigeons with a crust of bread they approached and pecked at. One, not so old, in a homely floppy velvet hat, he gazed at twice; in fact no more than a girl with a slender youthful body. He could stand a little sexual comfort but it cost too much. Holding the Madonna tightly to his chest, the painter hastened into the woodworker's shop.

Alberto Panenero, the proprietor, in a brown smock smeared with wood dust and shavings, scattered three apprentices with a hiss and came forward, bowing.

"Ah, maestro, another of your charming Madonnas, let's hope."

F unwrapped the wooden statuette of the modest Madonna.

The proprietor held it up as he examined it. He called together the apprentices. "Look at the workmanship, you ignoramuses," then dismissed them with a hiss.

"Beautiful?" F said.

"Of course. With that subject who can miss?"

"And the price?"

"Eh. What can one do? As usual."

F's face fell an inch. "Is it fair to pay only five thousand lire for a statuette that takes two weeks' work and sells on Via Tornabuoni for fifteen thousand, even twenty if someone takes it to St. Peter's and gets it blessed by the Pope?"

Panenero shrugged. "Ah, maestro, the world has changed since the time of true craftsmen. You and I, we're fighting a losing battle. As for the Madonnas, I now get most of the job turned out by machine. My apprentices cut in the face, add a few folds to the robe, daub on a bit of paint, and I swear to you it costs me one third of what I pay you and goes for the same price to the shops. Of course, they don't approach the quality of your product—I'm an honest man—but do you think the tourists care? What's more the shopkeepers are stingier than ever, and believe me they're stingy in Florence. If I ask for more they offer less. If they pay me seventy-five hundred for yours I'm in luck. With that price, how can I take care of rent and my other expenses? I pay the wages of two masters and a journeyman on my other products, the antique furniture and so forth. I also employ three apprentices who have to eat or they're too weak to fart. My own family, including a clubfoot son and three useless daughters, comes to six people. Eh, I don't have to tell you it's no picnic earning a living nowadays. Still, if you'll put a bambino in the poor Madonna's arms, I'll up you five hundred."

"I'll take the five thousand."

The proprietor counted it out in worn fifty- and one-hundred-lire notes.

"The trouble with you, maestro, is you're a perfectionist. How many are there nowadays?"

"I guess that's so," F sighed. "Don't think I haven't thought of selling the Madonnas to the tourists myself, but if I have to do that as well as make them where's my painting time coming from, I'd like to know."

"I agree with you totally," Panenero said. "Still, for a bachelor you're not doing too badly. I'm always surprised you look so skinny. It must be hereditary."

"Most of my earnings go for supplies. Everything's shot up so, oils, pigments, turpentine, everything. A tube of cadmium costs close to thirteen hundred lire, so I try to keep bright yellow, not to mention vermilion, out of my pictures. Last week I had to pass up a sable brush they ask three thousand for. A roll of cotton canvas costs over ten thousand. With such prices what's left for meat?"

"Too much meat is bad for the digestion. My wife's brother eats meat twice a day and has liver trouble. A dish of good spaghetti with cheese will fatten you up without interfering with your liver. Anyway how's the painting coming?"

"Don't ask me so I won't lie."

In the market close by, F pinched the tender parts of two Bosc pears and a Spanish melon. He looked into a basket of figs, examined some pumpkins on hooks, inspected a bleeding dead rabbit, and told himself he must do a couple of still lifes. He settled for a long loaf of bread and two etti of tripe. He also bought a brown egg for breakfast, six Nazionale cigarettes, and a quarter of a head of cabbage. In a fit of well-being he bought three wine-red dahlias, and the old woman who sold them to him out of her basket handed him a marigold, free. Shopping for food's a blessing, he thought, you get down to brass tacks. It makes a lot in life seem less important, for instance painting a masterwork. He felt he needn't paint for the rest of his life and nothing much lost; but then anxiety moved like a current through his belly as the thought threatened and he had all he could do not to break into a sweat, run back to the studio, set up his canvas, and start hitting it with paint. I'm a time-ravaged man, horrible curse on an artist.

The young whore with the baggy hat saw the flowers amid his bundles as he approached, and through her short veil smiled dimly up at him.

F, for no reason he could think of, gave her the marigold, and the girl—she was no more than eighteen—held the flower awkwardly.

"What's your price, if you don't mind me asking?"

"What are you, a painter or something?"

"That's right, how did you know?"

"I think I guessed. Maybe it's your clothes, or the flowers or something." She smiled absently, her eyes roaming the benches, her hard mouth tight. "To answer your question, two thousand lire."

He raised his beret and walked on.

"You can have me for five hundred," called an old whore from her bench. "What she hasn't heard of I've practiced all my life. I have no objection to odd requests."

But F was running. Got to get back to work. He crossed the street through a flood of Fiats, carts, Vespas, and rushed back to his studio.

Afterwards he sat on his bed, hands clasped between knees, looking at the canvas and thinking of the young whore. Maybe it'd relax me so I can paint.

He counted what was left of his money, then hid the paper lire in a knotted sock in his bureau drawer. He removed the sock and hid it in the armadio on the hat rack. Then he locked the armadio and hid the key in the bureau drawer. He dropped the drawer key into a jar of cloudy turpentine, figuring who would want to wet his hand fishing for it.

Maybe she'd let me charge it and I could pay when I have more money? I could do two Madonnas sometime and pay her out of the ten thousand lire.

Then he thought, She seemed interested in me as an artist. Maybe she'd trade for a drawing.

He riffled through a pile of charcoal drawings and came on one of a heavy-bellied nude cutting her toenails, one chunky foot on a backless chair. F trotted to the benches in the market piazza where the girl sat with a crushed marigold in her hand.

"Would you mind having a drawing instead? One of my own, that is?"

"Instead of what?"

"Instead of cash because I'm short. It's just a thought I had."

It took her a minute to run it through her head. "All right, if that's what you want."

He unrolled the drawing and showed it to her.

"Oh, all right."

But then she flushed under her veil and gazed embarrassed at F.

"Anything wrong?"

Her eyes miserably searched the piazza.

"It's nothing," she said after a minute. "I'll take your drawing." Then seeing him studying her she laughed nervously and said, "I was looking for my cousin. He's supposed to meet me here. Well, if he comes let him wait, he's a pain in the ass anyway."

She rose from the bench and they went together toward Via S. Agostino.

Fabio, the landlord, took one look and called her puttana.

"That'll do from you," said F, sternly.

"Pay your rent instead of pissing away the money."

Her name, she told him as they were undressing in his studio, was Esmeralda.

His was Arturo.

The girl's hair, when she tossed off her baggy hat, was brown and full. She had black eyes like plum pits, a small mouth on the sad side, Modigliani neck, strong though not exactly white teeth, and a pimply brow. She wore long imitation-pearl earrings and kept them on. Esmeralda unzipped her clothes and they were at once in bed. It wasn't bad though she apologized for her performance.

As they lay smoking in bed—he had given her one of his six cigarettes—Esmeralda said, "The one I was looking for isn't my cousin, he's my pimp, or at least he was. If he's there waiting for me I hope it's a blizzard and he freezes to death."

They had an espresso together. She said she liked the studio and offered to stay.

He was momentarily panicked. "I wouldn't want it to interfere with my painting. I mean I'm devoted to that. Besides, this is a small place."

"I'm a small girl, I'll take care of your needs and won't interfere with your work."

He finally agreed.

Though he had qualms concerning her health, he let her stay, yet felt reasonably contented.

•

"Il Signor Ludovico Belvedere," the landlord called up from the ground floor, "a gentleman on his way up the stairs to see you. If he buys one of your pictures, you won't have any excuse for not paying last month's rent, not to mention June or July."

If it was really a gentleman, F went in to wash his hands as the stranger slowly, stopping to breathe, wound his way up the stairs. The

painter had hastily removed the canvas from the easel, hiding it in
the kitchen alcove. He soaped his hands thickly, the smoke from the
butt in his mouth drifting into a closed eye. F quickly dried himself
with a dirty towel. It was, instead of a gentleman, Esmeralda's seedy
cugino, the pimp, a thin man past fifty, tall, with pouched small eyes
and a pencil-line mustache. His hands and feet were small, he wore
loose squeaky shoes with gray spats. His clothes though neatly pressed
had seen better days. He carried a malacca cane and sported a pearl-
gray hat. There was about him, though he seemed to mask it, a quality
of having experienced everything, if not more, that gave F the momentary shivers.

Bowing courteously and speaking as though among friends, he
was not, he explained, in the best of moods—to say nothing of his
health—after a week of running around desperately trying to locate Esmeralda. He explained they had had a misunderstanding over a few lire
through an unfortunate error, no more than a mistake in addition—
carrying a one instead of a seven. "These things happen to the best of
mathematicians, but what can you do with someone who won't listen to
reason? She slapped my face and ran off. Through a mutual acquaintance I made an appointment to explain the matter to her, with proof
from my accounts, but though she gave her word she didn't appear. It
doesn't speak well for her maturity."

He had learned later from a friend in the Santo Spirito quarter
that she was at the moment living with the signore. Ludovico apologized for disturbing him, but F must understand he had come out of
urgent necessity.

"Per piacere, signore, I request your good will. A great deal is at
stake for four people. She can continue to serve you from time to time
if that's what she wants; but I hear from your landlord that you're not
exactly prosperous, and on the other hand she has to support herself and
a starving father in Ficsole. I don't suppose she's told you about him but
if it weren't for me personally, he'd be lying in a common grave this
minute growing flowers on his chest. She must come back to work under my guidance and protection not only because it's mutually beneficial but because it's a matter of communal responsibility; not only hers
for me now that I've had a most serious operation, or both of us for her
starving father, but also in reference to my aged mother, a woman of
eighty-three who is seriously in need of proper nursing care. I understand you're an American, signore. That's one thing but Italy is a poor
country. Here each of us is responsible for the welfare of four or five
others or we all go under."

He spoke calmly, philosophically, occasionally breathlessly, as if his recent operation now and then caught up with him. And his intense small eyes wandered in different directions as he talked, as though he suspected Esmeralda might be hiding.

F, after his first indignation, listened with interest although disappointed the man had not turned out to be a wealthy picture buyer.

"She's had it with whoring," he said.

"Signore," Ludovico answered with emotion, "it's important to understand. The girl owes me much. She was seventeen when I came across her, a peasant girl living a wretched existence. I'll spare you the details because they'd turn your stomach. She had chosen this profession, the most difficult of all as we both know, but lacked the ability to handle herself. I met her by accident and offered to help her although this sort of thing wasn't in my regular line of work. To make the story short, I devoted many hours to her education and found her a better clientele—to give you an example, recently one of her newest customers, a rich cripple she sees every week, offered to marry her, but I advised against it because he's a contadino. I also took measures to protect her health and well-being. I advised her to go for periodic medical examinations, scared off badly behaved customers with a toy pistol, and tried in every way to reduce indignities and hazards. Believe me, I am a protective person and gave her my sincere affection. I treat her as if she were my own daughter. She isn't by chance in the next room? Why doesn't she come out and talk frankly?"

He pointed with his cane at the alcove curtain.

"That's the kitchen," said F. "She's at the market."

Ludovico, bereft, blew on his fingers, his eyes momentarily glazed as his glance mechanically wandered around the room. He seemed then to come to and gazed at some of F's pictures with interest. In a moment his features were animated.

"Naturally, you're a painter! Pardon me for overlooking it, a worried man is half blind. Besides, somebody said you were an insurance agent."

"No, I'm a painter."

The pimp borrowed F's last cigarette, took a few puffs as he studied the pictures on the wall with tightened eyes, then put out the barely used butt and pocketed it.

"It's a remarkable coincidence." He had once, it turned out, been a frame maker and later part-owner of a small art gallery on Via Strozzi, and he was of course familiar with painting and the painting market. But the gallery, because of the machinations of his thieving partner, had failed. He hadn't reopened it for lack of capital. It was shortly afterward he had had to have a lung removed.

"That's why I didn't finish your cigarette."

Ludovico coughed badly—F believed him.

"In this condition, naturally, I find it difficult to make a living. Even frame making wears me out. That's why it's advantageous for me to work with Esmeralda."

"Anyway, you certainly have your nerve," the painter replied. "I'm not just referring to your coming up here and telling me what I ought to do vis-à-vis someone who happens to be here because she asked to be, but I mean actually living off the proceeds of a girl's body. All in all, it isn't much of a moral thing to do. Esmeralda might in some ways be indebted to you but she doesn't owe you her soul."

The pimp leaned with dignity on his cane.

"Since you bring up the word, signore, are you a moral man?"

"In my art I am."

Ludovico sighed. "Ah, maestro, who are we to talk of what we understand so badly? Morality has a thousand sources and endless means of expression. As for the soul, who understands its mechanism? Remember, the thief on the cross was the one who rose to heaven with Our Lord." He coughed at length. "Keep in mind that the girl of her free will chose her calling, not I. She was in it without finesse or proficiency, although she is of course adequate. Her advantage is her youth and a certain directness, but she needs advice and managerial assistance. Have you seen the hat she wears? Twice I tried to burn it. Obviously she lacks taste. The same is true for her clothes, but she's very stubborn to deal with. Still, I devote myself to her and manage to improve conditions, for which I receive a modest but necessary commission. Considering the circumstances, how can this be an evil thing? The basis of morality is recognizing one another's needs and cooperating. Mutual generosity is nothing to criticize other people for. After all, what did Jesus teach?"

Ludovico had removed his hat. He was bald with several gray hairs parted in the center.

He seemed, now, depressed. "You aren't in love with her, are you, maestro? If so, say the word and I disappear. Love is love, after all. I don't forget I'm an Italian."

F thought for a minute.

"Not as yet, I don't think."

"In that case I hope you will not interfere with her decision?"

"What decision do you have in mind?"

"As to what she will do after I speak to her."

"You mean if she decides to leave?"

"Exactly."

"That's up to her."

The pimp ran a relieved hand over his perspiring head and replaced his hat. "The relationship may be momentarily convenient, but for a painter who has his work to think of you'll be better off without her."

"I didn't say I wanted her to go," said F. "All I said was I wouldn't interfere with her decision."

Ludovico bowed. "Ah, you have the objectivity of a true artist."

On his way out, he tossed aside the alcove curtain with his cane and uncovered F's painting on the kitchen table.

He seemed at first unable to believe his eyes. Standing back, he had a better look. "Straordinario," he murmured, kissing his fingertips.

F snatched the canvas, blew off the dust, and carefully tucked it behind his bureau.

"It's work in progress," he explained. "I don't like to show it yet."

"Obviously it will be a very fine painting, one sees that at a glance. What do you call it?"

" 'Mother and Son.' "

"In spirit it's pure Picasso."

"Is it?"

"I refer to his remark: 'You paint not what you see but what you know is there.' "

"That's right," F said, his voice husky.

"We all have to learn from the masters. There's nothing wrong with trying to do better that which they do best themselves. Thus new masters are born."

"Thank you."

"When you finish let me know. I am acquainted with people who are interested in buying fine serious contemporary work. I could get you an excellent price, of course for the usual commission. Anyway, it looks as though you are about to give birth to a painting of extraordinary merit. Permit me to congratulate you on your talent."

F blushed radiantly.

Esmeralda returned.

Ludovico fell to his knees.

"Go fuck yourself," she said.

"Ah, signorina, my misfortune is your good luck. Your friend is a superb artist. You can take my word for it."

·

How do you paint a Kaddish?

Here's Momma sitting on the stoop in her cotton housedress, awkward at having her picture taken, yet with a dim smile on the dry old snapshot turning yellow that Bessie sent me years ago. Here's the snap, here's the painting of the same idea, why can't I make one out of both? How do you make art of an old photo, so to say? A single of a double image, the one in and the one out?

The painting, 51 × 38, was encrusted in places (her hands and feet, his face), almost a quarter of an inch thick with paint, layer on layer giving it history, another word for thick past in the paint itself. The mystery was why in the five years he had been at it, on and off because he had to hide it away when it got to be too much for him, he hadn't been able to finish it though most of it was done already, except Momma's face. Five years' work here, mostly as he had first painted it, though he often added dibs and dabs, touches of brush or palette knife on the dry forms. He had tried it every which way, with Momma alone, sitting or standing, with or without him; and with Bessie in or out, but never Poppa, that living ghost; and I've made her old and young, and sometimes resembling Annamaria Oliovino, or Teresa, the chambermaid in Milan; even a little like Susskind, when my memory gets mixed up, who was a man I met when I first came to Rome. Momma apart and him apart, and then trying to bring them together in the tightly woven paint so they would be eternally mother and son as well as unique forms on canvas. So beautifully complete the idea of them together that the viewer couldn't help but think no one has to do it again because it's been done by F and can't be done better; in truth, a masterwork. He had painted her sad and happy, tall, short, realistic, expressionistic, cubistic, surrealistic, even in action splotches of violet and brown. Also in black and white, stark like Kline or Motherwell. Once he had molded a figure in clay from the old photo and tried to copy it, but that didn't work either.

The faces were changed almost every day he painted, his as a young boy, hers as herself (long since departed); but now, though for a year he had let the boy be, his face and all, he was still never satisfied with hers—something always missing—for very long after he had put it down; and he daily or nightly scraped it off (another lost face) with his rusty palette knife, and tried once again the next day; then scraped that face the same night or the day after; or let it harden in hope for two days and then frantically, before the paint stiffened, scraped that face off too. All in all he had destroyed more than a thousand faces and conceived another thousand for a woman who could barely afford one; yet couldn't settle on her true face—at least true for art. What was true for Bessie's old photo was true enough—you can't beat Kodak, but reduced on canvas, too much omitted. He sometimes thought of tearing up the old snapshot so he would have only memory (of it?) to go by, but couldn't bring himself to destroy this last image of her. He was afraid to tear up the snap and went on painting the face on the dumpy body on the chair on the stoop, little F standing blandly by her side knowing she had died though pretending, at least in paint, that he didn't; then scraping it off as the rest of the painting slowly thickened into a frieze.

I've caught the boy, more or less, and sometimes I seem to have her for a few minutes, though not when I look at them together. I don't paint her face so that it holds him in her presence. It comes out at best like two portraits in space and time. Should I stand him on the left instead of right? I tried it once and it didn't work; now I have this hard-as-rock-quarter-of-an-inch investment in the way they are now, and if I scrap either of them (chisel? dynamite?), I might as well throw out the canvas. I might as well scrap what's left of my life if I have to start over again.

How do you invent whoever she was? I remember so little, her death, not even the dying, just the end mostly, after a sickness they easily cure nowadays with penicillin. I was about six or seven, or maybe ten, and, as I remember, didn't cry at the funeral. For years that never bothered me much, but when Bessie sent me the snap and I began painting Momma's pictures, I guess it did. Maybe I held it against her, I mean dying; either that or I am by nature a non-mourner, born that way whether one wants it or not. The truth is I am afraid to paint, like I might find out something about myself.

I have not said Kaddish, though I could have looked up the words.

What if she were still a wandering figure among the stars, unable to find the Pearly Gates?

He hid the canvas and turned then to the statuette of the Madonna without child. Esmeralda liked to see the chips fly as the Holy Mother rose out of wood.

•

The girl had coffee with milk in the morning, slept on a borrowed cot in the kitchen alcove, and stayed out of his way while he was painting. The back of the canvas was what she saw when she came into the studio each morning for a few lire to shop with. It was understood she was not to try to look as he painted. "Malocchio," he said, and she nodded and withdrew on tiptoe. Because he found it uncomfortable to work with someone around, after a few days he had thought of asking her to leave, but when he considered how young she was, hardly grown up, like a young child's big sister, he changed his mind. Only once she indirectly referred to the painting, asking what was the snapshot he pored over so much. "Mind your business," F said; she shrugged and withdrew. In the kitchen she was slowly reading a love serial in a movie magazine. She shopped, cooked, kept the studio clean, although she did not bathe as often as he. In the kitchen, as he painted, she mended his socks and underwear, and altered her dresses. She had not much clothing, a sweater and skirt and two trollop's dresses, from one of which she removed two silver roses, from the other some rows of purple sequins. She sewed up the necklines and lowered the hems. She owned a tight black sweater that looked good on her because of her healthy bosom, long neck, dark eyes; also a few pieces of patched underwear, nothing enticing but a red chemise, not bad but too red, some baubles of jewelry she had bought on the Ponte Vecchio, and a modest pair of house shoes. Her gold high heels she had wrapped in newspaper and put away. How long for does she think? F thought. And the girl was a talented cook. She fed him well, mostly on macaroni, green vegetables cooked in olive oil, and now and then some tripe or rabbit. She did very well with a few lire, and all in all two lived cheaper than one. She made no complaints, though she could be sullen when, lost in his work or worry, he paid scant attention to her for days. She obliged in bed when he wanted her, could be tender, and generally made herself useful. Esmeralda once suggested she would pose for him in the nude but F wouldn't hear of it. Heavy-armed and long-footed, at times she reminded him of Bessie as a girl, though they weren't really much alike.

One October morning F sprang out of bed, terribly inspired. Before breakfast he got the painting out of its hiding place to finish off once and for all, only to discover that Bessie's snapshot was gone from the easel ledge. He shook Esmeralda awake but she hadn't seen it. F rushed downstairs, dumped the garbage bag on the sidewalk, and frantically searched amid the hard spaghetti strings and mushy melon rinds, as the landlord waving both arms threatened suit. No luck. Upstairs, he hunted through the studio from top to bottom, Esmeralda diligently assisting, but they found nothing. He spent a terrible morning, not a stroke painted.

"But why do you need a picture to paint from, it's all so ridiculous."

"Are you sure you didn't take it?"

"Why would I take it? It's not a picture of me."

"To teach me a lesson or something?"

"Don't be a fool," she said.

He trembled in rage and misery.

In his presence she searched through his chest of drawers—he had been through them a dozen times—and on top, under a book on Uccello he had been reading, discovered the lost snap.

F blushed.

"I forgive your dirty suspicions," she said, her eyes clouding.

"Not that I deserve it," he admitted.

After lunch she tried on the floppy hat she had worn when he met her, to see how she could alter it.

The sight of the velvet hat on her excited his eye. F had another inspiration.

"I'll paint you in it—at least a drawing."

"What for? You said it's ugly on me."

"It's unique is why. Many a master in the past was enticed by a hat to do a portrait of the face beneath. Rembrandt, for instance."

"Oh, all right," Esmeralda said. "It's immaterial to me. I thought you'd want to be getting back to your painting."

"The day's shot for that."

She agreed to pose. He did a quick charcoal for a warm-up that came out entrancing, especially the hat. He began then to sketch her in pencil, possibly for a painting.

As he was drawing, F asked, "How did you happen to fall into prosti—your former profession? What I mean is, was it Ludovico's doing?"

"Prosti—profession," she mimicked. "Once you've cackled, lay the egg."

"I was trying to be considerate."

"Try again. Keeping your mouth shut about certain things is a better consideration; still, if it's only your curiosity you're out to satisfy, I'll tell you why. Ludovico had nothing to do with it, at least then, although he was one of my earliest customers and still owes me money for services rendered, not to mention certain sums he stole outright. He's the only pure bastard I know, all the others have strains of decency, not that it makes much difference. Anyway, it was my own idea, if you want to know. Maybe I was working up to be an artist's mistress."

F, letting the sarcasm pass, continued to sketch her.

"One thing I'll tell you, it wasn't because of any starving father, if that's what he's told you. My father has a tiny farm in Fiesole, he stinks of manure and is incredibly stingy. All he's ever parted with is his virginity. He's got my mother and sister drudging for him and is sore as a castrated bull that I escaped. I ran away because I was sick to my teeth of being a slave. What's more, he wasn't above giving me a feel now and then when he had nothing better to do. Thanks to him I can barely read and write. I turned to whoring because I don't want to be a maid and I don't know anything else. A truck driver on the autostrada gave me the idea. But in spite of my profession I'm incredibly shy, that's why I let Ludovico pimp for me."

She asked if she could see the drawing of herself and, when she had, said, "What are you going to call it?"

He had thought, "Portrait of a Young Whore," but answered, " 'Portrait of a Young Woman.' I might do an oil from it."

"It's immaterial to me," Esmeralda said, but she was pleased.

"The reason I stayed here is I thought you'd be kind to me. Besides, if a man is an artist I figured he must know about life. If he does maybe he can teach me something. So far all I've learned is you're like everybody else, shivering in your drawers. That's how it goes, when you think you have nothing there's somebody with less."

F made three more drawings on paper, with and without the hat, and one with the black hat and Esmeralda holding marigolds.

The next morning he carved half a wooden Madonna in a few hours and, to celebrate, took Esmeralda to the Uffizi in the afternoon and explained some of the great works of art to her.

She didn't always understand his allusions but was grateful. "You're not so dumb," she said.

"One picks up things."

That evening they went to a movie and afterwards stopped for a gelato in a café off the Piazza della Signoria. Men looked her over. F stared them down. She smiled at him tenderly. "You're a lot more relaxed when you're working on the Madonnas. When you're painting with that snapshot in front of you, you haven't the civility of a dog."

He admitted the truth of it.

She confessed she had stolen a long look at his painting when he was downstairs going through the garbage bag for the snap.

To his surprise he did not condemn her.

"What did you think of it?"

"Who is she, the one without the face?"

"My mother, she died young."

"What's the matter with the boy?"

"What do you mean?"

"He looks kind of sad."

"That's the way it's supposed to be. But I don't want to talk about it. That can ruin the painting."

"To me it's as though you were trying to paint yourself into your mother's arms."

He was momentarily stunned. "Do you think so?"

"It's obvious to me. A mother's a mother, a son's a son."

"True, but it might be like an attempt on my part to release her from the arms of death. But that sort of stuff doesn't matter much. It's first and foremost a painting, potentially a first-class work if I ever get it done. If I could complete it the way I sometimes see it in my mind's eye, I bet it could be something extraordinary. If a man does only one such painting in his lifetime, he can call himself a success. I sometimes think that if I could paint such a picture, much that was wrong in my life would rearrange itself and add up to more, if you know what I mean."

"In what way?"

"I could forgive myself for past errors."

"Not me," Esmeralda said. "I'd have to paint ten great pictures." She laughed at the thought.

As they were crossing the bridge, Esmeralda said, "You're really nutty. I don't see why a man would give up five years of his life just to paint one picture. If it was me I'd put it aside and do something I could sell."

"I do once in a while, like this portrait of you I'm working on now, but I always go back to 'Mother and Son.' "

"Why does everybody talk about art so much?" she asked. "Even Ludovico, when he's not adding up his accounts, he's talking about art."

"Art's what it must be, which is beauty, and more, which is mostly mystery. That's what people talk about."

"In this picture you're painting of me, what's the mystery?"

"The mystery is you've been captured, yet there's more—you've become art."

"You mean it's not me anymore?"

"It never was. Art isn't life."

"Then the hell with it. If I have my choice I'll take life. If there's not that there's no art."

"Without art there's no life to speak of, at least for me. If I'm not an artist, then I'm nothing."

"My God, aren't you a man?"

"Not really, without art."

"Personally, I think you have a lot to learn."

"I'm learning," F sighed.

"What's so great about mystery?" she asked. "I don't like it. There's enough around without making more."

"Being involved in it."

"Explain that to me."

"It's complicated, but one thing would be that a man like me— you understand—is actually working in art. The idea came to me late, I wasted most of my youth. The mystery of art is that more is there than you put down and every stroke adds to it. You look at your painting and see this bull's-eye staring at you though all you've painted is an old tree. It's also a mystery to me why I haven't been able to finish my best painting though I am dying to."

"If you ask me," Esmeralda said, "my idea of a mystery is why I am in love with you, though it's clear to me you don't see me for dirt."

She burst into tears.

A week later Ludovico, come for a morning visit wearing new yellow gloves, saw the completed portrait of Esmeralda, 48 × 30, with black hat, long neck, and marigolds. He was bowled over.

"Fantastic. If you pay me half, I can get you a million lire for this work of art."

F agreed, so the pimp, crossing himself, left with the painting.

•

One afternoon when Esmeralda was out, Ludovico, breathing badly after four flights of stairs, appeared in the studio lugging a tape recorder he had borrowed for an interview with F.

"What for?"

"To keep a record for the future. I'll get it printed in *International Arts*. My cousin is assistant to the business manager. It will help you get a gallery for your first one-man show."

"Who needs a gallery if all I can show is unfinished canvases?"

"You'd better increase your output. Sit down here and talk into the microphone. I've turned it on. Don't worry about the machine, it won't crawl up your leg. Just relax and answer my questions candidly. Also don't waste time justifying yourself. Are you ready?"

"Yes."

LUD: Very well. Ludovico Belvedere speaking, interviewing the painter Fidelman. Tell me, Arturo, as an American what does painting mean to you?

F: It's my whole life.

LUD: What kind of person do you think an artist is when he's painting? Do you think he's a king or an emperor, or a seer or prophet?

F: I don't know for sure. I often feel like a constipated witch doctor.

LUD: Please talk with good sense. If you're going to be scatological I'll stop the machine.

F: I didn't mean anything bad.

LUD: As an American painter, what do you think of Jackson Pollock? Do you agree that he is a liberating influence?

F: I guess so. The truth is you have to liberate yourself.

LUD: We're talking about painting, not your personal psychology. Jackson Pollock, as any cultured person will tell you, has changed the course of modern painting. Don't think we don't know about him in this country, we're not exactly backward. We can all learn from him, including you. Do you agree that anyone who works in the modes of the past has only leavings to work with?

F: Only partly, the past is pretty rich.

LUD: I go now to the next question. Who is your favorite painter?

F: Ah—well, I don't think I have one, I have many.

LUD: If you think that's an advantage, you're wrong. There's no need of hubris. If an interviewer asked me that question, I would reply "Leonardo, Raphael, Michelangelo," or someone else but not the entire pantheon of painters.

F: I answered honestly.

LUD: Anyway, to go on, what is your avowed purpose in art?

F: To do the best I can. To do more than that. My momentary purpose is to create my uncreated masterpiece.

LUD: The one of your mother?

F: That's right, "Mother and Son."

LUD: But where is your originality? Why are you so concerned with subject matter?

F: I reject originality.

LUD: What's that? Please explain yourself.

F: Maybe I'm not ready, not just yet.

LUD: Mother of God! How old are you?

F: About forty. A little more.

LUD: But why are you so cautious and conservative? I'm fifty-two and have the mind of a youth. Tell me, what's your opinion of pop art? Think before you speak.

F: If it stays away from me, I'll stay away from it.

LUD: (*garbled*)

F: What did you say?

LUD: Please attend to the question at hand. I wish you would explain to me clearly why you paint.

F: With my paintings I try to stop the flow of time.

LUD: That's a ridiculous statement, but go on anyway.

F: I've said it.

LUD: Say it more comprehensibly. The public will read this.

F: Well, art is my means for understanding life and trying out certain assumptions I have. I make art, it makes me.

LUD: We have a proverb: "The bray of an ass can't be heard in heaven."

F: Frankly, I don't care for some of your remarks.

LUD: Are you saying the canvas is the alter ego of the artist's miserable self?

F: That's not what I said and I don't like what you're saying.

LUD: I'll try to be more respectful. Maestro, once you spoke to me of your art as moral. What did you mean by that?

F: It's just a thought I had, I guess. I suppose I mean that maybe a painting sort of gives value to a human being as he responds to it. You might say it enlarges his consciousness. If he feels beauty it makes him more than he was; it adds, you might say, to his humanity.

LUD: What do you mean "responds"? A man responds in rape, doesn't he? Doesn't that enlarge the consciousness, as you put it?

F: It's a different response. Rape isn't art.

LUD: An emotion is an emotion, no matter how it arises. In itself it is not moral or immoral. Suppose someone responds to the sunset on the Arno? Is that better or more moral than the response to the smell of a drowned corpse? What about bad art? Suppose the response is with more feeling than to a great painting—does that prove bad art is moral, as you call it?

F: I guess not. All right, maybe the painting itself doesn't have it, but putting it another way, maybe the artist does; that is he does when he's painting—creating form, order. Order protects us all, doesn't it?

LUD: Yes, the way a prison does. Remember, some of the biggest pricks, if you will excuse the use of this word, have been great painters. Does that necessarily make them moral men? Of course not. What if a painter kills his father and then paints a beautiful Ascension?

F: Maybe I'm not putting it exactly right. Maybe what I'm trying to say is that I feel most moral when I'm painting, like being engaged with truth.

LUD: So now it's what you feel. I speak with respect, maestro, but you do nothing but assault me with garbage.

F: Look, Ludovico, I don't understand, if you don't mind my saying so, why you brought this machine up here if all you want to do is insult me. Now take it away, it's using up work-time.

LUD: I am not a servant, maestro. I may have been forced into menial work through circumstance, but Ludovico Belvedere has kept his dignity. Don't think that because you are an American you can go on trampling on the rights of Europeans. You have caused me unnecessary personal discomfort and sorrow by interfering in a business relationship between this unfortunate girl and myself, and the lives of four people have been seriously affected. You don't seem to realize the harm you are doing—

END OF INTERVIEW

F had assaulted the tape recorder.

•

Each morning he awoke earlier to paint, waiting for dawn though the light from the streaked sky was, of course, impossible. He had lately been capable of very little patience with the necessities of daily life: to wash, dress, eat, even go to the toilet; and the matter became most inconvenient when his nervous impatience seeped into painting itself. It was a burdensome business to take the canvas out of its hiding place behind the armadio and arrange it on the easel, select and mix his paints, tack up the old snapshot (most unbearable), and begin work. He could have covered the canvas on the easel at night and left the snapshot tacked on permanently, but was obsessed to remove it each time after he put the paints away, soaked his brushes in turpentine, cleaned up. Formerly, just picking up a brush and standing in thought, or reverie, or sometimes blankly, before painting would ease interior constrictions to the point where he could relax sufficiently to enjoy the work; and once he had painted for an hour, which sometimes came to no more than a stroke or two, he felt well enough to permit himself to eat half a roll and swallow an espresso Esmeralda had prepared, and afterwards go with lit butt and magazine to the gabinetto. But now there were days he stood in terror before "Mother and Son" and shivered with every stroke he put down.

He painted out of anguish, a dark color. The canvas remained much the same, the boy as he had been, the fickle mother's face daily changing; daily he scraped it off as Esmeralda moaned in the kitchen;

she knew the sound of palette knife on canvas. It was then it occurred to F to use the girl as a model for his mother. Though she was only eighteen, it might help to have a living model for Momma as a young woman though she was touching middle age when Bessie took the photo, and was of course another sort of person; still, such were the paradoxes of art. Esmeralda agreed and stripped herself to the skin, but the painter sternly ordered her to dress; it was her face he was painting. She did as he demanded and patiently posed, sweetly, absently, uncomplaining, for hours, as he, fighting against his need for privacy in the creative act, tried anew to invent the mother's face. I've done all I can with imagination, I mean on top of the snapshot. And though at the end of the day he scraped her face off as the model wept, F urged her to be calm because he now had a brand-new idea: to paint himself not with Momma anymore but Bessie instead, "Brother and Sister." Esmeralda's face lit up because "then you'll stop using the snapshot." But F replied, "Not exactly," he still needed it to get the true relationship of them "in space as well as psychology."

As they were into the spaghetti at supper, the girl wanted to know if all artists had it so hard.

"How hard?"

"So that it takes them years to paint a picture?"

"Some do and some don't. What's on your mind?"

"Oh, I don't know," she said.

He slammed down his fork. "Are you doubting my talent, you whore?"

She got up and went into the gabinetto.

F lay on his bed, his face engulfed in a pillowful of black thoughts. After a while Esmeralda came out and kissed his ear.

"I forgive you, tesoro, I want you to succeed."

"I will," he cried, springing up from the bed.

The next day he rigged up a young boy's costume—blouse and knee pants, and painted in it to get to the heart of bygone days, but that didn't work either so he went back to putting Esmeralda into the painting and scraping her face off each night.

To live, to paint, to live to paint he had to continue carving Madonnas; being impatient he made them more reluctantly. When Esmeralda pointed out they had some sauce but no spaghetti, in three days he hurried out a statuette then hurried it over to Panenero's shop. The woodworker unfortunately couldn't use it. "My apprentices"—he shrugged—"are turning them out by the barrelful. Frankly, they model each stroke on yours and work fast. Eh, that's what happens to craft in these times. So the stuff piles up and the tourists won't be here till spring. It's a long time till the hackensacks and lederhosen come over the Alps, maestro. Still, because it's you and I admire your skill, I'll offer you two thousand lire, take it or leave it. This is my busy day."

F left without a word, in afterthought wondering whose yellow gloves he had seen lying on the counter. On his way along the riverbank he flung the Madonna into the Arno. She struck the green water with a golden splash, sank, then rose to the surface and, turning on her back, floated downstream, eyes to the blue sky.

He later carved two more Madonnas, finely wrought pieces, and peddled them himself to shops on the Via Tornabuoni and della Vigna Nuova. No luck. The shelves were crammed full of religious figures, though one of the merchants offered him six thousand lire for a Marilyn Monroe, nude if possible.

"I have no skill for that sort of thing."

"What about John the Baptist in shaggy skins?"

"What about him?"

"I offer five thousand."

"I find him an uninteresting figure."

Esmeralda then tried selling the statuettes. F wouldn't let her offer them to Panenero, so the girl, holding a Holy Mother in each arm, stood in the Piazza del Duomo and finally sold one to a huge German priest for twelve hundred; and the other she gave to a widow in weeds at Santa Maria Novella for eight hundred lire. F, when he heard, ground his teeth and, though she pleaded with him to be reasonable, swore he would carve no more.

He worked at odd jobs, one in a laundry, that tired him so he couldn't paint at night. One morning he tried chalking blue-robed Madonnas with Child, after Raphael, on the sidewalks before the Baptistery, Santa Chiara, the Stazione Centrale, where he was almost arrested. Passersby stopped to watch him work but moved on quickly when he passed the hat. A few tossed small coins upon the image of the Holy Mother and F collected them and went to the next spot. A brown-robed monk in sandals followed him.

"Why don't you look for productive work?"

"Advice is cheap."

"So is your art."

He went to the Cappella Brancacci and sat the rest of the day staring in the half dark at the Masaccio frescoes. Geniuses made masterworks. If you weren't greatly gifted the way was hard, a masterwork was a miracle. Still, somehow or other art abounded in miracles.

He borrowed a fishing pole from an artist neighbor and fished, amid a line of men with bent rods, off the Ponte Trinità. F tied the rod to a nail on the railing and paced back and forth, returning every few minutes to check his line as the float bobbed in the Arno. He caught nothing, but the old fisherman next to him, who had pulled in eight fish, gave him a one-eyed crippled eel. It was a cloudy November day, then rainy, patches of damp appearing on the studio ceiling. The cornucopia leaked. The house was cold, Fabio wouldn't turn on the heat till December. It was hard to get warm. But Esmeralda made a tasty crippled-eel soup. The next night she cooked a handful of borrowed polenta that popped in the pot as it boiled. For lunch the following day there was stale bread and half an onion apiece. But for Sunday supper she served boiled meat, green beans, and a salad of beet leaves. He suspiciously asked how come, and she admitted she had borrowed a few hundred lire from Ludovico.

"How are we supposed to pay him back?"

"We won't, he owes me plenty."

"Don't borrow from him anymore."

"I'm not afraid of him, he's afraid of me."

"I don't like him coming around. I'm at my most dishonest among dishonest men."

"Don't trust him, Arturo," she said, frightened. "He'd knife you if he could."

"He won't get the chance."

Afterwards she asked, "Why don't you carve a Madonna or two? Two thousand lire now and then is nothing to spit at. Besides you do beautiful work in wood."

"Not for the price, it's not worth my time."

The landlord, wearing a woman's black shawl, entered without knocking, shouting for his rent.

"I'll get the municipality to throw you both out, the puttana and you. You're fouling up this house with your illicit activities. Your friend told me what goes on here. I have all the necessary information."

"You know where you can stick it," said F. "If we weren't here the flat would go to ruin. It was empty six years before I moved in, you'll never rent it if I move out."

"You're no Florentine," Fabio shouted. "You're not even an Italian."

F got himself a badly paid job as journeyman in a woodworking establishment, not Panenero's. He worked long hours turning out delicate tapered legs for antique tables and did no painting. In the street, going back and forth from work, he looked for coins people might have dropped. He switched off the light after Esmeralda had washed the supper dishes, watched carefully what she cooked, and ate, and doled out shopping money sparsely. Once she sold six inches of her hair to a man with a sack who had knocked on the door, so she could buy herself some warm underwear.

Finally she could stand it no longer. "What are you going to do?"

"What can I do that I haven't?"

"I don't know. Do you want me to go back to my work?"

"I never said so."

"If I don't you'll be like this forever. It's what you're like when you're not painting."

He remained mute.

"Why don't you speak?"

"What can I say?"

"You can say no."

"No," he said.

"It sounds like yes."

He went out for a long walk and for a while hung around the palazzo where Dostoevsky had written the last pages of *The Idiot.* It did no good. When he returned he said nothing to Esmeralda. In fact he did not feel too bad though he knew he ought to. In fact he had been thinking of asking her to go to work, whatever she might do. It's circumstances, he thought.

Esmeralda had got out her black hat, the two dresses, and her gold shoes. On the velvet hat she sewed the silver roses. She raised the hems of the dresses above her knees and unstitched the necklines to expose the rounded tops of her hard breasts. The purple sequins she threw into the garbage.

"Anyway, I'll need protection," she said.

"How do you mean?"

"You know what I mean. I don't want those bastards hurting me or not paying in full. It's blood money."

"I'll protect you," F said.

He wore dark glasses, a black velour hat pulled low over one eye, and a brown overcoat with a ratty fur collar buttoned tight under the chin and extending to his ankles; he walked in white sneakers. He thought of growing a beard but gave that up. His bristly reddish mustache was thicker than it had ever been. And he carried a snappy cane with a slender sword inside.

They went together to the Piazza della Repubblica, almost merrily. "For art," she said, then after a moment, bitterly, "art, my ass."

She cursed him from the depth of her heart and then forgave him. "It's my nature," she said. "I can't bear a grudge."

He promised to marry her once he had finished the painting.

•

F paints all morning after Esmeralda has posed; she bathes, does her nails and toes, and makes herself up with mascara. After a leisurely lunch they leave the house and go across the bridge to the Piazza della Repubblica. She sits on a bench with her legs crossed high, smoking; and F is at a bench nearby, sketching in a pad in which he sometimes finds himself drawing dirty pictures: men and women, women and women, men and men. But he doesn't consort with the other pimps who sit together playing cards; nor does Esmeralda talk with the other whores, they call her hoity-toity. When a man approaches to ask whether she happens to be free she nods or, looking at him through her short veil, says yes as though she could just as well have said no. She gets up, the other whores watching her with their eyes and mouths, and wanders with her client into one of the crooked side streets, to a tiny room they have rented close by so there's no waste of man-hours getting back to the piazza. The room has a bed, water bowl, chamber pot.

When Esmeralda rises from the bench, F slips his drawing pad into his coat pocket and leisurely follows them. Sometimes it is a beautiful late-fall afternoon and he takes deep breaths as he walks. On occasion he stops to pick up a pack of Nazionale and, if he's a little hungry, gulps an espresso and a bit of pastry. He then goes up the smelly stairs and waits outside the door, sketching little pictures in the dim electric glow, as Esmeralda performs; or files his fingernails. It takes fifteen or twenty minutes for the customer to come out. Some would like to stay longer but can't if they won't pay for it. As a rule there are no arguments. The man dresses and sometimes leaves a tip if it has been most enjoyable. Esmeralda is still dressing, bored with getting in and out of her clothes. Only once thus far has she had to call F in to deal with a runt who said it hadn't been any good so no sense paying.

F enters with the sword drawn out of his cane and points it at the man's hairy throat. "Pay," he says, "and beat it." The runt, gone two shades white, hurriedly leaves assisted by a boot in the pants. Esmeralda watches without expression. She hands F the money—usually two thousand lire, sometimes three; and if she can get it from a wealthy-type client, or an older man especially fond of eighteen-year-old girls, seven or eight thousand. That sum is rare. F counts the money—often in small bills—and slips it into his wallet, wrapping a fat rubber band around it. In the evening they go home together, Esmeralda doing her shopping on the way. They try not to work at night unless it's been a bad day. In that case they go out after supper, when the piazza is lit in neon signs and the bars and cafés are doing business; the competition is stiff—some very beautiful women in extraordinary clothes. F goes into the bars and seeks out men who seem to be alone. He asks them if they want a pretty girl and, if one shows interest, leads him to Esmeralda. When it's rainy or freezing cold, they stay in and play cards or listen to the radio. F has opened an account in the Banco di Santo Spirito so they can draw from it in the winter if Esmeralda is sick and can't work. They go to bed after midnight. The next morning F gets up early and paints. Esmeralda sleeps late.

One morning F paints with his dark glasses on, until she wakes up and screams at him.

Later, when she is out buying material for a dress, Ludovico strides into the studio, incensed. His usually pallid face is flushed. He shakes his malacca at F.

"Why wasn't I informed that she had gone back to work? I demand a commission. She took all her instruction from me!"

F is about to run him out of the room by the worn seat of his overcoat but then has this interesting thought: Ludovico could take her over while he stays home to paint all day, for which he would pay him 8 percent of Esmeralda's earnings.

"Per cortesia," says the pimp haughtily. "At the very least 25 percent. I have many obligations and am a sick man besides."

"Eight is all we can afford, not a penny more."

Esmeralda returns with a package or two and, when she comprehends what the argument is, swears she will quit rather than work with Ludovico.

"You can do your own whoring," she says to F. "I'll go back to Fiesole."

He tries to calm her. "It's just that he's so sick is the reason I thought I'd cut him in."

"Sick?"

"He's got one lung."

"He has three lungs and four balls."

F heaves the pimp down the stairs.

In the afternoon he sits on a bench not far from Esmeralda's in the Piazza della Repubblica, sketching himself on his drawing pad.

.

Esmeralda burned Bessie's old snapshot when F was in the toilet. "I'm getting old," she said, "where's my future?" F considered strangling her but couldn't bring himself to; besides, he hadn't been using the photo since having Esmeralda as model. Still, for a time he felt lost without it, the physical presence of the decaying snap his only visible link to Ma, Bessie, the past. Anyway, now that it was gone it was gone, a memory become intangible again. He painted with more fervor yet detachment; fervor to complete the work, detachment toward image, object, subject. Esmeralda left him to his devices, went off for most of the afternoon, and handed him the lire, fewer than before, when she returned. He painted with new confidence, amusement, wonder. The subject had changed from "Mother and Son" to "Brother and Sister" (Esmeralda as Bessie), to let's face it, "Prostitute and Procurer." Though she no longer posed, he was becoming clearer in his inner eye as to what he wanted. Once he retained her face for a week before scraping it off. I'm getting there. And though he considered sandpapering his own face off and substituting Ludovico as pimp, the magnificent thing was that in the end he kept himself in. This is my most honest piece of work. Esmeralda was the now-nineteen-year-old prostitute; and he, with a stroke here and there aging himself a bit, a fifteen-year-old procurer. This was the surprise that made the painting. And what it means, I suppose, is I am what I became from a young age. Then he thought, it has no meaning, a painting's a painting.

The picture completed itself. F was afraid to finish it: What would he do next and how long would that take? But the picture was, one day, done. It assumed a completion: This woman and man together, prostitute and procurer. She was a girl with fear in both black eyes, a vulnerable if stately neck, and a steely small mouth; he was a boy with tight insides, on the verge of crying. The presence of each protected the other. A Holy Sacrament. The form leaped to the eye. He had tormented, ecstatic, yet confused feelings, but at last felt triumphant—it was done! Though deeply drained, moved, he was satisfied, completed—ah, art!

He called Esmeralda to look at the painting. Her lips trembled, she lost color, turned away, finally she spoke. "For me it's me. You've caught me as I am, there's no doubt of it. The picture is a marvel." She wept as she gazed at it. "Now I can quit what I'm doing. Let's get married, Arturo."

Ludovico, limping a little in his squeaky shoes, came upstairs to beg their pardons, but when he saw the finished painting on the easel stood stiff in awe.

"I'm speechless," he said, "what more can I say?"

"Don't bother," said Esmeralda, "nobody wants your stinking opinion."

They opened a bottle of Soave and Esmeralda borrowed a pan and baked a loin of veal, to celebrate. Their artist neighbors came in, Citelli, an illustrator, and his dark meager wife; it was a festive occasion. F afterwards related the story of his life and they all listened, absorbed.

When the neighbors left and the three were alone, Ludovico objectively discussed his weak nature.

"Compared to some I've met in the streets of Florence, I'm not a bad person, but my trouble is I forgive myself too easily. That has its disadvantages because then there are no true barriers to a harmful act, if you understand my meaning. It's the easy way out, but what else can you do if you grew up with certain disadvantages? My father was criminally inclined and it's from him I inherited my worst tendencies. It's clear enough that goats don't have puppies. I'm vain, selfish, although not arrogant, and given almost exclusively to petty evil. Nothing serious but serious enough. Of course I've wanted to change my ways, but at my age what can one change? Can you change yourself, maestro? Yet I readily confess who I am and ask your pardon for any inconvenience I might have caused you in the past. Either of you."

"Drop dead," said Esmeralda.

"The man's sincere," F said, irritated. "There's no need to be so cruel."

"Come to bed, Arturo." She entered the gabinetto as Ludovico went on with his confession.

"To tell the truth, I am myself a failed artist, but at least I contribute to the creativity of others by offering fruitful suggestions, though you're free to do as you please. Anyway, your painting is a marvel. Of course it's Picassoid, but you've outdone him in some of his strategies."

F expressed thanks and gratitude.

"At first glance I thought that since the bodies of the two figures are so much more thickly painted than their faces, especially the girl's, this destroyed the unity of surface, but when I think of some of the impastos I've seen, and the more I study your painting, the more I feel that's not important."

"I don't think it'll bother anybody so long as it looks like a spontaneous act."

"True, and therefore my only criticism is that maybe the painting suffers from an excess of darkness. It needs more light. I'd say a soupçon of lemon and a little red, not more than a trace. But I leave it to you."

Esmeralda came out of the gabinetto in a red nightgown with a black lace bodice.

"Don't touch it," she warned. "You'll never make it better."

"How would you know?" F said.

"I have my eyes."

"Maybe she's right," Ludovico said, with a yawn. "Who knows with art? Well, I'm on my way. If you want to sell your painting for a handsome price, my advice is take it to a reliable dealer. There are one or two in the city whose names and addresses I'll bring you in the morning."

"Don't bother," Esmeralda said. "We don't need your assistance."

"I want to keep it around for a few days to look at," F confessed.

"As you please." Ludovico tipped his hat good night and left limping. F and Esmeralda went to bed together. Later she returned to her cot in the kitchen, took off her red nightgown, and put on an old one of white muslin.

F for a while wondered what to paint next. Maybe sort of a portrait of Ludovico, his face reflected in a mirror, with two sets of aqueous sneaky eyes. He slept soundly but in the middle of the night awoke depressed. He went over his painting inch by inch and it seemed to him a disappointment. Where was Momma after all these years? He got up to look and, doing so, changed his mind; not bad at all, though Ludovico was right, the picture was dark and could stand a touch of light. He laid out his paints and brushes and began to work, almost at once achieving the effect he sought. And then he thought he would work a bit on the girl's face, no more than a stroke or two around the eyes and mouth, to make her expression truer to life. More the prostitute, himself a little older. When the sun blazed through both windows, he realized he had been working for hours. F put down his brush, washed up, and returned for a look at the painting. Sickened to his gut, he saw what he felt: He had ruined it. It slowly drowned in his eyes.

Ludovico came in with a well-dressed paunchy friend, an art dealer. They looked at the picture and laughed.

Five long years down the drain. F squeezed a tube of black on the canvas and with a thick brush smeared it over both faces in all directions.

When Esmeralda pulled open the curtain and saw the mess, moaning, she came at him with the bread knife. "Murderer!"

F twisted it out of her grasp, and in anguish lifted the blade into his gut.

"This serves me right."

"A moral act," Ludovico agreed.

✤ B M ✤

Man in the Drawer

A soft shalom I thought I heard but considering the Slavic cast of
the driver's face it seemed unlikely. He had been eyeing me in his
rearview mirror since I had stepped into the taxi and, to tell the truth,
I had momentary apprehensions. I'm forty-seven and have recently
lost weight but not, I confess, nervousness. It's my American clothes,
I thought at first. One is a recognizable stranger. Unless he had been
tailing me to begin with, but how could that be if it was a passing
cab I had hailed myself?

The taxi driver sat in his shirtsleeves on a cool June day, not
more than 50° Fahrenheit. He was a man in his thirties who looked
as if what he ate didn't fully feed him—in afterthought a discontented type, his face on the tired side, not bad looking—now that I'd
studied him a little, though the head seemed pressed a bit flat by
somebody's heavy hand even though protected by a mat of healthy
hair. His face, as I said, veered toward Slavic: broad cheekbones, small
firm chin, but he sported a longish nose and a distinctive larynx on
a slender hairy neck; a mixed type, it appeared. At any rate, the
shalom had seemed to alter his appearance, even the probing eyes.
He was dissatisfied for certain this fine June day—his job, fate, appearance—whatever. And a sort of indigenous sadness hung on or
around him, coming God knows from where; nor did he seem to mind
if who he was, was immediately apparent; not everybody could do
that or wanted to. This one showed himself as is. Not too prosperous,
I would say, yet no underground man. He sat firm in his seat, all of

him driving, a touch frantically. I have an experienced eye for details.

"Israeli?" he asked in a whisper.

"Amerikansky." I know no Russian, just a few polite words.

He dug into his shirt pocket for a thin pack of cigarettes and swung his arm over the seat, the Volga swerving to avoid a truck making a turn.

"Take care!"

I was thrown sideways—no apologies. Extracting a Bulgarian cigarette I wasn't eager to smoke—too strong—I handed him his pack. I was considering offering my prosperous American cigarettes in return but didn't want to affront him.

"Feliks Levitansky," he said. "How do you do? I am taxi driver." His accent was strong, verging on fruity, but redeemed by fluency of tongue.

"Ah, you speak English? I sort of thought so."

"My profession is translator—English, French." He shrugged sideways.

"Howard Harvitz is my name. I'm here for a short vacation, about three weeks. My wife died not so long ago, and I'm traveling partly to relieve my mind."

My voice caught, but then I went on to say that if I could manage to dig up some material for a magazine article or two, so much the better.

In sympathy Levitansky raised both hands from the wheel.

"Watch out, for God's sake!"

"Horovitz?" he asked.

I spelled it for him. "Frankly, it was Harris after I entered college but I changed it back recently. My father had it legally done after I graduated from high school. He was a doctor, a practical sort."

"You don't look to me Jewish."

"If not why did you say shalom?"

"Sometimes you say." After a minute he asked, "For which reason?"

"For which reason what?"

"Why you changed back your name?"

"I had a crisis in my life."

"Existential? Economic?"

"To tell the truth I changed it back after my wife died."

"What is the significance?"

"The significance is I am closer to myself."

The driver popped a match with his thumbnail and lit his cigarette.

"I am marginal Jew," he said, "although my father—Avrahm Isaakovich Levitansky—was Jewish. Because my mother was gentile woman I was given choice, but she insisted me to register for internal passport with notation of Jewish nationality in respect for my father. I did so."

"You don't say!"

"My father died in my childhood. I was rised—raised?—to respect Jewish people and religion, but I went my own way. I am atheist. This is almost inevitable."

"You mean Soviet life?"

Levitansky smoked without replying as I grew embarrassed by my question. I looked around to see if I knew where we were. In afterthought he asked, "To which destination?"

I said, still on the former subject, that I had been not much a Jew myself. "My mother and father were totally assimilated."

"By their choice?"

"Of course by their choice."

"Do you wish," he then asked, "to visit Central Synagogue on Arkhipova Street? Very interesting experience."

"Not just now," I said, "but take me to the Chekhov Museum on Sadovaya Kudrinskaya."

At that the driver, sighing, seemed to take heart.

•

Rose, I said to myself.

I blew my nose. After her death I had planned to visit the Soviet Union but couldn't get myself to move. I'm a slow man after a blow, though I confess I've never been one for making his mind up in a hurry about important things. Eight months later, when I was more or less packing, I felt that some of the relief I was looking for derived, in addition to what was still on my mind, from the necessity of making an unexpected serious personal decision. Out of loneliness I had begun to see my former wife, Lillian, in the spring; and before long, since she had remained unmarried and attractive, to my surprise there was some hesitant talk of remarriage; these things slip from one sentence to another before you know it. If we did get married we could turn the Russian trip into a sort of honeymoon—I won't say second because we hadn't had much of a first. In the end, since our lives had been so frankly complicated—hard on each other—I found it hard to make up my mind, though Lillian, I give her credit, seemed to be willing to take the chance. My feelings were so difficult to assess I decided to decide nothing for sure. Lillian, who is a forthright type with a mind like a lawyer's, asked me if I was cooling to the idea, and I told her that since the death of my wife I had been examining my life and needed more time to see where I stood. "Still?" she said, meaning the self-searching, and implying forever. All I could answer was "Still," and then in anger, "Forever." I warned myself: Beware of further complicated entanglements.

Well, that almost killed it. It wasn't a particularly happy evening, though it had its moments. I had once been very much in love with Lillian. I figured then that a change of scene for me, maybe a month abroad, might be helpful. I had for a long time wanted to visit the U.S.S.R., and taking the time to be alone and, I hoped, at ease to think things through, might give the trip additional value.

So I was surprised, once my visa was granted—though not too surprised—that my anticipation was by now blunted and I was experiencing some uneasiness. I blamed it on a dread of traveling that sometimes hits me before I move. Will I get there? Will the plane be hijacked? Maybe a war breaks out and I'm surrounded by artillery. To be frank, though I've resisted the idea, I consider myself an anxious man, which, when I try to explain it to myself, means being this minute halfway into the next. I sit still in a hurry, worry uselessly about the future, and carry the burden of an overripe conscience.

I realized that what troubled me most about going into Soviet Russia were those stories in the papers of some tourist or casual traveler in this or that Soviet city who is, without warning, grabbed by the secret police on charges of "spying," "illegal economic activity," "hooliganism," or whatnot. This poor guy, like somebody from Sudbury, Mass., is held incommunicado until he confesses, and is then sentenced to a prison camp in the wilds of Siberia. After I got my visa I sometimes had fantasies of a stranger shoving a fat envelope of papers into my hand, and then arresting me as I was stupidly reading them—of course for spying. What would I do in that case? I think I would pitch the envelope into the street, shouting, "Don't pull that one on me, I can't read Russian," and walk away with whatever dignity I had, hoping that would freeze them in their tracks. A man in danger, if he's walking away from it, seems indifferent, innocent. At least to himself; then in my mind I hear footsteps coming after me, and since my reveries tend to be rational, two husky KGB men grab me, shove my arms up my back, and make the arrest. Not for littering the streets, as I hope might be the case, but for "attempting to dispose of certain incriminating documents," a fact it's hard to deny.

I see H. Harvitz yelling, squirming, kicking right and left, till his mouth is shut by somebody's stinking palm and he is dragged by force —not to mention a blackjack whack on the skull—into the inevitable black Zis I've read about and see on movie screens.

The cold war is a frightening business. I've sometimes wished spying had reached such a pitch of perfection that both the U.S.S.R. and the U.S.A. knew everything there is to know about the other and, having sensibly exchanged this information by trading computers that keep facts up to date, let each other alone thereafter. That ruins the spying business; there's that much more sanity in the world, and for a man like me the thought of a trip to the Soviet Union is pure pleasure.

Right away at the Kiev airport I had a sort of scare, after flying in from Paris on a mid-June afternoon. A customs official confiscated from my suitcase five copies of *Visible Secrets*, a poetry anthology for high school students I had edited some years ago, which I had brought along to give away to Russians I met who might be interested in American poetry. I was asked to sign a document the official had written out in Cyrillic, except that *Visible Secrets* was printed in English, "secrets" underlined. The uniformed customs officer, a heavyset man with a layer of limp hair on a smallish head, red stars on his shoulders, said that the paper I was required to sign stated I understood it was not permitted to bring five copies of a foreign book into the Soviet Union; but I would get my property back at the Moscow airport when I left the country. I worried that I oughtn't to sign but was urged to by my Intourist guide, a bleached blonde with wobbly heels whose looks and good humor kept me calm, though my clothes were frankly steaming. She said it was a matter of no great consequence and advised me to write my signature quickly, because it was delaying our departure to the Dniepro Hotel.

At that point I asked what would happen if I parted with the books, no longer claimed them as my property. The Intouristka inquired of the customs man, who answered calmly, earnestly, and at great length.

"He says," she said, "that the Soviet Union will not take away from a foreign visitor his legal property."

Since I had only four days in the city and time was going faster than usual, I reluctantly signed the paper plus four carbons—one for each book—or five mysterious government departments?—and was given a copy, which I filed in my billfold.

Despite this incident—it had its comic quality—my stay in Kiev, in spite of the loneliness I usually experience my first few days in a strange city, went quickly and interestingly. In the mornings I was driven around in a private car on guided tours of the hilly, broad-avenued, green-leaved city, whose colors were reminiscent of a subdued Rome. But in the afternoons I wandered around alone. I would start by taking a bus or streetcar, riding a few kilometers, then getting off to walk in this or that neighborhood. Once I strayed into a peasants' market where collective farmers and country folk in beards and boots out of a nineteenth-century Russian novel sold their produce to city people. I thought I must write about this to Rose—I meant of course Lillian. Another time, in a deserted street when I happened to think of the customs receipt in my billfold, I turned in my tracks to see if I was being followed. I wasn't but enjoyed the adventure.

An experience I liked less was getting lost one late afternoon several kilometers above a boathouse on the Dnieper. I was walking along the riverbank liking the boats and island beaches and, before I knew it, had come a good distance from the hotel and was eager to get back because I was hungry. I didn't feel like retracing my route on foot—much too much tourism in three days—so I thought of a cab and, since none was around, maybe an autobus that might be going in the general direction I had come from. I tried approaching a few passersby whom I addressed in English or pidgin-German, and occasionally trying "Pardonnez-moi"; but the effect was apparently to embarrass them. One young woman ran a few awkward steps from me before she began to walk again.

Though frustrated, irritated, I spoke to two men passing by, one of whom, the minute he heard my first few words, walked on quickly, his eyes aimed straight ahead, the other indicating by gestures he was deaf and dumb. On impulse I tried him in halting Yiddish that my grandfather had taught me when I was a child, and was then directed, in an undertone in the same language, to a nearby bus stop.

As I was unlocking the door to my room, thinking this was a story I would be telling friends all winter, my phone was ringing. It was a woman's voice. I understood "Gospodin Garvitz" and one or two other words as she spoke at length in musical Russian. Her voice had the lilt of a singer's. Though I couldn't get the gist of her remarks, I had this sudden vivid reverie, you might call it, of me walking with a pretty Russian girl in a white birchwood near Yasnaya Polyana, and coming out of the trees, sincerely talking, into a meadow that sloped to the water; then rowing her around in a small lovely lake. It was a peaceful business. I even had thoughts: Wouldn't it be something if I got myself engaged to a Russian girl? That was the general picture, but when the

caller was done talking, whatever I had to say I said in English and she
slowly hung up.

After breakfast the next morning, she, or somebody who sounded
like her—I was aware of the contralto quality—called again.

"If you understand English," I said, "or maybe a little German or
French—even Yiddish if you happen to know it—we'd get along fine.
But not in Russian, I'm sorry to say. Nyet Russki. I'd be glad to meet
you for lunch or whatever you like; so if you get the drift of my remarks
why don't you say da? Then dial the English interpreter on extension
37. She could explain to me what's what and we can meet at your
convenience."

I had the impression she was listening with both ears, but after a
while the phone hung silent in my hand. I wondered where she had got
my name, and was someone testing me to find out whether I did or
didn't speak Russian. I honestly did not.

Afterwards I wrote a short letter to Lillian, telling her I would be
leaving for Moscow via Aeroflot, tomorrow at 4 p.m., and I intended to
stay there for two weeks, with a break of maybe three or four days in
Leningrad, at the Astoria Hotel. I wrote down the exact dates and later
airmailed the letter in a street box some distance from the hotel, whatever good that did. I hoped Lillian would get it in time to reach me by
return mail before I left the Soviet Union. To tell the truth I was uneasy
all day.

But by the next morning my mood had shifted, and as I was standing at the railing in a park above the Dnieper, looking at the buildings
going up across the river in what had once been steppeland, I experienced a curious sense of relief. The vast construction I beheld—it was
as though two or three scattered small cities were rising out of the
earth—astonished me. This sort of thing was going on all over Russia
—halfway around the world—and when I considered what it meant in
terms of sheer labor, capital goods, plain morale, I was then and there
convinced that the Soviet Union would never willingly provoke a war,
nuclear or otherwise, with the United States. Neither would America,
in its right mind, with the Soviet Union.

For the first time since I had come to Russia I felt secure and safe,
and I enjoyed there, at the breezy railing above the Dnieper, a rare few
minutes of euphoria.

•

Why is it that the most interesting architecture is from czarist
times? I asked myself, and if I'm not mistaken Levitansky quivered, no
doubt coincidental. Unless I had spoken aloud to myself, which I some-

times do; I decided I hadn't. We were on our way to the museum, hitting a fast eighty kilometers, because traffic was sparse.

"What do you think of my country, the Union of Soviet Socialist Republics?" the driver inquired, turning his head to see where I was.

"I would appreciate it if you kept your eyes on the road."

"Don't be nervous, I drive now for years."

Then I answered that I was impressed by much I had seen. Obviously it was a great country.

Levitansky's round face appeared in the mirror smiling pleasantly, his teeth eroded. The smile seemed to have come from within the mouth. Now that he had revealed his half-Jewish antecedents I had the impression he looked more Jewish than Slavic, and more dissatisfied than I had previously thought. That I got from the restless eyes.

"Also our system—Communism?"

I answered carefully, not wanting to give offense. "I'll be honest with you. I've seen some unusual things—even inspiring—but my personal taste is for a lot more individual freedom than people seem to have here. America has its serious faults, God knows, but at least we're privileged to criticize—if you know what I mean. My father used to say, 'You can't beat the Bill of Rights.' It's an open society, which means freedom of choice, at least in theory."

"Communism is altogether better political system," Levitansky replied candidly, "although it is not in present stage totally realized. In present stage"—he swallowed, reflected, did not finish the thought. Instead he said, "Our Revolution was magnificent and holy event. I love early Soviet history, excitement of Communist idealism, and magnificent victory over bourgeois and imperialist forces. Overnight was lifted up—uplifted—the whole suffering masses. Pasternak called this 'splendid surgery.' Evgeny Zamyatin—maybe you know his books?— spoke thus: 'The Revolution consumes the earth with fire, but then is born a new life.' Many of our poets said similar things."

I didn't argue, each to his own revolution.

"You told before," said Levitansky, glancing at me again in the mirror, "that you wish to write articles about your visit. Political or not political?"

"What I have in mind is something on the literary museums of Moscow for an American travel magazine. That's the sort of thing I do. I'm a freelance writer." I laughed apologetically. It's strange how stresses shift when you're in another country.

Levitansky politely joined in the laugh, stopping in midcourse. "I wish to be certain, what is freelance writer?"

I told him. "I also edit a bit. I've done anthologies of poetry and essays, both for high school kids."

"We have here freelance. I am writer also," Levitansky said solemnly.

"You don't say? You mean as translator?"

"Translation is my profession but I am also original writer."

"Then you do three things to earn a living—write, translate, and drive this cab?"

"The taxi is not my true work."

"Are you translating anything in particular now?"

The driver cleared his throat. "In present time I have no translation project."

"What sort of thing do you write?"

"I write stories."

"Is that so? What kind, if I might ask?"

"I will tell you what kind—little ones—short stories, imagined from life."

"Have you published any?"

He seemed about to turn around to look me in the eye but reached instead into his shirt pocket. I offered my American pack. He shook out a cigarette and lit it, exhaling slowly.

"A few pieces although not recently. To tell the truth"—he sighed—"I write presently for the drawer. You know this expression? Like Isaac Babel, 'I am master of the genre of silence.' "

"I've heard it," I said, not knowing what else to say.

"The mice should read and criticize," Levitansky said bitterly. "This what they don't eat and make their drops—droppings—on. It is perfect criticism."

"I'm sorry about that."

"We arrive now to Chekhov Museum."

I leaned forward to pay him and made the impulsive mistake of adding a one-ruble tip. His face flared. "I am Soviet citizen." He forcibly returned the ruble.

"Call it a thoughtless error," I apologized. "No harm meant."

"Hiroshima! Nagasaki!" he taunted as the Volga took off in a burst of smoke. "Aggressor against the suffering poor people of Vietnam!"

"That's none of my doing," I called after him.

•

An hour and a half later, after I had signed the guest book and was leaving the museum, I saw a man standing, smoking, under a linden tree across the street. Nearby was a parked taxi. We stared at each other—I wasn't certain at first who it was, but Levitansky nodded amiably to me, calling "Welcome! Welcome!" He waved an arm, smiling openmouthed. He had combed his thick hair and was wearing a loose dark suit coat over a tieless white shirt, and baggy pants. His socks, striped red-white-and-blue, you could see through his sandals.

I am forgiven, I thought. "Welcome to you," I said, crossing the street.

"How did you enjoy Chekhov Museum?"

"I did indeed. I've made a lot of notes. You know what they have there? They have one of his black fedoras, also his pince-nez that you see in pictures of him. Awfully moving."

Levitansky wiped an eye—to my surprise. He seemed not quite the same man, modified. It's funny, you hear a few personal facts from a stranger and he changes as he speaks. The taxi driver is now a writer, even if part-time. Anyway, that's my dominant impression.

"Excuse me my former anger," Levitansky explained. "Now is not for me the best of times. 'It was the best of times, it was the worst of times,'" he said, smiling sadly.

"So long as you pardon my unintentional blunder. Are you perhaps free to drive me to the Metropole, or are you here by coincidence?"

I looked around to see if anyone was coming out of the museum.

"If you wish to engage me I will drive you, but at first I wish to show you something—how do you say?—of interest."

He reached through the open front window of the taxi and brought forth a flat package wrapped in brown paper tied with red string.

"Stories which I wrote."

"I don't read Russian," I said.

"My wife has translated some of them. She is not by her profession a translator, although her English is advanced and sensitive. She had been for two years in England for Soviet Purchasing Commission. We became acquainted in university. I prefer not to translate my stories because I do not translate so well Russian into English, although I do it beautifully the opposite. Also I will not force myself—it is like self-imitation. Perhaps the stories appear a little awkward in English—also my wife admits this—but you can read and form opinion."

Though he offered the package hesitantly, he offered it as if it was a bouquet of spring flowers. Can it be some sort of trick? I asked myself. Are they testing me because I signed that damned document in the Kiev airport, five copies no less?

Levitansky seemed to know my thought. "It is purely stories."

He bit the string in two and, laying the package on the fender of the Volga, unpeeled the wrapping. There were the stories, clipped separately, typed on long sheets of thin blue paper. I took one Levitansky handed me and scanned the top page—it seemed a story—then I flipped through the other pages and handed the manuscript back. "I'm not much a critic of stories."

"I don't seek critic. I seek for reader with literary experience and taste. If you have redacted books of poems and also essays, you will be able to judge literary quality of my stories. Please, I request you will read them."

After a long minute I heard myself say, "Well, I might at that." I didn't recognize the voice and wasn't sure why I had said what I had. You might say I spoke apart from myself, with reluctance that either he wasn't aware of or chose to ignore.

"If you respect—if you approve my stories, perhaps you will be able to arrange for publication in Paris or either London?" His larynx wobbled.

I stared at the man. "I don't happen to be going to Paris, and I'll be in London only between planes to the U.S.A."

"In this event, perhaps you will show to your publisher, and he will publish my work in America?" Levitansky was now visibly uneasy.

"In America?" I said, raising my voice in disbelief.

For the first time he gazed around before replying.

"If you will be so kind to show them to publisher of your books— he is reliable publisher?—perhaps he will wish to bring out volume of my stories? I will make contract whatever he will like. Money, if I could get, is not an idea."

"Whatever volume are you talking about?"

He said that from thirty stories he had written he had chosen eighteen, of which these were a sample. "Unfortunately more are not now translated. My wife is biochemist assistant and works long hours in laboratory. I am sure your publisher will enjoy to read these. It will depend on your opinion."

Either this man has a fantastic imagination, or he's out of his right mind. "I wouldn't want to get myself involved in smuggling a Russian manuscript out of Russia."

"I have informed you that my manuscript is of made-up stories."

"That may be but it's still a chancy enterprise. I'd be taking chances I have no desire to take, to be frank."

"At least if you will read," he sighed.

I took the stories again and thumbed slowly through each. What I was looking for I couldn't say: maybe a booby trap? Should I or shouldn't I? Why should I?

He handed me the wrapping paper and I rolled up the stories in it. The quicker I read them, the quicker I've read them. I stepped into the cab.

"As I said, I'm at the Metropole. Come by tonight about nine o'clock and I'll give you my opinion, for what it's worth. But I'm afraid I'll have to limit it to that, Mr. Levitansky, without further obligation or expectations, or it's no deal. My room number is 538."

"Tonight?—so soon?" he said, scratching both palms. "You must read with care so you will realize the art."

"Tomorrow night, then, same time. I'd rather not have them in my room longer than that."

Levitansky agreed. Whistling through eroded teeth, he drove me carefully to the Metropole.

•

That night, sipping vodka from a drinking glass, I read Levitansky's stories. They were simply and strongly written—I had almost expected it—and not badly translated; in fact the translation read much better than I had been led to think, although there were of course some gaffes—odd constructions, ill-fitting stiff words, some indicated by question marks and taken, I suppose, from a thesaurus. And the stories, short tales dealing—somewhat to my surprise—mostly with Moscow Jews, were good, artistically done, really moving. The situations they revealed weren't exactly news to me: I'm a careful reader of the *Times*. But the stories weren't written to complain. What they had to say was achieved as form, no telling the dancer from the dance. I poured myself another glass of the potato potion—I was beginning to feel high, occasionally wondering why I was putting so much away—relaxing, I guess. I then reread the stories with admiration for Levitansky. I had the feeling he was no ordinary man. I felt excited, then depressed, as if I had been let in on a secret I didn't want to know.

It's a hard life here for a fiction writer, I thought.

Afterwards, having the stories around made me uneasy. In one of them a Russian writer burns his stories in the kitchen sink. Obviously nobody had burned these. I thought to myself, if I'm caught with them in my possession, considering what they indicate about conditions here, there's no question I'll be up to my hips in trouble. I wish I had insisted that Levitansky come back for them tonight.

There was a solid rap on the door. I felt I had risen a few inches out of my chair. It was, after a while, only Levitansky.

"Out of the question," I said, thrusting the stories at him. "Absolutely out of the question!"

•

The next night we sat facing each other over glasses of cognac in the writer's small, book-crowded study. He was dignified, at first haughty, wounded, hardly masking his impatience. I wasn't myself exactly comfortable.

I had come out of courtesy and other considerations, I guess; principally a dissatisfaction I couldn't define.

Levitansky, the taxi driver rattling around in his Volga-Pegasus, amateur trying to palm off a half-ass ms., had faded in my mind, and I saw him now as a serious Soviet writer with publishing problems. There are many others. What can I do for him? I thought. Why should I?

"I didn't express what I really felt last night," I apologized. "You caught me by surprise, I'm sorry to say."

Levitansky was scratching each hand with the blunt fingers of the other. "How did you acquire my address?"

I reached into my pocket for a wad of folded brown wrapping paper. "It's on this—Novo Ostapovskaya Street, 488, Flat 59. I took a cab."

"I had forgotten this."

Maybe, I thought.

Still, I had practically had to put my foot in the door to get in. Levitansky's wife had answered my uncertain knock, her eyes immediately worried, an expression I took to be the one she lived with. The eyes, astonished to behold a stranger, became outright uneasy once I inquired in English for her husband. I felt, as in Kiev, that my native tongue had become my enemy.

"Have you not the wrong apartment?"

"I hope not. Not if Gospodin Levitansky lives here. I came to see him about his—ah—manuscript."

Her eyes darkened as her face paled. Ten seconds later I was in the flat, the door locked behind me.

"Levitansky!" she summoned him. It had a reluctant quality: Come but don't come.

He appeared in apparently the same shirt, pants, tricolor socks. There was at first pretend-boredom in a tense, tired face. He could not, however, conceal excitement, his lit eyes roving over my face.

"Oh ho," Levitansky said.

My God, I thought, has he been expecting me?

"I came to talk to you for a few minutes, if you don't mind," I said. "I want to say what I think of the stories you kindly let me read."

He curtly spoke in Russian to his wife and she snapped an answer back. "I wish to introduce my wife, Irina Filipovna Levitansky, biochemist. She is patient although not a saint."

She smiled tentatively, an attractive woman about twenty-eight, a little on the hefty side, in house slippers and plain dress. The edge of her slip hung below her skirt.

There was a touch of British in her accent. "I am pleased to be acquainted." If so one hardly noticed. She stepped into black pumps and slipped a bracelet on her wrist, a lit cigarette dangling from the corner of her mouth. Her legs and arms were shapely, her brown hair cut short. I had the impression of tight lips in a pale face.

"I will go to Kovalevsky, next door," she said.

"Not on my account, I hope? All I have to say—"

"Our neighbors in the next flat." Levitansky grimaced. "Also thin walls." He knocked a knuckle on a hollow wall.

I indicated my dismay.

"Please, not long," Irina said, "because I am afraid."

Surely not of me? Agent Howard Harvitz, CIA—a comical thought.

Their small square living room wasn't unattractive but Levitansky signaled the study inside. He offered sweet cognac in whiskey tumblers, then sat facing me at the edge of his chair, repressed energy all but visible. I had the momentary sense his chair was about to move, fly off.

If it does he flies alone.

"What I came to say," I told him, "is that I like your stories and am sorry I didn't say so last night. I like the primary, close-to-the-bone quality of the writing. The stories impress me as strong if simply wrought; I appreciate your feeling for people and at the same time the objectivity with which you render them. It's sort of Chekhovian in quality, but more compressed, sinewy, direct, if you know what I mean. For instance, that story about the old father coming to see his son who ducks out on him. I can't comment on your style, having only read the stories in translation."

"Chekhovian," Levitansky admitted, smiling through his worn teeth, "is fine compliment. Mayakovsky, our early Soviet poet, described him 'the strong and gay artist of the world.' I wish it was possible for Levitansky to be so gay in life and art." He seemed to be staring at the drawn shade in the room, though maybe no place in particular, then said, perhaps heartening himself, "In Russian is magnificent my style—precise, economy, including wit. The style may be difficult to translate in English because is less rich language."

"I've heard that said. In fairness I should add I have some reservations about the stories, yet who hasn't on any given piece of imaginative work?"

"I have myself reservations."

The admission made, I skipped the criticism. I had been wondering about a picture on his bookcase and then asked who it was. "It's a face I've seen before. The eyes are poetic, you might say."

"So is the voice. This is picture of Boris Pasternak as young man. On the wall yonder is Mayakovsky. He was also remarkable poet, wild, joyful, neurasthenic, a lover of the Revolution. He spoke: 'This is *my* Revolution.' To him was it 'a holy washerwoman who cleaned off all the filth from the earth.' Unfortunately he was later disillusioned and also shot himself."

"I have read that."

"He wrote: 'I wish to be understood by my country—but if no, I will fly through Russia like a slanting rainstorm.' "

"Have you by chance read *Dr. Zhivago?*"

"I have read," the writer sighed, and then began to declaim in Russian—I guessed some lines from a poem.

"It is to Marina Tsvetayeva, Soviet poetess, good friend of Pasternak." Levitansky fiddled with the pack of cigarettes on the table. "The end of her life was unfortunate."

"Is there no picture of Osip Mandelstam?" I hesitated as I spoke the name.

He reacted as though he had just met me. "You know Mandelstam?"

"Just a few poems in an anthology."

"Our best poet—he is holy—gone with so many others. My wife does not hang his photograph."

"I guess why I really came," I said after a minute, "is I wanted to express my sympathy and respect."

Levitansky popped a match with his thumbnail. His hand trembled as he shook the flame out without lighting the cigarette.

Embarrassed for him, I pretended to be looking elsewhere. "It's a small room. Does your son sleep here?"

"Don't confuse my story of writer, which you have read, with life of author. My wife and I are married eight years, but without children."

"Might I ask whether the experience you describe in that same story—the interview with the editor—was true?"

"Not true although truth," the writer said impatiently. "I write from imagination. I am not interested to repeat contents of diaries or total memory."

"On that I go along."

"Also, which is not in story, I have submitted to Soviet journals sketches and tales many many times but only few have been published, although not my best. Some people, but only few, know my work through samizdat, which is passing from one to another the manuscript."

"Did you submit any of the Jewish stories?"

"Please, stories are stories, they have not nationality."

"I mean by that those about Jews."

"Some I have submitted but they were not accepted."

I said, "After reading the stories you gave me, I wondered how it is you write so well about Jews? You call yourself marginal—that was your word—yet you write with authority. Not that one can't, I suppose, but it's surprising when one does."

"Imagination makes authority. When I write about Jews comes out stories, so I write about Jews. Is not important that I am half-Jew. What is important is observation, feeling, also art. In the past I have observed my Jewish father. Also I study, sometimes, Jews in the synagogue. I sit on the bench for strangers. The gabbai watches me with dark eyes and I watch him. But whatever I write, whether is about Jews, Galicians, or Georgians, must be work of invention, or for me it does not live."

"I'm not much of a synagogue-goer myself," I told him, "but I like to drop in once in a while to be refreshed by the language and images of a time and place where God was. That may be strange because I had no religious education to speak of."

"I am atheist."

"I understand what you mean by imagination—as for instance that prayer-shawl story. But am I right"—I lowered my voice—"that you are saying something about the condition of Jews in this country?"

"I do not make propaganda," Levitansky said sternly. "I am not Israeli spokesman. I am Soviet artist."

"I didn't mean you weren't but there's a strong sympathy for Jews, and ideas are born in life. One senses an awareness of injustice."

"Whatever is the injustice, the product must be art."

"Well, I respect your philosophy."

"Please do not respect so much," the writer said irritably. "We have in this country a quotation: 'It is impossible to make out of apology a fur coat.' The idea is similar. I appreciate your respect but need now practical assistance.

"Listen at first to me," Levitansky went on, slapping the table with his palm. "I am in desperate situation. I have written for years but little is published. In the past, one, two editors who were friends told me, private, that my stories are excellent but I violate social realism. This what you call objectivity they called it excessive naturalism and sentiment. It is hard to listen to such nonsense. They advise me swim but not to use my legs. They have warned me; also they have made excuses for me which I do not like them. Even they say I am crazy, although I explained them I submit my stories *because* Soviet Union is great country. A great country does not fear what artist writes. A great country breathes into its lungs work of writers, painters, musicians, and becomes more strong. That I told to them but they replied I am not sufficient realist. This is the reason I am not invited to be member of Writers Union. Without this is impossible to publish." He smiled sourly. "They have demanded me to stop submitting to journals my work, so I have stopped."

"I'm sorry about that," I said. "I don't myself believe any good comes from exiling poets."

"I cannot continue anymore in this fashion," Levitansky said, laying his hand on his heart. "I feel I am locked in drawer with my stories. Now I must get out or I suffocate. It becomes for me each day more difficult to write. It is not easy to request a stranger for such important personal favor. My wife advised me not. She is angry, also frightened, but it is impossible to go on in this way. I know in my bones I am important Soviet writer. I must have audience. I wish to see my books to be read by Soviet people. I wish to have in minds different than my own and my wife acknowledgment of my art. I wish them to know my work is related to Russian writers of the past as well as modern. I am in tradition of Chekhov, Gorky, Isaac Babel. I know if book of my stories will be published, it will make for me favorable reputation. This is reason why you must help me—it is necessary for my interior liberty."

His confession came in an agitated burst. I use the word advisedly because that's partly what upset me. I have never cared for confessions such as are meant to involve unwilling people in others' personal problems. Russians are past masters of the art—you can see it in their novels.

"I appreciate the honor of your request," I said, "but all I am is a passing tourist. That's a pretty tenuous relationship between us."

"I do not ask tourist—I ask human being—man," Levitansky said passionately. "Also you are freelance writer. You know now what I am and what is on my heart. You sit in my house. Who else can I ask? I would prefer to publish in Europe my stories, maybe with Mondadori or Einaudi in Italy, but if this is impossible to you I will publish in America. Someday my work will be read in my own country, maybe after I am dead. This is terrible irony but my generation lives on such ironies. Since I am not now ambitious to die it will be great relief to me to know that at least in one language is alive my art. Mandelstam wrote: 'I will be enclosed in some alien speech.' Better so than nothing."

"You say I know who you are, but do you know who I am?" I asked him. "I'm a plain person, not very imaginative, though I don't write a bad article. My whole life, for some reason, has been without much real adventure, except I was divorced once and remarried happily to a woman whose death I am still mourning. Now I'm here more or less on a vacation, not to jeopardize myself by taking chances of an unknown sort. What's more—and this is the main thing I came to tell you—I wouldn't at all be surprised if I am already under suspicion and would do you more harm than good."

I told Levitansky about the airport incident in Kiev. "I signed a document I couldn't even read, which was a foolish thing to do."

"In Kiev this happened?"

"That's right."

He laughed dismally. "It would not happen to you if you entered through Moscow. In the Ukraine—what is your word?—they are rubes, country people."

"That might be—nevertheless I signed the paper."

"Do you have copy?"

"Not with me. In my desk drawer in the hotel."

"I am certain this is receipt for your books which officials will return to you when you depart from Soviet Union."

"That's what I'd be afraid of."

"Why afraid?" he asked. "Are you afraid to receive back umbrella which you have lost?"

"I'd be afraid one thing might lead to another—more questions, other searches. It would be stupid to have your manuscript in my suitcase, in Russian, no less, that I can't even read. Suppose they accuse me of being some kind of courier transferring stolen documents?"

The thought raised me to my feet. I realized the tension in the room was thick as steam, mostly mine.

Levitansky rose, embittered. "There is no question of spying. I do not think I have presented myself as traitor to my country."

"I didn't say anything of the sort. All I'm saying is I don't want to get into trouble with the Soviet authorities. Nobody can blame me for that. In other words the enterprise isn't for me."

"I have made at one time inquirings," Levitansky insisted. "You will have nothing to fear for tourist who has been a few weeks in U.S.S.R. under guidance of Intourist, and does not speak Russian. They sometimes ask questions to political people, also bourgeois journalists who have made bad impression. I would deliver to you the manuscript in the last instant. It is typed on less than one hundred fifty sheets thin paper and will make small package, weightless. If it should look to you like trouble, you can leave it in dustbin. My name will not be anywhere and if they find it and track—trace to me the stories, I will answer I threw them out myself. They won't believe this, but what other can I say? It will make no difference anyway. If I stop my writing I may as well be dead. No harm will come to you."

"I'd rather not, if you don't mind."

With what I guess was a curse of despair, Levitansky reached for the portrait on his bookcase and flung it against the wall. Pasternak struck Mayakovsky, splattering him with glass, shattering himself, and both pictures crashed to the floor.

"Freelance writer," he shouted, "go to hell to America! Tell to Negroes about Bill of Rights! Tell them they are free although you keep them slaves! Talk to sacrificed Vietnamese people that you respect them!"

Irina Filipovna entered the room on the run. "Feliks," she entreated, "Kovalevsky hears every word!

"Please," she begged me, "please go away. Leave poor Levitansky alone. I beg you from my miserable heart."

I left in a hurry. The next day I flew to Leningrad.

•

Three days later, after a tense visit to Leningrad, I was sitting loosely in a beat-up taxi with a cheerful Intouristka, a half hour after my arrival at the Moscow airport. We were driving to the Ukraine Hotel, where I was assigned for my remaining days in the Soviet Union. I would have preferred the Metropole again because it is so conveniently located and I was used to it, but on second thought, better some place where a certain party wouldn't know I lived. The Volga we were riding in seemed somehow familiar, but if so it was safely in the hands of a small stranger with a large wool cap, a man wearing sunglasses, who paid me no particular attention.

I had had a rather special several minutes in Leningrad on my first day. On a white summer's evening, shortly after I had unpacked in my room at the Astoria, I discovered the Winter Palace and Hermitage after a walk along Nevsky Prospekt. Chancing on Palace Square, vast, deserted at the moment, I felt an unexpected intense emotion thinking of the revolutionary events that had occurred on this spot. My God, I thought, why should I feel myself part of Russian history? It's a contagious business, what happens to men. On the Palace Bridge I gazed at the ice-blue Neva, in the distance the golden steeple of the cathedral built by Peter the Great gleaming under masses of wind-driven clouds in patches of green sky. It's the Soviet Union but it's still Russia.

The next day I woke up anxious. In the street I was approached twice by strangers speaking English; I think my suede shoes attracted them. The first, tight-eyed and badly dressed, wanted to sell me black-market rubles. "Nyet," I said, tipping my straw hat and hurrying on. The second, a tall, bearded boy of about nineteen, with a left-sided tuft longer than the right, wearing a home-knitted green pullover, offered to buy jazz records, "youth clothes," and American cigarettes. "Sorry, nothing for sale." I escaped him too, except that green sweater followed me for a kilometer along one of the canals. I broke into a run. When I looked back he had disappeared. I slept badly—it stayed light too long past midnight; and in the morning inquired about the possibility of an immediate flight to Helsinki. I was informed I couldn't book one for a week. I decided to return to Moscow a day before I had planned to, mostly to see what they had in the Dostoevsky Museum.

I had been thinking about Levitansky. How much of a writer was he really? I had read three of the eighteen stories he wanted to publish. Suppose he had showed me the best and the others were mediocre or thereabouts? Was it worth taking a chance for that kind of book? I thought, The best thing for my peace of mind is to forget the guy. Before checking out of the Astoria I received a chatty letter from Lillian, forwarded from Moscow, apparently not in response to my recent one to her but written earlier. Should I marry her? Did I dare? The phone rang piercingly, but when I picked up the receiver no one answered. On the plane to Moscow I had visions of a crash; there must be many nobody ever reads of.

•

In my room on the twelfth floor of the Ukraine I relaxed in a green plastic-covered armchair. There was also a single low bed and a utilitarian pinewood desk, an apple-green telephone plunked on it for instant use. I'll be home in a week, I thought. Now I'd better shave and see if anything is left in the way of a concert or opera ticket for tonight. I'm in a mood for music.

The electric plug in the bathroom didn't work, so I put away my shaver and was lathering up when I jumped to a single explosive knock on the door. I opened it slowly and there stood Levitansky with a brown paper packet in his hand.

Is this son of a bitch out to compromise me?

"How did you happen to find out where I was only twenty minutes after I got back, Mr. Levitansky?"

"How I found you?" The writer shrugged. He seemed deathly tired, the face longer, leaner, resembling a hungry fox on his last unsteady legs, but still in business.

"My brother-in-law was chauffeur for you from the airport. He heard the girl inquire your name. We have spoke of you. Dmitri—this is my wife's brother—informed me you have registered at the Ukraine. I inquired downstairs your room number and it was granted to me."

"However it happened," I said firmly, "I want you to know I haven't changed my mind. I don't want to get more involved. I thought it all through while I was in Leningrad and that's my decision."

"I may come in?"

"Please, but for obvious reasons I'd appreciate a short visit."

Levitansky sat, thin knees pressed together, in the armchair, his parcel awkwardly on his lap. If he was happy he had found me, it did nothing for his expression.

I finished shaving, put on a fresh white shirt, and sat down on the bed. "Sorry I have nothing to offer in the way of an aperitif but I could call downstairs?"

Levitansky twiddled his fingers no. He was dressed without change down to his socks. Did his wife wash out the same pair each night, or were all his socks tricolored?

"To speak frankly," I said, "I have to protest this constant tension you've whipped up in and around me. Nobody in his right mind can expect a complete stranger visiting the Soviet Union to pull his chestnuts out of the fire. It's your country that's hindering you as a writer, not me or the United States of America. Since you live here what can you do but live with it?"

"I love my country," Levitansky said.

"Nobody denies it. That holds for me, though love for country—let's face it—is a mixed bag. Nationality isn't soul as I'm sure you agree. But what I'm also saying is there are things about his country one might not like that he has to make his peace with. I'm assuming you're not thinking of counter-revolution. So if you're up against a wall you can't climb, or dig under, or outflank, at least stop banging your head against it, not to mention mine. Do what you can. It's amazing, for instance, what can be said in a fairy tale."

"I have written already my fairy tales," he said moodily. "Now is the time for truth without disguises. I will make my peace to this point where it interferes with my interior liberty; and then I must stop to make my peace. My brother-in-law has also told to me, 'You must write acceptable stories, others can do it, so why cannot you?' And I have answered to him, 'Yes, but must be acceptable to *me*!' "

"In that case, aren't you up against the impossible? If you permit me to say it, are those Jews in your stories, if they can't have their matzos and prayer books, any freer in their religious lives than you are as a writer? What I mean is, one has to face up to the nature of his society."

"I have faced up. Do you face up to yours?" he asked with a flash of scorn.

"My own problem is not that I can't express myself but that I don't. In my own mind Vietnam is a demoralizing mistake, yet I've never really opposed it except to sign petitions and vote for congressmen who say they're against the war. My first wife used to criticize me. She said I wrote the wrong things and was involved in everything but useful action. My second wife knew it but made me think she didn't. Maybe I'm just waking up to the fact that the U.S. government has for years been mucking up my self-respect."

Levitansky's larynx moved up like a flag on a pole, then sank.

He tried again, saying, "The Soviet Union preservates for us the great victories of our Revolution. Because of this I have remained for years at peace with the State. Communism is still to me inspirational ideal although this historical period is spoiled by leaders with impoverished view of humanity. They have pissed on Revolution."

"Stalin?"

"Him especially, but also others. Even so I have obeyed Party directives, and when I could not longer obey I wrote for drawer. I said to myself, 'Levitansky, history changes every minute and also Communism will change.' I believed if the State restricts two, three generations of artists, what is this against development of true socialist society— maybe best society of world history? So what does it mean if some of us are sacrificed to Party purpose? The aesthetic mode is not in necessity greater than politics—than needs of Revolution. Then in fifty years more will be secure the State, and all Soviet artists will say whatever they wish. This is what I tried to think, but do not longer think so. I do not believe more in partiinost, which is guided thought, an expression which is to me ridiculous. I do not think Revolution is fulfilled in country of unpublished novelists, poets, playwriters, who hide in drawers whole libraries of literature that will never be printed or if so, it will be printed after they stink in their graves. I think now the State will never be secure—never! It is not in the nature of politics, or human condition, to be finished with Revolution. Evgeny Zamyatin told: 'There is no final revolution. Revolutions are infinite!' "

"I guess that's along my own line of thinking," I said, hoping for reasons of personal safety to forestall Levitansky's ultimate confession —which he, with brooding eyes, was already relentlessly making—lest in the end it imprison me in his will and history.

"I have learned from writing my stories," the writer was saying, "that imagination is enemy of the State. I have learned from my writing that I am not free man. I ask for your help, not to harm my country, which still has magnificent socialistic possibilities, but in order to help me escape its worst errors. I do not wish to defame Russia. My purpose in my work is to show its true heart. So have done our writers from Pushkin to Pasternak and also, in his own way, Solzhenitsyn. If you believe in democratic humanism you must help artist to be free. Is not true?"

I got up, I think to shake myself out of his question. "What exactly is my responsibility to you, Levitansky?" I tried to contain the exasperation I felt.

"We are members of mankind. If I am drowning you must assist to save me."

"In unknown waters if I can't swim?"

"If not, throw to me rope."

"I'm a visitor here. I've told you I may be suspect. For all I know you yourself might be a Soviet agent out to get me, or the room may be bugged, and then where are we? Mr. Levitansky, please, I don't want to hear or argue anymore. I'll just plead personal inability and ask you to leave."

"Bugged?"

"By a listening device planted in this room."

Levitansky turned gray. He sat a moment in meditation, then rose wearily from the chair.

"I withdraw now request for your assistance. I accept your word that you are not capable. I do not wish to make criticism of you. All I wish to say, Gospodin Garvitz, is it requires more to change a man's character than to change his name."

Levitansky left the room, leaving in his wake faint fumes of cognac. He had also passed gas.

"Come back!" I called, not too loudly, but if he heard through the door he didn't answer. Good riddance, I thought. Not that I don't sympathize with him but look what he's done to *my* interior liberty. Who has to come thousands of miles to Russia to get entangled in this kind of mess? It's a helluva way to spend a vacation.

The writer had gone but not his sneaky manuscript. It was lying on my bed.

"That's his baby, not mine." Angered, I knotted my tie and slipped on my coat, then via the English-language number called for a cab.

A half hour later I was in the taxi, riding back and forth along Novo Ostapovskaya Street until I spotted the apartment house I thought it might be. It wasn't, it was another like it. I paid the driver and walked till I thought I had located it. After going up the stairs I was sure I had. When I knocked on Levitansky's door, the writer, looking older, distant—as if he'd been away on a trip and had just returned; or maybe simply interrupted at his work, his thoughts still in his words on the page, his pen in hand—stared at me. Very blankly.

"Levitansky, my heart breaks for you, I swear, but I am not, at this time of my life, considering my condition and recent experiences, in much of a mood to embark on a dangerous adventure. Please accept deepest regrets."

I thrust the manuscript into his hand and went down the stairs. Hurrying out of the building, I was, to my horror, unable to avoid Irina Levitansky coming in. Her eyes lit in fright as she recognized me an instant before I hit her full force and sent her sprawling along the walk.

"Oh, my God, what have I done? I beg your pardon!" I helped the dazed, hurt woman to her feet, brushed off her soiled skirt, and futilely, her pink blouse, split and torn on her lacerated arm and shoulder. I stopped dead when I felt myself experiencing erotic sensation.

Irina Filipovna held a handkerchief to her bloody nostril and wept a little. We sat on a stone bench, a girl of ten and her little brother watching us. Irina said something to them in Russian and they moved off.

"I was frightened of you also as you are of us," she said. "I trust you now because Levitansky does. But I will not urge you to take the manuscript. The responsibility is for you to decide."

"It's not a responsibility I want."

She said as though to herself, "Maybe I will leave Levitansky. He is wretched so much it is no longer a marriage. He drinks. Also he does not earn a living. My brother Dmitri allows him to drive the taxi two, three hours of the day, to my brother's disadvantage. Except for a ruble or two from this, I support him. Levitansky does not longer receive translation commissions. Also a neighbor in the house—I am sure Kovalevsky—has denounced him to the police for delinquency and parasitism. There will be a hearing. Levitansky says he will burn his manuscripts."

I said I had just returned the package of stories.

"He will not," she said. "But even if he burns, he will write more. If they take him away in prison he will write on toilet paper. When he comes out, he will write on newspaper margins. He sits this minute at his table. He is a magnificent writer. I cannot ask him not to write, but now I must decide if this is the condition I wish for myself for the rest of my life."

Irina sat in silence, an attractive woman with shapely legs and feet, in a soiled skirt and torn blouse. I left her on the stone bench, her handkerchief squeezed in her fist.

That night—July 2, I was leaving the Soviet Union on the fifth— I experienced massive self-doubt. If I'm a coward why has it taken me so long to discover it? Where does anxiety end and cowardice begin? Feelings get mixed, sure enough, but not all cowards are anxious men and not all anxious men are cowards. Many "sensitive" (Rose's word), tense, even frightened human beings did in fear what had to be done, the fear calling up effort when it's time to fight or jump off a rooftop into a river. There comes a time in a man's life when to get where he has to—if there are no doors or windows—he walks through a wall.

On the other hand, suppose one is courageous in a hopeless cause —you concentrate on courage but not enough on horse sense? To get to the point of the problem endlessly on my mind, how do I finally decide it's a sensible and worthwhile thing to smuggle out Levitansky's manuscript, given my reasonable doubts of the ultimate worth of the operation? Granted, as I now grant, he's trustworthy and his wife is that and more; still, does it pay a man like me to run the risk?

If six thousand Soviet writers can't do very much to squeeze out another drop of freedom as artists, who am I to fight their battle— H. Harvitz, knight-of-the-freelance from Manhattan? How far do you go, granted all men, including Communists, are created free and equal and justice is for all? How far do you go for art, if you're for Yeats, Matisse, and Ludwig van Beethoven? Not to mention Tolstoy and Dostoevsky. So far as to get yourself intentionally involved: the HH Ms. Smuggling Service? Will the President and State Department send up three cheers for my contribution to the cause of artistic social justice? And suppose it amounts to no more than a gaffe in the end?— What will I prove if I sneak out Levitansky's manuscript and all it turns out to be is just another passable book of stories?

That's how I argued with myself on more than one occasion, but soon I argued myself into solid indecision. What it boils down to, I'd say, is he expects me to help him because I'm an American. That's quite a nerve.

Two nights later—odd not to have the Fourth of July on July 4 (I was listening for firecrackers)—a quiet light-lemon summer's evening in Moscow, after two monotonously uneasy days, though I was still writing museum notes, for relief I took myself off to the Bolshoi to hear *Tosca*. It was sung in Russian by a busty lady and a handsome Slavic tenor, but the Italian plot was unchanged, and in the end Scarpia, who had promised "death" by fake bullets, gave in sneaky exchange a fusillade of hot lead; another artist bit the dust and Floria Tosca learned the hard way that love wasn't what she had thought.

Next to me sat another full-breasted woman, this one a lovely Russian of maybe thirty in a white dress that fitted a well-formed figure, her blond hair piled in a birdlike mass on her splendid head. Lillian could look like that though not Rose. This woman—sitting alone, it turned out—spoke flawless English in a mezzo-soprano with a slight accent.

During the first intermission she asked in friendly fashion, managing to seem detached but interested: "Are you American? Or perhaps Swedish?"

"Not Swedish. American is correct. How did you happen to guess?"

"I noticed, if it does not bother you that I say it," she remarked with a charming laugh, "a certain self-satisfaction."

"You got the wrong party."

When she opened her purse a fragrance of springtime burst forth —fresh flowers; the warmth of her body rose to my nostrils. I was moved by memories of the hungers of youth—dreams, longing.

During intermission she touched my arm and said in a low voice, "May I ask a favor? Do you depart soon from the Soviet Union?"

"In fact tomorrow."

"How fortunate for me. Would it offer too much difficulty to mail, wherever you are going, an airmail letter addressed to my husband, who is presently in Paris? Our airmail service takes two weeks to arrive in the West. I shall be grateful."

I glanced at the envelope addressed half in French, half in Cyrillic, and said I wouldn't mind. But during the next act sweat grew active on my body, and at the end of the opera, after Tosca's shriek of death, I handed the letter back to the not wholly surprised lady, saying I was sorry. I had the feeling I had heard her voice before. I hurried back to the hotel, determined not to leave my room for any reason other than breakfast; then out and into the wide blue sky.

I later fell asleep over a book and a bottle of sweetish warm beer a waiter had brought up, pretending to myself I was relaxed though I was concerned with worried thoughts of the departure and flight home; and when I awoke, three minutes on my wristwatch later, it seemed to me I had made the acquaintance of some new nightmares. I was momentarily panicked by the idea that someone had planted a letter on me, and I searched through the pockets of my two suits. Nyet. Then I recalled that in one of my dreams a drawer in a table I was sitting at had slowly come open, and Feliks Levitansky, a dwarf who lived in it along with a few friendly mice, managed to scale the wooden wall on the comb he used as a ladder, and to hop from the drawer ledge to the top of the table. He leered in my face, shook his Lilliputian fist, and shouted in high-pitched but (to me) understandable Russian, "Atombombnik! You massacred innocent Japanese people! Amerikansky bastards!"

"That's unfair," I cried out. "I was no more than a kid in college." That's a sad dream, I thought.

Afterwards this occurred to me: Suppose what happened to Levitansky happens to me. Suppose America gets caught up in a war with China in some semi-reluctant stupid way, and to make fast hash of it— despite my frantic loud protestations: mostly I wave my arms and shout obscenities—we spatter them, before they can get going, with a few dozen H-bombs, boiling up a thick atomic soup of about two hundred million Orientals—blood, gristle, marrow, and lots of floating Chinese eyeballs. We win the war because the Soviets hadn't been able to make up their minds whom to shoot their missiles at first. And suppose after this unheard-of slaughter, about ten million Americans, in self-revulsion, head for the borders to flee the country. To stop the loss of wealth, the refugees are intercepted by the army in tanks and turned back. Harvitz hides in his room with shades drawn, writing in a fury of protest an epic poem condemning the mass butchery by America. What nation, Asiatic or other, is next? Nobody in the States wants to publish the poem because it might start riots and another flight of refugees to Canada and Mexico; then one day there's a knock on the door, and it isn't the FBI but a bearded Levitansky, in better times a Soviet tourist, a modern, not medieval, Communist. He kindly offers to sneak the manuscript of the poem out for publication in the Soviet Union.

Why? Harvitz suspiciously asks.

Why not? To give the book its liberty.

I awoke after a restless night. I had been instructed by Intourist to be in the lobby with my baggage two hours before flight time, at 11 a.m. I was shaved and dressed by six, and at seven had breakfast—I was very hungry—of yogurt, sausage, and scrambled eggs in the twelfth-floor buffet. I went out to hunt for a taxi. They were hard to come by at this hour, but I finally located one near the American Embassy, not far from the hotel. Speaking my usual mixture of primitive German and French, I persuaded the driver by first suggesting, then slipping him an acceptable two rubles, to take me to Levitansky's house and wait a few minutes till I came out. Going hastily up the stairs, I knocked on his door, apologizing when he opened it, to the half-paja-maed, iron-faced writer, for waking him this early in the day. Without peace of mind or certainty of purpose I asked him whether he still wanted me to smuggle out his manuscript of stories. I got for my trouble the door slammed in my face.

A half hour later I had everything packed and was locking the suitcase. A knock on the door—half a rap, you might call it. For the suitcase, I thought. I was momentarily startled by the sight of a small man in a thick cap wearing a long trench coat. He winked, and against my will I winked back. I had recognized Levitansky's brother-in-law Dmitri, the taxi driver. He slid in, unbuttoned his coat, and brought forth the wrapped manuscript. Holding a finger to his lips, he handed it to me before I could say I was no longer interested.

"Levitansky changed his mind?"

"Not changed mind," he whispered. "Was afraid your voice to be heard by Kovalevsky."

"I'm sorry, I should have thought of that."

"Levitansky say not write to him," the brother-in-law said in a low tone. "When is published book, please to send to him copy of *Das Kapital.* He will understand message."

I reluctantly agreed.

The brother-in-law, a short shapeless figure with sad eyes, winked again, shook hands with a steamy palm, and slipped out of my room.

I unlocked my suitcase and laid the manuscript on top of my shirts. Then I unpacked half the contents and slipped the manuscript into a folder containing my notes on literary museums and a few letters from Lillian. I then and there decided that if I got back to the States, the next time I saw her I would ask her to marry me. The phone was ringing as I left the room.

On my way to the airport, alone in a taxi—no Intourist girl ac-

companied me—I felt, on and off, nauseated. If it's not the sausage and
yogurt it must just be ordinary fear. Still, if Levitansky has the courage
to send these stories out, the least I can do is give him a hand. When
one thinks of it it's little enough he does for human freedom during the
course of his life. At the airport if I can dig up a Bromo or its Russian
equivalent I know I'll feel better.

The driver was observing me in the mirror, a stern man with the
head of a scholar, impassively smoking.

"Le jour fait beau," I said.

He pointed with an upraised finger to a sign in English at one side
of the road to the airport:

"Long live peace in the world!"

"Peace with freedom." I smiled at the thought of somebody, not
Howard Harvitz, painting that in red on the Soviet sign.

We drove on, I foreseeing my exit from the Soviet Union. I had
made discreet inquiries from time to time and an Intourist girl in Leningrad had told me I had first to show my papers at the passport-control
desk, turn in all my rubles—a serious offense to walk off with any—
and then check luggage; no inspection, she swore. And that was that.
Unless, of course, the official at the passport desk found my name on a
list and said I had to go to the customs office for a package. In that
case—if nobody said so I wouldn't remind him—I would go get my
books. I figured I wouldn't open the package, just tear off a bit of the
wrapping, if they were wrapped, as though to make sure they were the
books I expected, and then saunter away with the package under my
arm.

I had heard that a KGB man was stationed at the ramp as one
boarded a plane. He asked for your passport, checked the picture, threw
you a stare through dark lenses, and, if there was no serious lack of resemblance, tore out your expired visa, pocketed it, and let you embark.

In ten minutes you were aloft, seat belts fastened in three languages, watching the plane banking west. Maybe if I looked hard I
might see in the distance Feliks Levitansky on the roof waving his red-
white-and-blue socks on a bamboo pole. Then the plane leveled off, and
we were above the clouds, flying westward. And that's what I would be
doing for five or six hours unless the pilot received radio instructions to
turn back; or maybe land in Czechoslovakia or East Germany, where
two big-hatted detectives boarded the plane. By an act of imagination
and will I made it some other passenger they were arresting. I got the
plane into the air again and we flew on without incident until we
touched down in free London.

As the taxi approached the Moscow airport, fingering my ticket and gripping my suitcase handle, I wished for courage equal to Levitansky's when they discovered he was the author of a book of stories I had managed to get published, and his trial and suffering began.

•

Levitansky's first story, translated by his wife, Irina Filipovna, was about an old man, a widower of seventy-eight, who hoped to have matzos for Passover.

Last year he had got his quota. They had been baked in the State bakery and sold in the State stores; but this year the State bakeries were not permitted to bake them. The officials said the machines had broken down but who believed them?

The old man went to the rabbi, an older man with a tormented beard, and asked him where he could get matzos. He feared that he mightn't have them this year.

"So do I," confessed the old rabbi. He said he had been told to tell his congregants to buy flour and bake them at home. The State stores would sell them the flour.

"What good is that for me?" asked the widower. He reminded the rabbi that he had no home to speak of, a single small room with a one-burner electric stove. His wife had died two years ago. His only living child, a married daughter, was with her husband in Birobijan. His other relatives—the few who were left after the German invasion—two female cousins his age—lived in Odessa; and he himself, even if he could find an oven, did not know how to bake matzos. And if he couldn't what should he do?

The rabbi then promised he would try to get the widower a kilo or two of matzos, and the old man, rejoicing, blessed him.

He waited anxiously a month but the rabbi never mentioned the matzos. Maybe he had forgotten. After all he was an old man burdened with worries, and the widower did not want to press him. However, Passover was coming on wings, so he must do something. A week before the Holy Days he hurried to the rabbi's flat and spoke to him there.

"Rabbi," he begged, "you promised me a kilo or two of matzos. What happened to them?"

"I know I promised," said the rabbi, "but I'm no longer sure to whom. It's easy to promise." He dabbed at his face with a damp handkerchief. "I was warned I could be arrested on charges of profiteering in the production and sale of matzos. I was told it could happen even if I were to give them away for nothing. It's a new crime they've invented. Still, take them anyway. If they arrest me, I'm an old man, and how long can an old man live in Lubyanka? Not so long, thanks God. Here, I'll give you a small pack but you must tell no one where you got the matzos."

"May the Lord eternally bless you, rabbi. As for dying in prison, rather let it happen to our enemies."

The rabbi went to his closet and got out a small pack of matzos, already wrapped and tied with knotted twine. When the widower offered in a whisper to pay him, at least the cost of the flour, the rabbi wouldn't hear of it. "God provides," he said, "although at times with difficulty." He said there was hardly enough for all who wanted matzos, so he must take what he got and be thankful.

"I will eat less," said the old man. "I will count mouthfuls. I will save the last matzo to look at and kiss if there isn't enough to last me. He will understand."

Overjoyed to have even a few matzos, he rode home on the trolley car and there met another Jew, a man with a withered hand. They conversed in Yiddish in low tones. The stranger had glanced at the almost square package, then at the widower, and had hoarsely whispered, "Matzos?" The widower, tears starting in his eyes, nodded. "With God's grace." "Where did you get them?" "God provides." "So if He provides let Him provide me," the stranger brooded. "I'm not so lucky. I was hoping for a package from relatives in Cleveland, America. They wrote they would send me a large pack of the finest matzos, but when I inquire of the authorities they say no matzos have arrived. You know when they will get here?" he muttered. "After Passover by a month or two, and what good will they be then?"

The widower nodded sadly. The stranger wiped his eyes with his good hand and after a short while left the trolley amid a number of people getting off. He had not bothered to say goodbye, and neither had the widower, not to remind him of his own good fortune. But when the time came for the old man to leave the trolley he glanced down between his feet where he had placed the package of matzos, and nothing was there. His feet were there. The old man felt harrowed, as though someone had ripped a large nail up his spine. He searched frantically throughout that car, going a long way past his stop, querying every passenger, the woman conductor, the motorman, but they all swore they had not seen his matzos.

Then it occurred to him that the stranger with the withered hand had stolen them.

The widower in his misery asked himself, Would a Jew have robbed another of his precious matzos? It didn't seem possible, but it was.

As for me I haven't even a matzo to look at now. If I could steal any, whether from Jew or Russian, I would steal them. He thought he would steal them even from the old rabbi.

The widower went home without his matzos and had none for Passover.

•

The story called "Tallith" concerned a youth of seventeen, beardless but for some stray hairs on his chin, who had come from Kirov to the steps of the synagogue on Arkhipova Street in Moscow. He had brought with him a capacious prayer shawl, a white garment of luminous beauty, which he offered for sale to a cluster of Jews of various sorts and sizes—curious, apprehensive, greedy at the sight of the shawl—for fifteen rubles. Most of them avoided the youth, particularly the older Jews, despite the fact that some of the more devout among them were worried about their prayer shawls, eroded on their shoulders after years of daily use, which they could not replace. "It's the informers among us who have put him up to this," they whispered among themselves, "so they will have someone to inform on."

Still, in spite of the warnings of their elders, several of the younger men examined the tallith and admired it. "Where did you get such a fine prayer shawl?" the youth was asked. "It was my father's who recently died," he said. "It was given to him by a rich Jew he had once befriended." "Then why don't you keep it for yourself, you're a Jew, aren't you?" "Yes," said the youth, not the least embarrassed, "but I am going to Bratsk as a komsomol volunteer and I need a few rubles to get married. Besides I'm a confirmed atheist."

One young man with fat unshaven cheeks, who admired the deeply white shawl, its white glowing in whiteness, with its long silk fringes, whispered to the youth he might consider buying it for five rubles. But he was overheard by the gabbai, the lay leader of the congregation, who raised his cane and shouted at the whisperer, "Hooligan, if you buy that shawl, beware it doesn't become your shroud." The Jew with the unshaven cheeks retreated.

"Don't strike him," cried the frightened rabbi, who had come out of the synagogue and saw the gabbai with his cane upraised. He urged the congregants to begin prayers at once. To the youth he said, "Please go away from here, we are burdened with enough trouble. It is forbidden for anyone to sell religious articles. Do you want us to be accused of criminal economic activity? Do you want the doors of the shul to be shut forever? So do us and yourself a mitzvah and go away."

The congregants moved inside. The youth was left standing alone on the steps; but then the gabbai came out of the door, a man with a deformed spine and a wad of cotton stuck in a leaking ear.

"Look here," he said. "I know you stole it. Still, after all is said and done, a tallith is a tallith and God asks no questions of His worshippers. I offer eight rubles for it, take it or leave it. Talk fast before the services end and the others come out."

"Make it ten and it's yours," said the youth. The gabbai gazed at him shrewdly. "Eight is all I have, but wait here and I'll borrow two rubles from my brother-in-law."

The youth waited patiently. Dusk was heavy. In a few minutes a black car drove up, stopped in front of the synagogue, and two police-men got out. The youth realized that the gabbai had informed on him. Not knowing what else to do he hastily draped the prayer shawl over his head and began loudly to pray. He prayed a passionate kaddish. The police hesitated to approach him while he was praying, and they stood at the bottom of the steps waiting for him to be done. The congregants came out and could not believe their ears. No one imagined the youth could pray so fervently. What moved them was the tone, the wail and passion of a man truly praying. Perhaps his father had indeed recently died. All listened attentively, and many wished he would pray forever, for they knew that as soon as he stopped he would be seized and thrown into prison.

It has grown dark. A moon hovers behind murky clouds over the synagogue steeple. The youth's voice is heard in prayer. The congre-gants are huddled in the dark street, listening. Both police agents are still there, although they cannot be seen. Neither can the youth. All that can be seen is the white shawl luminously praying.

•

The last of the stories translated by Irina Filipovna was about a writer of mixed parentage, a Russian father and Jewish mother, who had secretly been writing stories for years. He had from a young age wanted to write but had at first not had the courage—it seemed like such a merciless undertaking—so he had gone into translation instead; and then when he had, one day, started to write seriously and exul-tantly, after a while he found to his surprise that many of his stories— about half—were of Jews.

For a half-Jew that's a reasonable proportion, he thought. The oth-ers were about Russians who sometimes resembled members of his father's family. "It's good to have such different sources for ideas," he told his wife. "This way I can cover a varied range of experiences in life."

After several years of work he had submitted a selection of his stories to a trusted friend of university days, Viktor Zverkov, an editor of the Progress Publishing House; and the writer appeared at his office one morning after receiving a hastily scribbled cryptic note from his friend, to discuss his work with him. Zverkov, a troubled man to begin with— he told everyone his wife did not respect him—jumped up from his chair and turned the key in the door, his ear pressed a minute at the crack. He then went quickly to his desk and withdrew the manuscript from a drawer he first had to unlock with a key he kept in his pocket. He was a heavyset man with a flushed complexion, stained teeth, and a hoarse voice; and he handled the writer's manuscript with unease, as if it might leap up and wound him in the face.

"Please, Tolya," he whispered breathily, bringing his head close to the writer's, "you must take these awful stories away at once."

"What's the matter with you? Why are you shaking so?" said the writer.

"Don't pretend to be naïve. I am frankly amazed that you are submitting such unorthodox material for publication. My opinion as an editor is that they are of doubtful literary merit—I won't say devoid of it, Tolya, I have to be honest—but as stories they are a frightful affront to our society. I can't understand why you should take it on yourself to write about Jews. What do you know about them? Your culture is not the least Jewish, it's Soviet Russian. The whole business smacks of hypocrisy—of anti-Semitism."

He got up to shut the window and peered into a closet before sitting down.

"Are you out of your mind, Viktor?" said the writer. "My stories are in no sense anti-Semitic. One would have to read them standing on his head to make that judgment."

"There can be only one logical interpretation," the editor argued. "According to my most lenient analysis, which is favorable to you as a person—of let's call it decent intent—the stories fly in the face of socialist realism and reveal a dangerous inclination—perhaps even a stronger word should be used—to anti-Soviet sentiment. Maybe you're not entirely aware of this—I know how a story can pull a writer by the nose. As an editor I have to be sensitive to such things. I know, Tolya, from our conversations that you are a sincere believer in socialism; I won't accuse you of being defamatory to the Soviet system, but others may. In fact, I know they will. If one of the editors of *Oktyabr* was to read your stories, believe me, your career would explode in a mess. You seem not to have a normal awareness of what self-preservation is, and

what's appallingly worse, you're not above entangling innocent by-
standers in your fate. If these stories were mine, I assure you I would
never have brought them to you. I urge you to destroy them at once
before they destroy you."

He drank thirstily from a glass of water on his desk.

"That's the last thing I would do," answered the writer in anger.
"These stories, if not in tone or subject matter, are written in the spirit
of our early Soviet writers—the joyous spirits of the years just after the
Revolution."

"I think you know what happened to many of those 'joyous spirits.' "

The writer for a moment stared at him. "Well, then, what of those
stories that are not about the experience of Jews? Some are pieces about
homely aspects of Russian life. What I hoped is that you might personally recommend one or two such stories to *Novy Mir* or *Yunost.* They
are innocuous sketches and well written."

"Not the one about the two prostitutes," said the editor. "That con-
tains hidden social criticism, and is adversely naturalistic."

"A prostitute lives a social life."

"That may be but I can't recommend it for publication. I must advise you, Tolya, if you expect to receive further commissions for trans-
lations from us, you must immediately rid yourself of this whole
manuscript so as to avoid the possibility of serious consequences both to
yourself and family, and to the publishing house that has employed you
so faithfully and generously in the past."

"Since you didn't write the stories yourself, you needn't be afraid,
Viktor Alexandrovich," the writer said ironically.

"I am not a coward, if that's what you're hinting, Anatoly Boriso-
vich, but if a wild locomotive is running loose on the rails, I know
which way to jump."

The writer hastily gathered up his manuscript, stuffed the papers
into his leather case, and returned home by bus. His wife was still away
at work. He took out the stories and, after reading through one, burned
it, page by page, in the kitchen sink.

His nine-year-old son, returning from school, said, "Papa, what are
you burning in the sink? That's no place for a fire."

"I'm burning my talent," said the writer. He said, "And my integ-
rity, and my heritage."

❧ B M ❧

My Son the Murderer

He wakes feeling his father is in the hallway, listening. He listens to him sleep and dream. Listening to him get up and fumble for his pants. He won't put on his shoes. To him not going to the kitchen to eat. Staring with shut eyes in the mirror. Sitting an hour on the toilet. Flipping the pages of a book he can't read. To his anguish, loneliness. The father stands in the hall. The son hears him listen.

My son the stranger, he won't tell me anything.

I open the door and see my father in the hall. Why are you standing there, why don't you go to work?

On account of I took my vacation in the winter instead of the summer like I usually do.

What the hell for if you spend it in this dark smelly hallway, watching my every move? Guessing what you can't see. Why are you always spying on me?

My father goes to the bedroom and after a while sneaks out in the hallway again, listening.

I hear him sometimes in his room but he don't talk to me and I don't know what's what. It's a terrible feeling for a father. Maybe someday he will write me a letter, My dear father . . .

My dear son Harry, open up your door. My son the prisoner.

My wife leaves in the morning to stay with my married daughter, who is expecting her fourth child. The mother cooks and cleans for her and takes care of the three children. My daughter is having a bad pregnancy, with high blood pressure, and lays in bed most of the time. This is what the doctor advised her. My wife is gone all day. She worries something is wrong with Harry. Since he graduated college last summer he is alone, nervous, in his own thoughts. If you talk to him, half the time he yells if he answers you. He reads the papers, smokes, he stays in his room. Or once in a while he goes for a walk in the street.

How was the walk, Harry?

A walk.

My wife advised him to go look for work, and a couple of times he went, but when he got some kind of an offer he didn't take the job.

It's not that I don't want to work. It's that I feel bad.

So why do you feel bad?

I feel what I feel. I feel what is.

Is it your health, sonny? Maybe you ought to go to a doctor?

I asked you not to call me by that name anymore. It's not my health. Whatever it is I don't want to talk about it. The work wasn't the kind I want.

So take something temporary in the meantime, my wife said to him.

He starts to yell. Everything's temporary. Why should I add more to what's temporary? My gut feels temporary. The goddamn world is temporary. On top of that I don't want temporary work. I want the opposite of temporary, but where is it? Where do you find it?

My father listens in the kitchen.

My temporary son.

She says I'll feel better if I work. I say I won't. I'm twenty-two since December, a college graduate, and you know where you can stick that. At night I watch the news programs. I watch the war from day to day. It's a big burning war on a small screen. It rains bombs and the flames roar higher. Sometimes I lean over and touch the war with the flat of my hand. I wait for my hand to die.

My son with the dead hand.

I expect to be drafted any day but it doesn't bother me the way it used to. I won't go. I'll go to Canada or somewhere I can go.

The way he is frightens my wife and she is glad to go to my daughter's house early in the morning to take care of the three children. I stay with him in the house but he don't talk to me.

You ought to call up Harry and talk to him, my wife says to my daughter.

I will sometime but don't forget there's nine years' difference between our ages. I think he thinks of me as another mother around and one is enough. I used to like him when he was a little boy but now it's hard to deal with a person who won't reciprocate to you.

She's got high blood pressure. I think she's afraid to call.

I took two weeks off from my work. I'm a clerk at the stamp window in the post office. I told the superintendent I wasn't feeling so good, which is no lie, and he said I should take sick leave. I said I wasn't that sick, I only needed a little vacation. But I told my friend Moe Berkman I was staying out because Harry has me worried.

I understand what you mean, Leo. I got my own worries and anxieties about my kids. If you got two girls growing up you got hostages to fortune. Still in all we got to live. Why don't you come to poker on this Friday night? We got a nice game going. Don't deprive yourself of a good form of relaxation.

I'll see how I feel by Friday how everything is coming along. I can't promise you.

Try to come. These things, if you give them time, all will pass away. If it looks better to you, come on over. Even if it don't look so good, come on over anyway because it might relieve your tension and worry that you're under. It's not so good for your heart at your age if you carry that much worry around.

It's the worst kind of worry. If I worry about myself I know what the worry is. What I mean, there's no mystery. I can say to myself, Leo you're a big fool, stop worrying about nothing—over what, a few bucks? Over my health that has always stood up pretty good although I have my ups and downs? Over that I'm now close to sixty and not getting any younger? Everybody that don't die by age fifty-nine gets to be sixty. You can't beat time when it runs along with you. But if the worry is about somebody else, that's the worst kind. That's the real worry because if he won't tell you, you can't get inside of the other person and find out why. You don't know where's the switch to turn off. All you do is worry more.

So I wait out in the hall.

Harry, don't worry so much about the war.

Please don't tell me what to worry about or what not to worry about.

Harry, your father loves you. When you were a little boy, every night when I came home you used to run to me. I picked you up and lifted you up to the ceiling. You liked to touch it with your small hand.

I don't want to hear about that anymore. It's the very thing I don't want to hear. I don't want to hear about when I was a child.

Harry, we live like strangers. All I'm saying is I remember better days. I remember when/ we weren't afraid to show we loved each other.

He says nothing.

Let me cook you an egg.

An egg is the last thing in the world I want.

So what do you want?

He put his coat on. He pulled his hat off the clothes tree and went down into the street.

Harry walked along Ocean Parkway in his long overcoat and creased brown hat. His father was following him and it filled him with rage.

He walked at a fast pace up the broad avenue. In the old days there was a bridle path at the side of the walk where the concrete bicycle path is now. And there were fewer trees, their black branches cutting the sunless sky. At the corner of Avenue X, just about where you can smell Coney Island, he crossed the street and began to walk home. He pretended not to see his father cross over, though he was infuriated. The father crossed over and followed his son home. When he got to the house he figured Harry was upstairs already. He was in his room with the door shut. Whatever he did in his room he was already doing.

Leo took out his small key and opened the mailbox. There were three letters. He looked to see if one of them was, by any chance, from his son to him. My dear father, let me explain myself. The reason I act as I do . . . There was no such letter. One of the letters was from the Post Office Clerks Benevolent Society, which he slipped into his coat pocket. The other two letters were for Harry. One was from the draft board. He brought it up to his son's room, knocked on the door, and waited.

He waited for a while.

To the boy's grunt he said, There is a draft-board letter here for you. He turned the knob and entered the room. His son was lying on his bed with his eyes shut.

Leave it on the table.

Do you want me to open it for you, Harry?

No, I don't want you to open it. Leave it on the table. I know what's in it.

Did you write them another letter?

That's my goddamn business.

The father left it on the table.

The other letter to his son he took into the kitchen, shut the door, and boiled up some water in a pot. He thought he would read it quickly and seal it carefully with a little paste, then go downstairs and put it back in the mailbox. His wife would take it out with her key when she returned from their daughter's house and bring it up to Harry.

The father read the letter. It was a short letter from a girl. The girl said Harry had borrowed two of her books more than six months ago and since she valued them highly she would like him to send them back to her. Could he do that as soon as possible so that she wouldn't have to write again?

As Leo was reading the girl's letter Harry came into the kitchen and when he saw the surprised and guilty look on his father's face, he tore the letter out of his hands.

I ought to murder you the way you spy on me.

Leo turned away, looking out of the small kitchen window into the dark apartment-house courtyard. His face burned, he felt sick.

Harry read the letter at a glance and tore it up. He then tore up the envelope marked personal.

If you do this again don't be surprised if I kill you. I'm sick of you spying on me.

Harry, you are talking to your father.

He left the house.

Leo went into his room and looked around. He looked in the dresser drawers and found nothing unusual. On the desk by the window was a paper Harry had written on. It said: Dear Edith, why don't you go fuck yourself? If you write me another stupid letter I'll murder you.

The father got his hat and coat and left the house. He ran slowly for a while, running then walking until he saw Harry on the other side of the street. He followed him, half a block behind.

He followed Harry to Coney Island Avenue and was in time to see him board a trolleybus going to the Island. Leo had to wait for the next one. He thought of taking a taxi and following the trolleybus, but no taxi came by. The next bus came fifteen minutes later and he took it all the way to the Island. It was February and Coney Island was wet, cold, and deserted. There were few cars on Surf Avenue and few people on the streets. It felt like snow. Leo walked on the boardwalk amid snow flurries, looking for his son. The gray sunless beaches were empty. The hot-dog stands, shooting galleries, and bathhouses were shuttered up. The gunmetal ocean, moving like melted lead, looked freezing. A wind blew in off the water and worked its way into his clothes so that he shivered as he walked. The wind white-capped the leaden waves and the slow surf broke on the empty beaches with a quiet roar.

He walked in the blow almost to Sea Gate, searching for his son, and then walked back again. On his way toward Brighton Beach he saw a man on the shore standing in the foaming surf. Leo hurried down the boardwalk stairs and onto the ribbed-sand beach. The man on the roaring shore was Harry, standing in water to the tops of his shoes.

Leo ran to his son. Harry, it was a mistake, excuse me, I'm sorry I opened your letter.

Harry did not move. He stood in the water, his eyes on the swelling leaden waves.

Harry, I'm frightened. Tell me what's the matter. My son, have mercy on me.

I'm frightened of the world, Harry thought. It fills me with fright.

He said nothing.

A blast of wind lifted his father's hat and carried it away over the beach. It looked as though it was going to be blown into the surf, but then the wind blew it toward the boardwalk, rolling like a wheel along the wet sand. Leo chased after his hat. He chased it one way, then another, then toward the water. The wind blew the hat against his legs and he caught it. By now he was crying. Breathless, he wiped his eyes with icy fingers and returned to his son at the edge of the water.

He is a lonely man. This is the type he is. He will always be lonely.

My son who made himself into a lonely man.

Harry, what can I say to you? All I can say to you is who says life is easy? Since when? It wasn't for me and it isn't for you. It's life, that's the way it is—what more can I say? But if a person don't want to live what can he do if he's dead? Nothing is nothing, it's better to live.

Come home, Harry, he said. It's cold here. You'll catch a cold with your feet in the water.

Harry stood motionless in the water and after a while his father left. As he was leaving, the wind plucked his hat off his head and sent it rolling along the shore. He watched it go.

My father listens in the hallway. He follows me in the street. We meet at the edge of the water.

He runs after his hat.

My son stands with his feet in the ocean.

1968

Pictures of the Artist

Fidelman pissing in muddy water discovers water over his head. Modigliani wanders by searching by searchlight for his lost statues in Livorno canal. They told me to dump them in the canal, so I fucked them, I dumped them. Non ha viste? Macchè. How come that light works underwater? Hashish. If we wake we drown, says Fidelman. *Chants de Maldoror.* His eyeless face drained of blood but not yellow light, Modi goes up canal as Fidelman drifts down.

Woodcut. Knight, Death and the Devil. Dürer.

Au fond il s'est suicidé. Anon.

Broken rusting balls of Venus. Ah, to sculpt a perfect hole, the volume and gravity constant. Invent space. Surround matter with hole rather than vice versa. That would have won me enduring fame and fortune and spared me all this wandering.

Cathedral of Erotic Misery. Schwitters.

Everybody says you're dead, otherwise why do you never write? Madonna Adoring the Child, Mater Dolorosa. Madonna della Peste. Long White Knights. Lives of the Saints. S. Sebastian, arrow collector, swimming in bloody sewer. Pictured transfixed with arrows. S. Denis, decapitated. Pictured holding his head. S. Agatha, breasts shorn clean, running enflamed. Painted carrying both bloody breasts in white salver. S. Stephen, crowned with rocks. Shown stoned. S. Lucy tearing out eyes for suitor smitten by same. Portrayed bearing two-eyed omelet on dish. S. Catherine, broken apart on spiked wheel. Pictured married to wheel. S. Lawrence, roasted on slow grill. *I am roasted on one side. Now turn me over and eat.* Shown cooked but uneaten. S. Bartholomew, flayed alive. Standing with skin draped over skinned arm. S. Fima, eaten by rats. Pictured with happy young rat. S. Simon Zelotes, sawed in half. Shown with bleeding crosscut saw. S. Genet in prison, pictured with boys. S. Fidel Uomo, stuffing his ass with flowers.

Still Life with Herrings. S. Soutine.

He divideth the gefilte fish and matzos.

Drawing. Flights of birds over dark woods, sparrows, finches, thrushes, white doves, martins, swallows, eagles. Birds with human faces crapping human on whom they crap.

Wood sculpture. Man holding sacrificial goat. Cubist goat with triangular titties. Goat eating hanged goat.

The Enigma of Isidor Ducasse. Man Ray.

In this time Fidelman, after making studies of the work of Donatello, in particular of the Annunciation carved in stone for the Church of S. Croce, the S. George in armor, with all the beauty of youth and the courage of the knight, and the bald man known as Il Zuccone, from figures in the façade of Giotto's Campanile, about whom it was said the sculptor, addressing his creation, would cry out, Speak, speak: In this time the American began to work in original images dug into the soil. To those who expressed astonishment regarding this extraordinary venture, Fidelman is said to have replied, Being a poor man I can neither purchase nor borrow hard or soft stone; therefore, since this is so, I create my figures as hollows in the earth. In sum, my material is the soil, my tools a pickax and shovel, my sculpture the act of digging rather than carving or assembling. However, the pleasure in creation is not less than that felt by Michelangelo.

After attempting first several huge ziggurats that because of the rains tumbled down like Towers of Babel, he began to work labyrinths and mazes dug in the earth and constructed in the form of jewels. Later he refined and simplified this method, building a succession of spontaneously placed holes, each a perfect square, which when seen together constituted a sculpture. These Fidelman exhibited throughout Italy in whatsoever place he came.

Having arrived in a city carrying his tools on his shoulder and a few possessions in a knotted bundle on his arm, the sculptor searched in the environs until he had come upon a small plot of land he could dig on without the formality of paying rent. Because this good fortune was not always possible, he was more than once rudely separated from his sculptures as they were in the act of being constructed and, by the tip of someone's boot, ejected from the property whereon he worked, the hollows then being filled in by the angry landowners. For this reason the sculptor often chose public places and dug in parks, or squares, if this were possible, which to do so he sometimes pretended, when questioned by officials of the police, that he was an underground repairman sent there by the Municipality. If he was disbelieved by these and dragged off to jail, he lay several days recuperating from the efforts of his labors, not unpleasantly. There are worse places than jails, Fidelman is said to have said, and once I am set free I shall begin my sculptures in another place. To sum up, he dug where he could, yet not far from the marketplace where many of the inhabitants of the city passed by daily, and where, if he was not unlucky, the soil was friable and not too hard with rock to be dug. This task he performed, as was his custom, quickly and expertly. Just as Giotto is said to have been able to draw a perfect free-hand circle, so could Fidelman dig a perfect square hole without measurement. He arranged the sculptures singly or in pairs according to the necessity of the Art. These were about a braccio in volume, sometimes two, or two and a half if Fidelman was not too fatigued. The smaller sculpture took from two to three hours to construct, the larger perhaps five or six; and if the final grouping was to contain three pieces, this meant a long day indeed, and possibly two, of continual digging. There were times when because of weariness Fidelman would have compromised for a single-braccio piece; but in the end Art prevailed and he dug as he must to fulfill those forms that must be fulfilled.

After constructing his sculptures the artist, unwinding a canvas sign on stilts, advertised the exhibition. The admission requested was ten lire, which was paid to him in the roped-off entranceway, the artist standing with a container in his hand. Not many were enticed to visit the exhibition, especially when it snowed or rained, although Fidelman was heard to say that the weather did not the least harm to his sculptures, indeed sometimes improved them by changing volume and texture as well as affecting other qualities. And it was as though nature, which until now was acted upon by the artist, now acted upon the Art itself, an unexpected but satisfying happening, since thus were changed the forms of a form. Even on the most crowded days when more than several persons came to view his holes in the earth, the sculptor earned a meager sum, not more than two or three hundred lire at most. He well understood that his bread derived from the curious among the inhabitants, rather than from the true lovers of Art, but for this phenomenon took no responsibility since it was his need to create and not be concerned with the commerce of Art. Those few who came to the exhibit, they viewed the sculptures at times in amazement and disbelief, whether at the perfect constructions or at their own stupidity, if indeed they believed they were stupid, is not known. Some of the viewers, after gazing steadfastly at the sculptures, were like sheep in their expression, as if wondering whether they had been deceived; some were stony-faced, as if they knew they had been. But few complained aloud, being ashamed to admit their folly, if indeed it were folly. To the one or two who rudely questioned him, saying, Why do you pass off on us as sculpture an empty hole or two? the artist, with the greatest tact and courtesy, replied, It were well if you relaxed before my sculptures, if you mean to enjoy them, and yield yourself to the pleasure they evoke in the surprise of their forms. At these words he who had complained fell silent, not certain he had truly understood the significance of the work of Art he had seen. On occasion a visitor would speak to the artist to compliment him, which he received with gratitude. Eh, maestro, your sculptures touch my heart. I thank you from the bottom of my own, the artist is said to have replied, blowing his nose to hide the gratification that he felt.

There is a story told that in Naples in a small park near the broad avenue called Via Carracciola, one day a young man waited until the remaining other visitor had left the exhibit so that he might speak to the sculptor. Maestro, said he most earnestly, it distresses me to do so, but I must pray you to return to me the ten lire I paid for admission to your exhibit. I have seen no more than two square holes in the ground and am much dissatisfied. The fault lies in you that you have seen only holes, Fidelman is said to have replied. I cannot, however, return the admission fee to you, for doing so might cause me to lose confidence in my work. Why do you refuse me my just request? said the poorly attired young man, whose dark eyes, although intense and comely, were mournful. I ask for my young babes. My wife gave me money so that I might buy bread for our supper, of which we have little. We are poor folk and I have no steady work. Yet when I observed the sign calling attention to your sculptures, which though I looked for them I could see none visible, I was moved by curiosity, an enduring weakness of mine and the cause of much of my misery. It came into my heart that I must see these sculptures, so I gave up the ten lire, I will confess, in fear and trepidation, hoping to be edified and benefited although fearful I would not be. I hoped that your sculptures, since they are described on the banner as new in the history of Art, might teach me what I myself must make in order that I may fulfill my desire to be great in Art; but all I can see are two large holes, the one dug deeper by about a braccio than the other. Holes are of no use to me, my life being full of them, so I beg you to return the lire that I may hasten to the baker's shop to buy the bread I was sent for.

After hearing him out, Fidelman is said to have answered, I do not as a rule explain my sculptures to the public, but since you are an attractive young man who has turned his thoughts to becoming an artist, I will say to you what your eyes have not seen, in order that you may be edified and benefited.

I hope that may be so, said the young man, although I doubt it.

Listen before you doubt. Primus, although the sculpture is more or less invisible it is sculpture nevertheless. Because you can't see it doesn't mean it isn't there. As for use or uselessness, rather think that that is Art which is made by the artist to be Art. Secundus, you must keep in mind that any sculpture is a form existing at a point radiating in all directions, therefore since it is dug into the Italian earth the sculpture vibrates overtones of Italy's Art, history, politics, religion; even nature as one experiences it in this country. There is also a metaphysic in relation of down to up, and vice versa, but I won't pursue that matter now. Suffice to say, my sculpture is not unrelated, though not necessarily purposefully, to its environment, whether seen or unseen. Tertius, in relation to the above, it is impossible to describe the range of choices, conscious or unconscious, that exist in the creation of a single sculptured hole. However, let it be understood that choice, as I use the word in this context, means artistic freedom, for I do not in advance choose the exact form and position of the hole; it chooses me. The essential thing is to maintain contact with it as it is being achieved. If the artist loses contact with his hole, than which there is none like it in the universe, then the hole will not respond and the sculpture will fail. Thus I mean to show you that constructs of a sculpture which appear to be merely holes are, in truth, in the hands of the artist, elements of a conceptual work of Art.

You speak well, maestro, but I am dull-witted and find it difficult to comprehend such things. It would not surprise me that I forgot what you have so courteously explained before I arrive at the next piazza. May I not therefore have the ten lire back? I will be ever grateful to you.

Tough titty if you can't comprehend Art, Fidelman is said to have replied. Fuck off now.

The youth left, sighing, without his ten lire, nor with bread for his babes.

Not long after he had departed, as it grew dusk, the sculptor took down the banner of his exhibit and gathered his tools so that he might fill in the sculpture and leave for another city. As he was making these preparations a stranger appeared, wrapped in the folds of a heavy cloak, although winter still hid in its cave and the fields were ripe with grain. The stranger's nether limbs, clothed in coarse black stockings, were short and bowed, and his half-concealed visage, iron eyes in a leather face, caused the flesh on Fidelman's neck to prickle and thicken. But the stranger, averting his glance and speaking pleasantly, yet as though to his own hands, and in the accent of one from a foreign land, graciously prayed the sculptor for permission to view his sculpture, the effect of which he had heard was extraordinary. He explained he had been delayed on board ship and apologized for appearing so late in the day. Fidelman, having recovered somewhat from his surprise at the stranger's odd garments and countenance, is said to have replied it made no difference that he had come late so long as he paid the admission fee.

This the stranger did forthwith with a gold coin for which he neither asked nor received change. He glanced fleetingly at the sculpture and turned away as though dazzled, the which the sculptor is said to have wondered at.

But instead of departing the exhibit now that he had viewed it, however hastily, the stranger tarried, his back to that place where the sculpture stood fixed in the earth, the red sun sinking at his shoulders. As though reflecting still upon that he had seen, he consumed an apple, the core of which he tossed over his left shoulder into one of the holes of the sculpture; an act that is said to have angered Fidelman although he refrained from complaint, it may be because he feared this stranger was an agent of the police, so it were better he said nothing.

If you'll excuse me, said the stranger at last, please explain to me what means these two holes that they have in them nothing but the dark inside?

The meaning lies in what they are as they seem to be, and the dark you note within, although I did not plan it so or put it there, may be thought of as an attribute of the aesthetic, Fidelman is said to have replied.

So what then did you put there?

To wit, the sculpture.

At that the stranger laughed, his laughter not unlike the bray of a goat. All I saw was nothing. To me, if you'll pardon me, is a

hole nothing. This I will prove to you. If you will look in the small
hole there is now there an apple core. If not for this would be empty
the hole. If empty would be there nothing.

Emptiness is not nothing if it has form.

Form, if you will excuse me my expression, is not what is the
whole of Art.

One might argue that, but neither is content if that's what you
intend to imply. Form may be and often is the content of Art.

You don't say?

I do indeed.

The stranger spat on both of his hands and rubbed them together,
a disagreeable odor rising from them.

In this case I will give you form.

Since the stranger stood now scarce visible in the dark, the sculptor
began to be in great fear, his legs, in truth, trembling.

Who are you? Fidelman is said finally to have demanded.

I am also that youth that he is now dead in the Bay of Naples, that
you would not give him back his poor ten lire so he could buy bread for
his babies.

Are you not the devil? the sculptor is said to have cried out.

I am also him.

Quid ego feci?

This I will tell you. You have not yet learned what is the difference between something and nothing.

Bending for the shovel, the stranger smote the horrified Fidelman
with its blade a resounding blow on the head, the sculptor toppling as
though dead into the larger of the two holes he himself had dug. He-
who-Fidelman-did-not-know then proceeded to shovel in earth until
the sculpture and its creator were extinguished.

So it's a grave, the stranger is said to have muttered. So now we
got form but we also got content.

Collage. The Flayed Ox. Rembrandt. Hanging Fowl. Soutine.
Young Man with Death's Head. Van Leyden. Funeral at Ornans. Cour-
bet. Bishop Eaten by Worms. Murillo. Last Supper, Last Judgment,
Last Inning.

I paint with my prick. Renoir. I paint with my ulcer. Soutine. I
paint with my paint. Fidelman.

One can study nature, dissect and analyze and balance it without
making paintings. Bonnard.

Gouache. Unemployed Musician. Fiddleman.

Painting is nothing more than the art of expressing the invisible through the visible. Fromentin. Indefinite Divisibility. Tanguy. Definite Invisibility. Fidelman.

I'm making the last paintings which anyone can make. Reinhardt. I've made them. I like my paintings because anyone can do them. Warhol. Me too.

Erased de Kooning Drawing. Rauschenberg. Erased Rauschenberg. De Kooning. Lithograph. Eraser. Fidelman.

Modigliani climbs and falls. He tries to scale a brick wall with bleeding fingers, his eyes lit crystals of heroin, whisky, pain. He climbs and falls in silence.

My God, what's all that climbing and falling for?

For art, you cretin.

Thunder and lightning.

Portrait of an Old Jew Seated. Rembrandt. Portrait of an Old Jew in an Armchair. Rembrandt. It beats walking.

Then I dreamt that I woke suddenly, with an unspeakable shock, to the consciousness that someone was lying in bed beside me. I put my hand out and touched the soft naked shoulder of a woman; and a cold gentle little woman's voice said: I have not been in bed for a hundred years. Raverat. The Rat Killer. Rembrandt.

Elle m'a mordu aux couilles. Modigliani.

Mosaic. Piazza Amerina, Sicily. IVth Cent. A.D. All that remains after so long a time.

Susskind preacheth up on the mountain, a piece of green palm branch behind his head. (He has no halo, here the mosaic is broken.) Three small cactus plants groweth at his bare feet. / Tell the truth. Dont cheat. If its easy it dont mean its good. Be kind, specially to those that they got less than you. I want for everybody justice. Must also be charity. If you feel good give charity. If you feel bad give charity. Must also be mercy. Be nice, dont fight. Children, how can we live without mercy? If you have no mercy for me I shall not live. Love, mercy, charity. Its not so easy believe me.

•

At the bottom of the brown hill they stand there by the huge lichenous rock that riseth above them on the top of which is a broad tree with a twisted trunk. / Ah, Master, my eyes watereth. Thou speakest true. I love thy words. I love thee more than thy words. If I could paint thee with my paints, then would my heart soar to the Gates of Heaven. I will be forever thy disciple, no ifs or buts. / This is already iffed. If you will follow me, follow. If you will follow must be for Who I Am.

Also please, no paints or paintings. Remember the Law, what it says. No graven images, which is profanation and idolatry. Nobody can paint Who I Am. Not on papyrus, or make me into an idol of wood, or stone, not even in the sand. Dont try, its a sin. Here is a parable: And the Lord called unto Moses and spoke to him, Moses, come thou on this mountain and I will show Myself so thou mayst see Me, and none but thee; and Moses answered: Lord, if I see Thee, then wilt Thou become as a graven image on mine eye and I be blind. Then spake the Lord, saying, Thou art my beloved Son, in whom I am well pleased, and for this there is no Promised Land. / Whats the parable of that? Its more a paradox, Id say. / If you dont know its not for you. / Tell me, Master, art thou the Living God? Art thou at least the Son of God? / So we will see, its not impossible. / Art thou the Redeemer? / This could be also, Im not sure myself. Depends what happens. / Is thy fate ordained? / I act like I Am. Who knows my fate? All I know is somebody will betray me. Dont ask how I know, I know. You dont but I do. This is the difference. / It is not I, Master, I will never betray thee. Cast me out now if thou believest I speak not the TRUTH. / What happens will happen. So give up your paints and your brushes and follow me where I go, and we will see what we will see. This we will see. / Master, tis as good as done.

•

Fidelman droppeth into the Dead Sea all his paints and brushes, except one. These dissolve in the salted sea. (A piece of the blue sea is faded.)

•

(In this picture) As Susskind preacheth to the multitude, on the shore of the green Sea of Galilee where sail the little ships of the fisher men, as even the red fishes and the white fishes come to listen at the marge of the water, the black goats stand still on the hills, the painter, who hideth behind a palm tree, sketcheth with a coal on papyrus the face and figure of the Master. / If I could do a portrait of him as he is in this life I will be remembered forever in human history. Nobody can call that betrayal, I dont think, for its for the good of us all. / My child, why do you do that which I forbade you? Dont think I cant see you, I can. I wish I couldnt see what I see, but I can.

•

The painter kneeleth on his knees. (A few tesserae are missing from his face, including one of the eye, and a few black stones from his beard.) / Master, forgive me. All I meant to do was preserve thy likeness for a future time. I guess it gotteth to be too much for me, the thought that I might. Forgive, forgive in thy mercy. Ill burn everything, I promise, papyrus, charcoal, a roll of canvas I have hid in my hut, also this last paintbrush although a favorite of mine. / Listen to me, there are two horses, one brown, the other black. The brown obeys his master, the black does not. Which is the better horse? / Both are the same. / How is this so? / One obeys and the other does not, but they are both thoroughbreds. / You have an easy tongue. If I cant change you I must suffer my fate. This is a fact. / Master, have no further worries on that score, I am a changed man down to my toenails, I give thee my word.

•

Fidelman speaketh to himself in a solitary place in Capernaum. / This talent it is death to hide lodged in me useless. How am I ever going to make a living or win my spurs? How can I compete in this world if both my hands are tied and my eyes blindfolded? Whats so moral about that? How is a man meant to fulfill himself if he isnt allowed to paint? Its graven image versus grave damages to myself and talent. Which harms the most there is no doubt. One can take just so much. / He gnasheth his teeth. He waileth to the sky. He teareth his cheeks and pulleth out the hairs of his head and beard. He butteth his skull against the crumbling brick wall. On this spot the wall is stained red with blood. / Satan saith Ha Ha.

•

As Susskind sat at meat he spoke thus. Verily I say, one of you who eats now at this table will betray me, dont ask who. / His followers blusheth. Their faces are in shades of pink. No one blusheth not. Fidelman blusheth red. / But if he knows, it cant be all that wrong to do it. What I mean is Im not doing it in any sneaky way, that is, for after all he knows. / He that has betrayed me once will betray me twice. He will betray me thrice. / Fidelman counteth on his fingers.

•

He is now in the abode of the high priest Caiaphas. / (Here the mosaic is almost all destroyed. Only the painter's short-fingered hand survives.) Fidelmans heavy hand is filled with thirty-nine pieces of silver.

•

The painter runneth out to buy paints, brushes, canvas.

.

On the Mount of Olives appeareth the painter amid a multitude
with swords, staves, and lengths of lead pipe. Also come the chief priest,
the chief of police, scribes, elders, the guards with dogs, the onlookers to
look on. Fidelman goeth to the Master and kisseth him full on the lips. /
Twice, saith Susskind. / He wept.

.

He hath on his head a crown of rusty chain links. A guard smiteth
his head and spitteth on his eye. In mockery they worship Susskind. /
Its a hard life, he saith. / He draggeth the beam of the cross up a hill.
Fidelman watcheth from behind a mask.

.

12 12 12 12 12 12 12 12 12 12 12 12 12 12 12 12 12 12 12 12
369 369 369 369 369 369 369 369 369 369 369 369 369 369
veyizmirveyizmirveyizmirveyizmirveyizmirveyizmirveyizmirv
12369123691236912369123691236912369123691236912369123691236

.

Fidelman painteth three canvases. The Crucifixion he painteth
red on red. The Descent from the Cross he painteth white on white.
For the Resurrection, on Easter morning, he leaveth the canvas
blank.

.

P
t o tem
L
E
Suss
King

.

Je vous emmerde. Modigliani.

Oil on wood. Bottle fucking guitar? Bull impaled on pole? One-
eyed carp stuffed in staring green bottle? Clown spooning dog dung out
of sawdust? Staircase ascending a nude? Black-stockinged whore reading pornographic book by lamplight? Still life: three apple cores plus
one long gray hair? Boy pissing on old man's shoe? The blue disease?

Balding woman dyeing her hair? Buggers of Calais? Blood oozing from ceiling on foggy night?

Rembrandt was the first great master whose sitters sometimes dreaded seeing their portraits. Malraux. I is another. Rimbaud.

1. Watercolor. Tree growing in all directions. Nothing namable taxonomically speaking, like weeping willow with stiff spotted leaves, some rotted brown-green. Otherwise stylized apple-green-to-gold leaves. Not maple or sycamore same though resembling both, enlarged, painted to cover whole tree from roots to topmost spotted leaf. The leaves are the tree. Branches like black veins, thins to thicks, visible behind or through leaves. No birds in tree, not rook or raven. Impression is of mystery. Nothing more is seen at first but if viewer keeps looking tree is cleverly a human face. Leaves and branches delineate strained features, also lonely hollow anguished eyes. What is this horror I am or represent? Painter can think of none, for portrait is of a child and he remembers happy childhood, or so it seems. Exactly what face has done, or where has been, or knows, or wants to know, or is or isn't experiencing, isn't visible, nor can be explained as tone, memory, feeling; or something that happened in later life that painter can't recall. Maybe it never happened. It's as though this face is hiding in a tree or pretending to be one while waiting for something to happen in life and that something when it happened was nothing. Nothing much. 2. Triptych. Woodcut. It's about forbidden love. In the first black-and-white panel this guy is taking his sister in her black-and-white bathrobe. She squirms but loves it. Can be done in white-and-black for contrast. Man Seducing Sister or Vice Versa. The second panel is about the shame of the first, where he takes to masturbating in the cellar. It's dark so you can't see much of his face but there's just enough light to see what he's up to. Man Spilling Seed on Damp Cellar Floor. Then here in this third panel, two men doing it, each with his three-fingered hand on the other's maulstick. This can be inked darkly because they wouldn't want to be seen. 3. Then having prepared it for painting he began to think what he would paint upon it that would frighten everyone that saw it, having the effect of the head of Medusa. So he brought for that purpose to his room, which no one entered but himself, lizards, grasshoppers, serpents, butterflies, locusts, bats, and other strange animals of the kind, and from them all he produced a great animal so horrible and fearful that it seemed to poison the air with its fiery breath. This he represented coming out of some dark rocks with venom issuing from its open jaws, fire from its eyes, and smoke from its nostrils, a monstrous and horrible thing indeed. Lives of the Painters: Leonardo. 4. Figure; wood, string, and found objects. Picasso.

Incisore. The cylinder, the sphere, the cone. Cézanne. The impact of an acute angle of a triangle on a circle promises an effect no less powerful than the finger of God touching the finger of Adam in Michelangelo. Kandinsky.

Fidelman, etcher, left a single engraving of the series called A Painter's Progress. Originally there were six copper plates, drypoint, all with their prints destroyed, how or why is not known. Only a single imperfect artist's proof entitled "The Cave" survives. This etching represents a painter at work, resemblance to whom may easily be guessed. Each night, according to a tattered diary he had kept for a while, he entered the cave in question through a cellar he had the key to, when all the lights in the old clapboard house, several boards missing, were out, curtains thickly drawn over each narrow window. The painter in the etching worked all night, night after night, inch by slow inch covering the rough limestone surface of the voluminous cave at the end of a labyrinth under the cellar, with intricate designs of geometric figures; and he left before dawn, his coming and going unknown to his sister, who lived in the house alone. The walls and part of the roof of the huge cave that he had been decorating for years and years, and estimated at least two more to go before his labors were ended, were painted in an extraordinary tapestry of simple figures in black, salmon, gold-yellow, sea-green, and apricot, although the colors cannot of course be discerned in the three-toned engraving—a rich design of circles and triangles, discrete or interlocking, of salmon triangles encompassed within apricot circles, and sea-green circles within pale gold-yellow triangles, blown like masses of autumn leaves over the firmament of the cave.

The painter of the cave, wearing a leafy loincloth as he labored, varied the patterns of the geometric design. He was at that time of his life engaged in developing a more intricate conception of circles within circles of various hues and shades including copper red and light olive; and to extend his art further, of triangles within triangles within concentric circles. He drove himself at his work, intending when his labor was done to climb the dark stairs ascending to his sister's first floor and tell her what he had accomplished in the cave below. Bessie, long a widow, all her children married and scattered across the continent, her oldest daughter in Montreal, lived, except for occasional visitors, mostly the doctor, alone in the old frame house she had come to as a young bride, in Newark, New Jersey. She was, at this time, ill and possibly dying. Nobody he could think of had told her artist-brother, but he figured he somehow knew. Call it intuition. It was his hope she would remain alive until he had completed his artwork of the cave and she could at last see how it had turned out.

Bessie, he would say, I did this for you and you know why.

Fidelman worked by the light of a single dusty 100-watt bulb, the old-fashioned kind with a glass spicule at the bottom, dangling from a wire from the ceiling of the cave, that he had installed when he first came there to paint. For a long time he had distrusted the bulb because he had never had to replace it, and sometimes it glowed like a waning moon after he had switched it off, making him feel slightly uneasy and a little lumpy in the chest. He suspected a presence, immanent or otherwise, around; though who or why, and under what circumstances, he could not say. Nothing or nobody substantial. Anyway, he didn't care for the bulb. He knew why when it began, one night, to speak to him. How does a bulb speak? With the sound of light. Fidelman for a while did not respond, first because he couldn't, his throat constricted; and second, because he suspected this might be he talking to himself; yet when it spoke again, this time he answered.

Fidelman, said the voice of, or from within, the bulb, why are you here such a long time in this cave? Painting—this we know—but why do you paint so long a whole cave? What kind of business is this?

Leaving my mark is what. For the ages to see. This place will someday be crowded with visitors at a dollar a throw. Mark my words.

But why in this way if there are better?

What would you suggest, for instance?

Whatever I suggest is too late now, but why don't you go at least upstairs and say hello to your sister who hasn't seen you in years? Go before it is too late, because she is now dying.

Not quite just yet I can't go, said the painter. I can't until my work is finished because I want to show her what I've accomplished once it's done.

Go up to her now, this is the last chance. Your work in this cave will take years yet. Tell her at least hello. What have you got to lose? To her it will be a wonderful thing.

No, I can't. It's all too complicated. I can't go till I've finished the job. The truth is I hate the past. It caught me unawares. I'd rather not see her just yet. Maybe next week or so.

It's a short trip up the stairs to say hello to her. What can you lose if it's only fourteen steps and then you're there?

It's too complicated, like I said. I hate the past.

So why do you blame her for this?

I don't blame anybody at all. I just don't want to see her. At least not just yet.

If she dies she's dead. You can talk all you want then but she won't answer you.

It's no fault of mine if people die. There's nothing I can do about it.

Nobody is talking about fault or not fault. All we are talking about is to go upstairs.

I can't I told you, it's too complicated, I hate the past, it caught me unawares. If there's anything to blame I don't blame her. I just don't want to see her is all, at least not just yet until my work here is done.

Don't be so proud, my friend. Pride ain't spinach. You can't eat it, so it won't make you grow. Remember what happened to the Greeks.

Praxiteles? He who first showed Aphrodite naked? Phidias, whose centaur's head is thought to be a self-portrait? Who have you got in mind?

No, the one that he tore out his eyes. Watch out for hubris. It's poison ivy. Trouble you got enough, you want also blisters? Also an electric bulb don't give so often advice so listen with care. When did you hear last that an electric bulb gave advice? Did I advise Napoleon? Did I advise Van Gogh? This is like a miracle, so why don't you take advantage and go upstairs?

Well, you've got a point there. There's some truth to it, I suppose. I might at that, come to think of it. As you say, it's not everybody who gets advice in this way. There's something biblical about it, if I may say. Furthermore, I'm not getting any younger and I haven't seen Bessie in years. Plus I do owe her something, after all. Be my Virgil, which way to up the stairs?

I will show you which way but I can't go with you. Up to a point but not further if you know what I mean. A bulb is a bulb. Light I got but not feet. After all, this is the Universe, everything is laws.

Fidelman slowly climbs up the stone, then wooden, stairs, lit generously from bottom clear to top by the bulb, and opens the creaking door into a narrow corridor. He walks along it till he comes to a small room where Bessie is lying in a sagging double bed.

Hello, Bessie, I've been downstairs most of the time, but I came up to say hello.

Why are you so naked, Arthur? It's winter outside.

It's how I am nowadays.

Arthur, said Bessie, why did you stop writing for so long? Why didn't you answer my letters?

I guess I had nothing much to write. Nothing much has happened to me. There wasn't much to say.

Remember how Mama used to give us an apple to eat with a slice of bread?

I don't like to remember those things anymore.

Anyway, thanks for coming up to see me, Arthur. It's a nice thing to do when a person is so alone. At least I know what you look like and where you are nowadays.

Bessie died and rose to heaven, holding in her heart her brother's hello.

Flights of circles, cones, triangles.

End of drypoint etching.

The ugly and plebeian face with which Rembrandt was ill-favored was accompanied by untidy and dirty clothes, since it was his custom, when working, to wipe his brushes on himself, and to do other things of a similar nature. Jakob Rosenberg.

If you're dead how do you go on living?

Natura morta: still life. Oil on paper.

1968

❧ B M ❧

An Exorcism

Fogel, a writer, had had another letter from Gary Simson, the would-be writer, a request as usual. He wrote fiction but hadn't jelled. Fogel, out of respect, saved letters from writers but was tempted not to include Simson although he had begun to publish. I am not his mentor, though he calls himself my student. If so, what have I taught him? In the end he placed the letter in his files. I have his others, he thought.

Eli Fogel was a better than ordinary writer but not especially "successful." He disliked the word. His productivity was limited by his pace, which, for reasons of having to breathe hard to enjoy life, was slow. Two and a half books in fifteen years, the half a paperback of undistinguished verse. My limp is symbolic, he thought. His leg had been injured in a bicycle accident as a youth, though with the built-up shoe the limp was less noticeable than when he hobbled around barefoot. He limped for his lacks. Fogel, for instance, regretted never having married, blaming this on his devotion to work. It's not that it has to be one or the other, but for me it's one or none. He was, mildly, a monomaniac. That simplified life but reduced it—what else? Still, he did not pity himself. It amused Fogel rather than not that the protagonists of his two published novels were married men with families, their wounds deriving from sources other than hurt members and primal loneliness. Imagination saves me, he thought.

Both his novels had received praise, though not much else; and Fogel had for the past six years labored on a third, about half completed. Since he declined to write reviews, lecture, or teach regularly, he ran into money problems. Fortunately he had from his father a small inheritance that came to five thousand annually, a shrinking sum in an inflated world; so Fogel reluctantly accepted summer-school invitations, or taught, somewhat on the prickly side, at writers' conferences, one or two a summer. With what he had he made do.

It was at one of these conferences, in Buffalo, in June, and at another in mid-August of the same summer, on the campus of a small college in the White Mountains, that the writer had met, and later renewed a friendship with, Gary Simson, then less than half Fogel's age; a friendship of sorts, mild, fallible, but for a while satisfying; that is to say, possessing some of the attributes and possibilities of friendship.

Gary, a slight glaze in his eyes as he listened to Fogel talk about writing, wanted, he seriously confessed with a worried brow, "more than anything," even "desperately," to be a writer—the desperation inciting goose bumps on Fogel's flesh, putting him off for a full fifteen minutes. He sat in depressed silence in his office as the youth fidgeted. "What's the rush?" the writer ultimately asked. "I've got to get there," the youth replied. "Get where?" "I want to be a good writer someday, Mr. Fogel." "It's a long haul, my boy," Eli Fogel said. "Make a friend of time. And steer clear of desperation. Desperate people tend to be bad writers, increasing desperation." He laughed a little, not unkindly. Gary sat nodding as though he had learned the lesson of his life. He was twenty-two, a curly-haired senior in college, with a broad fleshy face and frame. On his appearance at the Buffalo conference he wore a full reddish mustache drooping down the sides of his thick-lipped mouth. He shaved it off on meeting Fogel and then grew it again later in the summer. He was six feet tall and his height and breadth made him look older than he was, if not wiser. For a while after his talk with Fogel he pretended to be more casual about his work, one who skirted excess and got it right. He pretended to be Fogel a bit, amusing Fogel. He had never had a disciple before and felt affection for the boy. Gary livened things up for the writer. One could see him in the distance, coming with his yellow guitar. He strummed without distinction but sang fairly well, a tenor aspiring, related to art. "Sing me 'Ochi Chornye,' Gary," Fogel said, and the youth obliged as the older man became pleasantly melancholic, thinking what if he'd had a son. Touch a hand to a guitar and Fogel had a wet eye. And Gary offered services as well as devoted attention: got books Fogel needed from the library; drove him into town when he had errands to do;

could be depended on to retrieve forgotten lecture notes in his room
—as if it were in compensation, though Fogel required none, for the
privilege of sitting at his feet and plying him with questions about
the art of fiction. Fogel, touched by his amiability, all he had yet to
learn, by his own knowledge of the sadnesses of a writer's life, invited
him, usually with one or another of his friends, to his room for a
drink before dinner. Gary brought along a thick notebook to jot down
Fogel's table talk. He showed him the first sentence he had copied
down: "Imagination is not necessarily Id," causing the writer when
he read it to laugh uncomfortably. Gary laughed too. Fogel thought
the note taking silly but didn't object when Gary scribbled down long
passages, although he doubted he had wisdom of any serious sort to
offer. He was wiser in his work—one would be who revised often
enough. He wished Gary would go to his books for answers to some
of the questions he asked and stop treating poor Fogel like a guru.

"You can't dissect a writer to learn what writing is or entails.
One learns from experience, or should. I can't teach anyone to be a
writer, Gary—I've said that in my lectures. All I do here is talk about
some things I've learned and hope somebody talented is listening. I
always regret coming to these conferences."

"You can give insights, can't you?"

"Insights you can get from your mother."

"More specifically, if I might ask, what do you think of my
writing thus far, sir?"

Fogel reflected. "Promise you have—that's all I can say now,
but keep working."

"What should I work most for?"

"Search possibility in and out and beyond the fact. I have the
impression when I read your stories—the two in Buffalo and the one
you've given me here—that you remember or research too much.
Memory is an ingredient, Gary, not the whole stew; and don't make
the error some do of living life as though it were a future fiction.
Invent, my boy."

"I'll certainly try, Mr. Fogel." He seemed worried.

Fogel lectured four mornings a week at eight-thirty so he could
spend the rest of the day at work. His large bright room in a guest
house close to a pine grove, whose fragrance he breathed as he wrote
on a cracked table by a curtained window, was comfortable even on
hot afternoons. He worked every day, half day on Sundays, quitting
as a rule around four; then soaked in a smallish stained tub, dressed
leisurely, whistling through his teeth, in a white flannel suit fifteen

years in service, and waited, holding a book before his nose, for someone to come for a drink. During the last week of the White Mountain
conference he saw Gary each night. Sometimes they drove to a movie
in town, or walked after supper along a path by a stream, the youth
stopping to jot down in his notebook sentences given off by Fogel,
chaff as well as grain. They went on until the mosquitoes thickened
or Fogel's limp began to limp. He wore a Panama hat, slightly yellowed, and white shoes he whitened daily, one with a higher heel
than the other. Fogel's pouched dark eyes, even as he spoke animatedly, were contemplative, and he listened with care to Gary though
he didn't always hear. In the last year or two he had lost weight and
his white suit hung on his shoulders. He looked small by Gary's side,
although he was shorter by only three inches. And once the youth, in
a burst of vitality or affection, his one imaginative act of the summer,
lifted Fogel at the hips and held him breathless in the air. The writer
gazed into Gary's gold-flecked eyes; that he found them doorless to
the self filled him with remorse.

Or Gary drove them in his noisy Peugeot to a small piano bar
by a crossroads several miles the other side of town, sometimes in the
company of one or two students, occasionally a colleague but usually
students; and this made it a fuller pleasure because Fogel enjoyed
being with women. Gary, who had a talent for acquiring pretty girls,
one night brought along one of the loveliest Fogel had ever seen. The
girl, about twenty-five, with streaked dyed-blond and dark hair wore
a red dress on her long-waisted body, the breasts ample, loose, her
buttocks shapely, sweet. A rare find indeed; but the youth, senseless,
sullen, or stoned, gave her scant attention. He glanced at her once in
a while as if trying to remember where he had met her. Sad-eyed,
she drank Scotch on the rocks, gnawing her lip as she watched his
eyes roving over the dancers on the floor. Too bad she doesn't know
how much I appreciate her, Fogel mused.

Where does he get so many attractive girls—he had been equally
effective in Buffalo—and why doesn't he bring the same one two
nights running? This blessed creature in red would last me half a
lifetime. The youth's taste in women could not be faulted—but he
seemed, after a short time, unmoved by them and yawned openly,
although it was rumored he enjoyed an active heterosexual life. He
has so many and goes through them so quickly—where does he think
one learns longing? Where does poetry come from? She's too good for
him, he thought, not knowing exactly why, unless she was good for
him. Ah youth, ah summer. Once again he seriously considered the

possibility of marriage. After all, how old is forty-six—not, in any case, *old*. A good twenty-five or thirty years to go, enough to raise a family.

On what?

For his companion Fogel had asked along a schoolteacher from his class, a Miss Rudel from Manhattan, unmarried but not lacking a sense of humor; nor did she take her dabbling in fiction seriously, a pleasant change from the desperate ladies who haunted the conference. But he looked her over and found her wanting, then found himself wanting.

Perhaps because the evening had acquired a sexual tone he remembered Lucy Matthews, a desperate writer presently attending his lectures. About a week ago, after going through a shoe box full of exasperating stories she had left with him, representing the past year's work, he had told her bluntly, "Miss Matthews, let's not pretend that writing is a substitute for talent." And when she quietly gasped, cracking the knuckles of one hand, then of the other, he went on: "If you are out to save your soul, there are better ways."

The lady gazed bleakly at Fogel; a slim woman with fair figure, tense neck, and anxious eyes.

"But, Mr. Fogel, how does one go about finding out the extent of her talent? Some of my former professors told me I write capable stories, yet you seem to think I'm hopeless." Tears brimmed in her eyes.

Fogel was about to soften his judgment but warned himself it would be less than honest to encourage her. She was from Cedar Falls and this was her fourth conference of the summer. He vowed again to give them up forever.

Lucy Matthews plucked a Kleenex out of her handbag and quietly cried, waiting for perhaps a good word, but the writer, sitting in silence, had none to offer. She got up and hurriedly left the office.

But at ten o'clock that night, dressed in a taffeta party dress, her hair brushed into a bright sheen, briskly perfumed, Lucy tapped on Fogel's house door. Accepting his surprised invitation to enter, after three silent sips of bourbon and water, she lifted her noisy dress over her head and stood there naked.

"Mr. Fogel," she whispered passionately, "you aren't afraid to tell the truth. Your work represents art. I feel that if I could hold you in my arms I would be close to both—art and truth."

"It just isn't so," Fogel replied as he fought off the feeling that he had stepped into a Sherwood Anderson story. "I would like to sleep with you, frankly, but not for the reasons stated. If you had said, 'Fogel, you may be an odd duck but you've aroused me tonight and I would gladly go to bed with you'—could you say that?"

"If you prefer fellation—" Lucy whispered tensely.

"Thank you kindly," he said with tenderness, "I prefer the embrace of a woman. Would you care to answer my question?"

Shivering around the shoulders, Lucy Matthews came to her finest moment at writing conferences.

"I can't truly say so."

"Ah, too bad," Fogel sighed. "Anyway, I'm privileged you saw fit to undress in my presence."

She slipped on the dress at her feet and departed. Fogel especially regretted the loss because the only woman he had slept with that summer, a young chambermaid in a Buffalo hotel he had stayed at in June, had hurt him dreadfully.

"Are you dreaming about something, Mr. Fogel?" Gary asked.

"Only vaguely," Fogel replied.

"An idea for a story, I bet?"

"It may come to that."

When the conference ended, Gary, waiting outside the lecture barn to take Fogel to the train, asked him, "Will I ever be a good writer, do you think, Mr. Fogel?"

"It depends on commitment. You'll have to prove yourself."

"I will if you have faith in me."

"Even if I have no faith in you. Who is Eli Fogel, after all, but a man trying to make his own way through the woods."

Fogel smiled at the youth and, though not knowing exactly why, felt he had to say, "One must grow spirit, Gary."

The youth blinked in the strong sunlight.

"I'm glad we're both writers, Mr. Fogel."

•

The next spring, a wet springtime, Fogel, wandering in a damp hat and coat in the periodical room of the New York Public Library, without forethought plucked off the shelf a college magazine and came upon Gary Simson in the table of contents, as the author of a story called "Travails of a Writer." He was surprised because they were in correspondence and Gary hadn't told him he had published his first story. Maybe it wasn't such a good one? Reading it quickly Fogel found it wasn't; but that wasn't why Gary hadn't mentioned it. The reason depressed him.

The story concerned a Mr. L. E. Vogel, a sarcastic, self-centered, although not thoroughly bad-natured middle-aged writer with a club-foot, who wore in summertime a white suit, the pants of which dripped over his heels, an old-fashioned straw hat, and the same yellow knitted necktie, day after day. He was a short man with a loud laugh that embarrassed him, and he walked a good deal though he limped. One summer he had taught at a writers' conference in Syracuse, New York. There the writer had fallen for a college girl chambermaid at the hotel he had lived in during his two weeks of lecturing. She had slept with him for kicks after learning he had published two novels. Once was enough for her, but Vogel, having tasted young flesh, was hooked hard. He fell in love with the girl, constantly sought her presence—a blond tease of twenty—with solemn offers of marriage, until she became sick of him. To get him off her back she arranged with a boyfriend to enter his room with a passkey and give him a bad time. Vogel, soaking in his afternoon tub, heard someone shout, "Fire, everybody out!" He climbed out of the bath, was grabbed by the arm and shoved into the hall by the boyfriend, who pulled the door shut after him and disappeared down the stairs. The naked writer wandered like a half-drowned animal in the huge hotel hall, knocking at doors that were slammed in his face, until he found an elderly lady who handed him a blanket to cover himself and phoned the manager for a key to his room. Vogel, heartbroken that the girl had done this to him—he understood at once she had contrived the plot and for what reason—packed and left Syracuse a full week before the conference had ended.

"Poor Vogel swore off love to keep on writing."

End of "Travails of a Writer."

Arriving home, Eli Fogel dashed a white pitcher of daffodils to the kitchen floor, and kicked with his bad leg at the shards and flowers.

"Swine! Have I taught you nothing?"

Incensed, humiliated to the hilt (the story revived the memory; he suffered from both), Fogel, in a rare rage, cursed out Gary, wished on him a terrifying punishment. But reason prevailed and he wrote him, instead, a scalding letter.

Where had he got the story? Probably it was rife as gossip. He pictured the girl and her friend regaling all who would hear, screaming over the part where the hairy-chested satyr wanders in a wet daze in the hotel hallway. Gary might easily have heard it from them or friends of theirs. Or perhaps he had slept with the girl and she had confided it directly. Good God, had *he* put her up to it? No, probably not.

Why, then, had he written it? Why hadn't he spared Fogel this mortification, though it was obvious he had not expected him to find the story and read it? That wasn't the point; the point was he had not refrained—out of friendship—from writing it. So much for friendship. He detested the thought that the boy had sucked up to him all summer to collect facts for the piece. Or possibly he had heard the story and been tempted by it, Fogel hoped, *after* the White Mountain conference. He had probably harbored the "idea" during the summer but did not decide to write it until he got back to San Francisco, where he went to college. All he had to do was salt the anecdote with some details of appearance, a few mannerisms, and the tale was as good as written, acceptable at once for publication in the college quarterly. Maybe Gary had thought of it as a sort of homage: this good writer I know portrayed as human being. He hadn't been able to resist. After a summer of too much talk of writing he had felt the necessity of having something immediately in print, no matter what. He had got it down on paper almost wholly as received. It invented nothing, in essence a memoir once removed.

When he felt he had regained objectivity, Fogel sat at his desk facing the landlady's garden behind the house and, dipping his fountain pen into black ink, began a letter to Gary: "I congratulate you on the publication of your first story although I cannot rejoice in it."

He tore that up and on another sheet wrote:

Your story, as is, signified little and one wonders why it was written. Perhaps it represents the desperate act of one determined to break into print without the patience, the art—ultimately—to transmute a piece of gossip into a fiction; and in the process, incidentally, betraying a friend. If this poor thing indicates the force and depth of your imagination, I suggest you give up writing.

L. E. Vogel, indeed! Yours truly, Eli Fogel.

P.S. Look up "travail." It's an experience not easy to come by.

After sealing the letter he didn't send it. We all have our hangups, Fogel thought. Besides, life isn't that long. He tore it up and sent a Picasso postcard instead, a woman with six faces sitting on a chamber pot.

Dear Gary, I read your story in *SF Unicorn*. I wish I could say it was a good story, but it isn't, not so good as the ones I read last summer that you couldn't get published. I wish I had had your opportunity to write about L. E. Vogel; I would have done him justice.

He received, airmail, a four-page, single-spaced letter from Gary.

To tell the honest truth I *was* kind of anxious about my writing. I couldn't finish a story for months after the W.M. conference, and without doubt took the easy way out. All I can say is I hope you will forgive and forget. Once I reread the story in the *Unicorn* I prayed that you wouldn't see it. If I have hurt our friendship, which I truly hope I haven't, I am willing to try to do better if you have the patience. I would like to be a better friend.

Also I recently read in an article about Thomas Wolfe that he said it was all right to write about other people you might know, but it's wrong to include their address and phone number. As you know, Mr. Fogel, I have a lot to learn about writing, that's for sure. As for what you could have done with the same material, please don't compare your magnificent powers with my poor ones.

I enclose a picture of my latest bride as well as one of myself.

In the envelope was an underexposed snapshot of a long-haired brunette in briefest bikini, sitting on a blanket by Gary's yellow guitar, on a California beach. Resting back on her arms, she stared distantly, certainly not happily, at the birdie; lost, as it were, to time and tide. She looked worn, cheerless, as though she had been had, and was, in her own mind, past having. She seemed to understand what she had experienced. She was, for Fogel, so true, lovely, possible, present, so beautifully formed, that he thought of her as a work of art and audibly sighed.

Gary, the hero himself of the other, overexposed colored snap, probably taken by the discontented lady herself, wore white bathing trunks, prominent genitals, and a handsome sunburned body; spare, dark, leaner than he was when Fogel had seen him last. His eyes staring blankly at the camera contradicted the smile on his face. Perhaps he was not looking at the unhappy lady but through her. The youth darkened in bright sunlight as the beholder beheld, or was Fogel prejudiced?

On the back of his picture Gary had scrawled, "You may not recognize me so well. I've changed, I've lost weight."

"What do you mean 'bride'?" Fogel wrote in the postscript of his reply forgiving Gary. He had urged patience in writing. "If you push time, time pushes you. One has less control."

"Not in the married sense," Gary explained when he appeared in person in Fogel's flat, in dungaree jacket and field boots, wearing a six-day growth of beard after driving practically nonstop across the country in a new secondhand station wagon, during the winter recess. He had brought his guitar and played "Ochi Chornye" for Fogel.

They were at first stiff with each other. Fogel, despite good will, felt distaste for the youth, but by degrees relented and they talked exhaustively. The older man had, more than once, to set aside the image of himself dripping along the hotel hallway before he could renew affection for Gary. The guitar helped. His singing sometimes brought tears to the eyes. Ah, the human voice, nothing like it for celebrating or lamenting life. I must have misjudged his capacity to relate, or else he does it better. And why should I bear him a grudge for his errors, considering those I make myself?

It was therefore freer talk than they had engaged in last summer, as though between equals, about many more interesting matters than when Gary was hastily taking it down to preserve for humanity. Yet as they conversed, particularly when Fogel spoke of writing, the youth's fingers twitched as though he were recording the older man's remarks in an invisible notebook, causing him later to say, "Don't worry if you can't remember word for word, Gary. Have you read Proust? Even when he remembers he invents."

"Not as of yet, but he's on my list."

There was still something naïve about him, though he was bright enough and gave the impression that he had experienced more than one ordinarily would have at his age. Possibly this was an effect of the size of his corpus, plenty of room to stuff in experience. Fogel was at the point of asking what women meant to him, but it was a foolish question so he refrained; Gary was young, let him find his way. Fogel would not want to be that young again.

The youth remained for three days in the small guest room in Fogel's rent-controlled flat in the three-story brick house on West Ninth Street. Gary one night invited over some friends, Fogel adding two or three former students, including Miss Rudel. A noisy crowded party flowered, especially pleasurable to Fogel when Gary sang, strumming his guitar, and a young man with a thin beard and hair to his shoulders accompanied him on a recorder. Marvelous combinations, inventions, the new youth dreamed up. The guests played records they had brought along and danced. A girl who smelled heavily of pot, dancing barefoot, kissed Fogel and drew him into the circle of her gyrations. The steps weren't so hard, he decided, really they were no steps, so he pulled off his shoes and danced in his black socks, his limp as though choreographed in. At any rate, no one seemed to notice and Fogel had an enjoyable time. He again felt grateful to the youth for lifting him, almost against his will, out of his solitude.

On the morning he left, Gary, bathed, shaved, fragrantly lotioned, in white T-shirt and clean cords, tossed a duffel bag into the station wagon and stood talking on the lowest stoop step with Fogel, who had come out to see him off. The writer sensed Gary was leading up to something, although he was ostensibly saying goodbye. After some introductory noises the youth apologized for bringing "this" up but he had a request to make, if Fogel didn't mind. Fogel, after momentary hesitation, didn't mind. Gary said he was applying for admission to one or two writing centers in universities on the West Coast and he sort of hoped Fogel would write him a letter of recommendation. Maybe two.

"I don't see why not."

"Hey thanks, Mr. Fogel, and I don't want to bug you but I hope you won't mind if I put your name down as a reference on other applications now and then?"

"What for, Gary? Remember, I'm a working writer." He felt momentarily uneasy, as though he were being asked to extend credit beyond credit earned.

"I promise I'll keep it to the barest minimum. Just if I apply for a fellowship to help me out financially, or something like that."

"That seems all right. I'll consider each request on its merits."

"That's exactly what I want you to do, Mr. Fogel."

Before the youth drove off, Fogel was moved to ask him why he wanted to be a writer.

"To express myself as I am and also create art," Gary quickly replied. "To convey my experience so that I become part of my readers' experience, so, as you might say, neither of us is alone."

Fogel nodded.

"Why are you writing?"

"Because it's in me to write. Because I can't not write." Fogel laughed embarrassedly.

"That doesn't contradict what I said."

"I wouldn't want to contradict it." He did not say Gary remembered his summer notes perhaps better than he knew.

The youth thrust forth his hand impulsively. "I'm grateful for your friendship as well as hospitality, Mr. Fogel."

"Call me Eli if you like."

"I'll certainly try," Gary said huskily.

Several months later he wrote from the Coast: "Is morality a necessary part of fiction? I mean, does it have to be? A girl I go with here said it does. I would like to have your opinion. Fondly, Gary."

"It is as it becomes aesthetic," Fogel replied, wondering if the girl was the brunette in the bikini. "Another way to put it is that nothing that is art is merely moral."

"I guess what I meant to ask," Gary wrote, "is does the artist *have* to be moral?"

"Neither the artist nor his work."

"Thanks for being so frank, Mr. Fogel."

In rereading these letters before filing them, Fogel noticed that Gary always addressed him by his last name.

Better that way.

In two years Fogel lost four pounds and wrote seventy more pages of his novel. He had hoped to write one hundred and fifty pages but had slowed down. Perfection comes hard to an imperfectionist. He had visions of himself dying before the book was completed. It was a terrible thought: Fogel seated at the table, staring at his manuscript, pen in hand, the page ending in a blot. He had been blocked several months last fall and winter but slowly wrote himself out of it. Afterwards he loved the world a bit better.

He hadn't seen Gary during this time, though they still corresponded. Fogel left his letters lying around unopened for months before answering them. The youth had written in November that he was driving East before Christmas and could he call on Fogel? He had answered better not until the writing was going well once more. Gary then wrote, "We must have some kind of mutual ESP, because the same thing has happened to me. I mean it's mostly because I have been uptight about future worries after I get my M.F.A. in June, especially money worries. Otherwise I've had two stories published, as you know, in the last year." (Both troubled Fogel: unrisen loaves. Gary said they had been "definitely invented." One was about a sex-starved man and the other about a sex-starved woman.) "And I've been thinking ahead because I want to get to work on a novel and wonder if you would like to recommend me to the MacDowell Colony for a six months' stay so I can get started on it?"

Fogel wrote: "Gary, I've recommended you for everything in sight because I thought you ought to have a chance to prove yourself. But I'd be less than honest if I didn't admit I've been doing it uneasily the last one or two times because there's such a thing as overextending good will. I'll think it over if you can send me something really good in the way of a fiction, either a new story or chapter or two of your novel."

He got in reply, hastily, Gary. The youth appeared several days later, as Fogel was in the street on his way to the liquor store on the corner. He heard the bleat of a horn, a dark green microbus drew up to the curb, and Gary Simson hopped out of the door and pumped the writer's hand.

"I have this new story for you." He held up a black dispatch case.

Though he smiled broadly he looked as though he hadn't slept for a week. His face was worn, eyes hardened, as if something in his nature had deepened. He was on the verge of desperate, Fogel thought.

"I'm sorry I couldn't warn you but I came up from the Coast suddenly, and as you know, you have no phone." He paused, suffering his usual opening stiffness although Fogel returned his smile.

"Have you had supper, Gary?"

"Not as of yet."

"We'll go upstairs and have a bit."

"Fantastic," Gary said. "And it's a pleasure to see you after all this time gone. You're looking swell but a little thin and pasty-faced."

"Vicissitudes, Gary. Not to mention endless labor, which is the only way I seem able to survive. One ought to be careful how he creates his life's order."

He was about to suggest calling a few people for a party but thought it premature.

They ate a simple meal. Fogel cooked a tasty soufflé. There was salad, Italian bread, and wine. Both ate hungrily and smoked Gary's cigars over coffee.

In Fogel's study the youth snapped open the dispatch case lock he had been fiddling with—too bad it wasn't the guitar—and they were at once alertly attentive to each other. Fogel detected an odor of sweat and Gary proved it by wiping his face, then twice around the flushed neck with his handkerchief.

"This is the first draft of a story I did the other day, my first in months. As I wrote you in my letter, I just wasn't making the scene for a while. I got the idea for this story the night before last. I was planning to drop in on you yesterday but instead spent the day on twenty cups of coffee in this girl's room while she was out working, and finally knocked off the story. It feels good to me. Would you care to hear it, Mr. Fogel?"

"A first draft?" asked Fogel in disappointment. "Why don't you finish it and let me read it then?"

"I would certainly do that if the closing date for my application wasn't hitting me in the eye this coming Monday. I'd really like to work on it another week at the very least, and the only reason I suggest reading it to you now is so you will have a quick idea of the merits of what I've done with it so far."

"Well, then let me read it myself," Fogel said. "I get more out of it that way."

"My typing isn't so hot, as you well know, and it'll be hard for you to make out the corrections in my lousy handwriting. I'd better read it to you."

Fogel nodded, removing his shoes to ease his feet. So did Gary. He sat cross-legged on the couch in tennis socks, holding his papers. Fogel, rocking slowly in his rocker, gazed melancholically at the pile of his own manuscript on the writing table. Remembering his youthful aspirations, the writer wanted Gary's story to be good.

The youth brushed his lips with a wet thumb. "I haven't got a sure title yet but I was thinking of calling it 'Three Go Down.'" He began to read and Fogel's rocker stopped creaking.

The narrator of the story was George, a graduate student at Stanford who had driven to New York and, having nothing to do one spring day, had looked up Connie, who had been in love with him last summer. She lived in the West Village, in an apartment with two friends, Grace and Buffy, pretty girls; and soon George, while eating with them, on learning that none of the girls was going out that night, had decided to sleep with each of them, one after the other. He wanted it to be a test of himself. Connie, he figured, he had been in before and knew the way back. Grace was uneasy when he looked her over, which he thought of as an advantage. Buffy, the best looking of the lot, seemed a cool drink of water, aloof or pretending it, maybe impossible, but he wouldn't think of her as yet. It was a long night and there was no hurry.

George invited Connie for a walk and later bought her a drink in a bar on Sullivan Street. While they were at the bar he told her he hadn't forgotten last summer in Bloomington, Indiana. Connie called him a shit for bringing it up. George, after saying nothing, said it had been one of the best summers of his life. He then became deeply silent. They had a second drink and in the street she softened to him and walked close by his side.

It was a warm airy evening and they wandered in the Village streets. George said it was his impression that Buffy was a pothead, but Connie said it was ridiculous, Buffy was the really stable one of them. She worked for a youth opportunity program as secretary in charge of anything. Her father had been killed in the Korean War and she was devoted to her widowed mother and two younger sisters in Spokane.

"What about Grace?"

Connie admitted that Buffy had a lot more patience with Grace than she had. Grace's problems, though she didn't say what they were, were more than Connie cared to contend with. "Even when she has a good time she comes home in a funk and pulls out some more of her eyelashes, one by one, while sitting at the mirror."

After a while George told Connie that he had loved her last summer but hadn't been willing to admit it to himself. His father had been hooked into an early marriage and he didn't want that to happen to him; the old man had regretted it all his life. Connie again called him a shit but let him kiss her when he wanted to.

When she said she would sleep with him George said there was a mattress in his bus and why bother going upstairs? Connie laughed and said she had never made love in a microbus but was willing to try if he parked in a quiet, private place.

In the bus he gave it to her the way he remembered she liked it.

Connie went to bed with a headache. She had said he could stay in the living room till morning and no later. "That's our rule and Buffy doesn't like it if we break it." George sat on the sofa, reading a magazine for a while, then looked into Grace's room. Her door was open and he went in without knocking. Most of Grace's eyelashes were gone. She wore a terry-cloth robe and said she didn't mind talking to George so long as he kept his machismo in his pants. She wasn't careful with her robe and he saw her large bruised breasts through the nightgown.

That's her bag, George thought.

He started talking sex with her and told her about some girl-friends he had in California who had given it to him in various interesting ways. She listened with slack mouth and uneasy eyes while drying her hair with a large towel.

George asked her where the gin was, he would make the drinks. She said she didn't want a drink. He asked her if she wanted to split a joint.

"I'm not interested," Grace said.

"What interests you?" George said.

"I'll bet you slept with Connie."

"Why don't you ask her?"

He then said he knew what interested her. George got up, and though she grabbed his hands, he freed one, forced her chin up, and French-kissed her. She shoved him away, her robe falling open. George, pretending he was a prizefighter, went into a crouch, ducked, then feinted with his left. With his right hand he grabbed her breast and twisted hard. Grace gasped and was about to cry. Instead, after wavering hesitations, searching his face, she swung to him, her eyes unfocused, grinning. When they kissed she bit his lip. George punched her between the legs. Grace came close again with a quiet moan. He began to pull off her robe but she caught his hands, then shut the door.

"Not here," Grace whispered.

"Put on your dress and meet me downstairs."

She came down in a green dress, wearing nothing underneath but her bruises. Grace stepped into the bus. "I love you," she said.

George handed her his belt and said she could hit him a few whacks but not too hard.

Buffy had been reading in bed. She said come in when he knocked but, seeing who it was, drew up her legs and asked him not to since it was late and she had to go to work in the morning. George offered her one of the joints he had got from Grace but Buffy said to cool it. He asked her if she would mind talking for a few minutes, then he'd go. She said she would mind. George then told her he was leaving for the war in the morning.

She asked him why was that, they were sending few draftees in.

"My draft board was saving me up. They were sore at all the postponements I had requested."

"Why don't you refuse to serve?"

He said he had been a physical coward all his life and it was time to get over it. She called it a useless, unjust war, but George said you only died once. He offered her the joint again and she lit up. Buffy smoked for a few minutes, then said it wasn't turning her on.

"Nor me either," George admitted. "Why don't you get dressed and come out for a walk? It's a nice night."

When she asked him hadn't he done enough walking with Connie and Grace, he told her she was the one who really aroused him.

"Before I left I wanted to tell you."

"I must be five years older than you."

"That doesn't change my feelings."

"What malarkey," she said.

George said goodbye. He thanked her for the supper and for talking to him. "See you after the war."

"Connie said you were staying here tonight."

He said he would be sleeping in his bus downstairs. He had to be at Fort Dix at seven, and before that had to deliver the bus to a friend who would drive him to Jersey, then keep it for him while he was away. He was leaving at 5:00 a.m., and no sense waking everybody in the house.

"Are you afraid of death?" Buffy asked him.

"Who wouldn't be?"

He shut her door and went down the stairs. In the bus George, plugging in the shaver, began to shave for the morning. There was a tap on the door. It was Buffy in skirt and sweater, ready for a walk. Her hair in a coil at the neck fell over her right breast. She wore a golden bracelet high up on her left arm.

When they returned it was still a warm breezy night. After talking quietly awhile they entered the microbus. George plowed her three times and the third time she finally came.

As they lay on the narrow mattress, smoking, she asked him whether he had also had Connie and Grace that night, and George admitted it.

"Three go down."

That was the story.

What have I fostered? Fogel thought.

•

"Ah," said the writer, his bad leg trembling. He stepped into his slippers to pour himself a drink and was angered by the empty bourbon bottle. He drank a long unsatisfactory glass of water.

Gary had finished strong and was at the edge of the couch, his feet turned inward. He was observing his tennis socks, occasionally darting glances at Fogel.

"You like?" he finally had to ask. "I don't mind if you slog it to me so long as it's the truth."

"I guess Connie's right in characterizing George as a shit?"

"Up to a point, an anti-hero is an anti-hero," George explained defensively. "What the story means is that's how the crow flies, or words of that effect. In other words, c'est la vie. But how do you like it is what I want to know."

Fogel sat motionless in his rocker.

"I wish you were more than a walking tape recorder of your personal experiences, Gary."

He did not accuse him of having lived the experience to record it, though the thought was distastefully on his mind.

Gary laced up his shoes, a glaze of annoyance in his eyes.

"I don't see what's so bad about that. You yourself once said that story material has no pedigree of any kind. You told me it depends on what the writer does with it."

"That's right," said Fogel. "To be honest, I would have to say that, all in all, this story seems an improvement over your last two. It's a compelling narrative."

"Well, that's a lot better, Mr. Fogel."

"As for the recommendation, I want to think about it. I'm not sure."

Gary rose, waving both arms. "Jesus, Mr. Fogel, give me a break. What am I going to live on for the next year? I have no father who left *me* a trust fund of five thousand bucks a year as you told me your father did for you."

"You have me there," said Fogel, rising from the rocker. "I've got to have a drink. I was on my way to the liquor store when you drove up."

Gary offered to go for the bottle but Fogel wouldn't hear of it.

The writer limped down the stairs in his slippers. At the curb stood the green bus. The sight of it nauseated him.

He's no friend of mine.

He went to the corner and on an impulse returned to the bus to try the door handle. The door was open. The back seats had been removed and on the floor lay a battered pink-and-gray thin-striped mattress.

In the liquor store Fogel bought a fifth of bourbon. Stepping into Gary's bus he pulled the door shut. The curtains were drawn. He did not flick on the light.

As he opened the whiskey bottle, Fogel, as though surprised by what he was about to do, told himself, "I have the better imagination."

On his knees, using a small silver penknife he kept to sharpen pencils, the writer thoroughly slashed the mattress and sloshed whiskey over it. He lit the soaked cotton batting with several matches. The mattress stank as it burned with a blue flame.

Fogel then went upstairs and told Gary he had entered his story to give it a more judicious ending.

After the firemen had extinguished the blaze and the youth had driven off in his smoky bus, the writer took his letters out of the folder in his files and tore them up.

He got one last communication from Gary, enclosing a magazine with the published "Three Go Down" much as he had written it in the first draft. Amid the pages he had inserted some leaves of poison ivy.

1968

❧ B M ❧

Glass Blower of Venice

Venice, floating city of green and golden canals. Fidelman floated too, from stem to stern. When the sirocco relentlessly blew in late autumn the island dipped on ancient creaking piles toward the outer isles, then gently tipped to the mainland against the backwash of oily waters. The ex-painter, often seasick in the municipal garbage boat, fished with a net out of the smelly canals, dead rats and lettuce leaves. He had come for the Biennale and stayed on.

November fog settled on the webbed-canaled and narrow-streeted city, obscuring campanile, church steeples, and the red-tiled roofs of houses tilted together from opposite sides of streets. Oars splashing, he skirted the mist-moving vaporetti, his shouts and curses opposing their horns and the tolling bell buoys in the lagoon. For Fidelman no buoy bells tolled, no church bells either; he kept no track of tide or time. On All Souls' Day, unable to resist, he rowed after a black-and-silver funeral barge and cortege of draped mourning gondolas moving like silent arrows across the water to San Michele, gloomy cypressed isle of the dead; the corpse of a young girl in white laid stiff in a casket covered with wreaths of hothouse flowers guarded by wooden angels. She waits, whatever she waited for, or sought, or hungered for, no longer. Ah, i poveri morti, though that depends on how you look at it. He had looked too long.

Fidelman, December ferryman, ferried standing passengers, their heads in mist, to the opposite rainy shore of the Grand Canal. Which-ever shore. The wet winter rain drummed on the crooked roofs of the façade-eroded palazzi standing in undulating slime-green algae; and upon moving clusters of black bobbing umbrellas in the dark streets and marketplaces. The ex-painter wandered wet-hatted, seeking in shop windows who knows what treat the tourists hadn't coveted and bought. Venice was full of goods he hungered for and detested. Yet he sought an object of art nobody would recognize but Fidelman.

In January the cold swollen tides of the Adriatic rose again over the Mole, swirling a meter deep on the Piazza and flooding the pavimento of San Marco. If you had to, you could swim to the altar. Gondolas stealthily glided over the Stones of Venice, wet Bride of the Sea, drowning greenly an inch or two annually as Fidelman, a cold fish in his thin pants, inch by inch also drowned, envisioning Tintoretto: "Venice Overwhelmed by Tidal Wave."

The rain blew away before the sunlit cold but not the pools and ponds, more than one campo alongside open water or canal, flooded. Fidelman staked a claim, having been fired from cross-canal transportation on the complaint of two patriotic gondoliers, and now did his ferrying piggyback for one hundred lire per person, skinny old men half price if they didn't grip him too tightly around the neck. He had once read of a fiendish beggar who had strangled and drowned a good samaritan carrying him across a flooded brook. Fat people he served last, after he had ferried across the others on line, though they roundly berated him for prejudice, or offered twice the going rate. One aristocratic huge old dame with a voice that rose out of a tuba belabored him with her slender silk umbrella.

Fidelman waded in hip boots through high water glinting like shards of broken mirror in the freezing winter sunlight, and deposited his customers on dry ground, whence they proceeded hurriedly along narrow streets and alleys. Occasionally while transporting a female he gave her a modified feel along the leg, which roused no response through winter clothing; still it was good for the morale. One attractive, long-nosed, almost Oriental-eyed young Venetian woman who mounted his back began at once to giggle, and laughed, unable to control it, mirthfully as he slowly sloshed across the pond. She sat on Fidelman, enjoying the ride, her rump bumping his, cheek pressed to his frozen ear, hugging him casually, a pair of shapely black-stocking legs clasped in the crooks of his arms; and when he tenderly set her down, his penis erect, athrob, she kissed him affectionately and hastily went her way. As Fidelman watched she turned back, smiling sadly, as though they had once been lovers and the affair was ended. Then she waved goodbye and walked on. He wished she hadn't, for he was after a while in love with her.

When the water receded as the bora roared, drying the city, uncovering here and there a drowned cat, the winter light sprang up crystal clear as Fidelman, once more jobless, holding on to his hat—you can't chase them on the canals—sought his lady, to no avail. He searched from the Public Gardens to the Slaughter House and on both sides of the humpbacked Grand Canal. And he haunted the little square of blessed memory where he had once carried her across the wet water, chain-smoking used butts from a pocketful in his overcoat as he watched a steam-breathed sweeper sweeping at the mud with a twig broom; but she never appeared. A few of his former clients passed by, all ignoring him but the large aristocratic lady, who called him a son-of-a-dog-in-heat. You can't win them all.

Afterwards, wandering along the Mercerie in the early evening, through a shop window hung with wires dripping strings of glass beads and trinkets, he had the sudden sense he had glimpsed her, saw himself reflected in her large dark eyes. If he was truly conscious she was standing behind a counter, this slim-bodied, slant-eyed, long-nosed, handsome Venetian, staring at him as though contemplating the mark of fate in the face of a stranger. Then taking another swift look and this time recognizing who he was, she lifted a frightened hand to her bosom and turned abruptly away. He ducked close to the glass under the beads, pawing the window as though to see her better, but she was no longer there; the shop was empty. Fidelman flung away a good butt and entered. The shop was crowded, its shelves laden with glass knickknacks, baubles, Madonnas, medallions, crap for tourists, which proved nothing, although he wondered if she had disappeared for reasons of taste.

Where the woman had been now stood a nearsighted man past sixty, in a gray suit, with puffy brows and potbelly, who gazed at the former ferryman in surprise, if not distaste—as though he knew he was there for no good cause—yet courteously inquired if he could assist him. Fidelman, secretly shivering, modestly priced a vase or two, politely listened to the verdict, nodded, bowed, casting a wild look through the open door into the rear room, where a corpulent glass blower sat at a table working with a small torch, in the process of creating a green glass snake; but no one else. After desperately trying to think what else to do, pretending to be thoughtfully counting the change in his pocket though they both knew he had none, then asking if he could use the gabinetto and being refused, Fidelman thanked the shopkeeper and left. He had visions of her disappearing in a mist. The next day, and every day for two weeks thereafter, he passed the shop seven or eight times daily. The shopkeeper once in exasperation thrust his arm at him in an obscene gesture but otherwise paid no attention. Fidelman never saw his dream girl in the shop. He had doubts he ever had: trompe l'oeil, mirage, déjà vu, or something of the sort.

He then gave her up, no easy trick if you had nothing. Like blowing kisses or kissing blows. Eh, Fidelman, you old cocker, there was a time you would have held on longer. On to what? I had nothing, I gave up nothing. Nothing from nothing equals nothing. Say more and it's confronting death. On the other hand spring came early that year: to his surprise flowers looking out of house windows. Young jewel-like leaves of myrtles and laurels rose above ancient brick walls in back alleys. Subtle pinks, apricots, lavenders streaked an underwater architecture of floating Gothic and Moorish palazzi. Mosaics glittered, golden and black, on the faces of churches. Sandali sailed under bridges, heaped high with eggplants, green peppers, mounds of string beans. The canals widened, golden light on green water, pure Canaletto all the way to the Rialto. A sense of sea enlivened the air, lagoon, and Adriatic under high blue sky above the outer islands. Fantasticando: Eastern galleons, huge battletubs approaching with cannons booming, star and crescent billowing on red sails, from Byzantium of mosaic saints and dancing dolphins. Boom, tara, War! History, the Most Serene Venetian Republic, Othello singing Verdi as Desdemona tussles in the hay with Iago under a weeping-willow tree. Fidelman, golden-robed Doge of Venice, though maybe better not since they garroted, stabbed, poisoned half the poor bastards. The Doge is dead, long live the dog that did him in! Boom, tara, yay! Fidelman III, Crusader on horse, hacking at Saladin and a thousand infidels! Fidelman in the Accademia! Ah Bellini, Giorgione, Tiziano, carissimi! The ex-painter wiped a wet eyelid, felt better, and decided he hadn't given her up after all. She is still present, lives in the mind. He kept an eye cocked for the sight of her and with surprise, though not astonishment, spied her in the glass trinket shop, which he now passed only once in a longing while. There she wasn't but if you looked again, she was.

Church bells.

Cannon scattering pigeons in San Marco.

Gondolas lit with Japanese lanterns.

Holy Mother, you have sent your Blessed Daughter. His heart, if he had a bit left, missed six beats and flapped like a mass of furled banners. He tapped on the window and out she came.

They talked quickly, intensely, searching one another with six eyes. She spoke her name: Margherita Fassoli, that made it real, an immediate commitment. She was herself real at last, no longer wild-goose shade he chased in a maze of dead-end canals, under low arches, and in alleyways. Breathless, she had only a moment; her uncle out for an espresso forbade her to be friendly with strangers. She had been ill for weeks—niente, a persistent virus—was better now, had hoped he would come by. He did not say how often he had, fruitlessly.

"Fidelman," he told her. "Where can we go, I have no money?"

She seemed momentarily stunned, hadn't given it a thought; then confessed she was a married woman—he knew—her husband a glass blower who worked in Murano, Beppo Fassoli. If nothing else he treated her kindly. "He gets annoyed about the kids sometimes but otherwise he's considerate. I'm sure you'll like him, he's wise about life."

"I can't invite you to my dump, Margherita," Fidelman said. "All it is is a lousy rathole with a bed that would collapse with two in it. And nothing else but a wine bottle to piss in. Should you open the window you have no idea of the stench of the canal."

She was desolated, squeezed her hands white but could not offer her place. They had four rooms and two boys, Riccardo and Rodolfo, eight and ten, little terrors. That made her around thirty or so, not a bad age for a woman. She was simple, spontaneous, direct—had already taken his hard hand and pressed it to her bosom. Her nose and eyes, pure Venetian. Her glossy hair, parted in the center, was rolled in braided circles over the ears. Her eyes were beyond him: the depth, light in dark, quiet enduring sadness—who knows where or from what. Whoever she was she knew who.

Margherita was urging him to go before her uncle returned.

"I will if you say when I can see you."

She gazed at him hungrily, eating with mouth, eyes. "Do you really want to, caro? There are so many better-looking women around."

"Passionately. But it's now or never, I'm frankly famished. Another day of dreaming and I'm a dead man. The ghost gives up."

"Oh my God, what do you mean?"

"I mean living on dreams. Sleeping with them. I can't anymore though I've accomplished nothing."

"Mio caro," she all but wept.

"Couldn't we go someplace you know? I haven't a lousy lira to rent a room. Do you happen to have a friend with an apartment we could borrow?"

She reflected hopelessly. Though her eyes lit she shrugged her shoulders.

"Maybe. I'll have to ask. But stop shivering as though you were in heat and take your hand out of your pocket. It doesn't look nice."

"I won't apologize for my passion. I'm hard up, it's now or never."

She finally agreed, asked him to meet her at the campanile after work. She would beg off around three.

"The boys come home from school at six and I've got to be there or they'll wreck the furniture. Beppo doesn't control them well enough. Usually he's not home before eight."

"All we need is a good hour."

"There's no need to rush, caro."

They kissed in the street. A passing tourist snapped a picture. The uncle hurried toward them, nearsightedly seeing nothing. Margherita disappeared into the shop as Fidelman walked quickly away.

This time is different, this one loves me.

They met at the bell tower, a dozen clucking pigeons at their feet. Margherita was tired around the eyes, a smudge of darkness, but worked up a listless smile; he blamed it on her recent illness. On the walk across the neck of the city she became animated again, showed him where Tintoretto had lived, in a Moorish section with turbaned figures and kneeling camels sculptured on stone plaques on house walls. Her matchstick street, take a few steps you were out of it, led into Fondamenta Nuove. In fact from her door he could see the island cemetery, thick with graves, across the water. They entered an old building, scabby masonry showing thin orange bricks, four stories high, terrazzi at the top floor loaded with potted plants—this house separated from the one it leaned toward across the narrow way by two or three buttresses at rooftop. She walked up the stairs, Fidelman at her direction trailing by two flights. He heard her open three locks with a bunch of keys. She left the door ajar for him.

"I'll undress, you come in after I'm in bed," she said.

"Wouldn't you want me to undress you?"

"I'm a modest person. I can't help it, don't press me."

But Fidelman, after quickly counting to a hundred and fifty, walked in on her anyway. She was standing in the semi-dark, the blinds down, but he found the light and snapped it on.

"You couldn't wait," she said bitterly.

"Painters love nudes, also ex-painters."

She was patient as he looked her over: heavier in the haunch and breasts than he had imagined; these were strong binding garments she wore. Her shapely legs were veined, splotched purple here and there. Slim at the waist but the stomach streaked with lesions of her pregnancies. She was forty if she was a day.

"Well, caro, are you disenchanted?"

"No more than usual," Fidelman confessed. "Still, you're not bad-looking although you play yourself down."

"At my age there's no pretending I'm in the first flush of youth."

She unbraided her hair. They sank into a deep bed with high head- and footboard and at once embraced.

"Why you're not hard at all," she said in surprise. He removed his member from her hand. "I'll get there myself, it won't take but a few minutes. Just act affectionate."

Her breasts were formless and he felt a roll of flesh above her hips. Fidelman snapped on the lamp. The same woman. He snapped it off.

"Do you mind if I get on top?" she asked. "It's hard to breathe since I had my illness."

"Be my guest."

They were tender to each other and both soon came, Margherita with vigor, making sounds of pleasure, Fidelman a while after in thoughtful silence. He fell asleep for a few minutes, had a quick dream which he couldn't recall. When he woke the blinds were up, Margherita filing her nails in bed. An old woman in a padded chair at the window was reading a folded newspaper.

The ex-painter sat up. "For Christ's sake, who is she?"

"Beppo's mother. She likes to read at that window. Don't worry, she won't say a thing. She's a deaf-mute in both ears."

"My God, she can write, can't she?"

"Don't get excited, she's not a suspicious type. I called a friend as you asked me to, but she couldn't accommodate us. I don't care for her sort anyway, she gives herself airs, so it's just as well. That's why I brought you here. Are you disappointed, amore mio?"

•

Beppo Fassoli, when Fidelman arrived one night famished for supper—he now supported himself by hawking corn for pigeons on the Piazza San Marco—gave his guest a glass rose with six red petals. The radio was blaring Cavaradossi singing, "L'arte nel suo mistero / Le diverse bellezze insiem confonde—" but Beppo snapped it off impatiently.

"The red in this rose is Venetian red. It is made from twenty-four-carat gold mixed in the formula."

"Real gold? You don't say." The ex-painter, touched by the gift, was embarrassed at being given since he had already taken.

"What do you make besides roses?"

The glass blower shrugged. "Fish, flasks of all sorts, the sentimental animals of Disney. Our craft has fallen to the level of the taste of the tourists."

"Eh," Fidelman agreed.

Margherita sat at the head of the table, ladling out plates of steaming ravioli to Rodolfo and Riccardo, quiet only while eating: otherwise slapping, kicking, shoving, incessantly testing each other's strength of arm, leg, lung. Beppo's old mother sat at the other end of the table attending her son at her right hand, Fidelman opposite him feeling terribly exposed. The deaf woman was up and down to supply the glass blower with ravioli, cheese, bread, white wine; she counted spoonfuls of sugar into his espresso, stirred the cup, and sipped a taste before he drank. Beppo ate slowly, paying little attention to his wife. He never once addressed her, except to throw her a look, with drawn thick brows—his eyes were green—when the boys were getting restless. She shut them up with a hiss and a glare. In that case, concluded Fidelman, nobody's cuckolding anybody. Beppo moodily picked his teeth with a fork tine. Their eyes met across two empty ravioli plates and both gazed away.

Though short of inches, the glass blower was a strong, muscular, handsome type, thick-shouldered, hairy. He appeared younger than his wife but Fidelman knew he wasn't. Maybe she looked older because he looked younger, an easy way to slap her in the face. If he was slapping; Fidelman wasn't sure. Did Beppo suspect him of usurping his rights as husband? Had the old deaf mother spelled it out on paper; she did not, after all, see with her ears, suspicious or not. He worried but Margherita assured him it was a waste of time.

"He doesn't know, just keep calm."

"He won't find out? I'd hate to hurt him—or vice versa. Mightn't he guess, do you think?"

"It's not his nature. His mind is usually occupied with other matters. There are men of that sort."

"What occupies his mind?"

"Everything but me. On the other hand, it's full of facts and fantasy. He also likes to live life. His father was the same but died young."

Beppo seemed to like the ex-painter's company. He liked, he said, the artistic viewpoint. Once he rowed Fidelman to Murano to see the glass factory where he worked, Vetrerie Artistiche. While they were there he blew Fidelman a small bird and set it in the cooling oven. The next night he presented it to him at supper to the applause of all at the table. He also invited the guest to go rowing in the lagoon Sunday with him and the boys. Beppo fished and caught nothing. The ex-painter, never having caught anything in his life, would not fish; he had vague thoughts of sketching but hadn't brought along pad or pencil. Fidelman enjoyed watching the floating city from the water. Venice, sober, dark, sank in winter; rose, a magic island giving off light, in summer. They rowed behind the Giudecca, the boys diving naked off the boat, their young asses flashing in sunlight before they splashed into blue water.

"Bravi, ragazzi," Beppo cheered. "Bello! Bellissimo! Non è bello, Fidelman?"

"Beautiful," murmured Fidelman, without innocence. He was spending more and more time with the glass blower, though it wasn't exactly easy to be sleeping with a man's wife and being friends with him. Still, somebody else might have made an effort to dislike him. Fidelman now visited Margherita one or two afternoons a week, depending on circumstances and desire—mostly hers; he was experiencing the first long liaison of his life. And he stayed often for supper because Beppo made it a standing invitation.

"I'm ashamed to leech on you."

"What's an extra plate of macaroni?"

He thought of Margherita's sex as an extra plate of something.

After supper they left the kids and dishes to the women. Beppo knew the cafés and liked the one the gondoliers frequented in Calle degli Assassini—away from the tourists, who had their own way of drowning the city. They drank grappa, played cards, sang, and told each other the day's adventures. When they were bored they watched television. The ex-painter, a butt in his mouth, liked to sketch the gondoliers in all poses and positions. When Beppo complimented him on one or two of the drawings, Fidelman confided to him the failures of his life in art. The glass blower listened at length with moody tender interest. It made Fidelman increasingly unhappy to be sleeping with Margherita and confessing irrelevancies to her husband; but the more he thought about it the more convinced he became that Beppo knew the situation and tolerated it. Is it because we're friends and he likes me? he asked himself, but then figured the man had a girl of his own somewhere, possibly Murano.

One day the glass blower confessed he slept with his wife on rare occasions, including her birthdays.

"Doesn't that make it hard all around?" the ex-painter asked thickly.

"Some things are harder than others."

Relieved of guilt, Fidelman all but embraced him.

That night, in a burst of inspiration and trust, he asked Beppo to come to his room on Sunday morning to look at his paintings—the few that remained. He had destroyed most but had kept a dozen perhaps justificatory pictures, and a few pieces of sculpture.

"I'll give you a private exhibition." He did not ask himself why; he was afraid of the answer.

"Do you like art, Beppo?"

"I love art," said the glass blower. "It comes to me naturally."

"What does?"

"Love for art. I never studied it at school. My taste formed itself naturally."

"This isn't classic stuff, if you know what I mean. It's modernist and you mightn't care for it."

Beppo answered that he had attended the last five Biennale. "My spirit is modern," he said haughtily.

"I was only kidding," Fidelman answered lamely, but the truth of it was he was no longer eager to show the glass blower his work and didn't know how to withdraw with grace, without insulting him more than he already might have.

Sunday morning, in a panic at his folly, he ran to Beppo's flat to tell him not to come, but Margherita, half-dressed, said he had already left. She invited Fidelman to stay for a half hour, the boys were in church; but the ex-painter was running with all his might and beat Beppo to his house. He seriously considered flight, hiding, not answering the bell; then Beppo knocked and entered, wincing at the disorder.

Fidelman apologized: he had changed his mind. "If you didn't like my paintings it'd make me feel bad, especially since you're a dear friend."

"I understand, Arturo, but maybe it's better to show me your work anyway. Who knows, I might be genuinely enthusiastic. Besides, if we're friends, we're friends for good or bad, better or worse."

Fidelman, touched, confused, not at all sure he knew what he was doing, or why, lifted a canvas and placed it on the kitchen table, against the wall, facing a small round window.

"This, you'll notice, has been influenced by Barney Newman, if you know who he is. The broad lavender band bisecting the black field at dead center is obviously the vital element organizing the picture. At the same time it achieves, partly through color, a quality of linear universality, in my case horizontal, whereas Newman does it vertically. Lately I've been sort of thinking maybe I could paint something more original based on a series of crisscrossing abstract canals."

Beppo nodded gravely. Leaning forward in somewhat the pose of Rodin's Thinker with a bit of belly, he sat on a half barrel Fidelman had in his room for want of a chair, his broad feet placed apart, his pants hiked up his hairy shins and calves, an unlit long cigar in his mouth. He gazed at the picture as if he were seeing it forever, with a shade of puzzlement and annoyance Fidelman noted and feared: half-stunned if it wasn't concentration—and occasionally Beppo sighed. It occurred to the ex-painter that he looked in his handsome way much like his mother. Who is this man? he thought, and why am I breaking my heart for him: I mean do I have to show him my private work? Why the revelation? He had then and there an urge to paint Beppo to his core, so much like a seizure he thought of it as sexual, and to his surprise found himself desiring Margherita so strongly he had to restrain himself from rushing out to jump into bed with her.

My life will end in calamity, Fidelman thought. Everything is out of joint again and I'm not helping by showing these pictures. You can pull up nails and let the past loose once too often.

Reluctantly, as if he were lifting pure lead, he placed a framed painting on the table.

"This is a spray job, an undercoating of apple-green acrylic resin, then a haphazard haze of indigo, creating a mood and a half before I applied a reconciling rose in varying values and intensities. Note how the base colors, invading without being totally visible, infect the rose so that it's both present and you might say evanescing. It's hard to explain a picture of this sort because it's something more than merely a poem of color. We're dealing with certain kinds of essences. In a way this and the other picture I just showed you are related, the other stating the masculine principle, this obviously feminine. Frankly, the inspiration is Rothko but I learned a trick or two from some of the things I've seen in *Art News* done by my contemporaries."

His voice at this point cracked, but Beppo's expression was unchanged and he still said nothing.

A scow passing by in the canal below agitated gem-like reflections of sunlit water on the ceiling. Fidelman waited till the rumble of the boat had disappeared into the distance.

"This," he said wearily, "is an old sculpture I did years ago, 'Fragment of a Head'—marble."

Beppo, as though smiling, nodded.

A broken head he responds to. Jesus God, whatever led me to do this? It'll all end in disaster.

In quick succession he showed a surrealistic landscape based on a frottage of tree bark, an old still life with rotting flowers, an old Madonna with old child, and an old sentimental self-portrait.

"These show me at various phases of development," Fidelman said, barely able to speak. "You needn't comment on each if you don't want to, though I would be interested in your overall impression."

Beppo sat silent, lighting his cigar.

"Here's a piece of pop sculpture, 'Soft Toilet Seat,' made out of vinylite. It was exhibited for two weeks in New York City. Originally I had a triptych of seats nailed on beaverboard more or less saying, 'Fuck all art, one must be free of the artistic alibi,' though I don't wholly subscribe to that. I can take just so much dada, so I cut it down to the single seat you see before you."

"Can you shit through it?" the glass blower ultimately asked.

"Art isn't life," Fidelman said. Then he said, "Don't be a wise guy, Beppo."

"Not that these things can't be done but you haven't done them. Your work lacks authority and originality. It lacks more than that, but I won't say what now. If you want my advice there's one thing I'd do with this stuff."

"Such as what?" said the ex-painter, fearing the worst.

"Burn them all."

"I thought you'd say that, you cruel fairy bastard."

Leaping up with Fidelman's kitchen knife in his hand, Beppo slashed the toilet seat and two paintings.

Fidelman interposed his body between the knife and the other canvases. "Have mercy!"

"Let me finish these off," the glass blower said hoarsely. "It's for your own sake. Show who's master of your fate—bad art or you."

Fidelman savagely struggled with him for the knife but at a crucial moment, as though a spinning color wheel had turned dead white, something failed in him and he relaxed his grip. Beppo quickly slashed up the other canvases. Afterwards they went downstairs and, in a corner of the junk-filled vegetable patch next to the smelly back canal, burned everything, including the fragmented marble head, which Beppo had smashed against a rock.

"Don't waste your life doing what you can't do."

"Why shouldn't I keep trying?"

"After twenty years if the rooster hasn't crowed she should know she's a hen. Your painting will never pay back the part of your life you've given up for it."

"What about Van Gogh? He never sold a single painting in his lifetime."

"You're not Van Gogh. Besides he was crazy."

Fidelman left the garden in a stupor; he wandered a day, his eyes glazed in grief. On Tuesday, somewhat calmer through exhaustion, though the weight of his emptiness dragged like a dead dog chained around his neck, he presented himself to Margherita, who, with tears in her eyes, embraced him, knowing what had happened.

"Come, tesoro," she said, leading him to the marriage bed. "For our mutual relief, me from my life and you from art."

As they were in the midst of violent intercourse, Fidelman on top, Margherita more loving than ever, the bedroom door opened and he glimpsed a nude hairy body wearing a horn or carrying a weapon; before he could rise he felt Beppo land on him. Fidelman cried out, expecting death between the shoulders. Margherita, shoving herself up with a grunt, slipped out from under them and fled out of the room. Fidelman rolled to the right and left to be rid of his incubus, but Beppo had him tightly pinned, his nose to the bedboard, his ass in the air.

"Don't hurt me, Beppo, please, I have piles."

"It'll be a cool job, I'm wearing mentholated Vaseline. You'll be surprised at the pleasure."

"Is your mother watching?"

"At her age she has no curiosity."

"I suppose I deserve this."

"Think of love," the glass blower murmured. "You've run from it all your life."

•

He stopped running.

Venice slowed down though it went on floating, its canals floating on Venice.

"Leonardo, Michelangelo," Fidelman murmured.

"If you can't invent art, invent life," Beppo advised him.

For good or ill Fidelman loved him; he could not help himself; he ought to have known. Beppo was handsome, hardworking, and loved to breathe; he smelled (and tasted) of oil and vinegar; he was, after all, a tender man and gentle lover. Fidelman had never in his life said "I love you" without reservation to anyone. He said it to Beppo. If that's the way it works, that's the way it works. Better love than no love. If you sneeze at life it backs off and instead of fruit you're holding a bone. If I'm a late bloomer at least I've bloomed in love."

"It's a good way to be," explained Beppo, "we're not like every-body else. I like it better with men because the company is more inter-esting and it's easier to be friends with somebody who speaks your language."

They were together as often as possible, everywhere except in Bep-po's house. Fidelman had stopped going there.

"Naturally," said Beppo. "It wouldn't be discreet."

"What does Margherita say?"

"She's said it before, I don't listen."

"Will you stay married to her?"

"Of course. I've got two boys and an old mother to think of."

"I guess so," said Fidelman.

Yet he was for once in his life on the whole serene; discontented only during the day when they were on separate islands, Beppo in Mur-ano and Fidelman selling pigeon feed on the Piazza San Marco. He spent most of his time thinking of Beppo, and the glass blower said he thought of him. They talked it over and one summer morning Fidel-man gave up his bird-food business and went with Beppo to Murano. At 6 a.m. they met at the Fondamenta Nuove. They stepped into Bep-po's rowboat and, each taking an oar, rowed past San Michele toward Murano. The water was calm and it took no more than twenty minutes to reach the island. Beppo spoke quietly to the assistant manager of the glassworks and got him to put on his friend as an apprentice and part-time man of all work. He was the oldest of the apprentices, some of them kids, but he didn't mind because Beppo, who was teaching him the rites of love, also taught him to blow glass.

Working with the hot molten glass excited Fidelman sexually. He felt creative, his heart in his pants. "With pipe, tongs, shears, you can make a form or change it into its opposite," Beppo said. "For instance, with a snip or two of the scissors, if it suits you, you can change the male organ into the female." The glass blower laughed heartily. Fidelman doubted he would be so minded; the thought evoked pain. Still it helped you understand the possibilities of life. And amid the possibilities was working with glass as an art form, though for certain reasons he did not say so to Beppo, who all day long, his face wet, armpits sweated, at in-tervals swigging from a beer or water bottle, blew varieties of fish and Disney creatures served up to him by an assistant from a wood or steel mold, for further shaping and decoration. For a change of pace he blew wine goblets, slim-waisted vases, flasks of odd shapes and sizes.

Fidelman, among other things, loved dipping the tapered blow-pipe into the flaming opening of the noisy furnace—like poking into the living substance of the sun for a puddle of flowing fire—Prometheus Fidelman—a viscous gob of sunflesh hanging from the pipe like a human organ: breast, kidney, stomach, or phallus, cooling as it gaseously flamed, out of which if one were skilled enough, lucky, knew the right people, he would create glass objects of expected yet unexpected forms. He blew gently into the red-hot glowing mass a single soft bubble of breath—it made no difference if the blower had eaten garlic or flowers—a small inside hole without spittle or seeds, a teardrop, gut, uterus, which itself became its object of birth: a sculptured womb; shaped, elongated by pendulum swing of pipe, the living metal teased and shorn into shape by tongs and scissors. Give the bubble a mouth and it became beaker, ewer, vase, amphora, or burial urn, anything the mouth foretold, or heart desired, or blower could blow. If you knew how, you could blow anything.

Not yet of course Fidelman, although he was learning. As apprentice he blew as Beppo shaped; or delivered the master fresh fish, birds-of-paradise, woodland creatures that he or another assistant blew into pristine form in molds; he also applied stems to vessels blown by Beppo, the stem shaped by a flick or two of his tool. To permit him to open and work at the mouth of any kind of container, Fidelman aimed a red-hot cone of glass at the bubble's bottom, Beppo gripping the gob with his tongs and leading it to the point of attachment. With his shears he creased the neck of the bubble and with a tap detached it from the blowpipe; he left Fidelman holding the openmouthed possibility: the open mouth. Every move they made was in essence sexual, a marvelous interaction because, among other things, it saved time and trouble: you worked and loved at once. When a glass object was completed, Fidelman hastily trotted to the cooling kiln in the rear with the thing on a wooden board, to stash away before it cracked. And he handed one tool or another to Beppo, who hardly looked at him during working hours, the assistant assisting for love's sake however he could. There were no spoken orders once you knew the process. He watched the glass blower and foresaw his needs, in essence a new experience for him. Otherwise he stood by, greedily watching the masters at other benches to absorb what they knew.

Impatient, agitated at times by all there was to learn, the variety of skills to master, Fidelman persuaded Beppo to stay on and teach him for an hour or two after the crowd of glass workers had gone home, the workshop talk and shouting silenced, five of the six furnace openings banked down, one blazing in a perpetual violet and lemon roar. He practiced then what he couldn't during the day, and though Beppo, eating an apple or smoking a butt, did not always encourage it, blew forms he had never blown before, or seen blown, evolving monstrosities of glass, so huge and complicated it took fifteen minutes to break their grip on the iron when he wanted to discard them. Many of Fidelman's creations cracked in midair, or against something on the workbench in a careless move. Those he completed intact stood (or fell) unbalanced, lopsided, malformed. But he worked for the first time in his life, instructed. Up to now he had taught himself and not got over it.

In the fall Margherita objected to the night work—it was killing her husband. Beppo's complexion had turned pale, his eyes were bloodshot, the skin around them dark and puffy. She was already half a widow, what more did they want? Abandoning the night sessions they came to work earlier, at half past four, leaving the Fondamenta bundled in overcoats against the stabbing wet cold, the fog cradled on the choppy water plopping against the boats at the dock, a star visible if they were lucky. They navigated by instinct—Beppo's—and made Murano usually on time, though once in a while they rowed in circles around the cemetery, lost in and breathing fog. "In the end we pay for everything," Beppo muttered. Suffering from loss of sleep he sometimes conked out at his work during the day, Fidelman having to wake him furtively; so in the end they decided that the apprentice himself would stay on alone nights, doing what he felt he had to do. Each assured the other it was for his benefit. "Though in a way it's mad," said the master to Fidelman; "the more you give up the more you undertake."

However, it was arranged and settled with the assistant manager, who had been assured it was all for the good of the company. Because Beppo left in the rowboat, and the vaporetto, before it expired at midnight, was fantastically slow making its stations, Fidelman considered renting a secondhand rowboat for himself; but then the thought occurred that taking a small room in a house on Murano, maybe with a little garden, would make more sense—be cheaper in the long run, and he could spend more time in the factory. Beppo could stay over when he felt like it, and they would as usual be together on Sundays.

Fidelman located a tiny room on Campo S. Bernardo, from which he could see the airport on the mainland and Burano and Torcello. But Beppo, when he heard, was infuriated. "You have no consideration for others, it's plain to see."

After he had calmed down, he said, "Why are you so fanatic about this accursed glass? After all, it's only glass."

"Life is short if you don't hurry."

"A fanatic never knows when to stop. It's obvious you want to repeat your fate."

"What fate do you have in mind?"

"Yours."

The apprentice sighed but hurried. For months he tried everything he saw others doing: cut glass in diamond patterns, carved glass as gems, practiced diamond point and acid engraving, flash painting with stains, gold and silver leaf applied in reverse: gods and goddesses in classic poses pretending left is right. In the spring he hungered to be involved with modern forms. Fidelman envisioned glass sculptures, a difficult enterprise, deciding first to experiment with compositions of mixed colors ladeled into and cast in molds. He invented objets trouvés—what better way to find what wasn't lost?—and worked with peacock's tails and Argus eyes in targets, casting concentric circles: amber / lavender / black / green. He fabricated abstract stained-glass windows, created Op Art designs of mosaics, collages of broken glass, and spent hours dripping glass on hot glass in the manner of Pollock.

Beppo from time to time watched, picking his teeth with an old toothpick.

"You're doing the same things you did in your paintings, that's the lousy hair in the egg. It's easy to see, half a talent is worse than none."

His criticism upset Fidelman so badly that he did not appear in the factory for a week. Is he wrong or am I? He went back one night to see what he had done and, when he saw, chopped it up with a hammer. He decided again, as he had more than once in the past, that he had no true distinction as an artist and this time would try not to forget it.

Fidelman cut out night work and spent the time with Beppo in the city. The glass blower asked no questions and made no comments. He was once again very tender and after a while Fidelman's heart stopped being a brick and began breathing. They drank with the gondoliers on the Calle degli Assassini and stayed away from painters and sculptors.

One day when they met by accident on the Rialto, Margherita, her large eyes vague, hair plaited in circles over her ears, her arms around a grocery bundle, stopped Fidelman and begged him to leave Venice.

"Listen, Fidelman, we've been friends, let's stay friends. All I ask is that you leave Beppo and go someplace else. After all, in the eyes of God he's my husband. Now, because of you he's rarely around and my family is a mess. The boys are always in trouble, his mother complains all day, and I'm at the end of my strength. Beppo may be a homo but he's a good provider and not a bad father when there are no men friends around to divert him from domestic life. The boys listen to his voice when they hear it. We have our little pleasures. He knows life and keeps me informed. Sometimes we visit friends, sometimes we go to a movie together and stop at a bar on our way home. In other words, things are better when he's around even though the sex is short. Occasionally he will throw me a lay if I suck him up good beforehand. It isn't a perfect life but I've learned to be satisfied, and was, more or less, before you came around. Since then, though there was some pleasure with you—I don't deny it—it ended quickly, and to tell the truth I'm worse off than I was before, so that's why I ask you to go."

In despair Fidelman rowed back to the factory and blew a huge glass bubble, larger and thicker than any he had blown before. He got it off the blowpipe with the help of an apprentice he had persuaded to stay over, and worked on its mouth in fear and doubtful confidence with tongs and a wet opening tool of smoking wood. Heating and reheating for several nights, he dipped, swung, lengthened, shaped, until the glass on his blowpipe turned out to be a capacious heavy red bowl, iron become ice. When he had cooled it without cracking he considered etching on it some scenes of Venice but decided no. The bowl was severe and graceful and sat solid, upright. It held the clear light and even seemed to listen. Fidelman polished it carefully and, when it was done, filled it with cold water and with a sigh dipped in his hands. He showed the bowl to Beppo, who said it was a good job, beautifully proportioned and reminding him of something the old Greeks had done. I kept my finger in art, Fidelman wept when he was alone. The next day, though they searched high and low with a crowd of apprentices, the bowl was missing and could not be found. Beppo suspected the assistant manager.

Before leaving Venice, Fidelman blew a slightly humpbacked green horse for Beppo, the color of his eyes. "Up yours," said the glass blower, grieving at the gray in Fidelman's hair. He sold the horse for a decent sum and gave Fidelman the lire. They kissed and parted.

Fidelman sailed from Venice on a Portuguese freighter.

In America he worked as a craftsman in glass and loved men and women.

1969

❧ B M ❧

God's Wrath

Glasser, a retired sexton, a man with a short beard and rheumy eyes, lived with his daughter on the top floor of a narrow brick building on Second Avenue and Sixth Street. He stayed in most of the day, hated going up and hated going out. He felt old, tired, and irritable. He felt he had done something wrong with his life and didn't know what. The oak doors of the old synagogue in the neighborhood had been nailed shut, its windows boarded, and the white-bearded rabbi, whom the sexton disliked, had gone off to live with his son in Detroit.

The sexton retired on social security and continued to live with his youngest daughter, the only child of his recently deceased second wife. She was a heavy-breasted, restless girl of twenty-six who called herself Luci on the phone and worked as an assistant bookkeeper in a linoleum factory during the day. She was by nature a plain and lonely girl with thoughts that bothered her; as a child she had often been depressed. The telephone in the house rarely rang.

After his shul had closed its doors, the sexton rode on the subway twice a day to a synagogue on Canal Street. On the anniversary of his first wife's death he said kaddish for both wives and barely resisted saying it for his youngest daughter. He was at times irritated by her fate. Why is my luck with my daughters so bad?

Still in all, though twice a widower, Glasser got along, thanks to God. He asked for little and was the kind of man who functioned well alone. Nor did he see much of his daughters from his first marriage, Helen, forty, and Fay, thirty-seven. Helen's husband, a drinker, a bum, supported her badly and Glasser handed her a few dollars now and then; Fay had a goiter and five children. He visited each of them every six weeks or so. His daughters served him a glass of tea.

Lucille he had more affection for, and sometimes she seemed to have affection for him. More often not; this was his second wife's doing. She had been a dissatisfied woman, complained, bewailed her fate. Anyway, the girl did little for herself, had few friends—once in a while a salesman where she worked asked her out—and it was possible, more and more likely, that she would in the end be left unmarried. No young man with or without long hair had asked her to live with him. The sexton would have disliked such an arrangement but he resolved, if ever the time came, not to oppose it. If God in His mercy winks an eye, He doesn't care who sees with two. What God in His mystery won't allow in the present, He may permit in the future, possibly even marriage for Lucille. Glasser remembered friends from the old country, some were Orthodox Jews, who had lived for years with their wives before marrying them. It was, after all, a way of life. Sometimes this thought worried him. If you opened the door a crack too much the wind would invade the bedroom. The devil, they said, hid in a cold wind. The sexton was uneasy. Who could tell where an evil began? Still, better a cold bedroom than one without a double bed. Better a daughter ultimately married than an empty vessel all her life. Glasser had seen some people, not many, come to better fates than had been expected for them.

At night after Lucille returned from work she prepared supper, and then her father cleaned up the kitchen so she could study or go to her classes. He also thoroughly cleaned the house on Fridays; he washed the windows and mopped the floors. Being twice a widower, used to looking out for himself, he was not bothered by having to do domestic tasks. What most disappointed the retired sexton in his youngest daughter was her lack of ambition. She had wanted to be a secretary after finishing high school and was now, five years later, an assistant bookkeeper. A year ago he had said to her, "You won't get better wages if you don't have a college diploma." "None of my friends go to college anymore," she said. "So how many friends have you got?" "I'm talking about the friends I know who started and stopped," Lucille said; but Glasser finally persuaded her to register at Hunter College at night, where she took two courses a term. Although she had done that reluctantly, now once in a while she talked of becoming a teacher.

"Someday I will be dead," the sexton remarked, "and you'll be better off with a profession."

Both of them knew he was reminding her she might be an old maid. She seemed not to worry, but later he heard her, through the door, crying in her room.

Once on a hot summer's day they went together on the subway to Manhattan Beach for a dip in the ocean. Glasser, perspiring, wore his summer caftan and a black felt hat of twenty years. He had on white cotton socks, worn bulbous black shoes, and a white shirt open at the collar. Part of his beard was faintly brown and his complexion was flushed. On the train Lucille wore tight bell-bottom ducks and a lacy blue blouse whose long sleeves could be seen through up to her armpits; she wore clogs and had braided her dark hair to about six inches of ponytail, which she tied off with a green ribbon. Her father was uncomfortable at an inch of bare midriff, her heavy breasts, and the tightness of her pants, but said nothing. One of her troubles was that, however she dressed, she had little to say, and he hoped the college courses would help her. Lucille had gold-flecked grayish eyes, and in a bathing suit showed a plumpish but not bad figure. A Yeshiva bocher, dressed much like her father, stared at her from across the aisle of the train, and though Glasser sensed she was interested, her face self-consciously stiffened. He felt for her an affectionate contempt.

In September Lucille delayed, then would not go to reregister for night college. She had spent the summer mostly alone. The sexton argued kindly and furiously but she could not be moved. After he had shouted for an hour she locked herself in the bathroom and would not come out though he swore he had to urinate. The next day she returned very late from work and he had to boil an egg for supper. It ended the argument; she did not return to her night classes. As though to balance that, the telephone in her room began to ring more often, and she called herself Luci when she picked up the receiver. Luci bought herself new clothes—dresses, miniskirts, leotards, new sandals and shoes, and wore them in combinations and bright colors he had never seen on her before. So let her go, Glasser thought. He watched television and was usually asleep when she got home late from a date.

"So how was your evening?" he asked in the morning.

"That's my own business," Luci said.

When he dreamed of her, as he often did, he was upbraiding her for her short dresses; when she bent over he could see her behind. And for the disgusting costume she called hot pants. And the eyeliner and violet eye shadow she now used regularly. And for the way she looked at him when he complained about her.

One day when the sexton was praying in the shul on Canal Street Luci moved out of the house on Second Avenue. She had left a green-ink note on lined paper on the kitchen table, saying she wanted to live her own life but would phone him once in a while. He telephoned the linoleum office the next day and a man there said she had quit her job. Though shaken that she had left the house in this fashion, the sexton felt it might come to some good. If she was living with someone, all he asked was that it be an honest Jew.

Awful dreams invaded his sleep. He woke enraged at her. Sometimes he woke in fright. The old rabbi, the one who had gone to live with his son in Detroit, in one dream shook his fist at him.

On Fourteenth Street, one night on his way home from Helen's house, he passed a prostitute standing in the street. She was a heavily made-up woman of thirty or so, and at the sight of her he became, without cause, nauseated. The sexton felt a weight of sickness on his heart and was moved to cry out to God but could not. For five minutes, resting his swaying weight on his cane, he was unable to walk. The prostitute had taken a quick look at his face and had run off. If not for a stranger who had held him against a telephone pole until he had flagged down a police car that drove the sexton home, he would have collapsed in the street.

In the house he pounded clasped hands against the wall of Lucille's room, bare except for her bed and a chair. He wept, wailing. Glasser telephoned his eldest daughter and cried out his terrible fear.

"How can you be so positive about that?"

"I know in my heart. I wish I didn't know but I know it."

"So in that case she's true to her nature," Helen said. "She can't be otherwise than she is, I never trusted her."

He hung up on her and called Fay.

"All I can say," said Fay, "is I saw it coming, but what can you do about such things? Who could I tell it to?"

"What should I do?"

"Ask for God's help, what else can you do?"

The sexton hurried to the synagogue and prayed for God's intervention. When he returned to his flat he felt unrelieved, outraged, miserable. He beat his chest with his fists, blamed himself for not having been stricter with her. He was angered with her for being the kind she was and sought ways to punish her. Really, he wanted to beg her to return home, to be a good daughter, to ease the pain in his heart.

The next morning he woke in the dark and determined to find her. But where do you look for a daughter who has become a whore? He waited a few days for her to call, and when she didn't, on Helen's advice he dialed information and asked if there was a new telephone number in the name of Luci Glasser.

"Not for Luci Glasser but for Luci Glass," said the operator.

"Give me this number."

The operator, at his impassioned insistence, gave him an address as well, a place on midtown Ninth Avenue. Though it was still September and not cold, the sexton put on his winter coat and took his rubber-tipped heavy cane. He rode, whispering to himself, on the subway to West Fiftieth Street, and walked to Ninth, to a large new orange-brick apartment house.

All day, though it rained intermittently, he waited across the street from the apartment house until his daughter appeared late at night; then he followed her. She walked quickly, lightly, as though without a worry, down the avenue. As he hurried after her she hailed a cab. Glasser shouted at it but no one looked back.

In the morning he telephoned her and she did not answer, as though she knew her father was calling. That evening Glasser went once more to the apartment house and waited across the street. He had considered going in and asking the doorman for her apartment number but was ashamed to.

"Please, give me the number of my daughter, Luci Glasser, the prostitute."

At eleven that night Luci came out. From the way she was dressed and made up he was positive he had not been mistaken.

She turned on Forty-eighth Street and walked to Eighth Avenue. Luci sauntered calmly along the avenue. The sidewalks were crowded with silent men and showily dressed young women. Traffic was heavy and there were strong lights everywhere, yet the long street looked dark and evil. Some of the stores, in their spotlit windows, showed pictures of men and women in sexual embrace. The sexton groaned. Luci wore a purple silk sweater with red sequins, almost no skirt, and long black net stockings. She paused for a while on a street corner, apart from a group of girls farther up the block. She would speak to the men passing by, and one or two would stop to speak to her, then she waited again. One man spoke quietly for a while as she listened intently. Then Luci went into a drugstore to make a telephone call, and when she came out, her father, half dead, was waiting for her at the door. She walked past him.

Incensed, he called her name and she turned in frightened surprise. Under the makeup, false eyelashes, gaudy mouth, her face had turned ashen, eyes anguished.

"Papa, go home," she cried in fright.

"What did I do to you that you do this to me?"

"It's not as bad as people think," Luci said.

"It's worse, it's filthy."

"Not if you don't think so. I meet lots of people—some are Jewish."

"A black year on their heads."

"You live your life, let me live mine."

"God will curse you, He will rot your flesh."

"You're not God," Luci cried in sudden rage.

"Cocksucker," the sexton shouted, waving his cane.

A policeman approached. Luci ran off. The sexton, to the man's questions, was inarticulate.

When he sought her again Luci had disappeared. He went to the orange apartment house and the doorman said Miss Glass had moved out; he could not say where. Though Glasser returned several times the doorman always said the same thing. When he telephoned her number he got a tape recording of the operator saying the number had been disconnected.

The sexton walked the streets looking for her, though Fay and Helen begged him not to. He said he must. They asked him why. He wept aloud. He sought her among the streetwalkers on Eighth and Ninth Avenues and on Broadway. Sometimes he went into a small cockroachy hotel and uttered her name, but nobody knew her.

Late one October night he saw her on Third Avenue near Twenty-third Street. Luci was standing in mid-block near the curb, and though it was a cold night she was not wearing a coat. She had on a heavy white sweater and a mirrored leather miniskirt. A round two-inch mirror in a metal holder was sewn onto the back of the skirt, above her plump thighs, and it bounced on her buttocks as she walked.

Glasser crossed the street and waited in silence through her alarm of recognition.

"Lucille," he begged her, "come home with your father. We won't tell anybody. Your room is waiting."

She laughed angrily. She had gained weight. When he attempted to follow her she called him dirty names. He hobbled across the street and waited in an unlit doorway.

Luci walked along the block and when a man approached she spoke to him. Sometimes the man stopped to speak to her. Then they would go together to a run-down, dark, squat hotel on a side street nearby, and a half hour later she returned to Third Avenue, standing between Twenty-third and -second, or higher up the avenue, near Twenty-sixth.

The sexton follows her and waits on the other side of the street by a bare-branched tree. She knows he is there. He waits. He counts the number of her performances. He punishes by his presence. He calls down God's wrath on the prostitute and her blind father.

1972

✿ B M ✿

Talking Horse

Q. Am I a man in a horse or a horse that talks like a man? Suppose they took an X-ray, what would they see?—a man's luminous skeleton prostrate inside a horse, or just a horse with a complicated voice box? If the first, then Jonah had it better in the whale—more room all around; also he knew who he was and how he had got there. About myself I have to make guesses. Anyway, after three days and nights the big fish stopped at Nineveh and Jonah took his valise and got off. But not Abramowitz, still on board, or at hand, after years; he's no prophet. On the contrary, he works in a sideshow full of freaks— though recently advanced, on Goldberg's insistence, to the center ring inside the big tent in an act with his deaf-mute master—Goldberg himself, may the Almighty forgive him. All I know is I've been here for years and still don't understand the nature of my fate; in short if I'm Abramowitz, a horse; or a horse *including* Abramowitz. Why is anybody's guess. Understanding goes so far and no further, especially if Goldberg blocks the way. It might be because of something I said, or thought, or did, or didn't do in my life. It's easy to make mistakes and easy not to know who made them. I have my theories, glimmers, guesses, but can't prove a thing.

When Abramowitz stands in his stall, his hooves nervously booming on the battered wooden boards as he chews in his bag of hard yellow oats, sometimes he has thoughts, far-off remembrances they seem to be, of young horses racing, playing, nipping at each other's flanks in green fields; and other disquieting images that might be memories; so who's to say what's really the truth?

I've tried asking Goldberg, but save yourself the trouble. He goes black-and-blue in the face at questions, really uptight. I can understand—he's a deaf-mute from way back; he doesn't like interference with his thoughts or plans, or the way he lives, and no surprises except those he invents. In other words questions disturb him. Ask him a question and he's off his track. He talks to me only when he feels like it, which isn't so often—his little patience wears thin. Lately his mood is awful, he reaches too often for his bamboo cane—whoosh across the rump! There's usually plenty of oats and straw and water, and once in a while even a joke to relax me when I'm tensed up, but otherwise it's one threat or another, followed by a flash of pain if I don't get something or other right, or something I say hits him on his nerves. It's not only that cane that slashes like a whip; his threats have the same effect—like a zing-zong of lightning through the flesh; in fact the blow hurts less than the threat—the blow's momentary, the threat you worry about. But the true pain, at least to me, is when you don't know what you have to know.

Which doesn't mean we don't communicate to each other. Goldberg taps out Morse code messages on my head with his big knuckle—crack crack crack; I feel the vibrations run through my bones to the tip of my tail—when he orders me what to do next or he threatens how many lashes for the last offense. His first message, I remember, was NO QUESTIONS. UNDERSTOOD? I shook my head yes and a little bell jingled on a strap under the forelock. That was the first I knew it was there.

TALK, he rapped on my head after he told me about the act. "You're a talking horse."

"Yes, master." What else can you say?

My voice surprised me when it came out high through the tunnel of a horse's neck. I can't exactly remember the occasion—go remember beginnings. My memory I have to fight to get an early remembrance out of. Don't ask me why unless I happened to fall and hurt my head, or was otherwise stunted. Goldberg is my deaf-mute owner; he reads my lips. Once when he was drunk and looking for company he tapped me that I used to carry goods on my back to fairs and markets in the old days before we joined the circus.

I used to think I was born here.

"On a rainy, snowy, crappy night," Goldberg Morse-coded me on my bony skull.

"What happened then?"

He stopped talking altogether. I should know better but don't.

I try to remember what night we're talking about and certain hazy thoughts flicker in my mind, which could be some sort of story I dream up when I have nothing to do but chew oats. It's easier than remembering. The one that comes to me most is about two men, or horses, or men on horses, though which was me I can't say. Anyway two strangers meet, somebody asks the other a question, and the next thing they're locked in battle, either hacking at one another's head with swords or braying wildly as they tear flesh with their teeth; or both at the same time. If riders, or horses, one is thin and poetic, the other a fat stranger wearing a huge black crown. They meet in a stone pit on a rainy, snowy, crappy night, one wearing his cracked metal crown that weighs a ton on his head and makes his movements slow though nonetheless accurate, and the other on his head wears a ragged colored cap. All night they wrestle by weird light in the slippery stone pit.

Q. "What's to be done?"

A. "None of those accursed bloody questions."

The next morning one of us wakes with a terrible pain which feels like a wound in the neck but also a headache. He remembers a blow he can't swear to and a strange dialogue where the answers come first and the questions follow:

I descended a ladder.

How did you get here?

The up and the down.

Which is which?

Abramowitz, in his dream story, suspects Goldberg had walloped him over the head and stuffed him into a horse because he needed a talking one for his act and there was no such thing.

I wish I knew for sure.

DON'T DARE ASK.

That's his nature; he's a lout though not without a little consideration when he's depressed and tippling his bottle. That's when he taps me out a teasing anecdote or two. He has no visible friends. Family neither of us talks about. When he laughs he cries.

It must frustrate Goldberg that all he can say aloud is four-letter words like geee, gooo, gaaa, gaaw; and the circus manager who doubles as ringmaster, in for a snifter, looks embarrassed at the floor. At those who don't know the Morse code Goldberg grimaces, glares, and grinds his teeth. He has his mysteries. He keeps a mildewed three-prong spear hanging on the wall over a stuffed pony's head. Sometimes he goes down the cellar with an old candle and comes up with a new one lit though we have electric lights. Although he doesn't complain about his life, he worries and cracks his knuckles. He doesn't seem interested in women but sees to it that Abramowitz gets his chance at a mare in heat, if available. Abramowitz engages to satisfy his physical nature, a fact is a fact, otherwise it's no big deal; the mare has no interest in a talking courtship. Furthermore, Goldberg applauds when Abramowitz mounts her, which is humiliating.

And when they're in their winter quarters the owner once a week or so dresses up and goes out on the town. When he puts on his broadcloth suit, diamond stickpin, and yellow gloves, he preens before the full-length mirror. He pretends to fence, jabs the bamboo cane at the figure in the glass, twirls it around one finger. Where he goes when he goes he never informs Abramowitz. But when he returns he's usually melancholic, sometimes anguished, didn't have much of a good time; and in this mood may mete out a few loving lashes with that bastard cane. Or worse—make threats. Nothing serious but who needs it? Usually he prefers to stay home and watch television. He is fascinated by astronomy, and when they have those programs on the educational channel he's there night after night, staring at pictures of stars, quasars, infinite space. He also likes to read the *Daily News*, which he tears up when he's done. Sometimes he reads this book he hides on a shelf in the closet under some old hats. If the book doesn't make him laugh outright it makes him cry. When he gets excited over something he's reading in his fat book, his eyes roll, his mouth gets wet, and he tries to talk through his thick tongue, though all Abramowitz hears is geee, gooo, gaaa, gaaw. Always these words, whatever they mean, and sometimes gool goon geek gonk, in various combinations, usually gool with gonk, which Abramowitz thinks means Goldberg. And in such states he has been known to kick Abramowitz in the belly with his heavy boot. Ooof.

When he laughs he sounds like a horse, or maybe it's the way I hear him with these ears. And though he laughs once in a while, it doesn't make my life easier, because of my condition. I mean I think, Here I am in this horse. This is my theory though I have my doubts. Otherwise, Goldberg is a small stocky figure with a thick neck, heavy black brows, each like a small mustache, and big feet that swell in his shapeless boots. He washes his feet in the kitchen sink and hangs up his yellowed socks to dry on the whitewashed walls of my stall. Phoo.

He likes to do card tricks.

In winter they live in the South in a small, messy, one-floor house with a horse's stall attached that Goldberg can approach, down a few steps, from the kitchen of the house. To get Abramowitz into the stall he is led up a plank from the outside and the door shuts on his rear end. To keep him from wandering all over the house there's a slatted gate to just under his head. Furthermore, the stall is next to the toilet and the broken water closet runs all night. It's a boring life with a deaf-mute except when Goldberg changes the act a little. Abramowitz enjoys it when they rehearse a new routine, although Goldberg hardly ever alters the lines, only the order of answer and question. That's better than nothing. Sometimes when Abramowitz gets tired of talking to himself, asking unanswered questions, he complains, shouts, calls the owner dirty names. He snorts, brays, whinnies shrilly. In his frustration he rears, rocks, gallops in his stall; but what good is a gallop if there's no place to go and Goldberg can't, or won't, hear complaints, pleas, protest?

Q. "Answer me this: If it's a sentence I'm serving, how long?"

A.

Once in a while Goldberg seems to sense somebody else's needs and is momentarily considerate of Abramowitz—combs and curries him, even rubs his bushy head against the horse's. He also shows interest in his diet and whether his bowel movements are regular and sufficient; but if Abramowitz gets sentimentally careless when the owner is close by and forms a question he can see on his lips, Goldberg punches him on the nose. Or threatens to. It doesn't hurt any the less.

All I know is he's a former vaudeville comic and acrobat. He did a solo act telling jokes with the help of a blind assistant before he went sad. That's about all he's ever tapped to me about himself. When I forgot myself and asked what happened then, he punched me in the nose.

Only once, when he was half drunk and giving me my bucket of water, I sneaked in a fast one which he answered before he knew it.

"Where did you get me, master? Did you buy me from somebody else? Maybe in some kind of auction?"

I FOUND YOU IN A CABBAGE PATCH.

Once he tapped my skull: "In the beginning was the word."

"Which word was that?"

Bong on the nose.

NO MORE QUESTIONS.

"Watch out for the wound on my head or whatever it is."

"Keep your trap shut or you'll lose your teeth."

Goldberg should read that story I once heard on his transistor radio, I thought to myself. It's about a poor cabdriver driving his sledge in the Russian snow. His son, a fine promising lad, got sick with pneumonia and soon died, and the poor cabby can't find anybody to talk to so as to relieve his grief. Nobody wants to listen to his troubles, because that's the way it is in the world. When he opens his mouth to say a word, the customers insult him. So he finally tells the story to his bony nag in the stable, and the horse, munching oats, listens as the weeping old man tells him about his boy that he has just buried.

Something like that could happen to you, Goldberg, and you'd be a lot kinder to whoever I am.

"Will you ever free me out of here, master?"

I'LL FLAY YOU ALIVE, YOU BASTARD HORSE.

We have this act we do together. Goldberg calls it "Ask Me Another," an ironic title where I am concerned.

In the sideshow days people used to stand among the bearded ladies, the blobby fat men, Joey the snake boy, and other freaks, laughing beyond belief at Abramowitz talking. He remembers one man staring into his mouth to see who's hiding there. Homunculus? Others suggested it was a ventriloquist's act even though the horse told them Goldberg was a deaf-mute. But in the main tent the act got thunderous storms of applause. Reporters pleaded for permission to interview Abramowitz and he had plans to spill all, but Goldberg wouldn't allow it. "His head will swell up too big," Abramowitz said for him. "He will never be able to wear the same size hat he wore last summer."

For the performance the owner dresses up in a balloony red-and-white polka-dot clown's suit with a pointed clown's cap and has borrowed a ringmaster's snaky whip, an item Abramowitz is skittish of though Goldberg says it's nothing to worry about, little more than decoration in a circus act. No animal act is without one. People like to hear the snap. He also ties an upside-down feather duster on Abramowitz's head that makes him look like a wilted unicorn. The five-piece circus band ends its brassy "Overture to *William Tell*"; there's a flourish of trumpets, and Goldberg cracks the whip as Abramowitz, with his loose-feathered, upside-down duster, trots once around the spotlit ring and stops at attention, facing clown-Goldberg, his left foreleg pawing the sawdust-covered earth. They then begin the act; Goldberg's ruddy face, as he opens his painted mouth to express himself, flushes dark red, and his melancholy eyes under black brows protrude as he painfully squeezes out the abominable sounds, his only eloquence:

"Geee gooo gaaa gaaw?"

Abramowitz's resonant, beautifully timed response is:

A. "To get to the other side."

There's a gasp from the spectators, a murmur, perhaps of puzzlement, and a moment of intense expectant silence. Then at a roll of the drums Goldberg snaps his long whip and Abramowitz translates the owner's idiocy into something that makes sense and somehow fulfills expectations; though in truth it's no more than a question following a response already given.

Q. "Why does a chicken cross the road?"

Then they laugh. And do they laugh! They pound each other in merriment. You'd think this trite riddle, this sad excuse for a joke, was the first they had heard in their lives. And they're laughing at the translated question, of course, not at the answer, which is the way Goldberg has set it up. That's his nature for you. It's the only way he works.

Abramowitz used to sink into the dumps after that, knowing what really amuses everybody is not the old-fashioned tired conundrum but the fact it's put to them by a talking horse. That's what splits the gut.

"It's a stupid little question."

"There are no better," Goldberg said.

"You could try letting me ask one or two of my own."

YOU KNOW WHAT A GELDING IS?

I gave him no reply. Two can play at that game.

After the first applause both performers take a low bow. Abramowitz trots around the ring, his head with panache held high. And when Goldberg again cracks the pudgy whip, he moves nervously to the center of the ring and they go through the routine of the other infantile answers and questions in the same silly ass-backwards order. After each question Abramowitz runs around the ring as the spectators cheer.

A. "To hold up his pants."

Q. "Why does a fireman wear red suspenders?"

A. "Columbus."

Q. "What was the first bus to cross the Atlantic?"

A. "A newspaper."

Q. "What's black and white and red all over?"

We did a dozen like that, and when we finished up, Goldberg cracked the foolish whip, I galloped a couple more times around the ring, then we took our last bows.

Goldberg pats my steaming flank and in the ocean-roar of everyone in the tent applauding and shouting bravo, we leave the ring, running down the ramp to our quarters, Goldberg's personal wagon van and attached stall; after that we're private parties till tomorrow's show.

Many customers used to come night after night to watch the performance, and they laughed at the riddles though they had known them from childhood. That's how the season goes, and nothing much has changed one way or the other except that recently Goldberg added a couple of silly elephant riddles to modernize the act.

A. "From playing marbles."

Q. "Why do elephants have wrinkled knees?"

A. "To pack their dirty laundry in."

Q. "Why do elephants have long trunks?"

Neither Goldberg nor I think much of the new jokes but they're the latest style. I reflect that we could do the act without jokes. All you need is a free talking horse.

One day Abramowitz thought he would make up a question-response of his own—it's not that hard to do. So that night after they had finished the routine, he slipped in his new riddle.

A. "To greet his friend the chicken."

Q. "Why does a yellow duck cross the road?"

After a moment of confused silence everybody cracked up; they beat themselves silly with their fists—broken straw boaters flew all over the place; but Goldberg in unbelieving astonishment glowered murderously at the horse. His ruddy face turned purple. When he cracked the whip it sounded like a river of ice breaking. Realizing in fright that he had gone too far, Abramowitz, baring his big teeth, reared up on his hind legs and took several steps forward against his will. But the spectators, thinking this was an extra flourish at the end of the act, applauded wildly. Goldberg's anger eased, and lowering his whip, he pretended to chuckle. Amid continuing applause he beamed at Abramowitz as if he were his only child and could do no wrong, though Abramowitz, in his heart of hearts, knew the owner was furious.

"Don't forget WHO'S WHO, you insane horse," Goldberg, his back to the audience, tapped out on Abramowitz's nose.

He made him gallop once more around the ring, mounted him in an acrobatic leap onto his bare back, and drove him madly to the exit.

Afterwards he Morse-coded with his hard knuckle on the horse's bony head that if he pulled anything like that again he would personally deliver him to the glue factory.

WHERE THEY WILL MELT YOU DOWN TO SIZE. "What's left over goes into dog food."

"It was just a joke, master," Abramowitz explained.

"To say the answer was okay, but not to ask the question by yourself."

Out of stored-up bitterness the talking horse replied, "I did it on account of it made me feel free."

At that Goldberg whacked him hard across the neck with his murderous cane. Abramowitz, choking, staggered but did not bleed.

"Don't, master," he gasped, "not on my old wound."

Goldberg went into slow motion, still waving the cane.

"Try it again, you tub of guts, and I'll be wearing a horsehide coat with fur collar, gool, goon, geek, gonk." Spit crackled in the corners of his mouth.

Understood.

Sometimes I think of myself as an idea, yet here I stand in this filthy stall, my hooves sunk in my yellow balls of dreck. I feel old, disgusted with myself, smelling the odor of my bad breath as my teeth in the feedbag grind the hard oats into a foaming lump, while Goldberg smokes his panatela as he watches TV. He feeds me well enough, if oats are your dish, but hasn't had my stall cleaned for a week. It's easy to get even on a horse if that's the type you are.

So the act goes on every matinee and night, keeping Goldberg in good spirits and thousands in stitches, but Abramowitz had dreams of being in the open. They were strange dreams—if dreams; he isn't sure what they are or come from—hidden thoughts, maybe, of freedom, or some sort of self-mockery? You let yourself conceive what can't be? Anyhow, whoever heard of a talking horse's dreams? Goldberg hasn't said he knows what's going on but Abramowitz suspects he understands more than he seems to, because when the horse, lying in his dung and soiled straw, awakens from a dangerous reverie, he hears the owner muttering in his sleep in deaf-mute talk.

Abramowitz dreams, or something of the sort, of other lives he might live, let's say of a horse that can't talk, couldn't conceive the idea; is perfectly content to be simply a horse without speech. He sees himself, for instance, pulling a wagonload of yellow apples along a rural road. There are leafy beech trees on both sides and beyond them broad green fields full of wild flowers. If he were that kind of horse, maybe he might retire to graze in such fields. More adventurously, he sees himself a racehorse in goggles, thundering down the last stretch of muddy track, slicing through a wedge of other galloping horses to win by a nose at the finish; and the jockey is definitely not Goldberg. There is no jockey; he fell off.

Or if not a racehorse, if he has to be practical about it, Abramowitz continues on as a talking horse but not in circus work any longer; and every night on the stage he recites poetry. The theater is packed and people cry out oooh and aaah, what beautiful things that horse is saying.

Sometimes he thinks of himself as altogether a free "man," someone of indeterminate appearance and characteristics, who is maybe a doctor or lawyer helping poor people. Not a bad idea for a useful life.

But even if I am dreaming or whatever it is, I hear Goldberg talking in *my* sleep. He talks something like me:

As for number one, you are first and last a talking horse, not any nag that can't talk; and believe me I have got nothing against you that you *can* talk, Abramowitz, but on account of what you say when you open your mouth and break the rules.

As for a racehorse, if you take a good look at the broken-down type you are—overweight, with big sagging belly and a thick uneven dark coat that won't shine up no matter how much I comb or brush you, and four hairy, thick, bent legs, plus a pair of slight cross-eyes, you would give up that foolish idea you can be a racehorse before you do something very ridiculous.

As for reciting poetry, who wants to hear a horse recite poetry? That's for the birds.

As for the last dream, or whatever it is that's bothering you, that you can be a doctor or lawyer, you better forget it, it's not that kind of a world. A horse is a horse even if he's a talking horse; don't mix yourself up with human beings if you know what I mean. If you're a talking horse that's your fate. I warn you, don't try to be a wise guy, Abramowitz. Don't try to know everything, you might go mad. Nobody can know everything; it's not that kind of world. Follow the rules of the game. Don't rock the boat. Don't try to make a monkey out of me; I know more than you. It's my nature. We have to be who we are, although this is rough on both of us. But that's the logic of the situation. It goes by certain laws even though that's a hard proposition for some to understand. The law is the law, you can't change the order. That's the way things stay put together. We are mutually related, Abramowitz, and that's all there is to it. If it makes you feel any better, I will admit to you I can't live without you, and I won't let you live without me. I have my living to make and you are my talking horse I use in my act to earn my living, plus so I can take care of your needs. The true freedom, like I have always told you, though you never want to believe me, is to understand that and don't waste your energy resisting the rules; if so you waste your life. All you are is a horse who talks, and believe me, there are very few horses that can do that; so if you are smart, Abramowitz, it should make you happy instead of always and continually dissatisfied. Don't break up the act if you know what's good for you.

As for those yellow balls of your dreck, if you will behave yourself like a gentleman and watch out what you say, tomorrow the shovelers will come and after I will hose you down personally with warm water. Believe me, there's nothing like cleanliness.

Thus he mocks me in my sleep though I have my doubts that I sleep much nowadays.

In short hops between towns and small cities the circus moves in wagon vans. The other horses pull them, but Goldberg won't let me, which again wakes disturbing ideas in my head. For longer hauls, from one big city to another, we ride in red-and-white-striped circus trains. I have a stall in a freight car with some non-talking horses with fancy braided manes and sculptured tails from the bareback rider's act. None of us are much interested in each other. If they think at all they think a talking horse is a show-off. All they do is eat and drink, piss and crap. Not a single word goes back or forth among them. Nobody has a good or bad idea.

The long train rides generally give us a day off without a show, and Goldberg gets depressed and surly when we're not working the matinee or evening performance. Early in the morning of a long-train-ride day he starts loving his bottle and Morse-coding me nasty remarks and threats.

"Abramowitz, you think too much, why do you bother? In the first place your thoughts come out of you and you don't know that much, so your thoughts don't either. In other words don't get too ambitious. For instance, what's on your mind right now, tell me?"

"Answers and questions, master—some new ones to modernize the act."

"Feh, we don't need any new ones, the act is already too long."

He should know the questions I am really asking myself, though better not.

Once you start asking questions one leads to the next and in the end it's endless. And what if it turns out I'm always asking myself the same question in different words? I keep on wanting to know why I can't ask this coarse lout a simple question about *anything*. By now I have it figured out Goldberg is afraid of questions because a question could show he's afraid people will find out who he is. Somebody who all he does is repeat his fate. Anyway, Goldberg has some kind of past he is afraid to tell me about, though sometimes he hints. And when I mention my own past he says forget it. Concentrate on the future. What future? On the other hand, what does he think he can hide from Abramowitz, a student by nature, who spends most of his time asking himself questions Goldberg won't permit him to ask, putting one and one together, and finally making up his mind—miraculous thought—that he knows more than a horse should, even a talking horse, so therefore, given all the built-up evidence, he is positively not a horse. Not in origin anyway.

So I came once more to the conclusion that I am a man in a horse and not just a horse that happens to be able to talk. I had figured this out in my mind before; then I said, no it can't be. I feel more like a horse bodywise; on the other hand I talk, I think, I wish to ask questions. So I am what I am. Something tells me there is no such thing as a talking horse, even though Goldberg, pointing his fat finger at me, says the opposite. He lives on his lies, it's his nature.

After long days of traveling, when they were in their new quarters one night, finding the rear door to his stall unlocked—Goldberg grew careless when depressed—acting on belief as well as impulse, Abramowitz cautiously backed out. Avoiding the front of Goldberg's wagon van he trotted across the fairgrounds on which the circus was situated. Two of the circus hands who saw him trot by, perhaps because Abramowitz greeted them, "Hello, boys, marvelous evening," did not attempt to stop him. Outside the grounds, though exhilarated to be in the open, Abramowitz began to wonder if he was doing a foolish thing. He had hoped to find a wooded spot to hide in for the time being, surrounded by fields in which he could peacefully graze; but this was the industrial edge of the city, and though he clop-clopped from street to street there were no woods nearby, not even a small park.

Where can somebody who looks like a horse go by himself?

Abramowitz tried to hide in an old riding-school stable but was driven out by an irate woman. In the end they caught up with him on a station platform where he had been waiting for a train. Quite foolishly, he knew. The conductor wouldn't let him get on though Abramowitz had explained his predicament. The stationmaster ran out and pointed a pistol at his head. He held the horse there, deaf to his blandishments, until Goldberg arrived with his bamboo cane. The owner threatened to whip Abramowitz to the quick, and his description of the effects was so painfully lurid that Abramowitz felt as though he had been slashed into a bleeding pulp. A half hour later he found himself back in his locked stall, his throbbing head encrusted with dried horse blood. Goldberg ranted in deaf-mute talk, but Abramowitz, who with lowered head pretended contrition, felt none. To escape Goldberg he must first get out of the horse he was in.

But to exit a horse as a man takes some doing. Abramowitz

planned to proceed slowly and appeal to public opinion. It might take months, possibly years, to do what he must. Protest! Sabotage if necessary! Revolt! One night after they had taken their bows and the applause was subsiding, Abramowitz, raising his head as though to whinny his appreciation of the plaudits, cried out to all assembled in the circus tent, "Help! Get me out of here, somebody! I am a prisoner in this horse! Free a fellow man!"

After a silence that grew like a dense forest, Goldberg, who was standing to the side, unaware of Abramowitz's passionate outcry—he picked up the news later from another ringmaster—saw at once from everybody's surprised and startled expression, not to mention Abramowitz's undisguised look of triumph, that something had gone seriously amiss. The owner at once began to laugh heartily, as though whatever was going on was more of the same, part of the act, a bit of personal encore by the horse. The spectators laughed too, again warmly applauding.

"It won't do you any good," the owner Morse-coded Abramowitz afterwards. "Because nobody is going to believe you."

"Then please let me out of here on your own account, master. Have some mercy."

"About that matter," Goldberg rapped out sternly, "I am already on record. Our lives and livings are dependent each on the other. You got nothing substantial to complain about, Abramowitz. I'm taking care on you better than you could take care on yourself."

"Maybe that's so, Mr. Goldberg, but what good is it if in my heart I am a man and not a talking horse?"

Goldberg's ruddy face blanched as he Morse-coded the usual NO QUESTIONS.

"I'm not asking, I'm trying to tell you something very serious."

"Watch out for your hubris, Abramowitz."

That night the owner went out on the town, came back dreadfully drunk, as though he had been lying with his mouth open under a spigot pouring brandy; and he threatened Abramowitz with the trident spear he kept in his trunk when they traveled. This is a new torment.

Anyway, the act goes on but definitely altered, not as before. Abramowitz, despite numerous warnings and various other painful threats, daily disturbs the routine. After Goldberg makes his idiot noises, his geee gooo gaaa gaaw, Abramowitz purposely mixes up the responses to the usual ridiculous riddles.

A. "To get to the other side."

Q. "Why does a fireman wear red suspenders?"

A. "From playing marbles."

Q. "Why do elephants have long trunks?"

And he adds dangerous A.'s and Q.'s without permission despite the inevitability of punishment.

A. "A talking horse."

Q. "What has four legs and wishes to be free?"

At that nobody laughed.

He also mocked Goldberg when the owner wasn't attentively reading his lips; called him "deaf-mute," "stupid ears," "lock mouth"; and whenever possible addressed the public, requesting, urging, begging their assistance.

"Gevalt! Get me out of here! I am one of you! This is slavery! I wish to be free!"

Now and then when Goldberg's back was turned, or when he was too lethargic with melancholy to be much attentive, Abramowitz clowned around and in other ways ridiculed the owner. He heehawed at his appearance, brayed at his "talk," stupidity, arrogance. Sometimes he made up little songs of freedom as he jigged on his hind legs, exposing his private parts. And at times Goldberg, to mock the mocker, danced gracelessly with him—a clown with a glum-painted smile, waltzing with a horse. Those who had seen the act last season were astounded, stunned by the change, uneasy, as though the future threatened.

"Help! Help, somebody help me!" Abramowitz pleaded. Nobody moved.

Sensing the tension in and around the ring, the audience sometimes booed the performers, causing Goldberg, in his red-and-white polka-dot suit and white clown's cap, great embarrassment, though on the whole he kept his cool during the act and never used the ringmaster's whip. In fact he smiled as he was insulted, whether he "listened" or not. He heard what he saw. A sly smile was fixed on his face and his lips twitched. And though his fleshy ears flared like torches at the gibes and mockeries he endured, Goldberg laughed to the verge of tears at Abramowitz's sallies and shenanigans; many in the big tent laughed along with him. Abramowitz was furious.

Afterwards Goldberg, once he had stepped out of his clown suit, threatened him to the point of collapse, or flayed him viciously with his cane; and the next day fed him pep pills and painted his hide black before the performance so that people wouldn't see his wounds.

"You bastard horse, you'll lose us our living."

"I wish to be free."

"To be free you got to know when you are free. Considering your type, Abramowitz, you'll be free in the glue factory."

One night when Goldberg, after a day of profound depression, was listless and logy in the ring, could not evoke so much as a limp snap out of his whip, Abramowitz, thinking that where the future was concerned, glue factory or his present condition of life made little difference, determined to escape either fate; he gave a solo performance for freedom, the best of his career. Though desperate, he entertained, made up hilarious riddles: A. "By jumping through the window." Q. "How do you end the pane?"; he recited poems he had heard on Goldberg's radio, which sometimes stayed on all night after the owner had fallen asleep; he also told stories and ended the evening with a moving speech.

He told sad stories of the lot of horses, one, for instance, beaten to death by his cruel owner, his brains battered with a log because he was too weakened by hunger to pull a wagonload of wood. Another concerned a racehorse of fabulous speed, a sure winner in the Kentucky Derby, had he not in his very first race been doped by his avaricious master, who had placed a fortune in bets on the next-best horse. A third was about a fabulous flying horse shot down by a hunter who couldn't believe his eyes. And then Abramowitz told a story of a youth of great promise who, out for a stroll one spring day, came upon a goddess bathing naked in a stream. As he gazed at her beauty in amazement and longing, she let out a piercing scream to the sky. The youth took off at a fast gallop, realizing from the snorting and sound of pounding hooves as he ran that he was no longer a youth of great promise, but a horse running.

Abramowitz then cried out to the faces that surrounded him, "I also am a man in a horse. Is there a doctor in the house?"

Dead silence.

"Maybe a magician?"

No response but nervous tittering.

He then delivered an impassioned speech on freedom for all. Abramowitz talked his brains blue, ending once more with a personal appeal. "Help me to recover my original form. It's not what I am but what I wish to be. I wish to be what I really am, which is a man."

At the end of the act many people in the tent were standing wet-eyed and the band played "The Star-Spangled Banner."

Goldberg, who had been dozing in a sawdust pile for a good part of Abramowitz's solo act, roused himself in time to join the horse in a bow. Afterwards, on the enthusiastic advice of the new circus manager, he changed the name of the act from "Ask Me Another" to "Goldberg's Varieties." And wept himself for unknown reasons.

Back in the stall after the failure of his most passionate, most inspired, pleas for assistance, Abramowitz butted his head in frustration
against the stall gate until his nostrils bled into the feedbag. He thought
he would drown in the blood and didn't much care. Goldberg found
him lying on the floor in the dirty straw, in a deep faint, and revived
him with aromatic spirits of ammonia. He bandaged his nose and spoke
to him in a fatherly fashion.

"That's how the mop flops," he Morse-coded with his blunt fingertip, "but things could be worse. Take my advice and settle for a talking horse, it's not without distinction."

"Make me either into a man or make me into a horse," Abramowitz pleaded. "It's in your power, Goldberg."

"You got the wrong party, my friend."

"Why do you always say lies?"

"Why do you always ask questions you can't ask?"

"I ask because I am. Because I wish to be free."

"So who's free, tell me?" Goldberg mocked.

"If so," said Abramowitz, "what's to be done?"

DON'T ASK, I WARNED YOU.

He warned he would punch his nose; it bled again.

Abramowitz later that day began a hunger strike which he carried
on for the better part of a week; but Goldberg threatened force-feeding
with thick rubber tubes in both nostrils, and that ended that. Abramowitz almost choked to death at the thought of it. The act went on as
before, and the owner changed its name back to "Ask Me Another."
When the season was over the circus headed south, Abramowitz trotting
along in a cloud of dust with the other horses.

Anyway I got my own thoughts.

One fine autumn, after a long hard summer, Goldberg washed his
big feet in the kitchen sink and hung his smelly socks to dry on the gate
of Abramowitz's stall before sitting down to watch astronomy on ETV.
To see better he placed a lit candle on top of the color set. But he had
carelessly left the stall gate open, and Abramowitz hopped up three
steps and trotted through the messy kitchen, his eyes flaring. Confronting Goldberg staring in awe at the universe on the screen, he reared
with a bray of rage, to bring his hooves down on the owner's head.
Goldberg, seeing him out of the corner of his eye, rose to protect himself. Instantly jumping up on the chair, he managed with a grunt to
grab Abramowitz by both big ears as though to lift him by them, and
the horse's head and neck, up to an old wound, came off in his hands.
Amid the stench of blood and bowel a man's pale head popped out of
the hole in the horse. He was in his early forties, with fogged pince-nez,

intense dark eyes, and a black mustache. Pulling his arms free, he grabbed Goldberg around his thick neck with both bare arms and held on for dear life. As they tugged and struggled, Abramowitz, straining to the point of madness, slowly pulled himself out of the horse up to his navel. At that moment Goldberg broke his frantic grip and, though the astronomy lesson was still going on in a blaze of light, disappeared. Abramowitz later made a few discreet inquiries, but no one could say where.

Departing the circus grounds, he cantered across a grassy soft field into a dark wood, a free centaur.

1972

The Letter

At the gate stands Teddy holding his letter.

•

On Sunday afternoons Newman sat with his father on a white bench in the open ward. The son had brought a pineapple tart but the old man wouldn't eat it.

Twice during the two and a half hours he spent in the ward with his father, Newman said, "Do you want me to come back next Sunday or don't you? Do you want to have next Sunday off?"

The old man said nothing. Nothing meant yes or it meant no. If you pressed him to say which he wept.

"All right, I'll see you next Sunday. But if you want a week off sometime, let me know. I want a Sunday off myself."

His father said nothing. Then his mouth moved and after a while he said, "Your mother didn't talk to me like that. She didn't like to leave any dead chickens in the bathtub. When is she coming to see me here?"

"Pa, she's been dead since before you got sick and tried to take your life. Try to keep that in your memory."

"Don't ask me to believe that one," his father said, and Newman got up to go to the station where he took the Long Island Rail Road train to New York City.

He said, "Get better, Pa," when he left, and his father answered, "Don't tell me that, I am better."

Sundays after he left his father in Ward 12 of Building B and walked across the hospital grounds, that spring and dry summer, at the arched iron-barred gate between brick posts under a towering oak that shadowed the raw red brick wall, he met Teddy standing there with his letter in his hand. Newman could have got out through the main entrance of Building B of the hospital complex, but this way to the railroad station was shorter. The gate was open to visitors on Sundays only.

Teddy was a stout soft man in loose gray institutional clothes and canvas slippers. He was fifty or more and maybe so was his letter. He held it as he always held it, as though he had held it always, a thick squarish finger-soiled blue envelope with unsealed flap. Inside were four sheets of cream paper with nothing written on them. After he had looked at the paper the first time, Newman had handed the envelope back to Teddy, and the green-uniformed guard had let him out the gate. Sometimes there were other patients standing by the gate who wanted to walk out with Newman but the guard said they couldn't.

"What about mailing my letter," Teddy said on Sundays.

He handed Newman the finger-smudged envelope. It was easier to take, then hand back, than to refuse to take it.

The mailbox hung on a short cement pole just outside the iron gate on the other side of the road, a few feet from the oak tree. Teddy would throw a right jab in its direction. Once it had been painted red and was now painted blue. There was also a mailbox in the doctor's office in each ward. Newman had reminded him, but Teddy said he didn't want the doctor reading his letter.

"You bring it to the office and so they read it."

"That's his job," Newman answered.

"Not on my head," said Teddy. "Why don't you mail it? It won't do you any good if you don't."

"There's nothing in it to mail."

"That's what you say."

His heavy head was set on a short sunburned neck, the coarse grizzled hair cropped an inch from the skull. One of his eyes was a fleshy gray, the other was walleyed. He stared beyond Newman when he talked to him, sometimes through his shoulder. And Newman noticed he never so much as glanced at the blue envelope when it was momentarily out of his hand, when Newman was holding it. Once in a while he pointed a short finger at something but said nothing. When he said nothing he rose a little on the balls of his toes. The guard did not interfere when Teddy handed Newman the letter every Sunday.

Newman gave it back.

"It's your mistake," said Teddy. Then he said, "I got my walking privileges. I'm almost sane. I fought in Guadalcanal."

Newman said he knew that.

"Where did you fight?"

"Nowhere yet."

"Why don't you mail my letter out?"

"It's for your own good the doctor reads it."

"That's a hot one." Teddy stared at the mailbox through Newman's shoulder.

"The letter isn't addressed to anybody and there's no stamp on it."

"Put one on. They won't let me buy one three or three ones."

"It's eight cents now. I'll put one on if you address the envelope."

"Not me," said Teddy.

Newman no longer asked why.

"It's not that kind of a letter."

He asked what kind it was.

"Blue with white paper inside of it."

"Saying what?"

"Shame on you," said Teddy.

Newman left on the four o'clock train. The ride home was not so bad as the ride there, though Sundays were murderous.

Teddy holds his letter.

"No luck?"

"No luck," said Newman.

"It's off your noodle."

He handed the envelope to Newman anyway and after a while Newman gave it back.

Teddy stared at his shoulder.

•

Ralph holds the finger-soiled blue envelope.

•

On Sunday a tall lean grim old man, clean-shaven, faded-eyed, wearing a worn-thin World War I overseas cap on his yellowed white head, stood at the gate with Teddy. He looked eighty.

The guard in the green uniform told him to step back, he was blocking the gate.

"Step back, Ralph, you're in the way of the gate."

"Why don't you stick it in the box on your way out?" Ralph asked in a gravelly old man's voice, handing the letter to Newman.

Newman wouldn't take it. "Who are you?"

Teddy and Ralph said nothing.

"It's his father," the guard at the gate said.

"Whose?"

"Teddy."

"My God," said Newman. "Are they both in here?"

"That's right," said the guard.

"Was he just admitted or has he been here all the while?"

"He just got his walking privileges returned again. They were re-voked about a year."

"I got them back after five years," Ralph said.

"One year."

"Five."

"It's astonishing anyway," Newman said. "Neither one of you re-sembles the other."

"Who do you resemble?" asked Ralph.

Newman couldn't say.

"What war were you in?" Ralph asked.

"No war at all."

"That settles your pickle. Why don't you mail my letter?"

Teddy stood by sullenly. He rose on his toes and threw a short right and left at the mailbox.

"I thought it was Teddy's letter."

"He told me to mail it for him. He fought at Iwo Jima. We fought two wars. I fought in the Marne and the Argonne Forest. I had both my lungs gassed with mustard gas. The wind changed and the Huns were gassed. That's not all that were."

"Tough turd," said Teddy.

"Mail it anyway for the poor kid," said Ralph. His tall body trem-bled. He was an angular man with deep-set bluish eyes and craggy fea-tures that looked as though they had been hacked out of a tree.

"I told your son I would if he wrote something on the paper," Newman said.

"What do you want it to say?"

"Anything he wants it to. Isn't there somebody he wants to com-municate with? If he doesn't want to write it he could tell me what to say and I'll write it out."

"Tough turd," said Teddy.

"He wants to communicate to me," said Ralph.

"It's not a bad idea," Newman said. "Why doesn't he write a few words to you? Or you could write a few words to him."

"A Bronx cheer on you."

"It's my letter," Teddy said.

"I don't care who writes it," said Newman. "I could write a message for you wishing him luck. I could say you hope he gets out of here soon."

"A Bronx cheer to that."

"Not in my letter," Teddy said.

"Not in mine either," said Ralph grimly. "Why don't you mail it like it is? I bet you're afraid to."

"No I'm not."

"I'll bet you are."

"No I'm not."

"I have my bets going."

"There's nothing to mail. There's nothing in the letter. It's a blank."

"What makes you think so?" asked Ralph. "There's a whole letter in there. Plenty of news."

"I'd better be going," Newman said, "or I'll miss my train."

The guard opened the gate to let him out. Then he shut the gate.

Teddy turned away and stared over the oak tree into the summer sun with his gray eye and his walleyed one.

Ralph trembled at the gate.

"Who do you come here to see on Sundays?" he called to Newman.

"My father."

"What war was he in?"

"The war in his head."

"Has he got his walking privileges?"

"No, they won't give him any."

"What I mean, he's crazy?"

"That's right," said Newman, walking away.

"So are you," said Ralph. "Why don't you come back here and hang around with the rest of us?"

The Silver Crown

Gans, the father, lay dying in a hospital bed. Different doctors said different things, held different theories. There was talk of an exploratory operation but they thought it might kill him. One doctor said cancer.

"Of the heart," the old man said bitterly.

"It wouldn't be impossible."

The young Gans, Albert, a high school biology teacher, in the afternoons walked the streets in sorrow. What can anybody do about cancer? His soles wore thin with walking. He was easily irritated; angered by the war, atom bomb, pollution, death, obviously the strain of worrying about his father's illness. To be able to do nothing for him made him frantic. He had done nothing for him all his life.

A female colleague, an English teacher he had slept with once, a girl who was visibly aging, advised, "If the doctors don't know, Albert, try a faith healer. Different people know different things; nobody knows everything. You can't tell about the human body."

Albert laughed mirthlessly but listened. If specialists disagree, who do you agree with? If you've tried everything, what else can you try?

One afternoon after a long walk alone, as he was about to descend the subway stairs somewhere in the Bronx, still burdened by his worries, uneasy that nothing had changed, he was accosted by a fat girl with bare meaty arms who thrust a soiled card at him that he tried to avoid. She was a stupefying sight, retarded at the very least. Fifteen, he'd say, though she looks thirty and probably has the mentality of age ten. Her skin glowed, face wet, fleshy, a small mouth open and would be forever; eyes set wide apart on the broad unfocused face, either watery green or brown, or one of each—he wasn't sure. She seemed not to mind his appraisal, gurgled faintly. Her thick hair was braided in two ropelike strands; she wore bulging cloth slippers bursting at seams and soles; a faded red skirt down to massive ankles, and a heavy brown sweater vest buttoned over blown breasts, though the weather was still hot September.

The teacher's impulse was to pass by her outthrust plump baby hand. Instead he took the card from her. Simple curiosity—once you had learned to read you read anything? Charitable impulse?

Albert recognized Yiddish and Hebrew but read in English: "Heal The Sick. Save The Dying. Make A Silver Crown."

"What kind of silver crown would that be?"

She uttered impossible noises. Depressed, he looked away. When his eyes turned to hers she ran off.

He studied the card. "Make A Silver Crown." It gave a rabbi's name and address no less: Jonas Lifschitz, close by in the neighborhood. The silver crown mystified him. He had no idea what it had to do with saving the dying but felt he ought to know. Although at first repelled by the thought, he made up his mind to visit the rabbi and felt, in a way, relieved.

The teacher hastened along the street a few blocks until he came to the address on the card, a battered synagogue in a store, Congregation Theodor Herzl, painted in large uneven white letters on the plate-glass window. The rabbi's name, in smaller, gold letters, was A. Marcus. In the doorway to the left of the store the number of the house was repeated in tin numerals, and on a card under the vacant nameplate under the mezuzah appeared in pencil, "Rabbi J. Lifschitz. Retired. Consultations. Ring The Bell." The bell, when he decided to chance it, did not work—seemed dead to the touch—so Albert, his heartbeat erratic, turned the knob. The door gave easily enough and he hesitantly walked up a dark flight of narrow wooden stairs. Ascending, assailed by doubts, peering up through the gloom, he thought of turning back but at the first-floor landing compelled himself to knock loudly on the door.

"Anybody home here?"

He rapped harder, annoyed with himself for being there, engaging in the act of entrance—who would have predicted it an hour ago? The door opened a crack and that broad, badly formed face appeared.

The retarded girl, squinting one bulbous eye, made noises like two eggs frying, and ducked back, slamming the door. The teacher, after momentary reflection, thrust it open in time to see her, bulky as she was, running along the long tight corridor, her body bumping the walls as she disappeared into a room at the rear.

Albert entered cautiously, with a sense of embarrassment, if not danger, warning himself to depart at once; yet stayed to peek curiously into a front room off the hallway, darkened by lowered green shades through which threadlike rivulets of light streamed. The shades resembled faded maps of ancient lands. An old gray-bearded man with thickened left eyelid, wearing a yarmulke, sat heavily asleep, a book in his lap, on a sagging armchair. Someone in the room gave off a stale odor, unless it was the armchair. As Albert stared, the old man awoke in a hurry. The small thick book on his lap fell with a thump to the floor, but instead of picking it up, he shoved it with a kick of his heel under the chair.

"So where were we?" he inquired pleasantly, a bit breathless.

The teacher removed his hat, remembered whose house he was in, and put it back on his head.

He introduced himself. "I was looking for Rabbi J. Lifschitz. Your—ah—girl let me in."

"Rabbi Lifschitz—this was my daughter Rifkele. She's not perfect, though God, who made her in His image, is Himself perfection. What this means I don't have to tell you."

His heavy eyelid went down in a wink, apparently involuntarily.

"What does it mean?" Albert asked.

"In her way she is also perfect."

"Anyway, she let me in and here I am."

"So what did you decide?"

"About what?"

"What did you decide about what we were talking about—the silver crown?"

His eyes roved as he spoke; he rubbed a nervous thumb and forefinger. Crafty type, the teacher decided. Him I have to watch myself with.

"I came here to find out about this crown you advertised," he said, "but actually we haven't talked about it or anything else. When I entered here you were sound asleep."

"At my age—" the rabbi explained with a little laugh.

"I don't mean any criticism. All I'm saying is I am a stranger to you."

"How can we be strangers if we both believe in God?"

Albert made no argument of it.

The rabbi raised the two shades and the last of daylight fell into the spacious high-ceilinged room, crowded with at least a dozen stiff-back and folding chairs, plus a broken sofa. What kind of operation is he running here? Group consultations? He dispensed rabbinic therapy? The teacher felt renewed distaste for himself for having come. On the wall hung a single oval mirror, framed in gold-plated groupings of joined metal circles, large and small; but no pictures. Despite the empty chairs, or perhaps because of them, the room seemed barren.

The teacher observed that the rabbi's trousers were a week from ragged. He was wearing an unpressed worn black suit-coat and a yellowed white shirt without a tie. His wet grayish-blue eyes were restless. Rabbi Lifschitz was a dark-faced man with brown eye pouches and smelled of old age. This was the odor. It was hard to say whether he resembled his daughter; Rifkele resembled her species.

"So sit," said the old rabbi with a light sigh. "Not on the couch, sit on a chair."

"Which in particular?"

"You have a first-class humor." Smiling absently, he pointed to two kitchen chairs and seated himself in one.

He offered a thin cigarette.

"I'm off them," the teacher explained.

"I also." The old man put the pack away. "So who is sick?" he inquired.

Albert tightened at the question, as he recalled the card he had taken from the girl: "Heal The Sick, Save The Dying."

"To come to the point, my father's in the hospital with a serious ailment. In fact he's dying."

The rabbi, nodding gravely, dug into his pants pocket for a pair of glasses, wiped them with a large soiled handkerchief, and put them on, lifting the wire earpieces over each fleshy ear.

"So we will make then a crown for him?"

"That depends. The crown is what I came here to find out about."

"What do you wish to find out?"

"I'll be frank with you." The teacher blew his nose and slowly wiped it. "My cast of mind is naturally empiric and objective—you might say non-mystical. I'm suspicious of faith healing, but I've come here, frankly, because I want to do anything possible to help my father recover his former health. To put it otherwise, I don't want anything to go untried."

"You love your father?" the rabbi clucked, a glaze of sentiment veiling his eyes.

"What I feel is obvious. My real concern right now mainly is how does the crown work. Could you be explicit about the mechanism of it all? Who wears it, for instance? Does he? Do you? Or do I have to? In other words, how does it function? And if you wouldn't mind saying, what's the principle, or rationale, behind it? This is terra incognita for me, but I think I might be willing to take a chance if I could justify it to myself. Could I see a sample of the crown, for instance, if you have one on hand?"

The rabbi, with an absentminded start, seemed to interrupt himself about to pick his nose.

"What is the crown?" he asked, at first haughtily, then again, gently. "It's a crown, nothing else. There are crowns in Mishna, Proverbs, Kabbalah; the holy scrolls of the Torah are often protected by crowns. But this one is different, this you will understand when it does the work. It's a miracle. A sample doesn't exist. The crown has to be made individual for your father. Then his health will be restored. There are two prices——"

"Kindly explain what's supposed to cure the sickness," Albert said. "Does it work like sympathetic magic? I'm not nay-saying, you understand. I just happen to be interested in all kinds of phenomena. Is the crown supposed to draw off the illness like some kind of poultice, or what?"

"The crown is not a medicine, it is the health of your father. We offer the crown to God and God returns to your father his health. But first we got to make it the way it must be made—this I will do with my assistant, a retired jeweler. He has helped me to make a thousand crowns. Believe me, he knows silver—the right amount to the ounce according to the size you wish. Then I will say the blessings. Without the right blessings, exact to each word, the crown don't work. I don't have to tell you why. When the crown is finished your father will get better. This I will guarantee you. Let me read you some words from the mystic book."

"The Kabbalah?" the teacher asked respectfully.

"Like the Kabbalah."

The rabbi rose, went to his armchair, got slowly down on his hands and knees and withdrew the book he had shoved under the misshapen chair, a thick small volume with faded purple covers, not a word imprinted on it. The rabbi kissed the book and murmured a prayer.

"I hid it for a minute," he explained, "when you came in the room. It's a terrible thing nowadays, goyim come in your house in the middle of the day and take away that which belongs to you, if not your life itself."

"I told you right away that your daughter had let me in," Albert said in embarrassment.

"Once you mentioned I knew."

The teacher then asked, "Suppose I am a nonbeliever? Will the crown work if it's ordered by a person who has his doubts?"

"Doubts we all got. We doubt God and God doubts us. This is natural on account of the nature of existence. Of this kind doubts I am not afraid so long as you love your father."

"You're putting it as sort of a paradox."

"So what's so bad about a paradox?"

"My father wasn't the easiest man in the world to get along with, and neither am I for that matter, but he has been generous to me and I'd like to repay him in some way."

"God respects a grateful son. If you love your father this will go in the crown and help him to recover his health. Do you understand Hebrew?"

"Unfortunately not."

The rabbi flipped a few pages of his thick tome, peered at one closely, and read aloud in Hebrew, which he then translated into English. " 'The crown is the fruit of God's grace. His grace is love of creation.' These words I will read seven times over the silver crown. This is the most important blessing."

"Fine. But what about those two prices you quoted me a minute ago?"

"This depends how quick you wish the cure."

"I want the cure to be immediate, otherwise there's no sense to the whole deal," Albert said, controlling anger. "If you're questioning my sincerity, I've already told you I'm considering this recourse even though it goes against the grain of some of my strongest convictions. I've gone out of my way to make my pros and cons absolutely clear."

"Who says no?"

The teacher became aware of Rifkele standing at the door, eating a slice of bread with lumps of butter on it. She beheld him in mild stupefaction, as though seeing him for the first time.

"Shpeter, Rifkele," the rabbi said patiently.

The girl shoved the bread into her mouth and ran ponderously down the passageway.

"Anyway, what about those two prices?" Albert asked, annoyed by the interruption. Every time Rifkele appeared his doubts of the enterprise rose before him like warriors with spears.

"We got two kinds crowns," said the rabbi. "One is for 401 and the other is 986."

"Dollars, you mean, for God's sake?—that's fantastic."

"The crown is pure silver. The client pays in silver dollars. So the silver dollars we melt—more for the large-size crown, less for the medium."

"What about the small?"

"There is no small. What good is a small crown?"

"I wouldn't know, but the assumption seems to be the bigger the better. Tell me, please, what can a 986 crown do that a 401 can't? Does the patient get better faster with the larger one? It hastens the reaction?"

The rabbi, five fingers hidden in his limp beard, assented.

"Are there any other costs?"

"Costs?"

"Over and above the quoted prices?"

"The price is the price, there is no extra. The price is for the silver and for the work and for the blessings."

"Now would you kindly tell me, assuming I decide to get involved in this deal, where I am supposed to lay my hands on 401 silver dollars? Or if I should opt for the 986 job, where can I get a pile of cartwheels of that amount? I don't suppose that any bank in the whole Bronx would keep that many silver dollars on hand nowadays. The Bronx is no longer the Wild West, Rabbi Lifschitz. But what's more to the point, isn't it true the mint isn't making silver dollars all silver anymore?"

"So if they are not making we will get wholesale. If you will leave with me the cash, I will order the silver from a wholesaler, and we will save you the trouble to go to the bank. It will be the same amount of silver, only in small bars, I will weigh them on a scale in front of your eyes."

"One other question. Would you take my personal check in payment? I could give it to you right away once I've made my final decision."

"I wish I could, Mr. Gans," said the rabbi, his veined hand still nervously exploring his beard, "but it's better cash when the patient is so sick, so I can start to work right away. A check sometimes comes back, or gets lost in the bank, and this interferes with the crown."

Albert did not ask how, suspecting that a bounced check, or a lost one, wasn't the problem. No doubt some customers for crowns had stopped their checks on afterthought.

As the teacher reflected concerning his next move—should he, shouldn't he?—weighing a rational thought against a sentimental, the old rabbi sat in his chair, reading quickly in his small mystic book, his lips hastening along silently.

Albert at last got up.

"I'll decide the question once and for all tonight. If I go ahead and commit myself on the crown I'll bring you the cash after work tomorrow."

"Go in good health," said the rabbi. Removing his glasses he wiped both eyes with his handkerchief.

Wet or dry? thought the teacher.

As he let himself out of the downstairs door, more inclined than not toward trying the crown, he felt relieved, almost euphoric.

But by the next morning, after a difficult night, Albert's mood had about-faced. He fought gloom, irritation, felt flashes of hot and cold anger. It's throwing money away, pure and simple. I'm dealing with a clever confidence man, that's plain to me, but for some reason I am not resisting strongly. Maybe my subconscious is telling me to go along with a blowing wind and have the crown made. After that we'll see what happens—whether it rains, snows, or spring comes. Not much will happen, I suppose, but whatever does, my conscience will be in the clear.

But when he visited Rabbi Lifschitz that afternoon in the same roomful of empty chairs, though the teacher carried the required cash in his wallet, he was still uncomfortable about parting with it.

"Where do the crowns go after they are used and the patient recovers his health?" he cleverly asked the rabbi.

"I'm glad you asked me this question," said the rabbi alertly, his thick lid drooping. "They are melted, and the silver we give to the poor. A mitzvah for one makes a mitzvah for another."

"To the poor you say?"

"There are plenty poor people, Mr. Gans. Sometimes they need a crown for a sick wife or a sick child. Where will they get the silver?"

"I see what you mean—recycled, sort of, but can't a crown be reused as it is? I mean, do you permit a period of time to go by before you melt them down? Suppose a dying man who recovers gets seriously ill again at a future date?"

"For a new sickness you will need a new crown. Tomorrow the

world is not the same as today, though God listens with the same ear."

"Look, Rabbi Lifschitz," Albert said impatiently, "I'll tell you frankly that I am inching toward ordering the crown, but it would make my decision a whole lot easier all around if you would let me have a quick look at one of them—it wouldn't have to be for more than five seconds—at a crown-in-progress for some other client."

"What will you see in five seconds?"

"Enough—whether the object is believable, worth the fuss and not inconsequential investment."

"Mr. Gans," replied the rabbi, "this is not a showcase business. You are not buying from me a new Chevrolet automobile. Your father lays now dying in the hospital. Do you love him? Do you wish me to make a crown that will cure him?"

The teacher's anger flared. "Don't be stupid, rabbi, I've answered that. Please don't sidetrack the real issue. You're working on my guilt so I'll suspend my perfectly reasonable doubts of the whole freaking enterprise. I won't fall for that."

They glared at each other. The rabbi's beard quivered. Albert ground his teeth.

Rifkele, in a nearby room, moaned.

The rabbi, breathing emotionally, after a moment relented.

"I will show you the crown," he sighed.

"Accept my apologies for losing my temper."

The rabbi accepted. "Now tell me please what kind of sickness your father has got."

"Ah," said Albert, "nobody is certain for sure. One day he got into bed, turned to the wall, and said, 'I'm sick.' They suspected leukemia at first but the lab tests didn't confirm it."

"You talked to the doctors?"

"In droves. Till I was blue in the face. A bunch of ignoramuses," said the teacher hoarsely. "Anyway, nobody knows exactly what he has wrong with him. The theories include rare blood diseases, also a possible carcinoma of certain endocrine glands. You name it, I've heard it, with complications suggested, like Parkinson's or Addison's disease, multiple sclerosis, or something similar, alone or in combination with other sicknesses. It's a mysterious case, all in all."

"This means you will need a special crown," said the rabbi.

The teacher bridled. "What do you mean special? What will it cost?"

"The cost will be the same," the rabbi answered dryly, "but the design and the kind of blessings will be different. When you are dealing with such a mystery you got to make another one but it must be bigger."

"How would that work?"

"Like two winds that they meet in the sky. A white and a blue. The blue says, 'Not only I am blue but inside I am also purple and orange.' So the white goes away."

"If you can work it up for the same price, that's up to you."

Rabbi Lifschitz then drew down the two green window shades and shut the door, darkening the room.

"Sit," he said in the heavy dark, "I will show you the crown."

"I'm sitting."

"So sit where you are, but turn your head to the wall where is the mirror."

"But why so dark?"

"You will see light."

He heard the rabbi strike a match and it flared momentarily, casting shadows of candles and chairs amid the empty chairs in the room.

"Look now in the mirror."

"I'm looking."

"What do you see?"

"Nothing."

"Look with your eyes."

A silver candelabrum, first with three, then five, then seven burning bony candlesticks, appeared like ghostly hands with flaming fingertips in the oval mirror. The heat of it hit Albert in the face and for a moment he was stunned.

But recalling the games of his childhood, he thought, Who's kidding who? It's one of those illusion things I remember from when I was a kid. In that case I'm getting the hell out of here. I can stand maybe mystery but not magic tricks or dealing with a rabbinical magician.

The candelabrum had vanished, although not its light, and he now saw the rabbi's somber face in the glass, his gaze addressing him. Albert glanced quickly around to see if anyone was standing at his shoulder, but nobody was. Where the rabbi was hiding at the moment the teacher did not know; but in the lit glass appeared his old man's lined and shrunken face, his sad eyes, compelling, inquisitive, weary, perhaps even frightened, as though they had seen more than they had cared to but were still looking.

What's this, slides or home movies? Albert sought some source of projection but saw no ray of light from wall or ceiling, nor object or image that might be reflected by the mirror.

The rabbi's eyes glowed like sun-filled clouds. A moon rose in the blue sky. The teacher dared not move, afraid to discover he was unable to. He then beheld a shining crown on the rabbi's head.

It had appeared at first like a braided mother-of-pearl turban, then had luminously become—like an intricate star in the night sky—a silver crown, constructed of bars, triangles, half-moons and crescents, spires, turrets, trees, points of spears; as though a wild storm had swept them up from the earth and flung them together in its vortex, twisted into a single glowing interlocked sculpture, a forest of disparate objects.

The sight in the ghostly mirror, a crown of rare beauty—very impressive, Albert thought—lasted no longer than five short seconds, then the reflecting glass by degrees turned dark and empty.

The shades were up. The single bulb in a frosted lily fixture on the ceiling shone harshly in the room. It was night.

The old rabbi sat, exhausted, on the broken sofa.

"So you saw it?"

"I saw something."

"You believe what you saw—the crown?"

"I believe I saw. Anyway, I'll take it."

The rabbi gazed at him blankly.

"I mean I agree to have the crown made," Albert said, having to clear his throat.

"Which size?"

"Which size was the one I saw?"

"Both sizes. This is the same design for both sizes, but there is more silver and also more blessings for the $986 size."

"But didn't you say that the design for my father's crown, because of the special nature of his illness, would have a different style, plus some special blessings?"

The rabbi nodded. "This comes also in two sizes—the $401 and $986."

The teacher hesitated a split second. "Make it the big one," he said decisively.

He had his wallet in his hand and counted out fifteen new bills—nine one hundreds, four twenties, a five, and a single—adding to $986.

Putting on his glasses, the rabbi hastily counted the money, snapping with thumb and forefinger each crisp bill as though to be sure none had stuck together. He folded the stiff paper and thrust the wad into his pants pocket.

"Could I have a receipt?"

"I would like to give you a receipt," said Rabbi Lifschitz earnestly, "but for the crowns there are no receipts. Some things are not a business."

"If money is exchanged, why not?"

"God will not allow. My father did not give receipts and also my grandfather."

"How can I prove I paid you if something goes wrong?"

"You have my word, nothing will go wrong."

"Yes, but suppose something unforeseen did," Albert insisted, "would you return the cash?"

"Here is your cash," said the rabbi, handing the teacher the packet of folded bills.

"Never mind," said Albert hastily. "Could you tell me when the crown will be ready?"

"Tomorrow night before Shabbos, the latest."

"So soon?"

"Your father is dying."

"That's right, but the crown looks like a pretty intricate piece of work to put together out of all those odd pieces."

"We will hurry."

"I wouldn't want you to rush the job in any way that would—let's say—prejudice the potency of the crown or, for that matter, in any way impair the quality of it as I saw it in the mirror—or however I saw it."

Down came the rabbi's eyelid, quickly raised without a sign of self-consciousness. "Mr. Gans, all my crowns are first-class jobs. About this you got nothing to worry about."

They then shook hands. Albert, still assailed by doubts, stepped into the corridor. He felt he did not, in essence, trust the rabbi; and suspected that Rabbi Lifschitz knew it and did not, in essence, trust him.

Rifkele, panting like a cow for a bull, let him out the front door, perfectly.

In the subway, Albert figured he would call it an investment in experience and see what came of it. Education costs money, but how else can you get it? He pictured the crown, as he had seen it, established on the rabbi's head, and then seemed to remember that as he had stared at the man's shifty face in the mirror the thickened lid of his right eye had slowly dropped into a full wink. Did he recall this in truth, or was he seeing in his mind's eye and transposing into the past something that had happened just before he left the house? What does he mean by his wink?—not only is he a fake but he kids you? Uneasy once more, the teacher clearly remembered, when he was staring into the rabbi's fish eyes in the glass, after which they had lit in visionary light, that he had fought a hunger to sleep; and the next thing there's the sight of the old boy, as though on the television screen, wearing this high-hat magic crown.

Albert, rising, cried, "Hypnosis! The bastard magician hypnotized me! He never did produce a silver crown, it's out of my imagination—I've been suckered!"

He was outraged by the knavery, hypocrisy, fat nerve of Rabbi Jonas Lifschitz. The concept of a curative crown, if he had ever for a moment believed in it, crumbled in his brain and all he could think of were 986 blackbirds flying in the sky. As three curious passengers watched, Albert bolted out of the car at the next stop, rushed up the stairs, hurried across the street, then cooled his impatient heels for twenty-two minutes till the next train clattered into the station, and he rode back to the stop near the rabbi's house. Though he banged with both fists on the door, kicked at it, "rang" the useless bell until his thumb was blistered, the boxlike wooden house, including dilapidated synagogue store, was dark, monumentally starkly still, like a gigantic, slightly tilted tombstone in a vast graveyard; and in the end unable to arouse a soul, the teacher, long past midnight, had to head home.

He awoke next morning cursing the rabbi and his own stupidity for having got involved with a faith healer. This is what happens when a man—even for a minute—surrenders his true beliefs. There are less punishing ways to help the dying. Albert considered calling the cops but had no receipt and did not want to appear that much a fool. He was tempted, for the first time in six years of teaching, to phone in sick; then take a cab to the rabbi's house and demand the return of his cash. The thought agitated him. On the other hand, suppose Rabbi Lifschitz was seriously at work assembling the crown with his helper; on which, let's say, after he had bought the silver and paid the retired jeweler for his work, he made, let's say, a hundred bucks clear profit—not so very much; and there really *was* a silver crown, and the rabbi sincerely and religiously believed it would reverse the course of his father's illness? Although nervously disturbed by his suspicions, Albert felt he had better not get the police into the act too soon, because the crown wasn't promised—didn't the old gent say—until before the Sabbath, which gave him till sunset tonight.

If he produces the thing by then, I have no case against him even if it's a piece of junk. So I better wait. But what a dope I was to order the $986 job instead of the $401. On that decision alone I lost $585.

After a distracted day's work Albert taxied to the rabbi's house and tried to rouse him, even hallooing at the blank windows facing the street; but either nobody was home or they were both hiding, the rabbi under the broken sofa, Rifkele trying to shove her bulk under a bathtub. Albert decided to wait them out. Soon the old boy would have to leave the house to step into the shul on Friday night. He would speak to him, warn him to come clean. But the sun set; dusk settled on the earth; and though the autumn stars and a sliver of moon gleamed in the sky, the house was dark, shades drawn; and no Rabbi Lifschitz emerged. Lights had gone on in the little shul, candles were lit. It occurred to Albert, with chagrin, that the rabbi might be already worshipping; he might all this time have been in the synagogue.

The teacher entered the long, brightly lit store. On yellow folding chairs scattered around the room sat a dozen men holding worn prayer books, praying. The rabbi, A. Marcus, a middle-aged man with a high voice and a short reddish beard, was dovening at the Ark, his back to the congregation.

As Albert entered and embarrassedly searched from face to face, the congregants stared at him. The old rabbi was not among them. Disappointed, the teacher withdrew.

A man sitting by the door touched his sleeve.

"Stay awhile and read with us."

"Excuse me, I'd like to but I'm looking for a friend."

"Look," said the man, "maybe you'll find him."

Albert waited across the street under a chestnut tree losing its leaves. He waited patiently—till tomorrow if he had to.

Shortly after nine the lights went out in the synagogue and the last of the worshippers left for home. The red-bearded rabbi then emerged with his key in his hand to lock the store door.

"Excuse me, rabbi," said Albert, approaching. "Are you acquainted with Rabbi Jonas Lifschitz, who lives upstairs with his daughter Rifkele—if she is his daughter?"

"He used to come here," said the rabbi with a small smile, "but since he retired he prefers a big synagogue on Mosholu Parkway, a palace."

"Will he be home soon, do you think?"

"Maybe in an hour. It's Shabbat, he must walk."

"Do you—ah—happen to know anything about his work on silver crowns?"

"What kind of silver crowns?"

"To assist the sick, the dying?"

"No," said the rabbi, locking the shul door, pocketing the key, and hurrying away.

The teacher, eating his heart, waited under the chestnut tree till past midnight, all the while urging himself to give up and go home, but unable to unstick the glue of his frustration and rage. Then shortly before 1 a.m. he saw some shadows moving and two people drifting up the shadow-encrusted street. One was the old rabbi, in a new caftan and snappy black Homburg, walking tiredly. Rifkele, in sexy yellow mini, exposing to above the big-bone knees her legs like poles, walked lightly behind him, stopping to strike her ears with her hands. A long white shawl, pulled short on the right shoulder, hung down to her left shoe.

"On my income their glad rags."

Rifkele chanted a long "Boooo" and slapped both ears with her pudgy hands to keep from hearing it.

They toiled up the ill-lit narrow staircase, the teacher trailing them.

"I came to see my crown," he told the pale, astonished rabbi, in the front room.

"The crown," the rabbi said haughtily, "is already finished. Go home and wait, your father will soon get better."

"I called the hospital before leaving my apartment, there's been no improvement."

"How can you expect so soon improvement if the doctors themselves don't know what is the sickness? You must give the crown a little more time. God Himself has trouble to understand human sickness."

"I came to see the thing I paid for."

"I showed you already, you saw before you ordered."

"That was an image of a facsimile, maybe, or something of the sort. I insist on seeing the real thing, for which I paid close to one thousand smackers."

"Listen, Mr. Gans," said the rabbi patiently, "there are some things we are allowed to see which He lets us see them. Sometimes I wish He didn't let us. There are other things we are not allowed to see —Moses knew this—and one is God's face, and another is the real crown that He makes and blesses it. A miracle is a miracle, this is God's business."

"Don't you see it?"

"Not with my eyes."

"I don't believe a word of it, you faker, two-bit magician."

"The crown is a real crown. If you think there is magic, it is on account those people that they insist to see it—we try to give them an idea. For those who believe, there is no magic.

"Rifkele," the rabbi said hurriedly, "bring to Papa my book of letters."

She left the room, after a while, a little in fright, her eyes evasive; and returned in ten minutes, after flushing the toilet, in a shapeless long flannel nightgown, carrying a large yellowed notebook whose loose pages were thickly interleaved with old correspondence.

"Testimonials," said the rabbi.

Turning several loose pages, with trembling hand he extracted a letter and read it aloud, his voice husky with emotion.

" 'Dear Rabbi Lifschitz: Since the miraculous recovery of my mother, Mrs. Max Cohen, from her recent illness, my impulse is to cover your bare feet with kisses. Your crown worked wonders and I am recommending it to all my friends. Yours truly and sincerely, (Mrs.) Esther Polatnik.'

"This is a college teacher."

He read another. " 'Dear Rabbi Lifschitz, Your $986 crown totally and completely cured my father of cancer of the pancreas, with serious complications of the lungs, after nothing else had worked. Never before have I believed in miraculous occurrences, but from now on I will have less doubts. My thanks to you and God. Most sincerely, Daniel Schwartz.'

"A lawyer," said the rabbi.

He offered the book to Albert. "Look yourself, Mr. Gans, hundreds of letters."

Albert wouldn't touch it.

"There's only one thing I want to look at, Rabbi Lifschitz, and it's not a book of useless testimonials. I want to see my father's silver crown."

"This is impossible. I already explained to you why I can't do this. God's word is God's law."

"So if it's the law you're citing, either I see the crown in the next five minutes or the first thing tomorrow morning I'm reporting you and your activities to the Bronx County District Attorney."

"Boooo-ooo," sang Rifkele, banging her ears.

"Shut up!" Albert said.

"Have respect," cried the rabbi. "Grubber yung!"

"I will swear out a complaint and the D.A. will shut you down, the whole freaking plant, if you don't at once return the $986 you swindled me out of."

The rabbi wavered in his tracks. "Is this the way to talk to a rabbi of God?"

"A thief is a thief."

Rifkele blubbered, squealed.

"Sha," the rabbi thickly whispered to Albert, clasping and unclasping his gray hands. "You'll frighten the neighbors. Listen to me, Mr.

Gans, you saw with your eyes what it looks like the real crown. I give you my word that nobody of my whole clientele ever saw this before. I showed you for your father's sake so you would tell me to make the crown which will save him. Don't spoil now the miracle."

"Miracle," Albert bellowed, "it's a freaking fake magic, with an idiot girl for a come-on and hypnotic mirrors. I was mesmerized, suckered by you."

"Be kind," begged the rabbi, tottering as he wandered amid empty chairs. "Be merciful to an old man. Think of my poor child. Think of your father who loves you."

"He hates me, the son of a bitch, I hope he croaks."

In an explosion of silence the girl slobbered in fright.

"Aha," cried the wild-eyed rabbi, pointing a finger at God in heaven. "Murderer," he cried, aghast.

Moaning, father and daughter rushed into each other's arms, as Albert, wearing a massive, spike-laden headache, rushed down the booming stairs.

An hour later the elder Gans shut his eyes and expired.

1972

B M

Notes from a Lady at

a Dinner Party

Max Adler, passing through the city in November, had telephoned his old professor of architecture, Clem Harris, and was at once cordially invited to dinner that night at his house in Hempstead to meet some good friends and his young wife, Karla.

She spoke of her husband's respect for Adler. "He says about you something he doesn't often say about his former students—that you deserve your success. Didn't you win an AIA national medal about two years out of graduate school?"

"Not a medal," Adler explained, pleased. "It was an Honor Award certificate for a house I designed."

Adler, at the time of the dinner party, was a loose-fleshed heavy man who dressed with conservative carelessness and weighed 210.

"That's what I mean." She laughed in embarrassment and he imagined that she often laughed in embarrassment. She was strong-bodied and plain, in an elegant way, and wore her brown hair pulled back in a twist. He thought she was twenty-five or -six. She had on a short green dress with sandals, and her sturdy legs and thighs were well formed. Adler, when she asked, said he was thirty-two, and Karla remarked it was a fine age for a man. He knew her husband's age was twice his. She was direct and witty, with a certain tensity of expression, and she told him almost at once that friendship meant a lot to her.

It was during dinner that Karla Harris let Adler know about the note in his pocket. They were six at the table in the large wood-paneled dining room, with a bay window containing a pebbled bed of chrysanthemums and begonias. Besides the hosts there was a middle-aged couple, the Ralph Lewins—he was a colleague of Harris's at the Columbia University School of Architecture; and maybe to balance off Adler, Harris's secretary, Shirley Fisher, had been invited, a thin-ankled, wet-eyed divorcée in a long bright-blue skirt, who talked and drank liberally. Harris, pouring wine liberally from a bottle in a basket, sat at the head of the broad neat table, opposite Karla, who was on the qui vive to see that everything went as it should; from time to time her husband smiled his encouragement.

Max Adler sat on her right, facing Lewin across the table, and on his right was Mrs. Lewin, a small luminous-faced, listening person. Karla, when Harris was ladling turtle soup into bowls out of a handsome tureen, and the conversation was lively, leaned imperceptibly close to Adler and whispered, "If you like surprises, feel in your left pocket when you can," and though he wasn't sure at once was the proper time, when she left the room to get the rolls that had almost burned, he casually reached into his suit-coat pocket and felt a folded slip of paper which, after a minute, he smoothed out and read in his palm.

If anybody at the table had noticed that Adler's head was momentarily lowered and wondered whether he was privately saying grace, or maybe studying his wristwatch with a view to catching an early train back to the city, it occurred to him he wouldn't have worried; he was politely reading the lady's note, had initiated nothing. The slip of yellow lined paper, in small printed handwriting, said simply, "Why do we all think we *should* be happy, that it's one of the *necessary* conditions of life?" and for a while Adler, who took questions of this sort seriously, didn't know what to say in reply.

She could quite easily have asked her question while they were having cocktails on the enclosed porch and he would have done his best with it; but she had seemed concerned about the dinner and had been in and out of the kitchen many times; dealing also with the girl sitter who was putting the children to bed, really too busy to sustain a conversation with any of her guests. Yet since she hadn't orally asked her question, Adler felt he had to respect the fact that she had found it necessary to write it out on paper and slip into his pocket. If this was the way she was moved to express herself, he thought he ought to answer with a note. He glanced at her husband, aged but still vigorous since he had seen him last, who was at the moment listening attentively to Shirley. Adler excused himself—he said to get his glasses—to scribble a note on a memo pad; and when he returned, though he wasn't comfortable in pretense, he covertly passed the paper to her, grazing her warm bare thigh, though he hadn't intended to, then feeling her narrow fingers, as he touched them, close on the note.

He had been tempted to say that happiness wasn't something he worried about anymore—you had it or you hadn't and why beat your brains blue when there was work to be done; but he didn't say that. He had quickly written, "Why not?—it's a short hard life if you don't outfox it."

Karla glanced at the paper in her hand, a fork in a piece of fillet of sole in the other, apparently not disappointed, her color heightened, expression neutral, a bit distant. She disappeared into the kitchen with an empty salad bowl and, when she was again seated at the table, secretly passed Adler another note: "I want you to see my babies." Adler solemnly nodded as he pocketed the paper. She smiled vaguely as her husband, who had once more risen to refill the wineglasses, gazed at her fondly. The others were momentarily quietly eating, not, apparently, attentive. Karla returned a resemblance of her husband's smile as Adler, wondering why she engaged him in this curious game, felt they were now related in a way he couldn't have foreseen when he had entered the house that evening. When Harris, behind him, pouring wine into his glass, let his hand fall affectionately on his former student's shoulder, Max, who had experienced a strong emotion on seeing his old professor after so many years, felt himself resist his touch.

Later he enjoyed talking with him over brandy in the living room; it was a spacious room, twenty-four by thirty, Adler estimated, tastefully and comfortably furnished, draped, decorated, with a glass bowl of golden chrysanthemums and Shasta daisies on the fireplace mantel and some bright modernist paintings on the wall. Karla was then in the kitchen, showing the sitter how to stack and operate the dishwasher, and Adler felt geared to anticipation, though not sure of what. He tried to suppress the feeling and to some extent succeeded. But as Clem Harris poured him a cognac he stealthily felt in his pocket and there were the two notes only.

The professor, a crisp tall man with a clipped grayish beard, faintly red, and thick gray sideburns, who wore a green blazer with an orange shirt and white bow tie, was lavish in his praise of Adler's recent work, some slides of which the architect had sent him; and Max once more expressed gratitude for the interest Harris continued to show. He had always been a kind man and influential teacher.

"What are you into now?" Harris asked. After two brandies he had gone back to Scotch-and-soda. His large face was flushed and he wiped his watery eyes with a pressed handkerchief. Adler had noticed how often he glanced up at the dining-room door in anticipation of his wife's reappearance.

"The same project you saw in the transparencies," Adler said. "How about you?"

"Renovating some slum units for a private low-income housing group. There's very little money in it. It's more or less pro bono."

"I ought to be doing more of that myself."

Harris, after observing Adler for a moment, asked, "Aren't you putting on more weight, Max?"

"I eat too much," Adler confessed.

"You ought to watch your weight. Do you still smoke like a chimney?"

"Not anymore."

"Bully. I wish I could get Karla to cut down."

When she reappeared his wife had brushed her hair. The green dress she had been wearing she had changed for a short crocheted strawberry mini, with white bra and half-slip showing through the weave. The warm color of the dress brought out a bloom in her face. She was an attractive woman.

"Ah, you've changed your dress," her husband said.

"I spilled at least a pint of gravy on it," Karla explained with an embarrassed laugh.

"I thought you didn't much care for this one."

"When did I say that?" she asked. "I do like it. I like it very much. It's the purple one I don't like—it's too damn harsh."

Harris, drinking from his glass, nodded pleasantly. Something else was on his mind. "I wish you'd get yourself more help when you need it."

"What kind of help?" asked Karla.

"In the kitchen, of course." His tone was affectionate, solicitous.

"Stephanie's cleaning up—that's the dirty work."

"It was a wonderful meal," said Max.

She thanked him.

"We ought to have a maid to help at dinner parties," Harris insisted. "Sometimes our guests barely get a look at you. I wish you'd be less a puritan about occasional luxuries. I hate for you to be too tired to enjoy your own parties."

"I'm enjoying this."

Max nodded.

"You know what I mean," Harris said.

"Clem, I simply don't like maids around at small dinner parties."

She told Adler that Stephanie was another of Harris's students.

"The father of us all," she laughed.

"Stephanie needs the money," Harris said.

Karla then asked Adler if he liked her in her crocheted dress. He said he did.

"Is it too short?"

"No," said Max.

"I didn't say it was," said Harris.

The phone rang, and when he answered, it was one of his doctoral candidates. Harris, good-humoredly wiggling his fingers at Karla, talked patiently with the doctoral candidate.

Adler and Karla were sitting on a love seat facing the flower-laden fireplace, when she whispered there was a note between the pillows. He recovered it as they were talking and slipped it into his pocket.

"I'll read it later."

But she had left the love seat as though to give him an opportunity to read what she had written. Karla plopped herself down next to Ada Lewin on the long beige sofa along the left wall, as Ralph Lewin, sipping a brandy, listened to Clem on the phone. Shirley Fisher then drifted over to talk with the visitor. She wore a low-draped white camisole with a slit midi and was openly flirtatious. When she crossed her legs a long thin thigh was exposed.

"Don't older woman interest you, Mr. Adler?" Her voice was slightly husky.

"I wouldn't call you old."

Shirley said she was charmed but then Karla returned. Harris was still patiently on the phone. Adler decided the colors he wore went well with the paintings on the walls. When Max was his student, Harris had worn gray suits with white shirts.

"Can you spare him for five minutes, Shirley?" Karla asked. "I want Mr. Adler to see the babies."

"Max," said Adler.

"Wouldn't they be sleeping now?"

"I want him to see them anyway—if he'd like to."

Max said he would.

He had managed to glance at her note: "Don't panic but I like you a lot."

"Enjoy yourselves," Shirley said, pouring herself a brandy.

"We will," Karla said.

As they were going up the stairs Adler said, "I wouldn't want to wake them up."

"They'll go right on sleeping."

She opened the door, switching on the light. Two children slept in cribs in a large nursery room with three curtained windows. At first Adler thought they were twins, but they weren't. One was a little girl with light-blond curls in a white crib, and the other was an infant boy in an orange crib. On the floor, in the corner, stood a circular canvas playpen strewn with dolls and wooden toys. A series of small-animal watercolors was framed on the walls; Karla said she had done them.

"I used to do such lovely watercolors."

Adler said they were charming.

"Not those, my watercolors from nature. I just haven't the time to paint anymore."

"I know what you mean."

"You really don't," she said.

"This is Sara," Karla said, standing by the white crib. "She's two. Stevie is just eleven months. Look at those shoulders. Clem thought we ought to have them close together so they would be friends. His first wife died childless."

"I knew her," Adler said.

The boy, in undershirt and plastic diaper cover, lay on his side, sucking the corner of his blanket in his sleep. He resembled his father.

The little girl, asleep on her back in a flowered yellow nightgown, clutching a stuffed doll, looked like Karla.

"They're lovely children," Adler said.

Karla stood at the little girl's crib. "Oh, my babies," she said. "My little babies. My heart goes out to them." She lowered the side of the crib and, bending, kissed Sara, who opened her eyes, stared at her mother, and was then asleep, smiling.

Karla withdrew the doll and the child released it with a sigh. Then she covered the little boy with his blanket.

"Very nice children," Adler said.

"My lovely little babies. My babies, my babies." Her face was tender, sad, illumined.

"Do I sound hokey?"

"I wouldn't say so." Max was affected by her.

She lowered the shades, switched out the lights, quietly closed the door.

"Come see my study."

It was a light-curtained lavender room with a desk, portable sewing machine, and a circle of snapshots on the wall before her. Her father, who had sold insurance in Columbus, Ohio, was dead. There he was, fifty, standing in front of his automobile. The sad-faced mother had posed in her flower garden. A shot of Karla taken in college showed an attractive, sober girl with wire-frame glasses, dark eyes and brows, firm full lips. Her desk was cluttered with books, sheet music, shopping lists, correspondence.

She wanted to know if Adler had any children.

"No." He told her he had been married a short time and divorced long ago.

"You never remarried?"

"No."

"Clem married me when I was very young," Karla said.

"Didn't you marry him?"

"I mean I hardly knew what I was doing."

"What was he doing?"

"Marrying me when I was very young."

She raised the shade and stared into the night. A streetlight in the distance glowed through the wet window. "I always give dinner parties on rainy nights."

She said they ought to go down to the others but then opened the closet door and got out a large glossy photograph of a one-family dwelling project she had done in her architecture class with Harris.

Max said it showed promise. Karla smiled wryly.

"Really," he said.

"I love *your* work," she said. "I love the chances you take."

"If they work out right."

"They do, they do." She seemed to be trembling.

They embraced forcefully. She dug her body into his. They kissed wet-mouthed, then she broke with an embarrassed laugh.

"They'll be wondering."

"He's still on the phone," Max said, aroused.

"We'd better go down."

"What's Shirley to him?"

"A tight-jawed bitch."

"To him, I said."

"He's sorry for her. Her fourteen-year-old kid is on LSD. He's sorry for everybody."

They kissed again, then Karla stepped out of his embrace and they went downstairs.

Harris was off the phone.

"I showed him our babies," Karla said to her husband.

"Showoff," smiled Harris.

"Lovely children," said Max.

Shirley winked at him.

I've lost the right to his friendship, the architect thought. A minute later he thought, Things change, they have to.

"Now please stay put for a few minutes," Harris said to Karla. "Catch your breath."

"First I have to pay Stephanie."

Harris went to his den and returned with a box of color transparencies of his renovation project for a slum-housing improvement group: before and after.

Max, his mind on Karla, examined the slides, holding each to the light. He said it was work well done.

Harris said he was gratified that Max approved.

Karla was paying Stephanie in the kitchen. Ralph Lewin, smoking a cigar, also looked at the slides, although he said he was the one who had originally taken them. Ada and Shirley were on the green sofa on the right side of the room, Ada seriously listening as Shirley went on about her son on LSD.

Karla carried in a silver trayful of bone-china cups and saucers.

"I'm always late with coffee," she remarked.

"Make mine tea," said Ralph.

She said she would get the tea in a minute.

As she handed out the coffee cups she slipped Adler a note with his.

He read it in the bathroom. "Pretend you're going to the bathroom, then go left in the back hall and you'll come out in the kitchen."

He went to the left in the hall and came out in the kitchen.

They kissed with passion.

"Where can we meet?"

"When?" Max asked.

"Tonight, maybe? I'm not sure."

"Is there a motel around?"

"Two blocks away."

"I'll get a room if you can make it. If not tonight, I could stay on till tomorrow noon. I've got to be in Boston by evening."

"I think I can. Clem and I are in separate bedrooms right now. He sleeps like dead. I'll let you know before you leave."

"Just give me a sign," Max said. "Don't write any notes."

"Don't you like them?" Karla asked.

"I do but they're risky. What if he sees you passing me one?"

"It might do him good."

"I don't want any part of that," Max said.

"I like to write notes," said Karla. "I like to write to people I like. I like to write things that suddenly occur to me. My diary was full of exciting thoughts when I was young."

"All I'm saying is it could be dangerous. Just give me a sign or say something before I leave and I'll wait till you come."

"I burned my diary last summer but I still write notes. I've always written notes to people. You have to let me be who I am."

He asked her why she had burned her diary.

"I had to. It beat me up badly." She burst into tears.

Adler left the kitchen and returned to the bathroom. He flushed the toilet, washed his hands, and reappeared in the living room. At the same moment, Karla, her face composed, brought in Ralph's tea.

For a while they talked politics across the room. Then the talk went to music and Harris put on a new recording he had bought of Mahler's "Songs of a Wayfarer." Despite the singing, Shirley talked earnestly to Ralph Lewin, who suppressed a yawn now and then. Ada and Karla were chatting about the Lewins' new house they were about to build in the spring, and Harris and Adler, on the long beige couch, discussed developments in architecture. "I might as well turn off the music," Harris said. After he had put the record away he returned and, resuming their conversation, characterized Adler's latest work as his most daring.

"That's a quality you inspired me to."

"In moderation."

Adler said he appreciated his mentor's sentiments. He felt for the first time he did not know what to say to him and it made him uncomfortable. He was now not sure whether to urge Karla to try to get out of the house tonight. On the one hand he had gratitude and loyalty to Harris to contend with; on the other he felt as though he were in love with her.

They managed to meet alone at the fireplace, when to his strange surprise she whispered, "Something's coming your way," and surreptitiously touched his hand with a folded slip of paper. Turning away from the company, Adler managed to read it, then thrust it into his pants pocket.

Karla's note said: "Can someone love someone she doesn't know?"

"We do it all the time."

"Partly I think I love you because I love your work."

"Don't confuse me with my work," Adler said. "It would be a mistake."

"It's on for tonight," she whispered.

As they stood side by side with their backs to the fireplace they reached behind them and squeezed hands.

Karla, glancing across the room at her husband, excused herself to go up to see if the babies were covered. Adler, after she had gone, tried to think of a reason to follow her upstairs, but the impulse was insane. It was past eleven and he felt nervously expectant.

When Karla came down from the nursery he heard her say to her husband, "Clem, I'm having some anxiety."

"Take a pill," Harris advised.

Adler then seriously wondered whether to tell her to cool it for tonight. It might be better to call her from the motel in the morning, when Harris was gone, and if she still felt she could they would meet then. But he doubted, if they didn't get together tonight, that she could make it in the morning. So he decided to urge her to come as soon as she was sure her husband was asleep.

She wants someone young for a change, he thought. It will be good for her.

Wanting to tell her the anxiety would go once they were in bed together, Max sat down beside her on the green sofa, where she was listening distantly to Shirley saying the drug situation had made her frantic. He waited impatiently for one or the other to get up so that he could say what he had to to Karla. Harris, standing nearby, conversing with Ada, seemed to be listening to Shirley. Karla pretended to be unaware of Adler by her side; but after a minute he felt her hand groping for his pocket. Without wanting to he moved away.

Adler, just then, expected his pocket to burst into flame. She'll write them forever, he thought; that's her nature. If not to me, then to the next one who comes into the house who's done something she wishes she had. He made up his mind to return the note unread. At the same time, with a dismaying sense of sudden loss, Adler realized he couldn't read it if he wanted to because the paper hadn't gone into his pocket but had fallen to the floor. The sight of the folded yellow paper at his feet sickened the architect. Karla was staring at it as though reliving a dream. She had written it upstairs in her study and it said, "Darling, I can't meet you, I am six months pregnant."

Before either of them could move to retrieve the paper, or even let it lie where it had fallen, Shirley had plucked it up.

"Did you drop this?" she asked Clem Harris.

Adler's head was thick with blood. He felt childlike and foolish. I'm disgraced and deserve it.

But Harris did not unfold the paper. He handed it to his former student. "It isn't mine, is it yours?"

"An address I wrote down," Adler said. He rose. "I have this early train to Boston to catch in the morning."

Ada and Ralph Lewin were the first to say good night.

"Bon voyage," said Shirley.

Harris brought Adler's coat and helped him on with it. They shook hands cordially.

"The air shuttle is the fastest way to Boston."

Max said he thought that was how he would go. He then said goodbye to Karla. "Thanks for having me."

"Love, marriage, happiness," Karla sang, standing in her crocheted short mini on the stairs.

She runs up to her babies in the nursery.

1973

❧ B M ❧

In Retirement

He had lately taken to studying his old Greek grammar of fifty years ago. He read in Bulfinch and wanted to reread the *Odyssey* in Greek. His life had changed. He slept less these days and in the morning got up to stare at the sky over Gramercy Park. He watched the clouds until they took shapes he could reflect on. He liked strange, haunted vessels, and he liked to watch mythological birds and animals. He had noticed that if he contemplated these forms in the clouds, could keep his mind on them for a while, there might be a diminution of his morning depression. Dr. Morris was sixty-six, a physician, retired for two years. He had shut down his practice in Queens and moved to Manhattan. He had retired himself after a heart attack, not too serious but serious enough. It was his first attack and he hoped his last, though in the end he hoped to go quickly. His wife was dead and his daughter lived in Scotland. He wrote her twice a month and heard from her twice a month. And though he had a few friends he visited, and kept up with medical journals, and liked museums and theater, generally he contended with loneliness. And he was concerned about the future; the future was by old age possessed.

After a light breakfast he would dress warmly and go out for a walk around the Square. That was the easy part of the walk. He took this walk even when it was very cold, or nasty rainy, or had snowed several inches and he had to proceed very carefully. After the Square he crossed the street and went down Irving Place, a tall figure with a cape and cane, and picked up his *Times*. If the weather was not too

bad he continued on to Fourteenth Street, around to Park Avenue
South, up Park and along East Twentieth back to the narrow, tall,
white stone apartment building he lived in. Rarely, lately, had he
gone in another direction though when on the long walk he stopped
at least once on the way, perhaps in front of a mid-block store, perhaps
at a street corner, and asked himself where else he might go. This
was the difficult part of the walk. What was difficult was that it made
no difference which way he went. He now wished he had not retired.
He had become more conscious of his age since his retirement, although sixty-six was not eighty. Still it was old. He experienced moments of anguish.

One morning after his rectangular long walk in the rain, he
found a letter on the rubber mat under the line of mailboxes in the
lobby. It was a narrow, deep lobby with false green marble columns
and several bulky chairs where few people ever sat. Dr. Morris had
seen a young woman with long hair, in a white raincoat and maroon
shoulder bag, carrying a plastic bubble umbrella, hurry down the
vestibule steps and leave the house as he was about to enter. In fact
he held the door open for her and got a breath of her bold perfume.
He did not remember seeing her before and felt a momentary confusion as to who she might be. He later imagined her taking the letter
out of her box, reading it hastily, then stuffing it into the maroon
cloth purse she carried over her shoulder; but she had stuffed in the
envelope and not the letter.

That had fallen to the floor. He imagined this as he bent to
retrieve it. It was a folded sheet of heavy white writing paper, written
on in black ink in a masculine hand. The doctor unfolded and glanced
at it without making out the salutation or any of its contents. He
would have to put on his reading glasses, and he thought Flaherty,
the doorman and elevator man, might see him if the elevator should
suddenly descend. Of course Flaherty might think the doctor was
reading his own mail, except that he never read it, such as it was, in
the lobby. He did not want the man thinking he was reading someone
else's letter. He also thought of handing him the letter and describing
the young woman who had dropped it. Perhaps he could return it to
her? But for some reason not at once clear to him the doctor slipped
it into his pocket to take upstairs to read. His arm began to tremble
and he felt his heart racing at a rate that bothered him.

After the doctor had got his own mail out of the box—nothing
more than the few medical circulars he held in his hand—Flaherty
took him up to the fifteenth floor. Flaherty spelled the night man at

8 a.m. and was himself relieved at 4 p.m. He was a slender man of sixty with sparse white hair on his half-bald head, who had lost part of his jaw under the left ear after two bone operations. He would be out for a few months; then return, the lower part of the left side of his face partially caved in; still it was not a bad face to look at. Although the doorman never spoke of his ailment, the doctor knew he was not done with cancer of the jaw, but of course he kept this to himself; and he sensed when the man was concealing pain.

This morning, though preoccupied, he asked, "How is it going, Mr. Flaherty?"

"Not too tough."

"Not a bad day." He said this, thinking not of the rain but of the letter in his pocket.

"Fine and dandy," Flaherty quipped. On the whole he moved and talked animatedly, and was careful to align the elevator with the floor before letting passengers off. Sometimes the doctor wished he could say more to him than he usually did; but not this morning.

He stood by the large double window of his living room overlooking the Square, in the dull rainy-day February light, in pleasurable excitement reading the letter he had found, the kind he had anticipated it might be. It was a letter written by a father to his daughter, addressed to "Dear Evelyn." What it expressed after an irresolute start was the father's dissatisfaction with his daughter's way of life. And it ended with an exhortatory paragraph of advice: "You have slept around long enough. I don't understand what you get out of that type of behavior anymore. I think you have tried everything there is to try. You claim you are a serious person but let men use you for what they can get. There is no true payoff to you unless it is very temporary, and the real payoff to them is that they have got themselves an easy lay. I know how they think about this and how they talk about it in the lavatory the next day. Now I want to urge you once and for all that you ought to be more serious about your life. You have experimented long enough. I honestly and sincerely and urgently advise you to look around for a man of steady habits and good character who will marry you and treat you like the person I believe you want to be. I don't want to think of you anymore as a drifting semi-prostitute. Please follow this advice, the age of twenty-nine is no longer sixteen." The letter was signed "Your Father," and under his signature, another sentence, in neat small handwriting, was appended: "Your sex life fills me full of fear. Mother."

The doctor put the letter away in a drawer. His excitement had

left him and he felt ashamed of having read it. He was sympathetic
to the father, and at the same time sympathetic to the young woman,
though perhaps less so to her. After a while he tried to study his
Greek grammar but could not concentrate. The letter remained in his
mind like a billboard sign as he was reading the *Times*, and he was
conscious of it throughout the day, as though it had aroused in him
some sort of expectation he could not define. Sentences from it would
replay themselves in his thoughts. He reveried the young woman as
he had imagined her after reading what the father had written, and
as the woman—was she Evelyn?—he had seen coming out of the
house. He could not be certain the letter was hers. Perhaps it was
not; still he thought of it as belonging to her, the woman he had held
the door for whose perfume still lingered in his senses.

That night, thoughts of her kept him from falling asleep. "I'm too
old for this nonsense." He got up to read and was able to concentrate,
but when his head lay once more on the pillow, a long freight train of
thoughts provocative of her rumbled by, drawn by a long black locomotive. He pictured Evelyn, the drifting semi-prostitute, in bed with
various lovers, engaged in various acts of sex. Once she lay alone, eroti-
cally naked, her maroon cloth purse drawn close to her nude body. He
also thought of her as an ordinary girl with many fewer lovers than her
father seemed to think. This was probably closer to the truth. He wondered if he could be useful to her in some way. He felt a fright he could
not explain but managed to dispel it by promising himself to burn the
letter in the morning. The freight train, with its many cars, clattered
along in the foggy distance. When the doctor awoke at 10 a.m. on a
sunny winter's morning, there was no awareness, light or heavy, of his
morning depression.

But he did not burn the letter. He reread it several times during
the day, each time returning it to his desk drawer and locking it there.
Then he unlocked the drawer to read it again. As the day passed he was
aware of an insistent hunger in himself. He recalled memories, experienced longing, intense desires he had not felt in years. The doctor was
concerned by this change in him, this disturbance. He tried to blot the
letter out of his mind but could not. Yet he would still not burn it, as
though if he did, he had shut the door on certain possibilities in his life,
other ways to go, whatever that might mean. He was astonished—even
thought of it as affronted, that this was happening to him at his age. He
had seen it in others, former patients, but had not expected it in himself.

The hunger he felt, a hunger for pleasure, disruption of habit, re-
newal of feeling, yet a fear of it, continued to grow in him like a dead

tree come to life and spreading its branches. He felt as though he was hungry for exotic experience, which, if he was to have it, might make him ravenously hungry. He did not want that to happen. He recalled mythological figures: Sisyphus, Midas, who for one reason or another had been eternally cursed. He thought of Tithonus, his youth gone, become a grasshopper living forever. The doctor felt he was caught in an overwhelming emotion, a fearful dark wind.

When Flaherty left for the day at 4 p.m. and Silvio, who had tight curly black hair, was on duty, Dr. Morris came down and sat in the lobby, pretending to read his newspaper. As soon as the elevator went up he approached the letter boxes and scanned the nameplates for an Evelyn, whoever she might be. He found no Evelyns, though there was an E. Gordon and an E. Commings. He suspected one of them might be she. He knew that single women often preferred not to reveal their first names in order to keep cranks at a distance, conceal themselves from potential annoyers. He casually asked Silvio if Miss Gordon or Miss Commings was named Evelyn, but Silvio said he didn't know, although probably Mr. Flaherty would because he distributed the mail. "Too many peoples in this house." Silvio shrugged. The doctor remarked he was just curious, a lame remark but all he could think of. He went out for an aimless short stroll and when he returned said nothing more to Silvio. They rode silently up in the elevator, the doctor standing tall, almost stiff. That night he slept badly. When he fell deeply asleep a moment his dreams were erotic. He woke feeling desire and repulsion and lay mourning himself. He felt powerless to be other than he was.

He was up before five and was uselessly in the lobby before seven. He felt he must find out, settle who she was. In the lobby, Richard, the night man who had brought him down, returned to a pornographic paperback he was reading; the mail, as Dr. Morris knew, hadn't come. He knew it would not arrive until after eight, but hadn't the patience to wait in his apartment. So he left the building, bought the *Times* on Irving Place, continued on his walk, and because it was a pleasant morning, not too cold, sat on a bench in Union Square Park. He stared at the newspaper but could not read it. He watched some sparrows pecking at dead grass. He was an older man, true enough, but had lived long enough to know that age often meant little in man-woman relationships. He was still vigorous and bodies are bodies. The doctor was back in the lobby at eight-thirty, an act of restraint. Flaherty had received the mail sack and was alphabetizing the first-class letters on a long table before distributing them into the boxes. He did not look well today. He moved slowly. His misshapen face was gray, the mouth slack; one heard his breathing; his eyes harbored pain.

"Nothin for you yet," he said to the doctor, not looking up.

"I'll wait this morning," said Dr. Morris. "I should be hearing from my daughter."

"Nothin yet, but you might hit the lucky number in this last bundle." He removed the string.

As he was alphabetizing the last bundle of letters the elevator buzzed and Flaherty had to go up for a call.

The doctor pretended to be absorbed in his *Times*. When the elevator door shut he sat momentarily still, then went to the table and hastily riffled through the C pile of letters. E. Commings was Ernest Commings. He shuffled through the G's, watching the metal arrow as it showed the elevator descending. In the G pile there were two letters addressed to Evelyn Gordon. One was from her mother. The other, also handwritten, was from a Lee Bradley. Almost against his will the doctor removed this letter and slipped it into his suit pocket. His body was hot. He was sitting in the chair turning the page of his newspaper when the elevator door opened.

"Nothin at all for you," Flaherty said after a moment.

"Thank you," said Dr. Morris. "I think I'll go up."

In his apartment the doctor, conscious of his whisperous breathing, placed the letter on the kitchen table and sat looking at it, waiting for the teakettle to boil. The kettle whistled as it boiled but still he sat with the unopened letter before him. For a while he sat there with dulled thoughts. Soon he fantasied Lee Bradley describing the sexual pleasure he had had with Evelyn Gordon. He fantasied the lovers' acts they engaged in. Then though he audibly told himself not to, he steamed open the flap of the envelope and had to place it flat on the table so he could read it. His heart beat in anticipation of what he might read. But to his surprise the letter was a bore, an egoistic account of some stupid business deal this Bradley was concocting. Only the last sentences came surprisingly to life. "Be in your bed when I get there tonight. Be wearing only your white panties."

The doctor didn't know whom he was more disgusted with, this fool or himself. In truth, himself. Slipping the sheet of paper into the envelope, he resealed it with a thin layer of paste he had rubbed carefully on the flap with his fingertip. Later in the day he tucked the letter into his inside pocket and pressed the elevator button for Silvio. The doctor left the building and afterwards returned with a copy of the *Post* he seemed to be involved with until Silvio had to take up two women who had come into the lobby; then the doctor slipped the letter into Evelyn Gordon's box and went out for a breath of air.

He was sitting near the table in the lobby when the young woman he had held the door open for came in shortly after 6 p.m. He was aware of her perfume almost at once. Silvio was not around at that moment; he had gone down to the basement to eat a sandwich. She inserted a small key into Evelyn Gordon's mailbox and stood before the open box, smoking, as she read Bradley's letter. She was wearing a light-blue pants suit with a brown knit sweater-coat. Her tail of black hair was tied with a brown silk scarf. Her face, though a little heavy, was pretty, her intense eyes blue, the lids lightly eye-shadowed. Her body, he thought, was finely proportioned. She had not noticed him but he was more than half in love with her.

He observed her many mornings. He would come down later now, at nine, and spend some time going through the medical circulars he had got out of his box, sitting on a throne-like wooden chair near a tall unlit lamp in the rear of the lobby. He would watch people as they left for work or shopping in the morning. Evelyn appeared at about half past nine and stood smoking in front of her box, absorbed in the morning's mail. When spring came she wore brightly colored skirts with pastel blouses, or light slim pants suits. Sometimes she wore minidresses. Her figure was exquisite. She received many letters and read most of them with apparent pleasure, some with what seemed suppressed excitement. A few she gave short shrift to, scanned these and stuffed them into her bag. He imagined they were from her father, or mother. He thought that most of her letters came from lovers, past and present, and he felt a sort of sadness that there was none from him in her mailbox. He would write to her.

He thought it through carefully. Some women needed an older man; it stabilized their lives. Sometimes a difference of as many as thirty or even thirty-five years offered no serious disadvantages. A younger woman inspired an older man to remain virile. And despite the heart incident his health was good, in some ways better than before. A woman like Evelyn, probably at odds with herself, could benefit from a steadying relationship with an older man, someone who would respect and love her and help her to respect and love herself; who would demand less from her in certain ways than some young men awash in their egoism; who would awake in her a stronger sense of well-being, and if things went quite well, perhaps even love for a particular man.

"I am a retired physician, a widower," he wrote to Evelyn Gordon. "I write you with some hesitation and circumspection, although needless to say with high regard, because I am old enough to be your father. I have observed you often in this building and as we passed each other in nearby streets; I have grown to admire you. I wonder if you will permit me to make your acquaintance? Would you care to have dinner with me and perhaps enjoy a film or performance of a play? I do not think my company will disappoint you. If you are so inclined—so kind, certainly—to consider this request tolerantly, I will be obliged if you place a note to that effect in my mailbox. I am respectfully yours, Simon Morris, M.D."

He did not go down to mail his letter. He thought he would keep it to the last moment. Then he had a fright about it that woke him out of momentary sleep. He dreamed he had written and sealed the letter and then remembered he had appended another sentence: "Be wearing your white panties." When he woke he wanted to tear open the envelope to see whether he had included Bradley's remark. But when he was thoroughly waked up, he knew he had not. He bathed and shaved early and for a while observed the cloud formations out the window. At close to nine Dr. Morris descended to the lobby. He would wait till Flaherty answered a buzz and, when he was gone, drop his letter into her box; but Flaherty that morning seemed to have no calls to answer. The doctor had forgotten it was Saturday. He did not know it was till he got his *Times* and sat with it in the lobby, pretending to be waiting for the mail delivery. The mail sack arrived late on Saturdays. At last he heard a prolonged buzz, and Flaherty, who had been on his knees polishing the brass doorknob, got up on one foot, then rose on both legs and walked slowly to the elevator. His asymmetric face was gray. Shortly before ten o'clock the doctor slipped his letter into Evelyn Gordon's mailbox. He decided to withdraw to his apartment, then thought he would rather wait where he usually waited while she collected her mail. She had never noticed him there.

The mail sack was dropped in the vestibule at ten-after, and Flaherty alphabetized the first bundle before he responded to another call. The doctor read his paper in the dark rear of the lobby, because he was really not reading it. He was anticipating Evelyn's coming. He had on a new green suit, blue striped shirt, and a pink tie. He wore a new hat. He waited with anticipation and love.

When the elevator door opened, Evelyn walked out in an elegant slit black skirt, pretty sandals, her hair tied with a red scarf. A sharp-featured man with puffed sideburns and carefully combed medium-long hair, in a turn-of-the-century haircut, followed her out of the elevator. He was shorter than she by half a head. Flaherty handed her two letters, which she dropped into the black patent-leather pouch she was carrying. The doctor thought—hoped—she would walk past the mailboxes without stopping; but she saw the white of his letter through the slot and stopped to remove it. She tore open the envelope, pulled out the single sheet of handwritten paper, read it with immediate intense concentration. The doctor raised his newspaper to his eyes, although he could still watch over the top of it. He watched in fear.

How mad I was not to anticipate she might come down with a man.

When she had finished reading the letter, she handed it to her companion—possibly Bradley—who read it, grinned broadly, and said something inaudible as he handed it back to her.

Evelyn Gordon quietly ripped the letter into small bits and, turning, flung the pieces in the doctor's direction. The fragments came at him like a blast of wind-driven snow. He thought he would sit forever on his wooden throne in the swirling snowstorm.

The old doctor sat in his chair, the floor around him littered with his torn-up letter.

Flaherty swept it up with his little broom into a metal container. He handed the doctor a thin envelope stamped with foreign stamps.

"Here's a letter from your daughter that's just come."

The doctor pressed the bridge of his nose. He wiped his eyes with his fingers.

"There's no setting aside old age," he remarked after a while.

"No, sir," said Flaherty.

"Or death."

"They move up on you."

The doctor tried to say something splendidly kind, but could not say it.

Flaherty took him up to the fifteenth floor in his elevator.

1973

Rembrandt's Hat

Rubin, in careless white cloth hat, or visorless soft round cap, however one described it, wandered with unexpressed or inexpressive
thoughts up the stairs from his studio in the basement of the New
York art school where he made his sculpture, to a workshop on the
second floor, where he taught. Arkin, the art historian, a hypertensive
bachelor of thirty-four—a man often swept by strong feeling, he
thought—about a dozen years younger than the sculptor, observed
him through his open office door, wearing his cap amid a crowd of
art students and teachers in the hall during a change of classes. In
his white hat he stands out and apart, the art historian thought. It
illumines a lonely inexpressiveness arrived at after years of experience.
Though it was not entirely apt he imagined a lean white animal—
hind, stag, goat?—staring steadfastly but despondently through trees
of a dense wood. Their gazes momentarily interlocked and parted.
Rubin hurried to his workshop class.

Arkin was friendly with Rubin though they were not really
friends. Not his fault, he felt; the sculptor was a very private person.
When they talked, he listened, looking away, as though guarding his
impressions. Attentive, apparently, he seemed to be thinking of something else—his sad life no doubt, if saddened eyes, a faded green
mistakable for gray, necessarily denote sad life. Sometimes he uttered
an opinion, usually a flat statement about the nature of life, or art,
never much about himself; and he said absolutely nothing about his
work.

"Are you working, Rubin?" Arkin was reduced to.

"Of course I'm working."

"What are you doing if I may ask?"

"I have a thing going."

There Arkin let it lie.

Once, in the faculty cafeteria, listening to the art historian discourse on the work of Jackson Pollock, the sculptor's anger had flared.

"The world of art ain't necessarily in your eyes."

"I have to believe that what I see is there," Arkin had politely responded.

"Have you ever painted?"

"Painting is my life."

Rubin, with dignity, reverted to silence. That evening, leaving the building, they tipped hats to each other over small smiles.

In recent years, after his wife had left him and costume and headdress became a mode among students, Rubin had taken to wearing various odd hats from time to time, and this white one was the newest, resembling Nehru's Congress Party cap, but rounded—a cross between a cantor's hat and a bloated yarmulke; or perhaps like a French judge's in Rouault, or working doctor's in a Daumier print. Rubin wore it like a crown. Maybe it kept his head warm under the cold skylight of his large studio.

When the sculptor again passed along the crowded hall on his way down to his studio that day he had first appeared in his white cap, Arkin, who had been reading an article on Giacometti, put it down and went into the hall. He was in an ebullient mood he could not explain to himself, and told Rubin he very much admired his hat.

"I'll tell you why I like it so much. It looks like Rembrandt's hat that he wears in one of the middle-aged self-portraits, the really profound ones. May it bring you the best of luck."

Rubin, who had for a moment looked as though he was struggling to say something extraordinary, fixed Arkin in a strong stare and hurried downstairs. That ended the incident, though it did not diminish the art historian's pleasure in his observation.

Arkin later remembered that when he had come to the art school via an assistant curator's job in a museum in St. Louis, seven years ago, Rubin had been working in wood; he now welded triangular pieces of scrap iron to construct his sculptures. Working at one time with a hatchet, later a modified small meat cleaver, he had reshaped driftwood pieces, out of which he had created some arresting forms. Dr. Levis, the director of the art school, had talked the sculptor into giving an exhibition of his altered driftwood objects in one of the downtown galleries. Arkin, in his first term at the school, had gone on the subway to see the show one winter's day. This man is an original, he thought, maybe his work will be, too. Rubin had refused a gallery vernissage, and on the opening day the place was nearly deserted. The sculptor, as though escaping his hacked forms, had retreated into a storage room at the rear of the gallery and stayed there looking at pictures. Arkin, after reflecting whether he ought to, sought him out to say hello, but seeing Rubin seated on a crate with his back to him, examining a folio of somebody's prints, silently shut the door and departed. Although in time two notices of the show appeared, one bad, the other mildly favorable, the sculptor seemed unhappy about having exhibited his work, and after that didn't for years. Nor had there been any sales. Recently, when Arkin had suggested it might be a good idea to show what he was doing with his welded iron triangles, Rubin, after a wildly inexpressive moment, had answered, "Don't bother playing around with that idea."

The day after the art historian's remarks in the hall about Rubin's white cap, it disappeared from sight—gone totally; for a while he wore on his head nothing but his heavy reddish hair. And a week or two later, though he could momentarily not believe it, it seemed to Arkin that the sculptor was avoiding him. He guessed the man was no longer using the staircase to the right of his office but was coming up from the basement on the other side of the building, where his corner workshop room was anyway, so he wouldn't have to pass Arkin's open door. When he was certain of this Arkin felt uneasy, then experienced moments of anger.

Have I offended him in some way? he asked himself. If so, what did I say that's so offensive? All I did was remark on the hat in one of Rembrandt's self-portraits and say it looked like the cap he was wearing. How can that be offensive?

He then thought: No offense where none's intended. All I have is good will to him. He's shy and may have been embarrassed in some way—maybe my exuberant voice in the presence of students—if that's so it's no fault of mine. And if that's not it, I don't know what's the matter except his own nature. Maybe he hasn't been feeling well, or it's some momentary mishigas—nowadays there are more ways of insults without meaning to than ever before—so why raise up a sweat over it? I'll wait it out.

But as weeks, then months went by and Rubin continued to shun the art historian—he saw the sculptor only at faculty meetings when

Rubin attended them; and once in a while glimpsed him going up or down the left staircase; or sitting in the Fine Arts secretary's office poring over inventory lists of supplies for sculpture—Arkin thought: Maybe the man is having a breakdown. He did not believe it. One day they met in the men's room and Rubin strode out without a word. Arkin felt for the sculptor surges of hatred. He didn't like people who didn't like him. Here I make a sociable, innocent remark to the son of a bitch—at worst it might be called innocuous—and to him it's an insult. I'll give him tit for tat. Two can play.

But when he had calmed down, Arkin continued to wonder and worry over what might have gone wrong. I've always thought I was fairly good in human relationships. Yet he had a worrisome nature and wore a thought ragged if in it lurked a fear the fault was his own. Arkin searched the past. He had always liked the sculptor, even though Rubin offered only his fingertip in friendship; yet Arkin had been friendly, courteous, interested in his work, and respectful of his dignity, almost visibly weighted with unspoken thoughts. Had it, he often wondered, something to do with his mentioning—suggesting— not long ago, the possibility of a new exhibition of his sculpture, to which Rubin had reacted as though his life was threatened?

It was then he recalled he had never told Rubin how he had felt about his hacked-driftwood show—never once commented on it, although he had signed the guest book. Arkin hadn't liked the show, yet he wanted to seek Rubin out to name one or two interesting pieces. But when he had located him in the storage room, intently involved with a folio of prints, lost in hangdog introspection so deeply he had been unwilling, or unable, to greet whoever was standing at his back—Arkin had said to himself, Better let it be. He had ducked out of the gallery. Nor had he mentioned the driftwood exhibition thereafter. Was this kindness cruel?

Still it's not very likely he's been avoiding me so long for that alone, Arkin reflected. If he was disappointed, or irritated, by my not mentioning his driftwood show, he would then and there have stopped talking to me, if he was going to stop. But he didn't. He seemed as friendly as ever, according to his measure, and he isn't a dissembler. And when I afterwards suggested the possibility of a new show he obviously wasn't eager to have—which touched him to torment on the spot—he wasn't at all impatient with me but only started staying out of my sight after the business of his white cap, whatever that meant to him. Maybe it wasn't my mention of the cap itself that's annoyed him. Maybe it's a cumulative thing—three minuses for me?

Arkin felt it was probably cumulative; still it seemed that the cap remark had mysteriously wounded Rubin most, because nothing that had happened before had threatened their relationship, such as it was, and it was then at least amicable. Having thought it through to this point, Arkin had to admit he did not know why Rubin acted as strangely as he was now acting.

Off and on, the art historian considered going down to the sculptor's studio and there apologizing to him if he had said something inept, which he certainly hadn't meant to do. He would ask Rubin if he'd mind telling him what bothered him; if it was something *else* he had inadvertently said or done, he would apologize and clear things up. It would be mutually beneficial.

One early spring day he made up his mind to visit Rubin after his seminar that afternoon, but one of his students, a bearded printmaker, had found out it was Arkin's thirty-fifth birthday and presented the art historian with a white ten-gallon Stetson that the student's father, a traveling salesman, had brought back from Waco, Texas.

"Wear it in good health, Mr. Arkin," said the student. "Now you're one of the good guys."

Arkin was wearing the hat, going up the stairs to his office accompanied by the student who had given it to him, when they encountered the sculptor, who grimaced in disgust.

Arkin was upset, though he felt at once that the force of this uncalled-for reaction indicated that, indeed, the hat remark had been taken by Rubin as an insult. After the bearded student left Arkin he placed the Stetson on his worktable—it had seemed to him—before going to the men's room; and when he returned the cowboy hat was gone. The art historian searched for it in his office and even hurried back to his seminar room to see whether it could possibly have landed up there, someone having snatched it as a joke. It was not in the seminar room. Arkin thought of rushing down and confronting Rubin nose to nose in his studio, but could not bear the thought. What if he hadn't taken it?

Now both evaded each other. But after a period of rarely meeting they began, ironically, Arkin thought, to encounter one another everywhere—even in the streets, especially near galleries on Madison, or Fifty-seventh, or in SoHo; or on entering or leaving movie houses. Each then hastily crossed the street to skirt the other. In the art school both refused to serve together on committees. One, if he entered the lavatory and saw the other, stepped outside and remained a distance away till he had left. Each hurried to be first into the basement cafeteria at lunchtime because when one followed the other in and observed him standing on line, or already eating at a table, alone or in the company of colleagues, invariably he left and had his meal elsewhere.

Once, when they came in together they hurriedly departed together. After often losing out to Rubin, who could get to the cafeteria easily from his studio, Arkin began to eat sandwiches in his office. Each had become a greater burden to the other, Arkin felt, than he would have been if only one was doing the shunning. Each was in the other's mind to a degree and extent that bored him. When they met unexpectedly in the building after turning a corner or opening a door, or had come face-to-face on the stairs, one glanced at the other's head to see what, if anything, adorned it; they then hurried away in opposite directions. Arkin as a rule wore no hat unless he had a cold; and Rubin lately affected a railroad engineer's cap. The art historian hated Rubin for hating him and beheld repugnance in Rubin's eyes.

"It's your doing," he heard himself mutter. "You brought me to this, it's on your head."

After that came coldness. Each froze the other out of his life; or froze him in.

One early morning, neither looking where he was going as he rushed into the building to his first class, they bumped into each other in front of the arched art school entrance. Both started shouting. Rubin, his face flushed, called Arkin "murderer," and the art historian retaliated by calling the sculptor "hat thief." Rubin smiled in scorn, Arkin in pity; they then fled.

Afterwards Arkin felt faint and had to cancel his class. His weakness became nausea, so he went home and lay in bed, nursing a severe occipital headache. For a week he slept badly, felt tremors in his sleep, ate next to nothing. "What has this bastard done to me?" Later he asked, "What have I done to myself?" I'm in this against my will, he thought. It had occurred to him that he found it easier to judge paintings than to judge people. A woman had said this to him once but he denied it indignantly. Arkin answered neither question and fought off remorse. Then it went through him again that he ought to apologize, if only because if the other couldn't he could. Yet he feared an apology would cripple his craw.

Half a year later, on his thirty-sixth birthday, Arkin, thinking of his lost cowboy hat and having heard from the Fine Arts secretary that Rubin was home sitting shiva for his dead mother, was drawn to the sculptor's studio—a jungle of stone and iron figures—to look around for the hat. He found a discarded welder's helmet but nothing he could call a cowboy hat. Arkin spent hours in the large skylighted studio, minutely inspecting the sculptor's work in welded triangular iron pieces, set amid broken stone statuary he had been collecting for years—decorative garden figures placed charmingly among iron flowers seeking daylight. Flowers were what Rubin was mostly into now, on long stalks with small corollas, on short stalks with petaled blooms. Some of the flowers were mosaics of triangles fixing white stones and broken pieces of thick colored glass in jeweled forms. Rubin had in the last several years come from abstract driftwood sculptures to figurative objects—the flowers, and some uncompleted, possibly abandoned, busts of men and women colleagues, including one that vaguely resembled Rubin in a cowboy hat. He had also done a lovely sculpture of a dwarf tree. In the far corner of the studio was a place for his welding torch and gas tanks as well as arc-welding apparatus, crowded by open heavy wooden boxes of iron triangles of assorted size and thickness. The art historian studied each sculpture and after a while thought he understood why talk of a new exhibition had threatened Rubin. There was perhaps one fine piece, the dwarf tree, in the iron jungle. Was this what he was afraid he might confess if he fully expressed himself?

Several days later, while preparing a lecture on Rembrandt's self-portraits, Arkin, examining the slides, observed that the portrait of the painter which he had remembered as the one he had seen in the Rijksmuseum in Amsterdam was probably hanging in Kenwood House in London. And neither hat the painter wore in either gallery, though both were white, was that much like Rubin's cap. The observation startled Arkin. The Amsterdam portrait was of Rembrandt in a white turban he had wound around his head; the London portrait was him in a studio cap or beret worn slightly cocked. Rubin's white thing, on the other hand, looked more like an assistant cook's cap in Sam's Diner than like either of Rembrandt's hats in the large oils, or in the other self-portraits Arkin was showing himself on slides. What those had in common was the unillusioned honesty of his gaze. In his self-created mirror the painter beheld distance, objectivity painted to stare out of his right eye; but the left looked out of bedrock, beyond quality. Yet the expression of each of the portraits seemed magisterially sad; or was this what life was if when Rembrandt painted he did not paint the sadness?

After studying the pictures projected on the small screen in his dark office, Arkin felt he had, in truth, made a referential error, confusing the two hats. Even so, what had Rubin, who no doubt was acquainted with the self-portraits, or may have had a recent look at them—at *what* had he taken offense?

Whether I was right or wrong, so what if his white cap made me think of Rembrandt's hat and I told him so? That's not throwing rocks at his head, so what bothered him? Arkin felt he ought to be able to figure it out. Therefore suppose Rubin was Arkin and Arkin Rubin— Suppose it was me in his hat: "Here I am, an aging sculptor with only one show, which I never had confidence in and nobody saw. And standing close by, making critical pronouncements one way or another, is this art historian Arkin, a big-nosed, gawky, overcurious gent, friendly but no friend of mine because he doesn't know how to be. That's not his talent. An interest in art we have in common, but not much more. Anyway, Arkin, maybe not because it means anything in particular—who says he knows what he means?—mentions Rembrandt's hat on my head and wishes me good luck in my work. So say he meant well—but it's still more than I can take. In plain words it irritates me. The mention of Rembrandt, considering the quality of my own work, and what I am generally feeling about life, is a fat burden on my soul because it makes me ask myself once too often— why am I going on if this is the kind of sculptor I am going to be for the rest of my life? And since Arkin makes me think the same unhappy thing no matter what he says—or even what he doesn't say, as for instance about my driftwood show—who wants to hear more? From then on I avoid the guy—like forever."

After staring in the mirror in the men's room, Arkin wandered on every floor of the building, and then wandered down to Rubin's studio. He knocked on the door. No one answered. After a moment he tested the knob; it gave, he thrust his head into the room and called Rubin's name. Night lay on the skylight. The studio was lit with many dusty bulbs but Rubin was not present. The forest of sculptures was. Arkin went among the iron flowers and broken stone garden pieces to see if he had been wrong in his judgment. After a while he felt he hadn't been.

He was staring at the dwarf tree when the door opened and Rubin, wearing his railroad engineer's cap, in astonishment entered.

"It's a beautiful sculpture," Arkin got out, "the best in the room I'd say."

Rubin stared at him in flushed anger, his face lean; he had grown long reddish sideburns. His eyes were for once green rather than gray. His mouth worked nervously but he said nothing.

"Excuse me, Rubin, I came in to tell you I got those hats I mentioned to you some time ago mixed up."

"Damn right you did."

"Also for letting things get out of hand for a while."

"Damn right."

Rubin, though he tried not to, then began to cry. He wept silently, his shoulders shaking, tears seeping through his coarse fingers on his face. Arkin had taken off.

They stopped avoiding each other and spoke pleasantly when they met, which wasn't often. One day Arkin, when he went into the men's room, saw Rubin regarding himself in the mirror in his white cap, the one that seemed to resemble Rembrandt's hat. He wore it like a crown of failure and hope.

1973

A Wig

Ida was an energetic, competent woman of fifty, healthy, still attractive. Thinking of herself, she touched her short hair. What's fifty? One more than forty-nine. She had been married at twenty and had a daughter, Amy, who was twenty-eight and not a satisfied person. Of satisfying, Ida thought: She has no serious commitment. She wanders in her life. From childhood she has wandered off the track, where I can't begin to predict. Amy had recently left the man she was living with, in his apartment, and was again back at home. "He doesn't connect," Amy said. "Why should it take you two years to learn such a basic thing?" Ida asked. "I'm a slow learner," Amy said. "I learn slowly." She worked for an importer who thought highly of her though she wouldn't sleep with him.

As Amy walked out of the room where she had stood talking with her mother, she stopped to arrange some flowers in a vase, six tight roses a woman friend had sent her on her birthday, a week ago. Amy deeply breathed in the decaying fragrance, then shut her door. Ida was a widow who worked three days a week in a sweater boutique. While talking to Amy she had been thinking about her hair. She doubted that Amy noticed how seriously she was worried; or if she did, that it moved her.

When she was a young woman, Ida, for many years, had worn a tight bun held together by three celluloid hairpins. Martin, her husband, who was later to fall dead of a heart attack, liked buns and topknots. "They are sane yet sexy," he said. Ida wore her bun until

she began to lose hair in her mid-forties. She noticed the hair coming
loose when she brushed it with her ivory-topped brush. One day the
increasing number of long hairs left in the comb frightened her. And
when she examined her hairline in the mirror, it seemed to Ida that
her temples were practically bare.

"I think the tight bun contributes to my loss of hair," she told
Martin. "Maybe I ought to get rid of it?"

"Nonsense," he had said. "If anything, the cause would be
hormonal."

"So what would you advise me to do?" Ida looked up at him
uneasily. He was a wiry man with wavy, graying hair and a strong
neck.

"In the first place, don't wash it so often. You wash it too often."

"My hair has always been oily. I have to shampoo it at least
twice a week."

"Less often," Martin advised, "take my tip."

"Martin, I am very afraid."

"You don't have to be," he said, "it's a common occurrence."

One day, while walking on Third Avenue, Ida had passed a
wigmaker's shop and peered into the window. There were men's and
women's wigs on abstract, elegant wooden heads. One or two were
reasonably attractive; most were not.

How artificial they are, Ida thought. I could never wear such a
thing.

She felt for the wigs a mild hatred she tied up with the fear of
losing her hair. If I buy a wig, people will know why. It's none of
their business.

Ida continued her brisk walk on Third Avenue. Although it was
midsummer, she stepped into a hat shop and bought herself a fall
hat, a wide-brimmed felt with a narrow, bright green ribbon. Amy
had green eyes.

•

One morning after Ida had washed her hair in the bathroom sink,
and a wet, coiled mass of it slid down the drain, she was shocked and
felt faint. After she had dried her hair, as she gently combed it, close to
the mirror, she was greatly concerned by the sight of her pink scalp
more than ever visible on top of her head. But Martin, after inspecting
it, had doubted it was all that noticeable. Of course her hair was thinner
than it had been—whose wasn't?—but he said he noticed nothing unusual, especially now that she had cut her hair and was wearing bangs.

Ida wore a short, swirled haircut. She shampooed her hair less frequently.

And she went to a dermatologist, who prescribed an emulsion he had concocted, with alcohol, distilled water, and some drops of castor oil, which she was to shake well before applying. He instructed her to rub the mixture into her scalp with a piece of cotton. "That'll stir it up." The dermatologist had first suggested an estrogen salve applied topically, but Ida said she didn't care for estrogen.

"This salve does no harm to women," the doctor said, "although I understand it might shrink a man's testicles."

"If it can shrink a man's testicles, I'd rather not try it," she said. He gave her the emulsion.

Ida would part a strand of hair and gently brush her scalp with the emulsion-soaked cotton; then she would part another strand and gently brush there. Whatever she tried didn't do much good, and her scalp shone through her thinning hair like a dim moon in a stringy dark cloud. She hated to look at herself, she hated to think.

"Martin, if I lose my hair I will lose my femininity."

"Since when?"

"What shall I do?" she begged.

Martin thought. "Why don't you consider another doctor? This guy is too much a salesman. I still think it could be caused by a scalp ailment or some such condition. Cure the scalp and it slows down the loss of hair."

"No matter how I treat the scalp, with or without medication, nothing gets better."

"What do you think caused it?" Martin said. "Some kind of trauma either psychic or physical?"

"It could be hereditary," Ida answered. "I might have my father's scalp."

"Your father had a full head of hair when I first met him—a shock of hair, I would call it."

"Not when he was my age, he was already losing it."

"He was catting around at that age," Martin said. "He was some boy. Nothing could stop him, hair or no hair."

"I'll bet you envy him," Ida said, "or you wouldn't bring that up at this particular time."

"Who I envy or don't envy let's not talk about," he replied. "Let's not get into that realm of experience, or it becomes a different card game."

"I bet you wish you were in that realm of experience. I sometimes feel you envy Amy her odd life."

"Let's not get into that either," Martin insisted. "It doesn't pay."

"What *can* we talk about?" Ida complained.

"We talk about your hair, don't we?"

"I would rather not," she said.

The next day she visited another skin man, who advised her to give up brushing her hair or rubbing anything into her scalp. "Don't stress your hair," he advised. "At the most, you could have it puffed up once in a while, or maybe take a permanent to give it body, but don't as a rule stress it. Also put away your brush and use only a wide-toothed comb, and I will prescribe some moderate doses of vitamins that might help. I can't guarantee it."

"I doubt if that's going to do much good," Ida said when she arrived home.

"How would you know until you've tried it?" Amy asked.

"Nobody has to try everything," Ida said. "Some things you know about without having to try them. You have common sense."

"Look," said Martin, "let's not kid ourselves. If the vitamins don't do anything for you, then you ought to have yourself fitted for a wig or wiglet. It's no sin. They're popular with a lot of people nowadays. If I can wear false teeth, you can wear a wig."

"I hate to," she confessed. "I've tried some on and they burden my head."

"You burden your head," Amy said.

"Amy," said her mother, "if nothing else, then at least mercy."

Amy wandered out of the room, stopping first at the mirror to look at herself.

Martin, that evening, fell dead of a heart attack. He died on the kitchen floor. Ida wailed. Amy made choked noises of grief. Both women mourned him deeply.

•

For weeks after the funeral, Ida thought of herself vaguely. Her mind was befogged. Alternatively, she reflected intensely on her life, her eyes stinging, thinking of herself as a widow of fifty. "I am terribly worried about my life," she said aloud. Amy was not present. Ida knew she was staying in her room. "What have I done to that child?"

One morning, after studying herself in the full-length looking glass, she hurried to the wigmaker's on Third Avenue. Ida walked with dignity along the busy, sunlit street. The wig shop was called Norman: Perukier. She examined the window, wig by wig, then went determinedly inside. The wigmaker had seen her before and greeted her casually.

"Might I try on a wig or two?"

"Suit yourself."

Ida pointed to a blond wig in the window and to another, chestnut brown, on a dummy's head on a shelf, and Norman brought both to her as she sat at a three-paneled mirror.

Ida's breathing was audible. She tried on the first wig, a light, frizzy, young one. Norman fitted it on her head as if he were drawing on a cloche hat. "There," he said, stepping back. He drew a light blue comb out of his inside pocket and touched the wig here and there before stopping to admire it. "It's a charming wig."

"It feels like a tight hat," Ida said.

"It's not at all tight," Norman said. "But try this."

He handed her the other wig, a brown affair that looked like a haircut Amy used to wear before she had adopted a modified Afro in college.

Norman flicked his comb at the wig, then stepped back. He too was breathing heavily, his eyes intent on hers, but Ida would not let his catch hers in the mirror; she kept her gaze on the wig.

"What is the material of this wig?" Ida asked. "It doesn't seem human hair."

"Not this particular one. It's made of Dynel fiber and doesn't frizz in heat or humidity."

"How does a person take care of it?"

"She can wash it with a mild soap in warm water and then either let it dry or blow it dry. Or if she prefers, she can give it to her hairdresser, who will wash, dry, and style it."

"Will my head perspire?"

"Not in this wig."

Ida removed the wig. "What about that black one?" she asked hesitantly. "I like the style of it."

"It's made of Korean hair."

"Real hair?"

"Yes."

"Oh," said Ida. "I don't think I'd care for Oriental hair."

"Why not, if I may ask?" Norman said.

"I can't really explain it, but I think I would feel like a stranger to myself."

"I think you are a stranger to yourself," said the wigmaker, as though he was determined to say it. "I also don't think you are interested in a wig at all. This is the third time you've come into this shop, and you make it an ordeal for all concerned. Buying a wig isn't exactly like shopping for a coffin, don't you know? Some people take a good deal of pleasure in selecting a wig, as if they were choosing a beautiful garment or a piece of jewelry."

"I am not a stranger to myself," Ida replied irritably. "All we're concerned about is a wig. I didn't come here for an amateur psycho-analysis of my personality." Her color had heightened.

"Frankly, I'd rather not do business with you," said the wigmaker. "I wouldn't care for you among my clientele."

"Tant pis pour vous," Ida said, walking out of Norman's shop.

In the street she was deeply angered. It took her five minutes to begin walking. Although the day was not cool she knotted a kerchief on her head. Ida entered a hat shop close by and bought a fuzzy purple hat.

That evening she and Amy quarreled. Amy said, as they were eat-ing fish at supper, that she had met this guy and would be moving out in a week or two, when he returned from California.

"What guy?" snapped Ida. "Somebody that you picked up in a bar?"

"I happened to meet this man in the importing office where I work, if you must know."

Ida's voice grew softer. "Mustn't I know?"

Amy was staring above her mother's head, although there was nothing on the wall to stare at, the whites of her eyes intensely white. Ida knew this sign of Amy's disaffection but continued talking.

"Why don't you find an apartment of your own? You earn a good salary, and your father left you five thousand dollars."

"I want to save that in case of emergency."

"Tell me, Amy, what sort of future do you foresee for yourself?"

"The usual. Neither black nor white."

"How will you protect yourself alone?"

"Not necessarily by getting married. I will protect myself, myself."

"Do you ever expect to marry?"

"When it becomes a viable option."

"What do you mean option, don't you want to have children?"

"I may someday want to."

"You are now twenty-eight. How much longer have you got?"

"I'm twenty-eight and should have at least ten years. Some women bear children at forty."

"I hope," said Ida, "I hope you have ten years, Amy, I am afraid for you. My heart eats me up."

"After you it eats me up. It's an eating heart."

Ida called her daughter a nasty name, and Amy, rising, her face grim, quickly left the room. Ida felt like chasing after her with a stick, or fainting. She went to her room, her head aching, and lay on the double bed. For a while she wept.

She lay there, at length wanting to forget their quarrel. Ida rose and looked in an old photograph album to try to forget how bad she felt. Here was a picture of Martin as a young father, with a black mustache, tossing Amy as a baby in the air. Here she was as a pudgy girl of twelve, never out of jeans. Yet not till she was eighteen had she wanted her long hair cut.

Among these photographs Ida found a picture of her own mother, Mrs. Feitelson, surely no more than forty then, in her horsehair sheitel. The wig looked like a round loaf of dark bread lying on her head. Once a man had tried to mug her on the street. In the scuffle he had pulled her wig off and, when he saw her fuzzy skull, had run off without her purse. They wore those wigs, the Orthodox women, once they were married, not to attract, or distract, men other than their husbands. Sometimes they had trouble attracting their husbands.

Oh, Mama, Ida thought, did I know you? Did you know me?

What am I afraid of? she asked herself, and she thought, I am a widow and losing my looks. I am afraid of the future.

After a while she went barefoot to Amy's room and knocked on her door. I will tell her that my hair has made me very nervous. When there was no answer she opened the door a crack and said she would like to apologize. Though Amy did not respond, the light was on and Ida entered the room.

Her daughter, a slender woman in long green pajamas, lay in bed reading in the light of the wall lamp. Ida wanted to sit on the bed but felt she had no right to.

"Good night, dear Amy."

Amy did not lower her book. Ida, standing by the bedside looking at Amy, saw something she long ago had put out of her mind: that the girl's hair on top of her head was thinning and a fairly large circle of cobwebbed scalp was visible.

Amy turned a page and went on reading.

Ida, although tormented by the sight of Amy's thinning hair, did not speak of it. In the morning she left the house early and bought herself an attractive wig.

The Model

Early one morning Ephraim Elihu rang up the Art Students League and asked them how he could locate an experienced female model he could paint nude. He told the woman speaking to him on the phone that he wanted someone of about thirty. "Could you possibly help me?"

"I don't recognize your name," said the woman on the telephone. "Have you ever dealt with us before? Some of our students will work as models but usually only for painters we know." Mr. Elihu said he hadn't. He wanted it understood he was an amateur painter who had once studied at the League.

"Do you have a studio?"

"It's a large living room with lots of light."

"I'm no youngster," he went on, "but after many years I've begun painting again and I'd like to do some nude studies to get back my feeling for form. I'm not a professional painter you understand but I'm serious about painting. If you want any references as to my character, I can supply them." He asked her what the going rate for models was, and the woman, after a pause, said, "Six fifty the hour." Mr. Elihu said that was satisfactory. He seemed to want to talk longer but she did not encourage him. She wrote down his name and address and said she thought she could have someone for him the day after tomorrow. He thanked her for her consideration.

That was on Wednesday. The model appeared on Friday morning. She had telephoned the night before and they settled on a time for her to come. She rang his bell shortly after 9 a.m. and Mr. Elihu went at once to the door. He was a gray-haired man of seventy who lived in a brownstone house near Ninth Avenue, and he was excited by the prospect of painting this young woman.

The model was a plain-looking woman of twenty-seven or so, and the old painter decided her best feature was her eyes. She was wearing a blue raincoat on a clear spring day. The old painter liked her face but kept that to himself. She barely glanced at him as she walked firmly into the room.

"Good day," he said, and she answered, "Good day."

"It's like spring," said the old man. "The foliage is starting up again."

"Where do you want me to change?" asked the model.

Mr. Elihu asked her name and she responded, "Ms. Perry."

"You can change in the bathroom, I would say, Miss Perry, or if you like, my own room—down the hall—is empty and you can change there also. It's warmer than the bathroom."

The model said it made no difference to her but she thought she would rather change in the bathroom.

"That is as you wish," said the elderly man.

"Is your wife around?" she then asked, glancing into the room.

"I happen to be a widower."

He said he had had a daughter once but she had died in an accident.

The model said she was sorry. "I'll change and be out in a few fast minutes."

"No hurry at all," said Mr. Elihu, glad he was about to paint her.

Ms. Perry entered the bathroom, undressed there, and returned quickly. She slipped off her terry-cloth robe. Her head and shoulders were slender and well formed. She asked the old man how he would like her to pose. He was standing by an enamel-top kitchen table in a living room with a large window. On the tabletop he had squeezed out, and was mixing together, the contents of two small tubes of paint. There were three other tubes he did not touch. The model, taking a last drag of a cigarette, pressed it out against a coffee can lid on the kitchen table.

"I hope you don't mind if I take a puff once in a while?"

"I don't mind, if you do it when we take a break."

"That's all I meant."

She was watching him as he slowly mixed his colors.

Mr. Elihu did not immediately look at her nude body but said he would like her to sit in the chair by the window. They were facing a back yard with an ailanthus tree whose leaves had just come out.

"How would you like me to sit, legs crossed or not crossed?"

"However you prefer that. Crossed or uncrossed doesn't make much of a difference to me. Whatever makes you feel comfortable."

The model seemed surprised at that, but she sat down in the yellow chair by the window and crossed one leg over the other. Her figure was good.

"Is this okay for you?"

Mr. Elihu nodded. "Fine," he said. "Very fine."

He dipped the brush into the paint he had mixed on the tabletop and, after glancing at the model's nude body, began to paint. He would look at her, then look quickly away, as if he was afraid of affronting her. But his expression was objective. He painted apparently casually, from time to time gazing up at the model. He did not often look at her. She seemed not to be aware of him. Once, she turned to observe the ailanthus tree and he studied her momentarily to see what she might have seen in it.

Then she began to watch the painter with interest. She watched his eyes and she watched his hands. He wondered if he was doing something wrong. At the end of about an hour she rose impatiently from the yellow chair.

"Tired?" he asked.

"It isn't that," she said, "but I would like to know what in the name of Christ you think you are doing? I frankly don't think you know the first thing about painting."

She had astonished him. He quickly covered the canvas with a towel.

After a long moment, Mr. Elihu, breathing shallowly, wet his dry lips and said he was making no claims for himself as a painter. He said he had tried to make that absolutely clear to the woman he had talked to at the art school when he had called.

Then he said, "I might have made a mistake in asking you to come to this house today. I think I should have tested myself a while longer, just so I wouldn't be wasting anybody's time. I guess I am not ready to do what I would like to do."

"I don't care how long you have tested yourself," said Ms. Perry. "I honestly don't think you have painted me at all. In fact, I felt you weren't interested in painting me. I think you're interested in letting your eyes go over my naked body for certain reasons of your own. I don't know what your personal needs are but I'm damn well sure that most of them are not about painting."

"I guess I have made a mistake."

"I guess you have," said the model. She had her robe on now, the belt pulled tight.

"I'm a painter," she said, "and I model because I am broke but I know a fake when I see one."

"I wouldn't feel so bad," said Mr. Elihu, "if I hadn't gone out of my way to explain the situation to that lady at the Art Students League.

"I'm sorry this happened," Mr. Elihu said hoarsely. "I should have thought it through but didn't. I'm seventy years of age. I have always loved women and felt a sad loss that I have no particular women friends at this time of my life. That's one of the reasons I wanted to paint again, though I make no claims that I was ever greatly talented. Also, I guess I didn't realize how much about painting I have forgotten. Not only that, but about the female body. I didn't realize I would be so moved by yours, and, on reflection, about the way my life has gone. I hoped painting again would refresh my feeling for life. I regret that I have inconvenienced and disturbed you."

"I'll be paid for my inconvenience," Ms. Perry said, "but what you can't pay me for is the insult of coming here and submitting myself to your eyes crawling on my body."

"I didn't mean it as an insult."

"That's what it feels like to me."

She then asked Mr. Elihu to disrobe.

"I?" he said, surprised. "What for?"

"I want to sketch you. Take your pants and shirt off."

He said he had barely got rid of his winter underwear but she did not smile.

Mr. Elihu disrobed, ashamed of how he must look to her.

With quick strokes she sketched his form. He was not a bad-looking man but felt bad. When she had the sketch she dipped his brush into a blob of black pigment she had squeezed out of a tube and smeared his features, leaving a black mess.

He watched her hating him but said nothing.

Ms. Perry tossed the brush into a wastebasket and returned to the bathroom for her clothing.

The old man wrote out a check for her for the sum they had agreed on. He was ashamed to sign his name but he signed it and handed it to her. Ms. Perry slipped the check into her large purse and left.

He thought that in her way she was not a bad-looking woman though she lacked grace. The old man then asked himself, "Is there nothing more to my life than it is now? Is this all that is left to me?"

The answer seemed yes and he wept at how old he had so quickly become.

Afterwards he removed the towel over his canvas and tried to fill in her face, but he had already forgotten it.

. **1983**

A Lost Grave

Hecht was a born late bloomer.

One night he woke hearing rain on his windows and thought of his young wife in her wet grave. This was something new, because he hadn't thought of her in too many years to be comfortable about. He saw her in her uncovered grave, rivulets of water streaming in every direction, and Celia, whom he had married when they were of unequal ages, lying alone in the deepening wet. Not so much as a flower grew on her grave, though he could have sworn he had arranged perpetual care.

He stepped into his thoughts perhaps to cover her with a plastic sheet, and though he searched in the cemetery under dripping trees and among many wet plots, he was unable to locate her. The dream he was into offered no tombstone name, row, or plot number, and though he searched for hours, he had nothing to show for it but his wet self. The grave had taken off. How can you cover a woman who isn't where she is supposed to be? That's Celia.

The next morning, Hecht eventually got himself out of bed and into a subway train to Jamaica to see where she was buried. He hadn't been to the cemetery in many years, no particular surprise to anybody considering past circumstances. Life with Celia wasn't exactly predictable. Yet things change in a lifetime, or seem to. Hecht had lately been remembering his life more vividly, for whatever reason. After you hit sixty-five, some things that have two distinguishable sides seem to pick up another that complicates the picture as you look or count. Hecht counted.

Now, though Hecht had been more or less in business all his life, he kept few personal papers, and though he had riffled through a small pile of them that morning, he had found nothing to help him establish Celia's present whereabouts; and after a random looking at gravestones for an hour he felt the need to call it off and spend another hour with a young secretary in the main office, who fruitlessly tapped his name and Celia's into a computer and came up with a scramble of interment dates, grave plots and counterplots, that exasperated him.

"Look, my dear," Hecht said to the flustered young secretary, "if that's how far you can go on this machine, we have to find another way to go further, or I will run out of patience. This grave is lost territory as far as I am concerned, and we have to do something practical to find it."

"What do you think I'm doing, if I might ask?"

"Whatever you are doing doesn't seem to be much help. This computer is supposed to have a good mechanical memory, but it's either out of order or rusty in its parts. I admit I didn't bring any papers with me, but so far the only thing your computer has informed us is that it has nothing much to inform us."

"It has informed us it is having trouble locating the information you want."

"Which adds up to zero minus zero," Hecht said. "I wish to remind you that a lost grave isn't a missing wedding ring we are talking about. It is a lost cemetery plot of the lady who was once my wife that I wish to recover."

The pretty young woman he was dealing with had a tight-lipped conversation with an unknown person, then the buzzer on her desk sounded and Hecht was given permission to go into the director's office.

"Mr. Goodman will now see you."

He resisted "Good for Mr. Goodman." Hecht only nodded, and followed the young woman to an inner office. She knocked once and disappeared, as a friendly voice talked through the door.

"Come in, come in."

"Why should I worry if it's not my fault?" Hecht told himself.

Mr. Goodman pointed to a chair in front of his desk and Hecht was soon seated, watching him pour orange juice from a quart container into a small green glass.

"Will you join me in a sweet mouthful?" he asked, nodding at the container. "I usually take refreshment this time of the morning. It keeps me balanced."

"Thanks," said Hecht, meaning he had more serious problems. "Why I am here is that I am looking for my wife's grave, so far with no success." He cleared his throat, surprised at the emotion that had gathered there.

Mr. Goodman observed Hecht with interest.

"Your outside secretary couldn't find it," Hecht went on, regretting he hadn't found the necessary documents that would identify the grave site. "Your young lady tried her computer in every combination but couldn't produce anything. What was lost is still lost, in other words, a woman's grave."

"*Lost* is premature," Goodman offered. "*Displaced* might be better. In my twenty-eight years in my present capacity, I don't believe we have lost a single grave."

The director tapped lightly on the keys of his desk computer, studied the screen with a squint, and shrugged. "I am afraid that we now draw a blank. The letter *H* volume of our ledgers that we used before we were computerized seems to be missing. I assure you this can't be more than a temporary condition."

"That's what your young lady already informed me."

"She's not my young lady, she's my secretarial assistant."

"I stand corrected," Hecht said. "This meant no offense."

"Likewise," said Goodman. "But we will go on looking. Could you kindly tell me, if you don't mind, what was the status of your relationship to your wife at the time of her death?" He peered over half-moon glasses to check the computer reading.

"There was no status. We were separated. What has that got to do with her burial plot?"

"The reason I inquire is, I thought it might refresh your memory. For example, is this the correct cemetery, the one you are looking in—Mount Jereboam? Some people confuse us with Mount Hebron."

"I guarantee you it was Mount Jereboam."

Hecht, after a hesitant moment, gave these facts: "My wife wasn't the most stable woman. She left me twice and disappeared for months. Although I took her back twice, we weren't together at the time of her death. Once she threatened to take her life, though eventually she didn't. In the end she died of a normal sickness, not cancer. This was years later, when we weren't living together anymore, but I carried out her burial, to the best of my knowledge, in this exact cemetery. I also heard she had lived for a short time with some guy she met somewhere, but when she died, I was the one who buried her. Now I am sixty-five and lately I have had this urge to visit the grave of someone who lived with me when I was a young man. This is a grave which everybody now tells me they can't locate."

Goodman rose at his desk, a short man, five feet tall. "I will institute a careful research."

"The quicker, the better," Hecht replied. "I am still curious what happened to her grave."

Goodman almost guffawed, but caught himself and thrust out his hand. "I will keep you well informed, don't worry."

Hecht left, irritated. On the train back to the city he thought of Celia and her various unhappinesses. He wished he had told Goodman she had spoiled his life.

That night it rained. To his surprise he found a wet spot on his pillow.

The next day Hecht again went to the graveyard. "What did I forget that I ought to remember?" he asked himself. Obviously the grave plot, row, and number. Though he sought it diligently he could not find it. Who can remember something he has once and for all put out of his mind? It's like trying to grow beans out of a bag of birdseed.

"But I must be patient and I will find out. As time goes by I am bound to recall. When my memory says yes I won't argue no."

But weeks passed and Hecht still could not remember what he was trying to. "Maybe I have reached a dead end?"

Another month went by and at last the cemetery called him. It was Mr. Goodman, clearing his throat. Hecht pictured him at his desk sipping orange juice.

"Mr. Hecht?"

"The same."

"This is Mr. Goodman. A happy Rosh Hashanah."

"A happy Rosh Hashanah to you."

"Mr. Hecht, I wish to report progress. Are you prepared for an insight?"

"You name it," Hecht said.

"So let me use a better word. We have tracked your wife and it turns out she isn't in the grave there where the computer couldn't find her. To be frank, we found her in a grave with another gentleman."

"What kind of gentleman? Who in God's name is he? I am her legal husband."

"This one, if you will pardon me, is the man who lived with your wife after she left you. They lived together on and off, so don't blame yourself too much. After she died he got a court order, and they removed her to a different grave, where we also laid him after his death. The judge gave him the court order because he convinced him that he had loved her for many years."

Hecht was embarrassed. "What are you talking about? How could he transfer her grave anywhere if it wasn't his legal property? Her grave belonged to me. I paid cash for it."

"That grave is still there," Goodman explained, "but the names were mixed up. His name was Kaplan but the workmen buried her under Caplan. Your grave is still in the cemetery, though we had it under Kaplan and not Hecht. I apologize to you for this inconvenience but I think we now have got the mystery cleared up."

"So thanks," said Hecht. He felt he had lost a wife but was no longer a widower.

"Also," Goodman reminded him, "don't forget you gained an empty grave for future use. Nobody is there and you own the plot."

Hecht said that was obviously true.

The story had astounded him. Yet whenever he thought of telling it to someone he knew, or had just met, he wasn't sure he wanted to.

1984

Zora's Noise

Here's this unhappy noise that upsets Zora.

She had once been Sarah. Dworkin, when he married her not long after the death of Ella, his first wife, had talked her into changing her name. She eventually forgave him. Now she felt she had always been Zora.

"Zora, we have to hurry."

"I'm coming, for godsake. I am looking for my brown gloves."

He was fifty-one, she ten years younger, an energetic, plump person with an engaging laugh and a tendency to diet unsuccessfully. She called him Dworky: an animated, reflective man, impassioned cellist—and, on inspiration, composer—with an arthritic left shoulder. He referred to it as "the shoulder I hurt when I fell in the cellar." When she was angry with him, or feeling insecure, she called him Zworkin.

.

I hear something, whatever do I hear? Zora blew her nose and listened to her ear. Is my bad ear worse? If it isn't, what are those nagging noises I've been hearing all spring? Because I listen, I hear. But what makes me listen?

The really bothersome noise had begun in April when the storm windows came off and the screens went up; yet it seemed to Zora she hadn't become conscious of its relentless quality until June, after being two months on a diet that didn't work. She was heavier than she cared to be. She had never had children and held that against herself too.

•

Zora settled on the day after her forty-first birthday, at the end of June, as the time when the noise began seriously to affect her. Maybe I wasn't listening with both my ears up to then. I had my mind elsewhere. They say the universe exploded and we still hear the roar and hiss of all that gas. She asked Dworky about that, forgetting to notice —Oh, my God—that he was practicing his cello, a darkly varnished, mellow Montagnana, "the best thing that ever happened to me," he had once said.

No response from him but an expression of despair: as though he had said, "I practice in the living room to keep you company, and the next thing I know you're interfering with my music." "Please pardon me," Zora said.

"The cello," he had defined it shortly after they met, "is an independent small Jewish animal." And Zora had laughed as though her heart were broken. There were two streams to her laughter—a full-blown humorous response, plus something reserved. You expected one and maybe got the other. Sometimes you weren't sure what she was laughing at, if laughing. Dworkin, as he seesawed his rosin-scented bow across the four steel strings, sometimes sang to his cello, and the cello throatily responded. Zora and Dworkin had met many years ago after a concert in L.A., the night he was the guest of the Los Angeles Philharmonic.

"My cello deepens me," he had told her.

"In that case I'll marry you both."

That was how she had proposed, he told friends at their dinner table, and everyone laughed.

•

"Do you hear that grating, sickening sound?" she had asked as they were undressing late one summer's night in their high-ceilinged bedroom. The wallpaper was Zora's, spread through with white cosmos pasted over the thickly woven cerise paper selected by Ella many years ago when she and Dworkin had first moved into this spacious, comfortable house. "Do you like it?" he had asked Zora. "Love it." She immediately had the upstairs sun deck built, and the French doors leading to it, giving her, she said, "access to the sky."

"What sickening sound?" he asked.

"You don't hear it?"

"Not as of right now."

"Well, it isn't exactly the music of the spheres," Zora responded. She had in her twenties worked in a chemistry laboratory, though her other interests tended to be artistic.

Zora was plump, in high heels about Dworkin's height; she had firm features and almost a contralto speaking voice. She had once, at his suggestion, taken singing lessons that hadn't come to much. She was not very musical, though she loved to listen and had her own record collection. When they were first married she had worked in an art gallery in Stockbridge. They lived in Elmsville, a nearby town, in a clapboard house painted iron-gray, with marine-blue shutters. The colors were Zora's own good colors. For Ella it had been a white house with black shutters. They were both effective with their colors.

Dworkin taught the cello to students in the vicinity and at a master class in the New England Conservatory of Music at Lenox. He had stopped concertizing a year after his fall in the cellar. Zora, who was not much tempted by travel, liked to have him home regularly. "It's better for your arthritis. It's better for me."

She said, referring to the noise, "I would describe it as absolutely ongoing, with a wobbly, enervating, stinky kind of whine."

That was in July. He honestly couldn't hear it.

•

At night she woke in slow fear, intently listening.

"Suppose it goes on forever?" She felt herself shudder. It was an ugly thrumming sound shot through with a sickly whine. She listened into the distance, where it seemed to begin, and then slowly drew in her listening as though it were a line she had cast out; and now she listened closer to shore. Far or near, it amounted to the same thing. The invasive noise seemed to enter the house by way of their bedroom, even when the windows were tightly shut, as if it had seeped through the clapboard and the walls, and once or twice frighteningly seemed to metamorphose into a stranger sitting in the dark, breathing audibly and evenly, pausing between breaths.

In the near distance there was a rumble of light traffic, though she knew no traffic was going through town at this time of night. Maybe an occasional truck, changing gears. The nearer sound was Dworkin sleeping, breathing heavily, sometimes shifting into a snore.

"Dworky," she said patiently, "snoring." And Dworkin, with a rasping sigh of contrition, subsided. When she had first taken to waking him out of a sound sleep to break his snoring, he had resented it. "But your snore woke *me* out of sound sleep," Zora said. "It isn't as though I had *planned* to wake you up." He saw the justice of her remark and permitted her to wake him if he was snoring. He would stir for a minute, break his galloping rumble, then more quietly slumber.

Anyway, if someone sat there, it wasn't Dworkin making dream noises. This was a quiet presence, perhaps somebody in the Queen Anne chair by the long stained-glass window in their bedroom, Ella's invention. Someone contemplating them as they slept? Zora rose on her elbow and peered in the dark. Nothing glowed or stank, laughed madly or assaulted her. And she was once more conscious of the unhappy sound she was contending with, a vibrato hum touched with a complaining, drawn-out wail that frightened her because it made her think of the past, perhaps her childhood oozing out of the dark. Zora felt she had had such a childhood.

"Zworkin," she said in a tense whisper, "do you hear this wretched noise I've been referring to?"

"Is that a reason to wake me again, Zora, to ask such a goddamn question? Is that what we've come to at this time in our lives? Let me sleep, I beg you. I have my arthritis to think of."

"You're my husband—who else will I ask? I've already spoken to the people next door. Mrs. Duvivier says the noise originates in a paint factory across town, but of that I'm not so sure."

She spoke in hesitation and doubt. She had been an uncertain young woman when he met her. She wasn't heavy then but had always been solid, she called it, yet with a figure and a lovely face, not fat. Ella, on the other hand, who could be a restless type, was always on the slim side of slender. Both had been good wives, yet neither would have guessed the other as his wife. As Zora gained weight her uneasiness seemed to grow. Sometimes she aroused in Dworkin an anguished affection.

He leaned on his arm and strained to listen, wanting to hear what she heard. The Milky Way crackling? A great wash of cosmic static filled his ears and diminished to a hush of silence. As he listened the hum renewed itself, seeming to become an earthly buzz—a bouquet of mosquitoes and grasshoppers on the lawn, rasping away. Occasionally he heard the call of a night bird. Then the insects vanished, and he heard nothing: no more than the sound of both ears listening.

That was all, though Dworkin sometimes heard music when he woke at night—the music woke him. Lately he had heard Rostropovich, as though he were a living element of a ghostly constellation in the sky, sawing away on the D-major Haydn cello concerto. His rich cello sound might be conceived of as a pineapple, if fruit was your metaphor. Dworkin lived on fruit, but his own playing sounded more like small bittersweet apples. Listening now, he only heard the town asleep.

"I don't hear anything that could be characterized as the whining or wailing you mention," he said. "Nothing of that particular quality."

"No steady, prolonged, hateful, complaining noise?"

He listened until his ears ached. "Nothing that I hear or have heard," he confessed.

"Thank you, and good night, my dear."

"Good night," Dworkin said. "I hope we both sleep now."

"I hope so." She was still assiduously listening.

•

One night she rose out of dizzying sleep, seemed to contemplate her blanket in the dark, and then hopped out of bed and ran to the bathroom, where she threw up. Dworkin heard her crying as she stepped into the shower.

"Anything wrong?" he asked, popping his head into the steaming room.

"I'll be all right."

"Something I can do for you?"

"Not just now."

He returned to bed and after a few troubled minutes drew on his trousers and a shirt, and in sneakers descended into the street. Except for a barking dog at the end of the block he heard only summer night sounds, and in the distance a rumble that sounded like traffic and might be. But if he concentrated, he could make out the whomp-whomp of machinery, indeed from the direction of the paint factory on the eastern edge of town. Zora and Dworkin hadn't been inconvenienced by the factory or its legendary smells until she began to hear her noise. Still, what she said she heard she no doubt heard, though it was hard to explain anything like a whine.

He circled the house to hear if one or another noise, by some freak of acoustics, was louder on the back lawn, but it wasn't. In the rear he saw Zora on the upstairs deck, pudgy in her short nightdress, staring into the moonlit distance.

"What are you doing outside in a nightgown at this time of night, Zora?" Dworkin asked in a loud whisper.

"Listening," she said vaguely.

"At least why don't you put on a robe after your hot shower? The night air is chilly."

"Dworkin, do you hear the awful whining that I do? That's what made me puke."

"It's not whining I hear, Zora. What I hear is more like a rumble that could be originating in the paint factory. Sometimes it throbs, or whomps, or clanks a little. Maybe there's a kind of a hum, but I can't make out anything else or anything more unusual."

"No, I'm talking about a different sound than you mention. How I hate factories in neighborhoods that should be residential."

Dworkin trotted up the stairs to bed. "It would be interesting to know what some of the other people on this street besides the Duviviers have to say about the sounds you are hearing."

"I've talked to them all," said Zora, "and also to the Cunliffes and the Spinkers."

Dworkin hadn't known. "What did they say?"

"Some hear something"—she hesitated—"but different things than I do. Mrs. Spinker hears a sort of drone. Mrs. Cunliffe hears something else, but not what I hear."

"I wish I did."

"I wouldn't want to afflict you."

"Just to hear it," he said.

"Don't you believe me, Dworky?"

He nodded seriously.

"It might have to come to our moving someday," Zora reflected. "Not only is there that zonky noise I have to contend with, which made me throw up, but the price of heating oil is way up. On the other hand, the real estate market is good, and maybe we ought to put the house up for sale."

"To live where?" Dworkin asked.

She said she might like to get back to city life sometime.

"That's news to me. I assumed you didn't care for city life anymore."

"I do and I don't. I'm forty-one and have been thinking I ought to be making changes. I think I'd like to get back into the art world. I'd like to be near a neighborhood of museums and galleries. That appalling noise all summer has made me honestly wonder if we shouldn't seriously be looking into the possibility of selling this house."

"Over my dead body. I love this house," Dworkin shouted.

•

As she was preparing a salmon soufflé for supper, the newsboy came to collect for the paper. After she had glanced at the first page, Zora uttered a short cry of surprise and sat down. Dworkin, who had been practicing in the living room, quickly laid down his cello and went to her.

"Here it is in cold print," Zora, her hand on her bosom, said. "Now I know I'm not going crazy."

Dworkin took the newspaper. An article described a class-action suit organized by several citizens in the eastern part of town against the D-R Paints Company "for pollution of the atmosphere." They cited "a persistent harrowing noise," and one of the women interviewed complained of "a sneaky sound that goes up and down like a broken boat whistle. I hear it at night, but I sometimes hear it during the day."

"I feel as though I have been reprieved from being thought mad," Zora said bitterly.

"Not by me," Dworkin insisted.

"But you never seemed to hear the whine I've been hearing."

"In good faith."

Zora began slowly to waltz on the rug in the living room. Dworkin's cello was resting on the floor, and he sat down and plucked strings to her dancing.

•

One rainy night, Dworkin in pajamas, vigorously brushing his teeth, heard an insistent, weird, thrumming whistle. "What have we here?" he asked himself uneasily. He had been attempting to develop a melody that eluded him, when a keen breeze blowing from afar seemed to invade his ears. It was as though he were lying in bed and someone had poured a pitcher full of whistling wind into both ears. Dworkin forcefully shook his head to dispel the uncomfortable sound, but it refused to disappear.

As Zora lay in bed perusing the paper—she complained she couldn't concentrate well enough to read a book—Dworkin went downstairs for a coat and rain hat and stepped out-of-doors. Facing toward the D-R Paints Company, he listened intently. Though he could not see the factory in the rainy dark, a few foggy, bluish lights were visible in the east, and he felt certain the plant was in operation. The low, thrumming wind in his ears persisted. It was possible that a machine had gone haywire in the factory and was squealing like a dying animal. Possible, but not highly likely—they surely would have found some means to shut it off, he thought irritably. Could it be that the experience was, on his part, a form of autosuggestion out of empathy for Zora? He waited for the droning whine to thin out and crawl off, but nothing happened. Dworkin shook his fist at the foggy blue lights and hurried inside.

"Zora, has your noise been sounding different lately?"

"It isn't only mine," she responded. "It's other people's too. You read that yourself in the *Courier*."

"Granted, but would you say it has increased in volume lately—or otherwise changed?"

"It stays more or less the same but is still with me. I hear it plainly enough. I hear it this very minute."

"In this room, or throughout the house?"

"There's no one place. I used to feel snug here and enjoyed reading in bed. Now I'm afraid to come up at night."

Listening affirmed it overwhelmingly—the ongoing intrusive sound—her keen wail, his thrumming whine.

Dworkin then told his wife about his own unsettling experience. He described what he was presently hearing in both ears. "It's an insult, to say the least."

But Zora responded jubilantly. "At least you've heard it. Thank God."

He was about to ask why that should make her so gay but didn't.

As if he had asked, she said, "If I seem relieved, it's simply because I feel that you can now confirm that what I heard, and was trying to get you to hear, last summer, was substantial and real."

"Whoever said it wasn't?"

Her lips trembled. Dworkin observed her watching him. When he coughed she cleared her throat.

•

In the morning he went to the music room and got his cello out of its case. It was like lifting a girl gently out of bed. The music room—Ella's name for it; she had named all the rooms in the house—was a large, white-walled room with a mellow pine floor. The eastern wall was rounded, containing four windows through which the morning sun shone warmly. It was a cold room in winter, but Dworkin had installed a wood stove. Here he practiced, composed, sometimes taught. After nervously tuning up he began the first bars of the Prelude to the Bach Unaccompanied D-minor Suite. He had played it in his sleep last night.

Dworkin crouched over the cello, playing somberly, slowly, drawing the sensuous melody out of his instrument. He played the Bach as though pleading with God. He speaks as a man stating his fate. He says it quietly and, as he plays, deepens the argument. He sings now, almost basso, as though he were someone imprisoned in a well singing to a circle of blue sky.

The music ceased. Dworkin, with bowed head, listened. He had been struggling to obliterate the whirling whistle in his head but it had effectively dirtied every note. He could not keep the Bach pure. He could not, past the opening measures, hear himself play. Gripping the cello by its neck, he rose from the chair with a cry.

"Zora," he called.

She arrived at once.

"What's happening?"

He said he could not go on with the suite. It was curdled by the disgusting whine in his ears.

"Something drastic has to be done."

She said they had already joined the class-action suit.

He threatened to abandon the accursed town if there was no quick improvement in the situation; and Zora, observing him, said that was entirely on his own head.

•

Away from home there was some measure of relief. Driving to Lenox for a class, he escaped the sound in his ears—certainly it diminished outside of Elmsville, but it worried him that he seemed still to be listening for its return. He couldn't be sure he was entirely rid of it. Yet just as he thought he had begun taking the noise with him wherever he went, the situation seemed to change.

One night in winter the *Courier* announced that the malfunctioning ventilation system at the plant had been replaced by a noiseless apparatus. Zora and Dworkin, as they lay in bed bundled in blankets, listened with two of the three windows wide open. She heard the same unhappy sound, he only the delicious country silence. But the noise had diminished a little, Zora admitted, and possibly she could stand it now.

•

In the spring, as she approached her forty-second birthday, she was restless again. She had gone back to the gallery where she had formerly worked and was in the process of arranging a show of two women painters and a male sculptor. During the day Zora wasn't home; Dworkin was—practicing and teaching. He was at work on a sonata for four cellos that was developing well. Four cellos gave it an organlike choral quality.

But Zora, after the gallery day, was impatient with herself, self-critical, "not with it."

"Why don't you tell me what's on your mind," Dworkin said one evening after they had had dinner out.

"Nothing much."

"Or is it the usual thing?"

"I can't burden you with my every worry."

She wiped her eyes but was not crying.

That night she woke Dworkin and, in a hushed, hesitant voice, begged him to listen. "I mean, just listen to what you hear in this room. What do you hear?"

He listened until he heard the cosmos, the rush of stars; otherwise he heard nothing.

"Not much, I'm afraid. Nothing I can lay a finger on."

On earth he heard nothing.

"Don't you hear," she asked, slowly sitting up, "a sort of eerie whine? This is drawn out as though at the far end of someone crying. I would call it a ghostly sound."

She held Dworkin tightly.

"Ghostly?" he said, trying to see her in the dark.

She listened keenly. "It has that quality."

"No," Dworkin replied after a good two minutes. "I don't hear any wail, whine, or whatever. I emphatically don't."

In the morning she firmly asked, "Would you move out of this house if it came to that, Dworkin? I mean if I asked you to?"

He said he would once he felt certain he heard the noise she was hearing. She seemed to accept that as fair.

•

Dworkin waited by the D-R factory fence in every wind and weather. He had talked to the owner, who promised him the problem was already solved. Zora said she didn't think so. They listened together on the bedroom deck, and Zora, pale-faced, raised a pale finger when she heard the noise especially clearly. "As though it were directly in front of our faces."

He wondered whether what she was hearing might be psychologically inspired. Zora had wanted a child but had never had one. Might she who can't conceive begin to hear a ghostly wailing?

Too simple, thought Dworkin.

Ella had taken her troubles in stride. Their baby was born dead, and she had not wanted another. But Zora could never conceive, though she had wanted to very much.

She agreed to have her ears tested when Dworkin suggested it. He reminded her that years ago she had had a disease of the middle ear, and she consented to see her former ear doctor.

Then Dworkin privately telephoned two of his neighbors and confirmed they no longer heard the noise Zora said she still heard.

"It's been solved for my husband and me with the new ventilation system they put in," Mrs. Spinker explained. "So we dropped the suit because nobody hears those noises anymore."

"Or echo thereof?"

"Not anymore."

Dworkin said he too would drop it.

Zora said she would try a new diet before visiting the ear doctor; but she promised to go.

•

The diet, after several weeks, appeared not to be working, and she was still hearing the quavering, eerie noise. "It comes up like a flute that hangs still in the air and then flows back to its source. Then it begins to take on the quality of a moaning or mystical sound, if that's what you can call it. Suppose it's some distant civilization calling in, trying to get in touch with us, and for some reason I am the one person who can hear this signal, yet I can't translate the message?"

"We all get signals we don't necessarily pick up," Dworkin said.

She woke him that night and said in a hushed voice, "There it goes again, a steady, clear sound, ending in a rising wail. Don't you hear it now?"

"I tell you I don't. Why do you still wake me?"

"I can't help wishing you would hear it too."

"I don't want to. Leave me the hell out of it."

"I hate you, Zworkin. You are a selfish beast."

"You want to poison my ears."

"I want you to confirm whether something I hear is real or unreal. Is that so much to ask somebody you are married to?"

"It's your noise, Zora—don't bang it on my head. How am I going to support us if I can't play my cello?"

"Suppose I go deaf," she said, but Dworkin was snoring.

•

"La la, la la," she sang to herself in the looking glass. She had been gaining weight and resembled, she said, an ascending balloon.

Dworkin, returning from Lenox that evening, complained he'd had trouble in his master class because the arthritis in his shoulder was taking a harder bite.

When he came upstairs before midnight, she was reading a magazine in bed, both ears plugged with wads of cotton. Her legs snapped together when he entered the room.

"The bedroom is virtually a sound box," Zora said. "It captures every earthly sound, not to speak of the unearthly."

I'd better stop listening, he thought. If I hear what she does, that is the end of my music.

•

Zora drove off in a station wagon for three days, traveling into Vermont and New Hampshire. She had not asked Dworkin to come along. Each night she called from a different motel or country inn and sounded fine.

"How's it coming?" he asked.

"Just fine, I suppose. I confess I haven't heard anything greatly unusual in my ears."

"No noises from outer space?"

"Nor from inner."

He said that was a good sign.

"What do you think we ought to do?" she asked.

"Concerning what?"

"About the house. About our lives. If I go on hearing noises when I get back."

He said after a minute, "Zora, I would like to help you extricate yourself from this misery. I speak with love."

"Don't make me feel like a crippled pigeon," she said. "I know I hear a real enough noise when I am in that house."

"I warn you, I love this house," he said.

•

On the night after her return from her trip alone, Dworkin, awakened by a burst of cello music in the sky, stood in yellow pajamas and woolen navy robe on the deck, staring at the clustered stars.

Spanning the knotted strings of glowing small fires across the night sky, he beheld, after its slow coming into sight, like a lighted ship out of fog, his personal constellation: the Cellist. Dworkin had observed it in childhood, and often since then, a seated figure playing his cello—somewhere between Cassiopeia and Lyra. Tonight he beheld Casals sitting in a chair constructed of six jeweled stars, playing gorgeously as he hoarsely sang. Dworkin watched engrossed, trying to identify the music; like Bach but not Bach. He was not able to. Casals was playing a prelude lamenting his fate. Apparently he had—for him—died young. It was hours past midnight and Zora slumbered heavily, exhausted by her lonely journey. After the stars had dimmed and the celestial cellist and his music all but vanished, Dworkin drew on a pair of knee socks under his pajamas, and in tennis shoes he went quietly downstairs to the music room, where he lifted the dark cello out of its hand-carved casket and for a moment held it in his arms.

He dug the end pin into the pockmarked floor—he would not use a puck, he had informed both his wives. Dworkin wanted the floor to move if the cello caused it to. Embracing the instrument between his knees, the delicate curved shell against his breast, he drew his bow across the bridge, his left fingers fluttering as though they were singing. Dworkin felt the vibrations of the cello rise in his flesh to his head. He tried to clear his throat. Despite the time of night and the live pain in his shoulder, he played from the andante of Schubert's B-flat major trio, imagining the music of the piano and violin. Schubert breaks the heart and calls it *un poco mosso.* That is the art of it. The longing heart forever breaks yet is gravely contained. The cello Dworkin passionately played played him.

He played for the space and solidity and shape of his house, the way it fitted together. He played for the long years of music here, and for the room in which he had practiced and composed for a quarter of a century, often looking up from his score to glance at the elms through the window of the arched wall. Here were his scores, records, books. Above his head hung portraits of Piatigorsky and Boccherini, who seemed to watch him when he entered the room.

Dworkin played for his gabled dark-gray, blue-shuttered house, built early in the century, where he had lived with both of his wives. Ella had a warm singing voice excellently placed and supported. Had she been braver she would have been a professional singer. "Ah," she said, "if I were a brave person." "Try," Dworkin urged. "But I'm not," said Ella. She had never dared. In the house she sang wherever she happened to be. She was the one who had thought of putting in the stained-glass windows of beasts and flowers. Dworkin played the allegro, and once more the andante of the heart-laden Schubert. He sang to Ella. In her house.

As he played, Zora, in a black nightgown, stood at the closed door of the music room.

After listening a moment she returned quickly to the bedroom. When he left the music room, Dworkin detected his wife's perfume and knew she had been standing at the door.

He searched his heart and thought he understood what she had expected to hear.

•

As he went along the hallway, he caught a glimpse of a fleeting figure.

"Zora," he called.

She paused, but it was not Zora.

"Ella," Dworkin sobbed. "My dearest wife, I have loved you always."

She was not there to assent or ask why.

•

When Dworkin got back to bed, Zora was awake. "Why should I diet? It's an unnatural act."

"Have you been lying there thinking of dieting?"

"I've been listening to myself."

"You hear something again, after being absolved in your travels?"

"I believe I am slowly going deaf," Zora said.

"Are you still hearing the whine or wail?"

"Oho, do I hear it."

"Is it like the sound of someone singing?"

"I would call it the sound of my utter misery."

Dworkin then told her he was ready to move.

"I guess we ought to sell the house."

"Why ought we?"

"It comes to me at this late date that it's never been yours."

"Better late than later." Zora laughed. "It is true, I have never loved this house."

"Because it was Ella's?"

"Because I never loved it."

"Is that what caused your noises, do you think?"

"The noises cause the noises," Zora said.

•

Dworkin, the next day, telephoned the real estate agents, who came that night, a man and his amiable wife in their sixties.

They inspected the house from basement to attic. The man offered to buy a child's fiddle he had seen in the attic, but Dworkin wouldn't sell.

"You'll get a good price for this place," the woman said to Zora. "It's been kept in first-rate shape."

When they were moving out in the early spring, Dworkin said he had always loved this house, and Zora said she had never really cared for it.

1984

In Kew Gardens

Once, as they walked in the gardens, Virginia felt her knickers come loose and slip down her ankles. She grabbed at her maidenhair as the garment eluded her frantic grasp and formed a puddle of cloth at her feet. Swooping up her underpants, with a cry of dismay she plunged into the bushes, shrilly singing "The Last Rose of Summer." As she stood up, the elastic knot she had tied snapped, and the knickers again lay limp at her feet.

"Christ, goddamn!"

Vanessa listened at the bushes.

"Don't be hysterical. No one will see through your dress."

"How can you be certain?"

"No one would want to."

She shrieked slowly.

"Forgive me, dear goat," Vanessa told her. "I meant no harm."

"Oh, never, no, never."

Insofar as I was ever in love I loved Vanessa.

George Duckworth, affectionate stepbrother, carried his tormented amours from the parlor to the night nursery. He nuzzled, he fondled, he fiddled with his finger. To his sisters he was obscenity incarnate. He touched without looking.

"I meant no harm. I meant to comfort you."

Virginia lost her underpants and wondered where she had been.

Her erotic life rarely interested her. It seemed unimportant compared with what went on in the world.

I was born in 1882 with rosy cheeks and green eyes. Not enough was made of my coloring.

When her mother died she tore the pillow with her teeth. She spat bleeding feathers.

Her father cried and raged. He beat his chest and groaned aloud, "I am ruined."

The mother had said, "Everyone needed me but he needed me most."

"Unquenchable seems to me such presence": H. James.

The father moaned, "Why won't my whiskers grow?"

As Virginia lay mourning her mother, dreadful voices cried in the night. They whispered, they clucked, they howled. She suffered piercing occipital headaches.

King Edward cursed her foully in the azalea garden. He called her filthy names, reading aloud dreadful reviews of books she had yet to write.

The king sang of madness, rage, incest.

Years later she agreed to marry Mr. Leonard Woolf, who had offered to be her Jewish mother.

"I am mad," she confessed to him.

"I am marrying a penniless Jew," Virginia wrote Violet Dickinson. She wondered who had possessed her.

"He thinks my writing the best part of me."

"His Jewishness is qualified."

His mother disgusted her.

She grew darkly enraged.

In fact, I dislike the quality of masculinity. I always have.

Lytton said he had no use for it whatever. "Semen?" he asked when he saw a stain on Vanessa's dress.

Vanessa loved a man who found it difficult to love a woman.

She loved Duncan Grant until he loved her.

She had loved Clive Bell, who loved Virginia, who would not love him. Virginia loved Leonard, who loved her. She swore she loved him.

When Julia, the mother, died, the goat threw herself out of a first-story window and lay on the ground with Warren Septimus Smith. "He did not want to die till the very last minute." Neither had she.

The old king emerged from the wood, strumming a lyre. A silver bird flew over his head, screeching in Greek.

A dead woman stalked her.

Janet Case, her teacher of Greek, loved her. She loved her teacher of Greek.

She loved Violet Dickinson.

She loved Vita Nicolson.

Leonard and she had no children. They lay in bed and had no children. She would have liked a little girl.

"Possibly my great age makes it less a catastrophe but certainly I find the climax greatly exaggerated."

Vanessa wrote Clive: "Apparently she gets no pleasure from the act, which I think is curious. She and Leonard were anxious to know when I had had an orgasm. I couldn't remember, do you?"

"Yet I dare say we are the happiest couple in England. Aren't we, Leonard?"

"My dear."

Leonard and Virginia set up the Hogarth Press but they would not print Mr. James Joyce's *Ulysses*. "He is impudent and coarse."

Mrs. Dalloway loved Warren Septimus Smith though she never met him.

"He had committed an appalling crime and had been condemned by human nature."

"The whole world was clamoring, Kill yourself, kill yourself for our sakes."

(He sat on the windowsill.)

He jumped. Virginia fell from the window.

As for *To the Lighthouse*, I have no idea what it means, if it has a meaning. That's no business of mine.

"[Lily Briscoe] could have wept. It was bad, it was bad, it was infinitely bad! She could have done it differently of course; the colour could have been thinned and faded; the shapes etherealised; that was how Paunceforte would have seen it. But then she did not see it like that. She saw the colour burning on a framework of steel; the light of a butterfly's wing lying upon the arches of a cathedral. Of all that only a few random marks scrawled upon the canvas remained. And it would never be seen; never be hung even, and there was Mr. Tansley whispering in her ear, 'Women can't paint, women can't write . . .'

". . . She looked at the steps; they were empty; she looked at her canvas; it was blurred. With a sudden intensity, as if she saw it clear for a second, she drew a line there, in the centre. It was done; it was finished. Yes, she thought, laying down her brush in extreme fatigue, I have had my vision."

All I need is a room of my own.

"I hate to see so many women's lives wasted simply because they have not been trained well enough to take an independent interest in any study or to be able to work efficiently in any profession": Leslie Stephen to Julia Duckworth.

"There has fallen a splendid tear/From the passion-flower at the gate."—Alfred, Lord Tennyson

"There was something so ludicrous in thinking of people singing such things under their breath that I burst out laughing."

The Waves.

The Years. The bloody years.

The acts among *Between the Acts.*

No one she knew inspired her to more than momentary erotic excitement throughout her life. She loved Shakespeare's sister.

Leonard gave up that ghost.

"They also serve."

She felt a daily numbness, nervous tension. "What a born melancholic I am."

They had called her the goat in the nursery, against which she tore at their faces with her tiny nails.

They had never found Thoby her dead brother's lost portrait. Vanessa had painted and forever lost it.

Her mother died.

My father is not my mother. Leonard is my mother. We shall never conceive a living child.

"I shall never grow my whiskers again."

She heard voices, or words to that effect.

"Maiden, there's turd in your blood," King Edward chanted in ancient Greece.

Her scream blew the bird off its one-legged perch and it flapped into the burning wood.

An old king strode among the orange azaleas.

For years she simply went mad.

She spoke in soft shrieks.

She wrote twenty-one books whose reviews frightened her.

"That was not my doing," said Leonard Woolf.

"Nor mine," sobbed her Greek tutor.

Perhaps it was mine, Vita Nicolson said. "She was so frail a creature. One had to be most careful not to shock her."

I loved Vita. She loved *Orlando.*

Virginia wrote a biography of Roger Fry. She did not want to write a biography of Roger Fry.

Leonard served her a single soft-boiled egg when she was ill.

"Now, Virginia, open your mouth and swallow your egg. Only if you eat will you regain the strength to write your novels and essays."

She sucked the tip of his spoon.

"Though you give much I give so little."

"The little you give is a king's domain."

At that time the writing went well and she artfully completed *Between the Acts*, yet felt no joy.

Virginia relapsed into depression and denied herself food.

"Virginia, you must eat to sustain yourself."

"My reviews are dreadful," Virginia said.

"I am afraid of this war," Virginia said.

"I hear clamorous noises in my head," Virginia said.

One morning, to escape the noises of war, she dragged herself to the river Ouse, there removed shoes, stockings, underpants, and waded slowly into the muddy water. The large rock she had forced into her coat pocket pulled her down till she could see the earth in her green eyes.

"I don't think two people could have been happier than we have been."

1984

❧ B M ❧

Alma Redeemed

Gustav Mahler's ghost.

Bruno Walter had seen it as Mahler conducted one of his last concerts. It waxed in music as the conductor waned. The ghost appeared, more or less, to Alma Mahler one or two years after her husband was dead. Alma did not believe in ghosts, but this one troubled her. It had got into her bedsheets but hadn't stayed long.

Can Jews haunt people?

Gustav was a rationalist nonbeliever. "In that clear mind I never detected any trace of superstition," Bruno Walter said. He spoke of Mahler—as Alma clearly remembered—as a "God-struck man," whose religious self flowered in his music, viz., "*Veni, creator spiritus,*" as it flashed in eternity in the Eighth Symphony. Alma felt that Mahler was too subtle a man to have believed simply in God, but that wouldn't mean he might not attempt to disturb her, although she was aware that some of her thoughts of Mahler had caused her more than ordinary fright. Might the fright have produced the ghost? Such things are possible.

In my mind, more than once I betrayed him.

Yet Mahler was a kind man, although an egotist who defined his egotism as a necessity of his genius.

"Gott, how he loved his genius!"

Now, all of Alma's husbands, a collection of a long lifetime including Mahler, Walter Gropius, Franz Werfel—and Oskar Kokoschka, the painter, made it a fourth if you counted in the man she hadn't married, whom Alma conceived to be her most astonishing (if most difficult) lover—they were all artists of unusual merit and accomplishment; yet Alma seemed to favor Mahler, even if she had trouble during her lifetime caring deeply for his music.

When she met Gustav Mahler, Alma stood five feet three inches tall and weighed 144 pounds. She loved her figure. Her deep blue eyes were her best feature. She drew men with half a glance. Alma never wore underpants and thought she knew who might know she wasn't wearing them. When she met him she felt that Mahler didn't know though he may have wanted to.

Alma, a lovely, much-sought-after young woman, one of the prettiest in Vienna in those days, felt Mahler was magnetic, but she wasn't sure she ought to marry him. "He is frightening, nervous, and bounds across the room like an animal. I fear his energy."

She wrote in her diary in purple ink: "At the opera he loves to conduct *Faust*."

She wanted Gustav. She felt she had snared him in her unconscious.

Yet his demands frightened her. "Is it too late, my dearest Almchi, to ask you to make my music yours? Play as you please but don't attempt to compose. Composition is for heroes."

"How can I make his music mine if I have loved Wagner throughout my life? What passion can I possibly feel for Mahler's music or even for Mahler?" These thoughts concerned her.

"You must understand, my tender girl, that my harmony and polyphony, for all their vivid modernity, which seems to distress you, remain in the realm of pure tonality. Someday your dear ears will open to the glories of my sound."

"Yes, Gustav," said Alma.

"Let us be lovers in a true marriage. I am the composer and you are, in truth, my beloved bride."

Mahler urged her to consult her stepfather and mother. "You must lay to rest your doubts, whatever they are. The matter must be settled before we can contemplate a union for life."

"Say nothing," Carl Moll, her stepfather, advised Alma. "Best get rid of the Jew."

"*Perhaps* get rid of him," said her mother. "I never trusted his conversion to Catholicism though he pleads sincerity. He became Catholic because Cosima Wagner insisted that no Jew be allowed to replace Richard Wagner at the Vienna Opera."

But Alma said she had thought about it and decided she loved Mahler.

She did not say she was already pregnant by him.

Mahler walked in his floppy galoshes to the church on their wedding day.

At breakfast the guests were spirited, although in memoirs she wrote many years later Alma wasn't sure of that. She had trouble defining her mood.

She was twenty-two, Mahler was forty-one.

"If only I could find my own inner balance."

Mahler whispered into her good ear that he loved her more than he had loved anyone except his dear mother, who had died insane.

Alma said she was glad he respected his mother.

"You must give yourself to me unconditionally and desire nothing except my love."

He sounded more like a teacher than a lover.

"Yes, Gustav."

"He is continually talking about preserving his art but that is not allowed to me."

Nothing has come to fruition for me, Alma thought. Neither my beauty, nor my spirit, nor my talent.

Does his genius, by definition, submerge my talent? My ship is in the harbor but has sprung a leak.

He did not lie in bed and make love to her. He preferred to mount her when she was deeply asleep.

His odor was repulsive. "Probably from your cigars," she had informed Mahler. He was a stranger to her, she wrote in her diary, "and much about him will remain strange forever."

She tripped over a paraffin lamp and set the carpet afire.

Mahler dreamed Alma was wearing her hair as she used to in her girlhood. He did not like her to pile her tresses on the top of her head. Gustav said her hairdo was Semitic-looking and he wished to avoid that impression. He assured his friends he was not a practicing Jew. Alma wore her hair long most of the time.

When their daughter, Maria, caught diphtheria and died, Mahler could not stand being alone. Memories of his daughter seared his life. He went from person to person with a new message: "Alma has sacrificed her youth for me. With absolute selflessness she has subordinated her life to my work."

Alma let Ossip Gabrilowitsch hold her hand in a dark room.

"To gain a spiritual center, my Alma, that's the important thing. Then everything takes on another aspect."

Alma found his impersonal preaching repellent and frightening.

Since her youth she had been nervous among strangers and very sensitive about her impaired hearing.

Mahler became frightened at the thought of losing his wife.

Mahler and Freud met in Leiden and walked for four hours along the tree-lined canals. Freud told him a good deal about the life of the psyche and Mahler was astonished though he had guessed much that Freud had told him.

"My darling, my lyre," he wrote his wife, "come exorcise the ghosts of darkness. They claw me, they throw me to the ground. I ask in silence whether I am damned. Rescue me, my dearest."

Mahler suspected that he loved Alma more than she loved him.

He was as strict now about her going back to her music as he had been nine years ago in insisting she give up composing.

One night she woke up and saw him standing by her bed like a ghost.

He dedicated his Eighth Symphony to her.

He feared his Ninth.

"Ah, how lovely it is to love, my dearest Almscherl. And it is only now that I know what love is. Believe me, Tristan sings the truth."

"Alma blossoms, on a splendid diet, and she has given up tippling Benedictine. She looks younger day by day."

One day she had a cold; Mahler invited the doctor who had examined Alma to look him over too.

"Well, you have no cause to be proud of that heart," the doctor said after listening for a minute.

The bacterial tests sealed his doom. Mahler insisted he be told the truth, and he said he wanted to die in Vienna.

He talked to Alma about his grave and tombstone. She listened gravely. He did not want to be cremated. He wanted to be there if people came to the graveyard to see him.

"Mozart," said Mahler, before he died during a thunderstorm. "Boom!"

•

Alma met the man who later became her second husband in a sanitarium, in Tobelbad, when, exhausted by Gustav's pace and striving, she was advised by a country doctor to take the cure.

Gustav displayed an unyielding energy she couldn't keep up with. She was the young one but he made her feel old. That's the trick, she thought. He wants me to match him in age.

At Tobelbad she met a handsome architect, Walter Gropius, age twenty-seven, who lived down the hall and stared at her in astonishment as she walked by. He gazed at Alma with architectural eyes and she was aware she had form.

They began to go for long walks. Gustav usually gave her short lectures in philosophy as they walked together, but this one talked on about nature and architectural masses; he seemed surprised that she did not throw herself into his arms.

Gustav, promoting his conducting career, hurried from city to city, writing to her from where he happened to be, one opera house or philharmonic society after another; but she was in no mood to respond. In his letters to his tender Almscherl he wrote, "I could not bear this depleting routine if it did not end with delicious thoughts of you. Regain your health, my precious dear girl, so that we may again renew our affectionate embraces."

In his letters Mahler tickled her chin and ladled out bits of gossip laced with pious observations. His pace was again frantic; yet wherever he went, he worried about her, though for reasons of scheduling, etc., he found it difficult to visit her at Tobelbad, yet surely she knew the direction of his heart?

He had asked his mother-in-law, Anna Moll, to write Alma a letter requesting news; and soon thereafter she paid her daughter a visit, but there was no news to speak of. "She is responding to her cure, not much more." Gropius was invisible.

Alma had put him out of her mind and returned home. No one knew whether they had become or had been lovers.

"When shall we meet again?" the handsome Gropius had asked.

She wasn't sure.

"Seriously, my dearest—"

"Please do not call me 'my dearest,' I am simply Alma."

"Seriously, simply Alma."

"I am a married person, Herr Gropius. Mahler is my legal husband."

"A terrible answer," Gropius replied.

" 'None but the brave deserves the fair.' " He quoted Dryden in English.

When he translated the line, Alma said nothing.

"Mahler met me at the Toblach station and was suddenly more in love with me than ever before."

One night when Mahler and Alma were in Vienna, before returning to their farmhouse in Toblach, Mahler, looking around nervously, whispered, "Alma, I have the feeling that we are being followed."

"Nonsense," said Alma. "Don't be so superstitious." He laughed but it did not sound like a laugh. He did not practice sufficiently, Alma thought.

Gropius then sent Mahler a letter asking his permission to marry his wife. Alma placed her husband's mail on the piano and shivered at lunch as Mahler slowly read the letter, whose writing she had recognized. She had wanted to tear it up but was afraid to.

Mahler read the letter and let out a gasp, then a deep cry.

"Who is this crazy man who asks permission to marry my wife? Am I, then, your father?"

Alma laughed a little hysterically, yet managed to answer calmly. "This is a foolish young man I met at the sanitarium. I do not love him."

"Who said love?" Mahler shouted.

Alma eventually calmed him, but he felt as though he had been shipwrecked and didn't know why.

That afternoon Alma saw Gropius from her car window as she drove past the village bridge. Gropius didn't see her.

She returned from her errand feeling ill and breathlessly told Mahler whom she had seen walking near the bridge: "That was the young man who was interested in me in Tobelbad although I did nothing to encourage him."

"We shall see." Mahler took along a kerosene lamp and went out searching for Gropius. He found him not far from their farmhouse. "I am Mahler," the composer said. "Perhaps you wish to speak to my wife?"

Gropius, scratching under his arm, confessed that intent. "I am Gropius."

Mahler lit the lamp. It was dark.

He called up the stairs and Alma came down.

"I come," she said.

"You two ought to talk," said Mahler. He withdrew to his study, where he read to himself in the Old Testament.

When Alma, white-faced, came to him in the study, Mahler told her calmly that she was free to decide in whatever way she wanted. "You can do as you feel you must." If he was conducting, no stick was visible.

"Thanks," said Alma. "I want him to go. Please let him stay until morning and then he shall go. I have spoken to him and explained that I will not tolerate bad manners."

Mahler went back to reading the Old Testament. He was thinking of *Das Lied von der Erde* though he had not yet written it.

Gropius stayed overnight and Alma drove him to his train to Berlin in the morning.

Gropius, holding his hat, said he was sorry for the trouble he had caused. Then he said, "When shall we meet again?"

"Never," said Alma. "I am a happy woman. Please stay away from my life."

"Never is *never*."

Gropius said none but the brave deserves the fair.

He got into the train and sent her a worshipful telegram from every station it stopped at.

Gustav, that night, collapsed outside Alma's bedroom. The candle he was holding fell to the floor and the house almost went up in flames.

Alma got him to bed; she put Gropius out of her mind, where he remained until years later, long after Mahler's death, when she felt she could no longer stand Oskar Kokoschka's wild fantasies and burning desires.

•

Mahler, leaning out of his window at the Hotel Majestic above Central Park, in New York City, heard "boom" in the street below. The boom was for a dead fireman in a horse-drawn funeral cortege.

Mahler wrote the muffled drumbeat into his Tenth Symphony: BOOM!

•

"I know I am lost if I go any further with the present confusion in my life."—Kokoschka

"May I see you?" he asked.

Alma loved men of genius.

He was worldly, sensuous. He needed love and money.

He came to visit and they went to bed. She woke him and said it was time to go home. When he left her he walked till dawn.

He signed her into his name: Alma Oskar Kokoschka.

"Read this letter in the evening."

He bought the Paris newspapers to check on the weather when she was there.

"Alma, I passed your house at one o'clock and could have cried out in anger because you see the others and leave me in the dirty street."

The women in his paintings resemble Alma.

Remembering Gustav and fearing that she was pregnant by Oskar, Alma worried about any Jew who might see her pregnant.

In view of the Jungfrau he painted her on a balcony.

Oskar's mother railed against his obsession. "She is like a high-society mistress, a whore without garters."

"Shut your black mouth," he told her.

Alma feared pregnancy. It was wrong to have had a child out of wedlock. Maria had died because Alma had become pregnant before her marriage to Mahler.

Oskar's mother threatened to shoot her.

Kokoschka went to Alma's house and found his mother walking around with a gun in her purse.

"Give it here."

She crooked her finger and said, "Boom."

"Those who sin will be punished," Alma said one night to Mahler's ghost.

Oskar: "I am not allowed to see you every day because you want to keep alive the memory of this Jew who is so foreign to me."

"I must have you for my wife or else my talent will perish miserably."

She said she would marry him only after he had created a masterwork.

"Alma, please don't send me any money. I don't want it."

Die Windsbraut is Oskar's painting of Alma and him. She sleeps with her head on his shoulder. He gazes into the distance.

"I dreamed that Gustav was conducting. I was sitting near him and heard the music but it clearly displeased me."

"How far behind me my life with Mahler seems."

"I need my crazy mystique of the artist and from this I always manage to fill my head. The whole world is ultimately a dream that turns bad."

In Kokoschka's painting at Semmering, Alma ascends to heaven in fiery immolation. Oskar is in hell, surrounded by sexy fat serpents.

Alma was pregnant. "She will marry me now": Kokoschka.

Gustav's death mask arrived in the mail. Alma unpacked it and hung it on the wall. She entered the clinic for an abortion.

Austria declared war on Serbia. Alma wrote in her diary: "I imagine I have caused the whole upheaval."

"I would like to break free from Oskar."

"God punished me by sending this man into my life."

"I would give up every man on earth for music."

"Wagner means more to me than anyone. His time will come again."

Mrs. Kokoschka picked up her clay pot and dropped it on the floor. She withdrew a blood-red string of beads she was holding for Kokoschka. Alma had given them to him as a memento of his love for her.

"Yesterday evening I ran away from Oskar."

"What of the Jewish question *now*? They need help and direction —brains and feeling from those of us who are Christians."

She wrote to Gropius.

"I will get him quickly. I feel this is, or will become, something important to me."

Walter's birthday fell on the day Mahler had died.

Alma went to see him. "Finally in the course of an hour he fell in love with me. We were where the wine and good food raised our spirits. I went to the train with him where love overpowered him so that he dragged me onto the moving train, and come what might I had no choice but to travel to Hanover with him."

Walter had the manners of a husband. He was talented, handsome, an Aryan. He was crazily jealous of Kokoschka. Alma married him.

"So married, so free, and yet so bound."

"I wanted to make my own music, or music about which I felt deeply, because Gustav's was foreign to me."

"Jews have given us spirit but have eaten our hearts."

"My husband means nothing to me anymore. Walter has come too late."

She had met Franz Werfel. "Werfel is a rather fat Jew with full lips and watery almond eyes. He says: 'How can I be happy when there is someone who is suffering?' which I have heard verbatim from another egocentric, Gustav Mahler."

•

Alma married Werfel. He was a Jew who looked like a Jew, yet passable. She had had half a Jew in Mahler, and Werfel made the other half. They had a lot to learn, these Jews. They needed a Christian quality. Gropius was a true Aryan, a fine gentleman, passionate in his way, though she had never loved him. She had given him up for Werfel. She often thought of Kokoschka but hated him. "He wants to annihilate me."

Werfel needed her. He lived in dirty rooms, his clothes uncared for, cigarette butts on the floor. He needed a wife. He already had fathered a son Gropius thought was his child. Walter guessed that out and departed. He had tried to keep their daughter, Manon, but Alma had fought him for her. Gropius retreated like a gentleman. Manon died and was buried next to her half sister, Maria Mahler.

Alma lived with Franz Werfel through her best days. He wrote *Verdi*, *The Song of Bernadette*, and *The Star of the Unborn*. He made money and they spent it freely. The only really bad time was when they were trying to find their way out of Europe as the Nazis sought them in Spain. Then an American diplomat assisted them and they got out of Portugal on a Portuguese ship and afterwards lived in Beverly Hills, U.S.A. Alma was feeling happy again.

But there is no beating out illness and bad health. Werfel died in his sixties. Alma did not attend his funeral though the guests had assembled and were awaiting her. Bruno Walter thrice played a Schubert impromptu as they waited for Alma to appear, but she had had it with funerals of three husbands. She was drinking Benedictine and never got to Werfel's funeral. She often felt that Kokoschka had been her best lover.

•

"Mahler had a long white face. He sat with his coat buttoned up to his ears. He looked like death masquerading as a monk. I told him this, hoping to exorcise my ghostly pangs of dread."

"Why do I fancy I am free when my character contracts me like a prison?": Mahler.

"Where is *my* truth?": Alma.

"He was always stopping on a walk to feel his pulse. I had always known his heart was diseased."

"The Jews are at once an unprecedented danger and the greatest good luck to humanity."

"I see Hitler as a genuine German idealist, something that is unthinkable to Jews."

"But fortunately he was stupid."

"Oh, my God, my God, why do you *so* love evil?"

"Werfel believed in the world revolution through Bolshevism. I believed that Fascism would solve the problems of the world."

Alma wore long necklaces with earrings and used dark lipstick. She drank Benedictine and ate little.

"Death is a contagious disease. That is the reason," Alma wrote in her diary, "why I will not place a photograph of a living person next to someone who is dead."

She thought she had met Crown Prince Rudolf of Austria on a mountaintop and he asked Alma to bear his child.

One night Mahler's ghost appeared, momentarily freezing her fingers.

"Alma, aren't you yet moved by my classically beautiful music? One can hear eternity in it."

"How can one love Mahler if she best loves Wagner?"

"My time will come."

Mahler diminished as he faded.

Alma felt he had handled her badly in her youth.

Yet there were moments she thought she still loved Mahler. She pictured him in a cemetery surrounded by his grave.

Alma favored cremation.

She was eighty-five when she died in 1964, older than King Lear.

•

Alma redeemed.

1984–85

APPENDIX

Bibliography of

Bernard Malamud's Stories

IF   *Idiots First*, Farrar, Straus and Company, 1963
MB   *The Magic Barrel*, Farrar, Straus and Cudahy, 1958
MR   *A Malamud Reader*, Farrar, Straus and Giroux, 1967
PF   *Pictures of Fidelman: An Exhibition*, Farrar, Straus and Giroux, 1969
PUS   *The People and Uncollected Stories*, Farrar, Straus and Giroux, 1989
RH   *Rembrandt's Hat*, Farrar, Straus and Giroux, 1973
SBM   *The Stories of Bernard Malamud*, Farrar, Straus and Giroux, 1983
TF   *Two Fables*: "The Jewbird" and "Talking Horse," limited edition, Banyan Press, Bennington College, 1978

ALMA REDEEMED. *Commentary*, July 1984.

AN APOLOGY. *Commentary*, November 1957.

ANGEL LEVINE. *Commentary*, December 1955. MB, SBM.

ARMISTICE. Written in Washington, D.C., in 1940; first appearance in PUS.

BEHOLD THE KEY. *Commentary*, May 1958. MB.

BENEFIT PERFORMANCE. *Threshold*, February 1943. PUS.

THE BILL. *Commentary*, April 1951. MB, SBM.

BLACK IS MY FAVORITE COLOR. *The Reporter*, July 18, 1963. IF, MR, SBM.

A CHOICE OF PROFESSION. *Commentary*, September 1963. IF.

A CONFESSION OF MURDER. Written in 1952; opening chapter of abandoned novel, *The Man Nobody Could Lift*. PUS.

THE COST OF LIVING. *Harper's Bazaar*, March 1950. IF, SBM.

THE DEATH OF ME. *World Review*, April 1951. IF, SBM.

THE ELEVATOR. *Paris Review*, Fall 1989. Written in Italy in 1957. PUS.

AN EXORCISM. *Harper's*, December 1968. Revised by the author for SBM but not included by author; in PUS.

THE FIRST SEVEN YEARS. *Partisan Review*, September–October 1950. MB, MR, SBM.

THE GERMAN REFUGEE. *Saturday Evening Post*, September 14, 1963. Title in the magazine was "The Refugee." IF, MR, SBM.

THE GIRL OF MY DREAMS. *American Mercury*, January 1953. MB, SBM.

GLASS BLOWER OF VENICE. First published in PF, 1969.

GOD'S WRATH. *The Atlantic*, February 1972. SBM.

THE GROCERY STORE. Written in 1943, first published in PUS.

IDIOTS FIRST. *Commentary*, December 1961. IF, SBM, MR.

IN KEW GARDENS. *Partisan Review*, double (anniversary) issue, Fall 1984 – Winter 1985. PUS.

IN RETIREMENT. *The Atlantic*, March 1973. RH, SBM.

THE JEWBIRD. *The Reporter*, April 11, 1963. IF, MR, SBM, TF.

THE LADY OF THE LAKE. First published in MB, 1958.

THE LAST MOHICAN. *Partisan Review*, Spring 1958. MB, MR, PF, SBM.

THE LETTER. *Esquire*, August 1972. RH, SBM.

LIFE IS BETTER THAN DEATH. *Esquire*, May 1963. IF, SBM.

THE LITERARY LIFE OF LABAN GOLDMAN. *Assembly*, November 1943. PUS.

THE LOAN. *Commentary*, July 1952. MB, SBM.

A LOST GRAVE. *Esquire*, May 1985. PUS.

THE MAGIC BARREL. *Partisan Review*, November 1954. MB, MR, SBM.

THE MAID'S SHOES. *Partisan Review*, Winter 1959. IF, MR, SBM.

MAN IN THE DRAWER. *The Atlantic*, April 1968. RH, SBM.

THE MODEL. *The Atlantic*, August 1983. SBM.

THE MOURNERS. *Discovery*, January 1955. MB, MR, SBM.

MY SON THE MURDERER. *Esquire*, November 1968. RH, SBM.

NAKED NUDE. *Playboy*, August 1963. IF, PF.

NOTES FROM A LADY AT A DINNER PARTY. *Harper's*, February 1973. RH.

PICTURES OF THE ARTIST. *The Atlantic*, December 1968. PF.

A PIMP'S REVENGE. *Playboy*, September 1968. PF.

THE PLACE IS DIFFERENT NOW. *American Prefaces*, Spring 1943. PUS.

THE PRISON. *Commentary*, September 1950. MB.

REMBRANDT'S HAT. *The New Yorker*, March 17, 1973. RH, SBM.

RIDING PANTS. Written in 1953; first published in PUS.

THE SILVER CROWN. *Playboy*, December 1972. RH, SBM.

SPRING RAIN. Written in 1942; first published in PUS.

STEADY CUSTOMER. *New Threshold*, August 1943. First book publication here.

STILL LIFE. *Partisan Review*, Winter 1962. IF, PF.

A SUMMER'S READING. *The New Yorker*, September 22, 1956. MB.

SUPPOSE A WEDDING. *New Statesman*, February 8, 1963. IF.

TAKE PITY. *America*, September 25, 1956. MB, MR, SBM.

TALKING HORSE. *The Atlantic*, August 1972. RH, SBM, TF.

A WIG. *The Atlantic*, January 1980. PUS.

ZORA'S NOISE. *GQ (Gentlemen's Quarterly)*, January 1985. PUS.